Same Face Different Place Pleasures

By Helen J. Christmas

To Susanna, Enjoy!

[signature]
x

INTRODUCTION

Pleasures is the third book of the series, Same Face Different Place, a powerful saga, which spans four different decades of British history.

Book 1, Beginnings is set in the criminal underworld of 1970s London - a mysterious conspiracy to end the life of a British MP has unleashed a chain of events, yet to be resolved.

Book 2, Visions, leaps into the 1980s - a decade where the face of Britain has changed forever. The characters join forces to help restore a beautiful English country house but find themselves drawn into a sinister plot which resurrects old enemies from the past.

Book 3, Pleasures continues throughout the 80s and into the 1990s. Characters good and evil from both Books 1 and 2 are thrown together in a battle to acquire a piece of land; but it is time to resolve the mystery which began in 1972 - and there is danger ahead.

No political opinions expressed by in this book are my own and I have used examples of real news events from the era around which some parts of the story are based.

Acknowledgements

I would like to express my thanks to everyone who helped and inspired me, including Jon Martin who advised me on the 'Black Monday' scene and especially Inspector Andy Kille of Sussex Police who was a wealth of information in helping me to expand on the finer details of police procedures and evidence. Lastly, a big thanks goes to my mother and my sister for all their encouragement and help - and to an American lady, known as Trenda whose valuable beta reading service was both constructive and positive.

Please note: This novel contains adult content which includes frequent strong language, scenes of a sexual nature, scenes of drug taking and violence.

CONTENTS

PART 1
THE BATTLE FOR THE LAND

Chapters 1-7

August 1987 - February 1988

Chapter 1

I

September 1987

"A future Prime Minister was blown up in a car bomb?" Elijah breathed, staring down at the newspaper, "and *this* is what my father witnessed?"

"Yes," Eleanor whispered fearfully, "but he also witnessed some very suspicious people hanging around beforehand…"

She broke off with a swallow and Elijah had seen that look before. In fact he had grown up, knowing precious little about his father, Jake. The one occasion his mother had even admitted he had been murdered had occurred on his 13th birthday; but she had refused to say any more. She had been looking at him in the same way as she was looking at him now. Elijah had seen the fear hiding in her eyes. Yet it was more than that. His mother had possessed an almost haunted look as if she feared something awful might happen to him - a feeling that had been reinforced by her words, *'you're all I've got left, Eli - I can't risk losing you too, please understand that…'*

They had been living at Westbourne House under the care of James Barton-Wells and his children. His step-father, Charlie, had been supervising the restoration of the building - a magnificent example of 17th Century architecture. He could clearly remember the months that followed; the depressive blackness that had stifled the atmosphere like a rain cloud before James finally lost his home - before the Hamptons had turned up. Elijah blinked. He didn't really want to think about them right now. What his mother was trying to tell him was far more important and he had waited many years to hear this.

So he listened in silence as Eleanor gently related Jake's story: the gruelling interview with Inspector Hargreeves, followed by a conspiracy to end his life. Jake had been seized by a gang of thugs and held prisoner, right up until the day Eleanor had rescued him. But the clock had always been ticking. Jake was destined to meet his death at the hands of a contract killer and in the weeks that followed, he explained the most obvious reason why someone must have wanted him dead.

"The IRA were blamed for the car bomb," Eleanor sighed, "but it seems Jake held a vital clue as to who might really have been responsible. He saw a blonde-haired man in a car, that's all - and neither of us had any idea who he was until this event…"

Her hand fell upon the surface of a blue foolscap folder titled 'Press Conference 1973.' She seemed hesitant.

"Go on," he prompted her.

"You have to swear to me, you will never repeat what I am about to show you," Eleanor urged him.

"Okay," Elijah muttered.

"Not even to Avalon or William?" Eleanor kept pressing him.

"I promise!" Elijah sighed, crossing his heart with his forefinger and this time, he meant every word, sensing her reluctance to move on until he had given her this reassurance.

Eleanor slowly peeled back the cover of the folder.

At first, all Elijah saw was a black and white photo which unveiled an elegant boardroom. His eyes studied the ornate ceiling and the pillars which lined the walls. Heavy velvet drapes poured from the pelmets crowning the top of each splendid arched window. The table was englobed in light diffused from a sparkling overhead chandelier.

"The Grosvenor Hotel," Eleanor whispered. This was the point when Elijah noticed the shadows of a few men seated around the table - the dark quality of the photo made them seem almost subliminal.

"That one there is Inspector Hargreeves," she added, pointing. Elijah could not ignore the bitter edge to her tone as he studied the man's hard features. "He brought along a couple of detectives who were involved in the murder enquiry. Do you recognise *him*?"

Elijah followed the path of her trailing finger and frowned. Yes, the polished profile of the dark haired man did seem oddly familiar. Yet his silhouette disguised the outline of a fifth man - barely visible within the cloak of shadow. All Elijah could see was a cap of pale blonde hair.

"I can't quite tell," he murmured, "right now, I'm more interested in the other man, the one you can't quite see!"

She released another sigh and brushing the photo to one side, revealed a second picture. This time, Elijah felt the breath catch in his throat, instantly recognising his mother. The flash of a camera had bathed her in a flood of white light - she looked stunning in a long, black evening dress, pearls around her throat, her river of glossy dark curls tumbling around her bare shoulders. She had been just 17 when this photo had been taken. Except this time, the camera had illuminated the mysterious blonde man - now undeniably recognisable.

"It's Perry Hampton," Elijah whispered. *A small part of him had always known.*

The camera had captured him mid-rant, his face engorged with fury - pale eyes blazing.

Elijah could feel his breathing deepening, conscious of every fear-filled gasp as it was dragged from his body. "Oh my God. How did you get hold of this photo?"

Eleanor threw him a calculating smile as she recalled the memory.

****

August 1987 - One Month Earlier

A slender Muslim girl slipped from the doors of the Community Centre, head down, her movements practised and slow as she took her first steps towards the pavement. Her head was submissively lowered as she had observed in Shajeda, their new community Liaison Officer. - her slender figure disguised beneath the enveloping folds of a long, navy Abaya, her hair wrapped in a veil. Even the warm hue of her complexion seemed befitting.

One side of the Community Centre had been cordoned off whilst its massive renovation was underway - Andrew was crouched by the scaffolding, rowing with Charlie about the height of the new windows. In the moment she drifted past, neither man had even given her a second glance. She kept walking; the only observer, a woman, also of Asian descent and strikingly attractive as she lingered in her car. Nothing in her expression betrayed suspicion. The first hurdle had been crossed.

She wandered on, making her way towards the station - tempted to quicken her pace though cautious not to. She had been studying Shajeda, as closely as Perry's spy had been watching her and after two months of careful scrutiny, she dared not risk anything which might blow her cover.

15 minutes later, she stepped aboard a train destined for London and to her delight, the beautiful Asian woman had refrained from following her. The train finally began to glide along the tracks and confident she had evaded her, Eleanor allowed herself a smile.

Half an hour later, she arrived at Waterloo Station; never able to forget a scene with Jake in 1972, unaware his assassins had been lurking there. And was it really only six months ago, she had travelled here with Charlie? They had only just got engaged. Yet she would never forget the appearance of Nathan - a man who Perry employed as a security guard. His role was to follow them, before Eleanor had led him on a wild goose chase across the London underground.

Her eyes darted round the area. It was hardly surprising, she had come to associate this station with terror. Though she hoped this time might be different - convinced she had evaded Perry's spies.

She stepped into a taxi and some 20 minutes later, found herself outside the chiseled beige walls of the Grosvenor Hotel where her contacts had booked a private conference room. Eleanor slid through the revolving glass door, impatient to meet them.

"Eleanor!" Joshua grinned as she pulled back her veil.

Joshua Merriman worked in the music industry while the man accompanying him had a long history of writing for 'New Musical Express' or 'NME' as it was better known. It was obvious that Adam Morrison would have changed - older, his frame rounder from many hours spent behind a typewriter and his glossy mop of light brown curls had receded slightly. Yet his glowing eyes were the same as Eleanor remembered from the 1973 press conference.

"What a pleasure it is to meet you at last," he purred, extending his hand. "If only we could have had this discussion 14 years ago. But I'm glad you came. I have something for you."

They settled themselves around an oak table, surrounded by high-backed chairs. The furnishings of this establishment were just as luxurious as she recalled before - despite the undercurrent of fear that had rippled the atmosphere. She forced herself to concentrate as Adam flipped back the top of a lever arch file.

"I kept the original transcripts," he began. "My fellow journalists took notes and I'll say one thing, Eleanor. Not one of us believed that police inspector - nor his creepy companion! We couldn't publish our suspicions until the fuss had died down. We even tried to trace you; specifically to hear *your* side of the story - but unfortunately you vanished."

"I had to," Eleanor said tightly. "Those men were very powerful. They had contacts in the criminal underworld and they threatened to harm my baby. I had to hide."

"Of course," Adam said gently.

"But eventually, I bumped into that *blonde man,*" she shuddered. "You know the one. He never actually introduced himself..."

"The one who totally freaked out?" Adam added. He gave a slow, crafty smile. "The clues are in my notes. His friend did *indeed* refer to him as 'Perry.' It was in the moment, Jess took a photo of you!" He released a chuckle. "*'Calm down, Perry'* - he'd just told her to put her *'effing camera away'* and luckily, she caught him in the same shot!"

Adam dipped into the file, rummaging through layers of typed transcripts mixed in amongst the wizened carbon copies. Eventually, he plucked out a hardback envelope containing the photographs. He handed it to her. Eleanor's initial reaction was disbelief - hit by the same bayonet of fear she would observe in her son in another month's time.

"That's him," she spluttered.

She could hardly speak as she realised the significance of what she was seeing. Perry's role at the press conference was unclear. Yet his reaction to her appearance had been unforgettable: a scene encapsulated in the photo, taken moments before she had leaked the truth. Jake's friend, Andries, had let it slip that *Jake witnessed something.* Fatal words which had changed everything.

"Could I possibly have a look at the transcript?" Eleanor urged him.

"Of course," Adam replied.

It took a few more minutes to glance over the notes. Angry tears shot to her eyes - it didn't take long to be reminded of the atrocious lies that had been smeared around that table.

"The police investigation was crap," she hissed under her breath. "Jake had no drugs in his possession. Do you want to know what *really* happened?"

"Go on," Adam urged her.

"The day Jake disappeared was the day he was summoned to Scotland Yard to give evidence about that car bomb. He spotted two men loitering by the minibus…" she could hardly bear to relate the rest about that interview - nor the shocking way Jake had been abducted. "We knew Hargreeves was involved. Jake told me his name. The same man visited me in hospital shortly after he was murdered."

"Do you know what became of him?" Adam pressed her.

"He was ousted from the police force for corruption," she smiled mirthlessly. "Though no charges were brought for his part in Jake's killing. It's clear he used his powers to cover up the truth. As for all those lies in the papers - it was Robin Whaley who started those. " The truth was harrowing. It had begun, several weeks before Jake had been shot. "He enlisted the help of a social worker, Bernard James…"

She broke off in dread. Poor Bernard! He had genuinely believed he was helping the police in securing the arrest of a dangerous drug dealer. She looked at the transcript again where Councillor Whaley's carefully practised lies swam in front of her '...*rumours came to my attention of a suspected drug dealer operating in the neighbourhood - a young man in his 20s with long dark, reddish hair…*' She felt a chill slip down her spine.

"Bernard told me everything. We discussed it at length, so I decided to write it all down. I never realised the importance of this but I do now. I needed some sort of log - as many details as I could remember before I forgot them. I had hoped there might be a trial…"

"Maybe one day, there will be," Joshua sighed. He touched her hand. "Doesn't Whaley practically live on your doorstep?"

"Yes," Eleanor sighed. How could she forget the day when he had unexpectedly reared up in front of her? The weeks of harassment... "He used the *same* underhand tactics to poison a community against me. He was desperate to get me out of Rosebrook."

"For what purpose?" Adam frowned. Even as an experienced journalist, he was finding all this a little hard to take in.

"They're scared I know the truth," Eleanor said bitterly, "and this is the problem. It's putting people I care about in danger, especially my son! Whaley dredged up my past - all that stuff about growing up in the criminal underworld."

"Was there ever any truth in that?" Adam probed.

"That my father worked for Sammie Maxwell?" Eleanor retorted. "Yes, it is true. It was only as I grew older, I began to suspect that Sammie was some sort of crime boss."

"Tell me about it!" Adam laughed. "He was a legend! The streets of

London were under much better control when he was around and you must of heard of his protection rackets."

"Though it shames me to say it, my father was involved in those protection rackets," Eleanor disclosed. "I had no idea what was going on! Not until a turf war arose which was the start of Sammie's demise. I don't suppose I need to ask you if you've heard of Dominic Theakston."

"Oh yes," Adam shivered. He looked troubled. "There were plenty of stories about *him* in the press, including the one where he was arrested for Jake's murder - and that was the only one we were interested in! So can I ask you if there was any truth in it?"

"Yes," Eleanor snapped. "Theakston was definitely a hit man. He'd been trying to hunt us down for months!" A strange coldness crept over her as she recalled the night of the murder. A tear slipped from her eye. "I try not to think too hard about it. It's still harrowing, even after all these years and I'm married to another man now. I mustn't dwell. Besides, the whole purpose of this meeting was to prove *Perry's* guilt. I know Theakston was paid to kill Jake - what I'm really curious to discover is who hired him to do it and why?"

She lifted up the photo and studied it as the two men sat in stunned silence; but she detected the occasional flicker of eyes - the way they exchanged glances. There was something lingering, something one of them was itching to say. Joshua opened his mouth and then closed it. He was staring at Adam intently.

"You might want to know something else," Adam said. He massaged his throat in a way Eleanor didn't like. "Jordaan didn't want to let this go either! He wasn't stupid - he guessed all that drug dealing stuff was a cover up and he knew Jake! He possibly knew him better than you did and that's the trouble! He went back to Holland, furious about the way Jake's murder had been handled. So he began his own investigation."

"Really?" Eleanor frowned. She settled the photo back on to the table. "Did he get very far? I mean - is there any chance Andries might have known something..."

"He's dead, Eleanor," Adam blurted before he could stop himself. "Jordaan Van Rosendal was killed in a hit and run accident. Police never did trace the perpetrators!"

"What?" Eleanor shrieked.

"I had to tell you," Adam's voice tolled into the room, "and that's not all. The other members of the band received death threats! One of them was so distressed, he committed suicide. It was Youf, the saxophonist - found hanged in his apartment. Matthias, the drummer, fled to the other side of the world and as for Andries - he is the only one of them who remained in Nijmegan but a fragile, damaged young man. He became something of a recluse..."

Eleanor stared into his intense dark eyes - eyes which sparked with outrage.

"I always suspected a conspiracy. Whoever these people are, they have got to be stopped. Every one of us could be under threat and this is the reason I agreed to help you..." He stabbed his finger down at Perry's enraged face. "So who is this man, Eleanor? How did you meet him and why are we *finally* talking about him after so many years?"

Eleanor pressed her eyes shut. Adam's last words had brought her nothing but horror. She had visited Nijmegan just the once - desperate to visit Jake's grave and to meet his family. They seemed subdued at the time, unwilling to discuss the murder. She put it down to grief. Yet even then, she found it a little strange how Jake's fellow band members had been absent.

"Perry was powerful in other areas," she whispered, "such as the building industry."

She took a gulp as the memories spiralled through her mind - Perry's sinister plot to overshadow the destiny of Westbourne House rose prominently.

"He was determined to seize James's property," she shivered. "It was heartbreaking! James and his kids were devastated and that was the day when Perry saw *me!*" She let out a sob. It was difficult to know where to stop as the awful visions discharged themselves.

"Take it steady, Eleanor," Adam's voice hummed softly. "We've got plenty of time."

Eleanor bit back her anguish, recalling the pivotal moment when Perry had approached her. He had always known she was living in Aldwyck and had never forgotten her secret file. There had even been an attempt to steal it.

But Perry had hissed a warning, that day: *'Don't ever dare to cross me again, Eleanor! You've already seen what I can do!'* She stared at Adam with dread.

"Finally, the worst happened - someone attempted to grab my son! We've got a pretty good idea who it was too. Nathan - some thug Perry employs as a bodyguard."

"I 'spect he's got a whole network of thugs working for him," Joshua said bitterly, "I mean who else would have issued those death threats? Or arranged Jordaan's accident?"

Eleanor's mind was reeling, unable to cast out the shock of hearing that news.

"It's unbelievable - and something else is coming back to me, something Theakston said..." the words were floating down the tunnels of her mind, taking her right back to the night of his murder. In fact, she could have borne testimony to every word that had echoed above those floorboards;

'...you're a marked man. There isn't a single place you could go where they wouldn't have followed you - not even Holland...'

"He was talking about Perry. He even warned *Charlie*, we had reason to be scared."

"Yeah, Theakston met her husband!" Joshua added guardedly.

Eleanor nodded, her hands curling into fists. "Perry's trying to muscle his way into *all* our lives and I don't think we'll ever be safe until we deal with him. This is what we pledged at our wedding - the reason I need this evidence! First, I want to prove Perry was at the press conference and these photos have given me that proof. Everything else here is a bonus and I hope you don't mind me asking - but is it possible I could file this material along with my other notes?"

"Absolutely," Adam smiled, "but if you ever need any more clues, I suggest you go back to Nijmegan. Just be careful - and I know I don't need to say this but can we agree this discussion stays secret." He gave a subtle wink, "at least for now."

"Of course," Eleanor answered, forcing a smile. "Why do you think I wore a disguise?"

She had passed through those doors disguised in the same tunic and veil, her head spinning so wildly, she staggered slightly. Perry's influence must have stretched way beyond the borders of Britain - filling her with a sense that even if they *had* escaped from London, Jake's enemies might still have caught up with them. It was as exactly as Theakston had taunted. *'He was a condemned man, Eleanor and he was never gonna escape from those who wanted him dead...'*

Eleanor sped along the pavement, eyes down - fearing the prospect, someone might see her. Just how many spies did Perry have? She knew about the Asian woman and Nathan but she could never assume there wouldn't be others. Was it possible that Holland too, had its own criminal underworld, granting Perry a whole nexus of International contacts?

Eleanor quickened her pace, keen to get back to Rosebrook. Victoria Station lurked invitingly around the corner and it was without delay, she had practically skidded across the polished floor to scan the overhead bill boards. She selected a train to Bromley.

She was glad to be out of the City. London was a place she would forever associate with menace - thoughts which finally abandoned her as she drifted into Marks and Spencer's. The rapid charge of her heart began to slow and with no further urge to rush, she bought herself a pretty summer dress. By the time Eleanor left the store, the Muslim tunic and veil were rolled up in the bottom of a carrier bag, leaving her free to step into Rosebrook with her identity restored. She resumed her normal gliding pace as she wandered towards the Community Centre and finally the almshouse, where to her even greater satisfaction, Perry's private detective seemed to have vanished.

Two weeks later, that daring trip to London seemed very much like a dream. It was 6:00 when she had unlocked the door and stepped inside. Charlie was already home. She stopped dead as her eyes fell upon him. He was seated at their lovely oak dining table, pouring over his plans; Margaret sprawled on the sofa watching television with their two adorable 5 month old tabby kittens nestling in her lap.

"You look nice," Charlie smiled up at her. "New dress?"

"Mmm," Eleanor murmured, "I've been to Bromley. How was your day?"

"Not great!" Charlie snapped - his eyes drifted back towards his architectural drawings, "mainly due to that arrogant son of mine who thinks he knows everything, yet can't seem to grasp the concept of sticking to an agreed plan! He went into a right strop. We ended up rowing!"

I know... The words had very nearly tumbled out of her mouth before she snapped it shut. She hated being so secretive, especially with her husband - his dark eyes clung to her and she knew right away, he must have sensed something. He knew her that well.

"Eli's gone to the pictures with William et al," he added, anxious to fill the pause which had stalled their dialogue. "Margaret didn't want to go - did you, love?"

"It's Robocop," Margaret scoffed without taking her eyes off the TV screen. "I hate those revolting, violent films."

"I quite agree," Eleanor sighed. "Now if you'll excuse me, I'm going upstairs to freshen up. I wouldn't mind a glass of wine, Charlie. I'll be down in a moment."

Charlie's eyes followed her as she spun from the lounge, noting the extra carrier bag - the way she hugged it to her chest. It seemed obvious she was hiding something. He was fighting against the urge to smile as he poured her a glass of rosé wine, left it on the table, then followed her up the stairs.

"So where have you really been?" he teased, poking his head round the door.

"Shut the door," Eleanor sighed, fearful they might be overheard. "Okay, there's no fooling you, is there? I've been to London."

"Did you see your solicitor?" Charlie frowned.

Eleanor shook her head. "Not this time. I did something much more exciting. Do you remember the last time we spoke to John? We discussed the idea of taking our investigation to NME..." Her features melted into a nervous smile. "I got something, Charlie and it's dynamite!"

"You're joking," he breathed, "well are you going to show it to me?"

"Of course," Eleanor consented. "Later - when I've had a chance to look at it myself." Her voice dropped to a barely audible whisper. "I've got proof of everything that happened at the press conference - but I discovered some other things…"

She took a deep swallow. It was as if her next words were entangled in her throat as she recalled the horrifying news of Jordaan and the other three band members. She couldn't bear to imagine the dangerous web she was drawing Charlie into. She reached up - tracing the strong contours of his face with her fingers, relishing the sheen of his sun-kissed skin. She felt a sudden weight in her heart.

His dark eyes remained fixed on her before he snatched hold of her hand. "Well I've got something to show you too. Remember how desperate I was to use up my last roll of film? I finally sent off the films from our honeymoon. The pictures arrived in the post today."

"Great!" Eleanor smiled, feeling her anxiety drop.

She waited for him to leave, glancing at her documents one last time before she locked them into a secure metal box. By the time she charged downstairs, she found him grinning over the photos - joined by Margaret who had abandoned her TV show as well as the kittens. Eleanor had never quite shed that overprotective feeling of love for her family, warmed by the scene; her husband and 12 year old step daughter laughing together at the table, as the kittens locked paws and started somersaulting around on the carpet in a play fight.

One month earlier, Charlie had whisked Eleanor away for a few days in Paris. Eleanor was already reminiscing over the pleasurable hours spent just ambling through the streets. Charlie had been unrestrained in his passion over the architecture. Right now, he was pointing to a row of hideous Gothic gargoyles leering over the North Tower of Notre Dame Cathedral.

"Ugh, they're so scary!" Margaret shivered. "They remind me of demons!"

"I think that was the general idea," Charlie nodded. "There was a full church service going on in there when we visited."

"It was also very beautiful," Eleanor smiled, leaning over Margaret's shoulder to look. "Did you take any pictures of the rose window, Charlie? Oh you did!"

Her eyes were drawn to a circular window glittering with an explosion of jewel coloured facets, the design so intricate, it resembled a tapestry.

She sunk into a chair next to Margaret, carefully examining each photo; from the Eiffel Tower stretching up into a cloudless blue sky to the exquisite design of each bridge captured on a boat trip along the river Seine. She found her thoughts wandering as she sipped her wine. It had been a pleasure to escape; to try and forget the pressing fears which seemed to have encroached on their lives again.

Her first concern was the children. She had been reluctant to leave them, given the lingering threat of their enemies. Fortunately, Peter Summerville had resolved that dilemma by inviting them to stay in his flat and of course, the kids were delighted - thrilled by the prospect of living in the upstairs of a

Fish and Chip shop for the next few days.

She closed her eyes as more and more memories came racing back to her; the warmth of Charlie's chuckle reminding her of one of the many conversations they had shared in the romantic seclusion of their hotel room: *'Do you think we might ever have a child, Charlie?'*

"I'm not sure, my love." His voice had been heavy with love. "Andrew might think he's an adult but he's by no means independent. I think we've definitely got our work cut out for a few years, don't you? Especially with a pair of growing teenagers..."

"I suppose you're right," she eventually conceded. They had snuggled into their king-sized bed, a luxurious cloud of softness - aware they had also sworn to look out for the Barton-Wells children. "I made a pledge to James, I would take care of them..."

She had broken off sleepily, unable to forget the trauma those kids had suffered. Yes, there were plenty of young people in their lives to look out for - even if a tiny part of her craved the possibility that she and Charlie may have a baby of their own one day.

Returning home to the kids was the least of their worries; although she was infuriated to arrive at the almshouse which Andrew had left in a right mess! Apparently, Margaret knew he'd been inviting his friends round for parties.

Elijah on the other hand, was inclined to shrug it off. At least they hadn't wrecked the place! What Eleanor didn't know was that her son guarded a secret. He knew Andrew was a dope smoker, but of a mind to keep quiet. He had already witnessed Andrew and his friends when they were stoned, unable to understand the appeal, lounging around like zombies with stupid grins on their faces. As far as he could see, it didn't make them violent and they didn't smash things up. It had only taken him a short while to realise, cannabis didn't affect people in the same way as alcohol.

There were times when Elijah *had* observed an uglier side of youth culture. Rosebrook enjoyed the reputation of being a small and tranquil town but it didn't prevent hoards of rowdy youths being discharged onto the streets at night time. He had awoken to the sounds of shattering glass and drunken brawls - cars ended up sprayed with graffiti - shop fronts vandalised. There had even been a morning when Eleanor was furious to discover an urn full of flowers tipped over, scattering her carefully planted flowers all over the grass.

Eventually, Charlie had divulged his own fears: Rosebrook was on the brink of extensive development. He knew about the lucrative piece of land at the back of the Community Centre - a derelict factory site which had captured the attention of two formidable contenders. One of them was Dominic Theakston. He had earmarked the site for a night club - a deadly enemy who never failed to strike at the heart of Eleanor's fear.

Yet their initial concern was overshadowed by someone far more sinister;

a man who had dealt a fateful blow in all their lives and that man was Peregrine Hampton. The thought of him acquiring the plot was a ghastly prospect, especially for William and Avalon. Perry was undoubtedly bitter, in so much as he had failed to get his hands on their father's land. Charlie suspected this was his way of making them suffer; to encroach on their neighbourhood *as well as* make himself a tidy profit. It was rumoured he was planning to develop an estate of exclusive, luxury homes.

As far as they could glean however, Westbourne House was picking up bookings - despite the fact that Perry had been refused planning permission to expand quite as quickly as he'd hoped. Thus the traditional country hotel continued to trade in much the same manner as its former proprietor, James Barton-Wells, had intended. Further more, they had started advertising for staff and this happened to be the one twist of fate which had drawn Eleanor's attention to the enigmatic Asian woman - or Alesha, as she would ultimately discover.

****

July 1987

In the aftermath of the honeymoon, Eleanor had gradually reconnected with her friends. It was with a sense of irony that the one woman she found herself spending more time with than anyone was Della. The two of them had shared a mercurial relationship. To think, it had begun in an East End brothel - then several years later, she had been astounded to bump into her in some rough neighbourhood where Charlie's family had lived. She had often wondered if their fate was entwined - especially when Della defended her from the scourge of Whaley's lies. It was a time when Della had finally confessed to the bleakness of her life - a notion which inspired Peter to suggest she should apply for a council house.

Three months down the line, Della had moved to Rosebrook. She was determined to protect her daughter, Lara, who had been drawn into the ranks of some fearsome gang and fallen pregnant. Della had never wanted her to throw her life away - and once she'd arranged a discreet abortion, she insisted Lara was to finish her education.

Once the school holidays got underway however, Lara started playing up again - ravaged by hormonal mood swings, ripped apart by the loss of her baby. Della had been unprepared for the violence of her emotions - until eventually she turned to Eleanor in despair.

The two of them had been enjoying a coffee outside one of Rosebrook's enchanting pavement cafés.

"What that girl needs is a job!" Della spluttered. "I'm gonna drag her to the job centre myself if I have to - 'fore we end up killin' each other!"

Eleanor had been delighted to accompany her, where Della had stumbled across the most interesting card in the hotel and catering section. Westbourne House had several vacancies for chamber maids and at £2.50 an hour, the pay was temptingly good.

Eleanor's first reaction was horror. "She can't work there! The family who run that place are evil!"

"But don't you see, it's perfect!" Della argued in a conspiratorial whisper. "My Lara's got eyes in the back of her head. She'll get you any juicy gossip you want!"

Eleanor very nearly divulged, they had Elliot for that role - only they hadn't heard from him in weeks. Lara's reaction had in fact, taken her very much by surprise. She could still picture her now, wallowing in the almshouse smiling to herself - eyes cast down as she painted her nails in alternate shades of black and shocking pink.

"I'm well up for it!" she grinned. "There ain't nowhere else I'm gonna earn £50 a week!" To someone who had spent a lifetime growing up in poverty, it seemed a fortune

"Okay," Eleanor relented, "just *please* be careful! Mr Hampton is not a nice man and his son is vile. Whatever you do, just try and avoid any contact with them."

III

Lara was recruited into the ranks of Westbourne House along with two other girls, leaving Della unwavering in her conviction that she had done the right thing. In the weeks that followed, Lara rose to the challenge - blown away by the stunning beauty of Westbourne House. They employed her for 5 days a week on alternative shifts. This in turn, allowed her to scrutinise the management of the hotel at different times of day and to get to know her employers better.

Occasionally, she dropped in at the almshouse to report her findings. It appeared to be Perry's wife, Rowena, who held the highest authority. Lara couldn't deny, she had been intrigued by this elegant woman who flaunted designer suits and carried an air of grandeur - schmoozing around guests and supervising the restaurant. Perry was often seen strutting around in the bar; a somewhat powerful looking man who struck Lara as frosty and business like. Yet she had only seen the son twice. The first time, she had been seized by an urge to duck behind the elegant staircase she was polishing. He had flounced through the door unannounced, cloaked from head to toe in tight, glossy black motorcycle leathers; accompanied by some menacing looking character - one who the other maids disclosed was his body guard.

Within that first week, Lara had identified all three members of the Hampton family without engaging in any contact. Everything had ticked along nicely for a few weeks - until that momentous day which had ruined everything.

She had only just finished cleaning the guest rooms - footsteps dragging as she padded along the carpeted hallway. She greeted a few new arrivals on route, before innocently wandering into the central section. If only she hadn't lingered! Yet the views from the windows were so magnificent, she couldn't help but savour the lush, wooded hills as they rolled down towards the pretty village below. She had never expected to bump into Ben - a little slow to notice him sauntering out from their family living quarters.

He bore down on her with a demeanour of arrogance; so typical of a young stock broker who had enjoyed an excellent day's trading - bottle of champagne tucked under one arm as his eyes latched onto her face.

"Well hello," he drawled, swinging towards the staircase.

Lara felt instantly self-conscious; dainty and dark-skinned, she possessed a wide forehead combined with high cheekbones which drew attention to her appealing brown eyes. She had been dressed in a typical maid's outfit - a simple navy dress worn with a frilly, white apron.

"Done my room, have you?" he smiled, stepping out in front of her.

Lara hesitated, her eyes dancing from side to side, searching for an escape route. Ben had planted his hand on the newel post, purposefully blocking her path.

"Yeah, this m-morning, Sir," she stammered quickly. "I'm done for the day…"

"Is that so?" Ben muttered. His eyes travelled down the length of her body. "Well don't go. I made a mint today, darling and in the mood for a little celebration. I bought some Dom Perignon…" He flaunted the bottle before her eyes. "Come and share it with me!"

Without waiting for an answer, he slid his arm around her shoulders and unexpectedly steered her across the landing. Lara blinked. Seconds later, she found herself propelled into his sumptuous bedroom, too nervous to protest.

She watched in disbelief as Ben lowered the champagne onto the bedside table. He flipped off his jacket, revealing an expensive-looking shirt worn with red braces - they were stretched tightly over his shoulders. In fact, he was in pretty good shape - wide shoulders sculpted with long, lean muscles. Lara felt her throat run dry, fearing where this was leading.

"I'm sorry, Sir, b-but I really gotta go," she protested. "I'll miss my bus…"

"No need to worry," Ben snapped, "I'll drive you home."

Lara glanced towards the door, knowing she should leave but he exuded such authority - a situation which rendered her speechless.

"Come on, sweetheart, relax," he added, dropping himself onto the bed.

She forced a smile, almost tempted to play along for a bit. There was no denying he was good looking - silky, white blonde hair flopping over a high forehead, matched by perfect features.

She had never wanted to make him angry. Yet she could no longer ignore the predatory bore of his gaze as he patted the spot right next to him - the shocking way he ran his thumb seductively over his belt buckle. Lara felt a sudden wave of fear.

"I-I can't," she finally found the strength to whisper. "I-I'm going home!" She had already begun to back towards the door

"Are you refusing me?" Ben retorted and straight away, she detected the ice in his tone.

"I'm sorry, Mr Hampton, but your father employs me as a cleaner n-not your p-personal maid."

His pale blue eyes flickered like warning lights. "Oh come on!" he sneered. "Clubs I visit in soho are full of girls like you - you little black bitches are gagging for it!"

"That's it," Lara gasped, fumbling for the door knob. "I ain't puttin' up with no racism…"

Ben had already sprung to his feet. He grabbed her arm - the violence in his expression unmistakable. "You're going to regret this," he whispered in hatred, "you nigger slut!"

Lara tore herself from his grip with a cry, hurling herself towards the door. Her hands shook as she practically wrenched it off its hinges before she charged downstairs.

Elliot had been shocked to discover her in the kitchens, her face wet with tears. But then again, James's former butler was fully aware of Ben's flawed personality - never able to forget the time when he had unleashed a fearful campaign against Avalon.

"Shh," he whispered gently. "Don't cry. Don't let him get to you…"

"What's going on?" a female voice boomed across the kitchen. "Lara Baker, what are you doing here? You should have finished your duties for today."

"Yeah and my duties don't include pleasurin' the boss's son!" Lara spluttered before she could stop herself, "and I don't like bein' insulted!"

Irene Fisher, a formidable battle-axe in her forties, was employed as Perry's general staff manager. Yet with new guests arriving, the last thing she needed was some hysterical chamber maid creating a scene - especially if it concerned Perry's son.

"I think, we'd better have a word with Mr Hampton, don't you?" she said coldly.

Lara stared at Elliot in panic. His gentle blue eyes betrayed a look of sympathy as Mrs Fisher guided Lara somewhat roughly towards the exit.

Lara was trembling at the prospect of facing Perry; an intensely cold man who's authoritarian manner had a way of hammering people into submission. From the moment she stepped into his office, his pale grey eyes raked over her - his florid face set like stone as Mrs Fisher repeated her allegations.

"Surely Ben's not the first man to make a pass at you, my dear?" Perry sneered. "He was probably just flirting with you…"

"He insulted me, Mr Hampton," Lara bleated, determined to stand her ground. "What's worse, he was makin' racist comments."

"I think you're overreacting," Perry said icily. "I very much doubt if my son's comments were *intended* to be racist."

"Excuse me!" Lara breathed in outrage, "but what part of callin' me a 'black bitch' a-and a 'nigger slut' ain't racist?"

Perry on the other hand, had a long history of knowing how to manipulate people. The glitter in his eyes intensified as he held her gaze. He extracted a wallet from his jacket. "I see no point in continuing your employment then," he taunted her. "I'll give you a months' wages - but in return, I expect you to keep silent!"

"Silent?" Lara whispered. "I could report Ben to the Race Relations Board, man…"

"You will do no such thing!" Perry hissed, rising to his feet. "Tell me - was there anyone else present when my son *allegedly* made these comments?" Lara froze, bolt-eyed. "Thought not!" he added softly. "You on the other hand, Miss Baker, are a slack worker or so I've been informed by Mrs Fisher here! Is it not true that on more than one occasion, she has pulled you up for the dawdling pace of your work?'

"Yes, b-but…" Lara mumbled.

"So you have already received a warning, young lady," Perry interrupted, "which means I am perfectly within my rights to fire you *without compensation!* Now take your wages and leave!" It was with no further argument, he had seized her hand, pressed several notes into her palm and directed her towards the door.

The bus journey back to Rosebrook seemed very long, that day, as Lara perched numbly in her seat, staring out of the window. Silent tears escaped down her cheeks. Though by the time she arrived at the almshouse, she was angry.

Eleanor was relieved no-one else had been home as Lara began pacing around the living room. Her story came out in torrents - punctuated with expletives. Eleanor, knowing exactly how dangerous Ben could be, said nothing - resigned to let her rant on until she eventually ran out of steam.

"Fucking arseholes," Lara finished, snapping to a standstill in front of the window.

"Lara, I'm so sorry," Eleanor croaked. "You can't say I didn't warn you. You're lucky you escaped, he might have hurt you…"

For several seconds, she had stood there fuming - letting all the hurt and humiliation drain out of her; her eyes inadvertently drawn to the silver VW

Scirocco pulling into the curb - to the ravishing Asian woman inside. Her eyes were lowered as she appeared to scribble something down. Lara spun from the window.

"Hey! I know her!" she hissed, "seen her at Westbourne House!" Her eyes lit up with sudden intrigue. "She and old Hampton seem *very* cosy. They pretend to be all business like but you should see the way she looks at 'im - I bet he's shagging her…"

"Step away from the window, Lara, now!" Eleanor ordered curtly.

Her tone disguised a warning which compelled her to obey. Then it all came flooding back.

Eleanor too had spotted the car; the first time, barely discernible beneath the shade of horse chestnut trees. Occasionally it lurked outside the Community Centre. As for the woman - she had assumed she was simply another community Liaison Officer.

"Who d'ya reckon she is?" Lara whispered numbly.

"I'm not sure," Eleanor sighed, lowering herself shakily into an armchair, "but if she's working for Perry and she's hanging around outside my home, it can only mean one thing. She must be spying for him."

The cogs in her mind kept turning. It all made perfect sense. This whole fearful scenario had begun from the moment Eleanor had clashed with Perry at Westbourne House. He had known she was living locally - his son had been visiting the 'Olde House at Home,' a memory which made her shudder. He had been just as vile - the flirting, the derogatory remarks. As if any girl would find that a turn on. Yet it was obvious Perry would keep her under careful scrutiny. She couldn't avoid thinking about those trips to London - the day she had recognised Nathan…

"Tell me," she murmured dreamily, "have you ever come across Nathan, Ben's security guard? Tall, nasty-looking guy - got one of those pencil thin beards…"

"Oh him!" Lara spat. "Once or twice! 'Cept he ain't got no beard and he's as bald as a coot. Why do you ask?"

"A bald man who wears shades?" Eleanor whispered to herself. She felt the spread of fear in her veins. "William's seen him - loitering around outside *his* house…"

"William?" Lara frowned.

"William Barton-Wells," Eleanor shivered. "He goes to your school, Lara, good looking boy with golden-brown hair - the one Margaret's got a thumping great crush on."

"Oh, you don't mean 'Posh Boy,'" Lara grinned tactlessly.

"Don't call him that," Eleanor whispered, coiling her arms around herself. "You may think he's some rich kid, born with a silver spoon in his mouth, but you've got no idea what he's been through… Nathan really hurt those kids. I don't think you realise just how evil these people are."

All traces of Lara's smile had faded, her brows drawing into a frown. "Perhaps I'd better go."

"No, stay!" Eleanor urged. She gazed deeply into her confused dark eyes. "The fact is, Lara, I'm telling you this to warn you! You've seen this lady liaising with Perry? Well there's a good chance she may have spotted you too. If she sees you now, word will get back. Yet we have the advantage. You've blown her cover and I can't thank you enough..."

"Okay, I get it," Lara agreed, nibbling her lip. "So why they spyin' on you?"

"I know something about Perry," Eleanor whispered fearfully, "and I need to find out more - but preferably without them knowing what I'm up to."

From thenceforth, Eleanor kept her on the radar. In the weeks that followed, she made a mental note whenever she appeared in the neighbourhood. She carefully chose the precise hour to step outside and water her plants - and without staring at her directly, she had felt a tug of caution *every time* that silver car had hovered on the shore of her vision.

It was in the first week of August, she received her first communication from Joshua Merriman. It had taken him six weeks to track down Adam Morrison - and with no wish to delay their meeting, Eleanor was driven by a powerful urge to evade this woman. So for the next few days, she had studied Shajeda.

It was in the privacy of her own home, she had posed in front of a full length mirror, imitating her movements - from her unhurried way of moving to the graceful tilt of her head. Finally, she had drawn both Shajeda as well as Peter into her confidence.

"I'm being watched," Eleanor whispered as the three of them took refuge in Peter's office. "I think this lady must be a private detective, Shajeda and I don't mean to be disrespectful - but I have got to get myself to London in disguise."

Eventually, they agreed to a plan: Shajeda would linger inside the Community Centre, whilst Eleanor - dressed in an identical Abaya dress and veil - would leave the premises at 3.00 in the afternoon, the usual time her colleague finished work. Shajeda was happy to remain inside the office adjoining the Information Centre - wait another hour - then eventually make her way home via a footpath at the back of the communal gardens; a plan which had been successful in its execution.

Reality blinked as Eleanor snapped herself out of her reverie. Charlie was still smiling over the photographs; the kittens had finally abandoned their game - miaowing in the kitchen, hassling Margaret for their food. Eleanor let out a sigh, yearning to look at those transcripts again. But she was reluctant to show them to Charlie, knowing they concealed a chilling truth. She hung her head, biting her lip. She had never divulged *everything* to him.

If she ever had explained Theakston's *true* role in Jake's killing, there was no telling what he might do. She knew Charlie. He was inclined to be a little hot-headed - never able to forget the horrific scenario Dominic had threatened for her son, if she dared mention his name. To think, her accusations were recorded in those very transcripts - a secret so lethal, it was a testimony which would bring nothing but danger...

Eleanor had no idea that in a very short time, her fears were about to be vindicated; an invisible force of acrimony was already rising and where the historic stone walls of Westbourne House were about to conceal a very clandestine meeting.

Chapter 2

I

Alesha had known something was wrong. She had lingered in her car for an extra 30 minutes, feeling her agitation rise. Where was Eleanor? Why hadn't she emerged from the Community Centre as one would have expected by now? It was out of pure frustration, she used a public telephone to ring the office - curious to learn if Eleanor Bailey was around. The news that she had already left brought an icy sensation of fear crawling over her.

"Oh shit," she muttered to herself, settling the phone back into its cradle. *How the hell was she going to tell Perry?*

By the time an hour had passed, she had left in a state of panic, slowly pushing her car towards London where she knew Perry awaited her. Her journey was fairly straight forward until she reached the other side of Bromley. She found herself immersed in a swelling tide of cars - struggling against the urge to blare her horn. Yet all the while she was stuck in traffic, it gave her time to think - as well as delay her dreaded meeting. Alesha shuddered, painfully aware that Eleanor had tricked her.

For two months she had been watching her, now fully acquainted with her day to day routine. On the days she worked at the hospital, she didn't need to hang around. Nurses were governed by a rigid timetable. No, it was Eleanor's voluntary work at the Community Centre which intrigued her; from helping some old lady in the tea bar to maintaining the gardens. On a day like this, Eleanor should have left at around 4.00. Yet she hadn't appeared and of even greater worry, where could she have sneaked off to?

At last, Alesha reached an elegant square in Pimlico - location of Perry's London residence. He had summoned her on a day when he knew his son wouldn't be around. For a moment Alesha could have smiled, guessing the secrecy behind his motive.

"Alesha," Perry breathed, drawing her inside.

She offered him a sweet smile, anchoring her thoughts to Rowena - anything to distract her mind from this nail-biting situation which had emerged. She watched with pleasure as Perry extracted two crystal wine goblets from an overhead cabinet, relieved to find him in a good mood.

Despite the fact, they shared a professional relationship, he had drawn her into his confidence with regards his marriage. Though it hadn't taken long to form her own opinion of Rowena; who she considered to be materialistic and forever clambering towards a higher social status. As if this beautiful, regency-style house in Pimlico wasn't enough! How hard Perry must have worked to acquire such a property. Yet Rowena had always wanted more. In her quest to be the envy of her friends, she had developed a yearning to escape the city in favour of an exquisite country house.

Their relationship over the years had become gradually more platonic. Perry confessed to having enjoyed the pleasures of a mistress tucked away in some exclusive Mayfair apartment. But in 1985, he had stumbled across the perfect property: Westbourne House - a building so old, it was starting show signs of structural decay. The owner had apparently been some doddering old man in his 60's. Rowena had yearned the opportunity of taking over the management of the hotel. Even better, it was surrounded by masses of land - located in an idyllic corner of Kent, soon to become a highly lucrative area for commuters. So Perry too, had grown obsessed with the idea of exploiting this situation for his own ends.

His original plan to bankroll the restoration had backfired. So Perry had set out to ruin the man; a plan which had involved several months of Machiavellian scheming - where Rowena had refused to allow him into her bed until he succeeded. Alesha couldn't help wondering why she had such a hold over him. Though she was never likely to get to the root of it.

"Sit down. Won't you take off your coat," Perry murmured, ushering her into his splendid lounge. He placed the glasses on a side table. "So how are things?"

Alesha took a deep swallow of wine. "Traffic was terrible."

"Anything else to report?" Perry smiled.

Alesha felt a grip of anxiety - she could not bear to confess to her failure. "Same as ever," she sighed. "What is your interest in that Bailey woman? Her life is so boring!"

"You know damn well," Perry replied harshly. "Those people are my enemies! Charles Bailey being one of them - not to mention the Barton-Wells pair who undoubtedly blame me for their father's death."

His face tightened visibly, giving way to a magenta flush. It was a look which turned Alesha cold. She stroked his hand. "So?"

"They are all connected to that Chapman woman," Perry barked.

"Bailey," Alesha corrected him.

"Whatever!" Perry whispered through gritted teeth. "The fact is, she is up to something! Remember the last time she saw her solicitor? Even *you* said she was in there for well over an hour! A little too long to be changing her will…" He broke off, fixing her with his intense stare - his eyes narrowed. "No, I suspect it had a lot more to do with that *secret file* of hers. My gut instinct tells me she's been adding to it. I've suspected it ever since she saw me in the bar."

Alesha took another gulp of wine, her heart pounding. "I see," she muttered softly.

"So you're absolutely sure she never went anywhere else today, are you?" Perry pressed.

She held his gaze steadily. "Absolutely," she said with conviction.

"Good girl," Perry nodded, his arm slithering around her shoulder. "Now drink your wine. I have something for you."

Alesha said nothing as she drained her glass although a small part of her had already guessed where this was leading. He had drawn the curtains. The light in the room was subtle - a warm golden glow had spread across the walls, leaving his face half masked in shadow. She felt his smile as he reached down and extracted a small carrier bag from the side of the sofa. He placed it gently in her lap.

Alesha peeped inside before her fingers sunk into the luxurious silk - pulling out a beautiful camisole, no doubt from one of the more expensive lingerie boutiques in London. It was a rich, plum red with a scalloped edging of black lace. It was still attached to its tiny hanger along with a matching G-string.

"It's beautiful," Alesha murmured.

"Put it on," Perry ordered softly, his voice thickening like treacle.

"Now?" she smiled up at him.

His hand slid around her jaw, tilting her face. "Yes - now, my darling. I have an important meeting at Westbourne House tonight, including some significant *allies* from the past. I need to mentally prepare myself - and I want to be able to picture you in that underwear..."

She saw no reason to resist him. Perry watched with immense pleasure as she peeled off her jacket before hastily removing her clothes - no doubt, devouring the sight of her youthful 28 year old body. The gleam of her fawn coloured skin looked particularly alluring against the burgundy red silk. She turned provocatively, conscious of the lacy G-string nestling in the cleave of her bottom, giving it the appearance of a firm, ripe peach. Seconds later, Perry had wrestled her down on to the carpet, manipulating her onto all fours before he ravished her greedily.

Alesha kept her eyes closed, grateful she didn't have to look at his face. She had so hated lying to him! She knew he could be ruthless and predatory, yet he was powerful. He paid her handsomely for her work as a private detective and the thrill of being drawn into an illicit affair was even more exciting, knowing he was betraying his pampered wife. It was after all, her obsession with Westbourne House that had ultimately put him at risk.

II

Unbeknown to Alesha, Perry harboured the same opinion. If it hadn't been for his passion to procure James's property, he might never have come into contact with that Chapman girl. He had learned of her existence in the village, shortly after he had invited the Barton-Wells family to dinner. In those days, she had possessed an air of vulnerability - a young woman living alone in a caravan with her son... he was convinced they had the ability to control her.

These thoughts prickled him as he swept along the winding country road towards Aldwyck, drawn through a familiar tunnel of trees which robbed his surroundings of light. Perry switched on his headlights. At the same time, he was buzzing - eager to meet up with the same two men who had been involved in the conspiracy from the start and where that last satisfying hour with Alesha had uplifted him, fuelling him with a renewed sense of power. By the time he steered his car into the driveway, it was dark. A thick bank of cloud had crawled across the sky and the air felt damp. He was gratified to see a glow of light behind the mullioned windows and stepping from his car, he released a shudder in anticipation of the night ahead.

It was 10.00 at night when the first of his guests arrived; a night when he knew the hotel would be quiet with only a few guests in residence. Most had retired to bed anyway. Rowena meanwhile, hovered in the restaurant, conversing with their talented new chef - he had left instructions with Elliot that the library was strictly out of bounds for the rest of the evening.

A sturdy knock resounded from the hall. He dismissed Elliot to the bar before striding across to answer it. Yet nothing could prepare him for the impact of seeing this towering figure of a man now dominating the doorway. He wore a long black raincoat. Its voluminous storm flap fluttered around his broad shoulders like a cape. Perry studied his face, observing the granite hard features beneath his cap of dark blonde hair. The man did not smile - and for a few seconds, Perry was stalled by the heat of his intense glare.

"Mr Theakston," he greeted him pleasantly. "How good of you to come."

"Hello Perry," the man snapped, seizing his outstretched hand. "Well - this is a surprise!" He sauntered casually into the entrance hall without waiting for an invitation.

"Please, this way," Perry muttered, steering him towards the library. "This room is more private. We will not be disturbed."

"Good," Dominic whispered icily, "'cos you might as well know, *Mr Hampton*, this ain't a meeting I'd normally choose to be part of! So what's going on? Far as I'm concerned, this business was put to bed years ago and I don't like dredging up the past."

"I respect your feelings," Perry said carefully, "but we *need* to talk. We each have our own personal goals - and there's only one person who stands in our way."

There was an electric pause. Dominic stood as still as a stature, drinking in his surroundings; seeing a cosy room whose walls were decorated a deep, burgundy red and terracotta brown. They were lined with bookshelves - volumes of encyclopedias stood alongside ranks of leather-bound books. The furniture possessed a priceless, antique quality - from the polished side tables, to the carefully arranged rectangles of leather Chesterfield seating.

"I've always adored this room," Perry sighed. "Won't you sit down?"

He watched as Dominic sank into a chair.

Perry switched on a table lamp - it illuminated his surroundings like the glow of a torch, encouraging him to dim the main light.

Seconds later, he was alerted to the door again. He offered Dominic a drink before momentarily abandoning him to attend to his next guest. Perry was not so cautious to exclude his butler, this time. Robin Whaley had attended Westbourne House on many occasions.

"Robin," his deep voice purred, "come through…" he seized the man's hand in a firm handshake. "I was just about to order drinks from the bar. Dominic has already arrived."

Once Perry had issued a request for coffee, a decanter of red wine and a Scotch whisky, they wandered back to the library where the other man awaited them. He exuded an air of menace as he lounged in his chair, head inclined, eyes dark as flints as they seared into Robin. For several moments, they exchanged pleasantries - but it wasn't long before Dominic became restless; the tiny flashes of movement were already starting to make Robin nervous as he shifted position in his chair, sipped his scotch, then finally picked up his coffee cup.

"Nice establishment, Perry," his soft voice broke into the lull of silence. "Never imagined you'd end up in the hotel game - thought your interest was in property."

"It is," Perry said smugly, "especially in a boom area like this. It was my wife who influenced me. She simply adored this house and location…"

"Yeah, well let's get down to business shall we?" Dominic interrupted. "Why did you summon us here, Perry?"

"You know why," Perry replied, keeping his voice steady. "Our connection lies in the past and I am sorry to 'dredge it up' but it is time to address our feelings about that Chapman woman - as well as the issue of her *secret file.*"

"I see," Dominic whispered, "well maybe you should explain why you're so worried!"

"I'm like a bloodhound," Perry retorted, "my intuition is telling me something's afoot. Eleanor is gathering allies including people from the village and the Community Centre. Two of them are former residents of this house, who already harbour vengeful feelings. Her husband, Charles, is also an enemy - the two of them have been embarking on several trips to London, recently…"

"So?" Dominic shrugged.

"To see her solicitor!" Perry finished. "I sensed an undercurrent of activity ever since she recognised me. She told Robin we had reason to be scared…" His voice adopted a bitter chill. "I took that as a veiled threat, gentlemen."

"What, you reckon she's gonna start stirring things?" Dominic sneered. "You sure you ain't being paranoid!"

"Perhaps we should look at this another way," Robin intervened, pale hands folded in his lap as he lured Dominic's attention. "We all want to carve our own niche in the business world. It would therefore be in our best interests to eliminate any *threat* which still exists."

"Exactly," Perry reinforced, fixing Dominic with his stare, "and I for one, am tired of looking over my shoulder, never knowing when she is about to strike."

"Yeah, so you said," Dominic scoffed. "Wasn't that the whole point of Robin finding me in the first place? What else are you hoping to achieve, Perry?"

"You know damn well!" Perry bridled, dismayed by his attitude. "Many years ago, Eleanor Chapman or *Bailey* as she's now known, compiled a secret diary; details of her boyfriend's murder. Further more, she disclosed that every single one of us was mentioned."

"And?" Dominic kept pressing him.

"I need to know what it says," Perry finished darkly, "in other words, it is essential we get our hands on it. Regrettably, there is only one way we will ever achieve that goal…"

"You're gonna go after her son again, aren't you?" Dominic hissed. "D'you think I didn't hear about your first bodged attempt? And as for you, Whaley…" he turned to him in anger, "you proper set me up there didn't you, you sly bastard?"

"What?" Robin gasped, hands shaking as he lowered his glass, "what are you talking about?"

"You got me to sneak up on her," he whispered in anger, "to remind her of *that threat!* Said you wanted her out of Rosebrook," his eyes spun savagely back towards Perry. "Never said anything about abducting her boy, did you? Hoping she'd pin it on me…"

"No, Dominic," Perry lied. He took a deep swallow of wine. "Didn't Robin explain? I intended to take matters into my own hands. Your role was to scare her back to her caravan, nothing more, which you did and I'm grateful for that."

"Bullshit!" Dominic spat. "Told you I wanted no further part in this! It's by the skin of me teeth I clung on the right to have access to me own kids - an' this could have fucked it up for me…"

"If you *must* know, she pointed the finger at my security guard," Perry persisted. "There is no way you were ever implicated."

"Right," Dominic snapped, shifting in his chair again, "'cos I ain't gonna be involved in no plot which involves Eleanor's kid, d'you hear?"

"Calm down, Dominic," Robin begged. "This is *not* the reason for this meeting."

"So what's your take on this?" Dominic rounded on him.

"I have to agree with Perry," Robin said silkily. "I fear Eleanor's file could destroy us and I wish no harm to her son but if holding him to ransom is the only way we can get her to surrender it…"

There was a long and chilling pause. The windows were shrouded in heavy velvet drapes but no-one could ignore the sound of the wind as it lashed against the panes. The light in the room flickered. Perry sat bolt upright, his florid face draining of colour.

"J-just the electrics playing up," he shivered, grabbing for his wine glass. "We've been having a few problems. I do apologise."

Dominic smirked. "What's up, Perry? Don't tell me this place is haunted." Perry glared at him. But it seemed he had not quite finished. "I dunno what you're worried about. Whatever's written in that file, it's just words! She can't prove nothing!"

"You don't know that," Robin said in a voice which reflected Perry's anxiety.

"I do," Dominic insisted. "There ain't a shred of evidence that proves, any of us were involved in Jansen's death - not even me. Cleared of that murder 14 years ago, I was. I told you how I felt about dragging up the past and I'm *not* turning back to crime. I've got too much to lose."

Perry's eyes turned frosty. "No one's suggesting that - though I confess, your connections in the criminal underworld would have been useful."

"Seems you've got your son to help you there," Dominic answered in a tone that was equally cold. "Did you know he joined my gym? Him and that leather-clad goon you employ as a bodyguard. Been quizzing me about organised crime - asking me if I'm still involved. Sounds to me like they're looking for an in road."

"Really?" Perry muttered, feeling a unexpected charge of excitement. "I expect he's just curious. I can't imagine my son turning to crime - he earns far too much as a stockbroker."

"Perhaps you should ask him yourself then," Dominic added. "Now cut the crap. Why *did* you invite me here? I severed my connections with crime and I'm fucked if I'm playing any part in grabbing that Jansen kid. So what do you want from me?"

"It's perfectly simple," Robin purred. "You've expressed an interest in the land behind the Community Centre - but have you looked at it recently?"

"Not since the day of the wedding," Dominic smirked.

"Any chance you could revisit the site from time to time?" Robin added guardedly. "Eleanor is bound to see you - she spends a lot of time in those gardens. A few more sightings would definitely make her feel a little more *nervous.*"

"It's not much to ask, Dominic," Perry added. "People are at their weakest when they feel vulnerable. It will give us an advantage…" The silence hung heavily. There was a subtle dimming of the lights again but this time, Perry ignored it. His eyes were pinned on Dominic. "It worked for me once - when we were plotting to get this house. We knew the owner couldn't restore it without my help, yet he opposed me. So we worked on his daughter,

Avalon...”

Dominic became very tense, his expression stony. “Who?” he demanded.

“Avalon Barton-Wells,” Perry whispered. “Ben was obsessed with her. She refused his advances, so he set out to terrify her instead.”

“She visits me at the Council,” Robin smiled. “She seems very close to Eleanor. It is only a matter of time before she reveals something she may not intend to.”

Dominic narrowed his eyes - it was as if something in his mind had just clicked.

“So what’s the deal with the land?” he frowned. “Come on, spill the beans - what are you two actually planning?”

“This is the second reason we are having this meeting,” Robin answered, unfazed by his distrust. “The time has come for you to submit a planning application. The council need to consider the best use for the land; residential or commercial. There’s likely to be strong opposition, either way and I will try to gauge everyone’s reaction. In the meantime, I’m in heavy consultation with Peter Summerville. His idea to set up a housing trust has appealed to the council. Whatever stance they take, there is little point in bidding for the land unless you can develop it as you wish.”

“Seems fair enough,” Perry nodded approvingly. “Do you agree with that, Dominic?”

“Okay,” he muttered, a cynical look carving its way into his features. “So you want me to have another scout around the land and that’s it?”

“Indeed,” Perry said in a voice of iron, “and keep an eye out for Eleanor! It will do no harm to approach her - drip a few words in her ears. The sooner she realises we’re on to her, the better.”

“Yeah, maybe,” Dominic sighed, his stance unwavering.

Perry’s knuckles tightened around his glass. To his regret, he felt the burn of anger in his face and there was nothing he could do about it. “Just what exactly is your problem, Theakston?” he snapped. “What gives you the right to be so damned cocky?”

Dominic knocked back the last of his scotch and with a smile of amusement which suggested he had the whip hand, he lowered it calmly to the table. “Listen, Perry - I ain’t gonna let this go. If you find any evidence, she’s a threat, well... I warned her once and I’ll warn her again; but you’re not my fucking paymasters. In fact, you ain’t got no hold over me whatsoever!”

Perry closed his eyes, forcing himself to remain calm. It was out of pure desperation, he started picturing Alesha. It seemed to do the trick, bringing an element of bliss to his tortured mind.

“There is no other choice,” he spluttered. “We’re in this together...”

“That’s where you’re wrong,” Dominic taunted. “Far as I’m concerned, I don’t have to play any more. You started this, Perry - maybe *you* should finish it.”

He started to rise - but Perry held one more trump card.

"Now you listen to me," he hissed. "You may think we have no hold over you - but I have something to say that will make you think again!"

Dominic froze and turned, just as Perry fired him a chilling stare.

"Whether you agree or not, Dominic, we *cannot* run the risk of being exposed. So you are not going to wriggle your way out of this - because if ever her testimony goes public, I will swear to the court that we commissioned *your gang* to carry out Jansen's killing. A fact which will no doubt, be corroborated in her file!"

Dominic's teeth flashed. "You're threatening me?"

"I'm afraid so," Perry finished coldly, "though I sincerely hope it won't come to that. So I suggest you play ball. As Robin says, you *could* go and have another look at that land."

"Why not carry out a survey?" Robin placated him. "Try and get some estimate as to how much the land is worth."

"And make sure you talk to the girl," Perry elaborated with undisguised malice. "Because when we do eventually corner that boy of hers - I want her to be scared."

They left together and Perry watched them go, relieved they had finally reached some compromise. Robin was right about Theakston. He had always been a cocky, arrogant bastard, forgetting it was powerful men like him who had forked out an enviable sum for his services. It was close to Midnight when he locked the doors of Westbourne House. Finally, the hall lay in silence.

The lights were still flickering but there was no storm. The black and white checkered floor tiles seemed to sway before his eyes and for a second, Perry felt giddy. He didn't like to confess how much this place unnerved him at times. His gaze crept towards the staircase where James had tumbled to his death - he had never quite got over the words that had spluttered from Avalon's shaking lips, *'I hope he comes back and haunts you!'*

Perry clenched his teeth, refusing to buckle under a burden of superstition; but the wavering lights were starting to bother him. It seemed to signify the presence of some 'haunting' energy triggered by James's spirit. There had been nightmares: dreams about James and even more chilling, dreams about Jake. Perry wished he could banish them but he couldn't. They crouched in the dark passages of his mind, waiting to spring - a regrettable aftermath of Avalon's curse, exacerbated by a tape he had found in the Orangerie. Perry shuddered, unable to forget his fearful reaction - the hideous prospect that Jake's song had drawn his spirit here.

He wandered a little further along the corridor. He would find no comfort in sleep just yet. His brain was still smouldering and he needed a brandy.

He momentarily admired his front lounge - a spacious room, furnished with their own choice of furniture. He quaffed back a brandy, then settled into a chair to ponder the finer details of the discussion. So Benjamin had joined Atlas Leisure - and yet Dominic had made it perfectly clear that he had no intention of resuming his dealings with organised crime. Maybe he was right. What if Ben really was seeking a route into the criminal underworld? It might even work out to his advantage; especially if his son could acquire a few contacts. Perry smiled, warmed by this revelation, just as the heat of the brandy spread through his chest. Perhaps the evening hadn't been such a disappointment after all.

III

Ironically, just a few miles away, Dominic's mind was hurtling towards the same topic as he sped towards London, seething with fury.

"Bastard!" he snarled under his breath, "fucking arrogant, puffed up piece of shit!"

It had taken all his inner strength to stop himself from slamming a fist into Perry's loathsome face - and how dare he wave that ultimatum!

He charged through the tunnel of trees towards the main road, where his main beams cut through the darkness like search lights. He had been desperate to get away and spend some quality time with his girlfriend, Pippa. Except he was so angry - it wouldn't be fair on her. She would be asleep by now. No, the next best thing he could do was to get himself up to Soho and find himself a high class prostitute. It was only as he kept driving, he had started thinking about his gym; a time when Ben Hampton and his sinister companion had first signed up as members.

He had questioned their motives. Why Swanley when there were plenty of gyms in London? Ben made some excuse, he didn't want to be recognised. Swanley was more rural and only a stone's throw from his parents' 'country residence' in Aldwyck. But Nathan disturbed him, bringing back a dim flicker of recognition. There was something about his face, he associated with his days in the criminal underworld. He planned to find out who he really was - but in the meantime, he accepted their membership, happy to be engaged as their personal fitness instructor - not that Nathan looked as if he needed it.

He was already a brute of a man, muscle bound from head to toe. Ben on the other hand, possessed the slender frame and soft hands of a city worker - his ambition to work on his shape and build up muscle tone which would in turn, allure him to the ladies. Dominic could not deny the cruel satisfaction in seeing the agony on Ben's face when he had forced him to endure one hundred abdominal crunchies.

"Want a six pack like mine, you have to pay the price," he smiled, patting the iron-hard muscles below the hem of his cropped singlet. "No pain, no gain!"

Yet Ben had not given up. If anything, he had pushed himself to the edge of endurance, starting with 5kg weights on the bench press before rapidly progressing to 10. He attended classes in circuit training - vigorous cycling workouts where he pumped the pedals like a man possessed. Dominic could not help but notice, his frame was already beginning to transform itself with well developed biceps and chest muscles.

"Rate he's going, he'll end up looking like the Incredible Hulk," Dominic sneered to his receptionist, Melanie. "Now do a bit of research for me will you, love? Find out who his friend is." The all pervasive sense that Nathan wasn't someone he wanted in his gym had never gone away.

What Ben hadn't revealed was the true purpose of his punishing workouts. He wanted to build up his strength - a secret which came to light in a most sinister conversation in the mens' changing rooms. Ben and Nathan had been the last to leave, that night. Unbeknown to them, Dominic had been observing them from a close circuit TV camera installed in his office. There had been a recent spate of theft - car keys and wallets had gone missing. So Dominic had taken the most obvious measure by installing some surveillance equipment; but what he overheard, that night, had turned him cold.

In the normal course of events, they would have changed and showered using the private cubicles. On this occasion, Nathan had quite unashamedly stripped naked in full view of Ben, momentarily posing in front of him. Ben stared at him in awe. He was like a well oiled machine; not an ounce of fat, just layer upon layer of well-honed muscle. His skin gleamed as if it had been buffed with boot polish. Nathan clocked his stunned expression and smiled.

"Wow," Ben breathed.

"Like what you see?" Nathan taunted, flexing his biceps. "Ever tried it with a man?"

"Pack it in, Nathan!" Ben snapped, "you know I don't go in for all that gay stuff. I don't swing that way. I prefer the seductive curves of a woman!"

"I've pleasured plenty of women in my time," Nathan bragged.

"Yeah, as a gigolo!" Ben smirked. "Now shut up! You know I like girls. The younger the better. In fact, there's only one girl I want right now…" his smile turned cold. "Reckon I'll be strong enough to handle that bitch on my own soon and then she'll get what's coming to her."

Dominic froze - watching in disbelief, as Ben's hand crept towards his neck, massaging an area he couldn't quite see. Yet the message was loud and clear. Further more, Dominic had done a little digging. It hadn't taken him long to figure out who Ben really was - or rather, Ben *Hampton*; the son of a man who had enlisted him to kill someone. Dominic shuddered, his outrage soaring. No wonder that kid had been plugging him for gossip about the past. He must have suspected some connection between him and his old man! Forever quizzing him about the 'old days,' a time when the East End was run by criminal gangs: *Didn't you used to be involved in all that stuff, Dominic? Rumour has it, you were some sort of crime boss...*' Stupid, yuppie bastard had even tried twisting his arm as to where he could get some cocaine.

In truth, Dominic found it all quite amusing. Let the kid play his stupid games. He was never going to get the real dirt on his Daddy. As if old Hampton would confess to arranging another man's murder - and here he was, parading around in his gym, attempting to be macho and build muscle. It was pathetic really. But that was *before* this fateful night; a night when he would discover something about his client, he really didn't like - his first insight into the particularly evil urges which hid inside this boy's mind.

"I'll probably leave it 'til winter," Ben rambled on casually. "It gets dark earlier. When Avalon gets home from work, I'll surprise her - I'll be hiding in the bushes dressed in black. I could even wear a mask... and when I've got her trapped in her own back garden, she's never going to know it was me." He released a chuckle as he stood in front of the mirror, combing his damp, fair hair. "This is my ultimate fantasy. I'm going to exploit every inch of her delightful body - teach her a lesson she will never forget..."

Dominic held his breath. So that's what this was all for! Ben wasn't just looking to get himself fit for any girl, he was actually planning to rape someone?

He should have banished them from his club there and then. Except he remembered something else - and it concerned Nathan or rather *Ethan Wadzinski*, as he was formally known; some East European pick pocket, who he had hired to run errands. No wonder they knew about his role as a crime boss. But he would bide his time with these two; keep them under close observation and hopefully, discover what they were really up to.

He guessed he'd been right. They were looking for a path into the criminal underworld. Yet he couldn't dispel the loathing he felt towards Ben - and he especially wanted to discover more about *Avalon*. To think how proudly Perry had disclosed, his son had been stalking her. Life was getting interesting and there was so much more he wanted to find out - just as the bright lights of the Capital lured him towards the sleazy back streets like a moth to a flame.

IV

Eleanor meanwhile, had barely stopped thinking about her meeting with Adam Morrison and Joshua. She couldn't help it - especially when Elijah had wandered so blithely through the door, that night. He was filled with all the boisterous enthusiasm of any teenage boy who had just returned from an action movie.

"You should have seen it," he was raving to Charlie, "it's gross - there's a bit when Robocop stabs some guy through the chin with a metal spike!"

Eleanor shivered. Her son had no concept of the barbarity which hid in the real world - some film, exploding with graphic, comic violence, had no significance. He had never experienced the trauma of another man's killing. It was surreal to him - a world that she inhabited but he did not. She had never fully got over the fatal shooting of his father - yet the revelation of Jordaan's death, coupled with Youf's suicide, had delivered fresh waves of horror.

It didn't take long for Elijah to sense her anxiety - the renewed sense of vigilance, he had witnessed his entire life. So she had finally admitted, his father had been murdered - but there was so much more he was hankering to know.

To escape her son's scrutiny, Eleanor eventually sought solace in the only place she felt at peace; the idyllic gardens behind the Community Centre. There was always plenty to do out here. Ornamental urns, bursting with begonias and fuchsias required constant dead-heading and in the wake of the recent gusts, some of her carefully arranged clematis had torn away from the trellis. Fortunately, the wind had dropped. The weather was mild but cloudy, starved of the sunshine which usually drew the crowds here.

She didn't mind the solitude. It gave her time to think as she gradually worked her way around the perimeter, tidying up the flower beds. Within an hour, she had gradually crept up to the rear where the sight of Margaret's herb garden brought a soft smile to her lips. Bushes of rosemary and sage stood dense with foliage - an assortment of terracotta pots flourished with parsley and tumbling threads of thyme. The aroma was heavenly as Eleanor plucked out the weeds. Then finally, she got to work on the clematis.

It wasn't long before her gaze drifted over the fence to the area of wasteland beyond. At least the ground was cleared of stinging nettles, the old textile factory just waiting to be demolished.

She was already remembering a day when Peter had first revealed this land; his altruistic proposal, the plot was perfect for affordable housing. Eleanor felt the first stirrings of anxiety, wondering if it was even possible to achieve that dream, given the might of the other interested parties. Then suddenly, she detected movement. A dark shadow sauntered into view and for a second, Eleanor froze. Her eyes were drawn to the tall, masculine figure whose back was momentarily turned as he stared up at the ruined factory building. He wore a long black raincoat draped with a storm flap. Yet there was something startlingly familiar about him, from the wide shoulders to the layers of dark blonde hair. Eleanor let out a gasp.

The man spun round. Their eyes met. Eleanor couldn't move as they continued to survey one another. It was with no hesitation, Dominic shoved his hands deep into the pockets of his raincoat and took those first strides towards her.

Eleanor dragged herself away from the perimeter fence and sought sanctuary behind the shrubs. Her hands were trembling as she continued to fasten the last spooling strands of clematis onto the trellis - her mind racing, praying he wouldn't come here.

She sensed his approach before she saw him - a long shadow spilled across the ground.

"Thought it was you," a male voice whispered into the silence.

She slowly turned, aware of the charge of her heart.

"Spying on me are you?" he added coldly.

"Not at all," Eleanor snapped. "I was already here. I didn't realise it was you. S-so what are *you* doing, snooping around?"

"What, you mean you haven't heard?" Dominic drawled, taking another step towards her. "Land's up for sale - but all that aside, I think it's time you and me had a little chat."

She could no longer fight the urge to back away. The light frame of the trellis reared up to meet her as she bumped into the fence.

Dominic offered her a cruel smile. He leaned in closer. The scene was horribly familiar - a snapshot of the railway tunnel flickering in her mind, bringing back an era she had hoped she would never have to be reminded of.

"Why won't you leave me alone," she hissed. "I told you I kept quiet. I've never once implicated you in Jake's killing - not even to Charlie. I only told him about your threats - you threatened to harm my son..."

"Yeah, don't I know it," Dominic's voice pulsed in her ears. "Thing is, one of us has to keep you under control. There's others, you know. *Someone's* got a particular interest in that file of yours. So tell me - do I need to be worried? You say you've never implicated me but is my name mentioned in that file?"

"Yes," Eleanor shivered. "Whoever ordered Jake's murder could have bumped me off too. That file is my insurance. And you can't deny, you were involved."

He impaled her with his stare and for a moment, she sensed his frustration. "Now you listen to me," he whispered, "we both understand the nature of that killing. It's what people like me were paid to do in them days."

"Jake was an innocent man," Eleanor shot back at him.

"When you're under contract to get rid of someone, you do it!" he spat. "You don't ask no questions and besides - I had a whole gang at me disposal. It wasn't as if I operated alone... so what exactly did you write about me, darling?"

Eleanor swallowed. She would never forget the night she had scrawled out her original notes. "That y-you were undoubtedly the man they hired to kill Jake - and you shot him dead."

She watched every muscle in his face harden, his eyes black with fury. She could no longer deny she was scared - just waiting for the axe to fall.

"And you're sure about that, are you?" he whispered, pressing his face in close. Eleanor squeezed her eyes shut - anything to block out his savage glare.

"Yes," she eventually mumbled.

She heard him sigh, sensing movement as he fidgeted. Suddenly he seemed restless. At the same time, she flinched to the sound of a door closing - recognising the squeak of its hinges. A rumble of voices rose from the other end of the garden. He had stepped away from the fence but in another flash of movement, he had coiled a fist around her arm, dragging her towards him.

"Let's walk," he ordered sharply. "Anyone asks, we went and had a butcher's at that land."

Eleanor did not argue as he steered her along the path towards the gap in the hedge and pushed her through. The instant they were out of sight, he spun her round.

"Now let's start again, shall we? Tell me, Eleanor - can you swear with absolute one hundred percent certainty that I killed Jake Jansen?"

Her eyes widened. "Yes! I heard you! You were in the bedsit all along - I'd recognise your voice anywhere...!"

"But did you see me?" he pressed. "Did you see me fire the lethal bullet?"

"Maybe not," Eleanor sighed, "but you've never denied it. You said *Jake was a condemned man*. If they hadn't have hired you, they'd have only found someone else to do it..."

Dominic gave a shrug. "What if I were to tell you, it wasn't actually me."

"What?" Eleanor gasped.

"I think it's time you knew the truth," Dominic continued. He proceeded to stroll across the grass, keeping close to the hedge and this time, Eleanor felt a compulsion to walk along beside him. "I never had nothing personally against your Jake. If anything, you were the one I had it in for! But we had to kill him. Orders from someone high up and on the night we finally captured him, there wasn't any time to piss around. Job had to be done."

Eleanor felt a surge of emotion - she took a gulp of air.

"When I said he had talent, I meant it. That's the trouble. Just didn't have the urge to pull the trigger! So one of me top men finished the job instead..."

"I don't believe you," Eleanor croaked. "Why are telling me this after all these years? Are you really that worried about my file?"

He released a bark of laughter. "D'you think I'm bricking it 'cos of your bloody file? You ain't got nothing on me! I was cleared of that murder and d'you know why? Well let me explain. They found evidence, see. Found a gun, not far from the place where we dumped him. It fitted the crime - even forensics confirmed it, from the calibre and the pattern of marks inside the barrel; this was the exact weapon used to finish him off..."

"So how does that prove anything?" Eleanor whispered, quickening her stride.

"You never let me finish," Dominic retorted. "Fingerprints! Killer might have been wearing gloves but the pattern of fingerprints proved something else. That gun was fired by a right-handed man. There was no way I could have been that person."

"What - so you're left handed?" Eleanor snapped.

"My right hand's fucked," Dominic whispered. He held it out in front of her and straight away, she could tell from the set twist of his thumb that he wasn't lying. She had worked in nursing for years and knew a damaged hand when she saw one. The flesh of his hand possessed a hard, withered quality - there was visible scar tissue. The moment he tried to wiggle it, only the inner three fingers moved. "Been paralysed like that since I was 17. I'll spare you the details. If you want proof, talk to the Police - ask for records of Jansen's murder. They'll confirm everything I told you."

Eleanor froze to a standstill, gaping at him in disbelief. They had reached the ruined shell of the factory building, yet she was too numb to take another step.

"So no, I ain't worried about your file," Dominic smirked, "but if I were you, I'd get rid of it before you land yourself in any more shit."

"What the hell is that supposed to mean?" Eleanor retorted.

"You should forget about Jake," he finished icily. "Nothing's gonna bring him back and I said much the same to your Charlie. If you care enough about your loved ones, let it go. They're the ones you should be worried about. 'Cos a little bird tells me you're stirring things."

"So that's it?" Eleanor gasped, "you're threatening me again?"

"It's just a warning. There's plenty of people who could do you more harm than me - and out of interest, who's the posh bird - the one with the double barrelled name?"

"Avalon!" Eleanor gasped before she could stop herself.

"Yeah, that's the one," Dominic nodded. "Sounds like she's made herself an enemy - might wanna consider getting her own security guard..."

Eleanor's mouth dropped open. "You're talking about Ben Hampton, aren't you?"

"Might be," he taunted, "him and that other bloke he hangs around with. Pair of 'em joined my gym, did you know that? I've already been hearing about their nasty little fantasies…"

"Why are you telling me this?" Eleanor blurted. "What's in it for you?"

"Quite simple. I'm after this bit of land. Wanna start me own entertainment complex, see and I'm guessing you lot are gonna be opposed to that!"

"Damn right," Eleanor said angrily. "This area is residential - nearly everyone will object."

"Really?" Dominic sneered. "Well it's gonna take more than a few 'nimbys' to stop this town from developing facilities. In which case, I'll ask you another question. Who'd you rather got this land? Me - or that cunt, Perry Hampton?"

A spark sprung to her eyes. "Are you trying to make some sort of deal?"

"Just asking you to think about it, Eleanor," he finished coldly. "I meant what I said. Your secret file don't bother me. But that don't mean I ain't keeping an eye on you - 'cos not everyone feels the same way if you get my drift."

"You're still working for them, aren't you?" Eleanor whispered.

She was chilled by the sinister glint in his eye, knowing there was little more to say, as she turned and fled back towards the Community Centre.

Dominic watched her go, observing her shrinking figure from a distance. He rammed his hands into the pockets of his raincoat with a sigh. A tiny part of him despised her for the chaos she had brought into his life - yet in another corner of his mind, lurked a desire so powerful... She had always had this effect on him and it reminded him of that fateful day in 1972 when he had cornered her in an East London brothel.

Part of the attraction, he put down to the fact that she was the daughter of a rival gangster; one he had sworn to avenge for the shooting of his right hand man. It was an encounter that had left him buzzing. Here was a girl who was not only a stunner but charged with an aura of fear, he found a real turn on! He had relished the fantasy - what it would be like to possess her delicious, teenage body. But at the same time, he had been brow-beaten into attending a meeting; one which not only included Inspector Hargreeves but that oily bastard, Whaley. It was a meeting which had ultimately sealed the fate of Jake Jansen.

Dominic had been scheduled to kill the boy - but unfortunately, Eleanor had got in the way. The two of them had escaped across London, not only denying him his pleasure but her actions had effectively destroyed any prospects of him carrying out his contract. This in turn, had brought the wrath of his paymasters crashing down on his shoulders. Dominic ground his teeth - the fury bit deep even now. He had been driven by a relentless urge to deal with both of them. Yet on the night they finally cornered Jansen, something inside him had changed.

Dominic sauntered towards the gates of the factory site, lost in his reverie. He could clearly remember the build up; the dismal days when he had loitered around Bethnal Green, knowing they were holed up in some basement - just waiting for the signal to go in and finish him.

The trouble was, the kid was a good musician. Dominic enjoyed many pleasures in life but music had always been his one guiltless passion. Jake possessed the raw talent which rivalled some of the best bands around. It was on that final day, his troubled mind had been caressed by one of the most beautiful songs he would ever hear - and there, sat cross-legged on a blanket, he spotted his victim, strumming a guitar. It was a scene that would always haunt him.

He never held any personal grudge against Jake and it was a feeling that had been exacerbated on that same pivotal night. Dominic was a ruthless killer who cared little about the lives of his victims. They were usually pretty

41

disgusting toe-rags anyway - slippery fraudsters who deserved everything they got. With Jake, it was different. The boy had witnessed a scene, no-one was meant to see; a killing sanctioned to silence him. Dominic had felt nothing but respect in the end. There had been no fear. He had faced death with a strength of character, Dominic had never before encountered. Previous victims usually wept, begged for mercy, pissed and shat themselves, yet Jake had looked directly into his eyes, knowing his life was about to be extinguished.

The memory chilled him even now. He had lowered his gun and stepped back from the chair, his left hand shaking so violently that if it *had* gone off, it would have made a hell of a mess! It took no more than a second for his partner, Dan Levy, to extract his own gun - and to coldly finish the deed. The rest was history.

In one way, Dan had done him a favour. He had fulfilled his contract, saving Dominic from the unthinkable scenario threatened by his paymasters. Hargreeves had enough dirt on him to put him away for life. Though he suspected, the idea had more likely been devised by that creep, Robin Whaley - ever determined to ingratiate himself to the man who'd ordered Jake's death.

Eleanor was right. They'd have killed her too. Her secret file *had* guarded her - because whatever Jake knew, she knew, leaving those at the top vulnerable. He could have smiled, if it hadn't been for the final role they had enlisted him for; never able to forget those threats whispered in the echoey confines of a railway tunnel. It had happened many years ago. Yet the thread of mystery surrounding Jake's murder was creeping its way back into their lives again; and it was a situation he wanted to use to his advantage.

He wanted this land and whatever else those slugs had in store for Eleanor, he would use his own sense of animal cunning to make sure he got it.

Chapter 3

I

"Charlie!" Eleanor shouted, racing towards him.

She kept on running - panic spreading through her mind like a fire. She pelted across the grass, unable to stop until she had reached the front of the Community Centre where fortuitously, she had spotted his familiar dark head.

"Charlie!" she shrieked again. "I need to talk to you!"

"What's the matter, love?" he frowned, catching her in his arms. "Jesus, you're shaking."

"Any chance we could pop home for a chat?" she panted.

He was speechless - fearing what might have happened to spark such fear. He held her tight, wary of the powerful crash of her heart. Yet he was engrossed in work and they were on a tight schedule. The new windows *had* to be fitted by the end of summer before the weather turned cold, exposing visitors to the elements.

"I'll have to find someone to cover," he spluttered, throwing a glance towards the building. "I was in the middle of a job..."

"I'm sorry," Eleanor gasped.

One by one, the ugly sash windows were being dismantled; the surrounding brickwork remodelled to accommodate the new mullioned windows, they had built by hand.

"Did you ever resolve your argument with Andrew?" she added numbly.

"Not really," Charlie grunted. "The windows have to be a certain height to adhere to our plan. I only wanted one more layer of bricks. Lazy little bugger just wanted to knock off early!"

Eleanor forced a smile and for a moment, they were distracted - thinking about the work ahead which would transform this dreary lump of a building into a design inspired by her own son. Once the windows were replaced, a layer of concrete cladding was to be applied to the outer shell like icing on a cake - a pattern of rusticated blocks scored into the surface - each window embellished with a decorative surround.

He had recruited a team of labourers which included his son. Luckily, it didn't take long to track down a work mate to finish the window he had been fitting. He snatched Eleanor's hand as they wandered away from the building - not missing the rapid side to side dart of her eyes, as if scanning the area for enemies.

"So, are you going to tell me what this is about?" he prompted her.

"Theakston's here," Eleanor whimpered. "He approached me again..." She stifled a sob. "I'm sorry, Charlie - but I'm still frightened of him!"

"What did he want?" Charlie demanded. "I hope he hasn't been threatening you again."

"Oh, where do I start?" Eleanor sighed, footsteps dragging.

They hovered beneath a horse chestnut tree as her eyes drifted towards the gardens. She briefly described the exchange - careful to omit any mention of Jake's killing.

"So he did threaten you!" Charlie snapped.

"Not directly," Eleanor sighed. "He's got a clever way with words - though it's obvious he's been in contact with Perry. This *someone* who's got an interest in my file... it *has* to be him!"

"I don't like this one bit," Charlie reacted. "I knew there was going to be trouble, I just didn't expect it this soon! First that spy hanging around and now this!"

"I know," Eleanor pondered, "and as for the land!' she nodded towards the communal garden, indicating the area beyond. "It's going to draw us all back into conflict."

"I think this is exactly what Whaley is hoping," Charlie said bitterly. "He's luring your enemies here. It's just another way of setting us at each other's throats. I wonder who'll actually win."

"Hopefully, Peter," Eleanor mused. "He's the only one with a plan that benefits the town. All Perry's interested in is profit!"

"Interesting what Dominic said," Charlie added. "Sounds like he really hates the guy. Given the choice, I don't think I could stomach someone like Hampton muscling in on our neighbourhood. Imagine the effect it'll have on James's kids..."

"Hmm," Eleanor pondered. "Though we definitely don't want a bloody night club either! Imagine all those drunken youths taking short cuts through the hedge and pissing in our front gardens. Eli's already worried about vandalism..."

"I guess we need to voice our fears," Charlie muttered as they strolled a little further up the path. "So why don't I have another chat with him? You know, on amicable terms - he seemed quite reasonable, the first time."

Eleanor nodded. "It won't hurt. Ask him to meet you in a pub or something. I'll catch up with Avalon. I think I should warn her about this threat - it sounded sinister."

"Maybe we *should* think about getting them some protection," Charlie added sagely, "and see if you can get them interested in the land. If I know those two, they'll fight like hell to make sure Perry doesn't get it."

"The only way they'll do that is by chatting up Whaley," Eleanor said. "Avalon could visit the council - or better still, William."

Her face had finally shed its fear, Charlie noticed - grateful to see the first glitter of excitement drawn back into her eyes.

By the time Eleanor drifted across the High Street, she was still thinking about Avalon. She would never forget the day Avalon had first enlightened

44

her about the Hamptons; Avalon, who had ultimately been robbed of her lovely home - followed by the tragic death of her father; Avalon, who on the night of their eviction, had been exposed to the mercy of Ben and Nathan - forced to witness a remorseless sexual assault on her 15 year old brother.

The ghastly details had gradually leaked out over time. Eleanor shuddered, having long sensed that Ben was a psychopath. If only they had sought justice. But William feared retribution - and now their assailants had joined Theakston's gym... The possibilities didn't bear thinking about.

Eleanor paused outside their idyllic Tudor-style house, drawing in the perfume of roses as they crowded around the porch. That final disclosure from Dominic brought back her worst fears. She took a deep breath, then rapped on the door.

"Eleanor!" Avalon exclaimed. Her lips curved into a smile of delight.

She looked rosy and sun-tanned, her luxurious curls braided into a thick plait. Eleanor was delighted that she and William had kept in contact with their dad's friends, the Fortescues. They had joined them for a week's holiday in the Dordogne. She also knew that Avalon had drifted back into an on-and-off relationship with their youngest son, George. She had obviously been topping up that glowing tan of hers in the seclusion of their cottage-style garden - she looked positively radiant.

"Day off?" Eleanor smiled back.

"I don't have to work on Saturdays any more," Avalon replied, ushering her inside the house. She was of course, referring to the large antiques company who were also the official auctioneers for the town. "Is everything okay?"

Eleanor bit her lip, lowering herself into their pretty, floral chintz settee. "Avalon, I don't mean to nag but didn't you ought to fit a chain to your door?" she found herself babbling. "I could have been anyone."

"I knew it was you," Avalon shrugged, "I saw you walking up the path. You're not worried about that Nathan are you? Shaven-headed or not, William would have recognised him anywhere!"

"So there have been no more sightings?" Eleanor pressed.

"No," Avalon shivered, "but you're right about security. Why are you worried, has something happened?"

"Not yet," Eleanor replied, choosing her next words carefully, "but there's no point keeping you in the dark. Charlie told me something and it's about that land at the back of the Community Centre..."

"I thought the Council were going to buy it!" Avalon interrupted. "Peter told us - even *Robin* was considering his idea."

"I know that," Eleanor said tightly, "but did you know Robin approached two other parties? Well this may come as a shock, Avalon, but one of them was Perry Hampton."

"No," Avalon gasped, sagging into her chair. "How do you know this?"

Eleanor watched the rosy bloom fade from her face, her hands knotting themselves together in her lap. Suddenly, there seemed no point holding back the truth.

"Avalon, I'm sorry! I should have said something earlier. Apparently, Perry is going to make a bid for this land with a view to building an estate of luxury homes. He's clearly cottoned on to the soaring value of property in this town - especially since he couldn't get his paws on your dad's land. He must be considering this as an alternative."

"He can't!" Avalon bleated. "Not here!"

"Avalon, this was the whole point of me mentioning security. We're worried, Perry will start visiting Rosebrook and you never know who he might bring along with him."

"So why hasn't *Robin* said anything?" Avalon snapped, her expression tightening to fury. "I thought he was on our side!"

"That's what he wanted you to believe - I always suspected, he would betray you. Put it this way, I'd be surprised if he *really* backed your campaign against Perry's plans..."

Avalon pressed a hand over her mouth. It was obvious, she would be jarred by memories; the ruthless quest to destroy the idyllic walled gardens, her father had spent years reinstating! Robin had promised to be her ally. Eleanor could already sense her conflicting emotions.

They were distracted by the sound of feet thundering down the stairs and seconds later, William materialised. At five foot seven inches tall, he possessed the long and supple figure of a growing adolescent, bronzed limbs on show in a striped rugby shirt and sawn off denim shorts.

"William!" Eleanor smiled warmly, "won't you sit down and join us?"

"Hello, Eleanor," he greeted her in his clipped public school accent. "What's up, Av?"

"It's Robin Whaley," Avalon fumed, "and his 'friendship' with Perry!"

William flicked up his shoulders in an exaggerated shrug. "So? We always knew he was an enemy from what Eli said! What's the problem?"

"Perry is bidding for the land behind the Community Centre," Eleanor explained, a second time, "but what I'm really after is some inside information - from Whaley - and you're the only two who might be able to butter him up a bit."

"Oh I see," William smirked. "What sort of information?"

It didn't take long to convince them.

There was only one way they might ensure, Peter could use the land for his housing trust - bid for it themselves. It was definitely preferable to Perry making himself a huge profit.

"Damn right!" Avalon whispered in disgust. "He must be loaded! Why is he doing this?"

"It's just greed, Avalon," Eleanor sighed, "though, I suspect he's doing it out of spite."

"Yeah," William nodded. "We stopped him demolishing the walled gardens. I bet he's livid. D'you know, I was speaking to Cyril. He says he wrote a killer of a letter! I'd love to see it."

"Well maybe you can," Eleanor smiled. She stared into his eyes before her own carefully planned words found an escape route. "All letters are kept in a file in the planning office. There's nothing to stop you asking if you can look at it."

"Me?" William frowned, "hasn't he always dealt with Avalon?"

"This is an opportunity for *you* to get to know him - and without making it obvious, I wonder if there's a way you can find out how much the land is worth."

She was still smiling, hoping her words would encourage him; unsure how Robin really felt towards Avalon. Yet she knew Robin masked a secret side - never able to forget a time, she had brought these kids to the Community Centre. It was in the wake of their harrowing eviction; a day when she had never seen such adoration in another man's eyes. She had long sensed, Robin had a soft spot for William - and there had to be a way they could exploit this.

II

The day William sauntered into the headquarters of Rosebrook Borough Council, he adopted a smarter dress code. A collar-less white shirt and classic waistcoat enhanced his boyish frame and he had abandoned his fraying cut-offs in favour of dark denim jeans. He loped his way through the pillared entrance with all the confidence he had acquired from public school. By the time he was approached by a security guard, his explanation was simple.

Upstairs in the planning office, Robin's ears pricked up to the words of his receptionist.

"Barton-Wells?" she threw an approving gaze in his direction. "That's right, it is Mr Whaley they usually deal with…"

With a smirk, Robin adjusted his tie. He had always been a well-preened man. "I take it, there's a young lady here to see me," he muttered softly.

"Not a young lady," the receptionist smiled, "a young man! He's downstairs in the foyer."

"I'll go," Robin said, feeling his pulse leap.

It had been a while since he had cast eyes on William Barton-Wells, but something about that boy had twisted his heart. He had sensed his torment - the terrible sadness reflected in his eyes and in the moment Peter had beckoned him, he had moved in a manner which didn't quite disguise his pain. On this occasion, Robin saw only a shadow of the cowering figure he remembered. William looked at him nervously - but it was as if a butterfly had burst from its chrysalis, his gelled hair shaped into smooth waves, his hazel eyes gleaming with warmth.

"Mr Whaley?" he faltered, extending his hand.

"You're William, aren't you," Robin smiled softly. He took the boy's hand and squeezed it. "It's a pleasure to meet you. Please, come with me."

He did not even question the nature of William's visit - nor did he express any surprise when William asked if he could view the file bulging with letters of objection to Perry's plan.

"I imagine, you're delighted it was refused," Robin said carefully; his pale hands were clasped on the surface of his desk. He had invited his visitor into his office, something he had never proposed to Avalon with whom he had always conversed in reception.

"Of course!" William said flippantly. "We've not long returned from holiday with one of Dad's friends. I'm dying to see what he wrote. He and Dad used to belong to some 'Heritage Society.' He said it was quite poisonous of old Hampton to try and ruin his estate!"

Robin almost winced, not used to hearing Perry maligned. He watched with growing unease as William sifted through the mountain of objection letters. Then at last, he froze.

Robin cleared his throat. "Did you find what you were looking for?"

"Yes," William replied.

It was over the next few minutes, Robin observed the changing emotions which spread across his face. At the same time, he could hear him muttering - a few damning phrases slipping from his lips as if by accident: *'Mr Hampton approached my friend, James Barton-Wells, in the autumn of 1985... he specifically said he was fascinated by older buildings...'* "That must have been the evening we met Ben! He hated me, even then."

"I'm sorry?" Robin frowned, struck with an unexpected chill.

"That's another story," William said quickly. *'I find it somewhat hypocritical of Mr Hampton to even consider destroying a feature of this estate which has stood for over 200 years.'*

"Your father's friend clearly felt very strongly," Robin responded ruefully.

"Oh Cyril knew everything!" William spat. He kept on reading - unable to resist narrating the little passages that focused on Perry's evil; *'the applicant cared very little... aware, this historic 17th Century house was undergoing restoration...'* his eyes blazed. Robin fiddled with his cufflinks, unable to meet his eye. Yet just before he finished, he detected a break in his voice.

"He was aware of Dad's declining health. He bankrupted him. *'His campaign to trick him into taking out a loan with his own finance company was an act of pure wickedness...'*" he let go of the letter, his hands shaking as it slid onto the desk.

Robin recognised the same vulnerable boy whose appearance at the Community Centre had evoked some deep, troubling emotion.

"Don't be upset, William," he whispered, his voice like honey.

"Sorry to be bitter," William snapped, "I shouldn't be telling you this. Perhaps I should go."

"No, stay," Robin pleaded. "I was about to take a coffee break - in fact, why don't you join me?" and without waiting for an answer, he leapt to his feet.

It didn't take long to brow beat a secretary into delivering a tray of coffee and biscuits. Robin couldn't deny, he was finding the whole business intriguing. William was so adorable - leaving him curious to wonder what these children *really* felt about Perry.

The conversation moved swiftly on to Peter and it was with no hesitation, William revealed he thought the world of him.

"You stayed with him, didn't you?" Robin smiled indulgently, just as William helped himself to another chocolate bourbon.

"Mmm," William found himself mumbling.

What Robin didn't realise was that in all this time, William had been carefully observing him too; monitoring every response, especially when he mentioned Perry. His reaction to Cyril's letter was no pretence - almost fated to rekindle his feelings of acrimony. But he was puzzled by Robin's tenderness - recognising the opportunity to expose what he really thought.

"Peter has a heart of gold. Moving in with him was the best thing Avalon and I could have done... I felt I could tell him anything."

"Peter is a good man," Robin nodded in approval.

"Yes," William sighed. "He is - and you've been meeting up with him a lot lately, haven't you? To talk about this piece of land up for sale. He told us about his dream. He's right, there isn't much affordable housing in town..."

"How do you know this?" Robin pressed.

William shrugged, taking another nibble of his biscuit, the reels in his mind turning. "My friends talk about it at school. Soaring rent - high mortgages. I think it's great what Peter's doing." He paused, mentally rehearsing his next words, his mouth dry. He took a sip of coffee. "I'd sooner he got the land than some greedy property developer. At least Peter's plan benefits the community."

"Well that's a topic up for discussion, young man," Robin replied with a flicker of a smile.

William nodded understandingly. "Good. Because he helped me through the worse time of my life, Mr Whaley. I'll always feel indebted to him."

"Do you mean your eviction?" Robin whispered, his gentle eyes almost hypnotic. "I don't mean to pry - but what exactly did happen?"

William felt the familiar chill snake through his veins. He had almost guessed Robin would ask this of him - though he was never going to confess the true dark reality.

He threw back the last dregs of his coffee. "We were attacked and threatened. One of the men was Ben's bodyguard..." he nibbled his lip, "but I won't say any more. It's been good to meet you, Mr Whaley and thanks for the coffee."

"My pleasure, William," Robin replied, "and call me Robin... I hope we can meet again."

He offered him one final reassuring nod before strolling lazily from his office.

Eleanor was intrigued to discover how William had got on; impressed he managed to touch Whaley's heart but without overdoing the charm. Between them, they discussed their next strategy. Now all Eleanor wanted to do was speak to Peter.

Her mind was cluttered with thoughts, as she drifted into the Community Centre in search of him. It seemed hard to imagine that nearly a week had slipped by since that incredible meeting in London. To think that in a short space of time, she had gathered a wealth of evidence against Perry. Yet she had also bumped into Dominic. Both encounters had sent powerful memories of Jake spooling through her mind. She was desperate to talk to Rosemary - convinced she was being drawn on to a trail which might finally unleash the mystery of his killing.

She paused on the threshold where the elderly visitors flocked - her senses impacted with the hubbub of voices, the clang of crockery and a pungent smell of cauliflower cheese. A flustered looking old lady in her 70s glanced up at her.

"Emily!" Eleanor called across, "is everything okay? You look worn out!"

"I'm fine, Eleanor!" Emily bellowed above the din, "nearly done for the day. Do you fancy a cup of tea?"

"Thanks, but I was looking for Peter!" Eleanor replied in earnest.

It emerged that Peter was caught up in a meeting. Eleanor wandered through the corridor and into the garden. She hadn't set foot here since her alarming clash with Dominic - dismayed to see, the grass needed cutting and the shrubs were looking straggly.

Yet the vision of her creation soothed her. The oppressive clouds had finally lifted, allowing a pool of sunshine to illuminate the flower beds. Eleanor breathed in their scent, closing her eyes as she savoured her environment. Today there were a few more visitors, some wandering along the paths while others lounged on wooden benches chatting and smoking.

Once again, she was drawn to the rear of the garden, suddenly curious to study the layout of the land. She gulped in the sweet air, bracing herself for the possibility that Theakston might be lurking. Fortunately, there was no sign of him.

She found herself staring across the vista of land - the old textile factory hung together in a tangle of rusting girders. The area revealed patches of tarmac, overgrown with weeds, which had once served as parking and delivery areas. Eleanor wondered how many acres the plot covered - trying to envisage how many dwellings could be accommodated.

Lost in her thoughts, she tensed to the murmur of voices emanating from somewhere behind the old factory carcass. It was at this point, she spotted Peter - his step unmistakable as he bounded into view. For several seconds she watched him, feeling the touch of a smile. His youthful grin was visible even from a distance as he conversed with his colleagues - tousled hair lit up like a silver coin in the glimmer of sunlight.

She leaned closer to the fence, hoping to catch his attention. She would have shouted and waved if it hadn't been for the gradual manifestation of the other men, especially when she identified Robin Whaley. Eleanor turned rigid as he strutted into view - head inclined, his characteristic dark suit so easily distinguishable. She felt a spiralling cord of hatred as she recalled her conversation with Charlie. *'He's luring your enemies here.'* She turned and marched away in the direction of the almshouses.

A metallic flash gleamed from the roadside as Perry's spy lingered in her car, scribbling away in her notepad. Eleanor was nearly tempted to jab two fingers up - but dismissing the urge to be so childish, she calmly let herself into her home.

She barely had time to gather her thoughts when she stopped dead in the middle of the lounge. An unpleasant mood stifled the air - her son coiled up at one end of the settee, while Andrew lay sprawled out at the other. It was obvious they had quarrelled.

"What's up, boys?" she queried, clocking the thunderous expression on Eli's face. "Are you not working today, Andrew?"

Andrew shrugged, his face turning stony. "What's the point? Seems nothing I do's good enough any more!"

"Andrew, don't tell me you still haven't patched things up with your dad," Eleanor moaned in dismay.

"He treats me like some shit-thick chippy!" Andrew protested, "not like old 'big brain,' over there!" he jabbed his thumb aggressively towards Elijah. "If it wasn't for your bloody drawings, we wouldn't be having this argument!"

Eleanor braced herself, feeling the sparks erupt between the two of them. For a second, she thought Elijah was going to leap up and punch him. His green eyes smouldered. Regrettably, Andrew was afflicted with a lingering sense of jealousy - it had started from the day Elijah had revealed his true visual creativity.

"Balls!" Elijah exploded. "You're working to Charlie's plan now! A professional architect! Why can't you just show a bit more respect?"

"Yeah, well I guess there's no loyalty between fathers and sons," Andrew finished coldly.

"You're lucky to have a father!" Elijah screamed, launching himself from the sofa. "I never got a chance to even meet mine!" He fled from the room, leaving a mantle of strained silence.

Andrew said nothing as he too shuffled from the lounge, slamming the door. Eleanor counted to ten - then crept up the stairs towards Elijah's bedroom. She tapped on the door.

"What!" Elijah grunted, wiping a tear from his face.

"Eli, don't get so worked up," Eleanor pleaded. She tried to coax him into her arms but he fought her off angrily. "I can tell you're upset but what else is troubling you?"

"Everything!" Elijah retorted. "Andrew, you - especially you! I thought you were going to tell me the truth about my father! You promised! At the wedding, remember?"

"Yes, I know," Eleanor protested. "It doesn't mean I've forgotten, I-I just don't know how to explain it to you..."

"But you know what happened," Elijah shrieked, "you were there!"

"Yes you're right, I was," Eleanor whispered, closing her eyes.

It was suddenly all so clear - the underground bedsit with its dingy yellow light. Jake playing his guitar as the cold bit into her shoulders. The pounding on the door... Eleanor started to cry. She would never forget that last kiss before Jake had covered her with the floorboards.

"Mum?" Elijah shivered, all the anger dried from his voice. "I'm sorry, I didn't mean to upset you. What is it?"

"They - they shot him," she gasped, "a-and there was nothing I could do to stop them..."

"Who shot him?" Elijah pressed. He seized her wrist, urging her to look at him.

"I don't know," Eleanor whimpered. "I didn't see..." she started shaking as the nightmare replayed itself. It was the words of a more recent conversation that haunted her; *someone's got a particular interest in that file of yours.'* Eleanor stared at her son, her eyes refilling with tears. It wasn't her misery that mattered, it was his safety. Perry's spies were everywhere.

"There is a file, Eli," she blurted before she could stop herself. "Everything I know about your father's death is in there. I'm trying to gather evidence - but right now, that file is our protection."

"What do you mean?" Elijah whispered.

"Oh, Eli," she gasped, twisting her head away. "I told Jake's killers. I swore it would be published if anything ever happened to me - and someone's after it..."

"Have you still got it?" Elijah pressed.

"Of course! And that's all I'm saying, so don't push it. I know you want the truth but I swore to your dad, I'd keep you safe - now does that satisfy you?"

"Yes," Elijah said guiltily, rising from the bed. "I'm sorry. I didn't mean to make you cry."

By the time Charlie walked in, the atmosphere had cooled slightly. Margaret too, had returned home - she had poured her brother a beer, detecting the friction.

"He *does* admire you," she whispered. "He told me he misses you - and like - no-one works as *well* as you do…"

She had even put some music on to lighten the mood; the last singalong notes of 'Who's that Girl,' by Madonna, resounding from the speakers.

"What's going on?" Charlie snapped, missing nothing.

"Never mind," Eleanor sighed. "Let's just say, there's a lot of tension in this house. We need a change of scenery. I wouldn't mind driving up to London to see the Merrimans."

Even Andrew seemed enthusiastic; he had always felt a certain allure towards London - the shops, the pubs, which seemed far more exciting than anything Rosebrook could offer. It was only a little later however, that Charlie expressed his reluctance.

"Are you sure this is wise," he nagged. "What if we're followed?"

"Don't think I haven't thought of that," Eleanor whispered, confident the kids were out of earshot. "I'm not about to put the Merrimans in danger!"

"Well, at least we'll recognise the car," Charlie sighed. He stretched his arms above his head, locking his fingers together to ease his tension. "But what if she *does* start tailing us? I suppose we'll need a backup plan - go sightseeing or something."

"I'd like to show Eli the park," Eleanor added, slipping her arms around his waist. "It's where I laid my tribute…"

"And then what?" Charlie sighed.

"I guess we just have to get on with our own lives," she murmured softly. She sunk her head into his shoulder, sensing a familiar creeping fear. "Find a way Peter can get permission to develop his housing trust…"

It was only a little later that Avalon paused outside the Fish and Chip shop located beneath the flat where Peter lived. She had spent a delightful hour in his company, curious to discover how his meeting had panned out; fully aware that he had been surveying the land, along with various decision-makers - including Robin.

She made her way up the high street, taking long swaying strides; graceful in a long, floral summer dress, her sun-streaked hair spiralling loose around her shoulders. She had only planned to pop out and buy a bottle of wine. Further more - and as Peter's company never failed to enliven her - she had invited him round for dinner in three days time. Avalon was gradually perfecting the art of cooking and to her delight, William was equally keen to learn. Several hours of daylight lingered as she wandered into the off-license. To her triumph, she spotted Robin.

"Avalon," he gushed, "how are things?"

"Good, thanks," she smiled. "I take it you met my brother…"

It was with no hesitation, she mentioned the dinner party - and in the light of his blossoming rapport with Peter, she seized the opportunity to invite him too.

Predictably, it was with no hesitation that Robin graciously accepted.

III

Before this most significant of dinner parties took place, the Baileys travelled up to London as planned. Charlie cruised along at a leisurely pace, constantly checking his mirrors for a glimpse of the mysterious silver VW Scirocco. He had purposefully prolonged his journey; first by pulling into a service station for petrol while the others congregated in the café. He then took the unusual decision to follow a slightly longer route via the new M25 motorway.

Eleanor's eyes were fixed rigidly ahead as they plunged through Blackwell tunnel towards East London, her thoughts rooted in the past. Her feelings of nostalgia intensified as Charlie pulled up in Commercial Road. Andrew hopped out, happy to make his own way to Central London by tube. Yet Eleanor's mind was elsewhere, her heart thumping as a familiar set of black railings loomed into view. She could see the glossy banks of laurel - the tiny gate where she and Jake had escaped and straight away, she felt the magnetic pull of his pendant. Her fingers crept towards it. *'I swear that one day, I will find out the truth…'* She had never forgotten her final whispered oath.

Snapping her mind back to the present, she directed Charlie a little further, finally recognising the turning that would take them to Forest Haven.

"She didn't follow us, then," Charlie muttered under his breath as he crawled the final leg of their journey. They had just spotted the towering, Victorian town house where Rosemary lived.

"Not this time", Eleanor frowned, "though we can never be sure he hasn't got others spying for him…"

"Well, I don't think anyone followed us," Charlie smiled, staring up at the house.

A moment later, Rosemary hurried them inside. Eleanor found herself gazing lovingly at the interior. The rustic lounge had undergone a dramatic change of decor since the 70s - the walls painted a sunny yellow, the eclectic mix of furniture replaced by a sumptuous corner suite upholstered in chintz cotton. The colours were warm and inspirational, though the original wooden shelves were just as she remembered, crammed with books, candles and ornaments. Eleanor breathed deeply, drawing in the evocative scent of incense and sandalwood. A delicious aroma wafted from the adjoining kitchen where Rosemary had prepared Sunday lunch.

It didn't take long for the youngsters to become completely absorbed in their surroundings, from the assortment of rooms arranged on three levels, to the magical garden at the back of the house and the railway embankment beyond. Elijah, who had been conceived in this house, forgot about his angst. Rosemary, as keen a herbalist as ever, offered them an infusion of mint tea - enchanted to hear about Margaret's herb garden.

It wasn't long (after they had feasted on a succulent roast dinner of turkey and nut cutlets) before Luke turned up. He was accompanied by his family, as well as Joshua, who seemed eager to reconnect with Eleanor. Once the lunch things were cleared away, Luke's wife, Sally and their eight year old twin boys, invited the children to join them for a leisurely stroll along the railway path. It was as if she sensed their need for privacy - leaving the five remaining adults settled around the stripped pine table over mugs of steaming tea.

"So the meeting with Adam was a success," Luke began gravely. "Have you got the photos? Can I see them?"

Eleanor pulled them from her bag where they lay hidden in the same envelope as the transcripts. She gazed deeply into his eyes before spreading them across table.

"Jesus!" Luke spluttered, grabbing for the photo which unmasked Perry's face. "That's him alright! So what now?"

"I've taken photocopies," Eleanor said, fearing their time was limited. "I just need to pass the originals on to my solicitor."

"Except she's being watched," Charlie added. "Perry's got spies."

"So maybe one of us could do it," Rosemary piped up. Her deeply tanned face creased into a smile. "I'm assuming this is what you're asking?"

Charlie laughed, warmed by her intuition. "Rosemary, that would be great. I don't think there's anyone else in the world we can trust."

At first, the entire conversation focused on the meeting - the tragic fate of Jordaan and the residual members of 'Free Spirit.' A sense of shock coiled into the atmosphere.

"Our enemies are without question very powerful," Rosemary shivered - the golden light practically draining from her face. "So what else has been going on?"

Charlie glanced at his watch. Sally had said they wouldn't be much longer than an hour. "I wish I knew where to start," he faltered, "but we're about to be drawn into a new conflict over some lucrative piece of land..." It was with no hesitation, he launched into a hasty explanation. "I might as well be truthful. I've decided to approach Dominic Theakston again!"

Luke and Joshua gawked at him in disbelief.

"I spoke to him before," Charlie shrugged. "Though to be honest, it's not him I'm bothered about so much as Hampton! I get the impression, Theakston doesn't like him very much..."

"What makes you say that?" Rosemary pressed.

Charlie glanced at Eleanor. "Call it intuition," she smiled, "but we've decided to approach this another way. Do you remember James's children? They've developed a close friendship with Peter. Next week, they're throwing a dinner party - and they've invited Robin Whaley."

"What?" Joshua spluttered, almost spilling his tea.

"Luke," she added. "You remember Perry - but is there a chance you remember the wine they chose? You know, when you served them at the press conference?"

"Of course," Luke spat. A look of contempt crept into his expression. "They chose a particularly expensive red from the Burgundy region. Why do you ask?"

"I'm wondering what Avalon might serve for their dinner party," Eleanor said.

"For Whaley?" Luke grinned. "Arsenic would be a good choice!"

Charlie let out a chuckle. Rosemary, on the other hand was not laughing.

"Are you sure this is a good idea? I don't mean to fuss - but I sensed something particularly nasty about that man. Have you considered this could be risky - especially for those adorable children?"

"It's okay, Rosemary, they know he's an enemy," she argued.

"But do they know what lies beneath the mask," Rosemary said, dropping her voice to a whisper, "and for that matter, do you?" she raised her eyebrows.

Eleanor said nothing more as the conversation fluttered around the table.

They were still discussing the land - the notion, they intended to put up a huge fight to stop Perry from getting his hands on it. Finally, the conversation drifted to Westbourne House - and ultimately to Aldwyck. Rosemary's sister, Marilyn, still lived in the farmhouse next to Eleanor's caravan - where Joshua was planning to spend the occasional weekend.

But there was something in Rosemary's words which left Eleanor troubled. She knew the extent of Robin's evil - never able to forget her first hand experience of his treachery. A tiny sliver of doubt had already started niggling - fearful she was about to lure James's children into danger.

IV

Avalon on the other hand, was charged with a heady blend of excitement and nerves. She had only ever conversed with Robin on a formal basis. She hummed softly to herself as she flitted around their spacious kitchen - comforted by the surround of creamy units. It was the type of kitchen friends envied; modern yet traditional where a checkered tile floor brought flashbacks of Westbourne House.

"Not nervous are you, Sis?" William piped up. He was carefully spooning prawn cocktail into some intricate crystal dishes.

"A little," Avalon answered, "though nothing could be as nerve-wracking as the time Dad invited *the Hamptons* over - and to think, I was dating Ben…"

"Don't talk about *him!*' William snapped.

"Sorry," Avalon whispered. Any further discussion was temporarily suspended by the clang of the doorbell. "I'll get it!"

She flew through the lounge towards the door, delighted to discover it was Peter. Avalon smiled, relieved he had turned up first. The light in the porch enhanced his gentle features, his complexion glowing. She seized his hands.

"Peter!" she beamed as he leaned in to peck her cheek. His silver hair had grown a little longer - it curled into the collar of his corduroy shirt. "I'm so glad you're here…"

Peter, restless as ever, followed her into the kitchen. "What are you cooking?" he quizzed, "it smells wonderful."

"Chicken with white wine and herbs," Avalon said, "it's a French recipe. Eleanor helped - but don't tell Robin that…"

"Of course not," Peter sighed, never able to forget the vindictive campaign Robin had spawned against Eleanor. He let out a sigh. In an earlier conversation, they had agreed to act as if they knew nothing of his 'friendship' with Perry.

"I feel like a complete traitor," Avalon whispered.

"Me too!" Peter chuckled, "but it's for a good cause - so relax!"

Ten minutes later, Robin was marching towards the same place, struck with an irrepressible sense of power. His cool blue eyes scanned the street for their house - he could hardly believe his good fortune! Perry had spelt out his desires, many months ago: to *ingratiate* himself with Peter Summerville and befriend the Barton-Wells children. Yet he was painfully aware of his motives. Perry was driven by his obsession to seize Elijah and perceived them as potential tools: *'We must bide our time - perhaps, enlist the help of someone he trusts…'*

Robin smiled, recalling that sinister conversation. How delighted would he be when he learned of this intimate little dinner party? He paused, staring at the house with its pure white walls slashed across with timbers. A large, silver tabby cat guarded the porch. Robin's smile softened as he stepped towards the door, reaching down to ruffle its fur. He actually quite liked cats and had one of his own - though he was a little surprised when the creature backed away from him before slinking into the bushes.

Seconds later, he found himself shepherded into a lovely lounge. Avalon looked gorgeous in a violet party dress - diamanté sparkling around her throat, her hair and makeup perfect.

"Your house is exquisite," he breathed, handing her a bouquet of flowers and a bottle of chilled, sparkling wine.

"Thank you," Avalon said shyly, coaxing him towards the sofa. "These flowers are beautiful." She gazed down at his gift, admiring the pink and crimson lilies interwoven with white carnations. "What can I get you to drink?

We've got red wine or white. Unless you'd prefer a beer."

He settled into the lounge, admiring the rich oriental rug spread across the floor - loving the furniture as well as the decor. He was further delighted to be joined by Peter and finally, William, who looked divine in a blue and white striped tunic worn loose outside his cotton chinos. For a moment, Robin's eyes were drawn to his long sun-tanned feet, strapped in sandals; his clothes trendy but casual, making him slightly self-conscious of his own formal attire.

Cautious of drinking too much too early, Robin politely requested a beer, prompting William to join him.

"So," he began, the moment the conversation lulled. "I hear you visited France with your father's friends." He gave a cool smile - he was still revelling in William's council visit.

It was an opening designed to encourage him to show off his photos as he plonked himself on the sofa next to him. His enthusiasm was relentless. The boy was right - the Dordogne was a most enchanting corner of France and straight away, Robin found himself admiring the medieval architecture. He also found himself studying photos of the kids.

"Is that your boyfriend?" he couldn't resist the urge to ask Avalon - eyes fixed on her lounging by a swimming pool in a skimpy bikini top and shorts, her face aglow with pleasure. Next to her hovered a boy of about 18 with haughty, aristocratic features.

"Mmm," Avalon murmured fondly. "George and I have known each other for years."

"We used to call him 'Wing Nut," William added with a laugh.

"You still do!" Avalon scolded, taking the photo from Robin.

She eventually arranged her guests around a light ash dining table and poured the wine. William hopped in and out of the kitchen, serving up his prawn cocktail with triangles of brown bread. For the next few moments, Robin was overwhelmed by their hospitality - relishing William's starter with its creamy sauce and succulent prawns. By the time he had finished his beer, William seemed eager to ply him with wine. He gratefully accepted a glass of the same sparkling white as the others were drinking.

"Impressive," Robin smiled at him.

"Okay, I confess, I cheated," he muttered furtively. "I got it from Marks and Sparks."

"William!" Avalon gasped.

"My cooking skills are still a bit amateurish," he shrugged.

"Well, it was beautifully presented," Robin enthused. He watched as William gathered up the dishes, his eyes transfixed on the back of his head. The soft light illuminated the brassy sheen of his hair, leaving him helpless to wonder what it would be like to run his fingers through it. "Are *you* dating anyone?"

"You could say I'm *between* relationships," William mused.

Avalon chuckled. "William, you're dating three different girls! All those years stuck in boarding school and now he's finally let loose on the female population!"

"I told him 'fighting girls off' would be his problem," Peter added with a grin.

"So what about you, Robin?" Avalon asked softly. "Have you ever been married?"

She caught Peter's eye and smiled. Robin didn't miss that doting look, every time she addressed him. At the same time, he could feel himself buckling under the weight of her stare - knowing she deserved an answer.

"I was married once, yes - but now I'm divorced."

"Oh," William responded in sympathy. "Did you love her?"

"Of course," Robin sighed. "Unfortunately, I stopped loving her." He gripped the stem of his wine glass, hating to be reminded. The wine had been gradually creeping up on him, releasing his inhibitions. "Theresa was 10 years younger than me and very pretty. Her family were Polish."

He momentarily closed his eyes where he could still picture her; a girl who's sparkling eyes and pale, freckled face left him spellbound. He would never forget the first time he had spotted her - he had mistaken her for a boy as she hovered by the photocopier. Her short, blonde hair was cut in the style of an Etonian schoolboy, matched by a narrow waist and tiny backside. Robin had experienced the magnetic draw of her presence where the discovery of her gender didn't deter him. He had fallen in love. He drained his glass, lowering it to the table.

"I wanted children," he added guardedly. "I was 40 but she didn't feel the same way - then she started seeing other men…"

"I'm sorry," Peter counselled him gently. "Relationships are a minefield. I've fallen in love and had my heart broken many a time! But let's not talk about it - not when there's so much else happening. What do you think of the work on the Community Centre?"

Robin smiled brightly, relieved Peter had changed the subject. "Magnificent," he breathed. "Your friend, Charlie, is very talented. He certainly knows how to drive a workforce."

Peter nodded, his eyes distant as if contemplating his next words. Robin was dimly aware of his hosts drifting around the table. Avalon had already plated up a sensational-smelling main course, whilst William eagerly poured him a goblet of red. He was still listening to Peter as he continued to rhapsodise about the building work. It was a discussion which continued over dinner where even the Barton-Wells children seemed unrestrained in their praise and keen to talk about the restoration of Westbourne House. Robin soaked up the information, delighted to be rewarded with these various snapshots into their lives. It was with no hesitation he added his support -

complimentary of Elijah's drawing.

"So how do you visualise your housing trust, Peter?" Avalon dropped into the discussion.

Robin frowned - recalling William's words.

"I can't be sure," Peter faltered. "I need to sketch out my ideas. It's something I want to discuss with Charlie and his son - and Elijah.'

"Elijah?" Robin frowned, feeling his heart skip a beat.

"Elijah wants to be an interior designer," Peter reflected.

Robin listened to their banter, whilst enjoying Avalon's mouth-watering chicken. He took a sip of wine, his taste buds further caressed by its smooth, well rounded berry flavour. It was without thinking, he gulped back a little more than he intended - momentarily distracted by William's hovering presence as he swooped in to top up his glass.

"The final decision rests with the council," Peter smiled. "So are they still willing to support my idea, Robin?"

William captured his stare - his eyes flared with hope.

"Peter, nothing is carved in stone," Robin shrugged. "Though it wouldn't hurt to put your plans on paper. The land is coming up for sale in a few months time - I am as keen for the council to purchase it as I proposed."

"And what do *you* want for this town?" Avalon pressed.

"To develop Rosebrook into something beautiful, of course," Robin smiled at her.

"Do you know of any other parties who are interested in the land?" Peter piped up.

Robin froze, his mind spinning - he was at a loss what to say. "Why do you ask?" he retorted, his voice a little harsher than he intended.

"I've been talking to Charlie," Peter shrugged. "He's been in the construction business for years. He reckons it's bound to appeal to property developers..."

"Did he now?" Robin whispered. He narrowed his eyes. "Well, it's possible he may be right. This land has huge development potential - both residential and commercial. It could ultimately be a shopping mall or even a leisure complex. This is the reason I am doing my utmost to persuade the council to buy it. So we can have the final say over what the land may be used for."

"What happens if somebody else wants it?" William chipped in.

The main course was finished and without delay, Avalon whisked away the plates before carefully setting down a board of cheese and biscuits. She sank into her chair, content to let them ponder. Peter glanced up at her and smiled. Yet still Robin paused - filled with a sense, the evening was about to turn a little more intriguing.

"The council has first refusal to purchase the land at its current market value," he murmured, "granting the vendor a quick sale and without complications."

"So what is its current value?" William's voice grazed against his ear.

"Around £30k…" He broke off, his knuckles white as he gripped his glass. *Jesus! He shouldn't have disclosed that!* He took another deep swallow of wine, fighting to retain his composure - his eyes cool as they slid towards William. "Why are you so interested?" he demanded, feeling the first flicker of anxiety.

"We've got land of our own, Mr Whaley," William shrugged, selecting a cracker before carving into the cheese. "It's handy to know these things."

Robin opened his mouth as if to speak, then closed it. Of course, he knew about the 2,000 acres of land in Aldwyck their father had bequeathed to them. Perry had been livid - especially when the girl refused to sell it to him.

"This is the land around Westbourne House," Avalon elaborated. "We should go over and look at it some time, William - think about what we could do with it."

"What sort of land is it?" Robin probed.

She gazed boldly back at him. "Rural land - farmland, woodland. Some of it's rented out for agricultural purposes but other than that, it's just a beautiful piece of countryside…"

"Why hang on to it?" Robin pressed, wondering if he could extract any further advantage from this evening. A smile crept onto his face. "What use is it to you?"

"We don't yet know," Avalon answered, her expression solemn, "but it means everything to us. This is the last legacy Dad left us; to retain a connection with Aldwyck."

"The locals are worried about future development," William said bitterly. "They wouldn't want someone like Hampton building all over it."

"Ssh, William," Avalon chided him gently. "We agreed not to talk about them."

Robin was still watching her, his smile lingering. He already feared, these children may know about his connection with Perry. Fortunately, they shied away from the subject - where it took the subtle intervention of Peter to draw the conversation back onto a safe, light hearted level.

By the time Robin left, his head felt heavy. He had consumed far too much alcohol and so, for that matter, had Peter. Avalon had further impressed him by making Irish coffee; carefully blending whisky and sugar - trickling the cream over the back of a spoon, so it floated in a velvety white layer. The evening had been divine, Robin reflected - charmed by the elegance of their home; their beautiful cat, Jim Beam, who had finally made an appearance. It ultimately reminded him that he needed to get home to his own cat; a blue-eyed Siamese pedigree.

He swayed on the doorstep, shaking Peter's hand - then William's. Their eyes locked in a way which made him falter - his emotions torn as he battled to fight his attraction. The boy's face was so exquisite. It was a moment he would have liked to suspend in time, so he could just keep staring.

Sensing the inappropriate nature of his thoughts, he dropped his hand. William disappeared inside the house and Peter too seemed to have vanished - they could hear him whistling to himself as he wandered down the darkening side street. Avalon giggled.

"This has been a most pleasurable evening," Robin smiled, clasping her hands. He leaned forward to peck her cheek - except his mouth discovered the sweetness of her lips. It was hard to ascertain who was the more surprised as he kissed her - where that powerful surge of affection had finally found an outlet. "You're so beautiful," he murmured, his voice slurring. "If I were only twenty years younger…"

"Oh, ssh now," Avalon teased. "Get yourself home, Robin and have a good sleep. It's been a lovely evening and I'm sure we'll bump into each other again very soon."

Robin wandered away and she watched him go. He threw her one last wave before he continued his journey. Except he didn't return home immediately - buzzing with the same sense of power as earlier, he found himself strangely drawn towards the almshouse.

The curtains were drawn yet he could see a dim shine of light. He stared at the house, despising its residents - disgusted to think that those sophisticated young people, back there, could possibly be so close to some half-caste whore like Eleanor - and William had divulged Elijah was his best friend. Robin thrust his bitter thoughts aside; struck with an idea, the situation might be useful one day - especially in the light of Perry's plans.

He allowed himself a smile then wandered a little further. The land at the back of the Community Centre lay beneath a cloak of shadow.

He stared across the yawning expanse, thinking about his own game; how he would endorse this plan of Peter's - persuade the council to grab the land while they were in with a chance. It would endear the council to the public: affordable housing for hard-working people, how could it fail? He would emerge from these early discussions, looking like some sort of saviour.

Except the council couldn't possibly afford to maintain such a scheme. As soon as the potential of Peter's housing plan was embraced, the value of the land would soar. He knew how badly the council needed funds. Especially if they wanted to keep on improving the town.

This would be the point when the council would be forced to consider other options, one of which would be Dominic's entertainment complex. Robin smiled again, envisaging the disruption this would cause the residents. Eleanor and her allies would oppose it and Robin would use *their* arguments to manipulate the council into rejecting it. Lastly, he would make sure

Dominic knew about it; and how sweet would be his victory, when it was discovered that *his dream to forge a night club* had been thwarted by none other than Eleanor Bailey.

No, there was only one person he wanted to acquire this land and that person was Perry. His scheme to develop an exclusive housing estate would bring wealth and prestige to Rosebrook. Perry would feel indebted to him - not to mention the council who would relish the extra revenue. In some ways, this evening had marked the start of a new era; one in which Robin found himself feeling more exhilarated than he had done in years.

Chapter 4

I

Before the month ended, the Baileys joined forces with the Barton-Wells children for a long overdue trip to Aldwyck. Alesha watched them go. She was parked at the far end of the Community Centre, hoping she was sufficiently concealed. It was only in the last week, she had reluctantly exchanged her lovely silver Scirocco for a black Ford Fiesta, now fearing Eleanor's suspicion. She had evaded her on at least one occasion; and neither did Alesha miss the glare she had flung at her, when she was momentarily captured in her wing mirror. She had almost ducked.

She kept a close watch as they emerged from the back of the almshouse in Charlie's Volvo. Eleanor was behind the wheel. It was to her even greater surprise that Charlie rolled up in a sleek MG sports car - the Barton-Wells children crammed in the back. Alesha followed, her intrigue growing as they left the town. Within minutes, they had poured onto the main road before disappearing down a country lane in the direction of Aldwyck. Alesha nibbled the inside of her lip, using her skill as a detective to keep a good distance behind; though it was fairly obvious where they were heading - a hunch that was confirmed 20 minutes later.

Alesha spun her car round and shot out of the village before they had a chance of seeing her. She got straight onto the phone to Perry.

"They're in the village," she breathed into the mouthpiece of her new mobile phone. Perry had insisted on this latest addition to her inventory, so she no longer had to rely on public phones. She stroked its black leather case and smiled. "I think we can safely leave this in your hands, Perry."

"Where are they now?" he demanded.

"Near the caravan. They appear to be visiting the people who live in the farmhouse."

"So keep an eye on them," Perry snapped, "update me on their movements."

He slammed down the phone, breathing hard. In some ways, Perry was looking forward to a stand off with those damned people! Robin had finally divulged the news of his little 'soirée' in the home of the Barton-Wells children; news which should have thrilled him - yet left him uneasy.

These thoughts pestered him, as he wandered through the patio doors and into the grounds where the last of the summer sun bathed the flowers in a blaze of light. Ever since Perry had moved here, he had been suffering from a rising sense of anxiety. The first few days had been hectic; both he and Rowena snowed under with tasks, which included completely refurbishing the ground floor. In the weeks that followed, they had been preoccupied with the recruitment of new staff, from chefs and bar maids to cleaners and gardeners.

But as the weeks sped by and they gradually grew accustomed to their palatial new surroundings, so Perry's sense of hubris began to wear off - and that was when the nightmares had started.

April had brought a tempest rolling into the grounds - his nights disturbed by violent winds and rainstorms; then James had started wandering into his dreams - every detail etched on the canvas of his mind, from his pale, gaunt face to the hazel eyes which shone with accusation.

It was throughout these dreams that James spoke to him; echoes of conversations which had been real. Even worse, were the scenarios where James had sworn retribution for the plight of his children. Perry was forced to remind himself, they were just dreams - his own mind playing tricks.

That was until early one morning, when he had been feeling restless and wandered downstairs to the library. The light of dawn was particularly pleasing - it flooded in through the column of large windows, throwing hazy shafts across the hall. He could never be sure if it had been a formation of dust motes, or had he really seen that tall shadow hobbling up the western staircase? Perry stood paralysed - struck by a memory of the day he had seen his victim limp across the bar. It was a terror that had sent him stumbling through the door and into the grounds, where James's gardens practically mocked him.

He had been gloating over his plans - determined to remodel the estate to accommodate new outbuildings for corporate events. By this time, he had already slammed in one planning application to demolish the Victorian walled gardens. He was even considering having the grounds re-landscaped as if to erase every last vestige of its former proprietor - but in the end, his conscience got the better of him. His wife particularly adored these gardens and perhaps, if he left well alone, James might stop haunting him!

Perry felt the clench of his jaw, as he strayed towards those wretched gardens; still angry that his planning application had been refused - not to mention the dwindling hotel business. It had only just started to pick up - despite the thousands he had splurged on advertising.

It seemed, Perry was not the only man with connections. James too, had retained a well-established 'Old Boy' network; people like Dr. Albany Price, who's client base hailed from the wealthiest echelons of society - Cyril Fortescue, who's contacts included cabinet ministers and heavy weight directors. It was hardly a wonder the usual clientele were boycotting the place.

Perry glared across the gardens where the orderly rows of vegetables flourished. It was out of pure spite, he had considered turfing over the whole lot; eradicate these fertile plots once and for all. Yet the impact of his heart seizure had forced him to endure a period of convalescence. And by the time he returned in July, troops of villagers were already invading the grounds, tending to their plots. Perry refused to tolerate it and using the intimidating might of his two security guards, he had steadfastly ordered them off his property.

Within a few days however, a barrage of villagers turned up in force, including Herbert Baxter and his solicitor, Nigel Patterson. The final straw came when Patterson had produced some antiquated document drawn up by James Barton-Wells himself, which clearly entitled his clients to hold on to their vegetable plots until the end of the year. It was an agreement which was legally binding, leaving Perry powerless to oppose it.

His gaze travelled over the landscape. There was no denying, Aldwyck was an enchanting village, yet Perry was driven by ambition. His plan to turn this traditional hotel into a gold mine was not quite working as he had hoped - and now it seemed, his enemies had returned here. He narrowed his eyes, picturing the farmhouse - the field where his most hated enemy had lived for all those years, sensing her power to destroy him even from a distance.

Eleanor had always adored Marilyn and Tom. Nothing brought more pleasure than to revisit their lovely farmhouse - the ceilings, striped with beams and the musty smell of flagstones. Marilyn's lounge had never been more crowded as the Barton-Wells kids, along with Eleanor and her family, competed for space on the various blanket covered sofas, chairs and floor rugs.

Yet at the same time as Perry was fuming over his failure to bar the locals, it seemed ironic that Tom was talking about the same thing.

"Damn lucky they had that contract! They're fully within their rights to manage those plots until January 1988 and there is nothing Hampton can do about it."

"I'm delighted," Charlie responded, casting a nod in Tom's direction, "and bloody well done to the villagers for standing up to that bastard! So what happens next?"

"It'll be the end of an era," Marilyn said sadly. "He's clearly going to get rid of those vegetable gardens. Horrible man!"

"Hmm," Eleanor pondered as her gaze flitted beyond the window. She could see the edge of the field, serene in a pool of sunshine - the small copse of trees which dappled the grass with shade. Her caravan lingered in peaceful isolation and suddenly another thought struck her. "Have there been any travellers camped here, over summer?"

Marilyn fired her a look of anxiety. "Funny you should ask. One or two vehicles did turn up but they didn't stay for very long..." she broke off, her expression strained. "It seems they were scared off. Usually within a day or two!"

"Who by?" Eleanor frowned. "Perry?"

"Not Perry," Tom muttered darkly. "His son, Benjamin..."

Eleanor felt Avalon flinch beside her.

"I saw them," Marilyn hissed feverishly. "Ben and that villainous body guard - both on motorbikes and I'll tell you something else. They brought some heavies down from London. At least, I assume that's where those *men* came from…"

"What sort of men?" Eleanor gasped.

"Black men," Marilyn whispered nervously, slanting her body closer, "they wore identical leather jackets. I got the impression they were some criminal gang!"

The atmosphere inside the lounge turned chilly. Elijah stared fearfully up at Eleanor.

"And you're sure about this?" her voice broke through the tension.

"Yes!" Marilyn insisted. "I don't mean to sound racist but you don't see many black faces in Aldwyck - at least, not since that poor girl lost her job…" she jerked her head in the direction of Westbourne House.

"Lara," Eleanor murmured. "I suppose you're right…" Her head snapped upright. "So Ben Hampton and that *creep*, Nathan, have been rolling up in the field with a gang of thugs - terrorising any travellers who turn up?"

"I'm afraid so," Tom nodded sagely. "We spoke to Inspector Boswell - but nobody seemed that bothered. Boswell never did like those hippies very much. I personally didn't find them a problem, apart from that dreadful lot who picked on Eli."

Andrew lowered his head. Eleanor too, felt tormented by the memory - recalling, it was Boswell's bully of a son, Gary, who'd spread the rumour that her son was a 'grass.'

"Doesn't mean those Hamptons can use bully-boy tactics!" William raged. "Who the hell do they think they are? It's not even their land!"

"I know," Marilyn sighed, "but what can we do? Tom and I are too old to take on people like that, William. I think you're just going to have to monitor your land a little better. I doubt if any of this would have happened if your father had been alive."

"Damn right it wouldn't," Avalon whispered, her eyes glittering with tears. "This is the first I've heard about it. We haven't been here for months - not even Elliot contacts us, these days."

"Elliot is under very close supervision," Marilyn placated her. "Perry has his own people working there - including that dreadful Fisher woman!"

"Well maybe you should consider an alternative use for the field," Charlie intervened.

Eleanor threw him a wily look. "In the light of what I've just heard, I'm wondering if the field could be used to set up some allotments."

"Brilliant idea!" William whispered, twisting his head round to smile at her.

"It is isn't it?" Tom smirked. "What's more, the villagers will love you for it! They're about to lose their plots at Westbourne House. It'll be a nice way of upholding a rural tradition."

"It's perfect," Avalon added numbly. "It's exactly what Dad would have wanted. You were right, Eleanor - this land anchors us to the village!" She raised her head - it was as if the true purpose of their visit had finally been realised.

"You may still have to apply to the council for permission," Charlie added gently.

"I know," Avalon sighed, "but I can't imagine there'll be a problem, can you? It's just an empty field. This is why it attracted travellers. You know Dad. His philosophy in life was to share - especially for those less fortunate…"

"You don't have to tell me that," Marilyn smiled. "This is the reason Rosemary rang me, all those years ago…" she cast a fond gaze towards Eleanor. "We knew James wouldn't have a problem with Eleanor living here. Rosemary always said 'it was meant to be.'"

"I know," Eleanor murmured dreamily, "which reminds me. Do you think this might be a good time to move Joshua on site?"

"I do," Marilyn nodded. "The sooner my nephew establishes a home here, the better. You haven't met his girlfriend, Lucy, have you? She's from Wales and misses the countryside dreadfully. They can keep an eye on the field and if there're any more problems concerning the Hamptons, they'll let you know about it."

"And *we'll* take our complaint to the police!" William added with confidence, "boot them off our land…" he released a chuckle.

Andrew, finally drawn out of his reverie, joined in his humour. "*Get orf moi Land!* Which reminds me - you said you wanted to go and visit Farmer Baxter!"

"Please be careful," Charlie nagged his son, who had only just passed his driving test. "Don't forget, you're not actually *insured* to drive William's MG…"

"Okay!" Andrew sighed, rolling his eyes. "It's not like William's ever gonna forgive me if I prang his precious sports car!"

"We're going up there to have a look at the woods Dad left to us," Avalon added, finally giving way to a smile. "We'll meet you a bit later."

"Meet us in the Olde House at Home," Eleanor beamed back. "Just promise, you'll take care of yourselves."

Five minutes later, Perry was summoned to the telephone. He caught a glimpse of his reflection as he marched into the lounge. A deepening red flush had crept into his complexion - whether it was from the glare of the sunshine or the fury which still bit deep into his heart, he was unsure.

He grabbed the receiver. "Any news?"

"Yes!" Alesha panted breathlessly. "They've split up!"

She had just spotted the Barton-Wells children leaving the farmhouse with

Charles Bailey's son. She assumed they would be drawn into the heart of the village. Yet they had swung left onto a concealed farm track. Perry's grip on the phone tightened.

"Herbert Baxter," he whispered icily. "They must be driving up to his farm…"

"It's just a tiny track," Alesha faltered, "I can't follow them - it'll be too obvious."

"Of course!" Perry snapped, "and the others?"

"Just pulled up outside the pub," Alesha replied.

Perry smiled. He could picture her now, hidden in one of the side roads. Her elevated position in the hills yielded a good view over the village, enhanced by powerful binoculars.

"Okay, you can leave this to me now, Alesha," Perry finished. "Just stay close to the main road. We can never be sure what they're up to." The moment the conversation ended, he turned to Rowena - the ghost of his smile lingered. "Come along, my dear," he murmured, "it's a beautiful day. Let's go and re-acquaint ourselves with the locals."

Charlie let out a sigh of pleasure as the familiar pub took shape. Eleanor followed his gaze where the usual array of barrel planters and hanging baskets exploded with flowers. Elijah shuffled along beside her with Margaret - a little disgruntled to be excluded from taking a ride with the others. Yet it had taken one glance at that deep, dark forest to remind them of the exhausting chase he had endured on the day those men had tried to grab him. Eleanor placed a protective arm around his shoulder, her eyes scanning the area. Some remote farm was the last place she wanted her son to be, right now, especially with their enemies lurking.

The pub's long serving landlord, Boris, caught sight of them. His face split into a grin.

"Eleanor," he gasped, "Charlie! Great to see you. How are things?"

He shook Charlie's hand and pleasantries were exchanged. It was almost as if they sensed time was short - maybe only a matter of minutes before Perry's spies started infiltrating the pub. "I've got something for you," he whispered, bobbing down behind the bar.

With a flash of movement so quick, it would have been miraculous if anyone had noticed, Boris slipped an envelope into Elijah's pocket, aware of Eleanor watching. "Don't move. It's from Elliot. There's a letter in there for James's kids - it'll explain everything."

"Half a cider please, Boris," Eleanor announced, sneaking a calculating glance at her son. He smiled back, his eyes glittering with intrigue.

Once they had ordered drinks and packets of crisps, Charlie engaged them in a cheerful repartee, updating Boris on everything that had transpired since the wedding; the blissful honeymoon in Paris - Peter's relentless enthusiasm over his potential housing trust.

"I'm pleased, folks," Boris sighed. "I wish I could say life was as rosy but there's been a lot of tension in this village since 'you know who' moved in…" His eyes swivelled towards the door then crashed to a halt. A look of dread swept across his face. "I say, w-why don't you folks go and sit in the beer garden…"

"No it's okay, we'll stay," Charlie said firmly. His eyes drifted towards the same door where Perry and his wife had just materialised.

Eleanor let out a gasp. She clutched Margaret's hand, horrified to notice the child's face turning pale. She had never stopped being scared of the Hamptons.

Rowena stepped forward, her eyes uncannily drawn to Margaret as if assessing her. She had changed since turning 12, Eleanor found herself thinking. Margaret was not only taller with the slender limbs and big feet of a growing adolescent but her delicate face was more pointed, accentuated by a shorter, feathery hair cut. She started to retreat. Elijah hovered just a few feet away and suddenly it was his turn to be the object of their scrutiny.

Elijah put on a brave face, staring openly back at them before Eleanor swung out in front of him like a tiger guarding her cubs.

"Go on, Eli, do as Boris says," she snapped. "Go to the beer garden with Margaret."

Perry's intense stare did not waver as he wandered towards them.

"What do you want?" Charlie sighed.

"I've got a bone to pick with you, Charles Bailey," Perry said in a voice of ice, "as well as *your dear wife* here!"

"Really?" Charlie drawled. He took a draft of beer. "Well go on then - I'm all ears."

Clouds of tension started to billow inside the pub, cooling the atmosphere.

"I had the electricians in," Perry continued. "Seems your expertise in the restoration of old properties wasn't that impressive after all…" he left his words dangling.

Charlie simply shrugged. "I don't know what you mean," he muttered, turning away.

"Really?" Perry sneered. "That damp course you installed in the basement was a shambles. Moisture crept in through the membrane and spread to the suspended timber floor. It's caused severe problems with the electrical circuits! The place has been blowing fuses left, right and centre!" His hand closed over his shoulder like a clamp. "It's not good enough, Bailey!"

"Take your hands off me, you arrogant turd!" Charlie hissed.

"Gentlemen," Boris said lightly, "could you please take your quarrel somewhere else…"

"You can shut up for a start!" Perry rounded on him. There was an electrifying pause before he turned his frosty gaze back to Charlie.

Charlie shook him off, refusing to be intimidated. "I didn't carry out that work. We drafted in a team of floor specialists from London. Take your issue up with them!"

"The air bricks were clogged with earth!" Perry continued to rant. "Only *you* would understand the consequences; with a lack of ventilation, it was never going to dry out - especially in the winter months. It's sabotage! You deliberately set out to cause me problems."

"No, I did not," Charlie said, forcing a calmer tone. "Despite what you think, I would never *set out* to ruin a property as beautiful as Westbourne House! Not like some I could mention."

Eleanor felt the coils of fear tightening as Perry continued to scowl at her husband. The interior of the pub had grown steadily quieter as more and more people strained to hear what was being said. She tugged Charlie's arm.

"Come on, let's go outside. We can't leave the kids on their own, they might not be safe."

Her eyes met Rowena's as she turned on her heel; but she sensed they were being followed. She bit her lip, stepping into the beer garden where the sun momentarily warmed her face. The kids were huddled on a bench, heads together in deep conversation. They glanced up. Yet again a wisp of fear passed across Margaret's face.

Eleanor spun round and for several seconds, the two women surveyed each another. She was immediately struck by Rowena's glamour; from her platinum blonde hair to a linen dress matched by a beautifully cut jacket. Perry followed, a purplish tinge seeping into his complexion.

"What did you say?" Rowena's voice lashed into the silence.

"You heard," Eleanor snapped. "Now stay away from us…"

"Why do you think your children might not be safe?" Rowena pressed.

Eleanor froze, conscious of Perry braced beside her. The two of them had her trapped. Her hand trembled as it clutched the glass; cider splashed over the rim and onto the paving stones, dilating into damp circles where it landed.

"You know why," she shivered. "Margaret's very sensitive. That *scene* in James's bar frightened her. As for my son…" she stared into Rowena's eyes. "You *know* he was nearly abducted."

"That had nothing to do with us!" Rowena spat back.

Charlie had moved to the table, where Margaret squeezed up against him.

"What are those horrid people doing here?" they heard her whimper.

Rowena's face twisted into a sneer. "Horrid people?"

"Oh yes," Perry's voice pulsed into her ears, "don't think we're not aware of your campaign to poison the community against us, Eleanor Bailey. Hoping to destroy my reputation are you?"

"I think you're doing that quite well, yourself," Eleanor said tightly.

"I see," Perry whispered. There was a moment of silence before he pressed his face right up against her ear. She breathed in the all-pervasive tang of his aftershave, wary of his power. "I know your game. I suppose you thought it amusing, leaving *that tape* in the Orangerie."

Elijah, who had been hanging onto every word, started to uncoil himself like a spring. Eleanor shot him a warning glance then turned to face Perry. "I have no idea what you're talking about!"

"Really?" Perry challenged. "You mean you didn't know? A recording taken from your lover's rock band..." his voice dropped even lower. "I warned you never to cross me again, *Eleanor* and I meant it."

She started to back away again but this time, Perry smiled.

"I've got my eye on you," he finished nastily. "Now go back to your family, Eleanor. Enjoy the rest of your day." His eyes were mocking as they purposefully locked with Elijah's.

II

Throughout the homeward journey, no-one could have felt more unsettled: It was only now, Elijah's fingers crept inside his pocket, feeling for the envelope Boris had smuggled him - but his thoughts were elsewhere.

He found himself recalling every episode connected to Perry. The scene in James's bar; a showdown he had never quite understood - at least, not until the day William and Avalon had mentioned it. Elijah had sensed something was afoot that day. Eleanor had scooped him into her car and sped back to the village. It was as if they had been escaping from someone - where eventually his mother revealed, her enemies had threatened her - or more specifically, *him*.

She had no idea he had listened to every word of her telephone conversation with Avalon; the notion, some gangster had been hired to put the frighteners on her. *'If I ever spoke a word of what I knew, they would snatch my son... more or less implied they would torture him...'*

Avenues of rolling countryside swept before his eyes - lush fields shimmering in the sun with the first golden hues of corn. The bordering woods seemed dark in comparison, reminding him of his near capture again. He pressed his eyes shut, picturing the men. It took his mind back to another conversation in one of the tranquil parks of Rosebrook. William suspected Nathan; the dreaded insinuation that Perry *was* involved.

By the time they pulled up outside the almshouse, his face was chalky white. Charlie roared to a halt behind them. The Barton-Wells children spilled out from the back.

"Eli!" Avalon breathed, rushing up to him. "What's up?"

It was only when they were hidden inside the almshouse, he finally extracted Elliot's letter. He looked at Eleanor. "Okay, so can we open it now?"

Avalon raised her eyebrows.

"It's from Elliot," Eleanor enlightened her. "It's even got a stamp on it. Boris must have intended to post it." She plucked the envelope from her son's hand and tore it open.

'Sorry I haven't been in touch. When I said Perry didn't know I attended the wedding, I was wrong. Word got back and it landed me in trouble. I'm going to London on September 15th to close the sale on Mother's house. We can't meet up but we can talk on the phone. Please pass my 2nd letter to A & W. Will explain everything. Miss you all, kind regards, E.S.'

One hour later, after Charlie had parked William's MG safely back inside their garage, Elijah chose to linger - curious to talk to the Barton-Wells children in the privacy of their own garden.

"Well, what did you make of that?" William pressed.

Elijah let out a sigh. They were resting in sun loungers, gazing over the garden - sipping glasses of orange juice and lemonade topped up with ice cubes.

"I don't know. I didn't like the way they just *turned up* at the pub - it was scary."

"So shall we see what's in the other letter?" Avalon suggested.

Both boys watched eagerly as she prised open the envelope. This one was a lot longer and written across several leaves of hotel note paper. Avalon took a deep breath. It was a letter which had been written over many weeks, judging from the occasional change of ink colour. The sight of Elliot's gentle, flowing handwriting brought a lump to their throats.

"He must have started this in July," she began, "he mentions the walled gardens; how the villagers were shooed off the property..." she released a sad smile. *'Perry has abandoned his plans to use the area for a conference centre. The wooden greenhouses and Orangerie also carry a listing so it will be impossible for him to get planning permission. Regrettably, he plans to rip out the vegetable gardens in the New Year and destroy the orchards...'*

"Bastard!" Elijah and William chorused in unison.

Avalon frowned. "He's going to turn it into a putting green - but listen to this, boys. It seems, Perry's been consulting with someone from the council. *'He's visited the house several times:- a very distinguished gentleman with greying, dark hair and blue eyes, always wears a suit.'* Now who does that remind you of?"

"Whaley!" Elijah gasped, rearing up in his seat.

"Let's talk about him in a sec," Avalon intervened as her eyes floated down the page. "It's not all doom and gloom. He says he gets on well with Rowena and most of the other staff. That is, all except the general manager, Irene Fisher who he describes as a right old dragon! *'Perry rewards those who spy and report any subversive activities. I should have been more careful when I came to the wedding but word got out. Someone followed me and reported me to Perry.'*

Avalon's eyes darkened - it was as if a veil of sadness had extinguished their light. *"He has banned me from having any further contact with you. He has me continuously under watch and I cannot even make a phone call in private…"* She let out a sob. "Oh Elliot!"

"Poor sod!" William grunted, quaffing back his drink. "I don't understand it. Why can't he just leave?" The ice in his glass jangled. The sound turned Elijah cold.

"I'm asking myself the same question," Avalon said miserably. *"I am so sorry to tell you this. Yet I feel a powerful allegiance to Westbourne House. All the while I am butler, I can keep an eye on your father's estate. Rowena confides in me, but Perry is very paranoid. She has spoken of his nightmares and he fears the place may be haunted…"*

"Excellent," William smiled evilly. "Let's go rattle chains outside his window."

"Ssh, William!" Avalon barked. "Listen to this! *There have been issues with the electricity. The lights in the hallway flicker and this unnerves him. Cracks started appearing in the outer walls again and on the night Perry suffered a heart seizure, a bulb exploded in the Orangerie.'* That's strange - nothing like that ever happened when we lived there."

"No," Elijah sighed, "but I don't understand why Elliot's afraid. He's known you for years, why doesn't he just contact you?"

"It's explained on the last page," Avalon said, unable to disguise the bubble of tears in her voice. *"I wish I could see you but I can't. Perry has me followed. He knows I have family in London. There are people I love who he has threatened…"* Avalon gulped.

"So what now?" William couldn't resist the urge to prod her.

"He thinks Perry's plotting something," she whispered fearfully. *"Whatever you do, I urge you to be vigilant. Perry has people in Rosebrook too and a very secret meeting took place recently. Perry made sure his guests were in the library, out of sight. One of them was the man from the council. The other, I'm not sure about but I did not like the look of him. I sensed he was some sort of villain. So please look after yourselves, Perry is a very dangerous man."*

"Well he's definitely got it in for my mum," Elijah shivered, catching Avalon's eye. "He used that same warning, you know. *'Don't ever try to cross me.'* I heard him!"

"Remember our oath?" William added, his eyes fixed on some invisible point in the distance. "We swore we'd find out what went on in the past!"

"I know," Elijah added, "and I will."

It was only then, he told them about the exchange in the beer garden, knowing exactly what he needed to do. He just needed to find an opportune moment.

III

September 1987

The opportunity arose, a week after the August Bank Holiday when Elijah had not long returned to school. He had just entered his fourth year; to his delight, he had been assigned to a different form room with a whole new set of classmates - no longer at the mercy of Gary Boswell whose barbed comments and bullying had been the bane of his school days.

It was on the 2nd Saturday that Charlie had been invited to a party. It was the 20th Wedding anniversary of his close friend, Christopher Farrin; a man who's friendship he had cherished - especially in the days when he had been unemployed. He had also been his best man.

Eleanor was scheduled to work an extra shift at the hospital and couldn't attend. Filled with the hope, they would be alone together for an entire afternoon, Elijah also chose to decline with the pretence he had a huge pile of homework. He felt a heaviness in his heart as he watched them leave. He hadn't seen Andrew or Charlie don suits since the day of the wedding. Margaret looked a picture in a pale pink party dress. It reminded Eli how dearly he loved his new family - that despite their ups and downs, life had improved vastly since their solitary days in the caravan.

It seemed hard to imagine that he would later find himself staring at that chilling photo of Perry, captured almost 15 years ago - but from the moment Eleanor stepped through the door, he had been hankering to know the truth.

"Couldn't you just explain a little of it?" he pleaded.

Eleanor closed her eyes, massaging her temples. It was guilt that finally got the better of her. For years, she had wrapped Jake's death in a shroud of secrecy. But Eli was 14 now; where that unfortunate clash with the Hamptons could only have piqued his anxiety.

"Follow me," she whispered, beckoning him up the stairs.

She uprooted her metal box, before carefully manipulating the digits on the lock. It was over the next half hour, she gradually revealed those first news clippings. He poured over them in silence - drinking in every line of print like there was no tomorrow.

"A future Prime Minister was blown up in a car bomb? And *this* is what my father witnessed?"

The shocking secrets were gradually leaked, one by one. She guessed he would have difficulty taking it all in, especially the role of the police officer.

"We lay low for nearly 2 months," she shivered, having briefly described the first section of Jake's story. "We found a place to hide. It was the Merrimans' house. But we were scared, Eli. We hardly dared set foot outside the door and when we did, we had to disguise ourselves. We knew there were people out there, hunting for us. I found this out from one of Sammie's bouncers."

"What sort of people?" Elijah whispered.

"You've heard of organised crime haven't you?" Eleanor sighed. "Protection rackets - contract killings? These people belonged to the same criminal gang who snatched Jake in the first place."

"And you couldn't go to the police?" he pressed her.

Eleanor shook her head, her face taut as she continued to articulate Hargreeves' role. By the time Jake had described his ordeal, there was no question Hargreeves was involved. He was the only police officer who had interviewed him. He had detained him for longer than necessary - releasing him at precisely the right moment, in readiness for his capture. Elijah harboured an expression of horror. It was obvious, he would be shocked to hear such ties existed between Scotland Yard and the criminal underworld.

"The IRA were blamed for the car bomb," Eleanor sighed, "but it seems Jake held a vital clue as to who might have really been responsible. He saw a blonde-haired man in a car, that's all - and neither of us had any idea who he was until this event."

Seconds later, Elijah found himself staring straight into the blazing eyes of Perry Hampton; the photo was clear in its detail - the mysterious blonde man undeniably recognisable.

The hands on the clock turned faster as he probed for more details. He was curious to know how she had acquired such a photo - and naturally, Eleanor was compelled to relate her story: the day she had evaded Perry's spy, disguised as Shajeda.

"You must be wondering why we organised the press conference," she murmured. Her voice sounded dreamy - her mind locked in the past. "But first, I need to explain the second half of our story…" Elijah watched numbly as her hand drifted towards the stone pendant dangling from her neck. He knew it belonged to his father. "We had to leave the Merrimans' house before they returned - at least, make *some* attempt to get out of London. I was pregnant, Eli, with you! Your father and I pledged we'd escape to Holland and get married and this is the most painful part of my story - because unfortunately, we never made it…"

Relating the story was clearly tormenting her - especially the episode when Theakston's men had closed in on them at Waterloo Station. "There was one man, Jake recognised and I'll never forget his face - tall, gaunt with dark hair and pale blue eyes. Eli, this might even have been the man who shot your father. Fortuitously, we escaped again. We went to a place called Toynbee Hall and met a man named Bernard James. It's also where I first bumped into Reginald Magnus?"

"Really?" Elijah gasped. "He met my father?" His forehead creased into a frown - he was thinking about Reggie, the cool-headed, somewhat diffident drugs counsellor who worked alongside Peter.

"Yes - but it doesn't matter," Eleanor said, yanking him out of his trance. "The fact is, they helped us. They found us a safe house. Though it was a horrible neighbourhood. Violence and crime were rife - which brings me to the worst part of my story."

She had adopted that haunted look again. She spoke of a time when the police had been seeking Jake's arrest - the sinister disclosure, he was alleged to be a drug dealer. It inspired her to dip into her box again, extracting a second set of news clippings.

"We had no idea," she shuddered, "so we kept ourselves well hidden. It was the first time I started disguising myself as a Muslim girl... There were times when I wished we could have made a run for it - split up, maybe - jump into a taxi and get ourselves as far away from London as possible. I even had the money Sammie left me."

"So why didn't you?" Elijah frowned.

"Jake was scared of being captured. He was worried about me and our baby - especially if those thugs got hold of us. We had the added burden of the police to worry about. Jake was convinced that if he was arrested, the police would hand him straight back to his killers - especially if Hargreeves was involved..."

"This is unbelievable!" Elijah spluttered, "why weren't the police helping you?"

"That's exactly what Bernard said," Eleanor sighed as the fury simmered in her eyes. "We went to see him one last time. We found a package containing drugs in Jake's pocket which someone had obviously planted. They were closing in on us and Bernard was the only person who was prepared to help us. He knew Jake wasn't a drug dealer..." She stifled a sob, running her hand over the news clippings yet to be revealed. "Bernard was due to drive us to the docks next day..."

"But his killers got to him first," Elijah finished tightly.

"Jake hid me under the floorboards," she choked. Elijah gripped her hand, knowing how the story would end. "He made me promise to protect myself - to keep *you* safe. Someone started banging on our door - we thought it was the police so I let him hide me. I thought there was a chance I could still save him.... b-but it wasn't the police."

She could no longer stifle the tremor in her voice as she described what she'd heard: the relentless splitting of wood, the smashing crockery. They had torn apart their bedsit, looking for her; yet it seemed insignificant compared to the doomed arrival of the gang leader. She closed her eyes, recalling the echo of Jake's final words - the dull thud of a gun shot.

She squeezed Elijah's hands in misery. "*Now* do you understand why I so much wanted to protect you?"

"Yes," Elijah whispered in horror, "but why did they have to kill him?"

"Because they were hired to," she retorted savagely. "The worse thing of all is the way they tried to cover it up…"

Elijah glanced through the second set of news clippings - charged with indignation, as he finally absorbed the propaganda used to malign his father.

"He was never a drug dealer!" he spluttered. "He was a rock star from Holland! All he ever did was perform a gig for the MP who was murdered - and no-one saw a connection?"

"Not at first," Eleanor answered, "and *this* was the reason for the press conference!"

"Right," Elijah murmured. He lowered his eyes. He had demanded answers yet somehow, he had never expected his father's death to be cloaked in so many lies! He stared at the photos again, sliding them apart. "Hampton was definitely involved then. So who is this other man?"

"Don't you recognise him?" Eleanor's voice brushed against his ear.

He felt a chill sweep down his back. Yes, there was something disturbingly familiar about the gentleman in the black dinner suit - the way he was perched in his chair, partially concealing the other one. He studied the flawless features - the gleam of his rippling, dark hair.

"Robin Whaley?" Elijah breathed.

"I'm afraid so," Eleanor said guardedly. "*Councillor* Whaley played a significant part in this conspiracy…" He gazed stonily up at her from beneath his eyebrows, causing her to falter. "Just don't ever let on, you know this. You have to live a lie, Eli. Show respect, despite everything - because if you cannot keep up the pretence then there is no way I am going to tell you."

Elijah gritted his teeth - it seemed obvious he was going to have to agree to this. "Alright, I promise!"

"And you're sure about that are you?" Eleanor pressed, "because if either of these men suspected you knew… the consequences wouldn't bear thinking about."

"Just tell me, Mum," Elijah snapped, "I swear I won't repeat it."

"It was Whaley who started the rumours. He informed the police *and* Bernard that Jake was a drug dealer!" She gripped the pages which contained the transcripts. "It's all here, Eli - the journalists took copious notes. It's the only evidence I've got, right now."

Eleanor took a deep breath. It was almost as if there was something else she had been hankering to tell him but she snapped her lips tightly shut. Elijah on the other hand, felt a blistering fury. Even his mother must have sensed how difficult it was for his young mind to piece this all together; but he was finally beginning to grasp some picture.

"So now you know," Eleanor sighed, scooping up her notes. "I suspect Perry was the ring leader and Whaley, his right hand man. As for Jake's killer - for years I believed it was the gang leader, one of the most feared men in

London and who's name I dare not repeat. This is the man who threatened me; swore he'd do terrible things to you if I repeated what I knew…" she broke off with a shudder. "I'll never know for sure unless I take my enquiry to Scotland Yard."

"Okay," Elijah fumed, "so what about the police inspector? You told me about Hampton and Whaley but what about Hargreeves? It strikes me, he played as big a part in my father's murder as any of them!"

"I don't know where he is, sweetheart," Eleanor mumbled, "he was thrown out of the police force for corruption…"

"Oh yeah?" Elijah thundered, rising to his feet. "So couldn't we track him down?"

Eleanor stared at him in consternation. Yet she could never have known what he was thinking, his mind was elsewhere.

He turned and glared out of the skylight. He could see the ugly brick wall of the Community Centre. But in his mind's eye, he was trying to imagine his father leaving the police headquarters - the stony faced police inspector who had spent hours grilling him, no doubt anticipating the lethal ambush about to be detonated.

He felt the burn of tears - forearmed with his own experience of how deceitful the police could be; never able to forget the day when those filthy new age travellers had set upon him, convinced he was a grass… and all along, it was Boswell's loathsome son, Gary, who'd set him up. Boswell had implicated him in that drugs bust for no other reason than to bolster his own prejudice against travellers - which included him and his mother.

He clenched his teeth, hating the police in their capacity to be so corrupt - where the truth of his father's cold-blooded murder had oiled the wheels of his fury.

"We have got to find him," he snarled, "he is just as responsible!"

"I know," Eleanor sighed. She placed a gentle hand on his shoulder, though his muscles remained tense. "We *will* bring your father's killers to justice - as soon as I've got enough evidence. But until that day, we have to live our lives as normal, without drawing attention… which means you can't mention any of this stuff, not even to James's children."

Elijah spun round, remembering their oath. "Why not?" he gasped. "They've got as much reason to hate Hampton as all of us!"

"I'm aware of that," Eleanor argued, "but you are *not* to involve them! We mustn't give Perry any further excuse to intimidate them."

Elijah pressed his eyes shut, recalling Elliot's letter. "You may be right, Mum - except it's too late. They've already cottoned on…"

"You mean you've been talking about this?" Eleanor gasped.

Elijah shrugged. "They saw the way Hampton behaved when you two recognised each other! They're not stupid."

"I see," Eleanor quivered. "Then don't say any more. It's important - not just for their safety but for yours. We're in this together, Eli and there's just one more piece of evidence I need. It's a secret James confided to me." She grasped his arms tightly, staring deep into his eyes. "When Albert Enfield was killed, your father wasn't the only witness! Someone else saw Perry, someone who knew him! Her name was Evelyn Webster. It seems, she bumped into him at a service station - just miles from the location of Albert's party; driving a black Daimler exactly as Jake described. You must understand what this means, Eli."

He encountered an initial fog of confusion before his eyes widened. Eleanor had only ever *heard* Jake's description of the man - she had never actually seen him and knew her testimony was unsubstantiated. She had however, *seen* Perry at the press conference and had the evidence to prove it. There was only one person who could provide the final link.

"We have to find her," Eleanor finished shakily, "because until that day comes - I don't think we will ever be able to resolve this."

IV

Over the next few days, Elijah was forced to bury his emotions.

It started from the moment Charlie came bursting through the door, jubilant from Christopher's party. It was almost dark and although he and Eleanor had long finished their discussion, Elijah's head was swimming. For years, he had been desperate to understand the mystery surrounding his absent father. Only now, did it finally make sense. No wonder she had fought so hard to protect him, given the injustice she had suffered!

He returned to school subdued - which fortunately no-one really noticed since he had always been one of the quieter boys. It was for reasons known only to himself that he had strenuously avoided William, weighted down by the shock of it all - while oblivious to the devastating conversation which was about to draw them back into contact.

Charlie had not forgotten about Elliot's note and by mid-September he was bracing himself for that long awaited phone call.

Elliot meanwhile, was in London where the darkness of the autumnal skies pressed down heavily. He had finally closed the sale on his mother's house - a buyer ready to move in as soon as the place was empty of her unwanted furniture. He had only just seen off the house clearance firm, now finally destined for Camden where his brother, Daniel, had agreed to put him up for the night. There was only one more person he had been longing to visit.

Elliot paused outside the pillared entrance of a beautiful Victorian terrace in West Brompton and knocked on the door - woefully oblivious to the deadly blue eyes that bore into him behind their mirrored shades. He hadn't really been paying much attention to the man who was following him, given his attire; where a black woolly hat disguised his shaven head and a thick donkey jacket gave him the appearance of a typical labourer.

An hour later, Nathan was still surveying the house, just as Elliot reappeared in the doorway. He couldn't fail to catch a glimpse of the man he had dropped in on - young, with floppy blonde hair combed into a side parting. He conveyed the look of an artist; casual but stylish in green cords and a flamboyant, loose fitting sweater. Designer knitwear was all the rage, these days. Nathan smirked, having *noticed* him before; working as a landscape gardener in the grounds of Westbourne House. He had vanished, not long after Perry had returned from his holiday in Cannes. Although he had seen enough to guess the reason for Elliot's affection.

He drew out his camera, adjusting the long lens; anything to furnish Perry with yet more ammunition to torment their butler with. The opportunity came within seconds. The blonde man stepped forward and the two of them embraced. Nathan took a couple of snaps, zooming in to capture the younger man's face. He watched as Elliot slid into his car and drove off.

But even though he could track Elliot's movements and monitor those he came into contact with, he could never have overheard his next conversation.

"Elliot!" Charlie breathed down the telephone. "How are you?"

"Relax, Charlie, I'm fine," Elliot said softly. "Have you spoken to James's children?"

"Yes!" Charlie snapped. "They showed me your letter. William's outraged! He was all for heading up to Westbourne House to have it out with those bastards..."

"You must urge him not to do that!" Elliot interrupted. "Like I say, Perry is a very dangerous man! He's convinced you're plotting some sort of uprising - you, Eleanor, the children, the villagers... That walled garden application was only the start. Something happened, shortly after and I'm not sure what but it seems to have unhinged him."

"Well, we knew about his heart seizure," Charlie muttered.

"Indeed," Elliot replied - thinking about the blissful interlude when Perry had been absent. "Unfortunately, his reaction was to stop us from having any further contact. Remember our day in London? He permitted me to accompany the children - but then you and Eleanor turned up."

"Eleanor was a beneficiary," Charlie started to protest.

"I know," Elliot continued, "but he guessed I must have told you about his planning application. He couldn't believe how powerful the opposition rose. He thinks we had it planned in advance - you know, *before* the application went public?"

"That's ridiculous," Charlie snorted. "We didn't voice our objections *until* it went public!"

"I know, but regrettably he found out about the wedding too - and that was the final straw…" he broke off, fighting to hang on to his composure - fearing Charlie would hear the desolation in his voice. He cleared his throat. "It's not all bad news though - Perry is right to be worried. I've discovered his weakness and this is why I wanted to talk to you."

Over the next few minutes, Elliot barely drew breath - keen to reveal how he had sabotaged the wiring in the basement. He had no qualms about boring into the cool stone wall to impair the damp course. The fact that it had precipitated a few new fractures in the outer wall was regrettable.

The sadness in his voice strengthened to steel as he went on to describe the rainstorms in April which had saturated the basement - how he had plugged up the air bricks without mercy.

"It was you?" Charlie spluttered in disbelief. "Perry thought it was me!"

"Charlie, I'm sorry," Elliot sighed. "My brother, Daniel's a builder too. I told him about the Hamptons. We plotted this together but do you know, I feel no shame. I wanted Perry to suffer! Especially for the way he treated those poor children! I will never forget the night he evicted them!"

"Elliot, calm down," Charlie soothed him. "Nobody blames you."

"I know," Elliot whispered gratefully. "The upshot is this; the electricity started short circuiting. Fuses blew on a regular basis and the lights flickered. Perry began to fear the place was haunted. He started having dreams about James. Rowena told me. Okay, so I confess to a little skulduggery but those nightmares were a product of his own twisted imagination."

"Elliot, you're a genius," Charlie laughed down the phone. "Do you have any idea what else might have upset him?"

"Not really," Elliot replied sadly, "but once he returned from Cannes, everything changed. Perry was on the warpath; determined to destroy every last thread of communication between me and those children…" His gentle eyes were drawn to the glow of the gas fire yet his heart dragged him down like a stone. "I miss them so much."

"So phone them!" Charlie insisted.

"I can't. And I don't want them to confront Perry. Because if they do and Perry finds out we've been in contact…" He heard Charlie's snort of protest but cut him off. "He threatened someone very dear to me, Charlie. His name is Alex; a sculptor by profession and he loves the great outdoors. He visited the house in early Summer - did a bit of landscape gardening. Unfortunately, that vile Nathan took photos. He guessed there was something between us and Perry drew his own nasty conclusions. So I sent Alex away - but they've discovered where he lives…" He felt a sob catch in his throat.

"I see," Charlie muttered uncomfortably, "and I'm guessing there's some sort of *relationship* between you and this man?"

"He's my son, Charlie," Elliot's voice cracked. "I fell in love with his mother over 30 years ago when I worked as a butler in London. She was from a wealthy family. They owned a second house in Buckinghamshire which was where we began our affair. Charlotte was betrothed to another - someone far more suited to a lady of her social standing, whereas I was just a servant. Our affair was hushed up through fear of causing a scandal. I lost my job - but Alex was our love child. I've always kept in touch with them, albeit in secret."

"Does he know you're his father?" Charlie whispered in astonishment.

"Oh yes," Elliot sighed, "but Perry does not. I have to protect him despite what they think - both Alex and his mother…" He closed his eyes, torn apart with fear. "I couldn't bear to bring them any grief. For Alex to be *permanently disfigured*' as Perry has warned…"

"That's monstrous!" Charlie hissed.

"I know," Elliot said in a resigned tone, "I just want you to understand why I can't risk breaking the rules. As for William and Avalon - tell them I miss them. I'm certain I'll see them again, one day. But there is danger ahead, Charlie."

"Yes, so you implied in your letter," Charlie said quickly, "you mentioned some clandestine meeting at Westbourne House."

"It was in August," Elliot whispered, dropping his voice even lower. "That man from the council turned up."

"Robin Whaley," Charlie said coldly. "Yes, so I gather - but you mentioned someone else."

Elliot paused, scouring the depths of his memory. He had caught only a glimpse of that menacing stranger but enough to leave a lingering impression; a tall, shadowy figure who's voluminous dark raincoat drew attention to his broad shoulders - those slow, forbidding footsteps. Elliot almost shuddered as he elucidated the details.

"They shut themselves in the library," he continued fearfully. "Perry gave orders, they were not to be disturbed but I overheard shouting. Their discussion was obviously a little heated."

"It's okay, Elliot, we're on to them," Charlie said wryly. "I've got a feeling I know who this other man is too. They're plotting to get their hands on some land behind the Community Centre and we are going to fight them!"

"Good for you," Elliot smiled, bolstered by the power in his voice. "As for me - if there is any consolation, my employment ties me to Westbourne House. I can keep my eyes and ears open - and I will always find a way to get a message to you."

Charlie did not see the glitter of tears as he gripped the receiver. Elliot knew he had been right in his decision to stay at Westbourne House. He had so much wanted to protect those children; where his absence on the night of their eviction had left him tortured. His contract of employment felt like some sort of penance - but he felt no loyalty towards Perry. His growing contempt smouldered like a fire and right now, he was thinking about the wedding - that pivotal moment when they had sworn to destroy him. He would never forget the charge of euphoria when they had joined hands across the table. It was like a pulse that throbbed in his veins, fuelling his resolve that he would do anything to help them fulfil that pledge.

By the time the conversation ended, Charlie was almost breathless - appalled by the things Elliot had told him. The final disclosure, concerning Perry's meeting left him stunned. He lowered the handset. Of course, he had already guessed who the third man was. It was Theakston! It had to be. There was no-one else who would have better fitted Elliot's description.

Eleanor might have been outwardly strong in her perseverance to rise above their enemies - but if Perry had Dominic Theakston in his back pocket, she was going to completely cave in. He let out a sigh, wary of Elijah's hovering presence just as Margaret too, appeared at the foot of the stairs. He couldn't speak - his mind working furiously, wondering what the hell they were going to do.

Dominic had already been surveying the land at the back of the Community Centre. A day in August. It might even have occurred shortly after that meeting. Charlie fiddled with the telephone wire. He had sworn he would find a way to communicate with him and on this occasion, Eleanor had agreed: '*Ask him to meet you in a pub, or something…*'

"What's up, Dad?" Margaret's voice piped. "Who was that on the phone?"

"It was Elliot," Charlie mumbled, nodding to himself. He was still numb from their conversation, whilst at the same time having reached an unequivocal decision.

Chapter 5

I

Before that day came, there were many milestones to be crossed as they tumbled towards the end of September faster than expected. The kids were immersed in their school lives. Margaret, at 12, was experiencing the first growing pains of adolescence; while Elijah, who had been wandering around in a daze for the past week, had finally settled into his studies. William had never really struggled with his school work but with 'O' levels imminent, he was of a mind to concentrate on his mock exams - though girls seemed to be a constant distraction.

He kept Elijah ceaselessly amused with his love life which fortunately took his mind off more pressing matters. William was currently going out with a girl named Vivienne who was, without a doubt, one of the prettiest girls in the school - yet he still had reservations.

"I don't know what to do," he whimpered as they wandered up the long driveway leading to the school. "It's not that I don't like Viv, I just find her a bit cold…" he let his words wither.

The truth was, the relationship was going nowhere. At nearly sixteen, William was desperate to lose his virginity; egged on by his classmates whilst incapable of ignoring the powerful hormonal urges that kept tugging him, especially around girls. Viv, being somewhat straight laced, refused to let him touch her which was perhaps the real reason his passion for her had cooled.

"If you don't feel anything in your heart, why not end it?" Elijah advised him sagely. "Don't lead her on - it's not fair."

He stared into the distance where the trees were just beginning to turn - a haze of green, already peppered with hues of gold, looming behind a veil of mist. It was a sight which inevitably drew his mind to Westbourne House, picturing its fabled beauty. He shivered despite the autumnal warmth.

"You do realise what day it is, don't you?" he muttered.

"Yeah, September 28th," William responded, glancing at the date on his digital watch, "and I know what you're thinking. It was around this time last year, those bastards showed up!" He raised his head, his eyes smouldering. "Did you ever manage to coax any more info out of your mum?"

Elijah shrugged. "Mum's very cagey. She's definitely trying to get some dirt on Perry but she has to be careful, he's having her watched."

"From what Elliot said, it sounds like he's having us *all* watched," William snapped, "but you're right, it seems strange looking back. It'll be my birthday next week…"

This was the second milestone. Elijah could almost sense what he was thinking; recollecting their heart-warming dinner party - the shimmer of candle-light, the champagne, the sumptuous food prepared by their two excellent chefs. There had been a trailing atmosphere of angst in the wake of the Hamptons' visit. Yet they had managed to throw the most uplifting celebration. It was one of the last occasions he had seen James alive.

"I wish we could have a dinner party like that again," William said, as if thinking out loud. "You moved into the almshouse next day," he added quickly.

It was good to reminisce yet at the same time, Elijah could remember what a painful era it had been. He had loved settling into their new home - blessed that James had donated some of his beautiful furniture. He would have smiled if it hadn't been for Perry's creeping deadline; the fear that the Barton-Wells family had *one month* to empty the house of their possessions and find a new home. It was an utterly heartless campaign and one that would never stop haunting them. He turned and glanced at William, knowing James had never reached that threshold.

"I'm sorry," he whispered. "I remember exactly what happened next."

William blinked, fighting to curb his emotions. "Yeah," he muttered. "I suppose we have to talk about it some time. It's coming up to the anniversary of Dad's death."

A look of agony flitted across his face and without a second thought, Eli's arm snaked around his shoulder. "It's okay," he whispered. "Hang in there. We'll talk about this later."

From the corner of his eye, he clocked the approach of Gary Boswell and his satellite of cronies; bracing himself for their insults, Elijah shoved William quickly through the door.

October 1987

Two weeks later, that conversation seemed like a dream. What William could never have guessed was that Avalon had organised a surprise birthday party. Finally, his troubled thoughts shifted. Avalon had given Elijah free rein over the decorations too; a futuristic theme which included metallic garlands interlaced with glittering fairy lights, added to a profusion of silver and blue balloons. William had been ecstatic. His friends even more so - especially over the delectable spread of food prepared under Eleanor's careful supervision.

Charlie meanwhile, was delighted with the progress they were making on the Community Centre. They had successfully completed the installation of all the new windows - confident their sturdy frames and double-glazed panes would withstand the worst of the winter weather.

A short distance away, Robin immersed himself in his scheme concerning the land behind the Community Centre. The dinner party with the Barton-Wells children seemed a very long time ago; though he had barely stopped thinking about it, unable to understand why Perry despised them. It was to his even greater surprise, Avalon had submitted a planning application of her own. It concerned the empty field where Eleanor's caravan lingered - she was hoping to establish a new allotment scheme, a notion that drew a smile to his face.

Perry on the other hand, continued to scrutinise everyone; gratified to hear that Elliot hadn't used his trip to London to collude with his enemies. Nathan's report had left him amused. So, he had visited that young man in West Brompton who Perry presumed to be his lover! Why else would two grown men display such affection? His vengeful thoughts had since switched to Eleanor.

Their recent encounter brought back the full force of his malevolence. He could almost taste her desire to destroy him, where the taunts of her son's abduction had stoked the fires of hatred.

Yet despite a prevailing air of menace, something was about to shake the edges of their world; something completely out of their control and not one of them could have predicted it...

II

10 days later Perry lay awake, plagued by an even deeper sense of anxiety. It had been several nights since Rowena had taken to sleeping in a different room, finally worn down by his nightmares. It was the room which had originally belonged to Avalon, positioned on the south east corner of the house and characterised by a blushing shroud of Virginia Creeper. His own room faced south, overlooking the grounds as well as the woods beyond. It was pitch black outside and the wind was getting stronger. For the last half hour, he had lain on his back, eyes closed, just waiting to cross the threshold of sleep - but the moment never came. His mind refused to switch off, conscious of the violent gusts which continued to swirl around the house and pummel the walls.

Perry opened his eyes, staring towards the window as it rattled in the wind. The London Met office had predicted a storm but they had never anticipated anything of this magnitude. The high winds had risen to gale force. He could hear them whistling through the trees. Then gradually, the whistling escalated to a roar. He clutched the bedclothes tightly, his body braced with tension. The storm spiralled upwards, building in intensity. Perry could hardly bear it.

Yet this was nothing compared to what was about to happen next.

As the wind grew, so the devastation began as a hurricane now advanced from the south coast, charging its way through the woods and into the grounds. Without warning, several tiles were torn from the roof. Some slid off the edge and tumbled; others, caught in a secondary blast, were flung mercilessly into the sky before they cannoned into the building, smashing a few window panes.

Perry discharged a shout of terror and fumbled for the light switch. For a second, his surroundings were illuminated by a subtle glow. Yet straight away, the light started flickering. He cursed under his breath. He'd only had the bloody electricians in last week! The light died abruptly; but in the splinter of time before the room sank into darkness, he was convinced he'd glimpsed a face in the mirror. It fluttered briefly, as subliminal as a shadow - the swish of a pony tail, the accusing stab of green eyes. It was a face he knew only too well - a face which never stopped torturing him.

"Go away!" he howled into the empty space, "just leave me alone…!"

He snatched a lacquered pill box without thinking and hurled it at the mirror, firing a radial crack into its surface. Perry covered his face with his hands. Fuck! Seven years bad luck on top of everything. It was with a growing sense of dread, he could no longer ignore what was going on outside. A hole in the window brought the high winds coiling into his room where the curtains were levitated by their force.

Just when Perry thought things couldn't get any worse, the most terrible groaning, splitting sound erupted from the grounds. He yanked back the curtains, feeling the icy blast slap against his face - watching in disbelief as one of their 50 foot oak trees was literally torn from the earth by its roots. He could see the shadow of another tree already buckled on the grass. Heavens knew what was going on in the woods up there. He watched, feeling utterly powerless as the next tree went crashing to the ground, knocking the stone fountain off its plinth. It plummeted onto the path with a sickening clang.

Perry backed away from the window and grabbing for his dressing gown, fled into the hallway where he came face to face with Rowena. She too looked petrified, dressed in a full length, silk kimono, her face white. Oddly enough, the lights in the corridor were still working.

"Perry!" she whimpered, "what on earth is going on?" She collapsed into his arms.

"Ssh, my darling," he whispered, forcing himself to remain calm despite the rapid charge of his heart. "Let's go downstairs. I expect some of the guests are already down there."

They were greeted by Elliot, fully dressed in his usual attire of formal black trousers and waistcoat. He offered Rowena a sympathetic smile - hovering in reception with a demeanour of calm as he held open the bar door. It was 3:30 in the morning.

Perry stepped into the bar, his face as pale as his wife's. He demanded a brandy. As predicted, several hotel guests were huddled in the area including the directors of a profitable, blue chip pharmaceutical company. This had been one of their first corporate bookings, Perry thought with dismay, aware of their animated conversation as the storm continued to ravage the grounds.

"It seems we've been hit by a hurricane," Elliot told them gravely.

"How do you know?" Perry snapped, fixing him with an angry stare. "Nothing was forecast!"

"I've been tuning into the radio," Elliot sighed. He lowered his eyes timidly. "It seems they got it wrong. A hurricane swept into the south coast at around Midnight and has moved its way up to London and the South East. It's chaos out there. They're saying London hasn't been hit by anything like this since the Blitz."

"London!" Rowena gasped, "Oh my God! Ben!"

"I'm sure Ben will be fine," Perry said softly, feeling his panic subside. In fact, Elliot's news brought a wave of relief. So this wasn't the manifestation of some *spirit* - though he was certain he had seen that face in the mirror. Maybe it was a product of his imagination, given the wind, the broken window, the light... yet just as he began to relish the thought, the lights dimmed, leaving the entire house swamped in darkness. He clutched Rowena's arm. She let out a petrified cry just as the men at the bar launched into an explosion of angry mutterings.

"What the bloody hell is going on?" Perry thundered.

"Haven't you heard?" a female voice boomed from reception. Perry's eyes were drawn to the beam of a torch as his hotel manager, Irene Fisher, strode into the bar. "That gale has brought down the power lines! We've got no electricity - and neither has anyone else in this village!"

It was one of the worse storms to have hit England in decades but the true extent of the devastation wasn't fully realised until next day. News bulletins reported winds of up to 90 miles an hour; trees had been uprooted, cars crushed and several main roads were blocked. For the next two days, Aldwyck was completely cut off from the outside world and much to Perry's fury. The grounds of Westbourne House lay ruined - the surrounding woods flattened. Yet there was nothing he could do. Even the train service had been cancelled due to a number of felled trees jamming the tracks, denying him any escape to London.

He did however, manage to get in touch with his son. It transpired, the Capital too, had been brought to its knees with no electricity and mass destruction everywhere. Ben, like his father, was plunged into a fit of despair and it had started when he made his first vain attempts to get to work, that morning.

Ben had awoken at around 6:00 where the other side of his bed lay cold. He had been dimly aware of a disturbance throughout the night - the lashing winds and rain, at times, punctuated by the wail of sirens. He found himself missing his girlfriend, Sasha, who was in Amsterdam for a few days. She had promised she would visit him later - hopefully equipped with some raunchy new sex toys. But that was Sasha all over; daring, risqué and best of all, daughter of the highly affluent stock broker who was not only his mentor, but thought the world of him. Ben possessed all the qualities Giles Dyer looked for in a trader; a sharp, calculating brain, a relentless sense of greed and utterly ruthless! Ben suppressed a smile, though he was still thinking about Sasha.

The first clue that something was wrong in the world, didn't actually register until he switched on the TV. The set remained lifeless. Ben frowned, testing the light switch, dismayed to discover there was no power. He dressed quickly, slipping into grey pin-stripe trousers before admiring his torso in the mirror. He resembled a Greek statue, his previously soft body sculpted into sleek, solid muscle. Ben smiled, glad of his sessions at the gym. He pulled on a white shirt, snapped on red braces and combed his hair which had grown slightly longer - enough to fasten it into one of those little pony tails which was a trend amongst yuppies.

He glanced at his Rolex watch, then shaved - pleased his shaver was battery operated. Finally he splashed on some Versace aftershave, a present from Sasha who adored its subtle, smoky fragrance. Just thinking about her gave him a hard on. It seemed incredible that they had been in a relationship for seven months. She was as shallow as he was, but they loved the same things; expensive restaurants, champagne, recreational drugs and sex. Best of all, they imposed no restrictions on each other. He knew Sasha slept with other men, same as she knew he picked up girls from night clubs. Yet when they were together, they relished each other's company. Ben put the success of their relationship down to the fact that they didn't inhibit each other.

By the time he stepped outside, he was starting to notice the wreckage - broken branches, bricks and crumbling stonework lay scattered all over the pavements. As he ventured away from the square, there seemed to be an unusual sense of panic in the streets. For a start, there was hardly any traffic. Though nothing prepared him for the shock of arriving at the Tube station, to discover there were no trains running either.

"Ain't you 'eard?" a news seller grunted as Ben bought himself a copy of the London Standard. "There's bin an 'urricane! Country's ground to an 'alt. You ain't gonna get no train today, son!"

Ben ground down his fury, feeling an onset of dread. How the hell was he supposed to get to work? He glanced at the paper where it was only just beginning to dawn on him, the entire Capital had been paralysed. Millions had no electricity and no phones but this was nothing, compared to the destruction some had suffered. Many had been forced to abandon their homes due to structural damage. Ben shuddered, glancing at his surroundings where the clearing up had only just begun. It appeared that fallen masonry was now the greatest hazard. It was like something out of the war! In the end, there was only one thing for it. Without delay, Ben marched home and ditched his beige trench coat for his motorcycle leathers. He leapt onto his Harley Davidson - then doggedly weaved his way through the debris until he had made it to the London Stock Exchange.

He was greeted by Giles, whose tanned face resembled a crumpled paper bag. "What the hell are you doing here?" he growled.

"Working, of course!" Ben protested. "Just because there's been a hurricane, it doesn't mean we have to stop trading."

"Well I wish you luck!" Giles sneered, throwing on his raincoat. "You won't get very far. Fucking power failure's crippled the computer systems!"

His boss was right. Those who *had* battled their way to work found themselves out on a limb as it rapidly emerged, the entire stock exchange would remain closed for the day. Ben cursed. He didn't want to go home, especially since he'd spent an entire morning trying to get here - though in the end, he really didn't have much choice.

By the time he let himself into the house again, his mood was black. So much so, he wasn't even remotely pleased to see Sasha sprawling on the fur rug in front of the fireplace. She was wearing tight, leather trousers and very high heels, while flipping through the latest Vogue magazine.

"You're early," she drawled. She didn't even look at him.

"What are you doing here?" Ben snapped, shrugging off his leather jacket, "I thought you were coming over this evening."

Finally, she raised her eyes. "What's the matter with you?"

"I've had a shit day," Ben retorted, "I need to get my head together!"

"What you need," Sasha purred, rising to her feet, "is a toot of coke and a bottle of bubbly…" she stepped right up to him, winding her arms round his waist. Ben froze, refusing to respond, his face wooden. "Oh for Christ's sake, will you snap out of it!" she added with a hiss.

"Fuck off!" Ben lashed back and without a second thought, he dislodged her from his torso and sent her stumbling to the floor.

She glared up at him in fury - her mouth angrily forming words which never found an escape. Ben turned on his heel and with no apology, stormed from the room. Sasha leapt to her feet and went charging after him. By the time they had reached the threshold of his bedroom, she had only just caught up with him.

"You bastard!" she screamed, pummelling him with her fists. "I've been away for three days and this is how you treat me?" her cat-like green eyes narrowed to slits, as she pressed her face up close. "I think what you need… is to be punished!"

"Now you're talking," Ben hissed back lasciviously. "So punish me!"

Five minutes later, he was kneeling on the floor, stripped to the waist. He held out his wrists around which she clamped some metal hand cuffs - waiting in anticipation as she clipped them to a chain. Ben smiled inwardly as the sound of clinking metal echoed around the room. The rings fixed to the wall had been his idea. If either of his parents asked, he would have sworn they were for hanging towels on.

He didn't take Sasha to Westbourne House so much, these days - not since the one time his mother had walked in on them. It had been embarrassing. It might not have been so bad if they had simply been in bed together - but he would never forget the disgust that had flared on Rowena's face when she was met by the sight of his girlfriend, naked, spread-eagled across his four-poster bed, wrists and ankles bound as he smeared her body with chocolate butter cream. Rowena had been furious so he had kept Sasha away. Though there were times when the sexual frustration had been unbearable - and possibly the only reason he'd tried it on with that pretty young black girl.

Nowadays, Ben kept their bedroom antics secret, where the things they got up to in this house were a lot more thrilling. If there was one thing which turned him on more than money, sex and power, it was pain - and there were times when Ben enjoyed being on the receiving end almost as much as he liked inflicting it. With his arms suspended high above his head, he watched with pleasure as Sasha moved towards him, swinging a cat-of-nine-tails. She was clad in glossy, black PVC hot pants and thigh-length boots, her honey blond hair scraped back into a high ponytail. Ben smiled - Christ, this was the sort of service judges and MPs paid a fortune for!

But Sasha was into everything and just as he relished the thought, the whip sang through the air and slapped across his bare shoulders, making him flinch. He bit down on his lip as she delivered one stroke after another, loving the sharp, tingling sensation of each lash.

"Do it harder," he breathed, gritting his teeth.

She willingly obliged. The next stoke made him yelp as the pain streaked across his upper arm. It continued for a few more minutes until he could take no more - where finally, he spluttered his own safe word, the signal for her to stop.

"*Avalon!*" He was breathing heavily - his skin was on fire.

With a cold smile, Sasha dropped the whip to the carpet. She was sweating from her exertion - further more, she was wet. At last, she unfastened the hand cuffs, her hand trailing down to his groin, delighted to encounter a rock hard erection.

"Time to pleasure you, my sweet," Ben panted, before hurling her across the bed.

III

If Ben thought things were tough in the aftermath of the 1987 hurricane, he was completely unprepared for the financial storm that would wreak havoc in his life. Three days later - and just as Avalon and William were mourning the anniversary of their father's death - something was about to happen and that day was 'Black Monday.'

Ben fought his way towards the sleek, grey shell of the London Stock Exchange. This could not be happening - how was it possible that the Dow

Jones Index in New York could plummet by 500 points in a single day? It seemed unreal - yet confirmed by the shouting conundrum of 100s of traders awaiting him on the trading floor. Ben surged to his desk and grabbed his telephone, his face white, as his gaze was drawn to the computer screens. Graphs and figures exploded before his eyes - world markets going into meltdown and there was nothing he could do to stop it. From that very first glance, Ben could see the FT100 index sinking - and after an incredible 5 year bull market where shares had been overvalued, their price was dropping like a stone.

"What the fuck is going on?" he bellowed to Giles as he strode past his desk.

"Market chaos!" Giles hollered over his shoulder. "It's all going off in Wall Street and Japan - traders selling in panic. It's wiping millions off share prices!"

Ben was already breathing heavily as the fear spread through his veins. He had his own portfolio to think about - not to mention the clients he invested for, including his own father!

"Oh shit," he whispered, running his hands over his face.

"Sell, sell, sell!" he could hear people braying all around him. The room swelled with panic.

It was with increasing horror, Ben knew he needed to offload some of his own shares before the market dived even lower. Yet he was reluctant. What if it bounced back? Throughout the day, prices were spiking up and down like yo-yo's - compounded by traders and institutions covering their long positions; a situation which was exacerbated by computer algorithms, designed to sell at certain prices as soon as the market felt the drop. It was with a sinking heart he left work that day, hit with the terror the index had slumped by more than 20%.

Ben hardly slept a wink that night and returned to work with nothing more than a cup of black coffee and a line of cocaine to fuel him. He felt sick. He had never known a crash like it and for the first time in his life, he was no longer the driver. His world had been turned upside down, spinning and falling like a roller-coaster, leaving him giddy. Dealers were still trying to gauge which way the markets would go; but UK share prices continued to be volatile and by the close of business, the index had slumped again - a repeat of Monday's record drop.

"What the hell am I going to do?" he gasped to Sasha. They had ordered a picnic box from Harrods, though food was the last thing on his mind. He was knocking back champagne as if his life depended on it, wondering if getting blind drunk was the best solution.

"Darling, stop worrying," she attempted to soothe him. "Daddy thinks it's just a blip. It's because we've got 24 hour trading - this is a huge over-reaction."

In some ways she was right - or rather, her father was. All this chaos in London had been a direct consequence of the panic in Wall Street. He knew share prices had been inflated - even small investors had profited from recently privatised markets like British Telecom. But the bubble had finally burst and it was a trauma which was felt by stock markets all over the world, bringing an end to the 80s boom. In some cases, computers were blamed. They had turned International trading into a gamble. But it brought him no comfort - and some 3 days later, the FT100 index was still tumbling.

A week later, Southern England was at last beginning to recover from the terrible winds that had lashed the nation. In the wake of the hurricane, torrential rain had followed, leading to mass flooding and where 1,000s of acres lay under water. The grounds of Westbourne House had been badly affected. Though Perry had just about eliminated the possibility of floodwater seeping into the house by using sandbags - whilst a team of structural repair specialists reinforced the damp course above the foundations.

Rosebrook ironically, survived better than most places and it was to Peter's heart-felt relief, the Community Centre had suffered hardly any structural damage. On this occasion, its squat, solid construction had been an advantage - along with the work Charlie and his son had undertaken to strengthen the roof. Yet the place had never been busier - gas ovens in constant use to heat up meals for those who were suffering from power failures.

Eleanor meanwhile, was rushed off her feet at the hospital - tending to victims who had suffered severe injuries, from being crushed in cars, to the bombardment of flying debris.

The clear-up in London progressed with incredible efficiency; the infrastructure rapidly restored, buildings repaired and the roads once again, teaming with traffic.

Back in Pimlico however, Ben was feeling practically suicidal. He had analysed the markets all wrong - sold shares which remained stable, whilst clinging on to those whose value continued to nosedive. Within days, he had lost a fortune and worse, his father was furious with him. Ben had consequently retreated to lick his wounds. He avoided contact with anyone, including Sasha - his mood so volatile, he feared he might do some serious harm if provoked! He even steered clear of Nathan - recalling the nights when they had slummed it in the rougher parts of the city. His Sloane ranger accent was a magnet for attracting trouble. Nathan thrived on it and with his powerful frame and thirst for brutality, he was the perfect ally. Yet Ben hungered for more than violence. He felt murderous, where the lure of the criminal underworld had never been stronger.

In the end, there was only one thing for it. Ben packed his gym bag and sped off to Swanley; struck with the notion that it would take a particularly gruelling workout to work off his rage - as well as afford him a further opportunity to work on Theakston.

The moment he changed, he got to work - warming up on the exercise bike, followed by 15 minutes pounding away on the treadmill. Atlas Leisure was busier than usual, as clusters of fit men and women threaded their way around the weight-training machines. He could hear the thump of music from an upstairs aerobics class. With a look of rabid fury, irritated that so many people were crowding his personal space, Ben strutted over to the free weights area and grabbed a pair of 12 kg steel-coated dumbbells - straining to lift them as he embarked on a series of lateral arm raises.

Seconds later, Dominic spotted him and without delay, wandered up casually before plucking the weights from his hands. Ben closed his eyes, fighting to suppress his frustration.

"What do you think you're playing at?" Dominic muttered, keeping his voice soft. "Trying to kill yourself? Those weights are way too heavy - here, use the 7.5 kilo."

"You don't understand…" Ben started to protest but Dominic cut him off.

"Now you listen to me, kid. You told me you wanted to get yourself in better shape, right? You're doing okay. But as your instructor, I'm telling you to use smaller weights and with more repetitions - unless you wanna end up looking like Arnold Swarzenegger."

"What if I do?" Ben argued, staring coldly into his eyes. "Women seem to like it!"

"Nah!" Dominic sneered. "They don't! If you're out to attract the girls then take it from me, they prefer a well-toned body, *not* bulging muscles - that's what the homos like!

"Fair enough," Ben snapped and without further argument, he resumed his workout.

"Why are you really here, Ben Hampton?" Dominic finally challenged. He was braced directly behind him, hands on hips, glaring at his reflection. "See - you said you wanted to get fit. So why do I get the idea, you're trying to turn yourself into the world's strongest man?"

Ben shrugged. "It doesn't do any harm to build up my strength but seeing as you ask, I've got enemies. Our family needs protection - apart from getting myself fit, I need contacts."

Dominic's eyes darkened before a sneer crept onto his face. "What sort of contacts?"

"Oh, you know," Ben said calmly, "the type of people you wouldn't want to meet in a dark alley. I lost a fortune on the stock market this week, I want to spread my wings, find *alternatives*."

Dominic released a harsh laugh. "Organised crime you mean?"

"Dominic, I don't mean to pry but you *must* know someone," Ben persisted. He rhythmically pumped the weights up and down, working on his biceps, the first sheen of sweat glistening on his forehead. "I won't repeat anything you say, I swear. I know you're very cagey about this but my father reckons you were a legend in the 70's. So why did you give it all up?"

Dominic on the other hand, was beginning to feel irritated, tempted to grab him by the throat, slam him against the mirror and tell him what he really thought of his fucking family! It was obvious Ben was never going to let this go; a concept which left him wondering whether to give him the in-road he hankered for. The boys who ran the criminal underworld, these days, were serious hard nuts and not worth messing with; but if Ben wanted to wander into a lions' den, that was his problem. At least it would get him off his back. They might take one look at him and give him a proper good kicking, teach the little prick a lesson!

"Why did I give it up?" Dominic echoed, "what - running a criminal gang?" He smiled evilly, suddenly proud to admit it. Ben's eyes glittered. "Let me tell you something, son. Those who stick with organised crime end up going one of two ways. Prison - or six foot under. When I was your age, I didn't give a shit but all that changed when I had a family of me own. Beautiful wife, couple of kids - something worth living for. I had my hay day. It was time to pass over the reins. So do you *really* wanna know who runs the show, nowadays…?"

"Go on!" Ben prompted him, lowering his weights - the excitement on his face was unmissable.

"Heard of Dan Levy?" Dominic whispered. "One of the hardest men in London - 'cept Dan's approaching 50. Been passing some of his *'business'* over to his son, Alan."

"I see," Ben responded, giving way to a smirk. "Any chance you could introduce me?"

Dominic let out a sigh - he shook his head. "No way. Alan's a nutcase and if this all goes tits up, I don't wanna be held responsible. You might as well know, his favourite tool's a scalpel - piss him off and he'll carve you up like a jigsaw. So I suggest you ask your friend, Wadzinski - seeing as he went to school with him."

"Thanks, Dominic," Ben nodded, finally dragged out of his brooding reverie.

IV

November 1987

It took that one fateful conversation to remind Dominic of something else he had been planning to do and before the month was up, he knew it was time to concentrate on the future - get the surveyors on board to assess that land behind the Community Centre.

Dominic didn't like to admit it but just the sight of Ben's cold, statuesque face had made his skin crawl. There was something about that kid, he couldn't quite put his finger on and it left him rattled. It drew his thoughts back to his loathsome father - that chilling meeting at Westbourne House; a memory which added yet another spark to the fire of his ambition. The thought of getting his mitts on that land, over Hampton, was suddenly too delicious to resist.

By November 3rd, Dominic had arranged a meeting with a firm of professional consultants, fully intent on getting an unbiassed opinion over the feasibility of his project. If the idea was met with approval, only then would he launch his outline proposal. This included a full estimate of costs, from initial calculations, to the final sum - along with any commercial risk assessment. But he was not the only person thinking about the land.

Peter, having been goaded by Robin Whaley, was simultaneously scribbling out his own plans - inspired to base his trust on three different property styles; from sheltered accommodation for the elderly, to a range of semi-detached family homes and apartments.

The weather outside had turned cold, although a weak glimmer of sunshine was trying to sneak its way through the cloud. Peter shivered, turning to adjust the heating. He opened the blinds to draw in the sunshine - yet the moment he paused, he stole a cursory glance across the garden. His eyes were instantly drawn to a group of men swarming around the land on the other side of the fence. Their dark suits and blue safety helmets suggested they were quantity surveyors - undoubtedly drafted in to assess the commercial potential of the site and to his further surprise, Dominic Theakston was among them.

Peter frowned. He would have recognised that tall, imposing figure anywhere, first by the way he moved; those slow, sidling steps, occasionally cut by flashes of animation. Dominic radiated a huge presence - his eyes wandering constantly as he monitored his surroundings.

Twenty minutes later, Charlie had joined him.

"Okay, so what do you suppose is going on?" Peter muttered.

"You met him, didn't you?" Charlie replied, "at the Community Centre open day..." He broke off, as if jarred by another memory. "Do you think he'd remember you?"

"He might," Peter frowned, "he seemed okay when Robin introduced us. Though Eleanor did warn me he was dangerous..." he turned to Charlie in dread. "Wasn't he some sort of *player* in the criminal underworld? She reckons he was sent here to frighten her - worked for the same people who killed Eli's father!"

"That's right," Charlie nodded, turning back to the window. There was a sudden clench to his jaw, his face set like stone. "What I'm curious to know is whether he still does!"

For weeks now, Charlie had been chewing over the possibility of approaching Theakston; especially in the light of Elliot's clue. His attendance at that *secret* meeting had left him troubled, wondering whether to phone him - or simply wander into his gym again. He knew he needed to tread carefully. The road ahead was a sea of egg shells - so how ironic that a golden opportunity appeared to be flaunting itself right in front of them!

"Shall we go and chat him up?" Peter gauged cheerfully. "I could take us to one of me favourite haunts - might even relax him a little."

Dominic's face bore a sardonic smile when the men first approached him. He recognised them instantly - guessing the reason they were here. There had never been any doubt that Eleanor would go blabbing to Charlie in the aftermath of their 'little chat' - so he must have known that he too, was about to launch a powerful campaign to grab this land for himself.

By the time his colleagues had packed away their surveying equipment, it was lunch time. Dominic could have laughed when Peter suggested they might like to continue their discussion in some Irish pub. But the lure was too hard to resist; especially if there was a chance he could glean some inside information - unaware they were planning exactly the same strategy.

30 minutes later, the three men were tucked inside the wood-panelled interior of the 'Castle Donoghue.' It lay hidden in one of Rosebrook's narrow side streets and possibly the last place on earth someone like Perry would visit. Peter found them an empty alcove which afforded them a degree of privacy. "Nice little place this, isn't it?" he smiled.

Charlie gazed at the intimate enclosure and nodded - loving the delicate mouldings that divided the stained-glass panels. A long bar lined with stools stood proudly between the walls - the cosy interior warmed by the gleam of brass lamps and where a crowd of regulars created a boisterous atmosphere.

"Yeah, got a bit more life than some of the gaffs round here," Dominic said scornfully. He lounged back in his seat, sipping tonic water. As Peter had observed, his eyes were everywhere.

"How did you find out about the land?' he quizzed him.

"Little bird told me," Dominic smiled.

"A little bird by the name of Robin Whaley?' Charlie added accusingly.

The smile dropped from Dominic's face. "How d'you know that?"

"Friend of mine's got connections in the building industry," he shrugged. "People talk."

"I see," Dominic whispered coldly. "Been in the building trade long have you, Charlie?"

"Long enough," Charlie replied, "do you seriously think you stand a chance of getting it? Do you know if Whaley's approached anyone else for example?"

It was the killer question and Charlie sensed he'd hit the nail right on the head, the moment he saw the suspicion flood Dominic's expression. His hand tightened around his glass.

"What makes you think that?"

"It's a prime piece of land," Peter muttered, drawing his head closer. "Robin admits that. It's bound to attract property developers. He told me he was trying to persuade the council to buy it."

"Keep talking," Dominic pressed.

"And if they do," Peter massaged into the conversation, "it gives *them* the power to decide what the land can be used for…"

"They've got that anyway!" Dominic retorted. "They're a Council. Whoever gets that land can't do fuck all unless they get planning permission!"

"So what do you think about our idea of using the plot for social housing?"

"Crap," Dominic sneered, "there ain't no money in it!" A look of hurt spread across Peter's face. Dominic released a sigh. "Look - no offence, but some low cost housing project won't generate much revenue."

"But this town is in crying need of affordable housing," Peter protested angrily.

"I know that," Dominic smirked, "but it's also in crying need of decent entertainment! So which one do you think'll bring more prosperity to Rosebrook?"

"You've really thought this through, haven't you?" Charlie broke in, tired of pussy-footing around. "See - for a moment I had you down as some sort of puppet doing Whaley's bidding."

"What the fuck are you on about?" Dominic hissed, looming up in his seat.

Charlie offered him a cunning smile. "I think you already know the answer. You spoke to my wife. She suspects you might be working for our enemies."

They knew they had him in a tight spot. His eyes shot round the pub and for a moment he looked murderous. He took Charlie's beer and pushed it to one side, slanting his body forward.

"Now you listen to me," Dominic whispered, "I don't work for no-one! *Especially* not Whaley. Okay - so it *was* him who let on about this land. He invited me to propose a use for it but at the end of the day, *he* doesn't own it!"

"What if it's a ploy to draw you to Rosebrook?" Charlie persisted, "you and someone else we both know…" he let his last words hang.

Dominic's eyes narrowed to slits - already Peter was fidgeting nervously in his chair.

"Charlie, let's not ruffle any feathers here," he said quickly.

"I'm not," Charlie said coldly. "I just *have* to ask you this, Dominic, then at least we know where we stand - are you operating on behalf of a man called Perry Hampton?"

"Is that what you think?" Dominic threw back at him, "I *told you* - I operate alone."

"That's okay, then," Charlie spluttered, snatching back his pint and draining it. "Now who's for another drink...?"

Dominic's fist closed over his wrist and for moment Charlie felt the first flutter of fear - struck with the sense, he might have been a bit tactless. Dominic's eyes had not yet lowered - still burning into him like lasers.

"Like I say, Charlie, I don't work for *no-one* - but that don't mean I'm on *your* side and no disrespect, Peter, but I ain't got no loyalty towards you neither. I'm looking out for number one here! As far as that land goes, it's every man for himself."

"Fair enough," Charlie nodded, feeling his panic recede a little. "I always knew you could be hard-nosed in business. I just wanted the truth - for my family's sake."

"Yeah and the last time we met, I told you I wouldn't cause you no problems provided you didn't cause me any," he persisted, "but situations change, Charlie. You tell that to your Eleanor. She needs to watch her back, 'cos I can't be held responsible for what'll happen if she steps out of line." He let go of Charlie's wrist. "Now you can get us a whisky, seeing as you're offering."

Charlie rose shakily to his feet, his heart crashing inside his ribs. He understood a veiled threat when he heard one, sensing Dominic had retained the upper hand. At least he had managed to glean the information he wanted. Maybe this 'secret meeting,' Elliot spoke of, had been purely to discuss the acquisition of the land and nothing more. Yet he didn't want to presume too much - where even Dominic had hinted that nothing was carved in stone.

Unforeseen by any of them, a girl breezed into the pub, heading straight for their table.

"Peter!" she twittered, "I thought I'd find you in here!"

She swooped down to peck his cheek, caught Charlie's eye and smiled. From the other side of the table Dominic surveyed her. Placing her at around 18, he was captivated by her striking features, from her generous lips and brown eyes to the coils of golden-brown hair tumbling around her shoulders. She moved in a way that was delicate and feminine. She was also well spoken. He flicked his gaze towards Peter, intrigued as to the nature of their relationship.

"Avalon! What an absolute delight!"

Dominic froze, recognising the name - recalling that hateful conversation in the men's changing rooms. He was dimly aware of some banter going on between her and Peter but for the next few minutes, he could barely take his eyes off her.

By the time Charlie returned from the bar, he too, seemed delighted to see her.

"Won't you sit down and join us?" he smiled, gazing warmly into her eyes.

"Can't stop," Avalon replied, "but I've had some great news - I just had to tell someone. The council have agreed to let us use that field for our allotment scheme!"

"Excellent!" Charlie beamed, giving her shoulder an affectionate squeeze.

"The villagers wrote in droves to support it!" Avalon raved. "Do you know, there was only one objection…" she let out a chuckle. "Bet you can't guess who that was. Perry! He thought the scheme would cause unnecessary congestion around the gates of Westbourne House."

Dominic tensed, sipping his whisky - his ears tuned in to their repartee like radar.

"William and I really ought to go over there again, Charlie - contact a local forestry management company about clearing up those forests."

"Of course," Charlie murmured, "but that's great news about the allotments. Well done!"

She gazed at him wistfully, then finally slipped a glance in Dominic's direction. Their eyes met. "Who's your friend?" she whispered nervously.

"Who Dominic?" Peter jumped in quickly. "He runs a health club. We were just talking about the land at the back of the Community Centre…"

"I see," Avalon mumbled. She offered him a shy smile. "Well, it's nice to meet you."

"Yeah," Dominic nodded knowingly, "you too. *Avalon*. Intriguing name…"

For a second she held his gaze - following it with a polite smile as she bid them farewell.

Little more was said about the exchange. Peter steered the subject back on course, wary of Dominic's preoccupation. Eventually, it was Charlie who rose. There seemed no other way forward than to finalise their outline plans for the council - unsure which stance they were likely to take and to simply await the outcome.

"Next phase should be interesting," Charlie finished, "whatever our plans, they'll be open to public view! Now, if you'll excuse me, I need to get back to work and grab a sandwich. It's been an interesting chat, Dominic." He extended his hand, if for no other reason than to demonstrate, there was no hard feeling.

Dominic grasped it firmly in his left and shook it. "Guess we'll be bumping into each other again soon then," he muttered coolly.

His eyes were fixed on Charlie's back as he squeezed his way through the crowd, towards the exit. Though for the next few minutes, Dominic chose not to leave. He lowered his empty whisky glass onto the table, observing Peter as he gulped back the remainder of his orange juice. He asked him if he could accompany him back to the Community Centre.

"Car's parked over that way," he added, as if he needed an excuse.

They wandered back up the same narrow street before turning into an alleyway - a short cut which would lead them back to the building but without having to pursue the main High Street. It made sense not to be seen together. Dominic was already wondering if the Hamptons had people on the lookout - and given Perry's paranoia, he couldn't overrule the possibility that he was putting himself at risk. He was due to visit his kids anyway, located just a mile away in a charming village called Farnborough. Though right now he wanted to talk about Avalon.

"Girlfriend of yours?"

"Good Lord, no!" Peter laughed. "I looked after her and her brother once. Those Hamptons treated them very cruelly."

Dominic shot him a sideways glance, his expression blackening. "Is that so? Well between you and me, Peter, I already know something about that girl. I probably shouldn't be telling you this but fuck it… you're some sort of counsellor, right?"

"I am indeed," Peter confessed. He glanced at him with a frown.

Dominic kept walking, his stride heavy but he was mentally picturing Ben. That last vision of him pumping iron in front of the mirror had lingered; those pale, pointed features, the clenched teeth, the obsessive loathing in his eyes. Dominic felt angry - especially now he had met this 'Avalon.'

It was a collation of thoughts which transported him right back to that covert meeting never able to forget Perry's smug face: *'Ben was obsessed with her. She refused his advances - so he set out to terrify her, instead.'*

"Where are they living now?' Dominic probed, his footsteps slowing.

"They've got a house in Rosebrook," Peter muttered. "Found themselves a nice quiet neighbourhood - close to the Community Centre so we can keep an eye on them."

"Hmm," Dominic nodded to himself. "Well listen, Peter, I'm gonna pass on a warning, but to you only. That girl's in danger. Get her to fit some powerful security lights and an alarm…"

They had just reached the junction in the alleyway where a small parade of shops lay directly opposite the Community Centre.

"Remember - you never heard this from me, okay? You're a decent bloke, Peter and I reckon you'll be a bit more discreet than Charlie. So don't go saying nothing! Just fix those kids up with some decent security."

"Thanks for the warning," Peter muttered. His eyes danced from one side of the street to the other, praying they wouldn't be spotted. "You'd best run along now," he added. "It was good to meet up again."

With a curt nod, Dominic rammed his hands into his pockets and streaked diagonally across the road without as much as a backward glance.

Chapter 6

I

Security was never far from Avalon's mind and those early warnings from Eleanor had not gone unheeded. Unfortunately, the ordeal of William's assault had never gone away. It had left her psychologically scarred - unable to forget, it had taken a single hammer blow for their attackers to gain access. The windows of their new home were at least double glazed and fitted with secure window locks - though she finally had some extra bolts fitted to the doors in addition to a chain and a spy hole.

She couldn't understand why Peter suddenly seemed so insistent on installing security lights - a statement which came right out of the blue. He admitted to being in a dark place; upset by the troubles in Northern Ireland which had culminated in the recent 'Poppy Day' bombing in the small town of Enniskillen. This callous attack, carried out by the IRA, had sent shock waves through the community; and with violence at the forefront of everyone's mind, he was adamant they needed to protect themselves better.

Avalon didn't argue. So by the middle of November, she invested in some high powered lamps whose incandescent beams were activated on approach. William too, was glad of the extra security measures - but William had troubles of his own.

It was regrettable he had attracted enemies from the ranks of his own school - a situation which had finally erupted into a fight.

It began on a typical journey home. Eli was in a thunderous mood and grumbling about his history project. It focused on immigration. He didn't much like his teacher, Ms Bloomfield, who with her cropped red hair and grannie glasses, was regarded as a bit of a weirdo. Elijah had never particularly relished her assignment to research his own ethnic origins. Yet when he naively disclosed that not only was his father Dutch - but Eleanor too, came from a mixed race background, Ms Bloomfield had been ecstatic.

"Silly cow didn't have to broadcast it in front of the whole class," Elijah snapped.

All the while, they were conscious of a trail of footsteps gradually catching up with them. It was Boswell of course - Boswell and his loathsome friend, Darren, Aldwyck boys. Even worse, they were accompanied by their usual gang of stooges. Then finally, they reached the almshouses.

William spun round. "Okay, so what do you want?" he spat, glaring at Darren.

Darren Jackson already despised him. Six foot tall, dark haired and blue-eyed, there was a time when Darren had revelled in the glory of being the class heart-throb. Ever since turning 15 however, his face had erupted in acne. William, with his dazzling good looks, had knocked him right off his perch. The two boys, dubbed as 'Gazza and Dazza,' made a formidable duo. Already Margaret looked nervous.

"Come on, spit it out!" William persisted. "It's obvious you're *dying* to say something."

"So where's your daddy now, Jansen?" Gary sneered, sidling up to Elijah. "Never knew he was from Holland! Though Dad always *did* reckon your mum was half coon!"

Margaret let out a whimper of shock.

"Shut up!" Elijah whispered, blushing scarlet. "Don't you dare talk about her like that!"

"Or you'll do what?" Gary retorted nastily.

"Oh piss off, Boswell!" William intervened, "you too, Jackson! What are you doing this side of town anyway? Shouldn't you be on a bus to Aldwyck?"

"All in good time," Darren muttered. He too, had wandered menacingly up to them where his eyes slid towards the almshouses. He smiled icily at Elijah. "So this is where you live is it?"

"What business is it of yours?" William demanded.

The satellite bullies giggled.

Darren sauntered towards him, his eyes filled with hate as he dipped his head lower. "You can shut up. You're not *Lord of the Manor* now, you know. Everyone knows your old man went bankrupt and you lost your big, fancy house."

"Get stuffed!" William snarled, the anger in him growing.

"Don't you talk to my mate like that," Gary broke in, shoving Elijah to one side, "William Farton-Smells!"

The others started braying with laughter - as if they had been the first in the school to think that one up! Margaret meanwhile, looked even more scared - tugging Elijah's arm, begging him to just hurry up and let them into the almshouse as the waves of hostility swelled higher.

"Yeah, yeah! Hilarious," William drawled in sarcasm. "Now fuck off, you tossers!"

"What did you say?" Gary hissed, his face darkening like beetroot.

"You heard!" William shouted back.

"Yeah and I thought I told you to stay out of this, you little poofter..."

His words were cut off abruptly as William hurled his fist into his face. The other boys gaped in shock - unable to believe he had hit him so hard. Gary flew backwards, spinning to regain his balance. Blood streamed from his nose. Already a small group of passers by had frozen and for a moment, time stood still. Yet the full force of William's rage had only just been discharged. He flew towards his victim.

"William, no!" Margaret screamed.

It was the catalyst Darren had been waiting for as he too, launched himself across the grass like a missile, knocking William off balance. Gary struggled to his feet, grimacing with pain and they started laying into William without mercy. William, having practised the art of boxing and fencing, did at least manage to dodge a few of their blows. Yet they seemed intent on teaching him a lesson - two against one, taking it in turns to grab his arms, alternately shelling him with punches. The others circled them like wolves, cheering them on.

"For God's sake, do something!" Elijah was heard yelling above the din. His cries fell on deaf ears as the violent fight continued, all three of them caught up in a frenzy of bloodlust.

With a sob, Margaret turned on her heel and charged into the Community Centre.

"Peter!" she screamed at the top of her voice. "Where's Peter?"

The area collapsed in silence as the crowds gathered to stare - Reginald Magnus among them, as well as his pious wife, Hilary. Peter peered through the crowd and jammed to standstill. There was something particularly heart-wrenching about the distraught schoolgirl who had just staggered into the hall, her eyes alight with panic, her blonde hair tousled.

"Come quickly!" she was sobbing. "They're gonna kill him!"

Within seconds, a group of adults had piled outside the doors where still, the fight hadn't abated. By this time, Gary had withdrawn; last seen hovering on the sidelines, his face bruised and bloody. William and Darren however, refused to back down - taking moments to pause before launching themselves, hammer and tongs, back into the affray.

"That's enough, boys, break it up!" Peter bellowed. "Where's Charlie?"

It took the might of four men to tear them apart. Yet William's eyes blazed, rabid with fury. Elijah and Margaret stared at each other. Never in their lives, had they seen their friend like this. It was as if he had been transformed into a monster. Margaret started to cry. She loved William, unable to bear seeing him so battered and dishevelled.

"What the bloody hell were you thinking of?" Charlie roared, some 30 minutes later.

To his utter dismay, Inspector Ian Boswell had been summoned - infuriated that his son was involved in a fight but even more appalled to find him battered to a pulp. The questions in the morning were going to be rife! In the meantime, Peter had finally tracked down Charlie; all three kids despatched to the almshouse where Margaret stood dabbing William's face with an ice-cold flannel.

"He called me a poofter!" William raged. Anyone could see he was still fuming.

"So what?" Charlie retorted. "You've been called worse things, surely! How could you behave like that? Your father would be ashamed..."

"I know that!" William screamed, "but my father's dead and if it wasn't for those pissing Hamptons, none of this would have happened!"

He appeared to be fighting tears now - where the only one in the room who could fully understand his torment was Peter.

"Charlie, stop this," he muttered. "There's no point being cross with him."

"Why not?" Charlie persisted. "We've all had to suffer because of those Hamptons! It doesn't give him the right to behave like a bloody hooligan!"

After a prolonged argument, it seemed that nothing was about to be resolved immediately and it was Andrew who agreed to escort William back home. Avalon awaited them, white faced. If only Eleanor had been around, Charlie found himself thinking.

"I knew his anger would come out one day," Peter whispered. "He's terrified, Charlie. You've got no idea what those people threatened..."

"But why would he behave like that?" Charlie kept grilling. "I don't understand!"

Peter took a nervous swallow - and all the while, Charlie was watching him, wondering if he knew more than he was prepared to let on.

"They threatened to do horrible things to him," Peter shivered, "things of a-a sexual nature... He's a good-looking boy, Charlie. He worries he might be a target."

Charlie started nodding to himself, pacified by his explanation. But it afforded him no solution as to how they would explain William's behaviour to the *rest of the community* and several days later, it was still a hot topic of conversation.

Alesha too, had witnessed the scene, where it was only a matter of hours before the news was leaked to Perry. Predictably, Perry was in his element - delighted to have finally derived some slur on the Barton-Wells family. Robin, on the other hand, was dismayed. He put the whole ghastly affair down to William's regrettable choice of school - firm in the belief that none of this would have happened if only he had set his sights a little higher.

Eventually the fuss died down. William, along with the other two were condemned to a week's detention. Yet the entire business left him embittered and even more determined to lose his virginity.

William knew he should have been concentrating on his mock exams as well as Avalon's up and coming 18th birthday. His relationship with Vivienne had fizzled, shortly after his party. But it was in the aftermath, that a series of whisperings began circulating among his school friends, now resolute in their encouragement; smuggling him porn magazines - pushing him into the path of some of the more promiscuous girls, except William was a little more choosy. He wanted his 'first time' to be special and preferably with someone he felt a degree of passion for.

That girl turned out to be Dawn. She had first caught his eye in his chemistry class and William found her divinely pretty; smoky grey eyes, a mane of glossy brown hair and a tiny, upturned nose inclined to wrinkle when she laughed. Dating her turned out to be more thrilling than anything he had encountered with Viv. Avalon had returned home, one day, to find them plastered together on the sofa, kissing hungrily. It was a sight which made her smile - and by the time Dawn left, cheeks flushing, William knew he was in love.

Their relationship developed smoothly after that; yet despite a powerful urge to go the whole way, William found he didn't want to rush things. He adored kissing her. By the 3rd date, she encouraged him to stroke her breasts - but it was on the 4th date, she had taken her bra off. William caught his breath - to hold them in his hands and caress them, a moment of pure bliss as he savoured their satin softness. His mouth lowered to her nipples before he could stop himself, further encouraged by her excited gasps of pleasure.

But Dawn was no virgin - she revelled in the fantasy of being William's first. It was Dawn who took their relationship to the next level, careful to choose an afternoon when Avalon was working late. From the moment they started kissing, she had seized his hands, resolute on dragging him upstairs. Gradually their clothes were peeled away. They took it in turns to pleasure each other, daring themselves to go further... until they tumbled into William's luxurious bed and she guided him skilfully inside her. It was an experience which levitated William to new heights of pleasure, his cries of ecstasy so loud, he was thankful Avalon *hadn't* been at home, that day.

As time progressed however, Avalon began to feel irritated by her brother's sexual antics. Hardly a day went by when she didn't come home to an empty lounge, knowing they were upstairs in the bedroom probably 'at it like rabbits!'

"You're supposed be revising!" she screamed. "If you fluff your exams, William, I swear I will cut your allowance!"

"That's not fair," William simpered. "I love her! And anyway, what about you and George? D'you think I didn't hear what you two were getting up to in France?"

"That was different," Avalon snapped, cheeks blazing. "We were on holiday... but that's not the point. I'm sick of being the only breadwinner! Why can't you get yourself a Saturday job?"

"Alright, I will!" William spat, thinking it might shut her up. It didn't.

"And another thing," she drawled. "We need to go to Aldwyck and sort out the woods. There's a lot of fallen trees up there and they're blocking the footpaths. It's dangerous."

"Okay," William mumbled. He bit his lip where the thought of Westbourne House brought a sudden dart of fear. He really didn't want to bump into the Hamptons. In some ways, he was still hurting - reminded of the *real* reason he'd triggered that fight. The anniversary of his father's death had left a deep and lingering pain.

"Is it okay if Dawn comes?" Avalon rolled her eyes. "Please!" he begged. "She'd love to see our old house… and so for that matter, would Eli!"

"Okay," Avalon finally relented, "they can both come! Just as long as you *promise* to do some revision!"

II

William was not the only one who was dreading the thought of returning to Aldwyck. Eleanor and Margaret too, were reluctant; unable to face the prospect of another run in with Perry. It was for that reason they declined to join them, leaving Charlie to escort the others.

It was the 3rd week in November and despite the devastation of the hurricane, he found himself drawn down a familiar country road. The spidery silhouettes of trees stretched overhead like a cage as the road twisted and dipped - the only evidence of damage appeared to be a few exposed craters where fallen trees had been excavated. The interior of the car ran silent as they approached the village and following Avalon's instructions, Charlie took the farm track which allowed them access to the land at the back of Westbourne House.

Elijah's face was taut as he stared out of the window. Charlie slipped a surreptitious glance in the driver mirror, guessing what he was thinking. He too, recognised the track where the surrounding woods seemed ominous. He knew they were probably going to bump into Herbert Baxter; the proud gentleman farmer who he had always found a little intimidating. Though he had expressed a surprising outburst of kindness towards James's kids - having pledged to protect their land *as well as* keep watch over Westbourne House.

The higher they climbed, the more the storm wreckage became evident. Charlie paused by a five bar wooden gate before Avalon stepped out to open it. She squinted into the distance and for a moment, she stood very still - perhaps, recalling the impenetrable forests tucked behind neat hedgerows and peppered with clouds of cow parsley.

Vast areas of forest now appeared to have been decimated.

Avalon clamped her hand over her mouth, fighting tears. "I can't believe it," she croaked.

Charlie crawled through the gateway before resuming his journey along the track. It ran adjacent to a stretch of farmland where cattle grazed peacefully - yet they could no longer ignore the jumble of flattened forests. Charlie veered left. They were still climbing as the area of woodland crept closer. William pressed his face against the window, as shocked as his sister.

He had known these woods since early childhood where they had enjoyed walks, picnics, climbing trees and playing hide and seek. "I wonder if the den's still there," he muttered to himself.

Those same woods lay devastated; fallen trees scattered on the forest floor like match sticks. Charlie tried not to look too hard, sensing the friction as he kept on driving. He was rolling towards the end of the forest where the track eventually led to Herbert's farm.

He pulled up outside another gate and this time everyone stepped out. Two identical barns lay ahead with a concrete track running between them. They could see a cluster of red-brick farm buildings beyond. The air felt chilly where the surrounding fields exuded a damp mist, as well as a strong smell of cow manure. Dawn shivered despite the warmth of her sheepskin jacket, prompting William to curl an arm around her shoulder - but before anyone had a chance to say another word, the sound of a tractor engine chugged into the silence, drawing their gaze towards the farm.

Eventually the tractor slowed. Charlie recognised Herbert Baxter from his vast bulk and florid face. Elijah gulped back his fear - though he had no reason to be nervous. Another man accompanied him, younger, dressed in the typical attire of a farmer; a waxed barbour jacket, cloth cap and thick corduroy trousers tucked into wellingtons.

"Good day to you," Herbert greeted them, climbing down from the tractor. He held out a meaty hand which Avalon grasped with affection.

"Herbert!" she breathed. "Allow me to introduce farmer Baxter and his son."

Charlie was the second to step forward. "I don't suppose you remember me..."

"Of course I do!" Herbert boomed, seizing his hand. "I met you at James's wake. Though I think we may have bumped into each other beforehand - arguing about those dreadful travellers. Though I gather you didn't like them much either. I apologise if I seemed rude."

Charlie felt his tension dissolve and turning to Elijah, drew him into the circle. "Well, I think it's safe to assume we're on the same side now. You know Elijah, of course. Oh - and if you hadn't guessed, this is William's girlfriend..." he grinned at William. "They can't bear to be apart."

"Oh, the joys of young love," the other man smiled. "I'm Toby."

With the introductions complete, the whole group trekked across the countryside to survey the land - first by approaching the largest area of forest before pursuing one of its many footpaths. It seemed only minutes before they came across the first of many obstructions. Avalon froze as a circular crown of tree roots reared up in front of her; a massive 40 foot beech tree, literally ripped from the earth, lying prostrate across the path.

"This is unbelievable," she muttered, running her hand over the trunk. Judging from its girth, it must have been hundreds of years old.

"Terrible, isn't it?" Toby sympathised. "Such a magnificent tree and this is what's causing problems. A lot of ramblers use the woods and most of these paths are impassable."

"I see," Avalon sighed, "so why was there so much damage? These woods have stood for centuries. I don't understand it…"

"We had a long, warm summer," Herbert intervened, "followed by a mild autumn. The trees were in full leaf when that storm struck which put up an unusual amount of resistance."

"We had a fair amount of rain too," Toby added, "which must have softened the ground. Added to 100 mile an hour winds, these trees were blown over like skittles."

Avalon stared at William in shock. Charlie shook his head.

"Terrible," he muttered. "So what now?"

"I've sourced a forestry management company to get the fallen timber cleared up," Toby replied. "We'll oversee it if you like. Don't worry - nature has a way of healing itself. Though once the dead wood is removed, you might need to think about having new saplings planted."

"Thank you," Avalon muttered, her voice hollow, "I'll pay you for your time of course…"

Herbert wagged his hand dismissively. "Don't be silly! It's nothing - we want to protect the countryside as much as you do. You've no idea how pleased we were, those bloody Hamptons didn't get ownership of it!"

They managed to weave their way around the beech tree before continuing a little further. Eventually they arrived at a four-way sign post where one of the paths was marked as a bridle-way. Yet as they ventured deep into the forest, so the condition of the land became worse. Nearly every access route was jammed with fallen timber, heavy branches split away from their trunks, the entire wood a tangle of destruction. Avalon caught Elijah's eye, her face alight with panic. This was *their* land, one of the last remnants of their family history - it seemed impossible to imagine how a single storm could ravage such a beautiful area of countryside.

"I think we've seen enough," William snapped.

"You're right," Avalon replied, "I don't think there's very much we can do right now, other than get the lumberjacks in."

"So shall we go and take a peak at Westbourne House?" William suggested. "It will be interesting to see if there's been any damage to the grounds…"

Nobody argued as he took Dawn's hand and gently led her towards the forest edge. Avalon blinked, trying not to cry as the historic grounds rolled out before her. As if to add to her heartache, she realised some of the ancient trees had gone - including one of her favourite Cedars. She felt the breath trickle from her lungs, relieved to see the faded brick walls of the Victorian kitchen gardens. They stood proudly in place, having fortuitously survived the hurricane - her father's formal gardens too, had changed very little. Then finally her eyes were drawn to the house.

"Wow!" Dawn gasped, breaking the silence. "What an amazing place!" she turned and smiled tenderly at William. "You used to live there?"

"It's been in our family for five generations," William said tightly.

"We were fortunate to live there, too," Charlie began reminiscing. "My son and I helped to restore that place - we actually managed to save it!"

Herbert nodded approvingly before turning to his son. Elijah watched them from the corner of his eye while the others continued to drink in the beauty of the house - it was as if something was about to be proposed.

"Nearly everyone in the village supports you, you know," Herbert then announced, "and we've been thinking - have you ever thought about forming a consortium? There are people who will do anything to protect Aldwyck from future development."

"Good idea," Charlie agreed, "though isn't it a shame Elliot couldn't be a part of it."

"We've found a way of communicating with Elliot," Toby smiled, "he's agreed to be our mole. But what I was leading to was this. Would you consider letting us buy some of the land? We could replant this side of the forest to retain the landscape. Although I wonder if the back might not be better assigned to farmland. Get the area cleared and ploughed. Use it for crops or grazing meadows. We'd like to expand our own farm - but only if you agree to it."

"No pressure," Herbert added sagely, "just have a think about it."

"It would be a shame to lose all this forest," Charlie nodded, "but it's a huge area to manage. To replant it in its entirety will cost you a fortune."

"Hmm," Avalon pondered, her eyes still fixed on Westbourne House.

She felt strangely disturbed without knowing why. From a distance, the beautiful house gazed back lovingly - threads of silver blue cloud were reflected in the glinting window panes. Its coat of dove grey tiles gleamed like fish scales, though several appeared to be missing. She turned and glanced at Herbert. His pale eyes twinkled behind his spectacles.

"Okay," she said dreamily, "what you suggest makes sense. Let's talk about it again in the Spring, once the ground's been cleared…"

She broke off abruptly, spinning back to the house. She could no longer deny, she felt a chill sweep over her. For a moment, she sensed they were being watched; a notion which compelled her to recede into the forest where the deepening curtain of shadow concealed them.

Perry had of course, known they were in the village - delighted Alesha was keeping him so well informed. She had been tailing Charles - though on this occasion, it appeared that his daughter, Margaret, as well as Eleanor had remained behind in the almshouse.

"Keep them under watch!" Perry insisted. "We can't dismiss the possibility, she might go sneaking off to London! I can always use Nathan as a backup."

His words had served as a painful warning - reminding her of the one and only time, Eleanor had slipped out of sight. Alesha had meekly obeyed, while Nathan, used to responding to Perry's orders without question, had immediately set out on his motorbike; surging into the hills towards a quiet country lane which provided the perfect vantage point. He saw them turn into the farm track, guessing they were heading towards Baxter's farm; a theory which turned out to be correct. Charlie's orange Volvo stood out like a beacon as it crept along the perimeter hedge - right up until the point, they had skirted around the side of the forest and were no longer visible.

Wasting no time, Nathan sped back to the house - but it was no longer Perry who was watching them from an upstairs window. It was Ben.

Ben had been keeping a considerably low profile; still pained by the disastrous outcome of 'Black Monday.' But despite that most illuminating discussion with Dominic, he was unsure which way to turn. His father had been utterly vile to him. Though Ben should have grown used to it by now, having suffered a lifetime of degradation. It was times like this when he hated his father more than anyone - yet he was probably the only man he respected. Ruthless and forceful, Perry always found a way of getting what he wanted, no matter how unscrupulous - his acquisition of this splendid house being an exceptional example.

Today, his father was at least being a little more civil towards him - and now he had shared the ultimate disclosure: the Barton-Wells children were in the village. He felt his pulse soar as Nathan described the route they had taken. Perry ordered him to keep the area under surveillance - forearmed with the knowledge, his enemies were marauding around in the very forests that surrounded their estate.

"At last!" Ben whispered.

He swung his binoculars to the left where a movement caught his eye. The first to appear was Herbert Baxter, recognisable by his barrel-like frame - he was tailed by another man dressed in the typical attire of a farmer. Then finally, a small party began to emerge from the depths of the forest. Ben's eyes flashed - recognising William, hand in hand with a girl! So the little pip-squeak had got himself a lady friend. Ben was convinced that with his 'pretty boy' looks, he would have attracted a different sort of attention.

Seconds later, Charlie appeared - Charles Bailey who's insults he would never forget. He had accused him of playing *'evil little mind games!'* He hadn't been wrong - where the subject of his sinister stalking campaign was finally drifting into view.

Ben's heart charged faster as he adjusted the lenses of his binoculars, increasing the magnification until he could see her clearly. In all these months, Avalon Barton-Wells had not changed. His eyes latched themselves to her distinctive face, as pale and strikingly beautiful as ever. Even from a distance, her eyes looked huge - glazed with anxiety.

Ben felt a powerful mixture of emotions. In some way he should have understood her panic. She had taken her reaction a little too far when she had punched him - but he would never *ever* forgive her for marking him! He felt the hatred creep into his soul as he touched his neck. The scars where her sharp fingernails had torn his skin were still there - a constant reminder.

The night Perry had sent him round to evict them was his chance for retribution - fully intent on screwing the bitch. Except that blasted kid brother had ruined things - so they'd taught him a lesson instead. His revenge would have been perfect, if it hadn't been for their miraculous escape on his motorbike.

Avalon turned to the group where she appeared to be in deep conversation. He had just spotted William's little friend who he guessed to be the Jansen boy. But before he had a chance to study his face, Avalon had whirled round again, peering back at the house - then vanished into the cloak of woodland just as abruptly.

"Those woods are ruined," Perry sneered. "I expect they only went up there to assess the damage. They could have saved themselves a whole lot of trouble if they'd just sold the land to me!"

Ben had joined him in the library where Nathan too, lounged among them. Perry threw him a cold smile. "Now, tell me Ben - what's all this I hear about you sniffing around, looking for a connection into the criminal underworld?"

Ben was taken aback. His father *knew* about the thugs they'd drafted in from Brixton to deal with the travellers - in fact, he had openly encouraged it!

"Why do you say that?" Ben stalled, wondering where this was leading.

"Oh come now, Ben, there is no need to be cagey," Perry pressed. "It was brought to my attention by *Mr Theakston* - who I gather, you are quite well acquainted with! He insists he has no further dealings with organised crime which comes as something of a disappointment; but this leads me on to my next point. Have you got very far?"

Ben shrugged. "I *did* finally manage to get a name out of him, yes. Why couldn't you just confide in me a little more…?"

"All in good time, Ben," Perry replied, his voice turning sinister. "Now answer my question."

Ben hesitated, shooting a sideways glance at Nathan. For a moment, even he looked furtive.

"Alan Levy," Ben finally divulged.

Nathan's eyes narrowed shrewdly. "I knew him when he was a kid, Perry. His old man took over from Theakston - but you wouldn't want to mess with either of them."

"I see," Perry muttered. "Well let me be the judge of that. Because if you *have* found an in-road, then I would like you to pursue it. It's useful to have such contacts. If you can successfully pull this off, then maybe I'll have reason to be proud of you again."

For the second time that morning, Ben was charged with a sense of euphoria - oblivious to the careful way his father was manipulating him. "Does this have anything to do with the Chapman woman?" he probed, unable to forget their campaign to grab her son. "Why is she such a threat to you? Isn't it time you explained…"

"Only when the time is right, Ben," Perry interrupted, rising from his chair. Ben watched with fascination as he strutted towards the window, head held high. At 51 years of age, his father possessed the dynamic energy of a man half his age - the powerful frame, the waves of thick white hair which showed no signs of receding. Power radiated off him like sparks and as he turned, Ben flinched at the glacial strike of his eyes. "Let's just say, she tried to destroy me once and I want to make sure she never tries it again, is that clear? If Theakston won't play ball, then we have to source an alternative…" He left the last words dangling - just waiting for Ben to respond.

"Okay I'll do it," he snapped. "If that's what you want." He smiled coldly at Nathan, resolute in his decision. "I hear you and Alan went to school together - any chance you could arrange a little reunion?"

III

Before that day came, Ben had another goal to achieve - that last fleeting vision of Avalon had not only refuelled his hatred, but stirred his desire. The evenings were a lot darker now, the time was right. So for the second time that week, he arrived at another momentous decision.

It was to his even greater satisfaction that Nathan had been carefully surveying the Barton-Wells kids, furnishing him with such details as the school William attended - the days he stayed behind for extra-curricular activities, leaving Avalon on her own. As for Avalon - he had already started stalking her again. He not only knew where she worked but discovered, she didn't get home until six on Fridays.

It had been raining outside. Avalon buttoned up her winter coat and grabbed her umbrella before stepping cautiously into the high street. They were always busier on Fridays - a day which drew in a lot more customers, armed with their most precious family heirlooms in advance of the weekly Saturday auction.

A couple of colleagues had asked her if she wanted to join them for a drink after work but tonight she declined. Right now, she was just looking forward to getting home. Eleanor was coming over later to talk about their land and she also wanted to discuss the allotment scheme. With so much on her mind, Avalon flew up the high street in a daze.

The cast iron Victorian lamp posts cast a shine across the wet pavements. Avalon felt inside her pocket for her key before she breezed up to the porch.

The front of the house was instantly illuminated in a blaze of bright light as she rammed her key into the door, paying little attention to her surroundings. She did not notice the dark shape that had materialised right on the corner of their house.

Within seconds, she had slammed the door shut again. Avalon shook out her umbrella and left it in the porch, then wandered into the kitchen. Her mind was still buzzing with activity as she poured herself a glass of white wine - her eyes drawn to a note left lying on the work surface.

'Hi Sis, Dawn and I have gone to the flicks, spag bol in microwave, love W.'

Avalon felt a smile touch her lips. William had been practising the art of cooking lately, ever keen to impress his new girlfriend; unfortunately, her reverie was shattered by a loud bang as Jim Beam launched himself through the cat flap like a torpedo.

He emitted a low growl, cowering by her feet. He was staring intensely in the direction of the garden, his grey and gold striped fur bristling with spikes.

"It's alright, baby," Avalon crooned, reaching down to stroke his head. *It must have been another cat, surely.* Her fingers briefly made contact with his fur before he glared up at the window - then surged from the room to hide.

Avalon followed his gaze and froze. She had already sensed someone might be out there, as a second security light was detonated. The garden was flooded with light without warning where the unmistakable shape of a man loomed into view; tall, wide-shouldered, dressed completely in black. He poised outside her window suspended in the glare - even more frightening, he appeared to be hooded and masked. Avalon could feel the malevolent bore of his eyes.

With a cry, she shot from the kitchen and into the lounge. Her hands were shaking as she grabbed for the telephone, knowing there was no alternative other than to dial 999.

"Police!" she spluttered. "Th-there's some scary man in my g-garden... Yes, a prowler! Please! Can you come quickly? I-I'm all on my own…"

Her heart was pounding. She inched her way towards the sofa, wriggling into the corner where she curled into a ball; something she hadn't done since the night of their attack at Westbourne House. Yet all those startling details were coming back to her again… the crash of breaking glass - the two men, formidable in their motorcycle leathers. Avalon closed her eyes where the images flared brighter; Ben's leering face followed by that fiendish assault on her brother…

By the time the police arrived, she was sobbing - she could no longer dismiss the possibility, it could be Ben outside her window. For what other reason would the character be masked?

The clang of the doorbell brought her unsteadily to her feet. She moved her eye towards the spy hole, the terror in her mind retracting slightly as a female police officer took shape. Avalon fumbled with the chain - conscious of the beam of torches cutting through the darkness as police officers began to scour the encircling bushes.

It was to her deeper regret, they returned fifteen minutes later - but with no success in finding the intruder. By 6:30, Eleanor too, had been summoned, shocked to find Avalon in such an inconsolable state. William returned a little later.

"We'll talk to the police in the morning," Eleanor comforted her.

Avalon could not stop crying. The demons of her past had stayed with her, refusing to shift.

"I'm sorry, Avalon, but there's precious little anyone can do. At least you're safe. Just thank God you had those security lights fitted!"

It was only now, they were left wondering why Peter had been so adamant about it!

With the concept of danger looming, Eleanor did not want to delay matters. She hadn't slept well - unable to dismiss that chilling warning from Dominic and now Peter too, had spoken to him. It left her with little doubt that the Hamptons were behind this. If Avalon was correct in her theory - that Ben *really* was up to his evil tricks again - the future didn't bode well, a concept which left her resolute in her decision to launch a deeper investigation.

Yawning and bleary eyed through lack of sleep, she turned to Charlie.

"Are you sure you don't want me to come with you?" he murmured, nuzzling his face against her neck. "You know - strength in numbers…"

Eleanor sank her fingers into his thick, dark hair, pressing her eyes shut. "No, Charlie," she whispered huskily. "Stay at home and look after Margaret. There's no point involving her. She's scared enough of the Hamptons as it is and I don't want to put *you* in the firing line either."

"What are you hoping to achieve?" Charlie kept pressing. He brushed a loose curl from her face before dropping a tender kiss onto her forehead.

"It's time we filed a complaint," Eleanor sighed, kissing him back. "Avalon can't live her life in fear - this has gone too far! If she could bring a prosecution against Ben, he might even be served with a court injunction. It's only now, I'm beginning to wish we'd gone to the police before…" she broke off quickly.

"What?" Charlie whispered, missing nothing. "You were going to mention the night of their eviction, weren't you?"

"That is not the reason I want to talk to the police?" she retorted. "Look - I'm sorry if I seem cagey but I'm only trying to protect people."

"I know, sweetheart," Charlie sighed, lowering his eyes, "and you're taking Eli."

"Eli specifically asked to come," Eleanor said defensively, wary her son felt as protective towards the Barton-Wells children as she did.

Two hours later, Eleanor glided into the police station accompanied by Elijah, Avalon and William. They were warmly greeted by the same female police officer who had consoled Avalon and shepherded into an interview room. They were each offered a chair and for several minutes, just waited. Then eventually, the door swung open and a man strutted into view.

Eleanor felt her heart sink. "Inspector Boswell," she greeted him softly. His intense dark eyes pricked into her - already she felt off guard.

"Mrs Bailey," Ian answered, lowering his heavy frame into the chair opposite. "I understand you wish to make a complaint."

"This isn't about me, it's about Avalon," Eleanor began, "a situation that's been bothering us for many months - and it concerns a man by the name of Ben Hampton."

"I see," Ian replied disdainfully, "and this relates to the incident yesterday, does it?"

"It was him!" Avalon broke in fearfully. "I know it was!"

Inspector Ian Boswell gazed at her with scepticism. "And you're sure about that are you, Miss Barton-Wells? Didn't you say the intruder was masked?"

"I just know!" Avalon shivered, coiling her arms around herself in fear. "It was the way he was stood there, staring - it reminded me of him!"

"I see," Ian muttered, making a note. "Well I can't really base an investigation on intuition. Do you have any evidence which might substantiate your claim?"

"Ben Hampton has been stalking Avalon since 1985," Eleanor broke in boldly.

Ian Boswell raised his eyebrows.

"It was around the time, the Hamptons started to take an interest in our home," Avalon added, forcing a gentler tone. "Ben and I were dating b-but I ended the relationship…"

Ian smirked. "A lover's tiff?" he mocked, "do you think he developed some sort of obsession?"

Tears swam in her eyes as she stared at him intently. Piece by piece, she stammered out her story. The dead flowers. She had foolishly discarded the packaging, hoping it was a one-off sick joke. The next parcel had contained a rabbit's skull.

"We went on a woodland walk together - there was one lying on the path. He kicked it away. He must have known I'd see a connection…"

"You assumed the skull was from him?" Ian interrupted.

"Well who else would have sent it?" Avalon gasped.

She shivered as she began to recall other things. How could she forget the spine chilling music pounding from his car? Music that had risen in the grounds, in the dead of night?

"Music in the grounds," Ian sighed. Even Elijah noticed he was beginning to look bored.

"He left a tape in the Orangerie," he finally plucked up the courage to say.

Ian threw him a look of irritation. "What did you say?"

"Creepy, electronic music," Elijah persisted. "I'll never forget it! She was terrified."

"I remember," William nodded. "It sounded like that German group, Kraftwerk."

"Well I'm not interested who it was by," Ian snapped, hurling him an even more contemptuous look. It was obvious he was still smarting from the pasting William had given Gary.

"The same music, Ben liked," Avalon added coldly.

"Mr Boswell, this *all* has relevance." Eleanor intervened. "We are trying to explain a prolonged campaign of terror. And there definitely seems to be a connection between the skull in the post and the music."

"And yet it never crossed your mind to report any of these *incidents*?" Ian frowned.

Avalon shook her head sadly. "Dad phoned Ben's mother. He urged Ben to stop upsetting me, otherwise he *would* call the police. I believe he did in the end - that day they came up to the house?"

"We were all there, Mr Boswell," Eleanor added. "The Hamptons confronted us in James's bar. It was a very unpleasant scene."

"Let's see," Ian muttered. He opened a loose leaf file, flipping through the pages. "Yes, your father did report something. He accused the Hamptons of behaving in a *threatening* manner. He specifically mentioned you, Miss Chapman - sorry, Bailey." His eyes narrowed. "Is there anything *you* wish to add to this story?"

"No," Eleanor said firmly. "This is about Avalon, not me." Once again, Ian's eyes seemed to bore right into her, searching for clues. Yet Eleanor had sworn to keep quiet about her feud with Perry - conscious of her son who had turned rigid.

"I see," Ian finally responded after a long, strained pause. "Well, up until now, I have a report of *one* incident where Mr Hampton's behaviour was threatening - but that's all. Is there any other reason you suspect he could have been your prowler?"

"Perry is after our land!" Avalon blurted. "He came round to my house once - asked me if I'd sell it to him... but he was nasty! He threatened me. He said he had people he could use to frighten me. I'm sure he was referring to Ben..."

Eleanor bit her lip, fighting against the urge to tell him what Dominic had said. *'Sounds like she's made herself an enemy...'* words which seemed to echo Avalon's.

"We visited our land recently," Avalon's voice kept piping. "I sensed we were being watched!"

"It is not impossible, Mr Boswell," Eleanor said, fixing him with her stare. "Is it?"

Ian cleared his throat in a manner which suggested he was beginning to feel pressurised. Already his face had turned a little redder. He shook his head.

"I'm sorry but this is pure fantasy! You *sensed* you were being watched. A masked man came prowling around your house - someone who was probably an opportunist burglar looking for a way in and yet you remain *convinced* it was Ben Hampton."

"This isn't make believe!" Avalon protested. To everyone's horror, she started to cry.

In all this time, Elijah too had been watching and listening - it was obvious the sneer on Inspector Boswell's face would enrage him.

"She's telling the truth!" he snarled under his breath.

"Do not take that tone with me, young man!" Ian barked.

"Avalon's my friend!" Elijah protested. "Why can't you take this seriously?"

"Eli, that's enough!" Eleanor gasped, her hand closing around his forearm.

"He didn't take my abduction very seriously!"

Avalon, pale as a ghost, wiped a tear from her face. She too was glaring at Ian, her eyes almost challenging. William, on the other hand, could no longer suppress his smirk.

"I base my investigations on evidence, boy," Ian hissed back, "and for your information, we *did* question Mr Hampton's security guard! The man you accused was in London, moving furniture - in advance of their move to Aldwyck! I saw a docket signed by Mr Wadzinski from the removal company - signed at 3:00 in the afternoon which is roughly the same time you were approached! He could not have been in two places at once!"

"Anyone could have produced that docket!" William drawled. "You had two witnesses, Mr Boswell - two people who identified Nathan as one of those men. You *could* have brought charges."

"And I could have brought charges against you, Mr Barton-Wells, for the assault on my son," Ian retorted fiercely.

"But *he* started that fight!" Eli gasped. "William was just trying to protect me...!"

"Boys, that's enough!" Eleanor snapped. "I'm sorry Gary was hurt! But we're not here to talk about the fight, nor Eli's abduction - and if there was insufficient evidence to convict Nathan, then we'll just have to live with that!" She took a deep breath, unnerved by the simmering fury in Ian's eyes. She chose her next words carefully. "Inspector Boswell, we are here to discuss Avalon's safety *and* William's. There's been a lot of nastiness concerning Ben... and if Avalon feels she's in danger I must urge you to look into this."

"And what do you hope to achieve?" Ian pressed.

"A court injunction which prohibits him from going anywhere near her," Eleanor said in a voice of steel. "The man is evil. She needs protection."

At first, Ian didn't reply. He appeared to mull over her suggestion. His eyes were still darting into her like bullets. He cleared his throat. "Okay - so try and understand this from my perspective. No crime has been committed. There is no clear evidence to prove Ben Hampton is a threat to you, Miss Barton-Wells. What I do see however, is a deep rooted family feud. I can sympathise, in so much as you lost Westbourne House - there was obviously some acrimony between the Hamptons and your father. But I cannot help wondering that if any future crime is committed, you are far more likely to incriminate *the Hampton* family than anyone."

"So that's it is it?" Elijah snapped in fury. "You're just gonna sit back and do nothing!"

"Eli, be quiet," Eleanor whispered again.

"No!" he gasped, erupting from his seat. "I won't! Avalon's in danger! I don't want to see her hurt!"

"Until I see some evidence, young man, there is very little we can do!" Ian shot back.

"Yeah, so you say," Elijah retorted, "or perhaps it's just easier to turn a blind eye to any crime that involves the Hamptons..." and refusing to be fobbed off for a moment longer, he turned and stormed out of the interview room.

By the time Eleanor found him, tears of anger burned in his eyes. There was a small parking area at the back of the police station which in turn, backed onto a surround of tall, brick buildings. Elijah clung to the railings, frozen like a statue. His heart ached with torment - where surely, Eleanor should have understood his rage.

"This is about Jake, isn't it?" she accused.

Elijah squeezed his eyes shut, desperately trying to claw together his composure.

"Look," she continued. "Inspector Boswell is not Hargreeves! You more or less insinuated there was some *corruption* going on!" She released a pitiful sigh, her hand tightening on his shoulder. "I told you, you had to live a lie - show respect to those in authority, even if you *do* suspect their motives. You are going to have to control yourself a lot better, Elijah."

"Mum, I'm sorry," he whispered, furiously blinking back his tears.

"I don't want you to be sorry, I want you to be careful," she added. Elijah recognised, for the first time ever, her voice sounded cold. "Carry on like this and we'll never get justice for your father. Now don't you ever speak to Inspector Boswell like that again."

Elijah swallowed, overburdened by a sense of defeat. He reluctantly nodded his head, still quaking at the thought of how badly Boswell had let them down - though finally understanding her dismay, as he followed her back to the car.

Chapter 7

I

February 1988

Avalon swallowed hard, staring at each set of display boards in amazement and with no concept that she was about to be an instrumental factor in the inception of Rosebrook's future.

An exhibition had been set up in the foyer of the Council headquarters. Plans for the land behind the Community Centre were finally being unveiled.

She was already familiar with the first display - the ambitious housing trust which enveloped Peter's vision. Charlie's professional drawings revealed an array of buildings positioned around a rectangular green; the first, an elegant terrace divided into purpose built retirement flats. These were situated closest to the Community Centre. On the facing sides of the green, stood the clusters of semi-detached homes more suited to families, complete with gardens and parking areas. While to the rear of the plot, another terraced row encompassed a complex of flats set on three levels, including some stylish roof apartments. Each would be available for low rent and specifically designed for young people struggling to get a foot on the housing ladder.

By 1988, house prices were alarmingly high but rented accommodation was scarce. Rosebrook, with its sophisticated architecture was a much sought-after place to live. Yet for the average worker, the choice was limited and this was where Peter's scheme was about to throw them a lifeline. Avalon nodded to herself, having long grasped the concept of his plan. An area near the green was already earmarked for a doctors surgery, as well as a library and grocery store. In fact, Peter and Charlie had put a lot of thought into their project - a plan which resembled a self-contained, miniature village with areas set aside for tree planting, a children's playground and plenty of green space for dog walkers.

She felt the touch of a smile; except it faded before it had a chance to flourish as she drifted towards the second display. The name, 'Falcon Properties' served as a chilling reminder of the company who had ruthlessly deceived her father. Just the sight of their aggressive logo depicting the head of a falcon seemed intimidating - from its deadly black eyes to the curve of its cruel and predatory beak, so symbolic of their enemy.

He had delivered a plan which revealed an alternative development - but with considerably less green space and nearly double the amount of dwellings. These exclusive 4-bedroom mansions were more suited to wealthy professionals and would undoubtedly be priced at the higher end of the market. Avalon gazed at the artist impression with contempt - the deluxe half-timber construction and most interestingly, a gated entrance which would only allow private access to the estate.

"Hello again, Avalon," a soft voice brushed against her ear.

She turned, meeting the serene, pale blue eyes of Robin Whaley.

"Robin," she greeted him sweetly. Her face folded into a smile. "I haven't seen you for ages."

It was no exaggeration. There had been very little communication since December. The last two months had disappeared in a flash. Avalon and William had at last, inaugurated their allotment scheme; and much to the delight of the locals who were heartbroken to lose their plots at Westbourne House. It marked the end of an era, Avalon reflected sadly.

"So how are you?" Robin added. "I trust there have been no more incidents - no prowlers?"

"No, thank God!" Avalon shivered - it was Peter who had informed him of the intrusion. She turned back to the display boards. Perry's logo loomed on the fringe of her vision like an omen.

"What do you think of the plans?" he pressed, keen to keep the conversation flowing.

Avalon gave a shrug. "Ostentatious - completely 'over the top' for this area of Rosebrook and obviously designed to make someone very rich! I'm not wrong am I? I still think Peter's is the best idea - it blends so much better with the neighbourhood!"

"You could well be right," Robin sighed. "Though the applicant has stressed, this town is undergoing expansion. A wider choice of property styles may prove to be popular."

"But unaffordable for the average working man," Avalon scoffed.

Finally, she wandered across to the 3rd display. Robin stood by in anticipation as if waiting for her reaction. Dominic's quantity surveyors had been exceptionally positive in their appraisal - all six hectares had now been cleared and the last remnants of the textile factory demolished.

The plan shimmering before them was impressive; a complex which depicted a long drive, lined with trees, rolling towards a futuristic looking night club. It was two storeys high, constructed from pure white blocks and intersected with panels of mirrored glass. A wide flight of steps led to the entrance. Pillars guarded a set of glass doors and the innovative sweep of its roof resembled a wave. Avalon raised her eyebrows, examining the paved pedestrian and parking areas set back from the trees; areas which had been artistically landscaped, sporting modern street furniture - two more sets of buildings indicated a scattering of restaurants and wine bars.

"Amazing," Avalon breathed, "it's almost en par with the Barbican! I'd be lying if I said that Rosebrook didn't need better entertainment facilities - who's the applicant?"

"Dominic Theakston," Robin replied smugly. "He's an entrepreneur from Swanley. Has your friend, Eleanor, never mentioned him?"

Avalon froze - clocking the glint in his eyes. Of course! She'd only met him very briefly in the 'Castle Donoghue.' Peter let slip they'd been discussing the land - and without knowing why, she suddenly guessed the secrecy behind that meeting.

"I don't think so," she murmured. "Have you had any dealings with him?"

"Not in the arena of planning," Robin said guardedly. He gave a tight smile, where the ice in his eyes had not quite receded. "His plan is bound to incite a degree of objection. Especially among the Community Centre people."

"I see," Avalon smiled back.

"Let's just say," Robin added, leaning a little closer to whisper, "the next few days are going to be interesting..."

"Have you seen the exhibition?" Avalon breathed.

She had not only managed to round up Eleanor, but Charlie and Peter too, before they slipped back to the almshouse, unnoticed.

"Go and have a look. The plans you came up with look great but I warn you, the others are just as impressive! Especially the night club and who is this man, Theakston? Who's side's he on?"

A flash of fear shot across Eleanor's face. Charlie lowered his eyes. Only Peter held her stare though even *he* seemed pensive.

"We're not sure," he broke in quickly, "but the thought of opposing his leisure complex is a bit nerve-wracking!"

"But why?" Avalon demanded.

"He used to be involved in organised crime," Eleanor spilled out before she could stop herself.

"Avalon, we have reason to believe this may be the man Elliot saw," Charlie sighed, "at that *very secret meeting* he mentioned, remember?"

"So he's in cahoots with Perry?" Avalon gasped, "but I saw you in the Castle Donoghue. What was all that about?"

"We were just testing the water," Charlie continued boldly. "Eleanor's seen a very different side to this man. We were wondering if Perry had some sort of hold over him - maybe using him in some way." He almost shivered. "Let's just say, he agreed to join us in the pub to talk about our plans - though none of us can fully trust him."

"Hmm - you did say Robin approached *two* other parties," Avalon said numbly.

"That's right," Charlie continued, "Robin has always used Peter's housing trust as a model; a means of persuading the *council* to buy the land - just as long as it appeals to the public. If one of these alternative plans proves to be more popular, they may reconsider."

"I see," Avalon nodded. "In that case, we have got to make sure Peter's housing trust gets the thumbs up - rally up as much objection as we can against these other plans."

"Indeed," Charlie said gravely, "but we're about to oppose two very powerful players here, Avalon, one of whom happens to be Perry Hampton. Are you still happy to back our fight?"

"You know I will!" Avalon snapped, rising to her feet. "William and I will do anything to stop him from getting it..." and snatching up the jacket she'd left draped across the arm of her chair, she slipped it over her shoulders. "Just go and look at the plans, Charlie. Then you'll get some idea of how much profit he's planning to make from this."

She gave a sad smile before withdrawing from the meeting.

"She seems very determined doesn't she?" Peter murmured.

"Avalon has more reason to hate Hampton than anyone," Eleanor sighed.

"At least we know the type of man we're up against," Peter added. "It's Dominic I'm worried about! We still don't really know who's side he's on! Although he *did* warn me about Avalon..."

"Ssh!" Charlie urged, "best we don't mention it. It's obvious he knows a lot more than he's letting on and he's also been very cagey."

"Ben and Nathan joined his gym!" Eleanor shuddered. "I got the impression he overheard something nasty." She gazed at Peter. "I wish we could have brought this up when we spoke to the police... but I suppose we have to consider the repercussions. Dominic said he only had one game plan; to get the land! It's obvious he's been liaising with both parties and if word got out..."

"He'd be seen as a traitor," Charlie finished somberly, "which would no doubt, put you straight back in the firing line."

"I see," Peter responded anxiously, "well at least the warning didn't come too late..."

The room fell silent as they mulled over his words. An advent of danger was finally spilling its way into their lives again and it was a situation which left them uneasy.

II

"Oh well, looks like D-Day has finally arrived!" Charlie announced over breakfast.

Was it really 8 months since he'd gleaned the first clues of this *sinister* conflict? It took him right back to the day of their wedding - and for a second, his eyes were drawn to a photo on the mantelpiece. Charlie and his bride looked so deliriously happy! Obviously, it had been taken *before* Christopher Farrin had taken him to one side - the chilling discovery that Perry, along with Dominic, had been approached by Robin Whaley. *'You could be up against a couple of giants here, Charlie! Hampton has already been likened to some sort of Mafia boss.'*

Charlie shivered. Christopher hadn't been wrong and now finally, here he was staring at a letter; an announcement of a public consultation where all three parties were expected to thrash out their proposals in front of an audience of spectators and decision makers.

On the face of it, Peter had nothing to fear. He only had to stress the plight of those living in Rosebrook who had been unfairly squeezed out of the housing market. Robin had pretended to back his proposal from day one and if he succeeded, the council would be seen as benevolent. Yet even Christopher had possessed the foresight to grasp the reality. The council could undertake a massive u-turn once the purchase was complete.

"So it's down to us to oppose the other plans?" Eleanor questioned fearfully.

Charlie gave a nod, his eyes on his daughter, soon to turn 13. "I'll do it," he said with conviction. "Dominic knows I'm backing Peter. And it should be obvious, we don't want Hampton muscling in on our neighbourhood."

"The Hamptons aren't coming *here* are they?" Margaret gasped, missing nothing.

"Not if I've got anything to do with it," Charlie soothed. He gave her a light peck on the cheek. "It's just a housing proposal, love. Now go and finish getting ready for school."

The moment she was out of earshot, Charlie sidled up to Eleanor. "Elijah seems keen to get involved. I guess he's been talking to the Barton-Wells kids."

"Did you know, Avalon is speaking publicly against Perry's plan?" Eleanor replied. "I've never known two kids so determined..."

The next few days were a blur as Charlie and Avalon worked on their speeches. Yet nothing had prepared them for the stringent new rules Robin was about to impose.

"I realise it's inappropriate for *me* to speak against his proposal..." Peter faltered.

"Indeed," Robin sighed, his expression betraying nothing.

"But how can you disallow Charlie?" Peter pressed, unable to disguise his shock.

"Charlie too, has a vested interest," Robin continued silkily. "He is the architect - the master builder who will be commissioned to carry out the work should we agree to it. It's obvious his views will be biassed against the opposing parties."

Charlie on the other hand, was fuming. "So who *is* permitted to speak?"

"Any member of the public who doesn't stand to profit from the outcome," Robin smiled, "such as your wife for example." His eyes were taunting as he stared directly at Eleanor.

They had paused outside the council chamber. Already Eleanor's pulse was racing. There was no question, Robin was pulling the strings - purposefully luring Eleanor into a web of conflict which was designed to enrage Dominic. Elijah looked confused - up until now, he had avoided all eye contact with Robin but suddenly he sensed a nip of friction.

"You can do it, Mum," he whispered, nudging her.

"Eli's right," Charlie snapped, unashamedly glaring at Robin. "Don't be scared, love. We've discussed our concerns against this night club! You can read out *my* notes."

"Fine!" Eleanor muttered with a flash of irritation. "It is after all, *the council* who decide, not me! I'm more than happy to voice the opinions of the residents."

They wandered into the council chamber where Eleanor took her seat. She looked almost ethereal, Charlie thought - admiring the folds of her cream-coloured tunic, its cowl neck which enhanced the sultry glow of her skin. Her gleaming, dark curls had been left to grow long again - tumbling past her shoulders, portraying an impression of fragile beauty that was almost magnified. So Whaley had prohibited him from being a spokesman - craftily pitching Eleanor into the arena to oppose her most feared enemy. In truth, he could have throttled him!

Before he had a chance to get a grip, his breath was cut short as Dominic, along with his entourage of surveyors, lawyers and planning consultants, rolled into the room. They formed a forbidding mob. He was aware of Peter nudging him - momentarily blown away by the might of his presence. He was in deep discussion with some suited man, whose sharp features and curling dark hair they recognised from the time they'd caught up with him on site - possibly one of the surveyors. It was also the first time any of them had seen Dominic in a suit; sharp and funereally black as if designed to depict his brooding nature. Charlie gave a shudder.

"Looks like the heavy mob have arrived," he muttered darkly. "Poor Eleanor! I hope they don't crucify her…"

After a brief resume from Robin, which was backed by the Head of Planning, Terry Griffiths, there seemed to be little hesitation in getting the ball rolling.

"We have a lot to discuss, ladies and gentleman," Terry announced pompously. "But first, I would like to invite Mr Peter Summerville to present his proposal."

With a smile, Peter bounded towards the lectern - he was engrossed in his pitch within seconds.

Up until a few years ago, Rosebrook had been an affordable location where its careful balance of accommodation catered for all classes. Encircled by housing estates, it offered an eclectic blend of the traditional and the modern; but come the mid 80s, the situation had changed as wealthy

Londoners flocked to the town, recognising its potential for commuting. Property prices had soared steadily - even council houses began to slip into the private sector; and as escalating property values drove up the price of rented accommodation, so a growing number of respectable, hard working people were finding it difficult to acquire a home.

"Here lies the reason, I'm so passionate about setting up a housing trust," Peter beamed. His eyes swept over the audience, his enthusiasm incandescent. "These dwellings are suited to couples and families, as well as older residents who need a little more care! My dream is to create a small community where people look out for each other; where facilities, such as a surgery, a library and children's playground will bring residents closer together. Its proximity to our Community Centre makes it ideal for the elderly..." He paused again, monitoring the mood. His eyes briefly met Avalon's whose tender smile inspired him. "Every one of you must know someone who is desperately seeking an affordable home - so I must urge you to support this scheme."

A brief rumble rose up from the audience before the floor was thrown open to comments. Some feared the low rent would attract a poorer class of society. Others questioned whether it was right to have youngsters living in the same neighbourhood as retired people - or where an influx of youths could be potentially drawn to crime and prey on the vulnerable.

It was Terry Griffiths who dispelled these fears; insisting that residents would be carefully monitored - the scheme was designed for hard working people on a low income, not those claiming state benefits.

With a sense Peter had gained a foothold, Eleanor felt she could relax slightly. Elijah was right. She had nothing to fear, where her gaze was unavoidably drawn towards Dominic's party. There was no question, the next part was going to be challenging - she had already clocked his cold, expressionless face as he lounged in his seat, unmoved by Peter's vision. A stunning young woman sat right next to him - well groomed and undeniably stylish in a short, close-fitting dress, tailored jacket and leather boots. Eleanor had heard it from Charlie that Dominic was divorced - this lady must have been his girlfriend, surely.

It wasn't Dominic who crept towards the podium however, but his accomplice - the same curly haired professional Charlie had already recognised. His name was Lawrence Goldblum, a commercial consultant. His comprehensive understanding of town and country planning gave him a formidable edge as he proceeded to outline his client's ambitious proposal.

Intricate plans swept before Eleanor's eyes from the twenty-page report the council had prepared in advance. She found herself staring in awe at the front and side elevations of the proposed night club - aware of the other man's voice ringing in the background.

"I understand there has been some resistance to this project - but I ask you, can the council of Rosebrook really afford to turn down such a spectacular complex? My client is looking to invest thousands of pounds in your town - build a state-of-the-art night club which will draw in visitors as well as provide an enviable source of entertainment for residents. There could potentially be 16 separate units available to rent - opportunities for local patrons to set up new businesses. Bars, restaurants, cafés, fast food outlets…"

Eleanor's eyes were drawn to the paved areas lining each side of the driveway and ultimately, the buildings set aside for this purpose. It was just as Avalon had described. No-one could deny, this project was ambitious and with additional benefits to Rosebrook's business community.

"Think of the possibilities for employment! This scheme will create hundreds of jobs. We intend to source local contractors - builders, decorators and electricians. There is no question of the prosperity this will bring to Rosebrook. This, ladies and gentlemen, is an investment which will serve your town for many years to come…"

Eleanor closed her eyes, rocked by his speech. How could she hope to oppose a man so charismatic? Dominic had cherry-picked his colleagues well.

"May we listen to the case *against* this proposal?" Robin's voice finally pulsed into the chamber.

Her eyes snapped open and for a moment she faltered. To her utter bewilderment, Robin was looking at her directly, his cold eyes piercing into her like spurs. She rose shakily, knowing they had her in a tight spot. Dominic followed his gaze.

"Mrs Eleanor Bailey," Robin smiled politely.

Eleanor stared at the circle of elected councillors positioned at the head of the room. Judging from their faces, they were as curious to hear her objections as anyone.

Charlie reached forward and squeezed her hand. "Don't worry, you'll be fine," he said softly.

"Good luck, Mum," Elijah added, offering his most encouraging smile.

Eleanor took her position at the podium and gripped Charlie's speech. The silence around her thickened. Everyone was waiting for her to begin and for a moment, she felt giddy. The crowd before her seemed to waver. Yet it was among that sea of faces she spotted Peter. She remembered his relentless passion for his housing trust - where just one glance at those sunny, Irish features brought a strength to her heart.

"Ladies and Gentlemen, I cannot imagine there is a single person in this room who isn't dazzled by the outline concept presented to you. But there are some concerns among residents as to whether this is suitable for the land we're discussing. Mr Whaley has asked me to voice these objections…" she flicked him a cool smile, despite her loathing.

She cleared her throat whilst scrutinising Charlie's notes. "This land lies within an area which is largely residential. There are elderly people as well as families with children. Many of you may have seen what the town centre is like on a Saturday night, especially when the club turns out. Streets overrun with youths, tanked up with alcohol. People worry about noise and disruption - anti-social behaviour such as drug taking and vandalism - graffiti on walls, people being sick, urinating in people's gardens and various sexual acts taking place..."

A chuckle rumbled through the audience, causing her to pause. For a moment, her eyes were unwittingly drawn to Dominic's - except he no longer looked so calm. He glared back at her with a force of hostility that was horribly familiar, his slanted eyes narrowed. Eleanor swallowed, feeling the first flutter of anxiety as she ceaselessly continued to recite Charlie's notes.

"Anyone can see this complex is impressive - but maybe better suited to an outlying area, as opposed to being slapped right in the middle of a residential neighbourhood! As for the design of the club - it is very ambitious! Obviously a great deal of thought has gone into it - b-but it doesn't really blend with the prevalent architecture. Rosebrook has always retained a traditional style. This building is futuristic - it looks like something out of the film, *Blade Runner*..."

Dominic let out an unpleasant laugh, turning to whisper in the ear of his consultant.

"If the council agree to our plan, the architecture can be modified!" Lawrence snapped rudely from the arena.

"Traditional architecture!" Dominic was heard to sneer. "She'll be suggesting we stick a bloody thatched roof on it next!"

"Would you kindly not interrupt, Sir," Terry Griffiths jumped in, much to Eleanor's relief. "Please continue, Mrs Bailey. What other objections do you have?"

"I-I hope I've sufficiently covered the issue of disruption," Eleanor rambled on nervously, staring at Charlie's notes, "and this is our principal concern! We have children of our own to consider. I have a 14 year old son and a step daughter, soon to turn 13. They've already been subjected to an incident which typified the nastier side of youth culture, where an excess of drink and drugs was involved... Yet we could be facing this type of anti-social behaviour on a regular basis! I conclude by expressing the widely supported view that an entertainment complex in this part of town is totally inappropriate. We urge Rosebrook Council *not* to embrace this plan..."

She barely had a chance to step shakily down from the podium when the silence was torn apart by a riot of comments. Though this time, the debate was a lot more heated.

"If a complex like this is built, it is going to compete with existing establishments!" one man bellowed. Charlie recognised him from the Chamber of Commerce. "Pubs, wine bars and restaurants are bound to feel the pinch!"

Another man had already sprung to his feet. "It'll destroy the *town centre* night club!" He had a shady look about him; untidy grey hair, scraped back into a ponytail - a shiny suit open just sufficiently to expose the glint of a medallion. There was no doubt in Charlie's mind, this character was probably the club's owner.

"What? That clapped out shit-hole, Tiffany's?" Dominic retorted nastily. "Yeah, been busted twice, it has! And our *dear lady* worries about an excess of drink and drugs…?"

Eleanor frowned, struck with a horror he was not exaggerating. Hadn't she read it in the papers that police *had* indeed carried out a number of drug raids on Tiffany's lately - where hard drugs including cocaine and amphetamines were reported to have been seized?

From the other side of the chamber, Robin stood very still.

"Can we have some order *please!*" Terry finally ranted, aware the meeting was becoming unruly. "You all have a chance to have your say and we still have one more plan to discuss!"

The arguments for and against the proposal continued to bounce around the auditorium until it was Dominic himself, who made the final closing comments. He rose to his feet and swaggered towards the edge of the chamber, not quite reaching the podium - then turned and stared directly at Eleanor.

"We understand the concern about noise!" he snapped, "but staff will be disciplined in handling rowdy behaviour. They'll ensure patrons leave quietly. There's gonna be paid security to handle trouble makers. Any offenders'll be barred. But there's no question, this enterprise'll go a long way towards providing employment - *additional* customers for pubs, takeaways and taxi companies who'd otherwise go to Bromley. Don't kid yourselves - this place ain't got great entertainment facilities. It's undergoing expansion anyway - so why not build your *housing trust* in another area of town. Don't deny Rosebrook something it hasn't got!"

She felt the hard blades of his eyes and for a moment, felt herself disintegrate into the terrified young girl she had been in the 70s, trapped inside that railway tunnel. She lowered her eyes. Yet the image of his face lingered, bringing back memories which had never really gone away.

"Well that was a personal attack!" she whispered as soon as she was back amongst her group.

"Ignore him, he's just trying to intimidate you," Charlie spat.

Dominic had wandered back to his seat where his girlfriend appeared to be congratulating him. Yet Charlie's eyes were on the council members, enthroned in a semi-circle of high backed chairs. They were nodding among themselves as if that final outburst from Dominic might have swayed them.

He felt his heart sink. If the council agreed to this leisure complex, they would no longer be considering the purchase of the land for Peter's housing trust; though before his despondency could drag him down any deeper, Robin was addressing the public again.

"We have one final proposal," he announced calmly, "from an illustrious property development company. Would the representative for Falcon Properties please present their case."

Charlie frowned at Avalon as a tall, silver haired man sidled up to the lectern and gazed over the crowd. Of slightly heavy build with a smooth, pink face, he portrayed a disturbingly smug demeanour. Charlie shrugged - oblivious to who this gentleman was, as he proceeded to eulogise over the exclusive accommodation his client was about to bring to Rosebrook.

"These houses will be exquisite! Stylish, meticulously designed with modern facilities - whilst retaining a *traditional* half-timber exterior which is in keeping with the local architecture..."

He had obviously been paying close attention to the last debate, Charlie fathomed.

"A private gated estate will allow residents better security," the man smiled, "the properties accessed through electronic coded gates... each property will have its own garage - a courtyard garden designed for low maintenance..."

Charlie could have yawned, wondering how much longer this nauseating spiel would go on for as he listed every grandiose feature - while cleverly interweaving objections against the other plans.

"It goes without saying, this site is *clearly* suited for housing - a residential area where any commercial development would seem out of place! But why have cotton when you can have silk? Rosebrook has already started to appeal to the commuter market with its excellent road and rail network - especially since the unveiling of the M25, a trend which is likely to continue. Professional, upper middle class residents will demand a high standard of accommodation and this development will go a long way towards satisfying that demand..."

Charlie shook his head, dismayed by the audacity of his speech. Peter would be heartbroken if the council denied him this one chance to introduce affordable housing into Rosebrook. For a moment, the man met his gaze. His eyes glittered. Then slowly, he stepped back from the lectern, leaving him with a sense, his face was already familiar to him. He barely had a chance to gather his thoughts however, when the floor was once again released to public opinion. Avalon had already leapt to her feet.

"This is a disgrace!" she raged. "We've seen hundreds of local people, unfairly priced out of the housing market thanks to this rising *commuter* market!"

"Miss Barton-Wells," Robin said softly and turning, he pressed his most benevolent smile, "I understand you have strong feelings against this property development."

"Yes I do!" Avalon responded stoutly, wandering up to the podium. She cast her gaze over the crowd and with a slight toss of her head, delivered her own carefully planned oration. "I have researched this proposal. A 'private estate of luxury homes' is a ridiculous scheme for this area." Her eyes drifted across to Peter. "What Peter proposes makes much more sense! He has devised a housing trust which blends well with the existing neighbourhood. And whilst our opponents have done an excellent job in convincing you that we must satisfy a demand for a wealthier class of society, I urge you not to abandon the needs of honest, hard working residents - people who make a valuable contribution to this town. Nurses and school teachers. Tradesmen and community workers, not to forget our undergraduates…"

Her words poured into the room as she continued to push her case; taking every opportunity to promote Peter's housing initiative - convinced there were other locations for the 'exclusive development' Perry had in mind. At one point, she stared straight at Dominic. To her surprise, he flashed her a cocky smile which further bolstered her confidence. She finished her speech almost breathless.

A chilling voice then rose up from the back of the hall. *"As emotionally charged as ever!"*

Heads had already started spinning. Eleanor let out a gasp as without warning, Perry reared up from the public arena. The room fell silent. No-one really knew quite how to react as he squeezed himself out from the row of seats and crept towards the chamber.

"Shit," Charlie muttered, "he must have been there all the time."

"So it would seem," Eleanor whispered in shock.

She was watching Avalon. Her face turned pale as Perry hovered on the edge of the chamber, now staring at her intensely.

"My name is Peregrine Hampton, founder of Falcon Properties!" his voice boomed across the audience. "I have listened to this debate with patience - but it has reached the point where the council has two choices. Designate this land for commercial development. Or retain it for residential purposes. But what do people here *really* want? More mediocre housing designed for the masses - or something more exclusive which puts Rosebrook on the map as a much sought after location?"

"It needs properties which cater for everyone!" Avalon shouted back.

"Oh, so young and idealistic!" Perry laughed. "As my colleague, Mr Booth has explained, rising house prices are a trend you cannot hold back. So why not go with the flow? Don't hold back the prosperity of this town for the sake of more cheap housing, of which there is plenty!"

"But there isn't!" Avalon argued, the passion in her voice swelling. "Affordable housing is dwindling! All your scheme is designed for is to make you rich! Peter is actually trying to help people!"

A murmur of consent rippled among the masses and for a moment, it seemed Avalon was winning them over. Perry's smile turned cold.

"In my day, young people and students took up house shares. I gather there is already an ample choice of rented accommodation!"

Eleanor stared at Charlie, aghast. She was squirming in her seat - ready to launch herself into the debate but Charlie touched her arm.

"Just let him keep ranting!" he breathed. "He's making a complete arse of himself! Look at the faces in the audience."

She knew he was right - though Perry's bumptious speech was not the reason for her anger.

"This area used to be deemed *the grotty end of town*. It has already undergone change. Have you not just revamped your Community Centre? Formerly a ghastly building which coupled with that rusting factory, degraded the entire town! It seems silly not to continue this progression - where surely, an estate of luxury homes must take priority over this rather dull housing trust initiative!"

"I think the council have heard enough of your ramblings," Eleanor interrupted, "in fact they have shown themselves to be somewhat hypocritical in allowing you to speak at all!" She glared at Robin. "Mr Whaley! You refused to let *my* husband object on the grounds of having a vested interest! This gentleman stands to gain even more if either proposal is refused. So why is *he* being allowed to voice his objections?"

"Mrs Bailey has a sound point," Terry Griffiths endorsed before Robin had a chance to argue, "and as a point of order, I must urge Mr Hampton to refrain from making any further comments against Mr Summerville's housing trust!"

A florid mauve flush swept across Perry's face as he turned towards Eleanor. It was with some reluctance, he moved away from the lip of the chamber - but his pale eyes flashed with more hatred than she could have imagined. The mood inside the room was tense. Robin looked uncomfortable, eyes lowered, though Eleanor could sense his fury. There was a rumble of discontent shifting around the hall and from their elevated position, even the council members seemed agitated.

"I think we've sufficiently covered the main arguments," Terry pressed almost apologetically. "There is a questionnaire included in the report for anyone who wishes to have a final say..."

"I have something to say," a new voice then piped into the room.

Everyone's attention was drawn to the softly spoken man who had just risen; young, possibly in his late 20s, he wore an expensive suit. His jet black hair and swarthy complexion suggested Asian descent. "This has been an interesting debate," he continued in the same polite tone. "My father was very keen to discover how you intended to use his land."

"I-I'm sorry, could you please introduce yourself," Robin stammered.

"Of course!" the man smiled. "My name is Abdul Nassar. Our family has traded in England for many years but in 1979, when the British textile industry declined, we took our enterprise to Bangladesh where business is booming. Almost all the spinning mills are privatised now and we want to expand!"

"You're here on behalf of the land owner?" Terry frowned.

"Yes! And I need to know if you still wish to purchase his land," Abdul continued. "For several months, he has been awaiting your decision. He has run out of patience."

"Mr Nassar, I understand your concern," Terry spluttered, "and I assure you, we are on the verge of making that decision."

"I see," Abdul snapped, lowering his eyes. "Well, I have a message for you. It seems, this is a highly sought after plot! Yet my father offered you *first refusal* at its current market price. You really should have grabbed it when you had the chance."

"What are you saying?" Robin gulped.

"This land is available to whoever wishes to make us an offer!" Abdul pressed relentlessly. "You have one week to submit your final bid - in writing to our estate agent - after which time, all offers will be considered and a buyer will be chosen."

Robin gaped at him in horror. "You mean... the land is to be sold in a sealed bid auction?"

"That is precisely what I am saying," Abdul finished. "Your council was too slow, Mr Whaley. We spoke to you over a year ago and you have dithered around for far too long! So hurry up and submit your bid. I wish you the best of luck."

He offered the council members a slight bow - then turned and strutted his way towards the exit before anyone had a chance to react to this unforeseen ultimatum. The room was left dangling in a gulf of silence. Robin looked outraged. Then Dominic started laughing - for all Robin's clever scheming, the negotiations had dissolved into a complete farce.

III

"What a shambles!" Charlie breathed, twenty minutes later, "so what now?"

"We've lost," Peter replied despondently, "that's what."

It was early evening. Their entire assembly had finally settled into the almshouse, where Eleanor had just opened some wine.

"That's not necessarily the case," she began, handing him a glass.

"Oh come on!" Peter sighed, "how can the council possibly outbid the others? They were only ever prepared to purchase the land at its basic market value! We discovered that much on the night we invited Robin round to have dinner with us!"

"Which was?" Eleanor pressed.

"£30k!" William broke in. "I'm sure that's how much he said it was worth!"

"Hmm - and that was six months ago," Charlie said. "It might have gone up a bit since then. I'm betting, Hampton'll bid double that amount!"

"So we're looking at somewhere around £60k?" Avalon pondered.

She sipped her wine, her expression dreamy and it was with no further doubt, she knew what she had to do.

She headed for London next day, determined to seek the opinion of George, or better still, his father. Much as she adored Peter, his pessimism was dragging her down. With so much negativity clouding everyone's judgement, Avalon was hankering for some honest advice - preferably from someone neutral, someone not so emotionally involved.

She allowed herself a smile, her hands light on the steering wheel of her classy, silver VW Golf. With her driving test imminent, both she and William had agreed to invest in a brand new set of wheels for her 18th birthday; something more suited to Avalon, who had ultimately fallen in love with it.

She cruised cautiously onto the main road, following the signs to London; still thinking about her 18th which in the aftermath of that fearful 'prowling' incident, had materialised into an almost magical affair. She was touched by the special dinner party organised in the tranquility of their home. If only her father had been there, it would have been perfect. Though Peter's company had gone a long way towards cheering her up and Eleanor's cuisine had been exquisite.

It was only as she entered London, she began to recall her second birthday treat. Avalon released a sigh, filled with more wonderful memories. George had booked them into a luxurious hotel, complete with tickets to see 'Les Miserables' in the West End. It was a memory she wanted to cling to forever; the enamel claw-footed bath tub where they had relaxed in an ocean of bubbles, the lighting soft, a champagne bucket set to one side; the sumptuous king sized bed where they had made exquisite love. It had been a night when George had asked her if she would consider moving up to London. Deep in her heart, she knew she could never agree to it - but nevertheless, said she'd think about it.

These thoughts stuck with her as she found herself creeping along in a line of traffic - moving gradually closer to the beautiful area of Kensington where George would be at home with his parents. The tall, regency house loomed up sooner than expected. Only on this occasion, she detected a difference in George. He was at university now - studying law. Even Avalon was not so deluded as to realise he wouldn't be surrounded by fleets of adoring females.

His response to her news however, left her stunned.

"Avalon, you can't be serious!" he breathed. "You're thinking of bidding for this land yourself? Why? What on earth are you likely to gain from it?"

She felt her cheeks burn - irritated with him for making her feel so foolish!

"This isn't how James would have wanted you to spend your inheritance," his father, Cyril, butted in gently. "I have to agree with George. A lack of affordable housing isn't really your problem. Residents of Rosebrook must decide for themselves what they want!"

"But you don't understand," Avalon whimpered, "our family have always supported local people. What about Dad's walled gardens?"

"And you carried on his good work by setting up some allotments," George smiled indulgently.

"Okay, so Peter's housing trust is something else I want to support," she persisted. Straight away, she saw his face tighten. Avalon frowned. "Look - it's not just Peter I'm thinking about, there's more to it than that. If we don't fight for this land, it'll be another victory for Perry Hampton!"

"Ah yes, now I understand your concern," Cyril sighed. He closed his eyes as if in deep thought, hands steepled together. Then finally, he gazed at her shrewdly. "I remain firm in my belief, this is *not* what your father would have wanted! His dream was for you and William to inherit Westbourne House. Unfortunately, that dream was destroyed by Perry Hampton, so please - don't let yourself be dragged into another war with him!"

"I'm not..." Avalon started to protest but Cyril raised a hand to silence her.

"I appreciate your campaign to stop *Hampton* from getting this land - but unless it affects you directly, don't get involved? Why not concentrate on what you could do with your own land?"

Avalon paused, unsure how to reply as the words sunk in.

"Of course," she whispered, "you're right. I'd almost forgotten..." She broke off, her mind strangely illuminated - where those last few words had triggered an idea.

She left at lunchtime, barely able to contain her excitement. George had been desperate to change the subject - convinced they had talked her out of this foolhardy idea; yet nothing could be further from the truth. She kissed him on the doorstep, knowing she was about to defy him.

"Why have you said nothing about moving to London?" he finally pressed her.

"My family's in Rosebrook," she sighed. "Like you say - we've got our own land to manage. Dad's grave is in Aldwyck and there's William's school..." The next time she gazed into his eyes, she could sense their relationship was dwindling. "Have you met someone else?"

George bit his lip. "I might have. I'm offering us a chance here,

Avalon…"

"Then I'm sorry to have to disappoint you," she finished sadly.

They had shared a few more words. Those tender, heart-felt phrases were still ringing in her ears as she guided her car into Aldwyck: *'We've had some wonderful times… our families will always be close…'* Tears blurred her vision as she steered her car up the farm track. She blinked them back, forcing herself to concentrate on her plan. It didn't matter. She had always been fond of George but it was only now, she acknowledged, she had never really loved him.

Ten minutes later, she was tucked inside the Baxter's farmhouse, her hands clasped around a heavy ceramic mug of tea. Herbert's son, Toby, was among them, as was his wife, Jane. Though for the first few minutes, Avalon could barely stop trembling.

"Were you s-serious about purchasing some of our land?" she whispered.

"Only if you agree," Herbert sighed. "What is it, Avalon - is something the matter?"

"I'm fine," Avalon said, forcing a smile, "it's just - I'm on the verge of making a very big decision; something I haven't discussed - not even with William - b-but I need to raise some money and fast! There is another plot I'm looking to buy, but without dipping into our inheritance. You mentioned a consortium..."

"That's right," Toby intervened. "Boris and Sue seemed very keen. So did the Harpers. Not to forget Nigel Patterson, our solicitor! How much are you trying to raise?"

Avalon felt her mouth turn dry. There was no turning back now. "Around £70,000," she blurted, "which will buy you approximately 500 acres - enough to cover the entire northern stretch of forest as well as the adjoining fields. What do you say?"

"We'd be delighted to take you up on your offer!" Toby jumped in, as if afraid she'd change her mind. "I promised you we'd take care of it and the pledge still stands! At current agricultural land prices, £70,000 seems very reasonable. I just need to check it out with the others."

"There isn't time," Avalon whimpered. "I've got 5 days to submit an offer for this land in Rosebrook - land Perry will also be bidding for a-and it's right on our doorstep!"

"5 days is enough time to approve our decision!" Herbert announced stoutly. "Put in your bid, Avalon! I am 100% certain the others will agree to it - you've got nothing to lose!"

IV

By the time Dominic left the meeting, he was buzzing - brain churning like an engine, as he swept through the gates of the stylish apartment block where he had established his home. It was modern in design with smoked glass windows and private balconies - a secluded development where a series of pale yellow walls wrapped themselves around a circular driveway.

Almost from the moment the meeting had reached its dramatic climax, he felt no desire to hang around. Pippa sat braced in the seat next to him and for the last few minutes, they had barely spoken; but Dominic hadn't been thinking about Pippa. His thoughts were latched on Eleanor, wondering how it was possible that one person could play such havoc with his emotions. Her speech against his proposal had left him crazed with anger. Yet it was only when she caught his eye, her words had started to falter. He had glimpsed the raw terror as it shimmied across her face - it not only charged him with a renewed sense of power but had been one hell of a turn on!

"You're very quiet, Dominic," Pippa snapped as he switched off the engine.

"Got a lot on me mind, love..." and wasting no time, he swung himself out of the driver seat and marched towards the entrance.

He headed straight for the fridge and uncorked a bottle of white, just as Pippa was switching on the oven. Nerves jangling, he poured out two glasses and quaffed down half his own before he even knew it. He found himself gazing at Pippa who had her back turned. She had thrown off her jacket yet his eyes honed in on her curves - crawling down the length of her long, shapely legs, right down to the heels of her black suede boots. He curled his arms around her waist.

"Let's go to bed," he murmured.

"I was just about to cook dinner..." she protested lightly.

"What we got?"

"Lasagne," Pippa smiled, flicking an adoring glance over her shoulder.

"Great," Dominic's voice grazed against her ear. "Stick it in the oven. Still gives us half an hour. About the only thing that's gonna relax me, babe..."

Moments later, they were in the bedroom, venetian blinds drawn as Dominic peeled off her dress. With his hands clamped around her upper arms, he pulled her towards him - his gaze drawn to her ample breasts swelling out from the cups of her designer bra. He pressed his face into her cleavage, savouring the warmth and smell of her skin, then reached around her back and expertly unclipped it. With their clothes hastily discarded, he pushed her down on to their king-sized bed without bothering to pull back the covers. The black, satin duvet felt slippery and cool.

A spotlight cast an amber glow over the top end of the bed but Dominic sank deep into the shadows. There was something about the subtle light which sent his mind spinning into the past; straight away, he imagined that brothel in the East End, a teenage Eleanor pressed into the corner - the stark fear in her eyes just as he'd witnessed a few hours ago. He held his breath, unable to shift the memory, his passion soaring as his hands swept up the inside of Pippa's thighs, driving them apart. He lowered his head, kissing her knee before his lips travelled upwards to explore her with his tongue. He could feel her flexing and her breath started to quicken - excited as he was, as she curled her feet around his back, now desperate for him to possess her. Unable to hold back for another second, Dominic plunged himself into her again and again.

The ring of the telephone didn't deter him - ensnared in a vortex of lust and fast approaching orgasm as they pounded together in synchrony. He tensed to the bleep of the answering machine but the moment he heard Whaley's whining voice resonating from the speaker, Dominic reached for the wire and yanked it out of the wall socket.

"Fucking prick!" he muttered without breaking rhythm.

It was only when they were settled in the dining room, hungrily devouring Pippa's lasagne, that he thought about that call. He smiled, secretly thrilled by the outcome of the meeting - having never imagined Robin Whaley would come out of it with so much egg on his smarmy face. The next call however, was from Lawrence.

"Right, let's get down to business," he barked after a few opening words. "Are you going to bid for that land or what? We're looking at a premium price of around £50,000."

"Bloody right, I am," Dominic hissed. "After all these weeks of planning, I ain't backing down now. I'll bid 60 if I have to - just to stop that fucker, Hampton!"

"That's up to you," Lawrence replied in a resigned tone, "though I wouldn't bid any higher. It's not worth it! This project will cost thousands and judging by the objections, you might not even get permission."

Dominic clenched his teeth. "Yeah, no thanks to Eleanor Bailey," he whispered.

"And nearly every resident in the neighbourhood," Lawrence added. "Her speech delivered no surprises. People's first concern is always going to be disruption and noise."

Eventually, the conversation dwindled. Dominic knocked back a second glass of wine - yet his heady sense of ambition was spiked with outrage. Of all the people to stand up against his spectacular new leisure complex, why did it have to be Eleanor bloody Bailey? Straight away, she was back inside his head again, her amber eyes huge and as startled as a fox caught in headlights. He clenched his fist on the table top, aware of Pippa staring.

"What is it with that Eleanor?" she demanded. "I mean, we even looked in on her bloody wedding! Are you sure there isn't something I should know about?"

"Don't even go there," he snapped, refilling his wine glass. "I told you - she's an enemy!"

As if to further torment him, the next call was from Charlie.

"Well aren't I the popular one," Dominic sneered, lowering himself into one of their luxurious, leather sofas, "what do *you* want?"

"Calm down, Dominic," Charlie reacted. "You always knew we were going to oppose you. We spoke in the pub, remember? You were the one who said 'it was every man for himself' and we were all gunning for Peter! Do you think Eleanor had any choice other than to voice our objections?"

"I couldn't give a shit!" Dominic snarled back at him.

"Well in that case, there is something you should know!" Charlie snapped. "Those were *my* notes she read out. I planned to be the spokesman, not her! It was Whaley who disallowed it, didn't you hear her say that? Did it ever occur to you, this whole thing was a game? Robin used that land as a means of getting you and Eleanor in the same place, tearing at each other's throats!"

"I hear you, Charlie," Dominic said coldly, "but I still want that land."

"So you'll be bidding for it, will you?" Charlie pressed.

"Course!" Dominic laughed. "What? You think that slimy Arab bastard was expecting us to pull out? I told you my plans - and nothing's changed!"

"So how much are you bidding?" Charlie whispered fearfully.

"That's none of your business," Dominic retorted.

"Okay, well let me put this another way," Charlie persisted. "What if you win and the council refuse you planning permission? 'Cos I bet you any money, they've got no intention of granting your wish - any more than they'd have sanctioned Peter's housing trust."

"Maybe I'll just flog it then," Dominic finished brutally, "to whatever property developer wants it most - including Hampton, who'll probably pay me double for it!"

"You're not serious," Charlie breathed. "Surely, even you wouldn't be that unscrupulous!"

Dominic smiled. "You listen to me, Charlie," he whispered evilly, "I never was renowned for having any fucking scruples!" and with nothing left to say, he slammed down the phone.

V

Two weeks later, Robin found himself staring numbly at a letter which had arrived in the last post. Nearly all his colleagues had gone home - but Robin had chosen to stay late on the pretence, he had some flexitime to make up. The meeting about to be arranged was completely unorthodox and he didn't want any staff lingering around to overhear.

He stared at the clock. It was almost 5:25 and time to set the wheels in motion. He stood up and slipped into a long, woollen overcoat before scooping up the letter and wandering into the planning reception area. The three proposals were displayed across the walls for additional public viewing. Robin stepped forward, his eyes honing in on just one of them. He positioned the letter on a desk - tilting it carefully, so it was visible below his chosen exhibition panel.

With everything in place, he took a deep breath, straightened his tie and made his way out of the council building. It was very dark outside where a chilly breeze nipped his cheeks. It was with no hesitation, he ambled a little further up the High Street. The shops were gradually closing - the neighbouring cafés and restaurants just shuffling into life. Robin's stare cut through the darkness, picking out the idyllic bistro where he knew William Barton-Wells worked, his mind overblown with memories.

Robin could have smiled, knowing it was down to his influence that William had even got that job! By the time Peter had updated him over the prowling incident, he felt a clawing desire to visit them again. Avalon had just celebrated her 18th birthday. William, having nearly finished his exams, had been seeking a part time job. Robin had revelled in the sound of his chirpy banter and 'Le Bon Plat,' tucked in an area known as 'Restaurant Row,' happened to be one of his favourite haunts. It had taken just a few quiet words with the proprietor to secure young William a job as a waiter. Jean Paul had been delighted to take him on - Robin even more so, relishing the prospect of drinking in his youthful beauty whilst enjoying the fine French cuisine.

He quickened his pace, dragging his eyes away from the bistro. He could no longer deny, the boy had become a bit of a distraction and it had started on the night of their dinner party. That last vision of William lay trapped in his thoughts. But those thoughts had led to darker fantasies where William materialised in a different guise - draped in the loose tunic and trousers of a concentration camp victim, his frightened young face pressed against a cruel barbed wire fence. Robin imagined himself as the domineering SS officer who would save him - but at a price and where this beautiful boy would finally be in his power.

He shuddered, reminded of himself at the same age. He would never forget the time he had passed *his* 'O' levels. His father had glowered at him with contempt, a father who felt no pride, only triumph in so much as it was time he 'stopped being a worthless parasite and got a job!' Robin sighed. He had never wanted to be another faceless worker. He wanted go to university but his working class thug of a father had laughed at him.

The likes of us don't go to university! Time you pulled your head out of your arse - start pullin' yer weight an' earnin,' like everyone else in this family!'

"I don't want to be like you!" Robin remembered yelling at him - for which his father had struck him across the face and taken a belt to him. He could have cried! The memory was harrowing, even now. In fact it was shortly after that nightmare, Robin had run away from home to spend the next few nights sleeping rough in a garden shed.

Eventually, his English teacher took pity on him. Robin would always remember those blissful days when this kind man had first invited him to come and live with him - never imagining, the special attention and the luxurious living standards might lead to something more sinister. All along, his teacher had been grooming him and Robin, utterly beholden to him, had surrendered - knowing this was his one and only chance to aspire to the academic life he craved.

His footsteps slowed as he drew close to the antique shop, guessing Avalon would be finished for the day. He was fighting to compose himself, his jaw tight, his hands balled into fists as he rammed them into the pockets of his coat. He was still thinking about that delightful dinner party - except everything seemed very different now. William had played him like a fool - plied him with wine, fully intent on getting him drunk in order to wheedle information out of him. Robin would never forget that most careless disclosure. He had revealed the value of that land; and it was only now, he had finally recognised their crafty little game plan.

"Avalon!" he called out, tethering his features into a smile. "I've been dying to talk to you! Can you spare me a moment? There's something I'd like to show you."

"What is it?" Avalon frowned, freezing to a halt.

"Follow me," Robin said smoothly and without waiting for an answer, he turned and strode back in the direction of the council headquarters. "Come along, we don't have much time…"

Avalon naively followed. It took just a few minutes to reach the steps. Robin hurled a glance towards the clock tower, now hurrying towards the entrance. The area was shielded by an imposing facade of pillars. Avalon did not notice the silhouette of a man lingering in the shadows. Robin held the door open, ushering her inside - the foyer hung in a mantle of gloom, illuminated by a few security lights.

"We won't be a moment," Robin called across to one of the security staff - too engrossed in reading his newspaper to glance up. He smiled as he guided his visitor towards the stairs.

"Where are we going?" Avalon whispered. The echo of her voice possessed an eerie quality.

"Planning office," Robin muttered politely. "I'm sorry if this all seems a little 'cloak and dagger' but I want it to be a surprise."

He took her by the hand before tugging her gently up the staircase and for that moment, Avalon had no reason to feel scared. They had travelled only half way up the stairs when an ominous shadow slipped into the elevator below - a man who was about to reach the planning office ahead of them where for the interim, he would be waiting.

"So here we are," Robin announced softly.

He let go of her hand and Avalon turned to smile at him - but the smile on her face withered as Robin quietly closed the door.

"What's going on?" she whispered, unable to disguise her anxiety.

"Take a look over there," Robin muttered. There was a sudden cold edge to his tone. "You haven't received your second post yet, have you, Avalon?"

She found herself staring at the plan outlining Peter's housing trust - her eyes inevitably drawn to the letter propped beneath it from Roland-Baron Estate Agents. Avalon let out a gasp.

"Congratulations, my dear," a deep voice tolled from some hidden corner. "It seems you played your game very well."

Avalon flinched, whirling round just as Perry crept into view. She released a cry of fear.

"That's right," Robin added, his expression changing. "Mr Nassar accepted your bid. It seems you are about to become the new owner of the land behind the Community Centre."

"What's *he* doing here?" Avalon hissed, backing away from Perry. "What the hell is going on?"

"Told you I wanted it to be a surprise," Robin said nastily.

Avalon scanned the sheet where the truth shone in black and white. The vendor had clearly accepted her bid as the most favourable - both in price and ability to proceed. Avalon gulped, forcing herself to stare at Robin but the frost in his eyes chilled her.

"You were in this together, all along!" she finally confronted them. "Admit it! You've known each other for years!"

"I cannot believe you weren't aware of that," Robin retorted. "Surely your dear friend, Eleanor, must have enlightened you!"

Avalon shook her head, heart pounding. "She never said much - though she did warn me you might still be friends. I didn't want to believe it but..."

"And what else did she 'warn you?'" Robin pressed.

"That one day, you might betray us," Avalon shuddered, "and she was right, wasn't she?"

"Betray?" Robin sneered. "Surely you are the one who betrayed us! That charming little dinner party was nothing more than a ploy to get information!"

Avalon closed her eyes in dread. "Stop this! Believe it or not, Robin, we respected you! You managed to convince us that you were *in support* of Peter's housing trust. So why did you lie?"

"I look after the interests of Rosebrook," Robin replied in the same contemptuous tone. "Peter's dream looked good on paper; at least, enough to persuade my superiors to consider the land purchase - but it was never going to bring prosperity to the town, was it?"

"We're wasting time," Perry snapped, taking his first steps towards her. "What I need to know is whether you intend to go through with this purchase!"

"Of course I do," Avalon shot back at him. "I've already raised the money."

"Oh yes," Perry smiled, "rumour has it, you sold some of your father's land! Do you know we even bid the same amount? Seventy grand! Yet Mr Nassar picked you!"

"It seems your stirring speech won him over," Robin added coldly. "He was moved by your passion! But you're not *really* going to bankroll Peter's housing trust are you?"

"I'm not backing out if that's what you think!" Avalon snapped. "William and I would rather go bankrupt than allow *you* to profit from that land!"

"So that's what this is about," Perry whispered. "Some petty vendetta. You silly girl! You should know better than to oppose me!"

Avalon had heard enough. With a furious sigh, she skirted around the walls, heading for the door - except Perry got there first. He had already stationed himself solidly against its frame, blocking her escape. Avalon froze, shocked by the familiar sneer which crept into his expression. His eyes were as cruel and rapacious as ever, reminding her of his logo.

"Let me out!" she spat. "I have nothing more to say to you!"

"But we have so much more to say to you," Robin's voice pulsed coldly from behind her. "You were foolish to betray us, Avalon. Neither of us are ever going to forgive you for this."

"I haven't betrayed anyone," Avalon whimpered, unable to tear her eyes away from Perry's. He looked dangerously evil as the terror churned inside her. She was struggling to find the right words yet in the end, they just came to her. "You just can't stand the fact that I beat you at your own game!" she started to sob, "and as for your veiled threats…"

"Threats?" Perry echoed. "I don't believe I've threatened you."

"What - *I should know better than to oppose you?*" Avalon challenged. "Didn't you say something similar to my dad? That he would *regret his decision?*"

"Oh I have no intention of threatening you, Avalon," he muttered. "Do you think I'd be so stupid as to arm you with any further ammunition to go whining to the police?"

"Police?" Avalon breathed.

"Didn't you accuse my son of sneaking around your house?" Perry's voice lashed back at her, "when he was at Westbourne House, all along? He has better things to do with his time, my dear. Though he has just made some very interesting new friends in London."

Avalon winced, remembering Marilyn's warning. *They brought some heavies down from London…'* "What are you talking about?" she shivered.

Perry smiled. "Let's just say we have plenty of time to plan our strategy. So go, play with your land! Let me know if you get bored. I may even consider relieving you of it."

He stepped away from the door. Yet for a moment, Avalon faltered -

compelled to turn and face Robin again. His face had not changed - the malice carved deep into his features. He had transformed into someone she no longer recognised.

"I'm deeply saddened by *your* response, Robin," she finished. "I had hoped it wouldn't come to this - b-but thanks for letting me know about the auction…"

Her bottom lip trembled and she thought she was going to cry - neither man said another word as she turned and made her way shakily back down the stairs.

The cold air hit her like a bucket of water. She was in shock - unable to think of anything better to do than charge up the High Street in the direction of the almshouse. Under normal circumstances, she would have gone home - yet she couldn't bear to be alone. Even William would have started his shift at the Bistro. *William!* She almost skidded to a halt, wary of her brother naively waiting on tables, oblivious to the truth.

Robin had effectively turned into the enemy.

Head down, she continued to march up the High Street. There was little she could do to warn him - she would just have to telephone the restaurant later. The Community Centre lay ahead of her; now an unbelievably stunning building, its revamp almost complete. She was barely looking where she was going as she almost collided with Elijah. He too was lingering on the pavement, gazing up at the building in awe, sketch pad in hand.

He froze as soon as he saw her. "What's up?" he gasped. He caught her by the elbows and for a moment they just stared at each other. Elijah was almost as tall as she was now with maybe another inch to catch up. His boyish face was partially masked in shadow.

"Eli!" Avalon panted, "you are not going to believe this b-but Perry was in the planning office with Robin Whaley! I-I didn't know he was there. We had words…" Her breath came in heavy, laboured gasps - anyone could see she was fighting tears.

"Let's go inside," Elijah said in a manner which seemed almost too adult for a boy his age. "Mum and Charlie are in there - you really need to tell them about this."

It took several minutes for Avalon to explain. Eleanor looked horrified. Charlie on the other hand, paced from one side of the room to the other, clearly confused.

"You mean, you actually bid for the land yourself?" he breathed.

"Well how else was Peter going to get it?" Avalon choked back.

Charlie turned to her, releasing a laugh, "and you won?"

"Yes!" Avalon announced. Finally, her lips twisted into a smile. "I'm sorry - do you know, this hasn't even sunk in yet. It must have arrived in the second post - that's why Robin was so cagey."

"They must be furious!" Eleanor said numbly. She gazed at her with pride before sweeping forwards to hug her.

"I can't wait to tell Peter," Avalon sniffed. "In fact, let's call him right now…"

No-one had a chance to say another word before there was a sudden pounding on the door. Margaret, who had been quietly sitting on the sidelines, leapt up to answer it.

It never occurred to her who it might be - though her eyes flared with surprise, as William materialised in the door frame. He looked livid. "Can I come in?" he snapped.

"Of course," Margaret mumbled, stepping aside.

He strode into the lounge, still dressed in the attire of a waiter.

"What are you doing here?" Avalon gasped. "Don't tell me you've been sacked…"

"Not at all!" William retorted. "I walked out! Can you *believe* that pompous toad, Hampton, rolled up with Robin Whaley, of all people! They ordered me to serve them wine! I could have poured it over their heads. Now will someone please tell me what's going on?"

"Sit down, William," Eleanor muttered. "Avalon's got some news…"

No-one could ignore the disturbed look on her face as she glanced towards the window. It was almost as if she had *sensed* the united power of their enemies, now creeping back into their lives.

PART 2
CRIME WAVE

Chapters 8-15

February 1988 - January 1989

Chapter 8

I

No-one really knew where they stood any more. Peter was enchanted by Avalon's selfless gesture, but could no longer deny, he felt uneasy; not quite sure how to proceed.

Charlie advised, they would need considerable financial back-up, but for the interim, they retained a low profile. They were wary of Robin's wrath; in the aftermath of a recent fall out with Peter, he had threatened to make future planning applications *'as difficult as possible.'*

Charlie had consequently approached Terry Griffiths, Head of Planning, dismayed by Robin's acrimony. He was eager to know if the council were still prepared to support their proposal and although the man seemed a little cagey, he did reveal that Peter's plan had received overwhelming public support.

A month later, Eleanor found Peter in his office, mulling over the plans. It seemed hard to imagine how this controversial plot could have ended up in the hands of the Barton-Wells children. Yet Peter seemed troubled - fearing the persecution this would bring for them. He had seen this *Perry* for himself in the Council chamber, wondering how those kids could possibly survive in the shadow of such a deadly enemy.

"What's up, Peter?" Eleanor coaxed him.

"Just bracing myself for the worst," he said softly. "I'm worried about Avalon. A small part of me wishes she had never got involved in this... There's enough violence in the world."

He let his forehead drop into his hands. Eleanor frowned - before her eyes drifted to a newspaper lying on his desk and only then, did she understand his anxiety.

It was the headline that startled her - dragging her mind back to the Enniskillen bombing, where the horrors of sectarian violence had brought a darkness into his world. It seemed, the IRA were preparing to step up the war outside Northern Ireland, by bringing it to mainland Britain.

She scanned the next few lines. The news had been rocked by a chain of events, starting with the three IRA terrorists gunned down at point blank range on the rock of Gibraltar. It was believed, they had been plotting to bomb a local changing of the guards ceremony - plastic explosives had been discovered.

A week later, a military style funeral took place in Belfast. Yet in a savage twist of fate, a Protestant gunman had materialised, opening fire into the crowd and hurling grenades. Both nationalists and loyalists traditionally respected sectarian funerals - which made this an unusual incident, although it had eventually emerged, the gunman was operating alone.

"What's the latest atrocity?" Eleanor whispered in horror.

"Two British soldiers were murdered," Peter shuddered. "They found themselves inadvertently caught up in the midst of an IRA parade; they were dragged from their car, beaten unconscious, then taken to some nearby wasteland and shot!"

"Horrific," Eleanor reflected sadly, "why are you so upset by this?"

"These are my countrymen!" Peter retorted. "It was this type of sectarian violence that caused the death of me own parents!"

"How come?" Eleanor kept pressing, desperate to reach out him.

"Armed rebels ambushed a military truck, close to my home. They were shooting at the windscreen - the lorry veered over to the other side of the road and both me Mammy and Da were driving the opposite way. They were killed in a head on collision."

"I'm sorry," Eleanor whispered.

He gazed back tenderly, as if fighting tears. He described how he'd been raised in a Catholic care home; that his two elder brothers had been shipped to Australia, his little sister adopted by some family in London.

"I went looking for her, once," he finished, lowering his eyes.

Eleanor nodded, hit with a wave of dread. She could fully appreciate why the news might have affected him - yet there was something she was hankering to know.

"Peter, I hate to ask - b-but..." her words faltered. "Do you know much about the IRA?"

He became very still, his expression furtive. "Listen, Eleanor, I came from a Catholic family. Everyone was expected to support *the Cause*. They came into the pub, rattling collection tins and no-one ever dared stand up to them. Anyone who didn't was considered a traitor."

"You were an IRA supporter?" Eleanor breathed.

Peter shrugged. "I had little choice back then... but violence sickens me!"

"Do you mind if I ask you something else?" Eleanor pressed. "Was the IRA responsible for the bomb that killed the politician, Albert Enfield?"

"Albert Enfield," Peter pondered. "Good question! 1972 wasn't it?" his eyes clouded over. He seemed lost in another world. "I remember the car bomb at the army barracks. Mr Enfield, we were never quite sure about..."

Eleanor felt a spark of hope. "So did they or didn't they?" she persisted, "and if so, why?"

"I can't answer that," Peter sighed. "No-one knows. It's a bit like the Protestant gunman. It could have been the work of a lone mercenary." A frown crossed his face. "Why are you so curious?"

"Peter, this is really important," Eleanor whispered, slanting herself forwards to hold his gaze. "Jake was present on the day it happened, see."

Peter's face froze. "What are you saying?"

"He saw someone hanging around by the minibus. A smartly dressed man in an expensive car! Now does that sound like the IRA?"

"I guess not," Peter whispered in shock, "so *this* is the reason Jake was killed?"

"Yes, but keep it to yourself, Peter. The fact that Jake saw the perpetrators of that car bomb is *exactly* the reason he was killed. It was to silence him."

"And you think I might have some inside information?" Peter added warily.

"If there was a way you find out, would you share it with me?"

He bit his lip and she could sense his dilemma. It lapped around the edges of his mind like waves on a seashore; he could never betray his countrymen but the murderous activities of terrorists appalled him - he wanted no more blood shed.

"Let's just say, I've got friends in Dublin who *know* people. IRA 'officials' who advocate a united Ireland by peaceful means; as opposed to the Belfast-based 'provisionals.' The IRA is split now, but people are bound to have connections. I could put out some feelers."

"Thank you," Eleanor whispered. "Because this begs one more question. If the IRA *weren't* responsible for the murder of Albert Enfield - then who was?"

"And you're hoping to solve the mystery?" Peter queried.

"I have to," Eleanor finished sadly. "I owe it to Jake and to our son. Jake could have brought Enfield's killers to justice - but I need to know who they were."

II

Perry meanwhile, was left floundering. Ben scrutinised him from afar, where he could almost sense his hatred spiralling. Twice these people had stood up to him; first, over the walled gardens and now this lucrative chunk of land! It was obvious, his father would want to teach them a lesson - a concept which ultimately drew his thoughts to own agenda.

On the evening Ben had sneaked into Avalon's garden, he had narrowly escaped arrest. That dark, drizzly night seemed a lifetime ago, although their plan was *extremely* well executed. Nathan had been lurking on standby. His black Ford XR3i with its tinted windows and wide wheels had provided a speedy getaway yet Ben was left dazed. How was he supposed to know the bitch had installed security lights? He remembered pulling off his mask, heart thumping - thankful he'd possessed the foresight to wear it.

Two days later however, Inspector Boswell had called - asking to meet him in person.

Ben had nothing to worry about. Everyone could have sworn, he was upstairs in his bedroom. He had faced Inspector Boswell with confidence - adamant, Avalon was lying. But while the experience served as a wake up call, it left him embittered. Avalon had once again evaded him, depriving him of his pleasure - and now she had spoken to the police; a situation which left him no choice other than to tread a little more carefully, to forget about Avalon. Ben knew he had far more important avenues to explore - where his failure was the catalyst which irrevocably propelled him into the nucleus of the criminal underworld.

A meeting had arisen, just days before that ill-fated council meeting.

They travelled by motorbike, sufficiently concealed in their black leather garb for anyone to really notice them. Nathan took the lead, heading straight for South London. Eventually, he led Ben down an unlit street, flanked by high brick walls. A succession of side streets branched in all directions, which in turn, penetrated a deeper neighbourhood. Nathan had turned his Harley Davidson into one of those side roads where a forbidding, dark tunnel loomed in front of them, drawing them into one of the grottiest parts of London Ben had ever visited.

Here, the walls were heavily sprayed with graffiti. Nathan was rolling towards a row of terraced houses hidden beneath the shadow of a high rise tower block. They lurked eerily in the dusk, guarded by cold metal railings and garages. Nathan dismounted, indicating to Ben to do the same, creeping right up to one of the garages before banging on the door.

"Christ, what a shit hole," Ben breathed.

"Shut up," Nathan whispered, "and let me do the talking. Don't try to impress him and for fuck's sake don't flatter him..."

His words were cut short as the garage door started to rumble. They were confronted by a man in similar leather clothing to their own. He possessed the craggy face of a hard drug user, the sides of his head shaved into a Mohican - his eyes appeared as narrow slits in the gloom. Without a word, he beckoned them into the garage where they were obviously meant to hide the bikes - then proceeded towards a second door.

Ben felt a slight chill. The door led down to a dimly lit basement. A pulse of reggae music infiltrated his senses, combined with a heady smell of marijuana smoke. Ben blinked, staring at a group of men camped out in the corner of this mysterious underground chamber - without really knowing why, he had guessed straight away which one was Alan Levy.

He was of smaller stature than Ben imagined and unlike the others, dressed in a pin stripe waistcoat and trousers which immediately distinguished him as the boss. His dirty blond hair was combed back from his forehead with gel. But Ben's eyes were unavoidably drawn to his face - the long scar which ran from the corner of his left eye right down to the edge of his mouth. He gave a twisted smile, his light blue eyes like icicles.

"Nathan!" he greeted him pleasantly. The two men seized hands. "Finally made it then! So who is this piece of shit?"

Ben felt a stab of tension - clocking the harsh, cockney accent.

"Ben 'ampton, eh?" Levy kept smiling. "What the fuck d'you think yer playing at, son? Some rich kid trying to worm yer way onto my turf?"

"Rich kid or not, Alan, he's offering to bring some business your way," Nathan barked.

"Shut it!" the other man snapped. His eyes slid to Ben. "Let's hear what the kid 'as to say!"

Ben opened his mouth to speak. He hadn't failed to notice that Levy was surrounded by some real hard nuts. A muscular black man, over six foot tall, towered directly behind him. The man stared at him with cold, dead eyes.

"What d'you want exactly?" Alan pressed.

"I need contacts, Mr Levy - Alan - what do folks call you…?"

"Usually, they call me Sir!" Alan smirked. The other men in the room started to snigger.

"Then let me just say this, *Sir*," Ben continued softly. "We have a circle of enemies who need to be kept in line! At some point, we may need to enlist your help with a burglary…" His plummy, Sloane Ranger accent grated into the room like nails down a blackboard.

"Really?" Alan drawled. The smile on his face died. "What's in it for me? See - no-one *enlists* our help! Only thing that gives me a buzz is profit!"

Ben's eyes had inadvertently flickered towards a sofa nestling in the corner. He could just about distinguish the shape of a hold-all, overflowing with thick bundles of cash. Yet his inquisitive stare had crept just that little bit further… He froze, knowing this was something he was never meant to see - but it was too late. He had clocked a stack of cubes, shrink wrapped in plastic; drugs - huge parcels of drugs, the sort of quantities men died for! Ben glanced back at the other man whose eyes gleamed cruelly.

"What? You thought the Yardies 'ad control of the cocaine market?" he hissed. "You stupid yuppie ponce! You better 'ave a fuckin' good reason for being 'ere..!"

"I have," Ben blurted. "I work in the financial district. I can get you customers from the wealthiest areas of the city. Doesn't organised crime usually go where the money is?"

Alan let out a sly laugh, shooting a glance at the gargantuan black man. Then everything seemed to happen in a flash. The man grabbed Ben's arms, twisting them behind his back - hoisting him several inches off the ground before he plonked him in the middle of the room. He saw Alan delve into his trouser pocket - there was a metallic hiss, as he flicked out a murderous looking scalpel.

"No!" Nathan shouted. "Don't hurt him!"

"What?" Alan barked, "you think we're just gonna let 'im go? No-one comes snooping round my ghetto and fucks off again! You're in shit up to your neck, son!"

"C'mon, guys!" Nathan snarled. "You agreed to meet him..!"

"Yeah, an' now I've met 'im, I wanna fuckin' kill 'im...!" Alan snarled back. "So talk to me, you shit head! Give me one good reason why I shouldn't slice you up like a salami?"

Ben let his emotions run cold, refusing to reveal his fear. It was a defence he had mastered well and an additional boost of cocaine had sharpened his senses. He inclined his head, eyes glazed, as he aimed them directly at Alan.

"I could cut out those baby blue eyes and use 'em as marbles!" his whispering voice mocked. "How 'bout we start off with a Chelsea grin?" He spun the scalpel between his fingers.

"I guess I can't stop you,' Ben shuddered, "but I meant what I said... I really *could* supply a whole new market for you; stockbrokers, business men, *yuppies* who enjoy the pleasures of coke..."

Alan hesitated, scalpel suspended. "What makes yer think I can't tap into them markets, anyhow?" Ben held his gaze, teeth gritted - braced for the flick of his blade; Alan gave a snigger. "You got some fuckin' cheek comin' ere! You cocky rich bastard! Gotta admire your balls!"

From the other side of the room, Nathan had been holding his breath. Yet still, Ben didn't waver. He continued to level Alan with a stare that was almost satanic.

"Do we have a deal or not?" he persisted.

"Yeah, 'as it 'appens, we do" Alan smiled coldly, "just so long as you realise, we ain't the sort of boys to mess with." He tucked away his weapon. "Let's smoke on it."

Ben smiled, convinced an alliance had been forged. Nathan could not get over his audacity. Lesser men had ended up scarred and yet, Ben had fearlessly faced him as an equal.

"You are one clever sod," he had spluttered when they had eventually abandoned Alan's haunt at around 2:00 in the morning. "How the fuck you pulled that off, I'll never know."

"Instinct," Ben nodded to himself as they paused outside Nathan's house. It lay close to an area known as Vauxhall Park - an unrelenting urban jungle where trains intermittently thundered across towering brick Viaducts. "I wanted him to know he was top dog - but I couldn't imagine he would turn his nose up! He wanted a lion's share of the market and I could tell he was hungry for it. There is one thing Theakston's right about though - he is a fucking nut case!"

Perry was delighted; confident Ben's liaison had given him an edge over his enemies. It was with some reluctance, he had ended his contract with Alesha, fearing that Eleanor must have noticed her by now. At the same time, he was congratulating himself. He had someone on the inside to take care of Alesha's role, in addition to Ben's sinister new contacts.

As winter drifted into Spring however, it gradually came to light that

Aldwyck had a new resident and at first, Perry had been too distracted to notice him.

The tidy up in the aftermath of the hurricane had preoccupied him and he became obsessed with making improvements to Westbourne House. Determined to make this hotel venture work, especially for Rowena, Perry had installed a beautiful new ornamental fountain in the gardens to replace the one that had smashed. He couldn't deny, he was soothed by the gentle tinkle of water from its three scalloped tiers - this in turn, had prompted him to extend the patio to create a permanent al fresco dining area.

Finally, the labourers had turfed over those wretched vegetable gardens; his ultimate plan, to hack down the orchards so they could maximise the area for a putting green. Yet other matters had distracted him and just at a time when he should have been concentrating on an aggressive new advertising campaign, he had poured all his energy into fighting for that land in Rosebrook.

Perry glared out of the window, his mind wrestling with the reality. So the villagers had been colluding - negotiating the purchase of land which should rightfully have been his! He had always known James's children would have no use for it but to think they had used it to defeat him, came as a particularly devastating blow. There was no doubt in his mind, Herbert Baxter had been the ring leader - though surprised their consortium included that retried couple in the farmhouse; people who had once been Eleanor's neighbours.

Perry eyes narrowed as they honed in on the field. The year had slipped into May quicker than he had expected, yet he could no longer ignore the truth. There was someone living in the caravan. He had revelled in his success in keeping out new age travellers - now acutely aware of this stranger who had drifted into the village; a young man who was already making himself popular with the locals and it was with no further hesitation, Perry was hankering to find out who he was.

III

Joshua Merriman had in fact, been visiting Aldwyck for several months.

It had started with an occasional long weekend as he gradually became acquainted with the village. Then one delightful day in April, both he and Lucy had finally moved into the caravan; a day when the cottage gardens blazed with sunny clusters of daffodils and just days before Eleanor's birthday. It was two years since she had celebrated her 30th in the Olde House at Home and with a yearning to repeat the tradition, she had taken the somewhat daring decision to go back there, keen to introduce her friends to the locals.

Joshua's bohemian looks initially drew suspicion; floppy, golden brown hair, loosely gathered in a pony tail - a trilby hat and waistcoat. It seemed ironic that out of all the people in Aldwyck, he would strike up a most amiable friendship with Toby Baxter.

The two men could not have been more different: Joshua, the habitual 'Londoner' who had travelled the world before pursuing a career in the music industry; Toby, the conventional farmer with his rosy face and receding hair - whose typical attire comprised an olive green waistcoat, tweed cap and cravat.

This most unusual camaraderie began when Boris hosted an evening's entertainment of lively folk music and real ale. A local group had huddled in one corner, where the energetic pulse of a tabor thudded in accompaniment to a guitar and the sweet notes of a violin. Joshua had been propping up the bar, tapping his feet - one arm slung round Lucy's shoulder as they engaged in a jovial banter. It was only a matter of time before he let slip that he too, was a musician.

The moment the band had grabbed a well-earned beer break, Boris joked that he might want to entertain them with a song of his own. Naturally, Joshua had been happy to oblige. Perched on a stool, strumming a guitar loaned from one of the folk artists, he enchanted them all. His cheeky grin had endeared him to his audience, as he took a bow then waltzed back to the bar for another pint.

"You're good," Toby breathed, sidling up to him. "You new around here?"

The two men ended up sharing their life stories, shored up by several glasses of ale. In fact, the Baxters took a real shine to Joshua and as an extension of their friendship, announced they were hosting a clay pigeon shoot the following Sunday and wondered if Joshua and his lady friend might like to join them.

It was the start of an enduring friendship. Joshua, who had never in his life used a shot gun, amazed everyone with his keen eye. Time after time, he had watched the tiny black disc as it arced across the sky before taking his shot - smiling as it shattered into fragments.

"Bloody good shot!" Herbert roared in approval and filled with a sense that he too, liked this quirky new resident, was amazed to discover he was Tom and Marilyn's nephew.

They had taken their hospitality one step further by inviting them indoors for a drink. Straight away, Lucy fell in love with their farmhouse. A country girl herself who'd grown up surrounded by fields of sheep, she struck up an instant rapport with Toby's wife, Jane, before Joshua clocked a line of Demi-Johns stacked along their shelf.

His eyes glittered. "You make wine! I've got a nice bottle of Elderberry picked from the hedgerows at the back of my mum's house. Drop by, some time."

With a shared love of countryside, folk music, real ale and country wines, Toby had started calling in at the caravan on a regular basis.

It wasn't long before Joshua's presence was warmly accepted. Even Herbert felt a little sheepish when he had eventually peeped inside the van. The hand-carved shelves were especially pleasing, as was the cosy furniture combined with the warmth of a wood burning stove.

It was a month later however, when Joshua made his first acquaintance with Perry.

He was tucked inside the caravan - too engrossed in making tea to notice the black Mercedes crawling up to the edge of the field. Lucy was crouched outside the door, tending to Eleanor's flower pots. It had been a pleasant Spring where the early rain showers had been replaced by rising temperatures, leading to a spate of warm, dry days. The tulips had withered - slender stems drooping, scattering petals all over the grass. Lucy had bought some non-stop flowering begonias to replace them - an ethereal figure who's mane of hair shone a rich Henna red in the sunshine.

Perry observed her from a distance, having already formed his opinion. Her skirt, spun from richly patterned cotton, flowed right down to her sandalled feet and as he wandered closer, he had already clocked the glitter of a nose piercing. Lucy looked up, dimly aware of the unfamiliar stranger sauntering towards her. His attire was markedly conservative; a sports jacket worn with pale grey trousers which matched his steely grey eyes.

"Well, hello there," she smiled up at him.

The man did not smile back. "Who are you?" he demanded icily.

Lucy paused, startled by his hostility. "My name's Lucy," she replied calmly. "We live here. Who are you, the local Gestapo?"

Perry's face tightened. "I am a resident like every other respectable member of this village."

Joshua tensed to the sound of voices before he cast his first casual glance out of the window. He almost dropped the mugs - jarred by the sinister, white haired man now hovering outside. He swung towards the doorway.

"Come inside, Lucy," he muttered. "I'll deal with this." She didn't argue.

"I don't believe we've met," Joshua greeted him coolly.

"I want to know who you are," Perry responded in the same menacing tone. "I thought we'd finally rid this village of hippies like you."

"There's no need to be rude," Joshua retorted. "We're not trespassing. We've got the full consent of the landowners to live here."

"I see," Perry whispered, his eyes fixed to his face and suddenly they possessed a searching quality. "You don't actually *come from* this village though, do you?"

Joshua froze, refusing to buckle as he battled to find an answer - anything to divert suspicion. "You're right," he finally laughed. "I hail from London; the lady in the farmhouse is my auntie! So does that qualify us to be residents?"

This time it was Perry who bridled, clearly toppled by Joshua's easy going nature.

"You haven't told us who you are," he added quickly, his smile mocking.

"Enough!" Perry hissed. "I suspect I know why you're really here. Tell me, do you have any connection with the caravan's former owner? A young lady known as *Eleanor Chapman?*"

Joshua's head was starting to spin. He could no longer hold back his fear as Perry's eyes carved into him - as if analysing his every response.

"Oh, Eleanor and I go way back," he shrugged carelessly. "She lived in London too, once - grew up there, same as me…" He knew he was faltering but couldn't help it. Perry's expression changed, from analytical to suspicious. Joshua's eyes widened.

"Interesting," Perry muttered, nodding to himself and with his eyes still latched onto Joshua's face, he gave a chilling smile. "You see, I'm sure I know you. Your face seems familiar…"

Eventually he retreated, leaving Joshua rigid with shock.

"Shit!" Joshua gasped, slamming the door. He collapsed into the seating area, his head in his hands, "Oh shit…"

"Josh, what's wrong?" Lucy frowned, lowering herself down next to him. "Who is he?"

Joshua could barely think straight. In all these years, Perry hadn't changed. His thick hair appeared to be more white than blonde - yet those icy grey eyes were unmistakable, hurling him 15 years into the past. What disturbed him even more was the memory of that photograph; a photo captured in 1973 where he could picture the same face glaring out of a circle of bright white light. The trouble was, would Perry remember him? He'd been no more than a gangly youth dressed in the uniform of a waiter. Joshua sat up, casting a glance at his refection. His features were a little more manly - but he remembered his hair, the same deep, golden brown as it had always been - how Luke's boss had made him tie it back with a rubber band.

He closed his eyes, recalling the press conference. If Perry ever *did* recognise him, he would know he was witness to every lie that had been fired around that table. He had captured Whaley's attention - as had his sister, Alison, never able to forget the moment they had tried to grab him: *'They're brother and sister…'*

Joshua's heart hammered faster. He had put himself right back in the firing line but it was too late to turn the clock back. The wheels of justice had been set into motion, the day Eleanor had agreed to meet Adam in London - a meeting, Joshua himself had inaugurated which proved beyond doubt that Perry had attended that press conference.

"Talk to me!" Lucy kept nagging, "you're not scared of that old ogre, are you?"

"No," Joshua snapped, "in fact, he can go to hell! I'm gonna talk to Eleanor!"

In some ways he was left wondering if he had anything to be scared of. Perry had a lot more to fear; but meeting him face to face had filled him with a yearning to discuss their strategy - struck with a sense, the man was still dangerous.

IV

"Joshua, that would be lovely," Eleanor purred into the telephone. "We'll come over this Saturday. I'll bring the kids."

She lowered the telephone, casting a gentle smile towards her step-daughter. Yet her widely spaced, brown eyes shone with tears. She bit down on her lower lip to stop it from trembling and straight away, Eleanor could tell she was trying hard not to cry.

"Margaret, what is it, love?"

"Don't wanna go back there," the girl mumbled, chewing her thumbnail.

"Don't be silly," Eleanor soothed her. "We're only popping round to the caravan. It will do you good to get some fresh air instead of hiding yourself away in here all day."

It hadn't taken long for Eleanor to realise that her step-daughter was desperately unhappy and very different to the girl she had been, a year ago. Since turning 13, Margaret had begun to suffer hormonal changes. Her ruler straight hair had turned oily - no longer suited to the shorter, choppy hairstyle that had likened her to a teenage Kim Wilde. Eleanor had eventually coaxed her to the hairdresser's to have it cut into a more flattering style. It swung around her shoulders like a brass bell. Her face however, had turned rounder and although she was gifted with the ample bosom of her late mother, Anna, she had filled out in other areas. Her clothes felt tight which only added to her misery; her complexion greasy and prone to spots.

"I bet Eli will come," Eleanor kept pressing her. "He loves his uncle Joshua…"

"What if we bump into the Hamptons?" Margaret shuddered.

"We won't. I only want to see Joshua, so stop worrying."

Margaret bit her lip again - a sight which tugged Eleanor's heart strings. She had never had a daughter. Yet Margaret was a worry; painfully lacking in self esteem, short of friends - and further more, she knew, some of the girls at school had been picking on her. Eleanor stood up and reached for her hand, already guessing what else was troubling her. Margaret not only suffered from pre-menstrual tension, but had a tendency to be weepy in the run up to her periods.

"C'mon, let's go and visit your herb garden," she smiled knowingly.

Margaret accepted her hand with a resigned sigh, allowing herself to be

160

hauled from the sofa. In times of despair, when she had no-one to turn to - not even her best friend, Holly - she was often drawn to these gardens where the tranquil solitude was soothing.

"Remember when we first planted these?" Eleanor whispered. "It was your idea."

"Oh yeah," Margaret said softly, dropping to her knees. She ran her palm over the curly leaves of parsley sprouting from one of the tall terracotta pots. "It was after James died... We were so sad. I wanted something to remind us of his walled gardens."

Eleanor closed her eyes - heartbroken to imagine, those gardens had been obliterated.

"It was a lovely idea," she whispered. "I'm so glad you kept it up."

She watched with pleasure as Margaret's face squeezed into a smile.

"I will. And I don't care what Holly says. She thinks gardening's a hobby for old farts!"

"Ignore her," Eleanor replied, feeling a spark of anger. It was all very well for Holly to scoff; Holly, who was blessed with the same petite frame as her mother and whose bright blue eyes and perfect skin attracted the boys like bees. Poor Margaret had never even had a boyfriend - still helplessly besotted with William. "I expect Holly's just jealous. This is something *you* enjoy where she's not the centre of attention. I don't suppose they've ever been to Westbourne House either."

"Actually, they have," Margaret surprised her by saying. "They went there for Reggie's 40th birthday! Had some really posh meal!"

"Really?" Eleanor pondered, picturing James's beautiful restaurant. "Then maybe we should go back there some day?"

Margaret rose to her feet. Despite the radiant flush to her face, Eleanor witnessed a flash of fear. "No way," she shivered. "Not with the Hamptons there! Have they still *got it in for us?*"

"What on earth makes you say that?" Eleanor frowned.

They had started to make their way back to the almshouse and all the while, Margaret was struggling to remember something Charlie had said. There had been another meeting - but then again, Charlie was always being dragged into meetings.

"Oh, I don't know!" she eventually spluttered. "I'm just so pleased, they're not gonna be building houses here! It was brave of Avalon to buy the land..." she broke off, her footsteps slowing. "I don't suppose she'll be coming to Aldwyck with us - she's terrified of them!"

"Probably not," Eleanor smiled, gladdened by the way she said 'us,' "but William will, so stop worrying. We'll have a really nice day out."

Come Saturday, Margaret had cheered up considerably, quick to bag herself the front seat of the car. She twiddled with the stereo to find Radio

One, where the interior was instantly bombarded with the 'Theme from S'Express.'

"Love this song!" she squealed, bouncing in time to the music.

"Turn it down!" Eleanor shouted. "What sort of music is this, anyway?"

"House Music!" William bellowed above the din. "D'you like 'The Jack that House Built?'"

Eleanor raised her eyebrows, feeling very much like a *boring parent*, as she turned down the volume. "I like to be able to hear myself think!" she added waspishly.

Elijah and William giggled, securely nestled in the back as Eleanor started the engine. She backed carefully out of her parking space before filtering into the High Street. She stole a glance in her mirror. Fortunately, no-one was following; a notion which left her confused, wondering what had happened to that glamorous Asian woman.

It seemed little time, before they were absorbed in the familiar wooded scenery, as the road wound its way towards Aldwyck.

"So how's your love life?" Elijah smiled.

"Non-existent," William snapped, "though I still miss Dawn…"

He broke off, biting his lip; hurt by the manner their four month relationship had ended.

The sad truth was that Dawn had turned out to be a bit of a gold digger. He had bought her the most beautiful silver bracelet as a birthday present. If only she hadn't been overheard complaining to her friend that with *his* wealth, she would have 'expected it to be gold!' Elijah nodded knowingly. The disclosure had come from the friend's younger sister, Mandy, who clearly had a crush on him.

"I don't know whether to go out with Mandy," William confided. "I suppose I should be concentrating on my O levels…" He slipped him a grin. "Why don't *you* ask her out?"

Elijah shifted in his seat, betraying the first hint of a blush. "You're joking. She's one of the school beauty queens! She wouldn't be interested in me…"

From the front seat of the car, Margaret was nibbling her lip again - filled with the fear that Mandy wasn't a very nice person either and one of the girls who taunted her at school.

Before she could dwell any further, Eleanor had cruised through the village and was pulling up by the farmhouse. Margaret blinked as if transported into another world. The stark field, which had only attracted travellers, contained a patchwork of vegetable plots. Neat rows of lettuces, carrots and corn flourished alongside circles of fruit bushes. Tall canes supported a network of runner beans and there were even a few garden sheds tucked around the edges.

"Wonderful, isn't it?" Eleanor smiled, following her gaze. "What a lovely tribute to the village!"

"Yeah, especially now Dad's gardens are gone," William said softly.

Margaret shot him a sympathetic gaze before stepping inside the caravan. It seemed a lifetime ago since they'd lived here and she instantly found herself comforted by the familiar cosy furniture and cushions. The same pretty shelves were heaped with ornaments; though Lucy and Joshua had added a few of their own trinkets; Greek vases, exotic seashells - a beautiful Aztec blanket draped over the bed. Joshua's guitar rested proudly in the corner.

Margaret turned to Lucy who had beckoned her towards the table - her eyes drawn to a carved wooden bowl filled with assorted beads.

"What are you making?" she piped up shyly, sinking into her favourite corner seat.

"Earrings," Lucy smiled back. Her fingers worked skilfully, as she threaded the tiny beads onto a loop of wire. "Would you like to have a go?"

Joshua was trying to make tea whilst the boys relentlessly quizzed him about his musical career. Eleanor helped - delving into cupboards for extra mugs and sugar cubes and by the time they were settled around the table, she turned her attention to Lucy.

"Where did you get the beads?"

"Rosebrook!" Lucy enthused. "There's a most idyllic arcade of shops tucked away in the back streets. Shilling Walk - do you know it?"

It was a statement that immediately drew grins to the boys' faces. Of course, they knew it! It was filled with the most unusual array of 'alternative hippy' shops, which included Andrew's favourite army surplus store. Elijah had seen the bead shop Lucy was referring to.

"It's a really cool place!" he shrugged. "There's loads of other weird stuff - crystals, incense, pipes..." he broke off quickly, clocking William's secretive smirk.

By 'pipes' they meant the *hubbly bubbly* kind; not to forget an abundance of little yellow stickers popping up everywhere with smiley faces, symbolic of a growing craze in LSD or 'acid'. They knew Andrew was a dope smoker - hence the reason he had been drawn to this place.

"Those shops sell some really cool clothes," Elijah added to plug the awkward silence. "Ethnic stuff and long Indian skirts - a little like the one Lucy's wearing."

"Sounds like the sort of place your mum'd like, Joshua," Eleanor said dreamily, "and Jake..." She slowly lowered her mug.

"Jake?" Elijah laughed, "as in my father?"

"Yes," Eleanor sighed, relishing the memories; his slightly hippy clothing - the coolness of his stone pendant as her fingers slipped over its surface, turning it. "This was his, you know."

"I've seen those type of pendants," Elijah added. "I'll have to get myself one."

With memories of Jake infused into the conversation, Eleanor found herself badly wanting to talk about him - conscious of Eli's innocent curiosity. It was comforting to know that some remnants of 70s hippiedom still existed in Rosebrook.

But right now, they needed to discuss more serious matters. The subject of Jake's murder loomed silently between them. Joshua caught Lucy's eye.

"I hear you wanted to visit the Baxters," Lucy beamed at William.

"Yes," William sighed, draining his mug, "see what they've done with our land."

"So let's walk!" Lucy suggested. "It's a gorgeous day. Joshua and I have already sussed the best footpaths." She gazed fondly at Margaret, who's brown eyes were filled with longing. "Come along, kids, the fresh air will do us good!"

For a moment they gazed at each other where the powerful memories were already beginning to surface. It was Joshua who lowered his eyes first.

"It's good to see you, Eleanor..." and moving towards the cupboard area, he uncorked a decanter of red. "For old times sake." Eleanor watched as he tipped a small amount into some dainty goblets. "It's elderberry. Mum and I never did give up making wine."

"Thanks, Josh," she sighed, swirling the wine in her glass; its dark crimson colour so intense, it was almost black. She took a sip. Its flavour was as earthy and rich as its colour. "Lovely!" she nodded to herself. "So you had the pleasure of meeting Perry..."

Joshua's expression changed to one of loathing. "What an absolute shit!" He shook his head. "Trouble is, I've got a feeling he recognised me - he said I looked familiar."

"Joshua, don't put yourself in any danger" Eleanor whispered, leaning in close. "You don't have to be involved in this…"

Joshua simply shrugged. "I *am* involved - always was. If anything, it's Lucy I'm worried about. If things ever did turn nasty, we may have to shoot back to London."

"That's fair enough," Eleanor insisted.

"So how's everything with you?" Joshua bounced back. "Any news?"

"Yes," Eleanor confessed. It didn't take long to explain how Eli had been badgering her. "I had to tell him the truth about Jake's murder… he wants me to find Hargreeves."

"And what about Theakston?" Joshua shivered.

"I'm not certain he was Jake's killer," She watched Joshua's face crease into a frown. "Forensic evidence," she continued warily, "apparently, the gun was fired by a right handed man. He showed me his hand - it looked as if it'd been crushed in an accident, it's paralysed."

"How do you know he's not lying?" Joshua spluttered.

"I could just *tell*," Eleanor mumbled. "Not that it matters. It was *his* gang who carried out the murder and this is what I was about to tell you. I wrote to Scotland Yard asking for details of the murder case - yet all I got back was a letter from the Home Office, demanding to know why I was interested."

"Seems odd," Joshua murmured, "so what did you tell them?"

Eleanor released a sad smile. "I said I owed it to my son - who never had a chance to meet his father. I haven't heard back but if I do, then the next step would be to visit my solicitor."

"So how does Charlie feel about this?" Joshua kept frowning.

"Charlie wants Perry brought to justice as much as we all do!" Eleanor said quickly. She closed her eyes - struck with a memory so powerful, it sent rivers of cold running over her skin. "That press conference was nothing. You should have seen the way he behaved when he finally got his hands on James's property…" she released a shudder. "I swore to James too, I would do whatever it took to bring him down - I made a pledge to both of them."

Joshua shook his head. "So even after the press conference, he continued to spread his evil!" he let out a cynical snort. "So what else has been happening?"

Eleanor was compelled to explain the outcome of the land issue; the dramatic meeting in the Council chamber where she had been pushed into the path of *all* her enemies.

"It's a miracle how Avalon pulled it off," she finished anxiously, "she sold a piece of their own land to buy that plot. I confess, we're all feeling a little nervous - but we're not giving up…" She threw back her last drop of wine. "There's only one way we'll be safe, Joshua and that's the day Perry is put behind bars!"

The others had meandered their way into the hills via the tranquil churchyard. William relished those few tender moments by his father's grave - but before anyone had a chance to feel melancholy, they had continued their hike. The footpaths circumnavigated a patchwork of fields separated by neat hedges. In contrast to the destruction of the previous year, the vegetation had burst back to life; the hedges lush with foliage and cow parsley whilst a profusion of creamy blossoms graced the slender branches of the elder trees. Lucy momentarily paused to admire them - explaining how the delicate blooms made a particularly pleasing wine.

Her love of the countryside was infectious. Margaret found herself completely absorbed as she observed the landscape through different eyes.

Elijah too, found himself equally enthralled. This was after all, the place he'd grown up as a boy, compelled to push aside his darker memories. They were approaching the woods that encircled Westbourne House, where the path curved its way towards a stile. On this occasion, the woods had been cleared of fallen timber. The few trees left standing allowed the sunlight to pour down in hazy shafts, illuminating the ground which lay scattered with the last withering blue bells.

"It looks a hell of a lot better than last time," William found himself explaining. They followed the path through the woods until it gradually trailed to a gate on the far side. They could clearly see Herbert's farm. The forest on this side had been completely excavated - the earth ploughed in readiness to be sown with grass seed. "It'll be so much easier to manage," he added.

They were warmly greeted by Toby and his wife, Jane, an amiable blonde who wore a flowery apron over her jeans.

Toby's eyes flickered to Margaret. "New lady friend?" he smiled.

"This is Margaret" Elijah jumped in to save any awkwardness. "My step sister!"

"And a very good friend," William added indulgently. "They lived with us, remember?"

Margaret lowered her head - conscious of the heat in her face which tinged her cheeks a soft, blushing pink. She was already a little out of breath from their hike. But the moment passed quickly, as did the next half hour.

Toby launched into an enthusiastic spiel over how they intended to use the land for grazing stock; intent on putting some goodness back into the soil, before turning it over to crops. It was inevitable they would end up inside their homely farmhouse, where straight away, Jane produced a bottle of elder flower cordial. Its floral taste was wonderfully refreshing - inspiring the kids to suggest, it would be a pleasure to pick some on the way back.

Jane loaned them a wicker basket just as they were leaving. In fact, their homeward stroll could not have been more blissful - pausing at intervals to pluck the lacy discs of flowers from the overhanging branches. They chose a slightly different route - and after the exertion of their steady up-hill climb, they continued to amble along the farm track which ultimately led to the road.

For the first time in a long time, Margaret felt deliriously happy - revived by her blossoming friendship with William. They had found so much to talk about in the end - to discover they had more in common than they thought. They loved the same music, where an era of house music had revolutionised the UK pop charts. They even liked the same films. It was a moment, she wished she could suspend in time, the feeling as if her heart would burst; except their footsteps slowed.

A breeze of tension rippled the air as without warning, a lone motorcyclist materialised on the track, just ahead of them. William froze, his features rigid - staring at the gleaming Harley Davidson. It looked horribly familiar, the rider indistinguishable; though his gleaming, black leather motorcycle suit spoke volumes.

"Oh fuck," he whispered beneath his breath.

"William, what's wrong?" Margaret whispered, picking up his anxiety.

"It's Nathan," William shuddered, "c'mon, we've got to go the other way! I-I don't know whether anyone told you this, Lucy, but that man…" he shot a quick glance at Elijah. "He works for the Hamptons - he's their hired thug. We reckon he even tried to snatch Eli once... "

"I think we should keep going!" Elijah announced boldly.

"Are you joking?" William gasped.

Elijah's face spread into devious smile. "Let's see if he tries to grab me now," he challenged, "with three witnesses present!"

"Eli!" Margaret breathed, "this is crazy. William's right we should turn back now!"

"What and prove we're scared of them?" Elijah sniffed. "We swore an oath, William."

"You're right, we did!" William snapped and with a look of defiance, he linked arms with Elijah. To Margaret's spiralling delight, he offered her his other arm while Lucy, swept up in an invisible tide of camaraderie, completed the chain. The motorcyclist did not move. The four of them stared fixedly ahead - now advancing down the track as a united team.

Yet it wasn't Nathan at all. It was Ben; a suspicion confirmed as soon as the rider dragged off his helmet. He shook out his sleek, fair hair, inclining his head. He fixed them with a blank, cold stare, meeting each of their eyes in turn.

"Well, hello there, folks," he drawled softly. His pale blue eyes wandered towards Lucy - he gave a twisted smile.

"Hi," she smiled back pleasantly.

William refused to meet his gaze. Elijah too, ignored him. Yet Ben's gaze was latched on Lucy, trailing over her feminine curves where his smile became flirtatious.

Then finally, he locked eyes with Margaret.

Margaret felt herself stiffen as they skirted past. He rolled his bike out of their path but for some reason, she found it difficult to tear her eyes away; her mind inexorably drawn into the past. She had been a child of just 9 when this leather clad demon had surged out of nowhere, almost running her down. Her heart pounded faster. She had never forgotten. The chill of his eyes had thrown her emotions into a state of turmoil, resurrecting a fear which had never really gone away.

Ben was still smirking. This was news for his father. So the girl who'd moved into the caravan and her hippy lover were undoubtedly from the enemy camp.

Perry already knew they had befriended the Baxter lot, so it was inevitable they would be in cahoots; but now he had seen proof for himself. Ben pulled on his motorcycle helmet and roared up the track, intent on returning to Westbourne House via a bridle way. At the same time, he was buzzing - thinking about his new connections again.

Alan and his gang were dealing in a new designer drug known as ecstasy -

a drug which was taking the nation by storm. These little pills had already begun creeping their way into the private parties and unlicensed clubs in London; a substance which appealed to all-night revellers who loved the slightly hallucinogenic, euphoric effects which sent the senses soaring.

Very soon, Alan would be introducing this new drug into Rosebrook, where its somewhat limited party scene was about to be revolutionised. Local youngsters would be hungry for it!

His smile was fixed, as their beautiful home loomed beneath an expanse of woodland - knowing his future was about to be more exhilarating than ever.

Chapter 9

I

The kids could hardly wait to tell Eleanor about their walk, including their unexpected clash with Ben. None of them could really fault his behaviour - only William had the courage to express what he really thought about him:

"Stay away from him, Lucy, he's a psycho."

Despite a lingering sense of foreboding, the visit could not have been more pleasurable.

They returned to the almshouse by early afternoon - in fact they only just jumped out of the car when a movement caught their eye. Eleanor spun round, instantaneously met by the vision of Hilary and her daughter rushing towards them.

"Well, hello!" she expressed with unusual sweetness. "How was your trip to Aldwyck?"

"Fine," Eleanor frowned. "How d'you know we went there?"

"Margaret told me," Holly piped up. She glanced at William from the corner of her eye and smirked before sliding her bright, blue eyes back to Margaret. "Enjoy yourself?"

"We had a great time," Margaret replied with more confidence than she had felt in months.

"Did you go to Westbourne House?"

"Not today," Elijah smiled shyly.

"Oh, but it's wonderful," Holly gushed.

"We know," Elijah nodded, his smile brightening. "We used to live there!"

William suppressed a chuckle, amused by the way she was staring wonderstruck at Elijah. He had decided to drift off home - but not before discreetly dragging his friend to one side. "Ask her out! Did you see the way she was looking at you? And she is dead attractive…"

"Shut up!" Elijah hissed. "Holly would never go out with me. She's way too popular…"

William strode off with a cheery farewell and Margaret waved him off. She unlocked the door - assailed by a rush of fur as both cats began weaving themselves around her legs. The silence was soothing as she wandered into the kitchen. The two young creatures followed; though the peaceful interlude didn't last. She had only just switched on the kettle, when a rumble of male voices emerged from the back of the house. The door burst open.

"Dunno why you put up with him, he's a fucking wanker!" Andrew spat as he and Charlie shoved their way in through the door. "Oh - hello, Maggie!"

"Andrew!" she beamed, ignoring the profanities.

"You've cheered up!" Andrew sniggered, "had a face on you like a slapped arse, lately!"

"Hello, love," Charlie added fondly, ruffling her hair. "Ignore him! How was your day?"

She smiled again - it had to be said, her brother was a lot nicer to her these days, since she had transformed into a teenager. "Who were you talking about just then?"

Charlie held her gaze. The warmth of his deep brown eyes was comforting - though Margaret had already witnessed a glitter of apprehension. He let out a sigh.

"We just popped into the pub for a quick one," he answered gently, "we bumped into that council officer, Robin Whaley."

"Oh," Margaret whispered in a tiny voice.

Suddenly she was remembering... something she had been trying to explain to Eleanor but couldn't quite call to mind. Her eyes were still connected to her father's. It was almost as if he could sense what she was thinking as he took a deep swallow.

Charlie felt a lump rise in his throat.

It had been a typical Monday when they had been summoned to an on site meeting. Various council employees had been present, including Terry Griffiths. Regrettably, Robin had also attended; a day when he had been at his most critical.

"These houses are packed too closely together. It poses a flood risk! Further more, you will need to invest in a new water main. It should be double the diameter..." and on and on he ranted where every new condition was leeching away Peter's confidence. Here they were, trying to do something positive; a proposal Robin had encouraged right up until the result of that fateful sealed bid auction. Charlie took one look at Peter's face - shocked to notice his sunny features clouded with dread. Something inside him had snapped.

"This is bullshit! Your friend, Hampton, was planning to stick double the amount of properties into this plot and with very little green space! Stop being such a bloody hypocrite!" Terry Griffiths almost choked - dismayed by such a serious allegation; but Charlie stood his ground. "I'm sorry but it's true. He didn't hide it from Avalon - did you, Mr Whaley?"

Robin had shot him a look of undisguised hatred but before the meeting ended, Terry warned him of the consequences: if Charlie's allegations were true, Robin would no longer have a say over any future planning application which concerned the Hamptons.

"You're going to regret this," Robin had whispered subtly, the instant the others were out of earshot, "especially when Perry gets to hear about it. Tell *that* to your wife..." and so a veil of malaise had been left lingering.

"What's he said now?' Margaret pressed, yanking his mind back to the present.

"Usual crap!" Andrew intervened savagely.

It would have been impossible not to detect the undercurrent of tension whenever Whaley was mentioned - only this time, Charlie had challenged him openly.

Margaret turned back to the kettle, conscious of the cats mewing at her feet. With a sigh, she reached for a tin before sprinkling some biscuits into their bowls. Both men had wandered into the lounge where the conversation shifted. Eleanor was enthusing about their day in Aldwyck and for the time being, nothing more was said about Whaley.

It was only a little later, Eleanor was finally drawn into Charlie's confidence. In truth, he didn't really want Margaret to grasp the reality of Whaley's loathing - it was possibly a little too much for her fragile young mind to handle, especially as they had just come face to face with Ben again.

"I'm sorry," Charlie whispered, coiling an arm around her shoulders. "I *had* to challenge him! They must be wondering how much I know. I thought it would clear the air."

"So how did this actually start?" Eleanor spluttered.

Charlie shook his head. The vision of the pub car park loomed; the silver Audi rolling up just as they were leaving, not to forget Robin's face.

"I suppose you think you've got one over on us. But I warn you - Peter's sentimental vision is never going to succeed without *my* influence."

"Don't you drag Peter into this!" Charlie thundered. "He's a good man! What exactly is your problem, Whaley?"

"You had no right to mention my relationship with Perry," Robin retorted. "It's got nothing to do with you! As for your wife - I warned Peter, she would bring trouble."

"What is it that really bothers you about Eleanor?" Charlie suddenly taunted him, wary of his son grinning in the background.

"More to the point, what's she been telling *you?*" Robin shot back evilly.

Charlie's face hardened. "Okay, so there's history! I gather, you knew Eli's father…"

"But what do you really know, Charlie?" he had whispered, his voice slipping so low that Andrew couldn't possibly overhear. "Has she mentioned her secret file for example?"

Charlie turned cold. He thought he had planned his next words carefully. "Yeah, she mentioned it. Eli's father was killed in London - she wrote an account of what happened."

"And you've read this *file* have you?" Robin's voice brushed against his ear.

"Of course not!" Charlie retorted. Robin's eyes flashed - but filled with a sense he could no longer escape his interrogation, Charlie had taken his defence one step further. "What are you really scared of, Mr Whaley? Are you worried that *you* might be mentioned? That you told lies at some press conference to malign Jake's character?"

"I was a councillor," Robin smiled. "My ward was in East London. What was I supposed to do when I picked up the rumours - just ignore them?"

"It doesn't matter," Charlie snapped, backing away.

"But it does," Robin kept smiling, filling him with a sense he was falling into a trap. "So she told you about the press conference. Did she mention *who else* was there?"

"Whatever went on in the past, you have no right to be so vile towards us!" Charlie shouted, pointing a finger in his face, "and that includes Peter and Avalon! Have you forgotten, he looked after those kids - after they were traumatised by *your* friends?"

"Be careful what you say, Charlie," Robin snapped. "I'm not a man you want to pick a fight with..."

The world had dissolved into darkness - those final words still spinning in his head and Andrew had heard them too; Andrew, who knew so little about the conspiracy to murder Eli's father. It seemed the best way, given the menace Robin had demonstrated.

"So, he knows we've been talking about this!" Eleanor gasped.

"I'm your husband. It's pretty obvious you must have said *something*!"

"Shit," Eleanor mumbled, turning her face away, "and you wondered why I was so cagey?"

Charlie shrugged. "So, let's keep on fighting. Don't cave in! If anything, they've got a lot more to be scared of than we have."

"That's what I'm worried about," Eleanor finished numbly.

II

By the middle of June, William sat his 'O' level exams and with a renewed sense of freedom, he was ultimately drawn into a relationship with Mandy Siddons. At first, he was reluctant, wary of her age. William, like his father, was bound by a strict code of honour. If he slept with her, he was effectively breaking the law - except Mandy had used her feminine wiles to seduce him and like any other red-blooded adolescent, William had fallen for it.

At 14, she was tall for her age with a figure most girls would die for - slender hips, a tiny waist and most alluring of all, a well-developed bust. The evening she invited William to a party, he was surprised to discover, the only other guests were a couple of friends and their partners. She had worn a tight, figure hugging blouse - top buttons undone, rewarding William with a good view of her cleavage. It seemed strange how her friends had discreetly made themselves scarce. Almost from the moment Mandy had him to herself, they had indulged in that slow, delicious kiss - several more buttons had miraculously slipped undone and shored up with cider, she had murmured in his ear, "do you want to see my tits, William...?" He didn't have to think twice. One thing led to another and before he knew it, they were an item.

Margaret observed them from afar. It was good to see him looking so happy yet on the other hand, she couldn't expel the pain in her heart. Girls like Mandy had it easy; bags of confidence, a great figure and pretty. It was inevitable, William would be bedazzled. Only Margaret knew that Mandy possessed a darker side and there were times when it leaked out of her like poison.

Tears sprung to her eyes as she recalled the morning her class had lined up outside, all set for a trip to the Tower of London; a day when there was no need to wear uniform and Margaret bravely turned up in tight, drainpipe jeans. Mandy had taken one glance at her and laughed.

"God, those jeans make your bum look big, Bailey!"

The entire crowd had erupted into laughter. She wanted to die. Regrettably, the experience turned out to be the catalyst that would drive Margaret into taking drastic measures with her diet.

She tried to do it sensibly at first - opting for salads and melon at lunchtime. But her weight refused to drop and it wasn't long before the very sight of food was starting to make her feel sick. She eventually started skipping school dinners altogether, resolute in her goal - her pack lunches consisted of little more than a couple of dry crackers and an apple.

"You'll make yourself ill," Holly commented in a rare display of compassion.

"So how else am I gonna lose weight?" Margaret sulked.

"It's puppy fat!" Holly snapped, "you'll grow out of it."

"So how come you don't have 'puppy fat!'" Margaret snapped and stormed out of the room.

Resisting food at home was even more problematic - mainly because Eleanor was such an excellent cook. She tended to pick at her food, psyching herself up into leaving most of it. It was hard, especially when the boys tucked in with such relish; the Sunday when she had abandoned her roast potatoes and Andrew had simply forked them off her plate without a second thought. It took the gentle intervention of Eleanor to persuade her to eat more, taking care to prepare healthy, low calorie meals. Though unbeknown to her, Margaret still skipped lunch.

It was a typical Monday however, when Margaret finished her grapefruit half - discreetly wrapping her toast in a napkin, ready to smuggle it into the bin. She slipped into her school uniform, overjoyed to discover it felt loose. She floated into school, delirious with joy, inspired to diet even harder. In a few weeks time, she might even be as slim as Holly. Though it was inevitable that a shortage of calories would leave her energy levels flagging - especially in PE, where her failure to perform on the athletics field was about to spark up a new wave of bullying.

William knew nothing of it. He luxuriated in the sunshine amongst the hoards of pupils camped out on the school field, where the usual spectacle of Sports Day took place. Mandy looked sensational in her sports kit - her dark hair pulled into high bunches, not to mention that tiny gym skirt which showed off her fabulous legs! His eyes were momentarily drawn to them, unable to shift the lingering vision of her sat astride him last night; those strong thighs pinning him to the mattress had taken him to new heights of ecstasy. William smiled to himself, feeling the first tug of an erection. He carefully rolled himself onto his side to conceal it; though in the next instant, the illusion was shattered as Margaret staggered onto the track.

"Oh God, here comes Snaily Bailey!" Mandy sneered.

William turned very still - all sexual fantasies forgotten. He hoisted himself up on one elbow and stared at her. "What did you say?"

Mandy let out a snigger. "Snaily Bailey! She always comes last! Do you know, someone in her year told me that whenever they pick teams for PE, she's the one no-body wants!"

"That's rotten!" William snapped, springing to his feet. He watched with growing trepidation as Margaret stood trembling in the ranks, ready for the next race. She looked terrified.

He could never have known how giddy she felt; she hadn't eaten a morsel all day and now, thanks to the absence of another pupil, she'd been roped into the 100 metre hurdles. She stumbled forwards, just about clearing the first - but then a second hurdle loomed. She barely had the strength to run, but nevertheless made a feeble effort. She never made it. Her foot caught on the edge and she tumbled, sending the hurdle crashing to the ground.

The crowd roared with laughter. Several teachers rushed to her aid, bellowing for silence as the unfortunate race continued. William couldn't speak - his dismay spiralling into shock as his friend lay huddled on the ground, clutching her ankle in agony.

"You're supposed to jump over them *not on top of them!*" Mandy chanted in delight.

"Stop it!" William hissed in fury, "just stop being so nasty!"

"What do you care?" Mandy rounded on him.

"She's my friend!" he retorted coldly. "A *very* close friend as it happens! So don't you dare call her names…" and turning away from her, he strode off.

"Margaret," he spluttered, rushing up to her, "are you okay?"

She stared at him in astonishment, unaware of what a mess she looked; mud smears on her hands and face, her hair a tousled birds' nest. Yet his smile was as warm as sunshine.

"Oh, William," she whimpered. "I'm such a klutz!"

Holly joined them - her face awash with concern as they escorted her, limping from the track.

But from the other side of the field, Mandy was spitting with fury -

dismayed, William had dared to show such concern; now set on a mission to make Margaret's life as miserable as possible.

It started within days. Mandy wasted no time; she ignored William for the rest of the afternoon and launched herself into a quest to find out as much about his 'friendship' with Margaret as possible. Before the day ended, she knew William had attended Charlie's wedding; they had lived together in some mansion in Aldwyck and more recently, spent a day there. Her jealously soared. William belonged to her now!

It seemed unnatural how one girl could develop such a consuming hatred; taking every opportunity to taunt Margaret, while her friends took sadistic delight in joining her. The playground, the sports field and the corridors became her personal battleground - especially the moments when pupils filed past each other in the hallways on the way to lessons. Mandy had chosen one of those occasions to swing right into Margaret's path, brutally elbowing her aside. Margaret banged into the wall, dropping her books. Elijah had witnessed the entire scene.

"Is she hassling you?" he gasped, helping her to her feet. He fired Mandy a filthy look.

"It's okay, Eli, I-I'm fine," Margaret spluttered and with her head drooping in shame, she continued shakily on her way.

Yet Mandy took her campaign further; whispering the vilest of insults, slipping her threatening notes and gradually reducing her self esteem. In the course of a week, Margaret disintegrated into a cowering wreck. Yet somehow, it still wasn't enough. William was in constant contact with her - it was time to drive a wedge between them.

She watched as Margaret wandered into the girls' lavatories and turning to her friends, gave a calculating nod. It was with no hesitation, they crept in after her.

For a few seconds, they waited. Margaret unlatched the cubical door, shocked to see them loitering. She let out a gasp. Mandy roughly grabbed the front of her blouse, yanking her out, yet her savagery had only just begun. Her cruel fingers entwined themselves into her hair, grasping it by the roots, before she proceeded to bang her head against the tiles again and again.

"You stupid, spotty, ugly cow!" she ranted.

"Please!" Margaret whimpered, "I haven't done anything…"

"You stay away from William Barton-Wells, you bitch!' Mandy kept hissing. "If I ever see you chatting him up again, I'll knock your teeth out! Not that it'd make you any uglier."

Margaret started to cry. "But William's my friend," she shuddered.

"You're not to speak to him again or even look at him," Mandy whispered evilly and to everyone's amazement, she locked her hands around Margaret's throat.

Margaret stared up at her, bolt-eyed, her face turning scarlet as she choked.

"Hey, don't strangle 'er, Mand!" one of the other girls tittered nervously.

Mandy's lips twisted into a pitiless smile. "He'd never fancy you in a million years," she finished nastily. "He thinks your fat, pimply and boring. In fact, the only reason he even talks to you is because you're Jansen's sister... now stay away from him!"

Finally she released her. Margaret staggered towards the door, the colour drained from her face, leaving the others sniggering in her wake.

Margaret tip-toed into the corridor. It was break time anyway, the hallways swarming with pupils. Yet her head was reeling - the sea of faces wavering and fearing the possibility she was going to faint, she kept walking, desperate to avoid eye contact. She passed the cafeteria and the library where she paused - the library had an external door which in turn, led into a courtyard.

It was with no delay, she sneaked away from the school premises. Though by the time she arrived home, she was sobbing. The attack had left her psychologically bruised. How could she cope with sitting out the last of her lessons with those hateful insults buzzing inside her head?   Margaret collapsed into a chair where the words echoed like a mantra - no wonder everyone hated her! Yet in the darkest corner of her mind crouched the most painful memory of all: 'He'd never fancy you in a million years.'

She let out a cry of misery - a shuddering wail which awoke both cats.

Sukey leapt lightly onto the arm of the chair. She was sobbing hysterically, yet nothing could ease her agony - not even the caress of cat fur. Her head throbbed; although it wasn't really the physical pain that bothered her. Her heart was bleeding!

She was no longer thinking straight when she wandered towards the booze cupboard. Margaret blinked, seeing her salvation as her eyes zoomed in on a half bottle of whisky. It was with a complete lack of resolve, she grabbed it, unscrewed the cap and poured herself a huge measure. She gulped it down without a care in the world and nearly gagged - yet by the time the feeling passed, she had already shakily refilled the glass.

Plagued with a sense she had nothing left to live for, she hurled it back. But of course, she had hardly eaten a thing all day. The alcohol surged straight to her head - her inner torment blissfully erased, as she gradually lost consciousness.

Eleanor was shocked to find her step-daughter home early. At first glance, she might have been sleeping - except there was something unsettling about the way she was slumped in her chair, mouth open, her cheeks encrusted with tears. Eleanor shook her gently but she was out cold; then finally, she noticed the glass on the table - the lingering trail of whisky fumes.

"Oh no," she whimpered, "Margaret! What have you done?"

She shook her more briskly. It was with a creeping sense of fear that Eleanor did the best thing she could think of and made a cup of strong, black coffee. The most obvious solution would be to take her to hospital - yet she really didn't want people knowing, her 13 year old step-daughter was intoxicated. She tapped her cheek - lightly at first, before the slaps became more forceful.

"Wake up!" Eleanor hissed, "for God's sake, say something!"

"He thinksh, I'm fat - boring..." she slurred drunkenly.

"Oh, sweetheart," Eleanor muttered sadly. "Let's get you to the kitchen - you need coffee."

It was a struggle to manoeuvre her into the kitchen, yet somehow they managed it. Margaret could barely stand as Eleanor held her by the sink, insistent on forcing her to gulp back some coffee, though she was violently sick within minutes. Eleanor held her jolting shoulders as she spewed into the washing up bowl, shocked to see nothing but liquid foam, tinged yellow with bile.

"God, Margaret, however much did you drink?"

As soon as it was over, Eleanor eased her onto the settee and covered her with a blanket. She placed a washing up bowl on the floor, knowing she would need it. Yet as she studied her tear stained face, she couldn't help but wonder what might have happened to provoke such a binge; her musings were cut short as Elijah, tailed by Holly, burst in through the door.

"It's okay, she's here!" Elijah spluttered in relief.

"What's going on?" Holly demanded, "we were supposed to have French and she didn't show up. The teacher's been doing her nut. It's not like Maggie to skive off."

Eleanor let out a sigh. "Do either of you know what's going on?"

Margaret opened her eyes a slit, clocking their arrival. She hauled herself into a sitting position; but the violent movement disturbed her. Before she could stop herself, she retched, clamping a hand over her mouth in horror.

"Bowl!" Eleanor bellowed, just as Margaret heaved over the side of the sofa. She shoved it in position just in time - both Holly and Elijah gaped at her in stunned amazement.

Mortified with shame, Margaret started to cry. "He doeshn't like me, I can't bear it..."

"Oh my God, she's drunk," Holly whispered to herself. "What are you going on about?"

Gradually the story tumbled out piece by piece.

By the time Margaret had finished, Eleanor was fuming. "I want a word with William, right now," she snapped curtly.

"But William would never say that!" Elijah protested, backing towards the door.

It was with no hesitation, he found himself racing towards William's house though already, he had guessed the truth. It was far more likely, William's toxic girlfriend had turned him against her! He thought about their day in Aldwyck - their enchanting walk, followed by that chilling moment they had crossed paths with Ben. By the time he rang the doorbell, he was angry; dismayed his friend could be so fickle.

It wasn't William who faced him, at first, but Avalon. She had already finished work - listening with escalating fury as Elijah spluttered out the details.

"I told you, Mandy was a nasty piece of work," Elijah could hear her whispering as the three of them marched back to the almshouse. "Jealous! Possessive! She even gives me the evil eye!"

By the time the three of them exploded through the door, their anxiety had reached fever pitch. Margaret was still sprawled on the sofa, barely conscious - her face the colour of cottage cheese.

Avalon stared defiantly at Eleanor.

"Okay, so what's going on?" she demanded, "because despite everything, I cannot *believe* my brother would deliberately set out to hurt Margaret!"

"I never said any of those things," William mumbled, "I swear it!"

Eleanor observed them; Avalon, sparking with indignation and clearly on the defensive. William on the other hand, looked as if he'd been slapped across the face.

"You'd better sit down," Eleanor sighed. "This poor girl has drunk herself into a stupor and from what Holly says, I'm worried she could be suffering from anorexia. So let's have the truth."

"William?" Margaret slurred fearfully.

Though William had already sailed over to her side, before anyone could stop him.

It was over the next half hour, the truth slowly dripped out. Holly had suspected for weeks, that Mandy Siddons was bullying her - now wondering if it was the 'big bum' taunt that had sent her hurtling towards anorexia. She had no idea, Margaret had been dumping her pack lunches and in all this time, Eleanor had been proud of her weight loss - horrified to discover the real reason she had shed all those pounds.

"Oh Margaret," she whispered, stroking her lank, dark blonde hair away from her forehead.

They moved to the sports day incident. Holly was quick to uphold that William *had* rushed over to help her. Elijah too, had his own story; recalling the vindictive shove in the corridor.

At first William said nothing, but it didn't take long for the sympathy in his eyes to darken to anger. By the time Holly left, Eleanor and Avalon had tucked Margaret into bed, filled with a horror that they were going to have to explain all this again to Charlie. But before Charlie arrived home, William begged for an opportunity to spend some time with her.

"I don't hate you," he whispered. Her lip started wobbling, he could see she was trying hard not to cry. He touched her hand. "I'm going to finish it with Mandy tonight. She's a bitch. I've always defended you. I had no idea she could be so nasty…"

"She's right, though," Margaret whispered, stifling a sob. "I *am* fat and spotty… How could someone like you ever love me…?"

"You're not ugly," he retorted, "and why shouldn't I love you?"

"What?" Margaret gasped.

William smiled tenderly. "What if I said, 'I did love you?' Not quite the way you want, but as a little sister. I value your friendship more than anything."

"So why don't you ask me out?" she blurted before she could stop herself.

"It's our age difference," William said quickly. "You're very young. Being a boyfriend wouldn't seen right - you must know what goes on in relationships." He lowered his eyes. "You're going to grow up into a beauty one day, Mags, I know it - and *then* I'll ask you out…"

He let her sleep, knowing his words brought her comfort - hoping things would be better and that no-one would blame him for the terrible condition she had been reduced to.

III

Charlie's first reaction was anger. His stress levels were already stretched to breaking point but as the truth of Margaret's predicament unfolded, he soon realised that his problems were nothing compared to hers. By the time he'd calmed down, he found himself staring at the nearly empty whisky bottle in dismay - ashamed he'd neglected her so.

"I don't know what to say," he sighed. "I can't *believe* all this was going on! More to the point, how come we never knew about it?"

"You *have* been engrossed in work," Eleanor placated him, "not to mention those meetings."

Charlie nodded, his face stony. He and Andrew had never been busier - where every dispute with the council was piling on extra pressure. The fact that Whaley was going out of his way to disrupt matters certainly wasn't helping.

"You're right," he nodded ruefully, "we haven't really been there for Margaret. This drinking binge was clearly a cry for help and do you know what? I think we need a holiday!"

"Really?" Eleanor whispered. Her golden eyes shone with hope.

"Yes," Charlie snapped, squeezing her hand. "Do you realise we've been together for more than 2 years and we have never taken the kids on holiday?"

"It's a lovely idea," Eleanor smiled with a shudder of delight.

Before any plans were made, they were compelled to tackle the school about the bullying; initially to explain Margaret's absence - but more importantly, to expose the relentless persecution which had left her emotions in shreds. It was a meeting which threw Eleanor's mind down past avenues - never able to forget the time when Elijah had been bullied. Though on this occasion, the staff were noticeably more sympathetic.

It gradually sprang to light, they were held in higher esteem than they realised: Charlie, revered for his architectural talent; Eleanor too, had been recognised for her voluntary work. Lastly, there was Elijah - a pupil who had bloomed into an incredible artist, one who's talent had not only inspired the new Community Centre design, but had earned the school some publicity.

People in the town looked up to them - where their ties with the aristocratic Barton-Wells children turned out to be a blessing. It was common knowledge, they had sold an entire stretch of forest to reserve a plot in Rosebrook for the benefit of local people. So as their reputation soared, there was no way the school were prepared to risk recrimination for such a shameful bullying incident - especially if it concerned the daughter of Charles Bailey.

"So where shall we go on holiday?" Margaret mumbled softly.

Charlie gazed at her with love, jarred by the muted tones of her voice. She was a shadow of her former self. "I'm not sure. Supposing we went camping! Purchase a couple of tents and just sneak away to Dover - catch a ferry."

"It'll be a mystery?" Margaret whispered, her face breaking into a smile.

"Yes," Charlie smiled back. "Let's just disappear for a week and not tell anyone where."

It was almost as if he had guessed, the idea of secrecy would excite her.

From another side of the town, Robin monitored them; simultaneously drip feeding news to Perry, as he stewed in his own hatred. It was the attitude of his manager, Terry Griffiths, that bothered him. He had been considerably cool, of late which would be disastrous for his promotional prospects; the ultimate goal that he would eventually take his place as Head of Planning. Terry didn't like the fact that he had kept his alliance with Perry secret. Nor did he like the way he was picking fault with Peter's housing project. It was a situation which left him fuming - resolute on destroying their little community by whatever means possible.

Perry on the other hand, was rejoicing. So, Charlie's little girl was being bullied - never mind the gossip they had tried so hard to hush up; that she had been discovered blind drunk in the almshouse! It all added to the fascinating shenanigans weaving around their community - dramas which included William Barton-Wells; a boy who was fast gaining the reputation of being a proper little Casanova.

But now it transpired, the Baileys were about to disappear on holiday for a week - even the older boy, Andrew, who Ben had since discovered worked at the 'Cat's Whisker's' wine bar. Perry smiled, thinking about the almshouse; picturing their beloved home, a perfect location for Eleanor's secret file. It was time to put the first phase of his long awaited plan into action.

IV

The plan to sneak away unnoticed, wasn't quite straight forward. Margaret's first concern was for the cats. She had originally asked Holly to look after them but Eleanor talked her out of it; Avalon and William had already offered them refuge. By the time Charlie managed to postpone a number of work projects and Andrew arranged leave from his bar job, their carefully planned 'escape' was scheduled for the final week in July.

Bags packed, sleeping bags crammed into the back of Charlie's old Volvo, the family set out at dawn before the sun had cast its first fiery rays onto the newly painted yellow walls of the Community Centre. Andrew who drove in convoy, had commandeered Eleanor's mini - although he had doggedly stipulated, he would only accompany them if he could invite his best friend, Matt; a regular festival-goer who's considerable camping experience was bound to come in useful.

They found a beautiful campsite in the Alsace region by mid-afternoon. It was on that first evening, they found themselves slumped on blankets - enjoying a bottle of Bordeaux within the peaceful surround of hills; a village where they had ultimately found a charming bistro to enjoy their first Continental supper.

Next day, they abandoned the alpine treasures of the Alsace Lorraine and crossed the border into Germany. At first glance, the terrain was not that different - until they were eventually drawn into a verdant plateaux of thickly forested mountains. After stocking up on provisions, they arrived in a town named Trier where they spent the next two nights. It was a place one could easily fall in love with; an ancient city scattered with Roman ruins, whose tidy city square was flanked by medieval buildings. Charlie was captivated by the architecture, Margaret, its exciting array of shops, whilst Eleanor and the boys seemed content to relax on the pavement cafés, sipping beer and generally watching the world go by. Yet it wasn't long before they were on the move again - unable to resist the lure of the Moselle Valley where Eleanor would be forever staggered by its beauty.

They were blessed with good weather. The sun beamed its light into the folds of endless mountains, striped with vineyards and cloaked with pine forest. The crystal waters of the river glittered - while most enchanting of all, were the fairy-tale castles perched high on a backdrop of hills. Most spectacular of all was Castle Cochem, with its conical turrets arranged around a central tower. It was a moment they stopped - tempted to enjoy a picnic on the river bank, whilst admiring this magnificent gem from below. Elijah immediately rummaged for his sketchpad, keen to capture its detail.

Eventually, they settled in Koblenz where they remained for the rest of their holiday.

It was a large campsite filled with a mixed clientele which included families and retired couples, thrown in amongst cycling enthusiasts and youth groups. It was here, they finally began to socialise. Andrew and his friend were quick to attract the attention of a group of German teenagers, where even Elijah and Margaret didn't feel out of place. The group leader was a young man named Klaus with whom they struck an instant rapport.

"Hey, English! Come, join us later for a beer, ya?"

Slender, hippy-like and sporting a goatee beard, it didn't take long to realise they had discovered a fellow 'toker.' Elijah took an instant shine to him. In some ways, he imagined him as an icon of his father - a musician who took his guitar everywhere. Even Margaret was delighted to join their camp - careful to avoid the strong German beer but happy to befriend the youngest member of the group, Sabina. Somehow, they all found common ground - whether it was a love of music, outdoor pursuits or simply because they were a gang of young people on holiday. By the end of the week, it was Margaret who was reluctant to leave; besotted with the youngest member of their group, Erik, whose chiselled Aryan looks combined blonde hair and startling blue eyes and with whom she had shared her very first kiss.

"Oh well, I guess all good things have to come to an end," Eleanor sighed.

She was squeezing the canvas of their tent into a tight roll, before Elijah helped her stuff it into a bag. His eyes possessed a misty quality.

"I've been looking at Klaus's map," he whispered, "do you know - we're not actually that far from Holland. Nijmegan - isn't that where my dad came from?"

"It was," Eleanor said dreamily, guessing what he was about to ask, "and if we had enough time, Eli, I would have suggested a detour..."

She saw his face fall a little. "Is that not possible?"

"Our ferry sails tonight, love," she told him truthfully. "That gives us just enough time to drive to Calais - but not through Holland. Maybe, next year..."

He smiled, fulfilled with that final promise.

They took a shorter route to the docks via Belgium, hankering for a last shop in Calais; a final chance to stock up on wine, French cheese, paté and the buttery golden pasties which somehow never tasted quite so fresh and light in England. Margaret bought gifts for everyone while Andrew and Matt bought as much duty-free tobacco as they could stuff into their rucksacks. By 5:30, they had boarded their ferry, waving good-bye to the Continent as the vessel surged its way across the English channel and the craggy white cliffs of Dover beckoned.

They returned to the almshouse by mid evening with enough daylight hours to empty both roof racks and lug everything indoors.

"I'll put the kettle on," Eleanor announced, sliding her weary body out of the car. "You'll pop in for a cuppa won't you, Matt? Unless you two are dying to go down the pub!"

"No, I'll stop," Matt grinned as he and Andrew started to unfasten the bungee ropes from the car roof. "Thanks, Mrs Bailey."

Eleanor left them to it as she shoved open the door - surprised to be obstructed by such a mountain of mail. She bent down to scoop it up, noting several letters from the council as well as the usual bills. Then her eyes fell to a familiar, cream coloured envelope bearing the frank mark of her solicitors, Sharp, Bancroft and Blackmore. She stuffed it into her pocket, not wanting the others to see it - struck with a familiar sense of excitement whenever she received this type of correspondence. Then finally she drifted through to the lounge.

She stopped suddenly. A whisper of cold swept over her neck - something wasn't right. She couldn't quite put her finger on it but as her eyes flitted around the lounge, she was experiencing an all-pervading sense of being 'spooked.'

"Is everything okay, love?" she heard Charlie holler from the back of the house.

His voice sounded unusually loud. Eleanor frowned. That was it! His voice actually sounded as if it was coming from *inside* the house - and he'd only just parked his Volvo around the back. Eleanor shivered, conscious that the air felt cold.

"Charlie?" she muttered, creeping towards the kitchen. She froze again, her eyes drawn to the light cotton curtains as they fluttered in the breeze. An entire window pane appeared to be missing; not broken but gone - cut clean out of the frame. "Charlie!" she shouted, her voice rising to a scream. She lunged towards the back door where a key still dangled in the lock - her hands trembling so violently, she was struggling to open it.

"What's wrong?" Charlie gasped, rushing towards her.

She collapsed into his arms, her breath coming in rapid gasps. "I think we've been burgled," she just about managed to splutter.

Within seconds, everyone shot into the house, eyes everywhere. The lounge looked more or less normal - until Andrew's eyes fell to the gap where the TV and video should have been.

"Shit," he breathed, "the telly's been nicked!"

Charlie closed his eyes in dismay. "We've got to phone the police," he muttered curtly.

"Now?" Andrew challenged him.

"Yes, now," Charlie sighed. "We need to report this immediately - get them to dust for fingerprints, so try not to touch anything..." Without another word, he lowered himself into a dining chair, his head tumbling into his hands.

"I-I'll make some tea, shall I?" Eleanor shivered.

"I'll do it," Elijah volunteered boldly. He squeezed Margaret's shoulder who was anchored to the spot, white faced. An atmosphere of shock curled into the living room.

"Christ, man, I'm sorry," Matt mumbled, slapping an arm around Andrew's shoulders.

"You two can make yourselves scarce if you want," Charlie said in a resigned tone. "Check your room first, Andrew. See if there's anything missing."

It was Elijah and Margaret who made the tea whilst Charlie got straight on the telephone. No-one knew what to say. It seemed a horrible situation to return to in the aftermath of such a blissful holiday. Margaret was fighting tears - knowing they had so much to do. Both vehicles lurked outside, still crammed full of their stuff.

By the time Andrew, Matt and Eleanor had gone through the downstairs, they were relieved to discover, nothing else was missing - not even Andrew's expensive 'Philips' stereo, which he'd bought on hire purchase.

"Thank God," Eleanor sighed and in a rare gesture of affection, they caught each other in a hug.

"Didn't you ought to check upstairs?" Andrew mumbled into her shoulder.

"Later," Eleanor whispered numbly. "We've got loads of unpacking to do first…"

Already her heart was thumping as she pondered over what else might have been taken - a terrible fear was winding itself through her mind, however hard she tried to ignore it.

It was over the next ten minutes, they methodically emptied the cars and hauled everything back indoors - hold-alls, suitcases and rolled up sleeping bags lay in a heap in the middle of the sitting room floor. They packed away the food. Though Charlie, exhausted by their long journey and whose inner resolve was finally beginning to crack, uncorked a bottle of red.

"I need a drink," he said bitterly just as a police car pulled up outside.

Eleanor stood by the door, watching, as two constables and a detective stepped from the car. They flashed their ID cards. It was with no hesitation, she stepped dazedly to one side. She was beginning to feel very tired now; her heart heavy with anxiety. One of the police officers was taking details. In fact, the whole scene was beginning to seem dreamlike.

She hovered at the foot of the stairs - where the final horror of this chapter was about to be unveiled. Her head spun as she placed a foot on the first stair and without wishing to delay the investigation, she tiptoed towards their bedroom.

Here the scene was very different. Every cupboard had been emptied, the bed tipped up at a peculiar angle. Clothes and underwear lay scattered on the floor, some still spilling over the tops of the gaping drawers. The wardrobe doors hung open, revealing an empty cavern of space. The entire room had been ransacked - and to her even greater shock, so had the children's.

"Oh God," Eleanor whimpered, sagging to her knees. Charlie and the police officers were already shuffling up the stairs. She stared at Charlie in panic. Then finally, she started sobbing.

Eleanor wiped away her tears; wary of the children, who knew nothing about the violation of their rooms. She was inclined to leave Charlie and the police to comb through the mess, knowing there was only one other person she could turn to. She drifted downstairs where Elijah and Margaret lingered in stunned silence. It was with little hesitation that she herded them together, clamping an arm around each shoulder.

"Pick up your bags," she told them sadly, "I'm taking you to Peter's."

"But why?" Elijah demanded. "What's going on?"

Eleanor squeezed her eyes shut - she couldn't lie. "I'm sorry but it seems, the burglars raided the upstairs. The police need to gather as much evidence as possible. You can't sleep up there tonight."

"No!" Margaret squealed in horror.

"Charlie and I will sort it out," Eleanor tried to soothe her. "Come on, let's go."

She banged on Peter's door, thankful to see a light on. In fact nothing could have brought her more comfort, as his cheery face materialised in front of them.

"Hi folks, how was the holiday...?" The smile dropped from his face. "Dear Lord, whatever's the matter?"

"Peter, is it okay if the kids stay with *you* tonight?" Eleanor gasped. "We've been burgled!"

Peter unwaveringly agreed to her request - quick to gather the children into the sanctuary of his flat before settling them onto his comfy sofa with a bag of crisps each.

His natural inclination was to console them; to ease their initial shock as only Peter knew how. They seemed happy to share the spare bedroom - and it wasn't long before they were beginning to look sleepy. Margaret's eyelids were drooping; although Eleanor was reluctant to leave them until they were placidly snuggled up in bed. She dimmed the light in the hallway then sidled back into Peter's lounge. He awaited her with patience.

"Oh, Eleanor," he sighed, guiding her towards a chair. "What a terrible thing..."

"Thank God, I asked you to protect it," she spluttered. It was only now, she finally allowed herself to embrace the truth. Those thieves, who had gone to incredible lengths to get inside their home, were after more than a TV - they were searching for her secret file. "Is it still here?"

"Of course," Peter muttered, his eyes bright with intuition. "I said I'd look after it - in case anything happened to you..."

Eleanor gave a nod, the gears in her mind turning. "I'm so grateful," she whispered tearfully, "but how could they have *possibly* known we were on holiday?"

"These enemies of yours are still around," Peter sighed, "they must have realised the house was empty. Did they steal anything of value?"

Eleanor shrugged, piecing together a scenario: the thieves had carefully picked their way through the downstairs - found nothing, so they had bagged a video and TV just for the hell of it; anything to make it look like a normal burglary. "Strange, they didn't touch Andrew's stereo," she reflected, "though we don't know if they took anything from upstairs." She closed her eyes, massaging her temples. "They must have lost patience... the way everything was flung all over the floor. I didn't want them to see it, Peter, it would have upset them!"

"Don't worry, they'll be fine with me. Take as long as you need. As for your file, do you want me to hang on to it for a little bit longer?"

"Would you mind?" Eleanor sighed, rising to her feet. She forced a smile. "I'd better get back. See if the police have found any clues. I'm sorry to rope you in like this, Peter, but you're the only person round here I can trust."

He led her downstairs where they paused on the doorstep. It was with a quick peck on the cheek, she thanked him for everything and wandered back home - ready to revisit the nightmare.

The police had gone. Charlie was slumped in an armchair, nursing a glass of wine though the expression on his face was dark with torment - it broke her heart.

"Oh Charlie!" she whimpered, sinking into their rich, leather sofa. "What now? Did the police manage to resolve anything?"

"Are the kids okay?" he interrupted her gently.

Eleanor nodded. He rose from his chair, grabbing the bottle of red wine and another glass before he joined her on the sofa. She watched in a daze as he filled up both glasses. He took a deep breath.

"The police suspect they were looking for jewellery. Anna's diamond wedding ring is missing." His face tightened. "I was hoping to pass that on to Margaret."

"I'm so sorry..." she started to say but Charlie cut her off again.

He clasped her hands. A sense of fear loomed silently between them.

"This was a highly sophisticated job. The police reckon a lot of planning went into it. It wasn't the work of some *passing thief* who would have broken in... these were professionals! That window was removed, using industry standard glass cutters." His eyes became more penetrating. "Eleanor, I suspect we both know what the intruders were *really* looking for."

Eleanor nodded again, besieged by a rising sense of dread. "My secret file. Don't think I haven't already thought of it - but the file is safe, Charlie."

"What - you mean, you hid it?" Charlie breathed.

"I had to," Eleanor snapped. She gripped his hands more tightly. "If there's one thing I learned when Jake and I were on the run, it was to be vigilant! There was no guarantee, something wouldn't happen to me - even abroad. I asked Peter to safeguard it for me."

She watched some of the tension drain from his face; his shoulders sagged heavily as he took a draft of wine. "Thank God! Though I guess, it confirms who's behind this."

"Perry?" Eleanor hinted without hesitation.

"I don't doubt it for a moment," Charlie agreed; his voice lowered to a snarl, "though I'm beginning to wonder if Whaley played a part! I mean - why was he so interested to know if I'd *seen* your file? I wonder if he guessed, you were keeping a copy here."

"Were there any clues?" Eleanor pressed. "Did the police find anything?"

Charlie banged his glass on the table. "Nothing. The detective discovered three sets of fingerprints but it seems, they were wearing gloves. It's even possible, they removed their shoes to avoid leaving any footprints! The detective searched for impressions on all the hard floor surfaces..." his gaze fell to their polished wooden floor boards. "Nothing showed up."

Eleanor stared at him in panic. "You realise what this means then. Perry - or whoever masterminded this burglary, must have some highly professional criminals working for them."

She dug into her pocket, where finally she unearthed the letter she had snatched off the doormat. It seemed a long time ago now - to think, their homecoming could have degenerated into such a nightmare. She stared at the letter and tore it open.

"It's from John," she shivered. "He wants to see me."

"Well, I suppose the timing is apt," Charlie sighed and topping up their glasses, he squeezed her thigh. "C'mon, let's go to bed! I've tidied the upstairs as much as possible. We'll just have to claim on the insurance."

"I'm sorry about Anna's wedding ring," Eleanor responded sadly. "Was it valuable?"

"It was to me," Charlie whispered. He kissed her gently on the lips. "But let's not dwell. Your file is safe and so are we. Let's go upstairs and relax. Do something to take our minds off it."

In a hidden corner of London, Alan Levy stared at Anna's wedding ring. He twiddled it in his fingers; watching mesmerised, as the spectrums of light bounced off its surface. He bit down on the stone as if to check it was real, defiling its priceless beauty.

"Pretty prize," he muttered. Nathan towered over him. "That all you got?"

Nathan shrugged. "Didn't have much worth nicking," he grunted. "You got a TV and a video, didn't you? And Ben paid your blokes handsomely for this job."

Alan looked at him with amusement and smiled, the scar on his face deepening to a crevice. "My boys don't normally do no burglary for just pocket money! Was expecting a little more booty!"

"At least you got *something* out of it," Nathan sneered, his eyes darkening. "My boss isn't happy. He didn't get what *he* wanted which means we'll have to resort to a different plan…"

"Go on!" Alan smirked, slipping the diamond ring into his pocket.

"Time you met Eleanor Bailey," Nathan said coldly. "There's only one way we're ever gonna get that file of hers - find a way she'll hand it to us willingly."

Chapter 10

I

Eleanor's family had drifted around the house in a daze, next day, engaged in the usual post-holiday tasks. A sense of suppressed shock tugged the atmosphere as Margaret helped her prepare their Sunday dinner.

They invited Peter. The children had been dying to present him with their gifts which finally launched them into an animated discussion about the holiday. It took their minds off the burglary, at least for a while; but the disquieting subject was never going to go away. It was like the creeping bind weed which lingered beneath the ground just waiting to coil its way into the conversation.

By Monday, news had swept through the neighbourhood as Police interviewed the residents.

It was with a sense of heartfelt pity that Avalon had contacted Elijah - wondering if they might like to join them on a walk which included a detour to the infamous 'Shilling Walk.'

It was here, Elijah and Margaret were finally seduced out of their shells. The area reminded them a little of Cochem with cobbled streets, leading to narrow passageways and a medley of shops. They differed from the neat, half-timber rows in Rosebrook High Street; small dwellings with artistic hanging signs and stucco walls, painted in an assortment of pastel shades. Their big glass frontages revealed an intriguing display of merchandise - rails of clothes lingered outside, crowding the pavements.

"Nice," Elijah nodded as he sifted through a selection of tunics spun from raw cotton. "I'm still on the look out for a pendant, you know - like the one my dad used to wear."

"Let's go inside," Avalon answered with a soft smile. Her eyes were fixed on Margaret, who was absorbed in another rail - admiring the dresses, printed in a myriad of delicate patterns. "Why don't you try a couple on," she added.

It had to be said, Margaret looked a lot better, these days. She had taken to exercising indoors with Holly, where an influx of fitness tapes had hit the nation by storm - from Jane Fonda to a faddish new workout known as 'Callanetics.' She was already developing firm limbs and undulating curves, where week of outdoor pursuits and sunshine had left her glowing.

"Yeah, go on," William indulged them, "treat yourselves."

It was a young person's paradise. Even William bought most of his clothes here. He guided Elijah towards the gemstone section, amused to see Avalon equally tempted; a long, crinkly skirt draped over one arm, as she fingered the delicate embroidery of a summer top. Its faded, sun washed fabric gave it an almost antique appearance.

"It'll look lovely on you," Margaret said sweetly. "Shall we go to the changing rooms?"

The boys left them to it. Elijah settled on a smooth pebble in onyx green which he immediately looped around his neck. William coaxed him outside. He wanted to buy some music, steering Elijah towards a record shop hidden in one of the side streets; he was hoping to find some mix tapes, featuring the revolutionary new acid house.

"I've been dying to ask this," he muttered as they stalked into the alleyway, "but did you ever manage to find much out about your dad's killers?" He glanced around furtively.

Elijah froze. "We haven't really talked about this much, have we?" Events of the last year flitted though his mind. It seemed like a *very* long time since his mother's file had been revealed to him. "You have to absolutely swear to keep this quiet," he added, pulling his friend aside, away from the drifting throngs of shoppers.

"Okay," William nodded. "I swear. What is it?"

"Mum kept records," Elijah whispered. "She's got this *secret file* - it's full of news clippings and photos. She wrote some sort of diary explaining everything that happened."

"And you saw it?" William breathed.

"Only some of it, but listen..." His voice dropped to an even softer whisper. "My father was shot by a criminal gang. Someone *hired* them - it was to cover up an even more horrible crime."

William's eyes stretched wide with disbelief. "Do you reckon it was Perry?"

Elijah offered him a subtle nod. "Perry was definitely involved. I saw a photo..." he broke off with a shudder. "Don't ever, *ever* let on I told you this, b-but so was *Robin Whaley...*"

"What?" William squeaked.

It was in the next few minutes, Elijah explained what Andrew had overheard; Robin had mentioned the file - asked Charlie if he'd seen it, leaving Eleanor convinced, the burglary might have been an attempt to steal it. In the dusky light of the alleyway, William looked pale.

"I even picked up some conflict during that *land* debate," Elijah whispered, "but there's someone else, someone Mum won't talk about. She like, totally clams up whenever his name crops up."

"Go on" William coaxed him.

"Theakston," Elijah muttered. "He was at the council meeting..." he broke off quickly, having just spotted the girls. "C'mon - let's go see what they're up to."

For the rest of the day, nothing else was said.

Jake's murder was in fact very much on Eleanor's mind. It had been two long weeks since the burglary and she was yearning to see her solicitor. Before she left however, she snatched a few quiet words with Peter, where an alarming new discovery could not have been better timed.

"I'm glad you came," he whispered, closing the door. "I've got something to tell you, sit down."

Eleanor didn't argue - she saw the troubled light in his eyes. "What is it?"

"You know I said I'd put out some feelers?" he continued, "ask me fellow men if they knew anything about Albert Enfield?"

Eleanor turned very still, her breath caught in her throat. "Yes?"

"The bomb was planted by a single terrorist," he sighed. "According to a friend, it was a member of an active IRA cell. He's currently serving a prison sentence for his part in a number of car bomb attacks across Britain."

"How could this 'friend' of yours possibly know this?" Eleanor gasped.

"The man confessed," Peter said darkly. "The IRA was split, you see, yet both sides talked." He dipped his head closer. "The greatest problem the IRA face is, they didn't actually sanction the attack. This person was operating alone."

"So who was he?" Eleanor spluttered,

"That is something Seamus wouldn't say," Peter said, lowering his gaze. "You must understand. He'd be deemed a traitor. Apparently, he overheard him bragging about it - he was known to be a mercenary. Seamus reckons he'd kill anyone for the right price."

"I see," Eleanor said numbly, "and when you say 'the right price' are you suggesting this - this - mercenary might have been *hired* to plant that bomb."

"I'm telling you this in the strictest confidence, Eleanor, because this is the *only* evidence that links the IRA to that bomb attack. Tell that to your solicitor friend."

She rose slowly. Peter's revelations had thrown her mind over a decade into the past, as the horror of Jake's story rose up to haunt her: she was imagining the minibus scheduled to ferry Enfield's party home before it exploded into flames. Eleanor shuddered. Could that mysterious pair of feet jutting out from under the minibus have been this same 'mercenary?' A man specifically hired by some mysterious, yet smartly dressed man to carry out the atrocity?

She drifted towards the door, unable to resist a final backward glance. Even James's friend, Evelyn, had mentioned a man in overalls. Eleanor felt a sudden chill. Somewhere, traces of this crime still existed; the truth that Jake's enemies had tried so hard to destroy, scattered like fragments of scorched paper in the aftermath of a bonfire. Now all she had to do was find them before they were obliterated forever.

"Thank you," she muttered, pausing by the door. "I won't mention your name - or put your friend in any danger. But what if the police latch on to this, what then?"

Peter shook his head. "The IRA will never admit responsibility," he finished gravely. "The only path left open would be to get this man to admit it! Let's see if you can bring your enemies to justice and then - if there's ever a trial - maybe the truth will find a way of outing itself..."

Eleanor nodded before sliding out of his office.

She made her way downstairs, hands tight around her carrier bag where the concealing Abaya dress and veil were already hidden. She dived into the toilets, ready to slip into the disguise. Taking no chances, she bolted the door then slipped the dress over her clothes. She lifted out the veil, wrapping it meticulously around her hair before she gradually emerged from the cubical.

The door swung open unexpectedly. Eleanor turned - shocked to find herself face to face with Hilary Magnus.

"Eleanor!" she gasped, "what on earth are you wearing?"

Eleanor's heart started hammering. "It's called an Abaya!" she smiled. "I-I'm off to London! I'm still looking for my dad, you know..."

"Dressed like that?" Hilary continued to grill her.

Eleanor found it difficult to meet her eye. "Have you not been to the East End lately? I-it's got a huge Muslim community. Better to be anonymous... in case of enemies."

Hilary let out a sniff. "I see. They're still around then?"

"Probably," Eleanor replied, nibbling her lip. "Now if you'll excuse me, I have to go."

She didn't wait for an answer. She had already clocked the suspicion in the other woman's eyes. She slipped out of the entrance, head lowered - almost a repeat of her performance, a year ago. Except this time, someone had identified her - someone, she really wished had *not*, knowing what a gossip Hilary was. Despite her gnawing unease, she drifted to the station. She still had Perry to worry about - praying the news wouldn't spread, as a train heaved itself up to the platform.

Hilary returned to her office. Her hand hovered momentarily over the telephone - she felt a pang of guilt but then Eleanor's behaviour was undeniably suspicious. Once again, her hand crept towards the handset, her decision unwavering as she dialled the number of Westbourne House. She closed her eyes, the memories sharp. She had of course promised to tell him everything - but he had been *so* persuasive!

It sent her mind reeling back to the night of Reggie's 40th; a night she had finally experienced the grandeur of this idyllic country house for herself. The house was indeed beautiful, though Hilary found herself mysteriously drawn to its proprietor, Rowena. Sophisticated, self-assured, she exuded class; she wore a silk designer suit in subtle shades of mauve which seemed to perfectly compliment her platinum blonde hair.

Hilary had ordered a bottle of champagne. It was after all, Reggie's birthday. Before the evening ended, they had ambled into the bar. Holly was content to flop in one of the richly upholstered sofas, drinking in the surroundings; Reggie, light headed on a single glass of champagne, seemed happy to keep her company. Hilary on the other hand, felt her inhibitions slide as she drifted towards the bar - keen to converse with Rowena who was the perfect hostess.

"So what line of work are you in?" Rowena asked her sweetly.

Hilary chose her words carefully. "My husband and I are professional addiction counsellors, at Rosebrook Community Centre."

It seemed a little strange how Rowena had latched on to her. "How very commendable! It seems, many of our clientele are involved in benevolent causes..."

Hilary felt her cheeks glow. She hadn't noticed the charismatic, white haired gentleman, at first, lounging in the shadow of a high backed chair. Yet there was something quite seductive about Rowena's interest - and in the time it took to order coffee, she found herself divulging everything there was to tell about the Community Centre. Information which included Peter and ultimately, Eleanor.

"I'd be interested to support you," Rowena oozed. "You could always book our ballroom, you know - a venue for a fund raising event, perhaps..."

Her eyes glittered, as they captured her gaze and for that moment, Hilary felt honoured.

She sensed a looming shadow as Perry sidled up to the bar. "Rowena, where is your charm? You haven't offered our guest a liqueur." He had turned and thrown her his most engaging smile. "I'm sorry, allow me to introduce myself. Perry Hampton - owner of this fine establishment." He thrust out his hand which Hilary accepted timidly.

She might have been slightly giddy from the champagne but that first impression was mesmerising - from the penetrating warmth of his hand, to the flash of his pale grey eyes. He exuded an almost magnetic power - for a second, Hilary felt overwhelmed. She accepted the complimentary glass of whisky liqueur - although it didn't take long for the conversation to adopt a slightly sinister tone.

"So," Perry started musing. "I understand my wife's interested in supporting your work, though I'm afraid I have my reservations..." Hilary watched in dread, as the smile slipped from his face. "Did I hear you say, you were a *friend* of Eleanor Bailey?"

"Not a *friend*," she babbled. "If it wasn't for Holly's relationship with Charlie's daughter, I'd have nothing to do with her." Her gaze drifted to

Holly who was giggling at something one of the boy waiters had said.

Perry nodded to himself as if contemplating his next words. "You see, I hate to disappoint you but if there were any ties between you and *that woman*, it would make any future alliance somewhat... *difficult*."

Hilary froze, caught up in her day dream - what it would be like to have someone as esteemed as Rowena as a patron of their good work! Yet she could sense the opportunity sliding, before she had a chance to seize it.

"To be honest, I don't really like her much! I've always thought of her as a bit of a trouble maker." She turned and offered Perry her sweetest of smiles.

Still, Perry did not smile. "She is more than a trouble maker," his deep voice pulsed. "She is a dangerous adversary and she is trying to ruin me."

"But why?" Hilary frowned.

He drew his head close, where she momentarily breathed in the sweet, woody scent of his aftershave. "Eleanor shared a close relationship with the hotel's *former* proprietor, James Barton-Wells. You must know, it was ultimately *my family* who took over the management."

Hilary frowned, assailed with distant memories. "Hmm, she told us about that business some while back. This James - didn't he fall victim to some *predatory loan shark*?"

A blaze of colour spread across his face and for a moment, Hilary wished she had kept her mouth shut. He fumbled with his cigars and released a chuckle, breaking the agonising tension.

"Loan shark! Is that what she said? Allow me to enlighten you, my dear. James was in financial difficulty and borrowed too much money. He got himself so deeply in debt, it was my company who bought the house - by way of bailing him out. James did not go bankrupt and as far as I am aware, his children are very well provided for."

Hilary was shocked - hanging on to every word as Perry proceeded to malign them; how he had tried so hard to turn this place into a thriving hotel - yet found himself continuously hampered by rumours and lies. Hilary in her befuddled state, was woefully oblivious to the truth. Rowena, on the other hand, seemed keen to support her - anything which would elevate them above this barrage of ill feeling. Buckling under the influence of Perry's deception, Hilary found herself easily swayed; unwittingly drawn into a devil's pact. She felt no allegiance towards Eleanor - irritated by her extraordinary beauty, the way Peter was forever fawning over her. Even Reggie had been inveigled into defending her once. She stared at Perry intently as the subject inevitably moved to the Barton-Wells children.

"They blame me for their father's death," Perry continued to drip evilly. "Eleanor is plotting a terrible revenge."

"So what is it you want?" Hilary whispered. "How can I be of help?"

"Help?" Perry smiled. "I want you to be my eyes and my ears. Pass on any information which may be useful and I promise, we will support any charity of your choosing."

A week later, Hilary had received a cheque for £1,000 - a donation towards a new rehabilitation centre which would provide an essential lifeline for their work. She hadn't disclosed who the donor was. For some reason, Perry insisted on keeping their alliance a secret. But the die was cast.

III

The telephone was answered on the 5th ring. It took only seconds to be connected to him.

"Hilary," Perry's voice emanated from the receiver, "how are you, my dear, any news?"

"You are not going to believe this," she responded breathlessly. "I've just seen Eleanor - dressed up as a Muslim! She's going to London…"

Perry gripped the receiver. His chest tightened and for a moment he felt a wave of giddiness. "What exactly is she wearing?" he snapped.

Hilary spilled out the details; the flowing robe, the concealing veil which would allow Eleanor to blend into a crowd unseen. "It's identical to an outfit, worn by one of our liaison officers," she added feverishly. "Her name is Shajeda!"

"Thank you, Hilary," Perry said softly and after pressing her for a few more details, he politely ended the call.

He had remained icily calm, up until now. So that was her game! Despite all his careful surveillance, Eleanor Bailey had been sneaking off to London in disguise. He could picture her now, floating from the doors of the Community Centre; indistinguishable, given what Hilary had said about this other girl. Perry clenched his teeth - he felt murderous.

It seemed ironic how busy Westbourne House had become. For the first time in a year, Perry had actually turned the business around; though right now, he was regretting it - fuming as he strutted down the staircase. The accommodation was fully booked, the staff rushed off their feet. Yet it all crumpled into insignificance in the light of this latest revelation.

"Tell Rowena, I've been called to London," he barked at a terrified looking girl on reception.

It was without another word, he marched out of the door.

His temper did not cool as he tore up the M25 motorway like a maniac. The killer question was, how many other times had that bitch deceived them? There was only one reason Eleanor would creep to the Capital in disguise: to visit her solicitor - a situation which rekindled another wave of panic. He was drawing close to the outskirts of London, where the traffic clogged densely around him. It was with a sense of dismay, he realised, it would take forever to fight his way to the centre. Forced to abandon his car in Poplar, Perry headed for the nearest railway station. He should have appointed Nathan for this mission - yet for some reason, this was one investigation he had genuinely wanted to undertake himself.

Eleanor sat patiently onboard the train for several minutes before it eventually hummed its way along the tracks, now fast approaching London. She found herself thinking about the route to High Holborn - the underground passage from Waterloo which would take her to Leicester Square then a quick changeover to the District Line. Yet her unexpected clash with Hilary had left her anxious; a feeling so powerful, she was already considering a change of plan.

She cruised up the escalator before stepping into the daylight, where a circle of parkland lay beyond. It hovered in a blur of foliage, encircled by wrought iron benches. She managed to flag down a taxi; in fact, she was in no hurry - relishing the opportunity to gaze out of the window as it crawled its way through the city. At last, she recognised High Holborn where a magnificent suite of offices soared into the sky. She politely requested if the driver would drop her outside before darting the final few yards to the door.

Despite the slightly longer journey, their meeting was swift and to the point.

There was still no word from the Home Office. John reassured her he would chase this up on her behalf, wondering why the police were being so cagey.

Eleanor was inclined to tell him about the burglary.

Though, it was overshadowed by that most *covert* piece of information, Peter had disclosed, concerning the IRA terrorist. It was a moment when John's interest peaked.

"This is a highly significant discovery," he muttered. He was clutching a small Dictaphone, where every word was recorded. "I understand the need for confidentiality but if we are ever to re-open the case of Jake's murder, this could be a vital piece of evidence."

"I know," Eleanor shivered. "I'm certain, we've identified at least *one* of the men Jake spotted by the roadside but if we were able track down the other man…"

John leaned back in his chair. There was a sudden wily glint concealed in his soft brown eyes. "We could be well on the way to resolving this mystery," he smiled, "which brings me to the most exciting news of all…" He nodded towards Eleanor's original file and it was only now, she noticed James's aged leather-bound diary resting right at the top. "This lady, your friend mentioned: Evelyn Webster. I've found her!"

Perry hated travelling by tube; condemned to endure the hot, stinking air, the crush of bodies from every nationality as he fought for space. Unfortunately, it was the fastest way to get to High Holborn. He had no choice - oblivious to whether Eleanor had even arrived yet. He finally made his way up an escalator before he was vomited onto the pavement amid a moving tide of commuters. Eventually he found a park bench nestling in a horseshoe of trees, grateful of this haven of green space; the sweeter air that cooled his flushed face. He wore very dark glasses. He had also thought to wear a Panama hat to conceal his white hair, confident he portrayed the image of any other respectable-looking tourist - though it was a good 20 minutes before he spotted her.

The charge of his heart accelerated as a black London cab cruised into the curb, directly outside the pristine building which accommodated the office of John Sharp. He watched as a slender young woman, dressed in the exact Islamic garb as described, slid out of the back, paid the driver then fled towards the door. A second later, she had disappeared inside.

"Treacherous bitch," he whispered under his breath.

There was nothing he could do but wait; find out exactly how much time she spent there and only then would he consider his options. The seconds had ticked by painfully - seconds which had multiplied into minutes. He would need a drink after this or better still, a screw, knowing exactly who he was going to call in on. But for the present, he lingered in solitude; filled with a familiar loathing as it bubbled inside him like a geyser.

Eleanor stared at John in amazement; she felt a rush of excitement. "You've actually managed to track down Evelyn Webster?"

John smiled. "She's been very reclusive. She and her husband moved abroad but they're divorced now. She lives in Bath with her son. I think the best way forward would be to contact her don't you? Ask her if she will agree to meet you."

"But what on earth are you going to say to her?" Eleanor whispered. She was already thumbing through James's diary; the yellowing pages etched with his testimony from 1972: *I couldn't believe what I was hearing as Evelyn described this gentleman she bumped into known as 'Perry' and in a service station in Surrey, just miles from that terrible car bomb incident...'* She felt her heart squeeze - moved by the way James spoke through his beautiful, flowing script. "Is it worth asking if she remembers James? Are you going to mention Albert Enfield?"

"I'll have to at some point," John sighed, "though the matter will be handled extremely delicately. We don't want to scare her off. Lets's just say you were doing some research; wondering just how contentious Albert's policies were and as this is an era of politics she'd remember, we would welcome her opinion."

Eleanor nodded to herself. "Okay. I suppose we have to try - but I won't deny, I'm scared. Can you *imagine* how Perry would react if he found out?" She shivered, despite the warmth of the sun streaming in through the window. "He warned me never to cross him, John."

With their pact well and truly sealed, Eleanor was happy to leave the matter in his hands. Their meeting only lasted 30 minutes yet she vacated the building more confident than she had felt in a long time. Already she was fantasising about meeting this *Evelyn*; an imaginary conversation where she might even coax her into disclosing everything James had told her. It would prove beyond doubt that Perry was the man Jake had seen by the roadside - where his appearance at the press conference had ultimately sealed his fate.

Eleanor was smiling. She hugged her handbag to her chest, whispering a silent prayer to Jake. Her face was elevated towards the sky, bathed in a glare of light reflected from hundreds of mirrored window panes; yet hidden in the shadow of the trees, lurked the very subject of her fear.

Perry was still braced on a park bench. He watched her wander into the sunshine, her face illuminated with joy. Hidden behind the lenses of his shades, his eyes possessed a flare of evil so intense, he could have killed her. Her face momentarily tilted in his direction.

He sprung from his seat. This day would be a disaster if she saw him - at worst, it would blow Hilary's cover. His sense of caution was acute as Eleanor shimmied into the distance, the slender robed figure gradually shrinking as she headed in the direction the tube station. Perry felt the breath pour from his lungs - now resolute in pursuing her.

He flitted into the tube station, quick to submerge himself into the crowds. The object of his scrutiny wandered ahead - her creamy veil distinctive against the descending surge of passengers. Perry clocked the direction she turned before he stepped onto the escalator. It took him by surprise; left as opposed to right. He could hear a whoosh of air as an underground train charged from the tunnel, now stealthily moving towards the same platform. It was just as he suspected. If Eleanor was planning her homeward journey, she would have chosen the Piccadilly Line to Leicester Square. But she had chosen the Central line.

Perry backed away from the passageway before whipping out a map of London. The train she had boarded extended *way* beyond central London. It travelled in a direction which would take her east and ultimately north, with every chance of arriving in South Woodford; a stone's throw from another location he was familiar with and that place was Forest Haven.

Perry glanced at his watch. It was 12:30 which left plenty of time to visit another acquaintance; gripped by an untiring motivation, as he strutted his way from the tube station to find a taxi.

"Perry!" Alesha gasped as he materialised on the doorstep of her idyllic Georgian terrace.

His smile was predatory as he stepped over the threshold. He seized hold of her hands before kissing her firmly on the lips. She smiled back, her eyes sparkling with pleasure.

"I've missed you," he whispered huskily, feeling that all too familiar flutter of the heart. He just about managed to conceal the tremor in his voice as he nudged her towards the staircase. He wasted no time. A moment later, they were in the bedroom.

"I've missed you too, Perry," Alesha simpered and without any prompting, she unbuttoned her dress. "How are things? Are you still keeping your eye on the Bailey woman?"

Perry concealed his emotions well. "Of course! In fact there's been an interesting development. I've finally figured out her game plan..."

He felt his throat turn dry as Alesha slid out of her dress, as lovely as ever. He found himself savouring the sight of her undulating curves - the firm breasts, her flawless skin, the colour of coffee. Without wasting a second, he tore off his jacket and unzipped his flies - he forced her down onto the bed and clambered on top of her.

Their coupling was as hasty as it was brutal, leaving Alesha looking slightly confused. He had been rougher than usual. He couldn't help it - by the time it was over and he collapsed panting on top of her, she was staring at the ceiling, perhaps wondering if anything else was wrong. It was without a word, he turned away from her. The minutes dragged by slowly.

"Darling, is something the matter?" Alesha whispered, struggling into a sitting position.

"There's something I need to ask you," Perry said coldly - he wasn't even looking at her now. "About this time last year, you visited me in Pimlico. I specifically asked you if the Bailey woman had gone anywhere. You seemed cagey."

Alesha shrugged. "I told you her life was boring," she smiled almost apologetically. "I'm *certain* she didn't go anywhere..."

She broke off - but Perry had already clocked the glitter of fear in her eyes. He felt a sneer twist his features as he swung back his hand and belted her hard across the face. The force of it sent her flying backwards onto the bed. She let out a cry of shock.

"You lying whore!" he roared. "You've got no idea where she went, have you?"

"Perry, please..." Alesha gasped, shielding her face with her hands.

"She disappeared without a trace and do you know why?" Perry hissed. "She's been dressing herself up as a Muslim! So let me ask you another question. Did you, per chance, see some girl in a long dress and a veil walk out of the Community Centre?"

"I-I can't r-remember..." she sobbed.

"You're useless," Perry berated her, "and you have failed me! I could destroy you for this, Alesha! See to it that you never work as a private detective again!"

"I'm sorry," she whimpered, "I'll make it up to you, I promise!"

He observed her with contempt. "Damn bloody right you will and this time you will not fail! I want you to research a family known as the Merrimans! They live in the north east corner of London in a place called Forest Haven. Have you got that so far?"

Alesha nodded dazedly, tears spilling down her face.

"These people share Eleanor's secrets. Many years ago, they helped her organise a press conference. It was very nearly the ruin of me."

His mind had already lapsed into the past - recalling that hippy family Eleanor had lodged with; two young people at the press conference, a boy and a girl, brother and sister. It was throughout the era Dominic had been surveilling them - the discovery that both boys worked at the Grosvenor Hotel. He relied on the hope, she would have lost touch with them but now he wasn't so sure...

"You are to uncover every scrap of information you can find," his autocratic voice barked. "Find out where they live, what they do for a living and preferably get photos! You are to build up your own dossier for me - do you understand?"

"Yes, Perry," Alesha agreed, in a resigned tone. "I'll do whatever you want."

"Good," he muttered evilly and the next time he moved towards her, it was to seize her by the chin, tilting her face upwards. "Don't cock up! I meant what I said, I will destroy you..."

He held her terrified stare for a few more seconds before marching from the room without a backward glance.

The possibilities of Eleanor's whereabouts continued to lash through his mind. He had no proof she had visited Forest Haven - it was only a hunch. On the other hand, where else would she have gone? That train was definitely destined for East London. Eventually his thoughts turned to Hilary, indebted to her for leaking that vital clue. He knew he needed to exercise caution. Even Robin had expressed his reservations: *Her husband, Reginald met Jake Jansen once...*

By the time he returned to his car in Poplar, he had calmed down. Robin was right. Reginald Magnus had always been a liability. Even Perry realised the situation was delicate.

Yet there were other ways he could penetrate their community, especially if he could take advantage of his son's menacing web of contacts. Perry smiled as the threads of an idea came to him. It was time to experiment with some slightly more unorthodox tactics.

The strangest coincidence took place, just as he returned to the car park. If he had stolen a glance towards the park on the opposite side of the road, he might even have spotted her again.

Eleanor wandered through the gate - drawn into a canopy of shrubs encircling the Garden of Remembrance. She hurried to the spot and dropped to her knees, searching for her tribute. It had become submerged a little deeper over time - but the moment her palms made contact with its cool, marble surface, she felt an immediate connection to Jake's soul. She used a tissue to wipe it clean where the words engraved on its surface were revealed;

My beloved Jake
Never to be Forgotten

She carefully lifted the stone, extracting a small wooden box. The veneer was mottled with age. Yet it had survived - its secret contents intact; a lock of hair snipped off in 1973 alongside a feather-soft wisp of baby hair. A neatly folded square of paper concealed a copy of Jake's last beautiful song - and although the paper had turned brown, traces of the words peeped through: *Our lives have been a mystery, where do we go from here? The net around us closing tight, like birds we disappear...*

Eleanor closed her eyes, cherishing his memory. It gave her time to reflect on every oath she had sworn since the day she had left London; the promise that she would bring his killers to justice. She wiped a tear from her face. There was no denying, she was on the way to accomplishing that goal. Finally, she thought of Elijah and all the others she had sworn to protect; the foundations of *a society where everyone could live together in safety*. Eleanor replaced the contents inside the box and pressed it back into the soil. She thought about everyone she held dear. Not only Jake, but her father, Oliver, her treasured friend, James and even Elliot - wondering what sort of life he led in the shackles of Perry's employment. Lastly she remembered Joshua, hoping he was avoiding Perry's scrutiny whilst establishing a foot-hold in the village.

Perry's theory however, was not wrong.

It was that final fleeting thought that yanked her to her feet to fulfil one more journey. She could not wait to tell Rosemary her news, almost shaking as she flitted to the bus stop. Rosemary would be ecstatic - though at the same time, fearful; with every step she took to unravelling the mystery of Jake's murder, it was gradually drawing her towards the flames of Perry's wrath. This was the only part of her plan which unsettled her.

It was a short visit but enough for Eleanor to pour out her news. She decided to abandon her Abaya dress and veil, rolling it up and stuffing it back inside her carrier bag. Two hours later, Eleanor returned to Rosebrook in her clinging summer dress, her luxurious dark hair pulled back from her face and fastened with a thick gold, banana clip.

"Charlie!" she breathed, slamming the front door.

She was relieved to see an absence of youngsters. They were probably out enjoying themselves together with the Barton-Wells kids - relaxing in their garden or browsing the eccentric shopping arcade known as Shilling Walk.

"You've had some news?" Charlie smiled, drawing her into his arms.

"John's tracked down Evelyn Webster," she whispered rapturously. "He's going to write to her - see if she'll agree to meet me..."

"Brilliant!" Charlie grinned, squeezing her even tighter.

Chapter 11

I

It didn't take long for Eleanor to pick up a hint that something sinister was afoot. She had just finished her shift behind the tea bar. She removed her apron and hair net, shaking out her gleaming dark curls before making her way towards the exit - momentarily distracted by two men as they swayed into her path, blocking her way.

Eleanor froze, staring up at them in dread; her eyes were drawn to one in particular. He had a long scar running down the side of his face and there was something about his icy, light blue eyes that unnerved her - a vision which shook up disturbing memories of the past.

"Can I help you?" she frowned.

He gave her a cool, lop-sided smile and eyed her up and down - devouring the sight of her long bronzed legs. His eyes settled on her face. "Any chance of a cuppa, darlin?'"

Eleanor froze, recognising the strong cockney accent. There was something about this entire scenario which brought flashbacks.

"Sorry, tea bar's closed," she responded coolly.

"Pity," Alan smiled and once again, his eyes travelled over her body.

"Do I know you?" Eleanor whispered. He reminded her of someone - yet who?

"Don't think so, love," the man joked in his menacing, sing-song voice.

"What happened to your face?" she couldn't help asking.

"What this?" He briefly touched his scar. "You don't wanna know. Happen, I just cut meself shaving."

Eleanor released a shudder - she barely noticed the younger man whose eyes had also briefly flickered over her. He offered her a subtle nod, then without another word, both men turned and sauntered towards the door.

She watched them go, conscious of them loitering. It was as if they had purposefully come here looking for her. It was with some reluctance, she finally edged her way out of the exit, waiting until they had gone before she sped towards the almshouse. She hurried inside and slammed the door, her heart crashing inside her ribs.

"Andrew, where are you going?" she gasped as her step son materialised in the lounge. He was already kitted out for work in a white shirt and formal black trousers.

"Cat's Whisker's, of course!" he snapped.

"But it's only just gone five!" she shrieked. "You don't start until six."

"So?" Andrew sneered petulantly. "Maybe I wanna see one of me mates, first."

"Don't go," she whispered, pausing by the door. "Not yet. There's something I need to talk to you about…"

"What?" Andrew sighed irritably.

The sad truth was, Eleanor didn't know what to say to him - unable to piece her feelings into words where suddenly, the town no longer felt safe any more. There was no denying, those men had reminded her of *gangsters*.

"Just be careful," she shivered. "I've got a feeling there might be some bad men hanging around Rosebrook. Don't forget, the police *still* haven't caught the thieves who burgled us."

"Oh for God's sake, chill out!" Andrew reacted with a cynical smile. "You're beginning to sound like Margaret." He didn't wait for a retort. He circled his way around her, completely unfazed, before flouncing his way out of their house.

Andrew resumed a more relaxed pace. His first destination lay south of the town centre. He swung left where the first of many elegant town houses reared up on both sides of the road. Grinning to himself, hands buried deep in his pockets, he navigated his way a little further until he was gradually drawn into the heart of bedsit land. It was here, his best friend, Matt lived.

Andrew knew he had less than an hour. Wasting no time, he slumped into one of Matt's threadbare armchairs and immediately rolled a cigarette. His friend made a cup of tea; except Andrew had more on his mind than just tea - fixated on the real reason he had dropped by.

"Any joy?" he muttered furtively.

Matt slid open a draw and fumbled around for a few seconds. He dug out a lump of cannabis resin, the size of an Oxo cube. "There you go! Quarter you wanted, wasn't it?"

Andrew's face lit up like a lantern. "Oh sweet!" he gasped. "Thanks mate, I owe you. What you doing tonight, anyway? You up for a toke later - after I've finished work?"

"Yeah, if you like," Matt nodded, sipping his tea, "be good to catch up."

By the time Andrew shot back into town to start his shift, his mood was elevated. He had been an addict for over two years; drawn to the delights of dope smoking when his family had briefly moved into Eleanor's caravan. It was a time when he had been disorientated and depressed, having never got over the untimely death of his mother. The mind numbing effects had offered him an escape route. He knew he could be a miserable sod at times but in the days when his supply ran dry, his mood blackened considerably, affecting all those around him.

He had been counting on the fact, his best friend would score; a day when he really didn't appreciate Eleanor holding him up. What was she even thinking? Blathering on about 'bad men in Rosebrook!' He had to admit, the burglary hadn't affected him quite so badly as the others but now she was just being paranoid! He could barely suppress his smile as he poured glass after glass of wine, pulled pints and occasionally mixed an exotic cocktail. Tonight he was on top form, already anticipating the pleasures that awaited him on the other side of his shift.

He left the Wine Bar, just after eleven where the dusk closed thickly around him. He could never have predicted he might be followed - oblivious to the predatory eyes zooming in on him, as he swaggered towards Matt's bedsit.

The limpid darkness was refreshingly cool; the streets quiet, apart from a distant hum of traffic added to the fading echo of voices and laughter as the pubs emptied out. A thump of music resounded from a nearby house. Andrew quickened his pace, driven by a sudden urgency to get to Matt's place. He was acutely aware of footsteps behind him - though nothing could have prepared him for the shock of being grabbed and slammed against a hard brick wall. He could feel the powerful grip of fists around his arms, before a leather-gloved hand was clamped across his mouth.

"Quiet," a voice whispered in his ear. To his spiralling dread, Andrew thought he heard the click of a flick knife. "Search 'im!" the same voice hissed.

Andrew pressed his eyes shut as the nightmare ensued. He could feel the alien fingers digging into his pockets - extracting his wallet, his keys and even his prized tobacco tin. He froze to the click of the latch being undone - it was followed by a chuckle that turned his blood to ice.

"Well, well, what have we got 'ere then?"

He could hear the tin being rattled, conscious of his precious dope stash.

"Don't hurt me..." he just about managed to whimper.

A moment later, he felt the impact of a fist as it was slammed into his back, chopping off his words.

Everything happened in a blur. He was flung to the ground, dimly aware of the three hooded youths crowding around him. Yet it seemed they had not quite finished. He tried in vain to roll over but instead, found himself staring up at the sole of a raised boot. The boot crashed down heavily, finding its mark. Andrew let out a gasp as it thudded against his chest, winding him. With a final snigger, they reached down and grasped his ankles, then dragged him into an alley way.

"One last thing," the voice penetrated into the darkness, "you see Ray Engel, tell him *Trev's boys are looking for 'im'* - and you won't be gettin' any more of this shit!" he heard the distinctive rattle of his tin again.

Andrew couldn't move as he flopped in the darkness, quaking with fear. Then at last, they backed away. He could hear their diminishing footsteps as they echoed down the alleyway. Heavy sobs escaped his chest, his torso throbbing. He had never been so frightened in his life.

Eventually, he found the strength to drag himself upwards. By the time he reached Matt's door, he practically fell against it, palm pressed against the doorbell until the continuous ring brought his friend running.

"What the fuck?"

"I've been mugged," Andrew gasped, staggering into the chilly hallway.

He was aware of his fellow lodgers poking their heads around the neighbouring doors. Matt urged them to stay out of it as he ushered his friend into his bedsit, bolting the door.

"It's okay, you're safe now," he whispered as Andrew hovered in the centre of his messy living room. "Sit down - I'll put the kettle on."

"Get a spliff together, will you?" Andrew breathed, sinking numbly into the same worn-out armchair. He was still clutching his chest - tender from the vicious stamp of that boot. For a moment Matt gaped at him. Andrew fired him a long and apologetic look. "They took my fucking ganja, mate."

"Oh shit," Matt sighed.

"You - you couldn't lend us a couple of toke's worth could you?" Andrew muttered miserably. "You know - 'til I can get my hands on some more?"

"Sure!" Matt muttered, fishing around for his papers. His fingers worked quickly as he speedily rolled a joint. "Didn't you ought to call the cops?"

"And tell 'em what?" Andrew snapped, "that they nicked off with my dope stash?"

Matt sparked up the joint and passed it to him. "Are you hurt?" he prompted him. "Did they take anything else?"

It took a good ten minutes for Andrew to splutter out every detail. By the time he had finished, Matt was staring at him with an even more pronounced expression of dread.

"They got your keys?" he shuddered. "What if they're planning another burglary? I mean, what the hell are your folks hiding in there, mate, the Crown Jewels?"

Andrew felt sick as the fragments of an earlier conversation slipped through his mind. Suddenly Eleanor's warning didn't seem so ludicrous.

"I don't know, Matt," Andrew gasped, "I really don't..." He broke off, his earlier fear racing back to him. "I'd better go home and warn them," he finished forlornly.

"I'm coming with you," Matt sighed, their tea well and truly forgotten as it sat, cold and stewing, in mugs. Without another thought, they rose shakily to their feet.

Andrew winced in pain as they lingered outside the almshouse, reluctant to ring the doorbell. It was nearly midnight. In the end, it was Matt who tapped lightly on the door.

They waited for the dim glow of the porch light to illuminate their surroundings - glancing for any crouching shadows, just as Charlie was opening the door.

Charlie froze. It took one look at his son to realise something bad had happened; his eyes set like two dark pools in the centre of an ashen face - in fact, he had never looked more scared.

"What happened?" he whispered, tugging the door open.

"I-I was attacked, Dad," Andrew whimpered miserably, "I don't h-have my keys any more - they took them!"

It had been a long time since Charlie had pulled Andrew into his arms and hugged him; but for a moment, he looked as if he could have burst into tears. "Come on in, son," he whispered softly, "you too, Matt. You look like you need a drink…"

"I don't like this one bit," Charlie whispered, some time later. "You don't think this has got anything to do with your trip to London do you? I mean - did anybody see you?"

"Only Hilary," Eleanor muttered naively, "but that doesn't overrule the possibility, there could be others keeping an eye open. I wore the disguise. Maybe someone sussed me out this time…"

Charlie let out a frustrated sigh. "So what now? I mean, we have got to get the locks changed but what about your file? I'm beginning to wonder if we should think about some other place to hide it. I don't think it's safe here any more."

Eleanor gazed at him. His eyes shone darkly in the subtle glow of candlelight as a similar thought ran between them.

"Maybe we should bury it."

She was imagining the scene in the park - hands scrabbling at the earth where the gleam of Jake's memorial plaque had finally peeped up at her. For some reason, the image had stayed with her.

"It's not a bad idea," Charlie muttered. "The question is where?"

"I'll think of somewhere," Eleanor whispered. She sank into his arms. "Just thank God, Andrew's okay. Though I suppose we'll have to inform the police."

He nodded silently and for the rest of the night, nothing more was said. Eventually, Charlie drifted to sleep. His troubled breathing deepened - though it was a long time before Eleanor's mind switched off, sensing the net of her enemies closing tighter.

II

It was two days before Andrew returned to work, grateful of a chance to recuperate. He had logged the crime with the police who actually took the matter very seriously - this was the second time the Baileys had been targeted.

Friday night at the 'Cat's Whiskers' was always busiest. 5:00-7:00 was Happy Hour where half price cocktails lured the youngsters in droves.

Andrew sighed, remembering his 18th birthday. From the other end of the bar, Lara Baker caught his eye.

"You okay, babe?" she smiled, fully up to speed with the mugging incident.

Andrew threw her a cheery nod, happy to have her working with him on this most challenging of nights. It was impossible to suppress the nightmare of his attack - yet the warmth of her alluring eyes had an instant soothing effect. He had known her for years. He liked her mum, Della too, conscious that she and Eleanor shared a somewhat clandestine past.

Up until the mugging, Andrew had been reasonably content with his life. He enjoyed working alongside his father as a builder - and this in turn, earned him a handsome wage. Andrew had become a lot more materialistic over the years. It went with the era where having pockets full of cash was a bonus. It inspired enough ribbing from his mates - even more so when a song titled 'Loadsamoney' hit the UK music charts and he found himself being likened to a character in 'Harry Enfield's TV show.'

He didn't have a steady girlfriend yet he never went short of female company. He found himself glancing at Lara, admiring her sexy figure. He could even remember an occasion where *they* had tumbled into bed together, wondering what she was doing after work. Her movements were quick and graceful as she lined up the glasses before spinning on her heel to mix each cocktail. She seemed in particularly good spirits; exuding a sparkle which made him wary of his own melancholy. It was in the next few minutes, he discovered the reason why.

"Have you met the new boy?" she murmured in his ear.

He followed her gaze. There were usually six people behind the bar on Friday but so far, this newcomer had gone unnoticed. It was only now, Andrew found himself observing him; feeling a spike of envy as an irrefutably slick, good looking black boy was gliding around the bar in full view. Andrew's eyes were drawn to his slender wrists and fake Rolex - the easy going smile which had the ladies melting in the palm of his hand. There was something about his fluid movements which reminded him of a cat.

"So who is he?" he snapped - conscious of the resentment slipping into his tone.

"Angel," Lara smiled, "at least, that's the name he goes by. What a dream boat!"

'Poser, more like,' Andrew thought savagely, biting back the retort.

For much of the evening, he ignored him. The place was heaving anyway, leaving no opportunity to talk. For the next two hours, the place became busier and noisier - customers four layers deep crushing their way forwards and competing for attention.

"Right, who's next?" Andrew bellowed above the din.

He kept on serving, eyes down, focused on his task. Another hour shot by. From the corner of his eye, he spotted Lara again. She was still swooning over the new guy - but in the next few seconds, something kicked off and it happened very quickly.

A group of youths sidled into the pub who looked undeniably thuggish. Andrew shot a look at them and tensed - they weren't the sort of blokes to mess with. Yet there was something very odd about the way this 'Angel' ducked behind the bar.

Andrew gaped at him. Their eyes met and there was no question, he looked scared. He held a finger to his lips, crouching so low that no-one could have spotted him.

"Swear you never saw me." Andrew thought he heard him whisper.

He paused, facing the bar where the youths swaggered up to him. Their leader appeared to be some breed of skin-head - he had a mean, rat-like face.

"What can I get you guys?" Lara beamed pleasantly, diving into the gap.

"We ain't 'ere for a drink," the youth growled. "We're looking for someone…"

"Yeah?" she murmured, hands working busily as she continued to serve customers. All the time, the youth's eyes were dancing up and down the bar, teeth clenched behind his thin lips.

"Some black bastard," he snarled, "goes by the name of Angel… no offence, darlin'"

Lara bristled - aware of Angel, slithering across the ground like a caterpillar, manoeuvring his way towards the kitchen.

"Ain't no-one like that in here," she snapped, glaring brazenly back at him.

They didn't stay for much longer. The leader shot another glance around the bar as his friends searched the lounge. He momentarily met Andrew's eye, grinned evilly then backed away. Andrew froze, clocking his heavy Doc Marten boots - a nasty, uneasy feeling curled right to the pit of his stomach.

"You okay, man?" Lara's voice drifted lazily past his ear.

"Tell you later," he spluttered, his eyes inexorably drawn towards the kitchen.

Andrew didn't waste a second. The instant they'd finished serving, he marched into the kitchen, where Angel was busily drying up glasses.

"Right, what's going on?" he demanded, "who were those louts?"

The new boy met his eye for the first time. He had an appealing face and gentle eyes, framed by thick, dark lashes. His eyebrows shot up slightly, giving him the appearance of a young puppy who'd been given a severe scolding.

"Bad news," he eventually muttered, "cheers for covering up for me."

Lara was next to slip through the door, her eyes accusing. "You're on the run, ain't yer?" she snapped, "you got some *big fish* comin' after you…"

"They ain't big fish!" Angel laughed, throwing down his tea towel.

Andrew frowned. "So what's your real name?"

No-one had a chance to respond as the manageress swept into the room. "What are you three doing in here - haven't you got homes to go to? You too, Raymond!"

Andrew wandered back to the bar, his mind reeling. The next time he glanced at the newcomer, everything locked into place. He felt exhausted yet exhilarated, his mind humming with questions.

"I wanna word with you," he challenged as they ambled their way out of the door. "Come on, who are you, really? You wouldn't happen to be *Ray Engel* by any chance?"

Angel gawked at him in panic, where Lara was quick to spring to his defence.

"What's the matter with you?" she hissed, "you ain't been the same since them guys came in."

"That's just it!" Andrew snapped, "I reckon it was *them guys* who attacked me the other night. So come on - you owe me an explanation!"

"Shit man, I'm sorry," Angel breathed. He lowered his eyes guiltily.

"Sorry?" Andrew spluttered. "They sneaked up on me, stole my wallet, my keys and what pissed me off more than anything, they stole my fucking ganja! I'd only just got that - Rosebrook's been a bit dry! They punched me, they stamped on my ribs and said they were looking for *you!*"

Angel looked horrified. "Like I say, I *am* really sorry. Word must've got out, I was working here. Maybe they followed you - but seriously, I'll make it up to you... I was gonna ask you back for a drink anyway. I owe you one!" The next time he turned to Andrew, his smile turned a little furtive. "If you wanna smoke, I've got some really nice weed..."

"Okay, you're on," Andrew nodded, just as Matt sauntered up to the door. "Mind if my mate joins us? I think it's about time we all got to know each other."

Angel didn't argue. He linked arms with Lara, quick to steer them towards the car park at the back of the Cat's Whiskers. He fished out a set of keys, unlocking his car - a sleek, navy Ford Sierra. Andrew and Matt exchanged glances - but nevertheless, slid into the back. Angel cruised up the high street. The pavements were thriving with young revellers; but Andrew wasn't really paying any attention to the unravelling party scene. He wanted answers - his mind charged with the same fears that had been troubling him, ever since the arrival of those thugs.

"So why were they looking for you?" he demanded before he could stop himself.

Angel shot a glance over his shoulder. "Not sure I wanna tell you that."

Andrew felt irritated, still bruised from his attack. "Look, cut the crap - 'cause you might as well know, I've already spoken to the police! I didn't know who my attackers were - but I'm guessing you do. Maybe I'll just pass 'em *your* details instead."

Angel shook his head. "Don't do that, man," he whimpered. "Look - I'll tell you but you gotta swear to keep it quiet. Those guys are from London - and yeah, I've landed myself in some shit…"

He steered his car into a quiet residential area. Andrew could still see his face reflected in the driver mirror - he looked scared again. It took little time to reach his flat which occupied the top floor of a converted terraced house. Angel switched off the engine.

"Bit posh, isn't it?" Andrew breathed, as they followed him upstairs.

"I like to keep a low profile," Angel shrugged, sliding a key into the door. "Most of my neighbours are commuters, so I don't actually get to meet many of 'em."

Moments later, they found themselves in a spacious lounge. It was the sort of place his parents might have chosen - tidy and minimalist; a sofa, draped with a stripy throw, two swivel armchairs and a bean bag. The one feature which seemed to dominate was a floor to ceiling unit in black ash, loaded with a state of the art stereo, TV, video, as well an impressive set of mixing decks.

"Take a seat," Angel said, flashing a smile at Lara. She looked gobsmacked. "Can I get you a beer? Got some 'Red Stripe' in the fridge."

"Great," Matt responded, crashing down onto the sofa. "I'll get a smoke together."

He fished out his tobacco tin and Rizlas. Angel looked amused - yet as time elapsed, it gradually emerged that he was no stranger to drugs. The moment they were settled, he delved into one of his cupboards and extracted a water pipe. It was similar to the ones they had seen in Shilling Walk - a glass chamber moulded from brightly coloured glass which billowed out at the base.

His chosen 'weed' appeared to be some leafy substance - it reminded Andrew of the herbs Eleanor stored in jars. A pungent, spicy fragrance was released into the lounge, fogging the atmosphere. Andrew sucked heavily from the pipe and coughed. The effects hit him almost instantly - but it was only as they became more intoxicated that Angel revealed a little about his own circumstances.

He explained how he had grown up in South London where he had earned a modest living, working at various clubs and bars - until he was ultimately seduced into drug dealing.

"The profits were massive," he confessed, gazing lovingly at his mixing decks. "How d'you think I managed to pay for those? I wanted to be a DJ!" But while drug dealing procured an enviable fortune, it incurred a risk - and this was where his true predicament began to emerge. He had been recruited by one of London's powerful drug lords. "Life was so much easier when I was operating small time. I got in deep - not supplying just anyone but the dealers themselves!"

"You're kidding!" Lara breathed, her eyes glazed from the effects of the cannabis.

"No, I ain't," Angel kept explaining, "I managed to stay out of trouble. Lucky I wasn't busted, the quantities I was shifting. It was the boss who controlled the drug gangs; my problems started when I accidentally crossed into the turf of one of them other gangs."

"And that's where those guys come in?" Andrew questioned. "They were a rival gang."

"Yup," Angel said frankly, "fuckin' racist bastards from Mill Wall. One of the brothers lived close to my gaff. I reckon they're in the National Front too, they hate black kids like me!"

He let his chin drop into his hands, planning his next words carefully, his expression guarded. "Please, don't *ever* say anything to the cops about them. They're after my blood."

"So how come you're living here?" Lara whispered in fascination.

"Boss dug me out the shit," he sighed. "Helps to have a major player in the criminal world. He made a deal. 'Get the fuck outta London and I'll put you in a town called Rosebrook, south of the border.' So here I am - duckin' and diving but still alive. I'm sorry you met them bastards. But I'll put the word out - make sure they don't give you no more bother!"

Andrew's head was spinning, trying to take it in - the flat which Angel was renting fully furnished; his aspirations to carry on working at the 'Cat's Whiskers,' as well as find some DJ work. This 'King Pin' had shifted him here to get him out of the way - as well as for his protection. He fully intended to continue a bit of drug peddling, knowing there was a whole new market just waiting to be exploited. But there was just one more question burning in Andrew's mind.

"So who is this 'King Pin' - the one who saved your arse?"

"I ain't telling you that!" Angel sputtered, rising to his feet and suddenly he couldn't meet his eye. "Seriously man, I could end up dead - worse, he could cut me up, bad!" he glanced towards the mirror on the opposite wall where his angelic face stared back at them. "I like this face…"

Andrew stared at him in horror, guessing he wasn't bluffing. He had never had dealings with the criminal underworld - yet it was a concept that scared him shitless! He had seen the fear in Angel's eyes. He possessed an air of vulnerability that stirred some deep troubling emotion; and while those thugs might not have hurt him *too* badly, it was enough. The notion of what they might do to Angel didn't bear thinking about. Andrew nodded to himself, knowing he had done the right thing.

In fact, Angel was one of the coolest people he'd ever met. He was enjoying the effects of his weed, his mind clouded with a pleasant sense of euphoria. The atmosphere was relaxed and dreamlike - his stereo system impressive with a beautiful, crystal clear sound. Angel had put on a CD where the uplifting rhythm of 'Bomb the Bass' penetrated his surroundings; the volume at low level so as not to disturb his neighbours. Andrew liked this guy, pleased he'd covered up for him.

They stayed until 2:00 in the morning by which time Andrew too, had shared his life story. "Nice smoke," he sighed, glancing at his watch. "I suppose we'd better make a move."

"It's Thai grass," Angel smiled warmly. "Here, have some..." and before Andrew could draw breath, he fished out a tin which he filled with the same green substance. "Should make up for what those fuckers took! You ever need any more, I'll get you some."

Matt caught his eye and grinned. "Brilliant," he muttered.

"You can't usually get this stuff outside London," Angel kept smiling, "but I can!"

"It's been nice, getting to know you," Lara purred, sidling up to him.

"So let's hit a club, tomorrow," Angel suggested. "You guys up for that?"

"Definitely," Andrew and Matt chorused, sensing the night had been a turning point.

III

The first time Eleanor met Angel, she wasn't entirely sure about him. He came across as charming, polite and of course no-one could ignore his flawless beauty. His adorable puppy dog eyes harboured a slightly doleful look. Although his slick mannerisms and confidence afforded him a maturity which seemed well advanced for the average 19 year old.

"Angel?" Eleanor mused, gazing at him with a mixture of admiration and suspicion. "Are you an angel? Or do I sense a little devilry?"

Angel laughed. "I ain't no saint!" he answered flippantly.

Eleanor smiled back, unsure what it was that unnerved her. A tiny warning light had started flickering, almost from the day Andrew had met him. He hailed from London; it tugged her mind back to the two menacing strangers who had appeared in the Community Centre and how strange, Angel had slipped into their lives just days after Andrew's mugging.

Yet it had to be said, Andrew possessed a certain glow. The introductions took place on the night they ventured to go clubbing at Tiffany's, Rosebrook's one and only night club; it was an evening which took Andrew right back to his 18th.

Two years down the line however, Tiffany's had gone downhill. The decor had always been a bit naff; yellow walls and bright blue leather seating which gave it the look of a cheap American diner. Those same walls were blemished with smoke stains, thinly disguised with a few dog-eared Athena posters. The furniture possessed a worn look with rips in the seating - the carpets grimy and peppered with cigarette burns. Even the music was awful. Andrew had never quite got into the new rave scene that was storming the nation - but

213

anything would have been better than the DJ's rather tired collection of UK chart toppers, which included the Pet Shop Boys, Kylie Minogue and a truly awful boy band known as Bros!

"This place is a dump, man!" Angel grunted as they departed, an hour before closing time.

The magnetic draw of his flat had never been more powerful. Angel was determined to bring his new friends up to speed with the current music scene - while showing off his DJ skills with a mind-blowing collection of underground music; rap, garage and finally the revolutionary new acid house, though Andrew was yet to be converted. Even stoned, he found it squelchy and weird. Then finally, Angel dropped the killer question.

"Perhaps you ain't taken the right drugs. You ever tried 'e?'"

"He means ecstasy," Matt grinned. "It's supposed to be wicked."

"I tried mushrooms once," Andrew mumbled, "I had a bad trip."

"You're confusing it with acid," Angel said gently. "It's not the same. This is a party drug. It just makes you wanna dance all night and have a good time..."

Andrew could remember very little else about that evening but a week later, his life was about to be transformed. They didn't bother with Tiffany's. Angel drove them up to London's West End, where they were destined to hit a club known as 'Planet-X.' Just before they went in, they had lingered on a park bench with bottles of mineral water. Angel slipped them a tiny round pill each.

"Go on then," Lara dared him.

"You first," Andrew whispered back.

"Why not, all together?" Matt suggested. "C'mon - one - two - three..."

Andrew was the only one who held back as they popped the pills into their mouths, gulping them back with water. Pricked with a sense, he was being a complete 'party pooper,' he reluctantly followed suit. The effects didn't happen immediately. They crept up twenty minutes later by which time, they were completely immersed in the club. This place was like nothing on earth; a swirling fog of dry ice, blended with the most stunning lighting effects - it presented a dreamy atmosphere in addition to the utterly stimulating acid house music. It wasn't long before Andrew found himself bouncing in time to its energetic beat - surrendering himself totally to the spiralling party scene which pulsated all around him. Everything and everyone looked beautiful and he had never felt so charged with energy in his life.

That night, Andrew lost all sense of time as Angel gently cruised back to Rosebrook. The sky was already beginning to lighten, giving way to a soft violet glow. He found himself gazing over the picturesque folds of countryside in a trance as the first golden rays of sunshine crept slowly over the horizon, draining away the shadows. An almost subliminal beat from

Angel's stereo permeated the car's interior - but nobody spoke, letting the intoxicating music wash over them while they drank in the atmosphere and the views. By the time he pulled up outside the almshouse, it was 5:00 in the morning yet strangely enough, Andrew didn't feel tired.

"That was incredible," he whispered as he slid out of the car. "That has got to be the best night of my life. I guess I'll be seeing you around then..."

"Yo!" Angel grinned, leaning out of the car window to clasp his hand, "pleased you enjoyed yourself, man - we should do it again."

It was the second week in August - a morning when Andrew seemed incapable of surfacing. Eleanor found herself in the company of the Barton-Wells kids, curious to know what their plans were. William was on the verge of getting his 'O' Level results where the new doors of opportunity were about to be thrown wide open.

"I've always wanted to join the army," he told her.

"But you're so young!" Eleanor protested. "You're not yet 17!"

It was his long term ambition - a decision they knew even James had supported.

"I don't want him to go," Avalon whispered, her eyes glistening with tears. "Oh William! Couldn't you stay at school for just a *little* longer? I never went in the 6th form. You could go on to university - join an Officer Training Corps, go straight in with a commission!"

William smiled softly. Anyone could see, she was heartbroken; the prospect of abandoning her for a life of army barracks seemed unbearable. It was too soon, given the turbulent storm of their lives - and there were other milestones to be crossed such as passing his driving test.

"This is something we've all been looking forward to," Eleanor coaxed him, "especially Eli! He loves having you around. So does Margaret. Is another 2 years really that long to wait?"

As the discussion continued, so William began to see sense. He wasn't unhappy at school. He was one of their highest achieving pupils. In truth, there was an awful lot to keep him in Rosebrook, especially their ongoing battle against the Hamptons.

"Okay," he grinned. "I'll stay - and I want to see how it goes with Peter's housing trust too."

No-one was more delighted than Elijah - thankful to hang on to his dearest friend for a few more years. There was only one more journey William was hankering to make and that was to visit his mother in America.

"I was beginning to think she'd forgotten she had a son!" he laughed. "She's just written to us. She seems to have given up trying to persuade me and Avalon to go and live with her - but a few weeks holiday would be nice. I've never been to the States."

William's flight was booked for the following week, although Avalon chose not to accompany him. It would have swallowed up all her annual holiday leave and like the others, she felt a powerful urge to stay at home, especially with another council meeting looming. As official landowner, she really needed to be present - wary of Robin's shenanigans.

She cherished the peace and quiet - at least, to begin with. Yet by the time they were creeping towards another weekend, Andrew was already enthusing about going clubbing again.

Eleanor pulled him to one side. "Why don't you invite Avalon?" she whispered. "She's all on her own, right now…"

Avalon could not deny, she was moved by his gesture - a chance to enjoy a good night out with friends. By the time the big night arrived, she was hit with a wave of excitement. She applied her makeup carefully while sipping a glass of white wine. It was a long time since she had been clubbing - also remembering Andrew's 18th.

The intense party scene at Tiffany's had dazzled her - it was the aftermath which had left her troubled; never able to forget those ugly, drunken scenes after closing time, the obscene language, the shock of being mooned at and finally, the alarming appearance of Ben Hampton. Avalon shivered. She lifted her wineglass and took a gulp, refusing to allow such dark thoughts to intrude.

She slipped into a flowing white dress which clung to her curves; her hair piled up messily, secured with a tortoiseshell spring clip - although a few wisps still managed to escape, spiralling around her neck in a way which looked sexy.

A moment later, she was alerted to the doorbell, knowing it was Andrew and his friends. Already, they seemed euphoric with smiles stretched right across their faces. Their mood was infectious and it was with no hesitation, she invited them in for a drink.

Once inside the club, however, she didn't stray far from Andrew or Matt. She too, couldn't have failed to notice the deterioration of Tiffany's. Yet there was something else. Avalon studied the crowd - some of the clientele seemed to have dressed down considerably; messy hair, torn jeans, T-shirts bearing that peculiar smiley face logo. They danced in a way which seemed odd; jolting to the music in an almost robotic fashion - glazed eyes, wild expressions glued to their faces…

What Avalon could never have known was that many of them were tripped out of their minds, from a mysterious flood of recreational drugs that had found its way into Rosebrook.

Neither was she aware of a number of plain clothes police officers milling around; searching for clues of the underground drug trade, alleged to have been peddled in the toilets. One of them was a gullible looking young man whose spiky, gelled hair gave him the appearance of a typical 18 year old. He had purchased one of these little round pills for a tenner, which he had surreptitiously dropped into his trouser pocket before slipping out of the doors, unnoticed.

The following Friday, the worst happened. At first, Andrew was oblivious to it as he toiled his usual shift at the 'Cat's Whiskers.' An excess of drugs and partying had finally taken its toll - it was betrayed in the inky shadows beneath his eyes, as well as his vacant, brooding expression. The after-effects of his last 'e' left him not only fatigued but depressed.

He glanced at Lara who was chatting up a couple of good-looking men at the bar. "So are you gonna ask her out or what?" he nagged Angel somewhat grumpily.

"All in good time," Angel smiled, "I'm besotted with someone else right now."

"Who?" Andrew couldn't resist quizzing him.

"Avalon," Angel whispered under his breath. "What a stunner, man! I got this feeling she's in need of a bit of tender loving…"

"Forget it!" Andrew snapped, "she's well out of your league!"

"Why d'you say that?" Angel protested. "I suppose you think I'm just some no good nig nog!"

Andrew slid him a withering look. "Don't you think *I've* thought about it? Her family's upper class. Something bad happened to them - their father died. Our folks have been looking out for 'em ever since, so don't fuck around with her, okay?"

Angel gave a shrug. "Okay."

Andrew clocked his crestfallen face and sighed. "She's seeing someone else, anyway."

It wasn't untrue. Just days after their clubbing venture, Avalon had started dating one of her work colleagues - a studious looking young man named Richard.

The crowds started to dwindle just before 11:00. Andrew was slipping on his denim jacket when Matt materialised in the doorway. He was moving tentatively towards the bar.

"Back to my place then, Yeh?" Angel nodded.

Andrew shook his head. "Not tonight, mate, I'm knackered…" He never got a chance to finish.

His eyes were drawn towards Matt, who seemed agitated.

It was not until they were outside, he told them why. "Have you heard?" he spluttered. "It's all kicking off at Tiffany's!"

They sped towards the club without delay. Their footsteps ground to an unexpected halt as the forbidding black building towered into view; though tonight, it was surrounded by police cars, the crowds of revellers swelling as they were evacuated from the doors. It had taken the police just one week to gather their intelligence - where various 'substances' had been analysed.

"The club's been raided!" Matt whispered excitedly.

They spotted Frank Pitman, the club's sleazy looking proprietor - grey ponytail swinging, as he fought off a pair of arresting police officers.

"They reckon he knew about it, all along!" Matt kept explaining, "but he turned a blind eye 'cos it brought in a lot of extra trade. Looks like they're arresting him..."

"Great!" Andrew muttered in fury, "I suppose that means they're gonna shut the club down!"

"We don't know that," Angel argued in a voice which seemed just a little too calm.

Andrew glowered at him in disbelief - saying nothing as the dramatic scenes kept unfurling.

"Please don't tell me, you had something to do with this!" he later accused.

Andrew had been adamant in his decision to go home, given the fatigue dragging on his mind and limbs. They wandered back in the direction of the almshouse where they had finally crashed out on the steps of the Community Centre.

"No way!" Angel protested. "This ain't got nothin' to do with me!"

Andrew's eyes narrowed, his senses sharp enough to realise how furtive his friend looked.

"You told me, you supplied the dealers," he kept accusing, "all that stuff about some 'drug lord.' And how come there's suddenly no shortage?"

"There's other dealers besides me," Angel snapped. "I told you. I came here to keep my head down and yeah, okay, I still deal - but only to my mates."

"You sure about that?" Matt pressed, aroused by Andrew's insinuations.

"Yeah, I swear!" Angel shrugged, "I said I'd get hold of anything you wanted and I will. You're my buddies, you've been good to me. I like you guys!"

Angel despised himself for lying to them yet by the time they parted company, he was assailed by an albatross of guilt. He had been honest about the drugs in Tiffany's. They genuinely *hadn't* been supplied by him - though he knew damn well who the real source was!

He closed his front door, that night and shuddered. If only they knew - except he would be a dead man. The boss had planted him here for a reason and that reason was to get to know Andrew; to infiltrate his exclusive circle of friends, where even from the first gathering, he had sussed who they bought their supplies from. One link in the chain led to another. The network kept branching; and by the end of that first week, he had figured out who the main dealers were.

All drugs originated from London and it was Angel who had guaranteed everyone a reliable new source. Provided everyone was careful, there was never likely to be a shortage. Angel had supplied names - but Levy's gang had done the rest. It was down to *their* intervention that any competition had been dealt with; before he began drip feeding his own supply into the town. Angel had no idea he was a pawn in their game, no more than the gang of skinheads. But he faced a dilemma. Now he had met Andrew and his mates, he had genuinely grown to like them. Avalon really was a stunner and so, for that matter, was Eleanor. It was a feeling which made him want to discard everything sordid in his life and unite with them; praying he wasn't putting anyone at risk as a result of his shady alliances.

Two weeks later, however, Tiffany's was closed down.

Frank Pitman might have narrowly avoided jail but he had inevitably lost his license to run a night club. On the night the police had raided Tiffany's, they had discovered ecstasy, LSD and cocaine. It left the clubbing fraternity of Rosebrook dumbfounded, with nowhere to party other than the outlying town of Bromley whilst the more adventurous headed for London.

It was also a year when the first of many illegal raves took place; a moving chain of parties hosted by various unlicensed clubs. This gradually mushroomed into a massive outdoor event which had lured revellers in their thousands.

Before the onset of autumn, William returned from America, pleased to be home and even happier to have passed his exams. He had loved spending time in the States with his mother and her new spouse but had missed his family and friends terribly. Avalon was enjoying the first flush of a new relationship yet clung to her unwavering devotion to Peter. Together they had endured one of the toughest council meetings ever where finally, Peter's housing trust was given the go ahead. The first stage of this extensive building project was scheduled to commence in the spring of 1989 - though before any foundations could be laid, deep ravines would be dug into the ground to install a new water main and gas supply.

As everyone grew more excited, so Robin continued to hover on the sidelines. There was bound to be a time when Tiffany's was placed on the market and a buyer found.

That buyer turned out to be Dominic Theakston. Whaley had been quick to leak any inside gossip, guessing that as soon as the opportunity arose, Dominic would pounce. It was a situation which couldn't have thrilled him more; Eleanor's most feared enemy had at last, established a foothold in Rosebrook.

Chapter 12

I

October 1988

Perry stared at the dossier in front of him. It wasn't much but it was a start. The notes did at least confirm that Rosemary Merriman was living in Forest Haven - the house Eleanor had inhabited in the aftermath of Jansen's murder, right up until the day Dominic had threatened her. Perry feared, this woman knew her secrets. His eyes narrowed. If only they'd possessed the foresight to deal with Eleanor once and for all.

But Alesha kept furrowing. Rosemary had been a widow for many years; a woman in her fifties who worked as a librarian, someone who liked to get herself involved in all sorts of campaigns: Friends of the Earth, Greenpeace - just the sort of hippy ideology Perry despised.

It emerged that only one of her children lived close by - a young man by the name of Luke who ran an exclusive wine shop. That left two others; a daughter who spent much of her time in America and a second son who remained even more elusive.

Apparently, he had spent many years travelling the world but had since settled back in London. All Alesha needed to do was to find out where - and hopefully glean some photos. Perry found himself gazing at a recent shot of Luke, wondering why this ruggedly handsome, dark haired man looked familiar. It filled him with a sense, they needed to do a little more digging.

In the mean time, he was delighted with Ben's accomplishments. It was down to his ties with the criminal underworld that the almshouse had finally been burgled - though what a pity there had been no trace of Eleanor's file. Perry clenched his jaw, further gratified by the news that Charles's son had been mugged; the discovery that he was a drugs user - the flood of recreational drugs which had found its way to Rosebrook, culminating in the closure of Tiffany's. Perry knew Levy's boys were behind it and as thrilled as Robin to think that Theakston was about to be the new owner.

It was a situation he would use to his advantage. Now if only there was a way he could get his claws on Eleanor's file, convinced it bore testimony that Dominic was Jake's killer. It was regrettable, Charles had been quick to change the locks - another chance to penetrate their home would have been useful. He was even wondering about having their phone bugged! How else was he going to discover where Eleanor's file was hidden - his curiosity was morphing into a phobia. He was convinced it concealed the skeletons of his crime and what else could she have reported?

Time was galloping by, where his nightmares continued to torment him. Yet even Perry had no idea of the terrible past that was about to be exhumed, a truth he had fought long and hard to bury and for which Jake Jansen had paid the ultimate price.

II

Perry had reason to be paranoid. On the same morning he was obsessing over that file, Eleanor found herself staring at a letter.

Dear Mrs Eleanor Bailey

I am in receipt of a letter from your solicitors, Sharp, Bancroft and Blackmore. Whilst it has been many years since I was involved in politics, I do of course, remember the MP, Albert Enfield, as well as the shocking event of his death.

I am more than happy to tell you a little more about his agenda. Though I cannot deny, I am curious to know the purpose of this discussion.

Please feel free to contact me via your solicitor, so we may agree a mutually convenient time to meet. I hope you understand the need for discretion.

Yours sincerely

Evelyn J. Webster

Eleanor knew what she had to do. In the first instance, she got straight on the phone to John where the first of many private conversations took place.

It was a secret she *had* to share with Charlie. He was as deeply immersed in this conspiracy as she was. It was Charlie who had sought out Albert Enfield's manifesto; Charlie who had urged her to go ahead and find this woman - alarmed, they had finally succeeded.

"Are you sure you don't want me to come with you," she remembered him whispering.

It was impossible. Eleanor gulped back her fear as she started the engine.

It was 3:30 in the morning and to her relief, the streets lay empty. No, there was no way Charlie could accompany her. Who would look after the kids? If they stayed with Peter, word would get out. Even if they did manage to slip away to Bath, there was every possibility they would be followed. Eleanor had long sensed the villains infiltrating their community - but she didn't know who they were, which left every one of them vulnerable.

So they had decided to pretend, she was ill; a particularly infectious bout of gastric flu that had confined to her bed for a few days. Even the children were forced to go along with it, but it wasn't easy. They were curious - which regrettably meant playing on their fear.

"We were burgled in July," Charlie reminded them gently. "Andrew was attacked. There's no question, we've got enemies..."

He accentuated the need to start an investigation - though Margaret needed a little more coaxing. Even Eli couldn't stress the importance of their mission highly enough; that it was essential to keep up the pretence, if they ever hoped to be safe.

Eleanor cruised the desolate streets, her mind blank - heading towards the M25 orbital road from where she would eventually join the M4 to Bath. It was crucial, no-one knew of her journey plans. If Perry picked up even the slightest hint where she was heading, he would immediately want to know who was living there. Eleanor felt her blood run cold. Even her trips to London no longer seemed so perilous - this was something different. She had no concept of what she was getting herself into where a different sense of danger loomed.

Eventually the signs to Bath began to crop up more frequently. Eleanor found herself being drawn into the Avon Valley where the enveloping wooded hills reminded her of home.

It was only now, she was beginning to feel anxious. Evelyn had been undeniably suspicious - though John's explanation was simple: Evelyn was the only political advisor they could find, who was allied to the Liberal Party - of which Enfield too, had been a member - at least, right up until the day he had switched loyalties. Eleanor was undertaking research into his assassination; curious to know why he had undergone such a massive change of heart before he had risen to power. She was curious to know why he had been targeted, yet at the same time, scared.

Eventually, Evelyn had accepted John's proposal. Eleanor would arrive at her house in the early hours, where a meeting would take place in secret.

It was 7:00 when Eleanor found her address, charmed by the sight of this beautiful Roman city with its sandy buildings stacked on many levels. She kept on climbing - until at last, she was drawn into a residential side street. She found herself gazing up at one of those distinctive stone houses in wonder. It nestled in a row, behind a series of walls, smothered in late summer flowers; the golden walls enveloped in a haze of autumnal light. There was hardly any traffic other than a milk float trawling along the road. Eleanor closed her eyes - her carefully rehearsed words running through her mind like a tape; though it was a good 30 minutes, before she wandered nervously up to the front door.

"Are you Eleanor?"

The woman who stood before her was of a small and wiry stature. She looked to be in her early 50's although her face was wreathed in lines. Eleanor imagined she must have been very beautiful in her younger days - her silver-blue eyes sparkled like gemstones and her features, though delicate in composition, suppressed a look of inconsolable sadness.

"Mrs Webster?" Eleanor smiled graciously, extending her hand.

Evelyn shook it, her touch feather light.

After the initial formalities were exchanged, Eleanor found herself being led into a spacious living room. The decor was reminiscent of Westbourne House where she had enjoyed those last heart-felt discussions with James. She felt a lump in her throat, struck with the knowledge that if he hadn't shared those secrets, she would never have ended up here. She lowered herself into one of the richly embossed settees where it didn't seem long before a discussion was underway. Evelyn offered her coffee, while a plate of home-made short bread rested on the table top. It seemed, she did not want to delay matters - inquisitive to know where Eleanor's curiosity lay.

"Why now? It's been sixteen years since Albert Enfield's murder!"

Eleanor stared into her eyes. "I'm not going to lie to you," she sighed. "I singled you out for a reason. You see, I'm not just doing this for myself - I lost someone very special..." It was with a nervous swallow, she dipped into her handbag. She had brought along some of her news clippings, as well as Jake's photo. "He lost his life because of this conspiracy."

She passed Evelyn the photo, watching her face as she studied it.

"What a very handsome young man," she mused. "Your boyfriend?"

"Yes," Eleanor smiled, "and we had a child. Jake was a very talented musician. His band, Free Spirit, was hired to play at Albert Enfield's birthday party."

She saw the twinkle vanish from Evelyn's eyes. "What happened?" she murmured numbly.

"Jake was murdered," Eleanor replied and it was with little hesitation, she passed her the article from NME.

It took several minutes for Evelyn to digest the information. Eleanor could already detect the underlying tension that was beginning to bite the atmosphere.

"Did he witness the explosion?"

"Yes," Eleanor stated factually.

Evelyn's face turned white. There was no mistaking what must have been trickling through her mind; Eleanor knew she needed to exercise discretion.

"I know it was reported as an IRA attack," she continued in the same neutral tone, "and I'll explain a little more about Jake's death in a moment. But is it possible you could tell me about Albert? I mean - why would anyone want to kill him? What was the nature of his politics?"

Evelyn passed the article back to Eleanor, her eyes glazed - she seemed lost in another world.

"Albert wanted to establish more equality. He spoke of improving education - get rid of the public school system. He held nothing but contempt towards a society which favoured those who hailed from elitist establishments like Eton - and do you know why?"

"Go on," Eleanor frowned.

A flicker of sadness passed across Evelyn's face. "Albert's only son went to a private school and he died in a tragic accident. There was a time when Albert was allied to the Liberal Party. He and his wife were members. They sent their son to an exclusive private school for many reasons. They didn't want him brought up by a succession of nannies - and they wanted him to receive a *good* education." Her eyes never left Eleanor's. "Even I questioned the morality of sending away someone so young - he was such a sweet little boy."

"How did he die?" Eleanor gasped.

"This is the question," Evelyn sighed. "The school were very cagey. He was found dead at the base of the school chapel. It's alleged, he fell from the top of a bell tower. Then gradually, it began to emerge that his death may have been suicide."

Eleanor shook her head, assailed by the sheer horror of it.

"Hard to imagine isn't it?" Evelyn added, "but then it came to light that Michael was being bullied, not physically, but psychologically - systematically terrified out of his wits! Even more outrageous, is the way the school tried to cover it all up!" She broke off with a shudder, reaching for her coffee. "Yet Albert wanted no secrets. The boy responsible *was* expelled but Albert started probing deep into his family history and he didn't like what he discovered! Anyway… I'm digressing. The fact is, Albert developed an intense loathing for the public school system and that's the reason he drifted over to the hard left. He was determined to fight the injustice of losing his only son."

"Jake and I had a son," Eleanor murmured. "I couldn't bear it if anything happened to him. So may I ask you another question - do you believe Albert was killed by the IRA?"

Evelyn froze. "It was quite typical of an attack the IRA might have carried out…"

"But no-one knew for sure did they?" Eleanor butted in. "Was there anyone else who might have been threatened by his politics?"

Evelyn stared back at her in horror - she couldn't speak. The room was choked with tension, prompting Eleanor to shuffle a little further along the settee. She was already sifting through her news clippings again.

"Jake didn't believe it was the IRA," Eleanor told her gently. "Do you want me to tell you what happened to him?"

"I think you better had," Evelyn said, paralysed in her chair; and it was over the next half hour, she absorbed the first half of Eleanor's story.

She chose her words carefully, omitting all mention of the blonde man to begin with. She instead concentrated on every other aspect of Jake's story - from the moment he had witnessed the car bomb explosion.

"Someone wanted Jake dead," she finished with a shudder. "Not just the criminal gang - but people at the top; people who pretended to help us and then betrayed us, not to mention the police inspector! It was a very carefully planned assassination and of course, they got him in the end..." a tear rolled down her cheek.

Evelyn touched her hand in sympathy. "I'm sorry, my dear," she whispered, "and you were pregnant. How dreadful. Yet you haven't told me what Jake witnessed."

"I was coming to that," Eleanor said huskily. She took a piece of shortbread, feeling suddenly giddy.

"Just tell me, Eleanor," Evelyn urged in a tone which seemed almost fatalistic.

Eleanor nodded. She bit into the shortbread, turning the words carefully over in her mind.

"Okay," she began. "I'm going to tell you what Jake told me. About half way through Albert's party, he slipped away to collect something from their van. It wasn't parked at the back of the hotel with all the other cars but on the road. He saw a man lurking about by the minibus; another man, wearing overalls, lying underneath who he couldn't quite distinguish. But the first man, he remembered clearly. Smart, stockily built with blonde hair - driving a black Daimler."

Her heart pounded as she spoke; Evelyn let out a sob. Her hands started shaking as she clung to her coffee cup. Eleanor plucked it gently from her hands and placed it on the table.

"You know who that man was don't you?" she whispered.

"Oh my God," Evelyn whimpered. She looked distraught - compelling Eleanor to rise.

She lowered a comforting hand on her shoulder. "Don't cry, Evelyn, please. I didn't come here to upset you. There's something else, see. You knew James Barton-Wells didn't you? You stayed at Westbourne House..."

"He told you, didn't he?" Evelyn's gasped, her voice wobbling.

"Yes," Eleanor sighed, "and this is where the story gets interesting. You see - I too, have a pretty good idea who this man is. I came face to face with him."

"Stop it!" Evelyn gasped, twisting her head away. "I can't bear it!"

"Evelyn, please..." Eleanor begged. Anyone could see, she was rapidly sinking into denial. It was out of sheer desperation, Eleanor snatched the photocopied sheet from James's diary before pushing it into her hand. "Just read what he wrote."

Evelyn stared at the sheet in panic, unable to ward off the quiver of her hands. *Evelyn described this gentleman she bumped into, known as 'Perry' and in a service station in Surrey...*' Eleanor's heart sank - fearing her reaction.

"I'm sorry," she heard herself whispering. "I just wanted to know if it was true."

III

Evelyn had momentarily left the room, filling Eleanor with a sense, she was walking across a forest of egg shells. The silence hung heavily, drawing her attention to the ticking clock. Yes, it was ticking away like a time bomb. In a few minutes, Evelyn would return - probably order her to leave and her mission would have been for nothing, leaving the trail well and truly cold.

By the time she wandered back into the living room however, she seemed much calmer. Eleanor studied her delicate features; the gentle, lined face, framed by wavy hair cut in the shorter style of a mature woman - hair that had once been dark and luxurious, now feathered with grey.

"I should have gone to the police," Evelyn began - her voice conveyed a dreamlike quality, "but you never knew him, Eleanor..."

Evelyn closed her eyes. She was imagining a small service station, just to the south of Dorking. She was paying for her petrol. It was a beautiful day. The sun shone down warmly, illuminating everything in its path - the shiny, black bonnet of a car which had just pulled up, where several flashes were reflected in the polished chrome bumper. She squinted, recognising the car - watching as a young man in overalls jumped out of the back. He gave the driver a nod which could only have been perceived as gratitude - then disappeared into a phone box. Evelyn was smiling, her eyes drawn to the driver. What in the world was that old devil doing out here?

"Perry?"

She had wandered back towards the pumps. His thick blonde hair gleamed like gold in the powerful sun rays. He whirled round suddenly, his face crimson. His light grey eyes emitted an unusual flare before a wolfish smile spread slowly across his face.

"What on earth are you doing out here in the sticks?" Evelyn laughed. They clasped hands. He was still smiling, albeit a little furtively. "Don't you live in London?"

"Don't say you saw me, please," Perry begged, his grip on her hands tightening. "Rowena mustn't know I was here - if you must know, i-it's because of Lavinia!"

"You're still seeing her?"

Evelyn had known Perry was embroiled in an affair. God only knew, there had been enough whispers in the corridors of Westminster. Perry was political advisor to the Rt. Hon. Lord Carrington, Secretary of State for Defence. He was also a regular spectator and lobbyist in the House of Commons and yet she had known him since their university days; never able to forget their own passionate romance. Even now, she felt her affection soar - she had never known anyone so charismatic and powerful.

"Who was that man?" she quizzed, her eyes swivelling towards the phone box. The man was no-where to be seen any more - he seemed to have disappeared without a trace.

"Oh, him!" Perry drawled dismissively. "No-one! Just some hitchhiker - I felt sorry for him!" he started filling his car with petrol - only a couple of gallons, she noticed. He rammed the petrol nozzle back into the holster with unexpected force.

"That's not like you…" Evelyn started to say, but he cut her off abruptly.

"Just leave it, Evelyn! I told you, he was a hitchhiker - now if you don't mind, it's been a long day. It's lovely to see you and we'll catch up again soon. Sorry, but I have to get back!"

She watched in disbelief as he turned and marched to the pay booth - recognising the dismissal and with no choice than to leave him in peace before making her way back to Dorking.

"That very same day, the story was on the news," Evelyn shivered. Her pallor had returned. She was clearly wracked with torment. "Even I didn't realise the connection - until the stories started filtering through the press. Finally, they named the village where the explosion took place!"

"Was it this story?" Eleanor added, holding up another one of her news clippings.

Evelyn glanced briefly at the headline and nodded. "Basil and I went to Westbourne House, shortly after. It was our wedding anniversary…"

James had been horrified. *"Didn't you ought to mention this to the police?"*

"I can't!" she remembered spluttering. "Perry's a friend! Apparently, he was out visiting his mistress, that day, he begged me not to say anything."

"I was talking about the hitch hiker. Don't you think this sounds a little suspicious? What if this 'person' had something to do with that car bomb?"

She remembered feeling a stab of alarm.

"I spoke to Perry the following week," she mumbled miserably. She twisted her hands together as she recalled the encounter - it was a memory that would haunt her forever.

"I take it you've heard the news," she began numbly.

They were back in Westminster.

An eerie sense of shock thickened the atmosphere; a whole nation reeling in horror as the fate of a man, who might have been the next Prime Minister, continued to rock the headlines.

"However much you despised him, Perry, he was a good man - but there's something I need to ask you. That man - the one I saw getting out of your car! Shouldn't you talk to the police?"

"I told you - he was a hitchhiker," Perry snapped.

"Yes, so you said," Evelyn argued, "but surely you remember what he looked like! This could be a vital lead..." she broke off, recognising the loathing that flickered in his eyes.

Perry closed the door. Before Evelyn could grasp what was happening, he turned the key in the lock. The next time he faced her, his face was suffused with anger.

"Shut up!" he whispered. "Don't say another word, Evelyn. If I go to the police, they are bound to want to know what I was doing in the area! I urged you to stay silent!"

"Oh no," Evelyn whispered, "you - you c-couldn't have... please don't tell me you had anything to do with this..." she released a sob, unable to prevent herself from backing away.

"Don't be bloody ridiculous!" Perry thundered.

"God only knows, you had an incentive!" Evelyn gasped back.

"What - and end up in jail? Even Enfield wasn't worth that risk!"

"If you have nothing to hide, then tell the police about that hitchhiker," she tried to reason with him, "because if you don't, I will!"

Perry wasted no time. He knew he had her trapped. Taking no chances, he marched right up to her, grasping the tops of her arms. She released a cry of fear.

"I will not put my marriage on the line because of that Communist bastard! Don't you think he's cost me enough?"

"I don't believe I'm hearing this," Evelyn sobbed, "six people were killed by that bomb..."

He pressed her hard against the wall. She could feel the force of his rage like flames from a furnace. For a second, she feared he was going to hit her.

"Six people who threatened to destroy this country with their revolting left wing politics," Perry continued to rant. "Did it never occur to you that there were others who wanted rid of Enfield?"

"You're insane," Evelyn breathed, twisting her head away, "let go of me!"

"Not until I can guarantee your silence," Perry said nastily, "because I swear, if you say one word about this to anyone - well - I'm afraid I might have to mention that massive tax fraud your husband pulled off so successfully."

Evelyn was beginning to feel giddy - the room swum with stars.

"He could have joined me in my investment in the nuclear industry," Perry smiled, "but he chose not to. Yet how much profit did he make from the sale of his north sea oil shares, I wonder? A fortune! So be careful what you say, Evelyn. Because if my marriage suffers, I'll see to it that yours does too - and it will be Basil who pays the ultimate price..."

Evelyn was forced to swallow the lie.

It was after all, claimed to be the IRA who were responsible for that car bomb. From that day onwards, she felt no further need to suspect Perry - at least, not until now.

Eleanor turned cold as Evelyn spilled out her story. She had come here looking for answers but never in her mind, imagined anything like this.

"I'm sorry," she kept on spluttering. "He would have ruined him! 5 years in jail, I couldn't bear it. I know I should have gone to the police and if I had, your Jake might not have died needlessly. But he was so evil! He swore he would make every member of my family suffer if *ever* I breathed a word that I saw him - and this is why I kept my silence!"

"I don't know what to say," Eleanor whispered in horror. Her hand drifted towards Jake's pendant, the memories resonating like a pulse. *So the man he saw, was definitely Perry!*

"So how did *you* meet him?" Evelyn's voice challenged, interrupting her reverie.

"At a press conference," Eleanor murmured. "You saw the cuttings. The stories about Jake's death were a complete cover up - people wanted answers."

It didn't take long to relate the dramatic night at the Grosvenor Hotel.

She had only very briefly mentioned her secret file. Yet by the time she had finished, there was a hardness to Evelyn's features.

"I'm glad you saw him," she said painfully, "were you not curious to know who he was?"

"Of course!" Eleanor gasped, "but it's like I said - there were others..." she squeezed her eyes shut, as tears sprung to the surface. It was with some difficulty, she divulged the final part of her story. "They sent the gang leader after me. He threatened me - warned me never to take on Jake's killers or they would snatch our baby boy. Even to this day, I'm still frightened!"

From the other side of the sofa, Evelyn looked horrified. "So what now?" she shivered.

Eleanor gazed at her and sighed. "I don't know. It sounds as if you're in as much danger as I am. But there is something you could explain. Why did Perry hate Albert Enfield so much?"

"Would it help your case if I told you?"

"I need to know if he had a motive," Eleanor persisted. "You see, to disagree with a man's politics is one thing - but to arrange his murder... there must have been something else."

"Oh, there was," Evelyn nodded. She pulled the collar of her cardigan tightly around her throat, as if to ward off a sudden chill - and then she started speaking again.

"It began in 1971," Evelyn continued darkly, "the same year Albert's son, Michael, was killed. It was feared, another pupil may have been responsible for his death," She looked at Eleanor with dread. "A pupil by the name of

229

Ben Hampton."

"No!" Eleanor gasped - a vision of Ben's face flickered briefly.

"There should have been an enquiry but there wasn't. The school did everything possible to cover it up. They were more concerned about protecting their reputation - though Albert suspected something more sinister; the Hamptons were a wealthy family which gave them certain powers."

Eleanor stared at her in disbelief, unsure how to react to that statement.

"The truth came out when Albert started talking to Michael's friends," Evelyn continued. "It was obvious he would challenge Perry at some point - and he did. Ben might have been expelled, but for Albert, it wasn't enough. He believed Perry's son to be dangerous and urged him to have him medically assessed. Even in the early 70s, people knew was a sociopath was..."

Eleanor had turned cold. Even *she* recognised the sinister undertones hidden in her voice.

"But Perry refused!" Evelyn sighed. "Albert had long recognised the hierarchy that governed the public school system; his family were regarded as no more than mediocre, middle class citizens. Whilst Perry, with his wealth and his allegiance to the elite, was held in higher esteem. Albert developed a deep loathing of such pecking orders and that's when his politics changed. He wanted justice for Michael, so he did a little digging. He probed deep into the Hamptons' medical records and he must have found something contentious!"

"Do you know what it was?" Eleanor queried, gripping the cushions of the sofa.

Evelyn shook her head. "Whatever it was, Albert threatened to expose it *unless* Perry stepped down from government. Albert swore that if ever a day came when Perry became an MP, he would tell the world what he knew about his family." She gave a mirthless smile. "Perry withdrew from the political front line and settled for a job as an advisor. He never stood for election again."

"Albert was blackmailing him?" Eleanor frowned.

"Yes - it was his dream to be an MP. Albert took that away from him."

"So what about Ben?" Eleanor shuddered. "I don't suppose anything ever *was* done! He grew up just like any other child and developed into a particularly nasty adult!"

"You know him?" Evelyn frowned.

"Oh yes," Eleanor whispered, "but please - finish your story. I need to understand what drove Perry into carrying out this atrocity."

"Perry despised Albert. We both attended Westminster, so it was impossible not to come into contact. Perry kept his loathing secret - b-but he confided in me at times. It was difficult."

Even Eleanor sensed her dilemma; allied to the Liberal Party of which Albert had formerly been a member - yet her relationship with Perry went deeper. They had known each other at University where they had been lovers. In fact, they had been close right up until the day Evelyn had bumped into him at that service station. No-one could fail to register the agony in her voice, given the horrible way their friendship had ended.

"Albert rose to power," she mumbled. "He clawed his way to the top and was unanimously accepted as leader of the Labour Party. It looked for all the world as if he would sweep the board at the next election. So Perry's hatred intensified. As if being denied the chance to be an MP wasn't enough - yet to see his rival rise to power... it was unbearable! He started a smear campaign."

"A smear campaign," Eleanor echoed, "that's more or less what James implied."

Every thread of communication was starting to come back: *We were led to believe that this man was about to start a revolution!'* Even Bernard had hypothesised that those in authority feared Enfield to be a socialist. The facts were finally coming together - fusing into a chilling truth.

"So those rumours," she continued, "they were started by Perry?"

"Yes," Evelyn confirmed, "and people started to believe them! Waves of fear were spreading across the nation - yet somehow, he rose above the rumours. He produced his own manifesto."

"I saw it," Eleanor mumbled, "my husband managed to get a copy."

"But in 1972 Albert discovered the source of the rumours - Perry started to panic…"

Evelyn lowered her eyes as the final piece of the jigsaw snapped into place.

Perry's face had been ghostly pale - devoid of its usual florid flush. *'He's going to ruin me, Evelyn! I'm finished!"*

"Then for God's sake make amends!" Evelyn had whispered. "It's not too late to have your boy assessed. Surely, they wouldn't lock him away in an asylum at his age!"

Perry was shaking his head, his hands balling into fists. "This isn't about Ben, this is about me!" he seethed. "I've been investing heavily in the nuclear industry. It's a growth industry. I tried to explain this to your husband but he wouldn't touch it with a barge pole!"

"Nuclear power?" Evelyn challenged him in her innocence.

"Nuclear weapons," Perry finished coldly. "Enfield's discovered my role in a private consortium; they're investing in a company who are developing a new, deadly first strike missile!"

Evelyn stared at him in disbelief, unable to make sense of it. "But why?"

Perry shrugged, the obsessive flare in his eyes growing. "Why not? At the end of the day, it would solve this country's problems - give us a profound edge over the Russians and generate more cash for the economy! I've always believed in a powerful defence strategy!"

"And Albert believes in unilateral disarmament."

"Albert is a supporter of the *Non-Proliferation Treaty*," Perry finished, "whose aim is to *halt* the spread of nuclear weapons and now he has prepared a press release..." He shook his head, his face darkening. "He intends to destroy my credibility once and for all."

She could still hear the echo of those fatal words.

"I've never before said this," she finished sadly, "but thank God, Perry never went into politics. Albert was right, the man was a megalomaniac - and that, my dear, is the reason Perry must have wanted him dead."

IV

They had been talking for nearly 3 hours by which time Eleanor was encumbered by such tiredness, it was impossible to take any more in. She had almost forgotten she had departed in the dead of night and driven until dawn to get here. It was Evelyn who insisted she should take a rest before guiding her upstairs to a cosy spare bedroom.

At the same time, Evelyn was driven by an all consuming impulse; all the while the flames of their startling dialogue were still burning, she decided to jot some of it down. At the very least, it would give Eleanor substance to add to her 'secret file' which they had only briefly touched upon.

From the moment Eleanor felt sufficiently rested, Evelyn insisted they took a stroll; a chance to show off the elegance of Bath and grab some fresh air. They proceeded towards the centre, passing row after terraced row of golden stone buildings. Eventually they wandered into Royal Crescent, one of Bath's landmarks - a semi-circle of townhouses arranged in a sweeping curve around an expansive lawn. Eleanor found herself drinking in its palatial splendour before Evelyn drew her a little further downhill to a secluded park.

"Royal Victoria Park," she enlightened her. "Would you care to sit down?"

The sprawling lawns dotted with mature trees reminded her of the park in Poplar. Already the leaves had turned autumnal where many had fallen, gathering on the ground in soft, crispy piles. They kept walking, following the winding path which led them to a park bench - and all the while, the conversation kept flowing as Eleanor began to tell her about her file.

"I didn't want Jake to be forgotten," she mused. "I was driven by an urge to write his story and I made sure *they* knew about it; if I ended up dead, like Jake, that file would go public!" She gave a sigh, reflecting the years the file had lay dormant.

It inevitably drew her thoughts to the era of James's fight to save Westbourne House. It was hard to convey the menace that had been infused into their world - the warnings from Charlie - the stalking, which was yet another branch of their ploy to seize James's property.

"Charlie always said that son of his was evil," Eleanor shivered, "and eventually, they turned up at the house..." she breathed deeply, her heart thudding. It was the first time she'd come into contact with Perry in 13 years, having recognised him instantly.

"From the press conference," Evelyn stated grimly.

Eleanor nodded. "He recognised me too - he warned me never to *cross him*." There was no stopping her now as the stories kept tumbling; the concentrated and ruthless acquisition which had ended with James's death. The only mercy Perry had ever shown, was to allow his children to stay for a few more months. "Even that ended horribly!" Eleanor whispered. "Perry sent his son to evict them..." she broke off, sparing Evelyn the details.

"Poor James!" Evelyn sniffed. "He was such a wonderful man. It is to my eternal regret, I never saw him again after that fateful evening. Basil and I moved abroad. Neither of us relished having to live under the shadow of Perry's threat. We're divorced now."

"I'm sorry," Eleanor whispered.

She closed her eyes, feeling the cold air prick her cheeks; *the shadow of Perry's threat...* It was only now, she was compelled to express the fearful reality of their own lives - finally understanding the scourge of his evil. There was not a single family member who had not been touched by it - from the burglary, to the terror of Andrew's mugging.

"He has got to be stopped," Eleanor finished boldly. "It's a pledge we made at our wedding. The reason I've been gathering all this evidence and even that carries a terrible risk."

"Be careful, Eleanor," Evelyn warned. "Perry is a very dangerous man. He finds ways of manipulating people. He did after all, find a way of making sure I kept my silence..." They had started walking again, aware of the sun dipping behind the trees as the encroaching shadows drew a bitter coldness to the air. "...I will never forget some hapless young councillor he had at his disposal - lovely looking man who Perry cherry-picked from university."

"Go on," Eleanor urged her.

"Poor boy was abused by his English teacher," Evelyn whispered, "it was a terrible scandal." She shook her head. "It's often said 'the abused can turn into an abuser.' Years later, I picked up rumours of this man's own *liaisons* with a number of teenage, male prostitutes. Even I could see, he had been seduced by power; by Perry - he promised to pave his path into politics but expected favours. I'm sure he was allied to him during his conquest to destroy Albert. Perry had the power to help this young man - yet at the same time, destroy him."

Eleanor felt a shiver of cold which had nothing to do with the air temperature - the man to whom she referred could be no other than Robin Whaley!

"Did he have a role in Albert's killing?" She muttered, thinking out loud.

"We'll never know, will we?" Evelyn sighed.

There was no question he had played a role in Jake's. It was only now, she started thinking about Robin - wondering if his soul was so corrupt, he would have been the *perfect* candidate for doing Perry's bidding. She had already guessed he was the co-ordinator of Jake's murder - a shadowy figure who had always been one step ahead of them. Even Rosemary sensed there was something inherently evil about him.

"Are you alright, my dear?" Evelyn piped up. "You seem preoccupied."

"I'm fine," Eleanor smiled, "I-I was just wondering if you could recommend a guest house."

Evelyn looped her arm through hers. "There's no need. Stay at my house! I have only just met you and there is so much more I want to talk to you about."

She brought a small overnight bag on the off-chance she would be spending the night here. It was a little later, they went out for dinner. Evelyn chose a tiny restaurant where the candle-lit tables dispensed a pleasing atmosphere; and although they spoke no more of their secrets whilst dining, they never ran out of conversation. Eleanor found herself recounting her son's inspired design for the Community Centre - their fight for the land and ultimately, Peter's housing trust.

It was only when they were nestled in the sanctuary of Evelyn's home again, the ugly subject of Perry loomed. "This file..." Evelyn probed, pouring them each a glass of Bailey's Irish Cream. "How much evidence have you collected and to what extent do you think you can use it?"

She was of course, referring to Jake's murder - where up until 1986, her file had only contained her own story, substantiated by a few news clippings.

"As soon as I recognised Perry, I added *his* name," Eleanor elaborated. "James gave me a copy of his diary." She swallowed, thinking about the other material. "I have a copy of Albert's manifesto and I'm trying to get a report from Scotland Yard - the details of Jake's murder..."

"But what are you actually planning to do?" Evelyn frowned.

Eleanor's expression turned steely. "We have *got to* reopen Jake's murder case but only if we can prove that Perry was behind it. That in itself could be tricky. We have to consider the other men involved. Robin Whaley. The police officer, Norman Hargreeves. There is only one man I'm worried about and that is the contract killer..." Even as she said it, she felt the coils of fear tightening. She had sworn never to mention Theakston's name - yet how could she not? His confession had thrown her into a minefield of uncertainty.

"Maybe you should talk to him," Evelyn suggested boldly, "is it not possible, he could verify that Perry hired his gang for the killing."

"I'm not so sure I can do that," Eleanor whimpered. "He frightened me very badly when I was a teenager and that fear has never gone away."

She stayed for one more day, where they embarked on another stroll around the city and took lunch in one of its many fine restaurants. Eventually, Eleanor left at midnight - filled with a sense, she had intruded on this woman's life for long enough. But it was just before she departed, Evelyn presented her with her own carefully typed manuscript; from the death of Albert's son, to the day she had confronted Perry in Westminster. And although she was putting herself at terrible risk, she reaffirmed her account of the day she had bumped into him, plagued by the notion, Jake's death had been organised to keep his testimony out of the news. It was as James had said all along - she would have made her own deductions.

"So Perry never did go back into politics," Eleanor frowned as they hovered in the doorway. "You'd think that once Albert was out of the way, he'd be hankering to get into Parliament."

"You would, wouldn't you! But something else happened - oh, the irony!"

"What are you talking about?" Eleanor whispered.

Evelyn smiled, despite the deep evil she had exposed in this man. "The press conference. Jake didn't die needlessly. He told you what he witnessed and eventually you came face to face with the man yourself. You made the connection!"

"But I didn't know who he was," Eleanor argued, "I told you - they threatened me!"

"Yes, but imagine if Perry *had* become a public figure!" Evelyn breathed excitedly. "Imagine his face in the newspapers and on TV... how long, before you *would have* identified him? Eleanor dear, it wasn't just Albert who kept Perry out of the political arena. It was you!"

IV

Hilary was humming softly to herself as she parked her car. She made her way towards the impressive entrance of Westbourne House as if floating on a cloud. Rowena had agreed to her request to leave some charity leaflets in reception. Even more wonderful was the proposal of a fund raising garden party in the grounds, next summer. Her heart fluttered as she tentatively pushed open the door. It was a very long time since she had felt this excited.

With the onset of autumn, the hotel seemed quiet. She hovered nervously by the door, then tip-toed up to the reception desk. It wasn't long before she became aware of an encroaching presence as Perry sidled up to the desk.

"Hilary," he breathed, "what an absolute pleasure." He leaned in to peck her cheek - the subtle fragrance of his aftershave instantly evoking memories of their evening here.

"Perry!" she smiled up at him. "How are things?"

It was with a furtive flick of the head, he ushered her into the restaurant. "First, I cannot thank you enough for enlightening me about Eleanor's disguise," he whispered.

"Did you find out what she was up to?" Hilary frowned. "Was she looking for her father?"

235

Perry smiled coldly. "Oh no. She was visiting someone of far greater significance."

"Go on!" Hilary pressed.

"People who pose as much danger as she does," Perry continued. "Anarchists; the family who originally moved her into that caravan and no doubt, encouraged all those other hippies. But I'm digressing. How is your delightful daughter? Holly, isn't it - such a pretty girl..."

Hilary swelled with pleasure. "Oh thank you! And she's got fleets of admirers. Do you know, even that *Elijah Jansen* asked her out?"

Perry paused, his gaze wandering towards the window - and if Hilary had been studying him more carefully, she would have clocked the cunning glitter in his eye.

"Did he now?" he muttered, "so are they an item?"

"Of course not!" Hilary sniffed. "My Holly could do far better!"

"Oh, come now," Perry smiled, curling an affectionate arm around her shoulder. "You can't discourage young love. He'll probably be the first of many boyfriends..."

She could never have known what Perry was *really* thinking - imagining the Jansen boy, swept up in a romantic fantasy world. What if they fell in love? Secret dates, walks in intimate locations, where his long term ambition to snatch this boy was creeping steadily back into his mind.

"Are you saying I should agree to this?" Hilary frowned.

"Why not?" Perry smiled. He gazed deep into her eyes. "What harm can it do?"

"We'll see," she sighed. She found herself following his gaze towards the window where the lawns rolled into the distance, fading, merging into a floating wall of mist. "Speaking of whom, I haven't seen Eleanor, all week..."

Perry snapped to a standstill. "What did you say?"

Hilary shrugged, oblivious to his changing mood. "She hasn't been seen in the Community Centre for days! I asked Emily, the old lady who runs the tea bar. She's not well, apparently."

"So, what's wrong with her?" Perry demanded, his posture stiffening. "Can you find out?"

Hilary faltered, unable to answer. She stared at him in disbelief. "What, call in on her? Won't that seem suspicious? She might think I'm spying on her."

"So, ask your daughter," Perry pressed, "she's Margaret's friend! The fact is, if Eleanor has been absent for a couple of days, I suspect she's up to something..."

"Oh for God's sake, what are you blathering on about?" Rowena's voice shot from behind them.

Perry spun round. "Rowena!" he announced, forcing another smile.

"If the girl is unwell, just leave it!" Rowena sighed. "Hilary has driven over to discuss other matters. Now if you don't mind, perhaps we can talk about this later?"

"Very well," Perry finished coolly, dragging himself away.

The moment he was gone, Rowena turned to Hilary. The restaurant was not yet open, despite the sounds of activity resonating from the kitchen. She offered her a chair.

"I apologise for my husband's behaviour," she sighed. "This whole business with Eleanor Bailey is turning into an obsession and made so much worse by his nightmares."

"Nightmares?" Hilary echoed.

"I shouldn't say this," Rowena whispered, "but shortly after we moved here, he wasn't well. He suffered a heart seizure. He thinks the place is haunted - a fear made *so* much worse by this awful sense of persecution..."

Hilary's eyes widened. "And this is down to Eleanor?"

"My husband blames Eleanor for a lot of things," Rowena sighed, "the truth is, I'm worried about him!" she touched her arm. "Do you know of anyone who could help him?"

"Peter Summerville," Hilary answered frankly. "He knows how to help people overcome *emotional* issues. The situation might be a little delicate, but why don't I talk to him? I'll be discreet. I don't have to mention Perry by name..."

"You're very kind," Rowena smiled, "and I'm sorry to burden you - now let's have a look at these leaflets!"

By the time Hilary left, she was buzzing, filled with a sense that she was turning into some sort of saviour; not only furnishing Perry with gossip, but Rowena had confided in her!

It was only a little later that Holly called round to see Margaret. For some reason, her mother seemed insistent in checking if Eleanor was at home. Yet Eleanor no longer needed to keep up the pretence. She was exhausted - eyes heavy from lack of sleep as she appeared at the foot of the stairs in a pink towelling dressing gown. She wore no makeup, her hair a tangled mess. Holly took one look at her sallow face, the dark shadows under her eyes and gasped.

"Was there something you wanted, Holly?" Eleanor murmured sleepily.

"Er - M-mummy wanted to send her 'get well' wishes," Holly stammered back, "a-and would you say to Eli - that I-I'd love to go out with him. Is it okay if I phone him a bit later?"

"I'm sure he'll be delighted," Eleanor smiled and without another word, she turned and shuffled back to bed.

Chapter 13

I

Several days later, Eleanor's mind was still spinning. Never in her life had she imagined Evelyn would be so candid; her manuscript practically smouldering as it rested in her file.

It was a truth she shared with Charlie - though she couldn't resist drawing Elijah into her confidence, if only to disclose a few fragments. It was over the course of an afternoon, she had gathered them together in secret. Margaret was at a school concert with Holly. Elijah should have been there too - barely able to keep the smile off his face since the day Holly had agreed to go out with him; yet unwilling to turn down the opportunity to delve so deep into this conspiracy.

"So Perry was definitely the man my father saw?" he whispered in bewilderment.

Eleanor nodded. He certainly had a motive. The fact was, her file concealed Perry's darkest secrets - filling her with an all consuming urge to hide it. These thoughts came to her as she carefully returned the manuscript to its folder. She lowered it into the secure metal box with all her other notes where it was ultimately protected by a combination lock.

"You're worried we might be burgled again, aren't you?" Charlie sighed.

"Well, aren't you?" Eleanor whispered. "It's not safe here, Charlie. We have got to bury it somewhere secret." She closed her eyes, having never forgotten the image of Jake's half submerged memorial stone. It had been a sign - as if his very soul had reached out and touched her.

Elijah had tentatively suggested burying it in the forests surrounding Westbourne House; but in the end, Charlie had an even better idea.

"Perhaps we could bury it underneath your caravan!"

Finally her face shed its anxiety. Joshua and Lucy were currently touring the West Country and due to return before the end of the month. Rosemary would have a pretty good idea when. It would provide a perfect opportunity for a rendezvous. Eleanor was all too aware how vital it was to deliver this latest material to her solicitor; a task either Luke or Rosemary would be honoured to fulfil, just as long as they were careful.

Later that night, Charlie cast a tender smile and moving towards her, seized her hands. No-one could have been more excited than he was. He was already contemplating the future, perhaps wondering if they had enough material to begin court proceedings.

But only one thing held her back.

It was only now she realised, there were many reasons to see John, other than to deposit Evelyn's testimony. They needed to discuss it - find a lawyer, find Hargreeves and chase up the police report. Eleanor blinked again where one more face rose up to haunt her - Theakston. She felt the onset of a shudder.

"Right - I'm well up for this if you are!" Andrew grinned at Angel.

It was a typical Saturday. No-one could have failed to notice the recent signs of building activity around Tiffany's. The club was clearly being revamped for a grand re-opening, leaving Angel hankering for a shot at becoming one of their DJs. Andrew had already been warned about the owner though - who according to his father, was renowned for being a hard bastard.

It was for this reason, they had invited Avalon round. She lingered in the lounge of the almshouse, a vision of modern-day loveliness in tight black jeans tucked into suede boots. Her tailored jacket clung to her figure, drawing attention to her waist and curving hips. No-one seemed to take much notice of Elijah who was lounging, feet up on the sofa, reading the latest issue of NME. He too, couldn't resist sneaking a few admiring glances over the tops of the pages.

Angel flashed his most engaging smile. "You happy to come along, Babe?" he simpered.

"Yeah, Dad said you already met this guy," Andrew elaborated

"What guy?" Avalon frowned.

"Theakston," Andrew announced naively.

A look of intense curiosity swept across her face as she caught Elijah's eye. He put down his magazine and stared at her. *Theakston.* Avalon gave a secretive smile.

"Okay, so let's all go? Eli too. You know - strength in numbers..."

Andrew paused. For a moment he looked as if he was about to protest - but with a casual shrug, he grabbed his coat and his keys and marched towards the door.

Moments later, they were threading their way through town, to where the night club lurked on the corner of a back street. At first glance, it resembled the same towering building; solid, rusticated walls painted black as coal. Though on closer examination, it appeared to have been fitted with new windows, finished with shiny metallic paint and mirrored panels. Avalon and Elijah lingered a short distance behind.

Elijah spoke softly. "All these secrets about my dad... I think he may have been involved."

"I know, William said," Avalon breathed, "and your mum is really scared of him..." She broke off quickly, glancing round. The next time she peered at Elijah, her eyes were lit with a furtive gleam. "I saw him in the pub with Charlie - I asked if he was an enemy."

"And?" Elijah pressed her, sliding his head close.

"Charlie wasn't sure, though he didn't relish the thought of opposing him.

Eleanor told me he used to be involved in organised crime - she's seen a very different side to him..."

"Oi, are you two coming or what?" Andrew bellowed from the other side of the street.

"Come on, let's just get this over with," Avalon muttered.

The doors were already open where the banging of a hammer resonated from within. They tiptoed into the corridor leading into the main lounge - pausing on the threshold as it yawned out in front of them. The first thing Andrew noticed was the floor. Gone were the shabby, worn out carpets with their pattern of cigarette burns; the dance floor completely refurbished with gleaming hardwood boards.

"Wow!" he exploded, before he could stop himself.

The echo of his voice hung in the silence. Two men glanced up; one obviously a builder, yet Andrew's eyes were drawn towards the second. He lingered in the background where he appeared to be studying a set of plans. There was a moment of tense silence before he swaggered across without warning. Elijah shrunk a little further back into the archway, still covertly studying him.

"Are you the boss?" Andrew mumbled nervously.

The man towered above them. Elijah stared at the hard planes of his face and nearly shivered - placing him somewhere in his forties with fine lines around his eyes and across his forehead. There was a set clench to his jaw, his mouth compressed in a tight line; most unnerving was the evil slant of his eyes. They stabbed into them in turn, before zooming in on Elijah.

"What d'you lot want?" he snapped.

Avalon stepped nervously forward. "Mr Theakston, isn't it?"

He gave a cynical smile. "I get it! Thought you'd rope in the local eye-candy to impress me… now answer my question!"

Angel took the lead. "Scuse us barging in, man. Just wondering if you were looking for a DJ."

"And that'd you, would it?" Dominic sneered.

"Yes Sir," Angel grinned. "I've been round some of the coolest clubs in London."

"I see," Dominic smiled, unfazed. "So name *five* of them clubs!"

Angel began reeling them off; he started with various establishments in south London before he dared to mention a club in Soho, where even the local King Pin hung out - a shady establishment known as 'Scarlet Moon.' Dominic's eyes flashed.

"Okay, I get your drift," he hissed dangerously. "What sort of genres?"

"All sorts, man," Angel said wistfully. "Disco, House, Techno, Hip Hop…"

"Right," Dominic snapped, plonking his hands firmly on his hips. "Well seeing as you're in tune with the current music scene, you can have a trial run.

Soon as the work's finished, I'm bringing the club's new manager over. She's the one you've gotta impress."

"Hey! Thanks man!" Angel nodded, stretching out his hand. To his surprise, Dominic grasped it.

"One last thing," he added softly. "When you say you're from London, I hope that don't mean you're mixed up with no shady stuff! I ain't having my club busted for drugs like that other prat."

"No way," Angel breathed. "I swear to you, the only thing I'm into is my music."

"Good," Dominic said, fixing him with an intimidating glare. It was Angel who lowered his eyes first. Andrew frowned; before it was his turn to be the object of scrutiny. "Who are you?"

"Who me?" Andrew mumbled anxiously. "Andrew Bailey - I-I'm a builder..."

"In other words, you're Charlie's son! Sent you round to have a good snoop, did he?"

"Not at all!" Andrew protested. "He doesn't even know I'm here..."

"Okay," he nodded, the beginnings of a smile playing around his mouth as if analysing them. His eyes slid to Avalon. "And what about you, love? Where do you fit into this little game?"

"It's no game," Avalon said defiantly. "We're friends. I've known Andrew for years! He and his dad helped my father restore our old home, Westbourne House..."

Dominic's eyes narrowed. He levelled her with the same probing stare just as another memory surfaced. *'We have reason to believe, he might have been the other man Elliot saw - from that 'very secret meeting.'* Avalon swallowed, finally understanding Eleanor's fear.

Finally, his eyes honed in on Elijah. "And what about you? Elijah Jansen? Met you once, at that Community Centre."

Elijah took a deep breath and stared him full in the face. "That's right, Mr Theakston."

"Shot up a bit, I see," Dominic kept whispering where the ice in his tone had returned. At 15, Elijah was the same height as Avalon - 5 foot 6 and as willowy as his father had been. "So what are you planning to do with *your* life?"

"I'm interested in architecture like Andrew's dad," Elijah said boldly, "but I want to be an interior designer. I might even get to decorate some of the flats for Peter's housing trust."

"Interior design," Dominic echoed. "So what would you do with this place? Go on, surprise me!"

Elijah glanced at his friends, hoping for a bit of moral support; Avalon gave his arm an affectionate squeeze though it was the slightly smug look on Andrew's face that got him scouring the depths of his imagination. It was a little like the time he had visualised the Community Centre. The picture came to him suddenly. For some strange reason, he was recalling a black and white photo his mother had showed him of the Grosvenor Hotel; the glamourous decor bathed in the sparkling light of a chandelier.

"Get rid of the mirrored pillars," he muttered quickly. "They're tacky. Black marble's more stylish - a-and black walls fitted with spotlights!" Elijah closed his eyes, engrossed in his reverie. "I think the seating should be velvet with a metallic bead trim. Anything that catches the light..."

"You've got some pretty sound ideas, kid," Dominic smirked, moving closer. "Ain't sure about the velvet..." The next time Elijah opened his eyes, he seemed to be leaning right over him, his eyes searching. "Now hop it, the lot of you! I'm a busy man. As for you..." he aimed his stare at Angel. "Call in at the club, Thursday night, 'bout eight. Never did catch your name."

"Ray," Angel beamed in gratitude. "Though everyone calls me Angel. Thanks a bunch, man!"

"Don't thank me yet," Dominic muttered. "And watch your backs, all of you."

No-one could ignore the ominous ring to his voice as his eyes bounced from each one of them in turn; but they ultimately lingered on Elijah.

"I reckon he's definitely a gangster!" Elijah spluttered as they loped away from the club. He shot a fearful glance over his shoulder. "Even when I met him at the open day, he seemed shady!"

"I think you might be on to something, bro'" Angel indulged him. "That place I mentioned - Scarlet Moon. I got a feeling, he knew it!"

"So what?" Andrew snapped petulantly as if sensing he was missing out on something.

"It's where all them mother fuckin' trouble boys hang out," Angel whispered out of the corner of his mouth.

"Yeah, right!" Andrew sighed, head down as he marched along beside him.

"Where've your folks gone today, anyway?" Angel quizzed.

"London - to see some old friends," Andrew remarked casually.

"Margaret's gone with them," Elijah added, "I would have gone too - but I've got a date with my girlfriend. I promised I'd take her to the pictures."

"Oh, sweet!" Angel muttered, flicking him a teasing smile.

"She's the prettiest girl in my year," Elijah couldn't resist the chance to brag, cheeks glowing.

He momentarily lapsed into a dream world. He could no longer deny, he adored Holly; enchanted by her delicate features, her tiny upturned nose and luxurious, silky hair, the colour of corn. Their relationship had thrown him into an era of bliss, he had never expected. Even at night, when he lay awake thinking about her, he was aroused by powerful inner stirrings he had never known existed. He loved holding her hand and he loved kissing her; just a polite peck on the cheek to begin with until eventually, she let him kiss her on the lips. He had savoured their softness which enkindled the strangest tingling sensation in his own.

They hadn't touched tongues yet - but Elijah didn't want to rush things. William, naturally couldn't resist teasing him, pressing him as to how far they'd got, before shamelessly sharing his own secrets. Elijah resisted - knowing exactly how he felt but too shy to push his luck. He respected Holly too much, filled with a yearning to let her take the lead.

"What film are you going to see?" Avalon asked him.

"Big," Elijah sighed blissfully, still swept up in his daydream. "It's about a boy who makes a wish and wakes up in the body of an adult - sounds like it might be a laugh."

II

Eleanor was basking in an almost synonymous sense of joy. It was early evening, the town immersed in a cool, velvety darkness. Everything was agreed. At the end of the month and on the day Joshua returned to Aldwyck, they would meet up after dark, intent on burying Eleanor's secret file deep underground, before the caravan was reinstated into position.

Margaret flopped down on the sofa, curling up with the cats. She adored the Merrimans as much as she loved their quirky home. She had been all too aware of some secret discussion in the garden, yet happy to spend time with Rosemary who kept her entertained, not to mention the antics of her grandsons, who at the age of 9 were a lively duo and made her laugh.

"You look cool!" she grinned at Elijah, back from his date with Holly.

It had to be said, her step-brother possessed a certain glow - dashing in his smart black jeans teamed up with a blue and green striped shirt. His clean hair shone like mahogany in the warm light of the room.

"Great film!" he muttered, helping himself to a glass of coca-cola from the fridge.

For the second half of the evening, they proceeded to swap stories.

Eventually Eleanor joined them. She closed her eyes - listening to the kids' banter with half an ear as they whittled away in the background.

"What else did you get up to today?" Margaret's voice hummed into the room.

"We visited that night club!" Elijah whispered feverishly. "Angel's desperate to get a job as a DJ. We spoke to the new owner!"

The words hovered on the periphery of Eleanor's senses. She sat very still - not liking the unpleasant chill that was gradually snaking over her shoulders.

"Avalon came," he added, casting a surreptitious glance in her direction. "She's met him before."

"Who are you talking about?" Eleanor interrupted.

"Theakston," Elijah confessed.

Eleanor froze, just as Charlie wandered into the room.

"What's up?" he demanded. "Christ, you could cut the atmosphere with a knife!"

"Eli, I want a word with you, right now," Eleanor snapped. "Upstairs!"

Margaret rolled her eyes. "Not more secrets!"

"Ssh," sweetheart," Charlie soothed, sliding his way onto the sofa to join her. "Whatever Eleanor has to say, it's only for his well-being." He too, hadn't failed to catch those final words - listening in dread, as the bedroom door clicked firmly shut from above.

"What on earth were you thinking?" Eleanor gasped, staring at her son in horror.

Even at 15, he possessed a demeanour of child-like innocence, his resemblance to Jake more pronounced than ever - and yet here he was, about to explain why he had guilelessly wandered into the domain of their most feared enemy!

He gave a shrug. "We just went to see him, Mum. Me, Avalon, Andrew and Angel!"

"What was he like?" Eleanor kept pressing him.

"Scary!" Elijah confessed. "Avalon said you were scared of him - we decided to suss him out for ourselves."

"He is a very bad man, Eli," Eleanor whimpered. She clasped the tops of his arms, gazing deep into his eyes - desperate to see some element of fear but there was none. He just looked at her blankly.

"So who is he?" he challenged. "Is he some sort of gangster?"

"Was," Eleanor whispered, pressing her eyes shut. The walls of the railway tunnel loomed in her mind - the monstrous threats. What was the point of keeping it a secret for any longer? "Eli, this is the man who threatened us!"

"What?" Elijah squeaked.

Eleanor sighed, grateful she had finally got through to him. She placed a finger to his lips, gently reminding him of the day they had sped back to the caravan; he had been furious - yet all she had been thinking about was his protection. "I thought we were safe - but the day, Theakston appeared at the open day, I panicked."

She could never have known of the thoughts drifting into his own mind.

Elijah turned very stiff, remembering it clearly. "You phoned Avalon," he whispered numbly, the memories accelerating: *'He was one of the most evil men in London... if I ever spoke a word, they would snatch my son... torture him.'* He collapsed, trembling on the side of the bed.

"Eli, I had to tell you," Eleanor sighed, settling down next to him. "Charlie spoke to him - he made him promise he would never hurt you... so how did he behave towards you?"

"He spoke as if he knew me," Elijah shuddered, "it was like - he was trying to warn me."

She nodded, tears glittering. "This is what I was worried about. I'm glad you understand. Now we're getting close to the truth... we're putting ourselves at risk"

"Is he mixed up with the people who killed my dad?" Elijah breathed.

Eleanor sighed. "I think it's time we found out, once and for all."

III

Later that night, Eleanor came to an irrevocable decision. It was something she chose not to share with Charlie. She was about to confront Dominic alone. If she could be absolutely sure, he had no further ties with Perry, only then would she continue her quest.

Monday came round quickly. She knew the club was undergoing refurbishment and with every chance the boss would be around, she decided to take a gamble. As soon as she finished her shift, she wasted no time - she made her way anxiously towards Tiffany's, clocking the gleam of a BMW parked outside - her heartbeat quickened, knowing who it belonged to.

Dominic however, was not in the best of moods.

He had spent the latter part of the afternoon visiting his kids; a visit that had left him disheartened. Almost from the moment his ex-wife's housekeeper let him in, the air had been spiked with hostility. A spacious lounge stretched out before him, where his son had glowered up at him. At 6 years old, Anton looked like his mother - the same aquiline nose and heart-shaped face. He possessed her large, soulful eyes - as dark as sloes like his own.

"Alright, kids?" he muttered.

4 year old Bella, had launched herself at him like a missile, hurling herself into his arms. "Daddy!" she squealed which immediately had his heart melting. They shared a closer resemblance; her dark eyes slanted as she smiled, her adorable baby cheeks pitted with dimples.

"Princess!" he smiled. "Good to see a cheery face!" his eyes flickered back to Anton. "What's up with you, misery guts?"

"I hate you!" Anton sulked. "You're really mean to us!"

"Aw, come on mate, that ain't fair," Dominic muttered, fighting to suppress his irritation.

He'd endured a prolonged argument, trying to explain; he still loved their mum - yet she was the one who'd ended the marriage. He couldn't deny, he was disappointed to hear that his son had turned more aggressive recently, under threat of suspension for thumping another pupil.

"She called me a little shit," Anton grunted, sticking out his bottom lip, "it's 'cos of you!"

245

Dominic released a sigh. How the hell was he supposed to retain any rapport with his kids if Crystal was drip-feeding this sort of crap into their ears?

Pushing aside his fury, he did his best to entertain them; blessed that at least his daughter was a credit to him but for how long was that going to last? The moment Crystal arrived home, he chose not to linger - driving from their magnificent mansion, steeped in resentment. That house had left little change out of a quarter of a mil and yet still his glamourous ex-wife kept moaning; so she had to get a job to pay for a nanny and a housekeeper - welcome to the real world, darling! It was *his* hard work, illegal or otherwise, that had paid for their luxurious living standards. She'd treasured the life of a gangster's moll and even in the aftermath of that bloody kidnapping, he had whisked her away to a better place. They could have enjoyed a great life if she hadn't been so possessive.

"Fucking women!" he snapped as he stormed into Tiffany's.

He was relieved to be back. The club did at least provide an exhilarating new challenge. The refurbishment was going well and in the next few days, he hoped to have the entire place rewired and refurbished.

Little did he know that another of his 'problems' was about to surface.

The builders had just gone, leaving him hovering on the dance floor, admiring their handiwork. He was just about to call it a day when without warning, Eleanor came drifting through the door, ethereal as an angel in her nurse's uniform. Dominic's face darkened to a scowl.

"What the fuck do you want?"

The tension sizzled between them. Dominic wasted no time - he had already taken his first strides towards her before he yanked her into the lounge. Eleanor let out a gasp.

"I-I only wanted a word..." she spluttered, fighting against his grip.

"Come on then, out with it!" he barked. "I'm all ears!"

"I hear, my son called in to see you the other day."

"Yeah," Dominic retorted. "Can't deny I was surprised! Handsome kid - just like his dad! Be a shame if he ended up in the same place!"

His words captured her in a spiral of fear. "What did you say?"

Dominic let out a sigh, the anger in his face simmering. "Sit down!" he ordered curtly.

Eleanor saw no reason to argue as she turned towards the old-style seating. Dominic plonked himself down opposite. "Be honest," she continued shakily. "Is my son in any danger?"

Dominic gave a shrug. "I ain't gonna lie. It's that file of yours - *someone* out there's prepared to resort to any underhand means to get their hands on it!"

"But are *you* involved?" Eleanor snapped. "I have to ask - b-but what exactly are you doing back in Rosebrook?"

Dominic smiled evilly. "Rosebrook's a thriving town - gives me easy access to me own kids."

"I see," Eleanor found herself nodding, "any other reason? The last time we spoke, you said you were only interested in the land."

"Okay, I'll come clean," he whispered. "It was Whaley's ploy to get me back in the loop! He wanted you to be scared - *so* scared, you wouldn't risk doing nothing stupid. It all goes back to that file. Last thing anyone wants is *you* stirring up shit again!"

Eleanor let out a sigh - tired of his games. "So how does this affect you? See, let's dispense with the *'someone.'* We both know we're referring to Perry Hampton."

She clocked the malevolent flash in his eyes. It compelled her to explain her fears: Perry was having her watched. There had been a spate of crime recently, resulting in the burglary of their home and somehow, their enemies had known when to strike.

"Could have been anyone," Dominic sneered.

"It was a highly professional job," Eleanor persisted. "That burglary had all the hallmarks of organised crime, *Dominic* and I know of only one person who'd have those connections."

"Wrong," Dominic spat. "I severed them *connections* years ago! Don't mean there ain't others…"

"I know and I think I may have met them," Eleanor said, "a man with a scar running down his face, cockney accent?" She knew she was playing with fire. "Sound familiar?"

"If it's who I think it is, you need to be afraid, love!" He shot a surreptitious glance towards the door before leaning in closer. "Sounds like one of London's top hard nuts. So before you make any further accusations, maybe I should ask *you* something - did you know *Ben Hampton* was looking for a route into the criminal underworld?"

Eleanor turned cold with fear.

Dominic smirked. "Surprised the kid pulled it off! Got more guts than I gave 'im credit for."

"And you gave him that in-road?" Eleanor gasped.

"Hampton kid joined my gym," Dominic hissed. Without warning, his hand closed over her wrist again. "Wanted to know who ran the criminal underworld so I told 'im. Happens that weirdo mate of his, Wadzinski, went to school with the guy!"

Eleanor raised her face. "Nathan?" she breathed. She felt giddy - the very concept of someone as evil as Ben mixing with gangsters was the most chilling scenario she could have imagined. "And you swore, you weren't allied to them…"

"I'm *not*," Dominic echoed, "but that don't mean I'm on *your* side! You're as much a threat as you ever were, Eleanor Bailey and do you know why?" his grip tightened. "If your file goes public, I've got as much to lose as Hampton!"

"You told me you didn't murder Jake," Eleanor shot back.

"That's right. 'Cept Hampton's gonna let loose it was *my gang*, recruited for the killing." His eyes burned black as they held her gaze, his expression dangerous.

"But they were!" she dared herself to whisper.

No more was said - the truth squatted darkly between them. Eleanor closed her eyes, pondering over Evelyn's words: the ultimate trump card lay on the tip of her tongue.

"Why not turn this around?" she challenged. "If he confesses this much, he's exposing his *own* guilt - *he* engineered Jake's murder!"

Dominic let out a cynical laugh. "You trying to cut a deal?"

"I've got nothing to lose. You said you were cleared of Jake's murder. Talk to the police, you said, ask to see the evidence - I'm still waiting..."

She watched his expression stiffen as if somehow he hadn't expected this. "Been doing a bit of digging have you?"

Eleanor swallowed. "I am willing to make a proposition. If I can see proof that you're innocent, I will erase your name from my file - that way, Perry will have no further hold..."

"You've got to be fucking joking!" he snarled.

"I'm not," Eleanor said coldly, "the only thing that bothers me is this: why couldn't you have let Jake go?"

"You ain't got a clue what it was like to have Hargreeves on your back!" Dominic argued. "Did you know he gave me the green light to terrorise Sammie's patch?"

Eleanor froze, unable to forget her father.

"Yeah, that's right," he sneered. "Said he'd turn a blind eye! Then used every crime me gang ever committed as a lever. We didn't have no choice. I never wanted to kill that kid - but I didn't relish spending the next 20 years behind bars either - no more than I do now."

"And you're worried that could happen?" Eleanor frowned, "despite everything I've said?"

"What - you think someone like Hampton will go down without a fight? If your file goes public, I'll tell you what'll happen! Perry will wriggle his way out. I'll end up being dragged through court, blamed for the murder and spend the rest of me life rotting in a prison cell!"

Eleanor sighed - of course, he had no idea of the evidence she had discovered about Perry!

"So what do you suppose I do?"

Finally his grip slackened. "There's only one sensible thing to do, darling. Give Perry what he wants and have done with it!"

"NO!" Eleanor gasped, tugging her wrist away, "I won't do that!"

"Why not?" Dominic pressed. "Seems obvious to me! Forget the past. Jake ain't never coming back. Concentrate on the future especially *your son's* future!"

"You don't understand," Eleanor whimpered. "We're not safe! Perry is evil. He ruined Charlie's life and you've no idea what Avalon went through!" she broke off with a sob. "I said I wouldn't implicate you - but I *can't* destroy my file!"

"Your choice!" Dominic snapped, "don't say I didn't warn you!"

"Warn me?" Eleanor added fearfully, struggling to her feet.

"I ain't making no deal," Dominic hissed, the evil creeping back into his expression, "so I'll tell you what's what! I swore to your Charlie, I wouldn't cause you no bother provided you lot didn't cause me any - but if go down for this, I swear I'll make him pay!"

Eleanor gasped - to think, they could have reached a truce. "You'd hurt Charlie?"

His chilling smile stuck deep. "That got your attention didn't it? Might have said I wouldn't harm your boy - but the day Charlie came barging into my gym, he put *himself* in the firing line."

Eleanor stared at him in stark terror, unable to believe what she was hearing. *He was threatening Charlie?*

"So I suggest you keep your mouth shut and drop this whole fucking business!" he finished brutally. "You came here looking for answers - well now you know the fucking score!"

IV

She left the night club in shock. Charlie had been *convinced* that Dominic was no longer a threat. How wrong he had been. Eleanor fought tears as she made her way slowly back home - memories of that horrific encounter in the railway tunnel loomed in her mind. She should have known better than to try and bargain with him.

Unfortunately, it had evoked a decision; she couldn't even dare to attempt bringing Perry to justice, given this new onslaught of threat. They had reached a terrifying stalemate, leaving her no choice other than to hide her file copy - at least for the time being.

On the last Sunday of October, Eleanor and Charlie slipped away from the almshouse, leaving Peter with the kids as they surreptitiously headed for Aldwyck. At least they weren't quite so conspicuous, Charlie thought to himself. He steered his new car towards the main road. He had finally said good-bye to his ageing orange Volvo in favour of a Vauxhall Cavalier in deep silver grey. That old car had been in his ownership for six years - but the Vauxhall was just as efficient, nothing flashy, just a solid, functional family hatchback. Its powerful engine felt smooth as it handled the various twists and gradients in the road, drawing them deep into the heart of the countryside.

There was little sign of activity in the village. Even the pub seemed dead; just a small cluster of cars parked outside, the doors closed, a subdued glimmer of light peeping from the windows. Charlie drew up to the field where Eleanor's caravan had sat for the last 15 years. It was a clear, frosty night. The final phase of a full moon encircled their surroundings in a cool blue glow. Charlie tucked his car tightly into the neighbouring copse of trees - its subtle shade masked by the shadows. Eleanor stepped from the car and shivered, immediately struck by the biting air as together, they tiptoed their way to the Harpers' farmhouse.

"Inside, quickly!" Marilyn urged, her voice a whisper.

She closed the door and turned to Eleanor. There was something feverish in her expression - her wide green eyes were not as intense as Rosemary's, yet they disguised a sparkle.

"Where's the caravan?" Charlie questioned.

"Hidden in the back yard," Marilyn replied. "Joshua came back early evening. We thought it best to hide it for now, just incase..."

Eleanor nodded. They had obviously thought this through carefully - all the while the field remained empty, Perry would have no reason to start snooping.

"Come through," Marilyn added warmly as they loitered on the chilly flagstones. "There's someone else who'll be pleased to see you."

They followed her, embraced by the homely warmth of their lounge. Joshua sprung to his feet, his face lit with a familiar boyish grin. His slightly longer hair swayed around his shoulders as they hugged like long lost siblings. Lucy too, stepped forward. Greetings were exchanged; then at last, Tom appeared in the doorway, his sagging face wreathed in smiles.

"Tom...!" Eleanor gasped. The salutation died on her lips, her gaze drawn to the man who accompanied him. She blinked as if she had seen a ghost. Those gentle features tore at her heart strings - the familiar blue eyes beneath a cap of snowy white hair; eyes which disguised an enduring suffering. "Elliot?"

"Hello, my dear," he smiled.

Eleanor almost fell into his arms, a sob rising in her throat.

"Elliot, you old devil!" Charlie laughed. "You managed to escape?"

"It's been a while since they kept me under close surveillance," Elliot said softly. "Your wedding was well over a year ago and I haven't stepped out of line."

"Does this mean they trust you?" Eleanor whispered in hope.

He cast her a look of resignation. "Not 'trust' exactly. I'm certain the phones are monitored; but Rowena took Perry to task - insisted he couldn't deny me a social life just as long as I don't stray beyond the village. If I do, someone usually follows me."

The hour flew by quickly - with so much to talk about, it would have been impossible to cover it all. Eleanor spoke to Joshua in the privacy of Marilyn's kitchen. Charlie stuck with Elliot. The conversation was inevitably drawn to the Barton-Wells children and he was compelled to mention the recent crime wave. "We can't help wondering if the Hamptons have recruited some highly professional criminals..."

He broke off, not wanting to divulge their true suspicions. The less people who knew about Eleanor's file, the better - where Joshua and Lucy were about to become the final trustees.

"Oh well, I can't hang around," Elliot sighed, "but I have a letter for you." He smiled sadly. "Pass it to Avalon and William when you've read it."

It was such a hurried flash of time, Charlie reflected - his heart heavy as he watched Elliot shuffle from the room. He gazed at his watch. 10:30 - it would be another 30 minutes before the pub emptied and Aldwyck would be sinking into its dormant state.

The village lay eerily silent; the trees crystallised into sharp silhouettes against a clear indigo sky. They manoeuvred the caravan carefully onto the road, watched by thousands of twinkling stars then finally eased it into the field. Joshua unhitched it from the tow bar.

For the next few minutes they just waited - the uninterrupted silence was comforting.

Eleanor gazed at the spot, the unmistakable rectangle of earth where no grass had grown for years. She was clutching a spade - satisfied, there was no-one watching as she ducked behind the caravan. Within seconds she started digging. The hole only had to be small yet deep, where regrettably, the spread of frost rendered the ground as hard as rock.

Charlie snatched the spade. It was with all his might he thrust downwards, stalwart in his attempt to hack through the unyielding earth. For several minutes, he worked steadily until he too, was panting from exhaustion. Then Joshua took his turn.

Eleanor's file was encased in its locked metal box. She had wrapped it in several layers of newspaper and lastly, a strong waterproof bag. It was with a loving smile, she lowered it into the earth, remembering Jake's memorial - struck with the sense, she was finally burying all their secrets. With the file tucked deep into its secret ravine, they refilled the hole and stamped down the earth before rolling the caravan over the area to conceal it.

"I can't imagine a better hiding place," Charlie sighed, collapsing into the seating area for a glass of wine. "I'm pleased that's done! Now perhaps we can relax a little."

"Let's just carry on as normal," Eleanor added sagely, "try to forget that any of this happened." She tapped Charlie's glass. "For now, the file protects us..."

"But what about justice?" Joshua pressed, his eyes glittering in the candle light.

Eleanor stared back wistfully - remembering the dramatic press conference; the records he'd acquired to prove Perry's attendance.

"We'll get there," she reassured him. "There may be enough material to condemn Perry - but we have no proof he was responsible for Jake's murder."

At the back of her mind lurked flashbacks of Boswell's cynicism. Eleanor knew what she needed to do - she needed to bide her time and keep a low profile. Intuition alone was never going to be enough. She needed hard evidence.

It was midnight by the time they left Aldwyck, guided by the silvery moonlit roads as they lured them back to Rosebrook. The little town had never seemed more placid beneath its glittering sheet of stars. For much of the journey, Eleanor was submerged in thought as the radio piped softly in the background. Then at last, they were approaching the High Street - Dominic's night club lurked behind the wall of shops and it was at this point, she decided to mention him.

"You went to see him?" Charlie breathed. "Why didn't you tell me?"

Eleanor bit her lip, knowing damn well why she hadn't mentioned it! The meeting had left her in a state of turmoil. She let out a sigh. "I needed time to digest some of the things he said… He didn't kill Jake, b-but he's worried he might be implicated."

"Who by, the police?"

"By Perry," Eleanor finished darkly, "which leads me to the scariest part of the conversation..."

The words echoed inside the car just as Charlie was pulling into his parking space.

He extinguished the engine - there was something hidden in her expression which unnerved him. It reminded him of the very first night she had told him about her file - her face frozen in a gleam of moonlight where those same beautiful eyes stared back at him. "What is it, my love?" he whispered, cupping a hand around her face.

"These criminals who've infiltrated their way into Rosebrook," she shivered. "They are allied to Ben Hampton. Apparently, he's been looking for a route into the criminal underworld - and now it seems, he's found it!"

Chapter 14

I

As Eleanor pondered over the most unsettling parts of their encounter, little did she know that Dominic was thinking about her. He knew he had over-reacted - his mind bombarded with the stress of the refurbishment. Yet by the time the week had ended, he'd found time to relax - to share a bottle of wine and a fine meal with his stunning girlfriend who was about to be manager of his new club. He was making love to her right now on one of their vast leather sofas.

But it was no longer anger that possessed him. It was regret. He closed his eyes where the vision of Eleanor's face reared up again; her eyes bright with panic, swimming with tears. Dominic clenched his teeth. He'd behaved like a complete shit! She had tiptoed into his club, offering to scratch his name from her file and all he had done was threaten her again. He opened his eyes, allowing them to travel over Pippa's glorious body as she writhed on top of him, her surgically enhanced breasts as round and smooth as two ripe melons. His eyes were heavy with lust as he pulled her head down to kiss her, hoping he could scatter away his demons.

By Monday morning, everything seemed different; a day where he found himself loathing Perry Hampton with a passion. It was his paranoia that lay at the heart of all this trouble, never to forget his ultimatum - it was a notion that left him hankering to put things right.

He was hoping to have the club fully refurbished by the end of October but there had been a delay. So the first thing he did was contact Charlie.

"Just need some new bar tops fitting," he snapped down the telephone. "Your son any good at carpentry? Tell him the job's his if he wants it!"

It was the first of a series of atonements. Charlie was stunned. So for that matter was Andrew; even more so when he received not only his pay packet, but a privilege membership pass. This entitled him to free admission on weekdays and 50% off at the weekend, provided he brought his friends along. Yet Dominic was full of surprises. He had even embraced one of Elijah's ideas. Andrew was quick to report, albeit begrudgingly, how they had chipped the mirror tiles from the pillars and applied a layer of gleaming black marble.

"Might as well tell the kid, I was swayed," Dominic remarked casually.

A huge disco ball was fixed to the ceiling - an array of LED lights oscillating around the walls and together they created a stunning lighting effect. Elijah was delighted. Angel even more so. It was as a result of their prospective visit that he too, had been recruited as one of their resident DJs.

It was over the ensuing weeks that Dominic chose to take his enterprise further - forever seeking ways he could expand the business. But it was a scenario that drew him back into contact with Rosebrook Council and ultimately, Robin Whaley.

Robin hid his feelings well, unable to deny he had been disheartened by the things he was hearing. His plan to lure Dominic into Rosebrook wasn't working quite as he hoped - wondering what the hell could have possessed him to enlist *Charlie's son* to finish the bar refurbishment.

"Kid's a skilled craftsman," Dominic drawled with some relish. "Charlie taught him well!"

Robin had only visited to see how things were progressing. He had initially marvelled over the marble pillars; the deep, buttoned leather seating which conveyed an impression of luxury. Yet the news that Elijah had influenced certain aspects of the design irked him even more.

"Says he wants to be an interior designer," Dominic shrugged, "no harm encouraging the young."

It was over the next few weeks, Robin allowed these thoughts to fester - until eventually the coils of fury started to unravel. Dominic was allying himself with the enemy. It was a situation that sparked his most Machiavellian nature - until finally an opportunity began to manifest itself and he couldn't wait to discuss it with Hilary.

"He's looking to convert the basement into an alternative dance floor," Robin smiled.

He had spotted her in town - quick to invite her to take tea with him.

"Why the basement?" Hilary whispered, "you don't supposed this has got anything to do with these 'underground parties' that have been on the news do you?"

Robin knew she would be suspicious as he continued to drip his poison. She was of course, referring to *acid house* parties - aware of the media storm that was gathering momentum. A lot of these 'so called parties' were held in basements and other secret locations such as warehouses. It hadn't been so long ago the club had been raided - and these parties were being linked to a designer drug called ecstasy.

"Reggie and I saw a documentary!" she whispered feverishly. "There's even a certain type of music associated with it. Youngsters call them dance parties. It's a euphemism. Where there are parties there are pushers."

Robin sipped his tea, his blue eyes fixed on her. "Do go on…"

"They say 'they just want to dance and have a good time,'" She sniffed. "It's a fallacy. This so-called 'good time' is linked to a mind altering high caused by the drugs they've taken. It's dangerous! They've no idea of the long term effects."

"I understand your concern as a drugs counsellor," Robin mused as if thinking out loud. "It's just that - I had a slightly different theory."

She was looking at him intently. Robin chose his next words carefully.

"I've known Dominic for a long time and I know the type of clubs he visits, especially in Soho. *Men's clubs.* You must have some idea, Hilary…" he stared deeply into her eyes. "Have you ever considered the possibility, he might be opening this club to such titillations as lap dancing?"

"Outrageous!" Hilary gasped. "Rosebrook is a respectable town!"

"It's only a theory," Robin murmured. "Dominic is an entrepreneur but his greatest weakness is women - and where there is sleaze, there is money to made."

It didn't take long before she was bristling with indignation; where the most obvious solution was to start a protest - exactly the reaction he had been hoping for.

"You should speak to Eleanor Bailey," Robin added silkily. "You must know she led the campaign against his last initiative. See if you can get her involved."

Hilary stepped from the café, charged with emotion; confident, she would have no problem enlisting Eleanor's support. But then again, she had been conversing with her a lot more, lately. It was impossible not to in the light of Holly's blossoming relationship with Elijah. Hilary had not been entirely happy at first, but as time progressed, she was forced to concede there was little to dislike about him. He was a sweet boy - academically minded and polite at all times.

And there was a plus side; all the while she was getting to know Elijah, she was gaining a deeper insight into his family life - and Eleanor's.

Hilary's curiosity had spiralled, hankering to find something shady - though he divulged nothing out of the ordinary. He spoke of her love of simple pleasures - walks, lunches out - that she was a wonderful cook; a shadow of the unworldly creature Hilary perceived from the early days, leaving nothing to fuel Perry's hatred. Her face tightened. She had seen no evidence of this so called 'hate campaign.' Maybe Rowena was right. Perry *was* suffering from some form of paranoia. Yet she didn't want to believe it. The Hamptons were high society people. They supported her charity work, leaving her with an insatiable desire to dig up something controversial.

These thoughts came to her as she wandered up the high street in the direction of the Community Centre. This newly revamped building served as yet another stark reminder of Elijah's talent. Holly was supposed to be taking him to a party later, but right now, she was hoping to catch Eleanor. Robin was right. It was Eleanor who had stood up at that council meeting, where her inner voice was now guiding her. It was with a sense of moral duty, she would do anything to oppose this basement expansion, shuddering at the thought of the vice that might be concealed there.

II

Elijah could never have known what was going on in Hilary's mind when he knocked on her door. He had other things on his mind, giddy with excitement at the thought of Holly dragging him along to a party. He had spent at least an hour shopping with William, grateful for his advice. He had treated himself to a crisp linen shirt with the wages he earned from his Saturday job, stacking supermarket shelves. It went well with his striped jeans - but according to William, the one garment that would really set him apart from the crowd was a waistcoat. The boutiques of Shilling Walk offered plenty; except he had been distracted - his eyes wandering over the jewellery, drawn to some really pretty earrings whose sapphire blue stones reminded him of Holly's eyes, so naturally, he had bought these too.

"Hello, Elijah," Hilary smiled coolly, inviting him into their plush living room. "Holly's upstairs." She drew her head close. "I was hoping to catch your mother earlier."

"Sorry Mrs Magnus, she's working a late shift," he answered her softly. "She'll be around tomorrow - said she needed to do a bit of tidying up in the gardens."

"Eli, is that you?" Holly's voice piped down the stairs, "is it okay, if he comes up here for a minute, Mummy?"

"No, Holly," Hilary barked in a tone which seemed unusually sharp. "You know we don't allow boys in your bedroom, dear. You can talk to him down here!"

Holly disappeared again, leaving Elijah in the company of her parents. Reginald was already perusing him through his vivid blue eyes. Elijah felt his cheeks turn warm, hopping from one foot to another, unsure what to say. He caught Reggie's eye - just as a strange pattern of thought came to mind: *You met my father - you were one of the last people to see him alive.* Eli was nearly tempted to ask him - banking up his courage. Then finally, Holly dashed downstairs.

The sight of her took his breath away. She wore a close fitting party dress in pink crushed velvet and although it almost reached her ankles, Elijah couldn't resist staring at her perfect feet, tucked into high heeled mules. She had been styling her hair with heated rollers, leaving it swirling round her shoulders in long, loose waves.

"Y-you look lovely," he smiled, the earrings tucked in one hand.

She glanced at him shyly - except, her eyes didn't quite contain the same twinkle. "Let's just go," she muttered quickly. "It's only round the corner."

The moment they were out of sight, she turned to him - her face grave.

"I bought you a present," Eli started mumbling, fishing out the earrings.

Her face lit up with an ecstatic smile. "They are beautiful," she breathed, stroking them. "Oh, Eli!" and without further prompting, she flung her arms around his neck and kissed him.

Elijah's head was reeling as she parted her lips and flicked her tongue inside his mouth. It was only very recently they had started 'French kissing' but the feeling was so deliciously nice, he never wanted it to end. By the time they broke apart however, that earlier look of anxiety had crept back into her expression and this time, Elijah was dying to know what was wrong.

"So who's party is this?" he said quickly.

"I didn't realise," she whimpered. "Janey invited me. She said the party was at her boyfriend's house, except it's Mickey Snyder... one of Gazza and Dazza's friends!"

"Oh," Elijah responded, feeling his heart sink. Everyone knew they were bitter enemies; even more so, since he'd started going out with Holly who Gary fancied like crazy!

"What if they don't let you in?" she added fearfully.

Elijah forced a smile. "I'll walk you there anyway - see what happens."

She threw him a look of woe and reluctantly agreed to let him escort her.

Five minutes later, they were wandering up the driveway of a smart semi-detached house with curving bay windows. It wasn't dissimilar to Holly's house. It was dark already but the porch was illuminated by lanterns. Several bunches of balloons flapped in the breeze where a steady thump of dance music resonated from inside.

Holly rang the doorbell. "Is Janey around?" she called, marching over the threshold with Eli in tow. He glanced around nervously, recognising faces from both Holly's year as well as his own. He knew Holly and Janey played the clarinet in the school orchestra, which was how they had forged their friendship. Suddenly, Elijah spotted her - a slender brunette whose animated face split into a smile. She was on the brink of yelling out a greeting when another boy reared up behind her. Elijah recognised his flat, deadpan face - eyes cold as they locked with his own. He had already grabbed Janey's arm before he swung out in front of her.

"It's okay, Mickey, Holly's with me," she simpered.

Elijah watched in dread as a sneer crept onto Mickey's face. He fired a glance over his shoulder, just as Gary Boswell swaggered into the hallway, practically filling it.

"Well look who's here," Mickey said nastily.

"You can fuck off for a start!" Gary hissed, barging his way towards the door.

"But he's my boyfriend!" Holly gasped. "Don't be like this... Can't we just come in?"

"You can!" Mickey snapped, "but I'm not having that gypsy scum in my home!"

"It's alright, I'm going!" Elijah muttered. He submissively lowered his eyes. "See you later, Holly - have a good time."

He bit back his emotions, aware of the heat flaring in his face as he spun round and wandered back down the driveway. He felt a tiny ray of hope when Holly came tottering after him.

She gazed sadly into his eyes. "Are you sure you don't mind?"

Elijah eased his lips into a smile, allowing his arms to snake themselves around her. He kissed her on the forehead. "Course I don't mind," he whispered. "Just enjoy yourself. You can tell me all about it in the morning…" he let out a mirthless chuckle. "They'd probably have played some horrible joke on me - like strip me naked and tie me to the fence or something…"

Holly laughed in sympathy. "Oh, Eli, I'm sorry. I'll make it up to you, I promise."

They kissed again and to Eli's delight, it was even more passionate than before; conscious of the door hanging open where the shadows of his enemies lurked like two bouncers. He pressed his lips hard against Holly's, relishing his audience before he unashamedly flicked up two fingers. He sensed Gary bristle, just as he released her.

Elijah didn't want to hang around. It was pitch dark, the streets empty, leaving him in a situation almost as perilous as the remote woods around Aldwyck. His senses were sharp, never able to forget his mother's warnings. He broke into a run, sprinting in the direction of his home. It only took a few minutes to reach the back door and it was only then, his anguish was detonated.

"Bugger them all to hell - bloody bastards…" Eli kicked the door in rage - only to be sent hopping in agony as he stubbed his toe. *"Shit!"*

"Eli?" Margaret gasped, rushing into the kitchen. "What's the matter?"

So he told her.

Charlie and Andrew had been watching 'Only Fools and Horses' blissfully unaware of their dialogue. By the time Elijah had finished his story, there were tears in Margaret's eyes.

"That's so mean," she mumbled. "If I was Holly, I would have left too!"

Elijah shrugged. "I guess, she didn't want to let her friend down. I'm worried though. I don't like to think of her alone in there with those tossers! What if one of them tries it on?"

"Don't worry," Margaret soothed him. "I'm sure she'll be fine. She wouldn't let Gary touch her if he paid her, she thinks he's gross!"

It was that last statement which finally drew a smile to his lips.

Eleanor too, had been a little concerned for Holly's safety, knowing how pious her mother could be - especially when she spotted her striding across the lawn towards her.

She had been tidying up the gardens. In the event of the frosts and the shorter daylight hours, many plants had withered, leaving a litter of bedraggled stems and blackened leaves. They needed digging up where the new winter varieties would take their place - the velvety white foliage of Cineraria which offset the vivid blooms of cyclamens so beautifully.

"Eleanor!" Hilary smiled tightly, "I've been meaning to talk to you..."

"Is Holly okay?" she interrupted breathlessly. "Only, you must have heard. Eli was barred from that party! He was so upset and yet he couldn't stop fretting about Holly."

"Oh, one of her friends' parents dropped her back," Hilary said airily, "but that isn't what I wanted to talk to you about. Have you met this *Dominic Theakston* character?"

Eleanor tensed; stung by her indifference towards her son's feelings. Though it seemed, she was harbouring opinions of a far more serious concern. The club had finally been opened. Its glitzy re-launch as 'Bella's Palace' had attracted media headlines. There was no doubt in Eleanor's mind that Dominic was about to be resurrected as a major player in this town and it left her uneasy.

"He's planning to build some private *underground club* in the basement!" Hilary sniffed. "What if it's used as a gambling den - or some disgusting strip joint?"

Eleanor continued to prune the shrubs, her movements slow as the information sank in. Hilary's principal fear revolved around the prospect of illegal 'acid house parties' and she was planning to start a protest. Yet her next words stunned her. "I was hoping you might join me."

"Oh no!" Eleanor protested. "There is *no way* I am getting involved."

"Why not, you did before!" Hilary said waspishly.

"That was different!" Eleanor retorted. "We stood against him as a community!"

Hilary let out a snort as she pressed ahead with her argument. And all the while, Eleanor kept on clipping at the shrubs, her face rigid; never able to forget, the objections she recited had been *Charlie's notes* - that it was *Robin Whaley* who had forced her into the arena. *Whaley!* She dropped her secateurs into an ornamental urn, turning to face Hilary directly.

"I told you, I don't care," she exhorted, "I am not going to be dragged into your campaign. I have more important things to worry about than the expansion of some night club!"

Before the day ended, it was Robin who felt the most dismayed. He could fully understand why Hilary chose not to pile *too much* pressure on Eleanor. The situation was delicate, his only intention to ignite that crucial spark. He knew he needed to be careful.

The planning department had started to empty yet Robin stayed behind. His hands fumbled for his dictaphone as he gazed at the file in front of him - the realms of notes collected from that volatile council meeting in February. Most important, was the speech Eleanor had read out; redrafted from an objection letter submitted by Charlie. *'Many of you may have seen what the town centre is like on Saturday night, especially when the club turns out…'*

His face twisted with disdain - he was all too familiar with the depravity which prevailed amongst the young. It lay just beyond his front door. *'People worry about noise and disruption - anti-social behaviour such as drug taking and vandalism…'*

Robin smiled. It was the last paragraph which captured his attention.

'We have children of our own… They've already been subjected to an incident which typified the nastier side of youth culture, where an excess of drink and drugs was involved…'

Robin calmly began to rephrase these points, using the tiny recording device in his hand.

Next morning, he summoned his secretary - he asked her if she would be so kind as to type out a report. The document was titled 'Objections against the Extension of Night Club Facilities.' It wasn't signed - but he made sure two of the names included in that report were Eleanor and Charles Bailey. He also arranged for the report to be back-dated so that it coincided nicely with the week Dominic's agent had submitted the planning application. Lastly, he surreptitiously slipped it into the applicant's file before closing the drawer, silently praying that Hilary would do her damnedest to furnish it with her own objections.

In another part of town, Holly felt terrible. It had been humiliating when Mickey had made that scene - whatever issues they had, Eli didn't deserve that sort of treatment! In some ways she was confused as to how she really felt about him. She couldn't deny he was handsome - his warm, blushing complexion was as smooth as velvet, devoid of spots, unlike many other boys. His soft, slightly pouting lips were a joy to kiss, his chestnut hair glossy - and he had such adorable eyes; they were predominantly green yet sparkled with a mosaic of colours.

The only problem with Eli was, he was *too* nice! It was clear, he was utterly besotted with her but painfully shy. He was forever plying her with gifts which in turn, forced her under even more pressure to return his affections - and those earrings really were stunning, his best present yet!

She closed her eyes - mortified, he had been banished from Mickey's party; yet any sympathy had been blown away, from the moment she found herself being chatted up by Ken Wilkinson. He was one of the school's top footballers - tall, blonde and divinely gorgeous. There wasn't a girl in school who didn't fancy him. She had even lied about getting a lift home.

It was Ken who escorted her - but there was no way, Holly was going to reveal what had really happened; how he had hauled her behind an overgrown Leylandii bush for a kiss.

The one thing she could never have known about was his wandering hands, the way he pawed her breasts, her bottom, kneading her like a lump of bread dough - yet somehow, it excited her. It felt incredibly naughty to be coiled up in a wave of such lust, only meters from her parents' lounge. They were so prudish. It was a small wonder they even allowed her to go out with Eli; though for some reason they trusted him, convinced he wouldn't take advantage - and in so many ways, they were right.

Ken by contrast, was an animal.

"Would you go all the way with me, Holly?"

He had ignored her for the next three days which left her floundering - even though it was rumoured, he already had a girlfriend. Ken was the ultimate 'bad boy.' He knew he was hero-worshipped. If only he hadn't slipped her that note - an invitation to meet in secret when he knew his parents would be out. A walk around their sprawling back garden seemed like such an innocent pastime until he coaxed her into the summer house. Holly flushed with shame. She was excited by the prospect of another kiss - but she had never expected to lose her virginity! She had been taken in like a fool, treated like a slut and to her utter horror, she now felt like one.

"Is everything okay, sweetheart?" her father's voice popped into the silence.

Holly blinked, staring at him in panic. "Of course!" she snapped, "why shouldn't it be?"

"No date with Eli tonight?" he teased.

It was with little delay, she rushed over to the almshouse. For a start, it would be nice to see Margaret - but the moment she stepped through the door, it was Eli who caught her attention.

His eyes glittered. "Holly," he whispered. "I thought you'd given up on me - you know, since I'm a proper 'Billy no mates.'"

"You're not!" Holly gasped, throwing her arms around him in sorrow. "You're one of the nicest boys in school! You've got tons more street cred than Boswell so stop worrying. He's a cretin!"

Ken might have used her, but he had awoken her innermost desires. She luxuriated in the warmth of Elijah's arms, passionate to push their relationship up to the next level.

III

They were fast approaching Christmas. In the aftermath of the first biting frosts, the weather turned uncharacteristically mild, robbing them of any chance of snow. William had predictably passed his driving test first time. He couldn't wait to take them for a spin in the beautiful vintage sports car James had bequeathed to him; his prospective 18th birthday gift. James's memory thrived in all their hearts as they tentatively ventured into Aldwyck to lay a wreath.

There was a certain desolation to the allotments and the field lay in silence. Joshua and Lucy had temporarily disappeared to London, to enjoy a traditional family Christmas. Yet the village retained its pleasing atmosphere - a place suspended in time where the romantic, picture postcard image materialised in a haze of mist. Avalon found herself comforted by the familiar sights - the village green hugged by its semicircle of cottages. The chalky white walls of the 'Olde House at Home' lingered opposite, tempting them inside.

But William didn't want to hang around - fearing the possibility, the Hamptons were lurking. Elliot's latest letter had disclosed that Perry was now a regular visitor - ever keen to keep abreast of any gossip circulating. It was said, he was even more paranoid than ever, obsessed with keeping them under observation. William didn't appreciate the notion of being watched. Though, he had no concept of how vindictive Perry had become since the discovery of Eleanor's secret trips to London.

Perry was actually gazing out of an upstairs window. He had already seen them - and all the while, the lingering vision of Eleanor's face still haunted him. Once again, he found himself disappointed with Alesha's efforts. She had discovered precious little else about the Merrimans that was of any use. But Christmas was approaching. It left him clinging to the hope, the family would be reunited. Alesha, equipped with her binoculars and powerful camera lens was under strict orders to keep their house under close surveillance; where maybe, he would finally gain some insight into the movements of Rosemary's absent children.

Elijah meanwhile, was whistling to himself as he set about the task of making garlands; the artificial ivy, carefully entwined with lengths of shiny green tinsel. He had applied a little extra glitter to capture the sparkle of candlelight - the final section carefully arranged around the hearth, interspersed with fairy lights, to create an effect which would have rivalled the best window displays in London. He had always loved Christmas where browsing around the magnificent West End had become something of a tradition. He flicked on the lights. Though the ambience of their lounge was not the only thing he was ecstatic about.

"It looks stunning," Eleanor whispered in pride. "Now are you sure you don't mind taking these mince pies to the Community Centre?"

"Course not!" Elijah beamed. "I'm meeting Holly - I probably won't be back until later."

Elijah buttoned up his black woollen coat, threw a scarf around his neck and backed out of the door, burdened with several Tupperware boxes. The tea bar was already swarming with elderly folk, in anticipation of a Christmas party arranged by Emily, Eleanor's fellow volunteer and friend.

On turning, he almost collided with Hilary, teetering on the edge of the communal hall - she was accompanied by Holly and Reginald.

"Holly," he smiled. "Looking forward to Christmas? When can we meet up?"

Holly nibbled her lip which always signified, something wasn't quite as straight forward. "I've been meaning to tell you - we're going away…"

"To my mother's," Hilary interrupted, with just a hint of smugness, "in Tunbridge Wells."

Elijah felt his smile drop.

"This is the reason I wanted to see you," Holly added, gazing deeply into his eyes. "We're going to church. I was wondering if you'd like to come with us."

Naturally, Elijah showed no reluctance. He knew Holly's family were devout Christians and happy to go along, where the notion of singing carols alongside his gorgeous girlfriend seemed like a lovely idea. It was an elegant church and even more splendid on the inside, especially in candlelight. It was only after the service had ended, Holly told him, he had a lovely singing voice - pitch perfect and every note as clear as crystal.

"Maybe I get it from my father," Elijah beamed proudly.

"What happened to him?" Holly frowned. "He's dead, isn't he?"

Elijah tensed, unsure how much to tell her. "I never knew him. He died when I was a baby."

Straight away, he sensed Reginald's attention. Elijah glanced back and for a moment, he could have sworn he saw him swallow. It was betrayed by the tell-tale ripple in his throat, leaving Elijah unsure what to say. He had witnessed his expression of horror and it disturbed him.

"I'm bored," Holly eventually whined, as the congregation flocked around the church hall. They were nearly all adults, Elijah noticed - engaged in heavy conversation amidst a seemingly never-ending flow of mince pies and mulled wine. "Can I go home, Mummy?"

Hilary bristled. "No you can't! I am not leaving you on your own!"

"She can always come back to the almshouse," Elijah offered politely. "Everyone's at home."

For once, Reginald chose to be diplomatic - almost impatient for them to leave.

Elijah on the other hand, had no idea what Holly was really planning. She ultimately hauled him through the door of her own house, with blatant disregard of her parents' wishes.

"I thought we were going back to my place," he whispered.

"Later," Holly smirked. "I wanted to give you your Christmas present."

Elijah was hardly thinking straight as she led him to her bedroom. Hilary would go mad if she discovered he was up here! Yet he felt like a moth unwittingly drawn to a flame, unable to tear his attention away from this beautiful girl, poised like an angel before him, her blonde hair tumbling around her shoulders, her eyes shiny with desire.

"Close your eyes!" she ordered.

Elijah did as he was told - but the sight she had in store took his breath away. Holly hovered before him, wearing nothing but a shell-pink satin bra and matching pants. "I want to go all the way," she smiled sexily. "I'm ready, if you are."

"Oh Holly," Elijah mumbled, staggering towards her. Before he even knew it, he almost tripped over, where the two of them crumpled on top of Holly's bed in a heap.

She dragged off his chunky knit sweater and teeshirt, admiring his body; the slender, supple limbs - the touch of his bare skin which was smooth and peachy all over. They had already started kissing and Elijah didn't hold back as their tongues connected. He wanted the moment to last forever. It was as if he no longer had any control over his desire - reaching around her back to unclip her bra. He stared at her breasts in wonder; small, firm, tipped with rosy pink nipples - he couldn't resist touching them, one in each hand, caressing them gently. The rest of their clothes were peeled away swiftly. Elijah closed his eyes, aroused beyond belief, the pressure in his groin building so much, it was almost painful.

It was in those few snatched moments, he started to remember everything William had shared with him - the secret of a girl's anatomy where finally, he was about to put theory into practice. He took one glance at the golden triangle of hair between her legs and blinked, careful not to hurt her as he slid his finger inside her. His heart charged even faster, stimulated by the feel of the warm, moist flesh which hid so many pleasures. Nevertheless, he bit back his longing - searching for the one special spot, William had told him about; delighted when his finger tip settled on a swelling. It felt like a small bead. He stroked it lovingly, hearing her breath turn heavy as she writhed and parted her legs - then a few minutes later, she was crying out in ecstasy.

The rest was a blur. Holly seized his shoulders, rolling him on top of her and from the moment he penetrated her, Elijah could no longer deny, it was the best feeling he had ever experienced as he too, quickly soared to a climax.

"Oh Eli, that was so nice," Holly sobbed, still shuddering from the intensity of her own orgasm. "I never imagined it would be that lovely!"

They lay together panting, where the only other sound in the room was the gentle ticking of the clock on Holly's bedside table. "It was magical," Elijah gasped, kissing her again. "That was the best Christmas present ever..." his words were cut short as his eyes flew towards the clock. The systematic 'tick-tock' conveyed a sudden mocking quality. "Oh no! What about your folks?"

Holly pressed her finger firmly over his lips. "They won't be home for at least half an hour," she soothed. "It's always the same at Christmas. They like to stay behind and chat. Though having said that, I suppose we should get ourselves over to your place."

Elijah felt deliriously happy as they stepped into the almshouse, hand in hand, unable to believe what had just happened. It was a shattering blow to think she was leaving, next day. He probably wouldn't see her until the new year. Yet the sight of his home, bedecked with its glittering decorations, brought another element of joy to his world; the room softened by a subtle gleam of candlelight, the banks of shadow almost masking him - where no-one could see the lusty glow in his cheeks.

Elijah sailed through the remaining days of Christmas as if in a dream.

Charlie watched him from afar, having already noticed the extra spring in his step - remembering a time when he had been that age and guessing the reason for this sudden upsurge in spirits. His step-son was in love! He smiled inwardly. These kids were growing up so quickly. All he could hope for now, was to secure them a better future; one where they would no longer be trapped in a web of fear. Elijah knew as many of his mother's secrets as he did by now - which inevitably drew his thoughts towards the pledge on their wedding day.

Before the year ended, they reflected on everything that had transpired: from the volatile land battle - to the rising tide of crime. In some ways, it felt like they were winning - in others, it seemed their enemies were growing more powerful. It was like a chess board. The pieces kept shifting: somewhere in the distance, Perry loomed, as did his evil son. Robin was tucked in the wings, determined to unhinge them - and floating between both parties, lurked the ever present threat of Dominic Theakston, leaving Eleanor unsure where the land lay.

She listened fearfully, as the clock stuck Midnight, with no idea what 1989 had in store.

Chapter 15

January 1989

Eleanor's concerns were not unfounded. None of them knew what had really been going on behind the scenes, as Robin continued to sow the seeds of treachery.

Charlie was engrossed in a meeting on site. He and Peter had joined forces with a team of construction engineers to discuss the first phase of the new infrastructure. Avalon and William too, had decided to join them - intrigued to discover how the land was being developed.

It stretched out before them; a blanket of naked earth carved into channels where the deep underground network of pipes was already under construction. The air felt damp but mild - the subdued winter sun low in the sky, casting long shadows as a haze of mist rolled into the distance. Avalon sighed, listening to the consultation with half an ear.

Charlie had just opened his mouth to speak when the violent slam of a car door ricocheted sharply into the atmosphere. She whirled round, alerted to the man striding towards them - recognising his towering frame and dark blonde hair. Dominic looked formidable in a black leather jacket - yet there was something about the set of his cold, deadpan face which sent the alarm bells ringing.

"Mr Theakston?" she greeted him tentatively.

He gave an abrupt nod, clearly making a beeline for Charlie. Avalon stared at her brother who gave a questioning flick of the eyebrow.

"Dominic," Charlie nodded. "Happy new year to you... is something wrong?"

"You could say that!" and before anyone knew what was happening, he had drawn Charlie aside, separating him from the group. "Just what the fuck do you think you're playing at?" he added, in a low and menacing growl.

The engineers were too absorbed in their evaluation of the pipe work to get involved. The others exchanged worried glances, instantly sensing conflict.

"I beg you're pardon?" Charlie spluttered.

"Just back from the planning office," Dominic continued, "me application to extend the night club's been refused - thanks to your bloody report!"

"I don't know what you're talking about!" Charlie muttered. "What report?"

Dominic took another step forward and grasped the front of his jacket. "A report that lists your same tired old arguments - why Rosebrook shouldn't expand its clubbing facilities. The noise, the disruption, the drugs - same shit, your wife read out at that meeting!" His eyes carved into him like daggers. "Come bleating, did she? Told you what I'd do if she stepped out of line?"

"What?" Charlie hissed, finally getting some gist of what he was saying. "She said she went to see you! Does this mean you've been threatening her again?"

"Dominic, please!" Peter intervened. "There's clearly been a misunderstanding!"

"Stay out of this, Peter," Dominic ordered, keeping his voice soft. "This is between me and Charlie. I was looking to expand me club, see and he just had to put the boot in…"

"Rubbish!" Charlie bellowed, struggling against his grip. It seemed, he was reluctant to let go; a situation which forced Charlie to grab him by the shoulders and after several seconds of wrestling, he managed to shove him away. "Get your hands off me…"

Once again, Dominic flew towards him - it looked for all the world as if he was about to hit him. This time it was William who surged into the melee with the same bullish determination he had demonstrated, the night Ben had attempted to rape his sister - forgetting the consequences.

"Don't you dare attack him," he yelled.

Dominic turned to him with a look of contempt, before he casually thrust him aside. It was regrettable that he would push him harder than he intended; given his slight frame and tender years, William was sent flailing to the ground. Avalon let out a sob.

"You bastard!" William screamed at him.

Sensing everyone was losing control, Peter helped him to his feet. "Will someone explain what the hell is going on!" he whimpered. His voice shook with emotion, his Irish accent thickening. He gaped at Dominic - yet the panic mapped across his gentle face seemed to be the one factor that froze them in their tracks.

"Okay, Peter, I'll tell you," Dominic snapped. He shot a guilty glance towards William. "Sorry, kid, but you shouldn't have interfered."

"And you shouldn't have gone for Charlie…" William retorted but Dominic raised a hand, commanding silence.

"All I wanted to do was refurbish the basement - to provide an alternative dance floor, but I gather there was some objection from *you lot!*"

"We had nothing to do with it!" Charlie exploded.

Dominic spun round. "What, you mean your Eleanor didn't start a campaign?" he accused, "along with that prissy drugs councillor from your Community Centre?"

"Hilary?" Charlie shot back. "That's ridiculous. They don't even see eye to eye!"

"Is that so? Well it seems, her objections were an even bigger load of shit! As if we're about to open some strip joint! Not to mention all the illegal acid house parties! And that, coupled with this *fantasy* of yours - that your kids are gonna be drawn down a slippery slide of drink and drugs…"

"This is bollocks!" Charlie retaliated. "It sounds as if the council have compiled their own report and cherry picked a few choice phrases from a letter I wrote, a year ago!" His eyes blazed. "That's it! I want to see this report for myself and I bet you any money, I know who's behind it!"

"Robin Whaley?" Avalon added coldly, still glaring at Dominic. "C'mon, William. It's time you and I paid a visit to the planning department. We'll get a copy for you, Charlie."

Dominic stared back at her, where none of the anger had abated from his expression. "You do that, darling," he hissed. "You see, for a moment I sort of hoped we could work together in this town - but I won't deny, that report's made me fucking angry!"

Eleanor stared at the report in horror. She had always known Hilary was about to start a protest. Yet she never imagined she would enlist half the congregation of her church; nor start a petition - filled with the signatures of dozens of naive elderly folk from the Community Centre. It was the way their individual concerns had been woven into the report that shocked her; a report prioritised by objections, she and Charlie had raised a year ago... it was pure deception!

Already she could feel a coldness slipping down her spine. Avalon sat opposite, her eyes glittering with outrage. She had already told her about the scene at the building site:

"He really went for Charlie!"

Eleanor felt her stomach churn, jarred by the thought of what this might have led to. It brought a sense of violence into her world - where Dominic's ultimatum now seemed horribly real.

"Are you sure you're okay, William?" she spluttered, grateful of his intervention.

He was slumped against the cracked leather cushions of their old Chesterfield sofa, though his face was a lot calmer than his sister's. He gave a nod.

"It was just a shove," he sighed. "I've been in worse situations. Bit of a thug, isn't he? And you reckon the report was deliberately engineered to stir things?"

"Definitely," Eleanor answered numbly, "and this time, I'm taking my complaint to the head of Rosebrook Council."

It was a pity they hadn't actually seen Robin - if only to watch him cringe. There was no doubt, this was his handiwork.

Charlie on the other hand, was fuming, finally understanding Dominic's rage. He had long recognised his entrepreneurial spirit, recalling the stunning interior of his gym. It was clear the man possessed a raging ambition. It had manifested itself yet again, in the refurbishment of the club - the plush leather seating, the sweeping bars which his own son had completed. All Dominic wanted to do was to expand; to create a second dance floor for alternative music. Charlie shuddered, unable to believe the way the application had been twisted - the mere hint of an underground club, designed to conceal a pit of sleazy activities. It was beyond belief!

He finally managed to track down Dominic at home. "You can always appeal, you know," he sighed down the telephone.

The conversation was short and to the point. At the very least, it ended with a begrudging apology. Unfortunately, it was too late. The conflict had injected a sense of ill feeling into the community - and to think, the refurbishment of the club had forged the start of an uneasy, but profitable bond. Bond any future connections had been severed, leaving Dominic no other choice than to take up the issue with the council.

As it happened, Robin could not have been more delighted. He knew it wouldn't be long before the sparks would fly, having heard about the furious intervention of the Barton-Wells children. It was fortunate he had been on a coffee break. But with accusations of skulduggery bounding their way around the planning office, it was time to speak to Dominic - time to express his sorrow, before offering his advice as to how the council could reach some compromise.

He smiled as he stepped into the night club, knowing the damage had been done. It was a few hours before the doors would be open to revellers - though the bar was already open. Robin drank in the surroundings with pleasure, unable to deny, there was something about the palatial but funereal dark furnishings which thrilled him.

"Could I trouble you for a gin and tonic?" he smiled politely to a glamourous young woman behind the counter.

Pippa glanced across at Dominic. He was neatly concealed in the shadows, just to the other side of the bar area.

"I think there's someone to see you, Dom," she smiled, pouring Robin's drink.

Robin flinched as Dominic loomed up from a horseshoe of black leather seating. He was dressed in a suit. In some ways, it made him appear even more like gangster-like and while his face appeared neutral, Robin thought he detected a glint of wrath in his eyes. It was obvious, he would be displeased.

For several minutes, they made small talk. Robin sipped his gin and tonic. By the time he had consumed almost half of it, Dominic glanced towards the back of the lounge.

"Never did take you on a tour round my club, did I?" he said softly. "Follow me - wanna show you something..."

With a shrug, Robin drained his glass, undeniably curious. A door led to a series of hidden rooms. He had never thought much about the inner workings of a night club. There was a storeroom for supplies, two cloakrooms and most interesting of all, a surveillance room. A set of TV screens revealed CCT footage of virtually every concealed area, including the lavatories.

"It's pretty much as I said," Dominic smiled. "Told you I'd invest in proper security. See any illegal drug dealing, we sort it. You with me, so far?"

"Impressive," Robin murmured, gazing in awe at the screens.

"Bouncers are built like brick shit houses. Won't necessarily stop the kids taking drugs *before* they come in - but any dodgy behaviour..." Dominic turned to face him directly, "anyone off their face, drinking too much, or causing any hassle gets the boot!"

He led Robin a little further down the hallway and pointed out the DJ cabin, where a set of ultramodern, metallic mixing decks shimmered under a faint glow of spot-lighting.

But as the hallway extended further, so the light became dimmer - and all the while, Dominic kept talking, never once breaking sentence.

"See, I never intended to encourage nothing seedy. No acid house parties, no gambling dens and definitely no strippers! All I ever wanted to do was run a decent establishment..."

The shadows seemed to swallow them, where one final office lingered at the end of the corridor. Already, Robin felt tense, hearing the ice creeping into Dominic's tone.

"Dominic, I am sorry the council refused your application," he leapt in quickly.

"Really?" Dominic sneered. He threw a quick glance over his shoulder - then turning to Robin, grabbed his arm and shoved him into the room. "By the way," he whispered evilly, "forgot to mention - CCTV footage doesn't cover *this* room."

Robin turned cold. "What's going on?"

"I might ask you the same question," Dominic smiled. He closed the door, trapping him inside. "You manipulative bastard! The Baileys had nothing to do with that campaign!"

"How can you be so sure?" Robin retorted.

"You ain't got a clue, have you?" Dominic laughed. "A few years back, you got me to put the frighteners on Eleanor again. Don't suppose you knew that Charlie paid me a visit!"

"What?" Robin hissed, hit with a jarring sense of panic.

"Yeah, that's right," Dominic kept taunting. "Happens, he knew I'd threatened Eleanor's kid! Another suggestion which came from your sick mind!"

"You've been communicating with them?" Robin whispered, feeling suddenly cheated.

"I knew they were gonna object to the leisure complex," Dominic sneered, "but they never had *no* problem with me extension. You used their speech for no other reason than to stir up shit."

"What if I did?" Robin spat. "You've got no idea how dangerous that woman is; sneaking around in disguise, visiting her solicitor, disappearing for days under the pretence of illness - and all the while, she's adding to her dossier of evidence…"

"How do you know that?" Dominic retaliated.

"Why the need for a disguise?" Robin pressed. "It's obvious, she's planning to re-open Jansen's murder case and if she succeeds… every one of us will go down, including you!"

"Yeah, don't I know it," Dominic nodded. "You're all riddled with paranoia…" In a second flash of movement, he gripped Robin by the lapels and slammed him against the wall. "Well let me tell you what I think! I'm guessing, Eleanor's not only got enough shit on Perry to prove he sanctioned Jansen's murder - but information that'll prove the *real reason* he had that kid killed!" He loosened his grip, as if satisfied by Robin's floundering panic.

"That's enough, Dominic," he shuddered. "There is no need for violence. Perry is only trying to protect us."

"Bollocks!" Dominic hissed, "Perry is trying to protect *himself* and using the two of us to save his arse! Well, I'm out! I want nothing more to do with this!"

"Your choice," Robin finished coldly. "Though don't say I didn't warn you. If we go down, you go down and Eleanor will have won her battle. Turn your back if you want, Dominic, but I won't. I should also warn you that Perry has enough contacts in the criminal underworld to fend off anyone who stands in his path - and that includes you…"

His words were cut short as Dominic spun round and slammed his fist into his gut. Robin let out a cry, his knees buckled and he collapsed to the floor in shock.

"Don't you threaten me, you slimy little shit," he snarled, his patience finally spent, "and as for these 'contacts.' If you mean Alan Levy, he ain't gonna lay a finger on me! His dad and I ran the criminal underworld. He was me right hand man and I've known the kid since he was a sprog!"

"That's an assault," Robin spluttered, struggling to his feet,

"I could do a lot worse," Dominic finished nastily, "now fuck off!"

Robin had no choice but to leave. His abdomen throbbed as he shuffled his way back up the corridor - frantically searching for the door before he burst into the main bar area. He braced his shoulders sharply, determined to resume some composure - aware of Pippa's scrutiny as he inched his way towards the exit.

The moment he was outside, he felt the breath pour from his lungs. In fact, he barely knew where he was going as he sped away from the club. Its back street location sent him on a wild, unplanned diversion. He clawed his way through the darkness until finally, he reached the edge of a field; the land, they had all bitterly fought over - the site of Peter's housing trust. Robin glared across the remote plain and felt a rise of nausea. He slumped against the chicken wire fence and threw up, leaving an unpleasant taste of gin and bile burning in his throat. He coughed, gripping the fence to haul himself upright, then staggered a little further - following the perimeter until at last, he discovered a gap which led into the Community Centre gardens.

Unsure what possessed him, he struggled through the gap. A tiny security light illuminated the area. Robin's eyes were drawn to it: seeing the decorative edge of a parapet framing the roof - the smooth walls which looked silver in the dusk. It had been over two years since he had persuaded the council to endorse this design - determined to make his mark by injecting an element of beauty into the town. His gaze became stony. Peter had been a fool to turn against him; but it wasn't Peter he yearned to avenge, it was Eleanor.

Robin blinked as his eyes adjusted to the darkness. He could just about make out the shape of the path; the tidy shrubs and magnificent stone urns silhouetted against the sky. He crept closer, gripping the edge of one of the urns. Dark ivy spilled over the rim and as he examined it more carefully, he could see the curling leaves of silver dust as well as the cyclamens. Soft plumes of petals rose from the centre, their pale pink shade only just discernible. In some ways, they reminded him of Eleanor - covert, yet undeniably beautiful.

Robin closed his eyes, forced to revisit that awful scene in the club. His plan had backfired; the one man, he had hoped would be their most offensive weapon was no longer at their disposal.

He felt his hatred rise, knowing the only solution left open to them. The notion to seize Eleanor's son hit him powerfully; only this time, he had no qualms. Like Perry, he was consumed by a gnawing urge to keep this community under control - knowing that sooner or later, they were bound to expose a weakness.

PART 3
ECSTASY AND AGONY

Chapters 16-25

February - July 1989

Chapter 16

I

Margaret had changed in the last six months. No-one could be absolutely sure she had overcome her brush with anorexia but she was a shadow of the plump, adolescent girl, Eleanor remembered from the previous year. She took the extra effort to ensure she was getting a healthy balance of foods; supplementing her lunch boxes with wholesome snacks, nuts and fruit. On the plus side, her spots had cleared up, unveiling a complexion which was dewy and fresh, warmed by the same soft flush as her mother, Anna.

There were times when Charlie felt his heart squeeze as other similarities came to light. She was thinner than Anna had ever been but she was definitely turning prettier - her face almost pixie-like, gifted with the same widely-spaced, brown eyes as his own.

Margaret had little concept of how she appeared to others; painfully lacking in confidence and grateful to have Holly as a friend. It delighted her that Holly was still going out with Eli, having already picked up the clue, they might have slept together. Holly admitted, she was too scared to invite him back to her house after school for fear of their nosy neighbours snitching.

The one thing Elijah had noticed, was how hard she tried to copy Holly's appearance; the long, floral skirts, worn with neat tops and cardigans. She had grown her hair long again. She had even persuaded Holly to help her lighten it by investing in a home highlighting kit. Elijah would never forget that day. How comical she looked in a tight plastic cap, while Holly tugged the strands of hair through with a hook. Though no-one could deny, the effect was stunning - her luxurious locks threaded with light, golden streaks.

It was her hair that captured the watery sunlight as she sauntered home, oblivious to the eyes that followed her. She was slowly making her way up the high street and if she had glanced across the road, she might have noticed the two Harley Davidson motorbikes loitering outside one of the town centre pubs. It was an establishment named the 'Rose and Crown' and popular amongst Rosebrook's working community; a traditional building set on two levels with tall, ornamental windows. But Margaret did not look up. She continued to wander in the direction of the almshouses, an ethereal figure who had snatched the attention of two men. One of them was Ben Hampton; the other, his ever faithful accomplice, Nathan.

"It's the Bailey girl," Nathan muttered, tugging Ben's sleeve.

"I know," Ben smiled. "C'mon, let's spy on her. Looks like someone else is sniffing after her too. This could be interesting..."

He had long recognised the boys who were steadily sneaking up on her - amused to wonder where this was leading.

By the time Margaret arrived home, she had no idea she was being tailed by Gary Boswell and a couple of his friends, including his evil sidekick, Darren.

She turned onto the path adjacent to the almshouses - but before she had a chance to slip her key in the door, she froze as a hulking shadow loomed up the wall. Margaret spun round - shocked to see Gary standing there. He seemed to have sprung out of no-where and yet there was something quite unpleasant about the way his mean, dark eyes were flickering over her.

"What do you want?" Margaret snapped.

"Just thought we'd drop by and say hello," Gary said snidely. "You on your own?"

Margaret looked scared - unaware, their real enemies were observing the entire scene from the seclusion of an alleyway, not far from the Fish and Chip shop.

"Gonna invite us in for a cup of tea, then?" Gary kept taunting. "You haven't got a boyfriend, have you? Thought you might like a bit of company."

She slowly met Gary's eye, clocking his leer. He was right - she had never had a boyfriend. They probably thought she was desperate; yet even she wouldn't stoop so low as to allow someone as vile as Gary Boswell to take advantage.

"Look - just leave me alone, okay," she spluttered. "I am not letting you in…"

"All in good time," Gary smirked. "How about a little kiss."

All three of them had sauntered right up to the door. Pitched against Gary's bulk, she felt tiny. Margaret let out a resigned sigh and hating herself for doing it, stretched up and planted a peck on Gary's cheek. "There!" she said, turning away to unlock the door, "now go away!"

She could hear the others whooping with laughter.

"Call that a kiss?" Gary sneered and planting a firm hand on her shoulder, he drew his lips right up to her ear. "Show us your fanny!" he whispered, "and I'll give you a pound…"

Margaret whirled back round, cheeks flaring - so appalled, she slapped his face.

"How dare you! I wouldn't go out with you if you gave me a thousand pounds!"

This time it was Gary who flushed, his face engorged with anger. He rubbed his cheek, then smiled nastily. "I wasn't asking you to go out with me. I'm more interested in your good looking mate. Not still going out with that waster, Jansen, is she?"

Margaret looked mortified. Gary's smile turned more spiteful.

"What - you didn't think I fancied *you* did you?" he let out an unpleasant snigger, glancing at his audience with amusement. His cruel eyes stabbed into her again. "You did?"

"I wouldn't touch you with a 12 foot barge pole, you great elephant!" Margaret screamed.

Gary turned puce. "What did you call me?" he hissed.

Margaret let out a sob, where the arrival of her brother couldn't have been better timed.

"What's going on?" Andrew hollered, drinking in the scene. He stood a short distance away, his denim jacket peppered with plaster dust. Whatever rivalry had existed between them in the past, there was no way he was going to tolerate these leering slobs giving her all this hassle.

"Andrew, thank God!" Margaret cried out.

Andrew strode towards Gary, grabbed him by the collar and yanked him away from the door.

"Piss off!" he ordered curtly, "and that goes for the lot of you!"

They were scattered like pigeons before they slunk their way back into the high street.

From their concealed position in the alleyway, Ben was still watching - his smile hidden behind the black visa of his helmet.

Charlie's initial complaint to Inspector Boswell however, did nothing to deter Gary and his cronies from moving their persecution to the school playground. One week on, Holly and Margaret were casually chatting to Elijah, until once again, they found themselves the objects of intimidation.

Boswell's gang encircled them like wolves. "Hi, Holly," he started crooning, "when are you gonna ditch gyppo boy and come on a date with me? What's *he* got that's so special?"

"He's better looking!" Holly snapped waspishly, "and he's a *very* good kisser!"

She threw Elijah her most enchanting smile - but had captured the attention of Mickey Snyder. He was surveying her coldly.

"Didn't stop you chatting up Ken Wilkinson at my party!" he sneered.

For a moment, Holly looked furtive. "We were only talking!"

"What - you mean, he didn't walk you home?" Gary smirked, taking his first menacing steps towards Elijah. "I knew you'd never hold down someone as pretty as Holly, you tosser!"

"Shut your trap!" Elijah hissed, his face flaring crimson. "Holly and I are just fine!"

"Really?" Gary smiled. "Well, rumour has it, she's a bit of a slag."

Elijah was shaking with rage, hands closing into fists as they hung stiffly by his sides. He shuffled on his feet. Everyone held their breath, just waiting to see if he would hit him. Gary's face had split into an evil grin. He held up his hands, then waggled his fingers as if egging him on, daring him to throw that first punch.

"Eli, leave it," Margaret hissed. "It's obvious he's trying to start a fight."

"You're right," Elijah snapped. He turned on his heel to walk away.

Except Darren Jackson had stuck his gangly leg right in his path, tripping him up. To his utter belittlement, Elijah went sprawling across the tarmac.

"You're a wimp, Jansen!" Gary was heard braying. "You wouldn't dare hit me! You haven't got the balls!"

Elijah leapt to his feet and limped away, burning with humiliation. It wasn't the first time. Even with the prestige of dating a beautiful girl like Holly, he was never going to shake off the stigma of his early life; some lowly 'diddicoy' living in a caravan. He felt the grip of torment, especially when Holly came dashing over - not to console him but to berate him!

"Eli!" she gasped. "He insulted me! Why didn't you defend me?"

"Why do you think?" Eli sulked, unable to meet her eye. "He's a giant! And I'm sorry, if you think I'm a *wimp*, but he would have flattened me!"

"Holly, that's really unkind," Margaret jumped in quickly. "It was five against one!"

"I'm sorry!" Holly snapped, pouting like a child, "but what if he tries it on, like he did with you, the other day?" Elijah gaped at her in horror, his emotions torn. Then finally, her face softened. "Oh, Eli… Why can't you just be a bit more… you know, macho?"

"I don't want to be *macho*," Eli whispered in her ear. "I love you."

She gave him a cool smile - yet didn't return the endearment.

II

Holly was beginning to feel irritated. She hadn't said anything, purely because she *didn't* love him. He was very sweet and had proven to be a good lover but the sad truth was, she wanted shot of him! She had started fancying someone else and finally in with a chance. So in the end, she devised a different strategy; one which would not only let Eli know the score, but boost her own female empowerment. Holly sneaked away from school, knowing exactly where she was heading. She licked her lips, feeling her confidence soar as she rang the doorbell.

"Holly!" William gasped. His face broke into a surprised smile. "What are you doing here?"

At 17, he was one of the school's most eligible sixth formers - his shoulders broad from the hours spent on the sports field as captain of the cricket team, his face as appealing as it had ever been, from the sweeping curve of his mouth to his enchanting hazel eyes.

"Oh William," Holly sighed. She stole a backward glance, as if she had expected to be followed. "Can I come in? You're the only person I can turn to, right now..."

He followed her glance, a frown etched across his face - but nevertheless, held the door open.

"It's Gary Boswell!" she simpered. "Did you know he made a pass at Margaret?"

William's eyes flashed. "Did he now?"

"Yes! But it's not *Maggie* he's interested in, it's me!" She started wringing her hands. "Is - is there any chance you could *scare him off* for me?"

His first response was to protest - until Holly reminded him of the pasting he'd dished out once before.

"Yeah and his dad's never forgiven me!" He sighed, "besides - shouldn't you be talking to Eli?"

Holly peered up shyly. "Eli hasn't got the nerve! He won't stick up for me."

William gaped at her in disbelief. A look of irritation flickered across his face.

"William, please…" Holly begged, springing to her feet. She allowed her arms to snake over his shoulders, marvelling at the ripple of muscle beneath his sweater. "You're so much more *manly* and I hate to say this - but you can't deny, Eli's a bit of a softie…"

"Enough, Holly," William snapped, shaking off her embrace. "Eli's my best friend, so don't you dare talk about him like that! Now, I really think it's time you left…"

"What?" Holly gasped. She clocked the contempt in his eyes, then finally lost her cool. "Fine! In that case, I'll tell Margaret, you're as big a chicken as he is…"

"Tell her what you like," William said coldly. "Margaret's worth ten of you! She'd never want to see Eli beaten to a pulp, for the sake of taking on Boswell."

Holly stared at him open-mouthed. "You prefer that little wallflower to me?"

William let out a cynical laugh. "Just listen to yourself. Forever banging on about how lucky she is to have you as a friend! You're lucky to have *her* - she's sweet, kind and will always be there for you. I bet the only reason you hang out with her, is to make yourself feel superior. And as for Boswell - if you don't want the attention, tell him yourself! Don't expect me or Eli to get our faces smashed in, charging to the rescue!"

Holly started to cry. She couldn't help it.

"Go home, Holly," he placated her and taking her arm, guided her gently to the door. "Dry your eyes, put something pretty on and go and see Eli. You're lucky to have him too, you know. He loves you and he would never, ever do anything to hurt you…"

Ten minutes later, Holly sat frozen by her dressing table as the waves of humiliation and hurt flooded over her. How dare William insult her! She had gone there looking for a champion and virtually offered herself on a plate. It

278

inspired her to take desperate measures; anything to restore her shattered ego and there was only one person capable of making her feel good about herself.

She re-applied her makeup - a sweep of brown eye shadow to draw out the azure blueness, a slick of lip gloss to enhance her pouting lips. She brushed her hair until it shimmered, then stepped into a figure hugging dress - loving the way it flared at the hem and nipped in her tiny waist. By the time she knocked on Elijah's door, his face was a picture.

"Let's go back to my place?" she whispered. It was to her utter dismay that Andrew was at home and so for that matter, was Charlie. "Please, Eli!"

He hesitated, conscious of the perils of being caught. It was in the split second of indecision, her eyes seemed to grow bigger. He could never have known that Holly wasn't thinking straight.

"Okay," he consented, hurling a glance towards the others. "Won't be long…"

"Be good," Andrew smirked, "don't do anything I wouldn't do!"

Holly ignored him and seizing Eli's hand, she practically dragged him to her house. They were barely through the door when she slid her arms around his waist, kissing him. Elijah felt the blood rush to his face as well as various other parts of his anatomy. Yet something didn't feel right.

"Holly, is something the matter?" he faltered - confused, as he wriggled away from her.

"No! Why should it be?" she snapped. "You're not giving me the cold shoulder are you?"

"Not at all," Elijah laughed, stroking his hands down the sides of her arms.

He gazed into her eyes, searching. There was no denying, she possessed a certain fragility; her eyes shining with some suppressed emotion - her lips trembling.

"L-let's go upstairs," she mumbled, "please, Eli - I need you…!"

Everything became a blur. Elijah felt a familiar glow spread through his body, allowing Holly to coax him upstairs - dreamy with desire, as she hauled her dress over her head. He watched as she reached round to unfasten her bra. It tumbled to the carpet with a flutter. She gave him a slow, seductive smile and arched her back, running her fingers through her luxurious hair, before flinging it behind her shoulders.

He lowered himself shakily onto her bed and removed his shoes and socks - he was still in his school uniform. She started tugging at the buttons of his shirt, easing it from his shoulders. Then finally, she unzipped his trousers.

"Holly, are you absolutely sure about this?" he whispered.

"Shut up and relax, will you!" she hissed, pushing him down onto the mattress.

Her fingers encircled themselves expertly around his penis. He let out a gasp, all reservations forgotten as they settled into a deep and loving kiss.

But the moment was short lived. It seemed only seconds before they heard the unmistakable crash of the front door - the patter of Hilary's feet as she stalked up the stairs.

Holly let out a squeak. "Oh my God, it's Mummy!" she whispered under her breath. "Hide - quickly..."

It was too late. The door flew open and in a single flash of movement, her mother swept into the room, just as Elijah was rolling off the bed - all set to dive under it.

"Gotcha!" Hilary snarled and without a moment's pause, she reached down and grasped Elijah by the roots of his chestnut hair, yanking his head upwards. "You disgusting, filthy boy!"

"Please," Elijah whimpered, "it's not what you think..."

"Think?" Hilary screeched. "I get home early - only to hear it from Mrs Julip that you two came sneaking in together and here you are, half naked in Holly's bedroom, taking advantage?"

"I'm not!" Eli gasped, wincing. "We love each other!"

Holly glanced up coolly, making no attempt to cover her nakedness. Hilary released him. She held her daughter's defiant stare for one more second, then slapped her hard across the face.

"You little slut!"

"Mummy, that's not fair!" Holly squealed, bursting into tears. "It's not *my* fault! I couldn't help it! He seduced me!"

Hilary spun to Elijah, who was struggling into his shirt. But it was on hearing those hateful words, he froze. "That is an absolute lie, Holly," he spluttered. "You know that's not true."

Hilary looked at him in disgust. "Get dressed," she ordered curtly.

Elijah gawked at her in shock, unable to believe Holly's duplicity. But there seemed little point in arguing. Hilary's eyes were narrow with scorn, her tiny mouth twisted into a sneer, leaving him wilting in shame as he hurriedly threw on the rest of his clothes.

The silence was heavy as Hilary practically frog-marched him to the almshouse. His heart thumped as she rang the doorbell. It was to his utter misery, she seized his collar, just as the door swung open and pushed him into the lounge as if he was some discarded piece of rubbish.

"What's going on?" Charlie breathed, erupting from his chair.

Eleanor stood in the kitchen doorway, staring at the unfolding scene with horror.

"I came home to find this - this *creature* in bed with my daughter!" Hilary's voice lashed.

Elijah felt chilled. "I-I'm sorry..."

Hilary gave a sniff, followed by an arrogant toss of the head. "Sorry? Did it never occur to you that Holly is underage!"

She was revelling in it - not even caring that Margaret was in the room.

It was with a self-righteous smile, she described the scene she had come home to. "He has broken the law, of course, seducing my little girl!"

"Hang on a minute!" Eleanor interjected. "Elijah's fifteen! Which means he's also underage. Did it never occur to you that these are two kids who maybe just got a bit carried away?"

Elijah felt himself sag with relief - at least his mother was on his side.

"I knew you'd say that," Hilary sneered, "but then you never did have any morals did you?"

Charlie's threw her a furious glare but his eyes were inevitably drawn back to Elijah. "What's your take on this, Eli?" he demanded.

"W-we're b-both to blame," he stammered miserably. "I-it's true. Hilary found us in bed together. I-I'm so sorry, Mrs Magnus…"

It seemed, Hilary was in no mood for forgiveness. "You will be! I forbid you to have anything to do with my Holly *ever* again! You're not to see her any more, do you understand?"

Elijah gave a sad but silent nod - his eyes burning with tears.

He slumped into a chair, paralysed. No sooner had Hilary left when Andrew came loping into the room, grinning. It was obvious he had heard every word.

"Told you not to do anything, I wouldn't do," he teased, with a light pat on the shoulder. "Does this mean you've been shagging her?"

Elijah's face crumpled. It was only now, the gravity of his feelings caught up with him. He covered his eyes with his hand - then suddenly, his shoulders started shaking.

"Shut up, Andrew," Charlie snapped softly. "Can't you at least, show a bit more tact!"

"I wasn't having a go," he protested. "I think it's excellent! Holly's a right stuck up bitch!"

Elijah let out a sob.

"Andrew, please…" Eleanor whimpered, rushing across to her son. "This is no laughing matter. Look at him! She's broken his heart."

It was no exaggeration. Elijah was inconsolable and sensing he needed some privacy, Eleanor led him to his bedroom where the bitter tears flowed freely. Never in her life, had she suffered this type of anguish. Jake had been her one and only. She had never experienced the trials and tribulations of young love as her son had today and her heart bled for him.

Charlie felt just as empathic. It had taken one glance at Hilary's protests against Dominic's extension, to realise what a truly sanctimonious crusader this woman believed herself to be. It left him little choice other than to discuss this latest fiasco with Peter; plagued by a nagging fear that in Hilary's eyes, Elijah had committed a sin beyond redemption.

It was several hours before Elijah felt any better - now begging to see William. Charlie took one look at his tortured expression and offered to drive him. They were taking *no* chances, where Eli's safety was concerned, especially after dark; but he also wanted a quiet word.

"Eli," he began gently, "I must say, I'm a bit shocked. I thought you'd be more sensible."

"I know," Elijah whispered, "I should have made us wait - I-I just couldn't resist her."

Charlie gazed at him - stirred by the sight of his forlorn face. "Did you take any precautions?"

"She said she was on the pill," Elijah mumbled, his cheeks flushing pink again.

"Thank God," Charlie breathed, staring up at the heavens. "Imagine if you got her pregnant! I've already got a feeling, Hilary's about to paint us as the black pariahs of the community!"

"Charlie, I am really sorry," Elijah croaked his voice refilling with tears.

"It's okay, son, we'll deal with it," Charlie said tightly. "Welcome to the world of manhood!"

Next, it was William's turn to console him - perhaps wondering if he alone, was responsible for Holly's rash behaviour. He finally came clean about her visit.

"She's a manipulative little tart," he hissed savagely, "thinks she can wrap boys around her little finger! You're better off without her, Eli, she'd have broken your heart, whatever..."

Regrettably, it was William's frankness that sent Elijah's misery hurtling even deeper; of a mind to completely obliterate his sorrow, as he helped himself to a little too much of Avalon's wine and ended up getting plastered.

It was Avalon who eventually got through to him, appalled to see him in such turmoil as she pulled up outside the almshouse - he was slumped in the passenger seat, white faced, now comatose with alcohol.

"Eli, look at the state of you," she whispered in horror. "Eleanor's going to kill me."

"Don't worry, I'll tell 'em it wa my fault," Elijah slurred.

He stared up at her. The moment their eyes connected, it was as if a tiny spark leapt between them. Avalon may have been a little older yet she had known Elijah, her entire life. At 15, he was still unbelievably timid but unlike Holly, she saw it as an asset. She didn't like boys who were big-headed; men like her colleague, Richard, who was particularly bullish and controlling. Avalon badly wanted to end their five month relationship and could no longer deny, she was finding Elijah's company a lot more pleasurable - even in his drunken state.

"Sorry I drank your wine," he spluttered. "I'll buy you another bottle..."

"Eli, stop worrying," Avalon chided, "I can tell you're hurting and know how it feels. Remember Hugh, who I dated a couple of years back? I found out he was two-timing me - it was like a knife being twisted in my heart." She let out a tinkle of laughter. "You'll bounce back. I did."

"Thanksh, Avalon," Elijah mumbled. He gazed into her eyes with an adoring a smile.

Back in the Magnus household, Hilary waited until Reginald had gone to bed; satisfied enough time had elapsed before she grabbed for the telephone.

It was with no hesitation, she proceeded to drip every morsel of this scandalous incident into the listening ears of Perry Hampton. All evening, her pent up anger had been spiralling.

"You were right all along," she spat into the mouthpiece. "An anarchist! No morals whatsoever. I can just imagine her living in that caravan. Some hippy commune. Probably had a string of lovers. I bet that boy grew up witnessing all manner of sexual activities!"

"I'm pleased you've seen her dark side," Perry said. He was practically purring, having just spoken to Alesha, who had some important news for him. He was meeting her in London, next day. "I always warned you, Eleanor would bring trouble," he massaged into the conversation.

"I know," Hilary sighed, "and so did Robin. I should have listened - all those connections with underground crime - prostitution…"

"Well, that's in the past," Perry snapped, feeling the heat darken his face. "What now?"

Hilary did not hold back - determined to sever her daughter's relationship with Elijah and at first, Perry listened with patience. In the grander scheme of things, the situation was regrettable; no moonlit walks - no secret kisses hidden in the trees of a public park, where the Jansen boy might have been vulnerable. He was as far from his reach as ever. Hilary meanwhile, was still ranting - despising the entire Bailey family and resolute in her desire to disassociate herself with the lot of them, including Margaret. It was the point where Perry bridled.

"Hilary, that would be extremely unwise! Have you considered the consequences? Without Holly's friendship, how can we hope to gain any more gossip about that woman?"

"Perry, I don't want her mixing with them!" Hilary sniffed.

"And jeopardise everything we've discovered?" he drawled. "Wasn't it *Holly* who found out about Margaret's binge drinking? Holly who visited, when Eleanor was unwell?"

"Are you saying I should allow their friendship to continue?" Hilary said disgustedly.

"Of course!" Perry boomed, "otherwise we sacrifice a vital source of information!"

By the time the conversation ended, Perry knew he had won her over. He lit a cigar - excited about the day to follow, despite his dismay towards Robin. He had never quite stopped fuming about his fallout with Dominic. But before he retired for the night, there was one more person he wanted to talk to - and that person was his son, who he knew he could rely on.

III

Elijah was determined to swallow his hurt. The only way he could do that was to remember the *real* danger in his life, his eyes fixated on the one and only photo of Jake, Eleanor kept on the mantelpiece. *He had died trying to hide from their enemies* - he could barely imagine the devastation his mother must have suffered on hearing that fatal gun shot.

He blinked back the last of his tears and walked into school, ready to face the world with a renewed sense of self-preservation - especially when he spotted Gary Boswell. In fact, the more he thought about Holly, the more he realised she wasn't a nice person - tarnished with the same superiority as her mother. He'd showered her with gifts, yet she hadn't even given him a Christmas card. He should have recognised her flaws - too shored up with the status of dating her.

The next time he faced Boswell, he could feel the steel developing in his core.

"You might as well hear it from me before you hear it from anyone else, but Holly and I split up. So go ahead - date her. She'll treat you like crap but do you know - it's not my problem!" and with a final look of rebellion, Elijah walked off and got on with the rest of his day.

It was only when he was home, he felt a trickle of melancholy slip back into his heart. He flipped through his sketchpad - haunted by Holly's beauty, as depicted in his many drawings. He had always captured her best assets; the shine of her hair, her pretty little upturned nose. There was only one sketch where she looked disdainful. They'd had a row, Elijah could remember it clearly.

Margaret sat sulking on the settee, flipping through one of her slimming magazines. Sukey sidled her way along the arm of the sofa but Margaret pushed her away. Elijah sensed her bad mood. It was obvious their lives would be different without Holly. He felt a moment of scorn, angered to think she had been such a dominating influence. He tore the sketch from the pad, screwing it into a ball then flung it across the floor towards the waste paper basket. He missed. Both cats instantly pounced on it, grateful for something to play with as they began to bat it around on the floor.

Margaret caught Elijah's eye and sniggered. "One of your sketches of Holly?"

"Might as well let the cats have some fun with it," Elijah muttered savagely. His eyes wandered to the magazine she was reading. "You're not still trying to lose weight are you?"

Margaret shrugged. "I always felt a bit of a trog next to Holly."

"Rubbish!" Elijah snapped, "in fact I wanna show you something…"

He rose from his chair and plonked himself down next to her, peeling back another page of his sketchpad. Margaret stared at the drawing. Neither girl knew anything about this sketch, snatched in a moment they had their backs turned. They were stood in the kitchen, side by side, pouring over some recipe, their long blonde tresses hanging down their backs. They could have been sisters.

"Okay, so tell me which one is you," Elijah ordered her softly.

"That one, of course!" Margaret sighed, pointing to the more curvaceous.

"Wrong," Elijah smiled. "Look closer - your hair's got darker streaks in it."

"There's no way I'm that slim!" Margaret argued.

"Yes you are!" Elijah pressed, the irritation in his voice rising, "you just can't see it! This is the trouble with Holly. She had a knack of making us feel inferior. I felt it too, you know! Whenever she was around, I felt like an oaf! At least we can be ourselves now."

Strangely enough, it was in the aftermath of that conversation, Margaret seemed to change overnight. The weekend had arrived and in a rare moment of boldness, she pulled on a pair of bleached denim jeans, threadbare in places and a colourful tunic from one of the boutiques in Shilling walk. She looked feminine, yet mutinous. Even when Holly approached her, her expression remained stony.

Holly stared at her in dismay - it clearly hadn't gone unnoticed, she was hand in hand with a new boyfriend. Yet she could not believe Margaret could snub her so icily.

"We can still be friends!" she bleated. "It's only *Elijah*, Mummy's banned me from seeing!"

"How could you do that to him?" Margaret whispered in hatred.

"I'm sorry," Holly simpered, "but I'm going out with Dave now."

They were lingering outside the Rose and Crown - one of her father's favourite pubs. There was even a chance he might be in there. Desperate not to succumb to Holly's wiles, Margaret stuck her nose in the air and sauntered inside.

"Maggie!" Holly called after her. She tightened her grip on Dave's hand, dragging him into the pub. "Talk to me, please…"

Margaret bit down hard on her lip as she shuffled towards the bar.

"I never meant to hurt Eli," Holly whispered, sidling right up to her. "I'm sorry about the way things turned out. It was embarrassing."

"Embarrassing?" Margaret hissed. "You broke his heart - and this isn't just about Eli. You went to see William; you flirted with him…" A sob caught in her voice. "You just had to try it on."

Holly backed away from the bar in shock, where it took one flick of her boyfriend's head to indicate there was nothing more to be said. They silently slipped out of the door.

Not one of them had noticed the smartly dressed man tucked in a corner, surveilling them. Margaret lingered by the bar, oblivious to the predatory eyes latched onto her. A tear trickled down her cheek - she wiped it away with a furious sweep of the hand, before staring up at the landlord.

"Can I have a glass of white wine please?" she requested boldly.

Joel, the landlord, took one look at her face and cocked his eyebrow. "Now then, young Margaret, you know I can't allow you to drink alcohol. I'd lose my licence."

"Better make it a Perrier then," she sighed.

She sensed the imposing shadow, before she caught her breath, clocking a smooth white hand resting on the bar top, tapping a leather wallet. His subtle but smoky aftershave wafted into the air, compelling Margaret to gaze up. She let out a startled gasp.

"It's okay, let me get this," Ben murmured in his practised upper class drawl.

Margaret couldn't move - mesmerised by the intense bore of his eyes. His blonde hair was cut into soft layers, cropped at the sides, which drew attention to his flawless features. Joel thought nothing of it as he poured out a small bottle of mineral water.

"Ice and lemon?" he grunted.

"Y-yes please," Margaret just about managed to whisper. For a second, she just stared at it.

Ben smiled, waving his hand towards the glass. She faltered for a few more seconds, then reluctantly reached out to grab it, her hand shaking.

"I'll have a glass of Chardonnay," he added mockingly. He was still gazing at Margaret who had no choice other than to accept the drink - terrified she might cause offence. "Would you care to join me?" he added gently.

"I-I can't," she whispered under her breath. "You're the enemy…" She gulped, turning to meet his eye again. "Why are you doing this?"

Ben shrugged. "Why not? I was enjoying a drink anyway - now all I want is a pretty girl to keep me company."

Margaret felt her cheeks turn warm, unable to believe this was real! Just one look at his clothes told her he was loaded. An expensive looking roll neck in the softest slate-blue cashmere - crisp, tailored trousers. She couldn't fail to notice his pewter watch which seemed almost too chunky for his slender wrist. He turned, beckoning her towards his table. It was situated in the most covert area of the pub, secluded by a mass of tropical plants.

"Sit down," he insisted, waving her towards a chair.

His beige trench coat was already draped over one arm. Margaret numbly obeyed. She took a swig of Perrier, just as Ben surreptitiously pushed his glass towards her.

"The wine was for you too," he added with an element of mischief. "Margaret isn't it?"

"Yes," she whispered, "and you're Ben Hampton. How could I forget...?" She closed her eyes, where the same sinister face flashed in her mind - she could hear the roar of his motorbike, her mother's scream. "Y-you nearly ran me over once..."

Ben let out a sigh. "I remember. I was a reckless fool in those days! Even your father called me a hooligan!" he laughed lightly. "How old were you?"

"Nine," Margaret replied. She stared at the wine, poised temptingly in front of her.

"Hmm," Ben nodded to himself as if mentally calculating her age. "I am truly sorry, you know. Can you ever find it in your heart to forgive me?"

His mouth curved into a smile. He was a monster - yet Margaret offered a shy smile in return, unable to stop herself. It wasn't in her nature to be stand-offish.

"Do you - you - still have the bike?" she mumbled, "a Harley Davidson wasn't it?"

"I've still got a Harley Davidson," Ben said, "but not the same one."

Even now, the memory of this incident left her chilled; it was the day, their lives started to go horribly wrong. Charlie and Andrew had lost their jobs. They had lost their home and somehow, it all seemed to be connected to the Hamptons. She took a sip of wine without thinking.

"What else is bothering you?" Ben murmured silkily.

Margaret took a second draft to steady her nerves. Her thoughts were naturally drawn to Westbourne House - leaving her no choice but to explain the horror she had experienced.

"Ah, I thought we might come to that," Ben nodded, his expression somber. He lowered his eyes. "What can I say? My father fought hard to get that house. Even I admit, we behaved badly."

"Badly?" Margaret breathed, finally banking up the courage to protest. "James was ill! You took away his home!"

"Wrong," Ben jumped in, "James went bankrupt. Did you know he borrowed more money than he could afford to pay back? The house would have been repossessed anyway. My father did not *take away his home*, he bailed him out."

Margaret shook her head. "Dad thinks we could have saved James's house - you deliberately set out to ruin him."

"Not me, Margaret, my father," Ben berated her softly. "You have no idea... Though I understand how you must feel, especially seeing as your father restored the house so beautifully."

The memories were flooding back fast, whirling in her mind like a sand storm. She could still remember the evil embedded in his face - the moment he had crept towards Avalon; the vicious threat towards William. It made her want to cry.

"I'm sorry," Ben kept interrupting, "we behaved like savages. My father went there to gloat over his success and I guess, we all got a little carried away..."

"So what about now?" Margaret pressed. There was no doubt in her mind, Ben was dangerous. He hadn't threatened her but she was still scared of him. "I thought your family *had it in for us?*"

"Whatever makes you say that?" Ben frowned, nudging his chair a little closer.

"A lot of bad things have happened. W-we were burgled. My brother was mugged..."

"Really?" Ben mused, "and you think this had something to do with *my* family?"

Margaret flushed - aware of how silly it sounded. She drained her wine almost sub-consciously, eyes darting sideways. She didn't like the probing nature of his questions. In fact there was something quite creepy about the way he was chatting her up like this.

"I have to go," she whispered fearfully, "I shouldn't be talking to you..." She rose as if to leave, but in a single flash of movement, Ben grabbed her hand.

"Don't go," he urged. "Please - whatever my family have done in the past, I wish I could make it up to you. Now sit down - there's so much more I want to say to you."

With a sigh Margaret surrendered, hypnotised by his stare.

Ben smiled inwardly, sensing her terror. In fact, he was enjoying himself. She was a far cry from the skinny child he had almost mown down, all those years ago. He had bumped into her more recently - recalling a day they had crossed paths on a remote country lane; a plump, pubescent girl who had stared back at him with her big, doe eyes. Yet she had blossomed into a beauty, he found himself thinking; studying the fragile blonde braced in front of him with her pretty, heart-shaped face - her frightened brown eyes, which he had to admit, were quite alluring.

"What is it you want with me?" she mumbled, squirming in the spotlight of his scrutiny.

"A chance to get to know you better," he replied.

It wasn't a lie - more than anything, he was yearning to gain her trust.

"I just want us to be safe!" she shuddered. "Your family got Westbourne House and there's not much we can do about that. But I can't forget... the things you said to Avalon, to William..."

"I can't change the past," Ben sighed, staring at her empty glass -

wondering how long it would be before the alcohol rushed to her head. "Don't dwell on it. Can I get you another drink?"

"N-no, it's okay, I'm f-fine," Margaret stuttered, a sudden flush pouring into her cheeks again. "I h-hope you're not trying to get me drunk..."

"Not at all," Ben purred. He laid his hand gently over her own, his head swooping closer. "Even I know that would be irresponsible! Though I'd be delighted to take you out to dinner..." He lifted his eyes, trapping her gaze - watching with pleasure as her face coloured even brighter.

"I can't!" she gasped. "You're older... if my dad ever found out, he'd kill you!"

"Hmm," Ben pondered, a smile playing around his lips. "I appreciate, he doesn't think very highly of me but I'm glad we had this chat." He squeezed her hand, sensing her imminent departure and yet still, she hesitated. "Any chance we can be friends?" he added gently.

"I-I don't know," Margaret shuddered, snatching her hand away, "but thanks for the drink."

He held her stare, reluctant to let her go - charmed by her innocence, yet conscious of his father's game plan. He was right in so many ways. Eleanor's community had grown stronger; and according to Perry, this *sweet little girl* was the weak link. It was a situation he wanted to use to his advantage, pleased to have established an initial bond of acquaintance.

Just as he was cherishing the thought, Margaret erupted from her chair. She threw him a final wistful glance, then practically shot towards the door.

The instant she was outside, the cold air felt refreshing.

Her heart was nonetheless, pounding. There was no question, she was as terrified of Ben as she had ever been but today, she had seen a different side to him. She sensed the magnetic pull, unable to deny, there was something menacing about him - but at the same time, something dangerously attractive.

Chapter 17

I

As the sullen winter skies began to recede, so the first overture of bird song penetrated the dawn. It was accompanied by a light breeze as it whispered through the tree tops - the haunting cries of rooks sailing across the distant fields. It was not quite light; the sky still hung with a translucent indigo veil and yet somewhere, beneath this pleasurable resonance, echoed the incessant whine of a chain saw.

Joshua sat bolt upright. He cast a hasty glance at Lucy who was sleeping peacefully beside him. Careful not to wake her, he slid gently from the bed before slipping into his clothes. He threw a thick, hooded sweatshirt over his head, stuffed his feet into heavy boots and grabbing his car keys, tiptoed outside. He craned his head, listening for the sound - jarred by the familiar drone as it rose again in the distance; only this time there was no doubt, it was emanating from the grounds of Westbourne House.

Wasting no time, he climbed into his Land rover in pursuit of the track that led to the Baxter's farm. The passage of vehicles had carved deep ravines in both sides - the ground muddy, jostling him from side to side as he skidded his way up into the hills. He already knew the best vantage points, as he raced along the edge of the field to reach the forest on the other side.

With the Land rover tucked in the mouth of the forest, Joshua pulled up his hood and set off on foot. He strode along the woodland path - secure in the knowledge, the trees would conceal him until finally, Westbourne House peeped into view. Joshua froze, sensing movement in the grounds. He lifted his binoculars. Snapshots of the gardens and grounds swung past the lenses but Joshua kept on searching. Then at last, he discovered the source of the noise. His eyes focussed on the dangling branch of a mature oak tree - watching in horror as the vibrating blades seared into its girth and with a final shudder of protest, it tumbled to the ground.

He absorbed the scene for a few more seconds; seeing an area to the left of the trees, newly excavated and flattened. Joshua gulped in the cool, damp air as a creeping sense of dread entered his mind.

"Wasn't it always Hampton's plan to get another building in the grounds?" he found himself pondering, a short while later.

Joshua had chosen not to hang around. It was with no hesitation, he bounded back to the Land rover before continuing his journey towards the farm. Toby was already up and about, cheeks flushed from the cold. He had ushered Joshua into the kitchen where they huddled around the table, hands cupped around mugs of steaming tea.

"That's right," Toby said darkly. "His original plan was to demolish the walled gardens to make way for a conference centre - but there was an outcry.

Planning permission was refused."

He exhaled a sigh, describing the desolation when Perry had ruthlessly torn away the gardens, along with James's beautiful orchards - how an endearing tradition had been lost.

Yet Perry's plan to create a recreational green for putting and croquet had not been without problems. The immaculate lawn had sunk in several places, due to the crumbly nature of the soil. A month earlier, the green had been ravaged by moles. It was a scenario which made the villagers smile - but only reinforced Perry's belief that Westbourne House was cursed! It seemed, he had turned even more cantankerous, determined to make his mark on the property.

"It's fortuitous, Westbourne House is a historic building," Toby continued. "The house and outbuildings carry a grade II listing - which means they can't be destroyed. But if I know James, I bet he protected the grounds in some way. Some of those trees must be hundreds of years old. There's even a chance they'll carry a preservation order."

"Then what are we waiting for?" Joshua insisted, swigging back his tea. "Let's get straight on to the council and report this!"

"How do you know they're not just pruning that tree?" Toby frowned.

"They're not," Joshua snapped. "They're felling it! My father was a lumberjack - he explained it to me when I was a boy. If this was just a responsible bit of tree surgery, they wouldn't be lopping off the main branches at crown level..." His eyes widened. "And why is the work being done at this time of day? My guess is, they're getting an early start in before any of us realise what's going on. I'll put money on it, come midday, that tree will be gone!"

Toby glanced at his watch. The darkness had faded, giving way to a chilly grey dawn. Yet Joshua's words left him floundering, knowing he was on to something. The area sounded like a prime site to install a new building. Perry had been clever - he was getting the ground works done early. By the time he applied for permission, his chosen site would be ready, leaving Rosebrook Council no reason to object. It was unlikely they had any concept of how the grounds looked in their present state - especially in the aftermath of the 1987 hurricane. They needed to act fast.

"What time do you reckon the council office opens?" Toby muttered. "9:00? There might be someone around at eight - our best bet would be to drive there."

"Okay," Joshua nodded. "Meet me at the caravan in five minutes. I'll wake up Lucy and if you want to bring your dad, it'll be a bonus."

They gave each other a mutual nod, knowing that if the council were reluctant to investigate, only Herbert would possess the gumption to urge them to take this seriously.

Toby's intuition was spot on. According to records confirmed by a council arborologist, the majority of trees were indeed protected. In Perry's case, this included the beautiful mature oak, his lumberjacks had nearly destroyed; a scattering of ancient beech trees, just budding into leaf, so no-one could claim they were diseased. Thus, the preservation order was enforced, prohibiting Perry from having any more trees felled.

No-one wanted to hang around in the aftermath - fearing the wrath about to descend on them. Boris, on the other hand, couldn't resist beckoning everyone back to the pub for a swift pint to celebrate.

"Very well done, folks," he muttered, as they gathered inside the Olde House at Home.

Joshua and Lucy squeezed themselves into a corner - choosing one of the upright barrels which served as a makeshift table. Joshua hoped they would be sufficiently hidden behind Herbert's vast bulk as he propped up the bar, still crowing over their victory.

"I swore to those kids, we'd keep an eye on the place!" he smirked, raising his beer glass.

"That was on the day of James's funeral," Boris reflected dreamily. "It seems you upheld your pledge, Herbert."

"And not without a tip off from our young friends here!" Herbert proclaimed. He threw an approving nod in Joshua's direction, "what are you two hiding for, anyway?"

"Please, Herbert," Lucy breathed. "We really don't want any attention…"

Her apprehension was not unfounded as the pub door swung open. Perry strutted in without warning, his cold eyes sweeping around the room like searchlights. Rowena wandered in after him and to Boris's even greater surprise, Elliot. Herbert stood his ground, turning on his heel, now resolute in protecting Joshua from his probing stare. Toby was quick to follow his lead and without knowing why, they all suddenly felt a little scared for them.

"Celebrating something are we?" Perry drawled.

"What's it to you?" Herbert snorted.

Perry ignored him, his gaze honing in on Boris. He had a tendency to look nervous when he was trying to hide something.

"And what have you got to say about this, Boris?" he muttered; except Boris never had a chance to reply. Perry's eyes had already swivelled back to Elliot who remained placidly by Rowena's side. He was looking for clues, they realised - checking for the slightest, furtive flicker of eye contact, where thankfully there was none. "Colluding again?"

"I don't know what you're talking about," Boris said disdainfully.

"What?" Perry snapped. "You had no idea, I was going to be visited by some jack-booting council enforcement officer with regards the pruning of my trees?" His eyes jabbed into Herbert.

"We've done nothing wrong," Herbert shrugged. "Those trees are protected! Some of them have stood for centuries! What gives you the right to just arbitrarily hack them down?"

"Do I take it that *you're* the one who stirred up all this trouble?" Perry demanded.

He wandered right up close, now braced just inches away. Herbert puffed himself up like a toad, determined to stand his ground; but Perry's eyes were still roaming - moving along the bar to where Joshua and Lucy huddled in silence. Finally, his scrutiny had found its mark. Joshua raised his eyes where the temperature inside the pub seemed to plummet several degrees.

"Ah, I see you had a little help…" Perry added in a deep and sinister tone.

For the next few seconds, nobody spoke. The tension kept building - and all the while, Perry was staring fixedly at Joshua, never once breaking eye contact.

"We're just enjoying a quiet drink," Lucy announced.

"That's right," Toby intervened, placing a gentle hand on her shoulder. "So don't pin this on them! For your information, us farmers get up early! You might want to bear that in mind, the next time you call the lumberjacks in because you could hear those chain saws right across the valley!"

Eventually, Joshua could no longer handle the tension - chilled by the intensity of Perry's glare. Rowena said very little; haughty and majestic as ever, as she lounged in an elegant, high-backed chair positioned by the hearth. A log fire flickered gently, dispensing some of the hostility as it gnawed the atmosphere. Elliot, attentive as ever, behaved like her personal servant - wandering from the bar, drink in hand, politely asking if she was warm enough.

"Let's just get out of here," Joshua whispered to Lucy.

Perry watched them go, his mind still ticking. It was several weeks since Alesha's comprehensive dossier had been revealed - where right now, he couldn't take his eyes off Joshua. He wondered why he had recognised those clear, grey eyes. This was undoubtedly Rosemary Merriman's younger son - a boy, he had first spotted at the press conference in 1973.

He rose to his feet, determined not to lose them. Alesha had done a lot more than simply lurk around the Merrimans' house, taking photos. She had uncovered their entire family tree. There were pictures of Luke, along with his pretty wife, Sally and their twin boys. Yet at the core of her findings, lay those final photos of Joshua - his complexion golden in the winter sunlight, his head thrown back in laugher. Perry had glared at the images - mentally despising his unconventional clothing, the long dark overcoat and trilby hat which didn't conceal the long hair flopping around his shoulders. He felt his hatred escalate.

As for Rosemary - there was no question, she was a collaborator! Alesha had followed her on many occasions - but even Perry had never expected her to go waltzing into the clean white office block where Eleanor's solicitor was based. Perry raked through the possibilities - wondering if she was delivering some message. And now he had unearthed the most shocking truth of all; never imagining, this elusive 'younger son' of hers would be the same young man who had infiltrated his way into Aldwyck.

'The lady in the farmhouse is my auntie.' Alesha had discovered that Rosemary had a sister; a sister by the name of Marilyn. Joshua had almost given the game away. If only Perry had been sufficiently enlightened to make the connection.

"Stay here," he said to Rowena. He shot an icy glance towards Elliot. "Keep her company," he added, before he turned and left the pub.

He could still see them as they made their way stealthily along the pavement in the direction of the caravan. Perry's eyes narrowed. He called the house, using his mobile phone - knowing he would need backup. He allowed them a little space, careful to remain about 50 meters behind. There was no point in panicking them just yet - he would save that pleasure for later.

They were only yards from the caravan. Perry quickened his pace.

"I know who you are, Joshua Merriman!" he called out, relishing the moment.

They whirled round, just as Perry came striding across the field towards them - pausing to a standstill outside the caravan. Joshua froze with fear.

"What do you want?" Lucy hissed. "Toby spoke the truth! We *all* heard those chain saws!"

"Oh, this is no longer about illegal tree felling," Perry smirked. "In fact, I think it's time we got to know each other on a more personal level, don't you - *Lucy!*" Her face turned rigid. "Let's start again, shall we. What are you two *really* doing in this village?"

She opened her mouth as if to speak; any next words suspended as the roar of a motorbike ruptured the silence. Joshua backed away - staring in disbelief at the leather clad figure sat astride a powerful Harley Davidson. He felt frantically in his pockets for his keys but it was too late. The rider had surged right up to them - enjoying the effect of his advance as he revved the engine. He could sense Lucy flinching beside him.

"What's going on?" she spluttered, "who the hell *are* these people?"

"Easy, Nathan," Perry kept smiling. "In fact, you may as well introduce yourself!"

The man obligingly tore off his motorcycle helmet. Joshua took one glance at his granite hard features and shuddered. Nathan had regrown his hair. It stood up in short, gelled spikes, a startling peroxide blonde which enhanced his deeply tanned complexion and the dark splinter-like eyes.

"My security guard," Perry added icily. "So let's have no more lies. It *was* you who reported those lumberjacks. You are undeniably in cahoots with Eleanor Bailey, not to mention the Barton-Wells children…"

Lucy stared at him open-mouthed. "I don't know what you mean…" she started to say.

"Last year, my son saw you on a country walk, young lady!" Perry barked, his eyes searing into her. "You, the Jansen boy and William Barton-Wells!" His expression turned more threatening. "Show you the best views, did he? The prime observation point for spying on my property - right on the edge of that forest?"

"You're crazy!" Joshua gasped. "They only went for a walk!"

"Unless you hadn't noticed," Lucy added sarcastically, "Aldwyck is surrounded by beautiful countryside."

"Yeah," Joshua nodded, "and as for spying - it seems the villagers don't need us for that. They're already on to you."

As if to mirror his words, the Baxters came chugging up the road in their Range Rover, pulling up sharply by the edge of the field. Joshua almost smiled. Perry could never have anticipated, the local farming community would be looking out for them.

"What's going on?" Herbert bellowed, staggering from his vehicle.

"Stay out of this!" Perry shot back in fury. "This is none of your business!"

"If you're giving our friends hassle then it bloody well is our business!" Toby retorted.

Somehow, both men had expected to find Perry here but not this thug of a security guard. Nathan was bearing down on them like some sort of cavalry - leaving Joshua virtually pinned against the caravan. The two farmers advanced with no further delay.

They had only taken a few steps when Nathan spun his bike around, engine still ticking as he deliberately swerved it into their path.

"You were saying?" Perry pressed, satisfied their rescuers were sufficiently held at bay.

Joshua couldn't move. "W-we're not here to cause any harm," he mumbled.

"You're lying," Perry whispered evilly. "You're associated with my enemies. The guilt's written all over your face and as for reporting those lumberjacks. That's just the tip of the iceberg."

Joshua frowned, unsure what he was rambling on about - distracted by the arrival of a second vehicle, only this one was a classic Jaguar. Rowena stepped out from the passenger seat.

"Know anything about the destruction of my bowling green, do you?" Perry growled. A familiar purple flush loomed in his face. In final fit of anger, he grasped the front of Joshua's coat, ramming him hard against the caravan. "You've been sent here to ruin me haven't you? I bet you even had something to do with those moles!"

"I've never heard such rubbish!" Herbert roared above the rumble of Nathan's motorbike. "You can't introduce moles to an area! Chances are, those pests found themselves a nice, well-watered bit of lawn and were attracted by the grubs! Shows how little *you* know about country matters!"

"Let go of him!" Lucy shouted hysterically.

Rowena had been wandering nearer and nearer to the melee and at first, Perry was oblivious to her presence - his face pressed dangerously close to Joshua's.

"I want you out of this village!" he hissed. "We crossed paths before, *remember?*" his eyes carved into him like blades. "I told Eleanor never to cross me and if you've got any sense, boy, I suggest you leave immediately!"

He flicked another warning glance in Nathan's direction. He was still rolling his bike relentlessly back and forth, with every attempt Toby made to dart past him. In all this time, he had placed an effective barrier between them, giving Perry free reign to interrogate them. But it was no longer just Nathan lingering in the field. Finally, Perry clocked Rowena's presence.

"Get your hands off me!" Joshua shuddered. "We're not going anywhere!"

"That's right!" Lucy howled, finally breathing her Welsh fire. "This is our home! How dare you come here and bully us! You're not the bloody land owner!"

Perry turned puce; then suddenly, Rowena snapped.

"That's enough, Perry!" she shrieked. "You're being ridiculous - what's worse, you're making a fool of yourself!"

Even Nathan knew not to argue and with a final rev of his bike, he turned and tore away from the field. It was with some reluctance, Perry too backed off. Yet his eyes were blazing, his expression filled with loathing and it was a vision that would haunt Joshua for a very long time.

II

There was no question the villagers would be revelling in this! Rowena slid into the back seat of Elliot's Jaguar, surveying the scene with dismay; Herbert Baxter and his son marching into the field - mouths snapping at the air as they launched into an animated dialogue - and just as the car slid through the ornamental gateposts, she had seen them *all* disappear inside that caravan.

"Well, that's going to go down well!" she sniped, "after all my hard work trying to improve public relations - all my charity work..."

"Just leave it, Rowena!" Perry's voice lashed from the front, "and as for you, Elliot! I trust you'll know better than to breath a word about this."

"You know you can always rely on my discretion, Perry," Elliot answered him gently.

It was only when they were settled back into the luxurious confines of

Westbourne House, Rowena began to consider her options. Perry had disappeared for a walk in the grounds - possibly to work off his rage; though it seemed even more likely, he would be scrutinising the land, in advance of his next devious scheme to get another building in there. She settled herself into one of their deep sofas - her eyes following him from behind the patio doors, just waiting until he drifted out of view. She turned pleadingly to Elliot.

"Would you like some tea?" he asked her courteously.

Rowena shook her head. "Not tea, Elliot, advice. Sit down for a moment will you..."

It was over the next 10 minutes, she explained what was troubling her. She closed her eyes, the cogs in her mind turning. She had heard nothing more from Hilary. Yet a tiny part of her hankered to meet this enigmatic 'Peter' - unable to deny that if it wasn't for Perry's torment, her life would be perfect. She had tried the gentle approach. She had even urged him to see a doctor but he had shaken her off somewhat brutally - insisting that his recurring nightmares were hardly a matter which required medical attention.

Deep down, Rowena knew otherwise. She knew exactly what demons lingered in Perry's mind and it was an admission that left her cold. Perry inhabited an imaginary world where his victims lived on. She trod a path of fear, knowing he was becoming more irrational; but this was not a concern she could share with her close-knit circle of lady friends. So she suffered in silence.

Despite her beautiful dream home which Perry had fought so hard to acquire, he found it impossible to share her bliss: forever engrossed in work - or dreaming up new ways he could make a fortune out of the place. That was, when he wasn't driven by his obsession with Eleanor!

Rowena was desperately lonely - so in the end, she sought solace in Elliot.

"Would you care to drive me to Rosebrook tomorrow?" she sighed. "Perry won't suspect a thing, not if you're escorting me..." She smiled coolly. "I could always make an appointment at the beauty salon. I'm long overdue a facial."

"Except Perry knows, you usually go to Covent Garden," Elliot faltered.

"So I'd like to go somewhere local," Rowena insisted.

The conversation didn't last long. The solid oak door boomed shut, signifying Perry's return.

They left next day as planned. Except Rowena hesitated, just as Elliot was easing his car into a parking space by the Community Centre. She stared up at the beautiful building in awe; stunned by the facets of design which revealed such obvious architectural similarities to Westbourne House - and then she remembered its originator.

"I can't go in," she whispered. "I almost forgot - we're on enemy territory."

"Would you like me to make some enquiries on your behalf?" Elliot suggested lightly.

She gave a nervous swallow. But Elliot could never have known the real reason for her hesitance; the possibility that Hilary would be in there. If she spotted her now, she might be tempted to stop for a natter - and what if Eleanor was to materialise? Rowena felt the onset of panic, finally recognising the risk of blowing her cover. Perry would be incandescent!

"Just find out if it's possible to consult with a counsellor known as Peter," Rowena spluttered, "see what help is available."

"It will be my pleasure," Elliot responded. He gave her a conspiratorial smile.

"Oh and Elliot," Rowena added crisply. "I'm sure I can trust you - but please don't do anything treacherous. I *do* know who else lives around here..."

She left the last words dangling. Elliot had long recognised the authority behind that tone. He watched her go - observing her over-confident stride as she swept down the high street in the direction of Rosebrook's premier beauty salon.

The more he thought about it, the more he couldn't believe his good fortune! It had taken less than two years to win her confidence, unable to forget the harrowing months when the Hamptons had first taken up residence. Rowena had eventually warmed to him and he had nurtured their camaraderie - despite the smouldering hatred he felt for her husband. There was no denying that Perry's soul had turned more and more corrupt, as his fixation to destroy his enemies consumed him. Yet Rowena had flourished like a rose.

She had ultimately revealed that *she* was the one who had fallen in love with Westbourne house; and how tirelessly Perry had campaigned to get it for her.

Elliot's smile faded as he stepped inside the Community Centre. He would of course, *never* forgive them for what they had done to James. These thoughts confronted him now as he stealthily made his way through the crowd in the direction of the tea bar. He saw Eleanor. She turned - almost dropping the tray of cups she was carrying as he ambled towards her.

"What are you doing here?" she breathed.

"I don't have long," Elliot muttered, "but is there a chance I could talk to Peter - in private?"

Eleanor froze, head spinning, as he hastily explained his reasons.

After the furore over Dominic's nightclub extension, their lives had quietened down. Yet from the moment Elliot began to describe Perry's delusional paranoia, she sensed the tide was about to change.

She wasted no time. She led him upstairs to Peter's office - throwing a sharp glance over her shoulder just to check the Magnus's weren't lingering. Ever since their fallout, Hilary had been cool but polite. Eleanor was struck with a sense that she always seemed to be watching her but right now the coast was clear - in fact, she was banking on the possibility that both Hilary and Reginald would be engrossed in their work until noon. If only she could have stayed - but her duties prevented her. She couldn't deny she was curious.

How strange that Rowena would seek the console of Peter and more to the point, how might Elliot have influenced her?

"I only have an hour, myself..." Elliot was pondering. "I mentioned the nightmares, many months ago when I wrote to the children. Something happened on the evening he suffered a heart seizure."

He released a sigh, keen to reveal everything he had witnessed - culminating with that unmistakably threatening scene outside the caravan.

"Who do you suppose is haunting him?" Peter frowned, tilting one eyebrow. "The children's father, perhaps - James wasn't it?"

"Not just James," Elliot whispered darkly, "a young man, Eleanor lost in her youth."

Peter stared back at him with an expression of disbelief. "Jake?"

"I've often overheard him mention a singer," Elliot elucidated, "slim, auburn haired..." He eyed him shrewdly, wondering if it was possible to delve deep into Perry's past.

Peter stroked his chin. "And what sort of advice is Rowena hoping I can give you?"

"She's hoping you might be able to recommend some form of help," Elliot confessed. "This sense of persecution seems to be getting worse - it makes him nasty. That business yesterday upset her, which is the reason she sent me round here."

"Elliot, this requires help beyond anything we can offer here," Peter enlightened him. "All I can suggest is some form of *psychotherapy* which tunnels deep into a person's past. Though if I'm honest - I think he should see a psychiatrist."

With the turmoil of Perry's mental state under discussion, Avalon found herself drifting towards the Community Centre. Her eyes stopped dead as a familiar black Jaguar shimmered in the sunlight. Her father's old car? It couldn't be! The car was of course, willed to Elliot. Yet it seemed just as unlikely that *he* would be here, given the constraints of his employment. She found herself backing away, unable to make sense of it.

Right now, she had so many problems that she too, craved a quiet word with Peter.

The sight of Elliot's car had thrown her, forcing her to lower herself onto a street bench. She breathed deeply as finally, her heart began to slow itself -

wondering how it was possible, her relationship with Richard could have descended into such chaos.

She could no longer deny, she had become increasingly unhappy, as his behaviour became more and more controlling. He condemned her devotion to Peter's housing trust - just as George Fortescue had done, a year earlier. She couldn't understand it! What was so *wrong* about trying to accomplish something worthwhile? Something which didn't rely on making profit?

"William and I always wanted Peter to have that land!"

This inevitably led to her having to explain the time, Peter taken care of them; their eviction from Westbourne House - though she couldn't bear to divulge the details. Sadly, Richard was the jealous type, suspicious of Peter's motives. He was suspicious of anyone who radiated compassion, especially those engaged in social work.

"Hypocrites and charlatans!" he exhorted. Yet the one thing that offended her most, was his insinuation that Peter was grooming her for his bed. "Why else do you think he invited you to live with him?" he would gush with that odious, self-satisfied smirk. "You and William are a couple of nice looking kids..."

It was the allegation that Peter was some sort of paedophile that finally drove her over the edge. Avalon clasped her hands together in her lap to stop them trembling.

She had tried to end their relationship so many times but somehow, he always managed to wheedle his way back. First came the apologies, then the flowers, the tears, the threat of what he might do to himself: *'I just can't bear to let you go...'* and finally the invitation to dinner *'to talk things through.'* Though even that was never straight forward! Richard had an infuriating habit of enthusing over some fancy dish which he would insist on ordering for her too. She couldn't stand it and today, the situation reached boiling point when he had started making his snide little digs at work.

The ordeal of working under the same roof was excruciating. She had endured it right up until her coffee break, then fled from the antique shop, fighting tears. She darted up the high street, terrified he might follow - but progress was slow. It was market day; the pavements already thronging with shoppers. Avalon picked her way carefully through the masses, firing an occasional glance over her shoulder - hoping she was sufficiently submerged in the crowd to be invisible.

There was still no sign of him and for a few minutes, she resumed her journey at a slightly more leisurely pace. The next time she looked up, she paused - a smile touched her lips as a familiar head of chestnut hair gleamed in the middle distance. It was the home furnishings stall. She might have guessed he'd be drawn to it with his passion for interior design.

"Eli!" she called out as the slender figure turned to move away. She surged forwards, desperate to catch up, until eventually her footsteps slowed. "Eli?"

The chestnut-haired figure spun round. Avalon caught her breath - shocked to discover, the object of her scrutiny appeared to be female.

"S-sorry," she stammered, "I thought you were someone else..."

Mortified with shock, Avalon wandered towards the Community Centre. On the one hand, she was aching to see Peter whose warmth and compassion never failed to melt away her anxiety. Yet for that moment, she had felt an insatiable urge to confide in Elijah; never able to forget the night he had poured his heart out, in the aftermath of his own break up.

Avalon released a sigh, as the shadow of her father's Jaguar hovered on the shore of her vision. She remembered Elliot, now hankering to wonder what he was doing here.

Avalon rose, rushing towards the pillars that were guarding the entrance. Only this time, it was a reflection in the doors that halted her. She froze for a second time. The top end of the high street shimmered in the glass - but captured in that image was a woman she knew only too well; an unmistakable flash of white blonde hair as she marched in her direction. Wasting no time, Avalon hauled open the door and shot inside the Information Centre.

She watched as Rowena Hampton loomed closer. It was only now, she feared for Elliot. She could still see her though the window blinds.

It was a moment later, she knew her fears had been groundless. Elliot cruised into the hallway and pushed his way out of the same glass doors. She could clearly see the back of his snowy white head. Even more gratifying was Rowena smile. It implied, she knew he would be here. She felt her heart lift as Elliot held the car door open. Yet at the same time, her mind was blazing with questions; her bitter feud with Richard almost forgotten.

III

By the time the day drifted into evening, Avalon found herself stretched out on the sofa. She had calmed down considerably by now - though it was no longer a sense of numbness that possessed her, it was anger. *How dare that creep, Richard, go sneaking to the manager and report her for leaving the premises.* This was the first time, her suitability for employment had come under fire. Her jaw clenched - sorely tempted to hand in her notice. But she had more important things on her mind and it was out of sheer mutiny, she had invited Peter round to dinner.

William came bounding into the room. He had changed into denim jeans and a T-shirt, emblazoned with a yellow smiley face and captioned 'Acid is Music not Drugs.'

"So tell me about Elliot!" he breathed, grabbing a beer from the kitchen. "You actually saw him outside the Community Centre? With Rowena Hampton!"

"Yes," Avalon sighed, massaging the spot between her eyebrows, "I'm sure Peter will explain everything. Oh - and incase you didn't know, I've finally dumped Richard!"

"Don't know why you don't give Angel a shot," William smiled. "He fancies you like mad."

"You know why," Avalon protested. "Lara is totally in love with him! It wouldn't be fair."

She smiled inwardly - her brother thought Angel was the coolest guy in Rosebrook. Never in his life, had he imagined he would hit upon such a rich new source of contemporary, underground music. It was inevitable, he would be lured to Angel's regular Friday night slot at Bella's, alongside Andrew and his friends.

Avalon stretched her arms high above her head - intrigued by the prospect of what Peter was about to tell them. She had lit some candles; the lighting low, casting a warm glow around the walls. A glass of chilled white wine sat seductively on the side table as Jim Beam settled down next to her, purring thunderously.

Peter was already hurrying his way towards the house, guided by the street lamps as the darkness closed in. There was no denying, Elliot's visit had left him cold.

Come midday, Eleanor had been eager to talk to him, so they had sneaked across to the almshouse for lunch. It was the only place they could guarantee any privacy - Eleanor was particularly anxious that someone like Hilary might burst in on them.

Peter bit his lip. How could he forget that some time before Christmas, Hilary had made an unusual approach? He could virtually recall the conversation word for word - her concern for some *friend*: *'Her husband is afflicted by nightmares; a sense of persecution, the fear of being haunted...'*

Peter bit back his fear. This was a matter he really needed to discuss with Hilary - woefully aware of the acrimony that existed between she and Eleanor. Yet even *he* couldn't imagine that Hilary would be so duplicitous as to mingle with their enemies... would she?

He had faced Eleanor with a strength of steel - fearful of what he was about to tell her.

"Perry believes he is being haunted by Jake?" she breathed in shock.

"So Elliot reckons," Peter nodded. "Do you have a picture of him, Eleanor?"

Almost from the moment he studied Jake's photo, a sense pain pierced into his heart. It was a face that reflected such innocence - marble white skin moulded to a face whose exquisite bone structure bore an uncanny resemblance to Elijah's. Peter took note of the long, auburn hair, the smiling mouth. The photo even possessed a slightly yellowish hue which threw him right back to the 70s. He felt quite chilled.

"Do *you* believe in ghosts, Eleanor?" he remembered whispering. "Do you wonder if it is possible that on the night Jake died, some trace of him was left behind…"

Her eyes filled with tears. She told him about a park in Poplar - a memorial stone that she had installed there; how every time she visited, she could almost imagine Jake's spirit lingering.

Peter braced himself outside Avalon's front door.

He could still hear the echo of his final words; the notion that Perry was becoming dangerously unstable. Though between them, they had agreed not to mention anything about this to the Barton-Wells children.

Avalon served a simple supper; succulent, spicy prawns, fluffy rice - nothing pretentious as Richard would have expected. Yet Peter praised her efforts to the roof tops. Right now, they were devouring the last crumbs of a shop-bought lemon meringue pie. Avalon hadn't enjoyed herself so much for a long time - delighted to indulge her brother in his own choice of music, where the electronic pulse of Inner City's 'Big Fun' was pounding from the speakers without drawing criticism.

She betrayed a tiny smile. She had even taken the phone off the hook, filled with a sense that Richard might phone; unable to bear the prospect of having to listen to his sanctimonious voice in the midst of such an intriguing night. Feeling utterly sinful, she made Irish coffee, determined to make the most of Peter's visit.

"I still miss Elliot," she brooded, her eyes glassy from a little too much wine. It was only now, the true sentiment of her feelings were laid bare.

"Charlie told me he bumped into him at the Harpers'," William mused. "We should ask them to invite him for a cuppa! Especially if we're going over there, this weekend."

"I don't know, William…" Avalon faltered.

A candle started flickering. Its wick was drowning in molten wax, leaving the walls dancing with shadows. Avalon struggled to her feet to extinguish it. She was still contemplating William's words. If only they hadn't been interrupted by a sudden thumping on the door.

"Oh no," Avalon groaned, rolling her eyes.

"Didn't you ought to answer that?" Peter muttered, as the pounding grew more insistent.

Avalon did not have to guess who it was; bitter words of anger were already forming on her lips as she peeped through the spy-hole. Richard loomed outside, armed with an enormous bouquet of roses. She studied his arrogant face - the small beard which in some way, enhanced his pious expression - and something inside her snapped.

"Avalon, for God's sake!" he whined. "We need to talk…"

She slowly unfastened the latch - yet before she even had a chance to open it, Richard was attempting to push the door open, determined to barge his way in.

"I've got nothing to say to you!" she shrieked. "Now go away!"

"Not until I've said what I came to say," Richard smiled. "I am not going to let you push me away, my darling…" his words were cut short as Peter materialised in the hallway.

The mask slipped. His eyes blazed dark in their sockets against his pale, slightly sweaty complexion - his nostrils flared.

"What's *he* doing here?" he hissed, his voice flooded with hatred. "I should have known! You're a fool, Avalon. How can you be taken in by that - that - *pervert?*"

"How dare you!" Avalon screamed. "Peter's more honourable than you'll ever be! Now take your flowers and get stuffed!" and without any further regret, she slammed the door in his face.

Avalon knew she shouldn't have let this minor event ruin the evening but it had! Richard's intrusion had blown away the soothing ambience they had created, leaving a nasty air in its wake. He was loathsome. She glanced at William and Peter's worried faces - these were the people who really mattered. It had taken the patchwork of events from this day, to fully appreciate the powerful camaraderie they shared. Peter was as much involved in their fight against the Hamptons as anyone - and today, Avalon refused to let some hollow relationship stand in the way of that.

"Stay," she whispered as he lingered by the door.

It was almost midnight. William had gone to bed, ready to face another school day. Suddenly, she found herself alone with Peter - craving his solace more than ever.

"Avalon, I have to go," Peter consoled her gently. "You get a good night's rest, now."

"But I don't want you to leave," she protested, taking another step towards him.

She slid her arms around his waist, tilting her head back to stare at him. Their eyes connected and for a second, he held her gaze, his expression filled with longing.

"Spend the night with me," Avalon pleaded.

His blue eyes shone with undisguised passion, but it was infused with a look of sadness. "I can't. Imagine what people will think." He stroked her face lovingly. "You're very beautiful," he kept murmuring, "if only I was ten years younger… but I have to think of my position. People will talk. It'll be nasty! A little like your ex-boyfriend insinuated - I'd be seen as some sort of *sexual predator.*"

"Ignore Richard, he's a prat!" Avalon snapped.

He smiled tenderly. "We've had a wonderful evening," he placated. "Let's just cherish that for now. Oh - and he left your flowers, by the way…"

"You have them," Avalon sulked, letting him slip from her arms.

He moved resolutely towards the door - and yet still she watched him as he wandered into the folds of darkness, before completely disappearing from sight.

Chapter 18

March 1989

Strangely enough, Avalon was not the only one who had been presented with flowers recently - especially when the most magnificent display turned up at the almshouse on Valentines Day. Eleanor could hardly believe it; mesmerised by the mass of roses in almost every pastel shade imaginable, from pearly whites to soft blushing pinks, interspersed with delicate fountains of gypsophila.

"You must have a secret admirer," Charlie smiled over her shoulder. He pulled back the lustrous wrapping then froze. "Actually, they're for Margaret!"

Margaret had been dumbstruck. She'd never in her life even had a card, never mind flowers!

These thoughts came back to her as she sat squashed in the back seat of William's sports car, cruising along the road in the direction of Aldwyck. Those flowers had certainly caused a stir. Andrew in particular, had been intrigued. They clearly cost a lot more than the average schoolboy could afford; though deep down, Margaret was hit by an eerie suspicion as to who the sender *really* was.

A small part of her was reluctant to join the others today, fearful she might bump into him. Yet she felt a strange tug of attraction. It had been a while since they had ventured into the village and with Elijah securely ensconced in the back seat with her and the Barton-Wells siblings in the front, she felt very much part of their gang. Andrew cruised behind in the mini. He in turn, had enlisted the fellowship of Matt and Angel, who seemed especially keen to chaperone them. Safety in numbers, they agreed and together they felt invincible.

Eventually, the small entourage crept past the village sign. Andrew noticed Angel's eyes were everywhere, drinking in their surroundings. It had rained heavily in the last hour, the sky bulging with leaden clouds. Water dripped from the roof of the 'Olde House at Home,' spreading in puddles outside the door, where the tables shone wetly in the gloom. He glanced to the right, clocking the idyllic, chocolate box cottages encircling the green. Angel's mouth curved into a smile. The image possessed a misty, eerie quality like something out of an old film. Having spent his entire life as a city boy, it must have looked surreal. A lone gardener, meanwhile, stood outside one of the cottages as if frozen in time - her eyes fixed on their convoy as it trundled slowly past.

In all the time Andrea Marsh had lived here, she had never had reason to take much notice of visitors, at least not until now. She observed the distinctive sports car with interest - recognising it as the vehicle that belonged to the Barton-Wells boy.

It had been over two years since she and her husband feared, they may have lost their dream cottage to some wealthy stockbroker from London. Yet in September 1987, Ben's father astounded them with his 'white knight' gesture to let them rent it.

Unfortunately, accepting favours from someone like Perry came with conditions. The Marshes felt indebted - forever anxious that he might double the rent at the drop of a hat. So as the years drifted by, they sensed an underlying obligation to pander to his every whim, which included keeping an eye out for the Barton-Wells children.

Andrea stood very still, trowel in hand. She had been planting primroses in one of the hanging baskets outside her door, just as William's car crept into view. She waited for it to pass, then turned and vanished inside the cottage. She knew who she needed to telephone. But it wasn't Perry she was connected to; it was Ben.

William parked outside the farmhouse. Within seconds, they were all squeezed inside the caravan where Lucy had cleared some space on the bed to make extra room.

"This is wicked!" Angel announced, his grin growing broader. "I've met folks like you at festivals - what line of work you into?"

Elijah observed them in contemplative silence - Lucy and Joshua smiled, clearly warmed by the company of their friends. It was over the next few minutes, Joshua described his career in music journalism. Everyone seemed impressed. Andrew had only ever met Joshua briefly. Yet he too, was captivated by this couple - loving their eclectic lifestyle, their colourful attire as well as Joshua's dedication to music.

"You get to travel to gigs and interview bands?" he was musing. "That sounds cool!"

"What made you wanna move out here then?" Matt's voice rolled lazily into the discussion.

Elijah smiled shyly, overwhelmed by the mass of people crammed inside his old home. And of course, Joshua had to tell them.

The conversation hopped from limb to limb and everyone had their story to tell. It was inevitable they would move on to the saga of Westbourne House - the restoration, the Hamptons heartless takeover. It was at this point, a cloud swept across Avalon's face; and all the while, Elijah sensed Angel's interest - he was avidly listening whilst at the same time, covertly observing her.

"The Hamptons," she eventually sighed. "It's the activities of the aforementioned, we came here to talk about... I gather you had some aggravation from Perry."

"That's right," Joshua said tightly.

Gradually, the news came spilling out.

The caravan lapsed into near silence - the only intrusion, the persistent patter of rain which had resumed outside. It seemed to echo the disturbing nature of their discussion - the more they thought about it, the more they realised that Perry had been blatantly hostile from the start.

"We had the pleasure of meeting his security guard," Joshua added coldly, "some guy on a motorbike - goes by the name of Nathan…"

William nodded, his face tight. "This is exactly as Elliot described," he muttered anxiously. "It wasn't long ago, they were recruiting gangs of thugs to scare away travellers. If they give you any more hassle, you should get straight onto the police!"

"That's right," Avalon snapped, her eyes flashing with defiance. "I was going to talk to Marilyn. I mean, you're not even on the phone! We were thinking, maybe we should get a line installed."

"Are you serious?" Joshua frowned.

"There's a line to the farmhouse," Andrew added, peering out the window. "Shouldn't cost much to fit an extra one. D'you want me to check this out?"

"Thanks, mate," Joshua mumbled, forcing a smile, "'cos if I'm honest, Lucy and I don't particularly wanna go - we've established a home here. This place suits us…"

As the conversation progressed, it seemed clear that everyone was determined to protect them and stand up against Perry. Elijah felt a strong sense of rebellion too; but then, none of them had any idea what he *really* knew about Perry. He fought against an urge to smile, especially when Lucy uncorked a bottle of elder flower wine.

"You never did get to taste it," she laughed, tipping a drop into several tiny glasses.

By the time they had resolutely agreed to install a telephone in the caravan, the conversation moved on. No-one appeared to notice that Margaret had said very little - her eyes dreamy as they drifted beyond the window.

The allotments lay beneath a mantle of drizzle. She closed her eyes, as the heady floral fragrance of elder flower took her right back to the day they had gathered them; their delightful walk in the hills - the return journey along the farm track. But it was here, the romantic illusion was shattered, as she recalled the lone motorcyclist, the chill of Ben's eyes. She almost shivered. It hadn't taken long for the conversation to remind her just how evil the Hamptons were. She closed her eyes, struggling to overcome her more recent encounter with Ben. There was no denying, it had thrown her emotions in turmoil - and it took William's next words to finally coax her out of her reverie.

"There's going to be a couple of rather special birthdays, this year!"

"Your 18th," Avalon smiled indulgently.

"And Andrew's 21st!" Margaret gasped, where at last, her sweet lips curled into a smile.

"That calls for a big celebration!" Angel exploded. He had been resting on the edge of the bed, letting the conversation roll over him - he suddenly uncoiled himself into a sitting position.

"We could throw a *joint* party..." William started to say.

"With Joshua's connections, you wanna plan something bigger," Angel smiled in his assertive, slick-talking manner. "Set up a stage, speakers. I could be your DJ!"

"An outdoor event," Joshua mused.

"Yeah. You must have heard of the 'Sunrise Group,' right? They've organised some seriously cool parties!" He turned back to Joshua. "You ever come across any of them dudes?"

"Maybe," Joshua said softly. A smile flickered around his lips. "When were you thinking?"

"William's birthday's in October," Andrew reflected, "mine's at the end of May."

"So we could organise something for mid-summer," Avalon suggested.

The ideas kept circulating, the discussion effervescent, until gradually the caravan was beginning to turn stuffy; the windows steamed up, blocking out the lush countryside. Joshua flung the door open to dispense some of the heat. The welcome rush of cool air felt invigorating where finally, the rain had subsided, exuding a fragrance of damp grass into the atmosphere. William dug into his pocket for his car keys.

"Let's go for a spin in the countryside - have another look at our woods. Who's coming?"

"I'm up for that!" Andrew leapt in, catching Matt's eye.

"Me too," Angel smiled, where his earlier enthusiasm showed no signs of abating.

They hauled themselves to their feet, just as Margaret wistfully asked if she could accompany them. "Of course," William smiled, almost surprised she had asked.

Lucy was reluctant; Avalon resolute in her decision to visit the Harpers.

"We may as well take two vehicles," Joshua volunteered, "we'll follow in the Land rover."

One by one, they stepped out of the caravan where the rain held off for another hour.

Not one of them could have detected the cold, crazed eyes, surveying the scene through the powerful lenses of Perry's binoculars. Ben didn't waste a second, glad of his decision to spend another weekend here. The more his father was willing to involve him in his conspiratorial plans, the more Ben felt an overwhelming desire to appease him.

Right now, they were positioned high in the hills and on the bend of a tiny road; Nathan's favourite vantage point. They wore dark clothing and with the addition of an enveloping cape of trees, they were well concealed. He watched William hop down from the caravan before bounding towards his sports car - a far cry from the precocious child Ben had met in 1986. His binoculars wobbled slightly as they honed in on the blonde-streaked head of Margaret, his expression softening as he relived their delicious encounter. He would *so* much liked to have seen her reaction, the day those flowers had arrived - his father seemed convinced that if they played their cards right, there would come a time, she would ultimately slip some vital clue about her step-brother.

Almost on cue, Elijah wandered into view. Ben smiled, clocking his appealing young face, the sweep of his slender brows above those mysterious eyes. He might have sprung a little taller, but his looks hadn't changed. Even the reddish gleam of his hair was discernible, despite the gloom that sapped the colour from the landscape. Elijah clambered into Joshua's land rover, followed by two boys he didn't recognise: one of them hippy-like with long, mousy hair, tied in a ponytail - the other, some casual-looking black youth who's loping strides reminded him of a panther. The Land rover lurched from the field, heading towards the all familiar track which led to the forests around Westbourne House. They were almost fated to end up there.

"Perry'll be pissed off when he hears about this," Nathan's voice cut through his reverie.

Ben shrugged. "What makes you say that?"

"Didn't have any joy with Alan's lot then - putting the frighteners on those hippies?"

"No," Ben answered him lightly, "I'm afraid not. He's worried about Boswell and his connection with the Met - he doesn't want the risk of it being traced back to his boys…"

Ben trailed off, content to let him make his own observations as the convoy sped up the track. He had expected to see the Barton-Wells kids - but it appeared, they had brought a whole gang along. It suggested collaboration on a much grander scale where no-one knew what they were plotting. Nathan was right, his father was not going to be happy. He let out a sigh, thinking about Alan again - disappointed by his refusal to have anything to do with Joshua's *eviction* as his final, hissing words echoed in the chambers of his mind.

"You listen here, *shit head* - you recruited my boys for a burglary! Ain't my fault they didn't find what you were after." He had pressed his chilling smile. "You wanted me to plant a drug dealer in Rosebrook. Kept my end of the bargain there too, didn't I? I told you - no-one uses my boys whenever they feel like it, otherwise word gets out! I ain't your fuckin' lackey!"

How Ben held on to his nerve, he never knew.

"Oh come now, Alan - I've given you more channels for your drugs cartel than you could have dreamed of. You're raking it in!" It was true - Alan was shifting bigger quantities of cocaine than ever, mainly due to Ben's network of wealthy yuppies.

"Yeah and gettin' a nice cut of the profits as middle man," Alan sneered, "not to mention a few extra 'spies' on yer own turf!"

"Does that include the drug dealer?" Ben probed.

Alan shook his head, his icy, light blue eyes like splinters. "Engel's mine. Always was, always will be. I dug that kid out the shit. I could pluck him outta Rosebrook, as fast as I planted 'im in, you got that?"

Ben understood all too clearly when he was being given the brush off. He was lucky to have Alan; the man was as volatile, as he was lethal and Ben knew when to call it a day.

There was however, one more lead he had been hankering for; if Alan's thugs weren't at his disposal was there anyone else, lower down the chain, they could count on? Several days later, it transpired that Alan was willing to release a new contact to Nathan - regrettably, it was none other than the ring leader of the skin-head gang who'd mugged Andrew Bailey.

Yet still, Alan was biding his time. "Gimme a *worthwhile* reason why I should call the 'eavies in," he smiled nastily, "and maybe, I'll give our mutual friend that lead. Couple of hippies ain't worth the bother. Deal with 'em, yer fuckin' self!"

Ben shivered. He no longer needed binoculars to observe the small party. They paused by the forest, before tumbling out of the vehicles in succession.

Nathan, on the other hand was smirking - clocking Andrew's mates as they passed around cigarettes. He had a hunch about that charismatic black kid; already filled with some notion of who he was. If his theory turned out correct; that this was the boy, Alan had enlisted to infiltrate Bailey's circle - it would seem, he was a lot cosier with the enemy than Perry would have liked.

"What the fuck are they up to?" he muttered as if thinking out loud.

"What, other than surveying their precious land?" Ben sneered, snatching back the binoculars.

It suddenly occurred to him that Avalon wasn't there - a pattern of thought which inevitably drew his stare back to the caravan.

It lay placidly in its field, lonely against a backdrop of allotments and there, side by side, stood the two girls, engrossed in conversation. Ben felt his heartbeat quicken, unable to shake off that irrepressible surge of desire. His eyes fell upon Avalon; drinking in the sight of her long legs in drainpipe jeans, her luxurious hair, coiled into a plait. He could see her delicate nose - the swell of her rose-pink lips fluttering in speech whenever she turned sideways. Ben swallowed, shifting his attention to the other one. Dear God, she was a stunner too! The henna tones of her hair glowed as Elijah's had - bright as a flame against her soft English rose complexion.

From the other side of the valley meanwhile, Angel appeared to be gazing in awe at the enveloping folds of woodland - perhaps imagining what the area would look like in summer.

Joshua was following his gaze, remembering their earlier conversation. He felt his interest soar, especially in the moment they locked eyes - Angel grinned back knowingly.

Chapter 19

Elliot didn't call in at the farmhouse as William had hoped, despite a heartfelt plea from Marilyn. He might have earned Rowena's trust but even *he* understood the risk of chancing a visit in broad daylight - especially on a day when the Barton-Wells children were in the village.

Avalon was ardent in her decision to visit Marilyn, if for no other reason than to pass on a letter. But she also wanted to press home her warnings to ensure Joshua and Lucy's safety.

"Please keep an eye on them," she whispered, the moment Lucy vanished to use the bathroom. "We're going to fix them up with a telephone..." She didn't need to say more. Tom and Marilyn already sensed they were in danger and swore to be vigilant.

It was no secret that Perry was campaigning to have the couple banished from the village. Already, a succession of rumours had begun dripping their way among the villagers who were split in their opinion. Some questioned whether it was right to allow some 'hippy couple' to camp in a field - worried it would compromise the character of their charming village. Inspector Boswell was undecided - worried such people could be trouble makers. Boris on the other hand, fought to defend them along with every other long standing resident. No-one was more furious than Toby - quick to exhort that they were a much-liked couple who had done no harm!

Elliot had no choice but to stay out of it, convinced there was little Perry could do.

Marilyn was finally able to give him Avalon's letter though she too, was outraged to hear of this relentless campaign of bigotry against her nephew. "They are perfectly within their rights to live here," she sighed, "but I won't deny, nearly everyone is worried about them."

"I wish there was something I could do," Elliot said softly as he tore open the letter.

His life at Westbourne House might have been a little more harmonious but nothing filled his heart with more joy than this newsy letter from Avalon.

Elliot closed his eyes. There had been precious little he could advise Rowena; Perry's progressive paranoia couldn't be cured with counselling and it was going to take a far deeper level of psychiatric intervention to get to the root of his problems.

Rowena bit back her hurt, reluctant to share Elliot's opinion. Perry was openly disdainful of any form of help - but she had no idea what was really brewing in the dark catacombs of his mind.

No, there was only one way he could vanquish the ghosts that were the scourge of his life and that was to destroy Eleanor Bailey, along with everything she knew about him.

It was a matter he felt a compulsion to discuss with his own allies; Ben, Nathan and Robin. He chose a night when the hotel was quiet. The sky hung pregnant with cloud, the air damp, where the only sound was the rain sluicing down on the patio. The drapes in the library were tightly drawn.

Ben smiled inwardly - relishing the news he had imparted recently.

Eleanor was clearly gathering more allies, including that slightly bohemian couple who inhabited her caravan. His father swore they were connected to her past and it all seemed to be tied up with some clandestine era in the 70s when he had felt at his most vulnerable.

"Robin knows exactly who I am referring to," Perry whispered, his cruel stare fixed on him. "Don't you, my friend?"

Robin fiddled with his tie, his face ashen. Perry had shown him nothing but contempt since his fall out with Dominic. "Of course," he answered submissively. "How could I forget? Joshua Merriman infiltrated a press conference in 1973. He was witness to every accusation your father's enemies made, Ben. He could be as dangerous as Eleanor."

"I see," Ben replied coolly. "So how do you hope to get shot of him? The villagers are divided, the Harper woman's a relative and the field belongs to those kids!"

"I'm disappointed with the villagers," Perry snapped. "There was a time when someone like Baxter would have backed us! But it's too late - they've befriended them. There is little more we can do, other than to resort to more *underhand* tactics..."

The persistent lash of rain seemed to echo the sinister undertones in his voice. Nathan shifted uncomfortably in his chair.

"Our *criminal* contacts aren't interested, Perry," he added ominously.

"Then I'm afraid this very much relies on you two," Perry whispered. "So come on, Ben, don't look so despondent! We all know you're an expert when it comes to injecting fear into people."

"Like this *Joshua* person's going to take any notice of me," Ben drawled.

"I was referring to the female!" Perry's voice hissed. There was a moment of chilling silence, before a smile touched his lips. "Have you forgotten Avalon?"

"Of course," Ben responded coolly.

Perry's eyes glittered. "So I want you to work on Lucy. It's what you do best, Ben. There's bound to be a time when she will be alone..."

Ben nodded, already lapsing into one of his darker fantasies. He couldn't deny the lust he'd felt, when he had seen those two girls together; and where Avalon was out of reach, he relished the idea of having someone new to play with. "Okay," he consented, his smile lingering. "Now when are you going to tell me about *Eleanor*? She is after all, at the centre of all this..."

314

"She is," Perry muttered furtively, "and I swore I'd explain everything when the time was right; but that is not going to happen until we get our hands on her boy."

A look of hatred wound its way into his expression and suddenly, the atmosphere felt chilly. He was running out of patience. It had been over two years, since their first attempt to snatch Elijah and in all that time, Perry had existed on a tightrope of anxiety.

"This is the reason we are having this meeting," his voice throbbed into the silence. "It is time to double our efforts. We failed in our efforts to get the land..." he shot an accusing glare at Robin, "and to think, it was right at the heart of their community."

"We have the Barton-Wells girl to thank for that!" Robin intervened coldly.

Perry's glare intensified. "And what have *you* done? You've had more opportunity to keep watch over their community than any of us. How is it, you still know so little about that Jansen boy?"

"What else is there to know?' Robin sighed, the panic in his expression growing. "He attends the same school. He has a tight-knit circle of friends who he sticks very closely to and he occasionally helps his mother out in those gardens. What more can I tell you?"

From another shadowy corner of the room, Nathan was watching them - not quite able to shift the sneer from his face, as Robin squirmed beneath the chill of Perry's gaze.

"That kid is *never* on his own, Perry," he intervened.

Perry slammed his wine glass down onto the side table, finally recognising the deadlock they were caught up in. "Then we have got to set a trap," he finished icily. "There is no other way."

"There is always Peter," Robin added, desperate to win back his favour. "I'm certain Dominic let slip, the boy was keen to get involved in his housing trust."

"Then I suggest you keep your finger on the pulse," Perry whispered, "especially if the council are intending to finance some of it. Why not show a little more interest?"

"Of course," Robin agreed, "I won't let you down..." He held his stare for a few more seconds. "It would help if we could bug their telephone," he finished silkily.

Perry threw him a look of disdain. "Now that's a job for which we *will* need a professional," and as if to further deride him, he followed it with an appraising smile towards Nathan.

Robin knew when he was being maligned. No-one could have missed the mockery in Perry's eyes when he had dared to repeat the suggestion of phone bugging. If only he could find his own ally but he had been distracted; his life encumbered with a few personal problems - and it took him right back to a life-changing event that had occurred a few weeks back. The rain kept streaking down, caught in the gleam of headlights. He stared ahead as if hypnotised.

These troubles first came to light when he had decided to use up some of his annual holiday leave. He was warmed by the memory of those first few days; waking up in a hotel room - momentarily gazing down at some graceful, dark skinned boy he had spent the night with. Robin knew exactly the right places to seek out the pleasures he craved - cautious to choose towns where nobody knew him. Brighton was perfect with its thriving gay community and choice of clubs - a place where rent boys like Carlos were easy to find.

Any lingering feelings of sexual gratification were blown from his mind however, when he had embarked on his second journey to London. He had known his sister was desperate to talk to him; unprepared for the sight of her blotchy pink face, her eyes swollen from crying.

"I can't cope any more!" she had sobbed, sinking into his arms.

Robin knew of her plight. Their mother (fast approaching 80) had been diagnosed with Alzheimer's. Jenny had made every effort to look after her; seduced by the charming bungalow in West Ham they would ultimately inherit. Yet her condition had reached a stage where it was essential to transfer her to a nursing home. They had been forced to sell the bungalow to pay for it - and cruellest of all, was the way the rest of the family were condemning her for it.

Robin clutched her as she wept, feeling his fury soar. Their two elder brothers had done nothing! Alfred like his father was a slovenly brute - he had even served time in prison for a spate of football hooliganism. Timothy wasn't much better, although he did at least have a job as a car mechanic.

"So what about Gavin?" Robin seethed, remembering Jenny's husband.

"He's left me, Robin!" Jennifer wailed, sobbing even harder.

It had been a very unpleasant hour as the story came spluttering out. Robin had initially been pleased when his sister had married an academic. Though Gavin hadn't treated Jennifer particularly well and a long standing affair with a former student had been a constant source of unhappiness.

"I'm no longer any use to him, now we've sold the bungalow!" she sniffed. "We're getting divorced. It hasn't been great for the kids, either!"

This was the point, Robin's eyes had wandered towards his niece. She hovered in the kitchen, her expression truculent. Yet she had transformed into an arrestingly lovely young lady; sharp blue eyes - a face which disguised a calculating air of intelligence. She was the only family member who had possessed any drive and ambition. In fact, she reminded him very much of himself.

"Naomi's becoming a right handful," Jennifer whispered, fighting tears again. "She's dropped out of college - some of the girls were picking on her, calling her a lesbian…" her face crumpled. "I've just about reached the end of my tether, Robin…"

"So why doesn't she come and live with me?" Robin responded. He levelled her with a tender smile. "She could work for the council! There's even a vacancy in Leisure Services. They're advertising for an admin assistant in the Parks and Gardens department."

Within seconds, Jennifer started nodding, relishing a solution. It would at least, resolve *some* of their worries. Naomi loathed where they lived and had very few friends.

The first few weeks were a challenge. Having never had kids of his own, Robin was slightly nervous when his niece moved in - wary of the willful teenager, about to disrupt the tranquillity of his home. Apart from a few early spats however, they tumbled into an awkward harmony. It was only now that Robin cherished her company; someone who cooked occasionally, happy to discuss a political debate or a science documentary. The only cloud lingering on the horizon was this perpetual acrimony with Perry.

By the time he let himself in, he felt drained - his face white in the reflection of the window. He poured himself a measure of whisky before collapsing into his favourite chair. From the other side of the room, Naomi watched him.

"Why are you upset? Has this got anything to do with this *Perry* who keeps phoning?"

"I couldn't even b-begin to explain…" Robin faltered.

For once, it seemed Naomi would not give up. She couldn't understand why Perry had this effect on him. Robin closed his eyes as she sidled closer, now easing herself onto the arm of his chair as he sipped his whisky. Her hand on his shoulder felt soothing.

"I can't tell you," Robin kept whispering. "It happened in the past; something I got caught up in, something evil. I fear, you would think very badly of me…"

She allowed him to finish his whisky before cajoling him into telling her. Robin let out a sigh. He began to tell her about an era, he had first entered into politics. It was the concept of what Perry could do to him that trapped him in a web of fear. This man was his mentor. At the same time, he was drawn into a conspiracy - one that was guaranteed to elevate him to new heights of power; a mission so compelling, it had been impossible to refuse.

"You didn't know him," Robin choked, "you have no idea how manipulative he was!"

Naomi fixed him with her mesmerising blue eyes. "So what *was* this mission?" She released a soft sigh. "Don't tell me you had someone *killed*…"

Robin clawed the arm of his chair, his face turning rigid.

"Oh my God!" Naomi sniggered. "Really?"

"I-it's not what you think!" Robin spluttered in panic. His hands started shaking - she couldn't possibly understand... a conspiracy which combined the joint forces of a senior ranking police officer and hired hit man. Robin had been indispensable - someone Perry had relied upon to ensure the job was completed. "Our plan should have been perfect," he finished guiltily.

He broke off with a shudder, his knuckles white around his empty glass. Naomi slid herself down from the armchair and drifted over to the mahogany drinks cabinet. By the time she sat down, she had plucked out the whisky bottle, along with a second glass.

"So who was the victim?" she pressed, topping up both glasses.

Robin chose his words carefully. He couldn't possibly confess it all - but he told her about Jake; a boy who'd visited Scotland Yard to pass on some particularly damning evidence about Perry.

"He was a liability. He had to die - but someone got in the way!" His voice slurred with menace as he continued the story, right up until the night of Jake's murder.

The room contained a sudden chill. Naomi no longer looked so calm.

"So why didn't they deal with her, too?" she eventually gasped.

Robin gave a mirthless laugh. "My dear girl, Eleanor Chapman was more dangerous to us dead, than alive! She compiled a dossier of notes - every detail of our conspiracy; a document which will no doubt rear its ugly head - and this is what Perry is afraid of."

"So what was *your* role?" Naomi snapped, the anxiety in her voice growing.

"I set a trap," Robin whispered. "I sent them to a place where they would find sanctuary. Toynbee Hall..." He felt no shame in confessing his betrayal - but on the night Jake died, Eleanor had seen him. He had yet to tell her about the press conference; that fateful evening when Eleanor had finally locked horns with Perry... "and now we have to set a trap for her son," he shivered, his resolve splintering. "This is the only way Eleanor Bailey will ever reveal the location of that file! Perry is obsessed with getting hold of him - to use him as a bargaining tool and until that day comes, he is going to make my life hell..." he broke off with a sob.

Naomi rose. She clocked his fear as well as the tears glittering in his eyes. She had never seen a grown man cry - a sight that was as pathetic as it was harrowing.

"Bloody bitch," he seethed. "Why couldn't she have just disappeared and moved on, but no! She had to end up in Rosebrook..."

"Then we have to find a solution," Naomi said, a thread of steel slipping into her tone. "Get Perry what he wants - then maybe you can live your life without fear."

"You can't mean that!" Robin breathed, "Naomi - do you have any idea what you're getting yourself into?"

"I've heard enough to know it's time you resolved it," she muttered. "I'm glad you confided in me - I'll do whatever I can to help you see this nightmare through to the end."

She collapsed into his arms and they hugged each other - and finally, he had found his ally!

II

As the months wore on, it gradually occurred to Ben that any opportunity to intimidate Lucy was not as forthcoming as he'd hoped. As ever, he prioritised his life around his busy stockbroking career. The portfolios of his clients mattered more than anything. Neither could he ignore the sizzling party scene he was swept up in; the private mansions of London's richest business tycoons. Ben's popularity had soared, since he had unlocked a reliable new source of cocaine.

This in turn, brought him into regular contact with Alan Levy. Much of their communication was done using mobile phones these days. And Ben had no intention of abandoning his long standing girlfriend, Sasha, either; another draw on his time.

On each occasion he kept watch, he had been dismayed to discover that Lucy was rarely alone. The advent of Spring had brought a trickle of people to the allotments; whatever the time of day, there always seemed to be *someone* milling around. In fact, it wasn't until early May, shortly after Elijah's 16th birthday, he finally stumbled across a window of opportunity.

According to Perry's sources, Joshua worked as a journalist which occasionally drew him to London - Lucy, the very subject of Ben's obsession, enjoyed a part time job making jewellery for a boutique in Rosebrook. It was by pure chance, that on a day he visited Andrea Marsh to collect the rent, his eyes had been drawn to an unusual pendant she was wearing; one of Lucy's designs.

He studied the exquisite moonstone wrapped in a spiral of wire and smiled. "Stunning - perhaps I could commission a piece for my girlfriend in Pimlico... do you have Lucy's number?"

Andrea unsuspectingly handed him one of Lucy's cards; apparently, a whole pile of them had been spotted in the 'Olde House at Home' recently - but Ben was hardly listening, his mind ablaze with possibilities.

It was a little later that day, Lucy had received the first of many obscene phone calls. She had never wanted to tell Joshua - until an evening he returned home to find her in tears.

"So what did they say?" he pressed. "Just tell me - we can go to the police."

He clung to her tightly as she wept - the incident had left her trembling.

"I don't think I c-can bear to - to tell you," she sniffed.

How could she reveal the utter vileness of that call? The muffled, distorted voice, the crackle of a bad line which somehow added that extra spur of menace. They always started in the same manner; an enquiry about *wanting a special piece of jewellery...*'

"And?" Joshua kept pressing.

Lucy pressed her eyes shut, recalling the voice that spurted lasciviously from the ear piece. *'I'd do anything to see your 'treasures,' my angel... I'd like to lick you all over... make you suck my cock...'* she flared crimson. "I wish we'd never had the bloody thing installed! I won't answer it!"

Eventually, they found a solution.

From that day onwards, they embarked on a system of coded calls. Joshua would let the phone ring three times, hang up, then immediately call again. It was a secret they passed to everyone who knew them and of course, Ben had known nothing about it.

Several days later however, Joshua was called to London at short notice; he was regrettably coerced into attending a rock concert, the very same evening.

"Another journalist called in sick, baby," he simpered down the telephone, "you can always scoot up to London and join me!"

Lucy was reluctant. There was no way she felt like venturing out this late. The sunlight was dwindling, the last golden rays draining away from the landscape. She could see a small scattering of villagers gathering up their tools, as an advancing line of shadow spread across the allotments. Lucy watched them go, fearful of the encroaching dusk.

Joshua didn't want her to be on her own. Even the Harpers had gone to the pub.

Ben, on the other hand, was fuming; frustrated by her refusal to answer the phone. It left him wondering what other means he could use to torment her as he snatched a final glance at the caravan.

He pointed his binoculars towards the field, clocking the twinkle of light in her windows - the absence of the Land Rover rekindled a sudden spark. Ben glanced across at Nathan and smiled. Did they dare risk it?

Dusk finally closed in, blotting out the silhouettes of the trees. Lucy could hear the melodic flute of a blackbird in one of the overhead branches. She was just settling down with a book when she tensed to the rumble of a motorbike. She sat very still, praying it would fade away. Yet it was creeping into their field, edging closer and closer to the caravan. She sunk deep into the cushions - anything to make herself less visible as the throaty roar intensified; every belch of its engine bringing back the horror of Perry's confrontation.

The bike began to circle the caravan. It swerved in an arc almost parallel to the place where she was sat, huddled in terror. The glare of a headlight poured through the window. Lucy blinked - dazzled like a hare caught in the path of a car. A cry escaped her throat as she leapt up and closed the curtains.

Though it seemed, her ordeal had only just begun.

The bike edged around a little further before the same intense light flared outside a second set of windows. Lucy grabbed hold of the curtains again, yanking them shut. Thank God the windows were protected by metal grills! Obviously, Eleanor must have felt a need to protect herself.

She repeatedly shut the curtains as the motorcyclist continued to stake her out from every angle. Yet still he lingered. Despite the fact that she was fully hidden from view and had extinguished the light, the unrelenting throb of the engine kept on taunting her,

Lucy crept back towards the bed and closed her eyes. For several minutes, she lay completely still, her breath coming in shallow gasps until finally, it seemed her tormentor had nothing more to gain. It was to her ultimate relief, he moved away.

She sat up with a gasp, staring at the telephone. She snatched for the handset, punching in Marilyn's number - waiting to hear a ring tone but there was nothing but silence. She stared at the device with a frown, then swiftly tried again but the response was the same. Lucy felt her panic rise as her fingers stabbed at the buttons a third time. She dialled 999. Nothing! A new wave of fear swept over her. The telephone line was dead.

Lucy grabbed her coat, pressing her ear against the door. The air had fallen uncannily silent with no further trace of the motorbike. She bit her lip, wondering if it was safe to venture outside. Yet she was desperate to talk to someone. The farmhouse sat temptingly, a few meters away and if she couldn't talk to Marilyn, she would sprint to the pub. How she wished, she'd agreed to join Joshua up in London - but it was too late now.

She crept from the caravan towards the road, then flew across to the farmhouse. She started pounding on the door, but the silence mocked her. Lucy felt her heart sink, dreading the thought of staggering her way through the village in darkness. The hum of a few cars reassured her - the village was not completely barren; it was Friday night and there were bound to be a few people around. It was a thought which lingered on the edge of her mind for a few more seconds, before a loan figure materialised by the gates of Westbourne House. Lucy stopped dead, staring at the handsome, blonde man who seemed to be observing her.

"Lucy, isn't it?" his soft voice oozed into the silence, "are you alright?"

Lucy started to back away. She forced a smile, no longer relishing the idea of walking those extra few yards to the pub, especially with this sinister new stranger in her wake. She had recognised him straight away, of course.

"Hi," she said quickly, "you're Mr Hampton's son, aren't you? I-I was after Marilyn... but on second thoughts, I think I'll just go home."

"I'll walk you back," Ben dropped out casually and before Lucy could argue, he had fallen into step beside her. A curtain of silence hung between.

By the time they reached the caravan, Lucy felt a surge of relief as she turned to unlock the door, conscious of him loitering. She cast him a friendly but dismissive smile.

"Aren't you going to invite me in for a drink then?" Ben whispered in her ear.

Everything happened in a blur. Before Lucy could argue, he had leapt up the steps and pushed her through the door, kicking it firmly shut behind him.

"What are you doing?" Lucy screeched.

"Shut up!" he hissed, "and don't make another sound! It's time you and I got to know each other a little better..." He gripped hold of her arm, now yanking her towards the bed.

His eyes darted frantically, as if searching for something - his grip strengthening as he pressed her wrist against one of the metal poles fixed to the bunk beds.

Before Lucy could make any sense of it, she felt the click of some sort of catch mechanism. He was using handcuffs! Not just any handcuffs but a velvet, padded variety, designed to restrain, without leaving marks. Lucy felt sick. What sort of weirdo carried this type of inventory? He manoeuvred her onto the bed and with her wrist shackled firmly to the bed post, he hoisted himself astride her, using his body weight to pin her down.

"Please!" Lucy sobbed, "don't hurt me!"

He clamped his other hand over her mouth, his eyes cold. "I won't," he whispered, "not this time. Keep quiet, don't struggle and everything will be okay, my angel."

My angel! Lucy froze, remembering the obscene calls as he leered down at her; woefully conscious of her gypsy-like dress, undeniably feminine with its floral print and elasticated bodice threaded with tiny buttons. It was with escalating dread, she knew what he was about to do. He removed his hand from her mouth and gently unfastened each button, tugging back the folds of the fabric to exposed her pale breasts.

The smile on his lips became twisted. "Beautiful," he murmured.

"It was you!" Lucy gasped, "you made those disgusting phone calls!"

Ben let out a sigh. "My father told you to leave the village but you chose to be defiant! He urged me to give you a little more... *persuasion.*"

He stroked her cheek, then lowered his head. Lucy writhed beneath him - wincing in disgust as he ran his tongue slowly over her breast. It made her skin crawl, her horror spiralling to a peak as his teeth clamped over her nipple. He wasn't hurting her but the threat hovered.

"No lover boy, tonight?" he chuckled.

"Get off me, you pervert," Lucy whimpered, "or I swear I'll go to the police."

Ben jerked himself upright. "Oh no!" he snapped. "You're not going to do that, Lucy - 'cos if you do..." he calmly reached into his pocket and drew out a pack of cigarettes.

The evil sparked in his eyes as he extracted one and lit it. He took a drag of smoke and blew it into her face in a long, coiling stream. Lucy coughed; but it was nothing compared to the panic that assailed her, as he lowered the glowing tip towards her nipple. For a second, she felt its radiant heat. His expression was satanic - Lucy started to cry.

"Shame to spoil such perfection," he whispered. "Maybe I'll save that pleasure for another time! But I'm warning you, don't go to the police, Lucy. I'm an expert in pain. My girlfriend's quite a masochist, you know - and I prefer inflicting pain to receiving it."

"You're sick!" Lucy started to sob. "Let go of me!"

"All in good time," Ben sneered, "there's just one or two conditions…" He took another puff of his cigarette, whilst fumbling under the skirt of her dress. Lucy's eyes widened, as he thrust the fabric upwards to expose her lacy, black knickers. "Very nice," she heard him drawl.

She closed her eyes; conscious of the creeping fingers inside the fabric before he savagely yanked down her pants. She was exposed. She could sense the lust in his eyes, as they latched themselves onto her pubic hair. "As I was saying," his voice echoed into the caravan, "my father wants you out of the village! You can either slip away quietly - otherwise expect another visit and next time, I won't be so merciful!"

Seconds later, her wrist was released from the hand cuff. Ben rose to his feet and with a final smirk, he sauntered towards the door before slipping away into the shadows.

Lucy hastily restored her modesty, her shock so pronounced she felt giddy. He might not have raped her, yet she felt utterly violated. A sense of threat lingered inside the caravan, added to the translucent veil of cigarette smoke. It was a very long time before she dared move.

Eventually, she staggered to the door, making sure it was locked before yanking the bolts across. She dialled Marilyn number again - but the line was infuriatingly defective. Her sobs came before she could stop them - her craving for Joshua's return so fierce, it tore her heart like a wound.

It was over the next hour, she made several fitful attempts to use the phone; until mercifully, after what seemed like an eternity, the line was restored. Lucy felt a stab of hope as the phone rang on and on, wondering how on earth it could have died on her, just when she needed it most.

But still, there was no reply. With a moan of anguish, she slammed down the handset, her sobs coming harder. The next number she dialled was the 'Olde House at Home' though by the time she got through, she was nearly hysterical.

"Lucy, calm down, Love," Boris consoled her. "Just tell me what's wrong."

He was staring at the Harpers, whose expressions were filling up with dread. Marilyn shot to her feet and within seconds, Tom followed, abandoning the last of his beer.

"Best you get home," Boris finished tersely. "I'm going to call the police."

It so happened that Inspector Boswell was on duty. A strange thread of anxiety curled its way into his mind as he remembered Avalon's tearful disclosures. He could no longer ignore what his gut instinct was telling him. There was something undeniably shady about Ben Hampton.

They managed to entice Lucy gently away from the caravan and into the farmhouse where Ian desperately furrowed for the details - but it was impossible. She was in so much shock.

"He-he warned me not to talk to the p-police," she shivered, white-faced.

Of course, Ian was all too aware of the rumours Perry had been smearing around the village. Lucy might have been portrayed as some rebellious hippy, but as he observed the fragile girl braced in front of him, he formed his own opinion.

Wasting no time, he roared off to join the second squad car, destined for Westbourne House - satisfied to see it outside the entrance, blue light flickering. As usual, the grounds were basked in a silence that seemed unearthly. He found Rowena lingering in the hall with two police constables, the expression on her face disdainful.

"My son is in London, attending a very prestigious party!" she snapped irritably.

Ian's eyes zoomed in on her, searching for clues. Yet not a flicker of guilt was evident. She even supplied an address.

It then transpired, Ben definitely *was* in London - a situation which came to light as the result of a wider investigation carried out by the Metropolitan Police.

Deep down, Ian was hankering to make an arrest - driven by an urge to interrogate him. Except Ben had friends in high places; all of whom were emphatic in their claims, they had been enjoying the pleasure of his company, all evening. Ben had a rock solid alibi and Ian knew when he was bashing his head against a brick wall.

He would have liked to have spoken to Perry - though even he was strangely absent. Rowena was almost smug in her disclosure that he was engrossed in some property deal around the London dock land area. By the time Ian left, he could no longer deny he felt troubled. There were just too many unprecedented tales concerning the Hamptons and it was a notion which left a nasty aftertaste.

It was nearly 11:30 by the time Joshua returned; incensed to have been delayed and even more shocked to discover the caravan empty. He clocked the police car lurking by the farmhouse - sprinting towards it, his heart leaping.

"It's okay, son, she's asleep," Tom had eventually placated him. "Sit down."

Everyone was perched in the sitting room where the comforting sag of furniture, cloaked in its medley of woollen throws, did nothing to banish the tension that resonated in the atmosphere.

WPC Jepson had taken as many details as Lucy could bear to impart - yet her face drooped with regret. "She's scared out of her wits; b-but it seems, she doesn't want to press charges..."

The whole world turned black. Joshua saw stars as he listened with mounting dread to the unbelievable scenario being presented to him. "No-one saw this Hampton gentleman," the woman's voice echoed ominously. "There were at least twenty people willing to vouch that he was at a party, all evening - including the son of an eminent Tory MP..."

"They're lying," Joshua snapped. "There's no way Lucy would make any of this up."

"Mr Merriman, I believe her," Ian sighed uncomfortably. "I wish there was more I could do - but with the absence of evidence, there isn't a court in the land who can prove Ben's guilt."

III

There was no question about Joshua staying the night. Lucy clung to him. It was throughout those long, dark hours, she revealed the truth - and while Joshua said very little, he was hit with a thirst for retribution so powerful, he barely slept a wink.

They had no choice but to face the reality, next day - yawning as they crept their way back to the caravan. Lucy closed her eyes, allowing the clean country air to waft over her face; drinking in the delightful scent of the grass, now glistening with dew. An enchanting chorus of birdsong was ringing from the trees and for that moment, they lingered in an aura of such tranquillity, it brought tears to her eyes. Joshua's face tightened as he hunkered down to examine the telephone wire. It seemed obvious, someone must have unplugged it. He bit his lip, gazing sadly at Lucy; unable to cast out the vision of her alone in there with that *monster*.

"I loved this place," she gasped huskily, gazing around their adorable home for the last time. "B-but there's no way we can stay here..."

Joshua picked up the phone. "I'm gonna ring Mum," he snapped, as Lucy lowered herself shakily down onto the bed. "Ask her if you can have Alison's room. At least you'll be safe."

"But what about you?" Lucy squeaked.

She looked haunted - it was as if their home had been defiled.

"I guess, I'll be leaving at some point, baby," he reflected, "but I've gotta pack up our stuff." He forced a smile. "Besides that, I've got some unfinished business - I wanna talk to Toby. I'm gonna make sure every person in this village knows about this..."

Already, she was shaking her head in denial - the horror in her eyes unmissable.

"Okay, so I won't go into the details," Joshua spluttered, sliding onto the bed to join her, "but he threatened you! He sent his thug round to intimidate you..." He bit his lip. "Sorry. I'm as pissed off about leaving as you are but there's no reason why we can't stay in touch with everyone!"

How could he forget the last occasion they had ventured into the woods? A day when William and his gang had visited? If the Hamptons thought they were going to quietly disappear, they were wrong. He was going to leave his mark on this village - where the threads of an idea were already fusing.

Joshua watched Lucy's train disappear into the distance, feeling utterly disheartened. He had spent his whole life floating on a cloud of optimism. Yet something inside him had changed in the last few hours. It was only now, all that bigotry and hostility unleashed a wave of hatred. His gentle features hardened like stone as he picked up the telephone. He dialled Eleanor's number.

"We're leaving," he told her icily

Eleanor listened to his story in horror.

"We thought we'd be okay - especially with the villagers on our side - but there's something else..." He took a deep swallow, fighting to contain his emotions. "Lucy's expecting a baby."

"Oh, Joshua," Eleanor whispered numbly, "congratulations..."

"Which is why we can't stay," he blurted. "She's terrified - it's not good for her condition! What's more, the police are powerless - we haven't got much choice!"

"I'm sorry," Eleanor shivered, "b-but why can't the police *do something?*""

"There wasn't a mark on her," he shivered. "He threatened her with a lit cigarette, Eleanor! You'd think he might have dropped a bit of fag ash, but no! He covered his tracks - and with enough rich friends to bail him out!" He felt the coils of fury tightening, hating Ben Hampton with such intensity, he felt murderous. His eyes shot towards the window. Somewhere up there, Westbourne House lurked on the horizon like an enemy fortress.

He let out a sigh. "Boswell's not happy, though. He brought a policewoman... trouble is, there's no proof! Just promise me one thing, Eleanor! Swear to me, you'll keep fighting - you'll use whatever evidence we've got to put that fucker, Perry, in prison!"

"You know I will," Eleanor whispered.

"So why the delay?" Joshua snapped in a voice which seemed uncharacteristically harsh.

"Joshua, we are very nearly there..." she protested.

From the other side of the phone, Eleanor squeezed her eyes shut as the tears of frustration surfaced. The memory of her meeting with Dominic swirled darkly - it was like the oily black tar clinging to the wings of a sea bird.

"There is just one thing holding me back. Do you remember when I said, I couldn't be absolutely sure it was Theakston who shot Jake? I need evidence, so I can scrub his name from my file. He threatened my son, Joshua - but more recently, he swore he'd hurt Charlie if *ever* he was implicated in that killing!"

"You're kidding!" Joshua exploded.

"No. I wish I was!" Eleanor sighed, "but this is the stalemate situation we're caught up in. I'm going to chase it up with my solicitor - I think it is time we upped our campaign."

"Yeah, damn right," Joshua reacted, the ice returning to his tone. "Just one last thing - is Eli there? I wanna to talk to him about Andrew and William's birthday bash."

Moments later, Eleanor numbly handed her son the phone.

"We need to talk!" Joshua whispered hastily. "You, William, Angel... Can you organise a meeting somewhere private - in other words, no parents?"

"We could meet up at Avalon's," Eli mumbled. He glanced surreptitiously towards the kitchen, handset pressed against his ear. "When?"

"Soon as possible," Joshua finished. "Ring me," and with no further word, he hung up.

A meeting took place the next evening. Even Elijah couldn't ignore the subtle hint that something sinister had happened. The only one excluded was Margaret, who was dragged down with period pain. Yet for some reason, Joshua saw it as a blessing.

"She's young," he sighed, staring into the golden depths of his apple juice. "Best she doesn't know..."

They had congregated in the garden, where an assortment of garden chairs and loungers encircled the patio. Joshua's tale left an ominous chill - despite the warmth of the evening sun.

"Bastards!" Andrew hissed, fumbling for his cigarettes.

"We thought you'd be okay," William said numbly, "especially with a phone."

"Yeah, me too," Joshua nodded - he swilled the ice cubes in his glass, his expression troubled. "Anyway, it's over. Lucy's staying at Mum's and I'll be joining her soon - but before I go, I wanna leave with a bit of a blast! And we've got a party to arrange..."

"Weren't we thinking about some outdoor event?" Angel broke in, his expression grave.

"We were," Joshua replied, revealing a shadow of a smile, "and I think you and I may have had the same idea - when we were up in them woods, remember?" His gaze settled upon William. "How d'you feel about putting that land of yours to a different use?"

"What - you mean, throw a party up there?" William frowned.

Joshua's eyes narrowed. "I was thinking more along the lines of a rave..."

There was a moment of silence - the sentence left trailing.

"Yes!" William hissed. His hand coiled into a fist as it rested on the table top. He stared at Avalon. "Can't you see? It's perfect! We said we'd do something special. Can you think of anything more fitting than a massive party in the woods?"

"No," Avalon smiled back, "and you're right, it is perfect. This is *exactly* where we'd have celebrated your 18th if Dad had been alive - if we hadn't lost Westbourne House! Best of all, can you imagine how much this is going to annoy the Hamptons?"

A shudder of excitement began to disseminate around the circle; a sense, they were finally about to get their own back.

Chapter 20

I

June 1989

It began on the evening of June 24th; the secret vein of activity was launched by a progression of vehicles and trailers as they snaked their way into the hills.

The villagers had of course, been alerted a month earlier - a time when they were still reeling in the aftermath of Lucy's ordeal, especially when Joshua marched into the 'Olde House at Home' to announce their departure.

"So what happened?" Boris had sighed as he hastily filled a glass with Joshua's favourite ale. People seemed to have forgotten it was Boris who had answered Lucy's panic-stricken call.

"Ben Hampton was in the village," Joshua said bitterly, "despite all that *bullshit*, he was supposed to be at some party."

He told them about the obscene phone calls. A pile of Lucy's cards lingered innocently on the bar top - a devastating clue as to how Ben might have discovered their phone number.

"And he threatened her?" Toby said disgustedly.

Joshua gave a shudder. He couldn't bear to impart the rest, sickened by the thought of Ben shackling her to the bed post, brandishing his cigarette. "I'm sorry - I just thought you should know… and this is why we're leaving - but not without making some form of protest."

The fact that Lucy was pregnant made the whole business seem even more appalling.

"What are you planning?" Toby eventually whispered.

The two men had disappeared into the beer garden. Joshua told him about the party.

"So let me get this right?" Toby mused, "the Barton-Wells kids are thinking of organising a rave in the woods - and you're going to help them?"

"Avalon and William have got more reason to hate the Hamptons than anyone," Joshua sighed, "and in the light of what happened to my Lucy... Do you have any objection?"

"I don't," Toby grinned, "but I warn you, my father isn't going to be too happy! What date have you got in mind?"

"Midsummer's Day," Joshua muttered, drawing his head closer.

"Tell you what," Toby winked, "organise it the following weekend and my folks will be away in Madeira - so they won't have cause to complain."

Gradually, the news fed its way to the villagers; the concept of a secret rave party gently dripped into the ears of Boris, the Harpers and a select group of allies who would forever remain loyal to the Barton-Wells family;

locals who worked the allotments - people who had demonstrated their support for Joshua and Lucy when Perry was vehement in his campaign to drive them out.

Toby however, was not wrong about Herbert. "Bloody ridiculous idea!" he thundered.

"You won't even be here," Toby bristled, "and besides - can you *imagine* how much this event'll infuriate the Hamptons?"

The next time they visited the pub, Joshua wanted to glean a little more gossip - determined to make sure Perry was in residence.

"Seems a shame to disrupt the harmony if that bastard's not around!" he whispered to Boris.

Boris laughed heartily, just as Marilyn sidled up to the bar.

"Oh, don't you worry about that," she snapped, "he's always around at the weekend. But I'll see if I can grab a quiet word with Elliot."

A day later, Marilyn returned to the pub with even better news. "Your timing is perfect," she smiled, folding an affectionate arm around Joshua's shoulder. "They're hosting an important conference. Elliot leaked it. Apparently 20 delegates from the Institution of Agricultural Engineers are going to be in residence *and* hosting a gala dinner in the ballroom." Her mouth was drawn into a hard line, Joshua noticed, not missing that tiny glint of spite in her eyes.

There wasn't a person in their circle who felt anything but disgust over the fate of her nephew. The Harpers demonstrated their outrage more than anyone - especially when Perry had next appeared.

"You should be ashamed of yourself!" Marilyn spat with all the ferociousness of a tiger protecting her cub. "Sending your son round to terrorise that poor girl…"

Perry froze in front of her. "You have no proof of that!" he sneered, "but then, I suppose you lot will believe any cock and bull story levelled against my family!"

"Lucy wouldn't lie!" Marilyn yelled, in a voice which shook with emotion, "what's more, she's pregnant!" Even Perry faltered - though the scorn in his eyes showed no sign of abating. "That's right," she finished with an element of satisfaction. "Your son is *evil*, Perry Hampton!"

"Except there were no witnesses," Perry challenged her icily. "It's her word against his."

The small cluster watched in disbelief as he turned and routinely ordered a glass of wine. He strutted towards a chair, calmly unfolding his newspaper. There was not a person in that pub who couldn't have sensed the ripples of hatred spiralling around the walls. Perry exuded a demeanour of arrogance they found repulsive - his florid face set like stone, devoid of all humanity. Suddenly, no-one had any qualms about the illegal 'acid house party' that was about to explode in the depths of his neighbouring woods - and with one month to go, they awaited the night with relish.

If anyone had a vital role to play, it was Angel - who in the run-up to the rave, was hopping around town as if walking on hot coals. Having played the field for nearly a year, he had finally settled into a relationship with Lara. The two of them not only shared a passionate love bond but he had assigned her the job of getting some fliers printed: a mission which lured her to London. They wanted it to remain secret, almost right up until the advent. It was only a little earlier in the week, she had dropped a batch round to Avalon and William's place.

"These look amazing!" William breathed.

He gazed at the colourful printed sheet with pleasure - loving the swirling new age, fantasy art set against the silhouette of an oak tree. The words "Midsummer Night Dreamscape" were emblazoned across the centre in 3D lettering.

Angel kept in regular contact with Joshua who was at the nucleus of its success. Using his connections, he recruited a small team of event organisers. Within weeks, they had managed to co-ordinate the hire of a mobile stage and a powerful PA system, encompassing huge speakers, microphones and a 12-channel mixer capable of pumping out over 100 decibels of sound. The glittering concept of the event gradually took shape - where the addition of a portable lighting stand with sound activated strobe light, blue and green lasers, as well as a smoke machine were about to transform the woods into something as magical as the image on their flier.

Angel was so excited, he was buzzing - knowing he was their prime DJ. The only potentially regrettable situation arose, when one of the fliers accidentally found its way into Bella's Palace.

Dominic pulled him to one side. "What's all this about a rave?" he demanded.

It was a while since Angel had seen the boss. Dominic spread himself thinly, only popping into Rosebrook when he was needed; the gym in Swanley was his main business priority. He had grown his hair a little longer which in some ways, resurrected the hardened villain he had been in the 70s. His face bore more lines, the slant of his eyes as malevolent as ever.

Angel gazed back at him in consternation. "It's in honour of Andrew and William BW," he shrugged. "They've got special birthdays, this year. We wanted to organise something cool."

"Where is it?" Dominic snapped.

When Angel reluctantly betrayed the location, Dominic's first reaction was to laugh. "Are you mad?" he spluttered. "You do realise Hampton will have the police out in force - if he don't set a load of guard dogs on you, that is - an' I'd never put it past him..."

Angel's eyes turned stony. "You don't need to tell us who we're dealing with, man, they're fucking bastards, the lot of 'em."

"You'll get yourselves nicked," Dominic sneered. "Hope you got a plan B."

"Don't let on," Angel pleaded. "This is important to us, man - but seein' as you ask, we could always move the party on to your place... you know, if things get heavy."

Dominic's eyes shed none of their malice. "You think I'm gonna be happy about a load of pilled-up kids turning up at my club?"

"Aw come on, Boss!" Angel whined, "it's the closest place to where the party is!"

Dominic offered him a cold smile. "Just as long as they pay the entry fee. But you watch your back, son, 'cause I doubt if any of you *really* know who you're taking on, here."

Angel was tempted to ask how he knew so much about the greatly-feared Hamptons; filled with a sense, he was actually on their side, but without understanding why.

Unfortunately Dominic wasn't wrong. If he knew Perry, it was virtually fated their party wasn't going to run quite as smoothly as they anticipated - but who was going to listen?

II

It was still daylight when the first vehicles were crawling round the forest, to an open area of grass land on the other side of the trees. By this time, Joshua had been revelling in the sheer scale of the operation; the stage erected, an electricity generator already up and running as the final fixtures were about to be put into place. He felt as if his heart was on fire.

The weather was fortuitously on their side. It had been dry for the last two weeks and the temperature had rarely dropped below 20 degrees, leaving a haze of warmth floating in the air. Tonight, just 3 days after the Summer Solstice, the hills were cloaked in a warm golden light - the sun spreading the last of its rays up to the forest edge, where Joshua stood gazing over the landscape. It brought a lump to his throat, knowing that as soon as the rave was over, he would be leaving Aldwyck. He watched, as a couple of girls dressed in floaty, chiffon dresses, darted among the trees, threading fairy lights into the branches. Come nightfall, the area would be illuminated by a harlequin of colour. It was going to be breathtaking, Joshua thought - delirious with excitement as he turned and made his way back to his Land Rover. He had agreed to take a trip into Rosebrook to pick up some spare bulbs - an excuse to rendezvous with the kids, before dropping them round to the Barton-Wells' house.

With Joshua set to pick them up at around 8:00, Elijah and Margaret had just finished preening themselves, hopping downstairs in silent anticipation of the night ahead.

Eleanor and Charlie lingered in the lounge. They too, were dressed up and about to celebrate their wedding anniversary. Charlie had booked the same delightful restaurant where he had originally proposed to her - wary the kids had organised something else; though the precise details remained top secret, even now.

"Dressing down?" Eleanor smiled, observing Elijah's long-sleeved baggy top, worn loose outside his black chinos - a hooded jacket was slung casually over his arm.

"Party's gonna be outside," he mumbled. "Might be a bit chilly later."

He shot a quick glance at Margaret. She had braided her golden hair into plaits and despite the application of make-up, she looked disturbingly innocent in tight jeans and a pretty cardigan. It clung to her bosom but flared at the hem in a way which enhanced her slender waist.

Charlie and Eleanor had no idea what was about to kick off - having assumed their party was at Avalon's, where they were also spending the night. They heard Joshua pull up outside the almshouse.

"See you later then!" Elijah called, skipping to the door with Margaret in tow.

But before either of them had a chance to jump into the Land Rover, they froze as Holly sidled up to them. She seemed to have materialised out of no-where. Margaret flashed her a warm but furtive smile - it had been impossible to stay angry with her forever.

"Where are you going?" Holly asked wistfully. "Eli?"

"Hi, Holly," Elijah muttered curtly, inching his way towards the Land Rover.

Holly hopped out in front of him. "Is it a party?" she kept bleating. "Can I come? How come you don't talk to me any more? Look - I-I'm sorry if I upset you..."

Margaret laughed lightly as if on the verge of reassuring her, but Elijah stepped in first.

"Holly, you didn't just *upset me,* you busted my heart! You treated me like crap - worst, you lied to your mum about us." He couldn't stop himself - all the pent up hurt finally leaking out of him. He was about to participate in possibly the biggest rave in the county - damned if he was going to let Holly manipulate him like this.

"I'm sorry - we can still be friends..." she persisted.

Elijah's face softened. "I know," he sighed, "and I'd like that - but your mother told me to have nothing more to do with you, remember?" He stroked her cheek.

"It's a private party," Margaret spluttered, "sorry - invitation only."

"But where is it?" Holly gasped, outraged to be excluded.

"It's a secret!" Elijah and Margaret chorused in union, before scrambling into the Land Rover.

Andrew had left earlier. He had been assigned to round up Matt, Lara and finally Angel; oblivious to the fact that his friend had been picking up a large consignment of ecstasy tablets, courtesy of Alan Levy's network. By the time they caught up with him, he was outside his flat, lugging two leather cases packed with his enviable vinyl collection.

You're what this party started, right!" they heard him singing tunelessly.

He looked irrefutably slick in a corduroy bomber jacket, baseball cap plonked on back to front over his close-cropped curls.

"I gotta go, you guys," he added sharply, hauling the cases into his car.

"I thought we were gonna rendezvous at Avalon's," Andrew argued.

Angel glanced at him shrewdly then winked. "You go," he whispered, slipping a tiny plastic bag into his hand. "Here's your supplies, man, I'll see you up there. Gotta get my set ready."

Naturally, Lara wanted to accompany him. She looked gorgeous, Andrew thought; her hair a mass of glossy, black tendrils from a recent spiral perm. She was swathed in a purple silk top and matching trousers - a leather jacket slung across her bare shoulders.

The moment they piled inside the Barton-Wells' house, William poured everyone a beer, his cheeks flushed, bronze hair tousled as he jogged around the lounge in a familiar loose fitting tunic and jeans. With the exception of Angel and Lara, everyone was dressed for comfort.

"Might as well get a drink in," William smiled, raising his glass to the sound of one of his own mix tapes belting from the speakers. "It won't be a boozy affair!"

"No, I guess not," Andrew muttered and fishing Angel's tablets out of his pocket, he extracted one of the tiny pills, holding it between forefinger and thumb. "Who's up for a tab?"

"Is that ecstasy?" William gasped. "I'm up for it!"

Avalon looked anxious. "I don't know, William - neither of us have ever tried anything like this before. Does it make you hallucinate?"

"You'll have the best time of your life," Andrew grinned wickedly, "music'll sound brilliant and you won't wanna stop dancing. This is supposed to be a rave, right?"

William numbly held out his hand and glanced at Avalon.

She gave a nod. "How much?" she whispered - hazel eyes brimming with uncertainty.

"Ten quid a tab," Andrew replied, slipping them a pill each.

"Can I have one?" Margaret piped up.

It was as if everyone had forgotten their two youngest members.

"No, you can't," Andrew snapped, "you're way too young, Dad'll kill me."

"So we don't tell him!" Margaret insisted, "I'm not your stupid little kid sister any more, I'm 14! And I thought we were in this together - otherwise what's the point of us coming?"

"Okay, you can have half," Andrew relented, snapping one of the pills along the seam.

"I'll have the other half," Elijah jumped in quickly, unfolding his palm.

"Fine," Andrew sighed, "just make sure you drink plenty of bottled water. You'll have a mouth as dry as a nun's tits, otherwise!"

The hands on the clock were turning faster. 9:00 approached and every one of them except William, had popped their pill.

"All for one and one for all!" he exulted, thrusting his empty glass high in the air. "I'll take mine when we get there!"

They bounded out of the house where William's lovely, glacier-blue sports car sat invitingly in the drive. Avalon jumped into the passenger seat, Elijah slithered into the back and eventually, they cruised up the High Street with the others in convoy.

Twenty minutes later, William steered his car into one of Herbert Baxter's empty barns, just as the fiery embers of a sunset were sinking below the horizon.

Evening tipped into nightfall - the party was about to begin.

Elijah blinked, absorbing the scene as the mind-altering chemical high from the ecstasy took effect. The mouth of the forest glittered like a fairies grotto; colourful lights dangling from the trees, glowing in his vision like fireflies. A succession of bulbs oscillated around the stage in time to the music, infused with billowing waves of smoke - and right at the front, illuminated in a halo of bright white light, stood Angel. He was in his element - a set of black leather earphones wrapped around his head, his face split into a euphoric smile as he spun the records with his hands, using the channel mixer to blend them seamlessly.

Elijah's eyes travelled further - spotting the various 'chill-out' tents where revellers could periodically flop down for a rest. Andrew was probably sprawled under one of those canopies right now, he thought, getting a spliff together. His eyes kept wandering - drawn to the catering vans parked just outside the forest entrance. An assortment of mouth-watering smells coiled into the cool night air which reminded him of a fairground - hot dogs, chips, onions. He was tempted to buy an ice cream though for now, he settled for a bottle of chilled water.

It was very dark and yet the forest had come alive - a growing crowd of people thrown together en mass, throbbing in time to the music. Elijah was reminded of some giant pulsating dragon, his eyes glazed as he filtered his way dreamily into the heart of it. Periodically, a troupe of dancers took to the stage, beautifully choreographed to the pounding waves of music. It seemed that everyone was dancing - he could feel their energy, yearning to be a part of it as he threaded his way through the mass of people in search of his friends.

He had only just caught up with them when the most amazing light show erupted from the stage. A whoop rose up from the crowd as a fan of lasers shot into the sky - the woods around them flickering in alternate shades of blue and green. Elijah caught his breath, as he danced alongside Margaret and William - then finally, his eyes leapt towards Avalon.

She was dancing so beautifully - completely enraptured in the scene; her hips writhing like a snake, her arms coiled high above her head, painting strange patterns in the air. A beautiful smile lingered on her face as she stared up into the sky, dazzled by the lasers - and for the next hour, he could barely take his eyes off her.

III

Less than a mile away, guests at Westbourne House were enjoying their gala dinner. The plates had been cleared away by now, the tables pushed against the wall to make room for dancing.

Staff had been rushed off their feet, serving up a most exquisite three course dinner; too busy to notice any unusual activity in the area, as dozens of vehicles continued to creep their way up the tracks and into the hills. Wine flowed copiously. Everyone seemed to be enjoying themselves as a lively band kept them entertained with a succession of golden oldies.

Perry was among them, puffing joyfully on a cigar as he surveyed the exuberant scene inside his ballroom. Dozens of smartly dressed couples were swinging each other around the dance floor - the ladies beautiful in their ball gowns while their partners adhered to a protocol of formal black tie.

Elliot lingered on the periphery, happy to chaperone anyone who wanted to step outside for a breath of fresh air or a cigarette. Tonight, he was of a mind to keep the guests at the front of the house - away from the grounds that stretched towards the forests; the very place, he feared the rave was happening right now. It was a blessing, the amplified base and vocals emanating from their own event sufficiently masked any alternative sound in the distance.

Even Ben had joined the party - buoyed up on champagne which inspired him to chat up some of the prettier females. It was unbeknown to anyone, he had even smuggled a couple into his bedroom which was also positioned at the front of the house. It was from here, he did most of his spying, still revelling in his triumph over Lucy. Though she was a dim flicker of a memory, compared to the two little firecrackers who had shared his bed for the last half hour.

They slipped surreptitiously back to the party where the final hour passed quickly; the band gradually winding down and finishing with a few crooning numbers that had everyone back on the floor for a last dance. From the moment they started packing away their instruments, people began to disperse. It was around midnight when the hotel finally lapsed into tranquillity.

"What a wonderful success!" Rowena was heard crowing as she proceeded to wander upstairs.

Elliot closed and locked the main door, just as the final couples were heading towards the car park. He didn't fail to witness the sudden jerk of their heads as they turned and stared into the hills. His heart leapt. There was suddenly no mistaking, something was happening up there.

Unfortunately, it was only moments before Perry realised it too.

Elliot watched as if in a dream as he sauntered into the lounge, cigar dangling loosely from his fingers. His face was flushed from the heat. He threw open the patio doors to draw in the cool night air and then he heard it - a solid boom of music resonating from the woods.

He braced to a standstill. "What the bloody hell...?"

"Dad!" Ben shouted, tearing into the lounge. "You are never going to believe what's going on in the woods up there!"

"I know," Perry growled, "I can hear it!"

"You need to see it from the upstairs landing," Ben urged him.

They stormed from the room, leaving Elliot frozen in the shadows; terrified for the Barton-Wells children, as he silently prayed for their safety.

Perry meanwhile, stood braced on the first floor landing, glaring across the grounds. He could see the silver flicker of strobe lighting above the tree tops. At first glance, it could have been lightning - until he also saw the interconnecting spikes of blue and green dancing towards the heavens.

"Someone's holding an illegal rave," Ben whispered dangerously.

Guests were already complaining. They had barely let themselves into their rooms before the heady pulse of rave music became impossible to ignore. Windows had been left open - it was after all, a very warm night.

"No-one's going to get a wink with all that racket going on!" One of the more senior guests was heard grumbling as he headed back downstairs towards the bar. It was the chairman of the Institution of Agricultural Engineers; the eminent figurehead who had selected Westbourne House for their conference. Perry turned back to Ben, his eyes smouldering.

"That's it," he snarled, "I'm calling the police!"

"Ssh!" Ben hissed. "Think about who owns the land up there. Might explain whose party it is!"

"The Barton-Wells children," Perry muttered. "Little bastards..." He was finding it hard to suppress his rage - yet it was in a splinter of time, they arrived at the same conclusion; if the Barton-Wells children were organising a dance party, somewhere deep in those forests…

"I wonder who else could be up there," Ben was musing.

"Elijah Jansen," Perry finished evilly.

"Indeed," Ben smiled. "So why don't we hold off the police for now. Leave this in Nathan's hands. There's even a possibility he might be able to rope in a few of Alan's thugs. He said he'd give us a lead, if we gave him good reason."

Within an instant, Nathan was straight on the case.

It took no more than 20 minutes to track down the gang, Alan had hinted he could spare in an emergency; and in another secluded part of Aldwyck, Nathan eagerly awaited them.

If there was one thing William had never counted on, it was that people were prepared to travel miles to these events. By 11:00 there must have been over 250 people milling around in the forest, but that number steadily rose to over 600 as a seemingly never-ending stream of vehicles threaded their way up the tracks, in search of an illegal rave rumoured to be tucked in the hillside. Even from a distance, the mesmerising light show lit the area up like a beacon.

In fact it was impossible for the event to stay secret. Stories of 'some big party in the woods' had already circulated among pupils in their school year; boys like Gary Boswell, who came lumbering towards the forest entrance with Darren in his wake.

"What are you doing here, Boswell?" William snapped, "you're not invited!"

"Oh yeah?" Gary sneered, "then maybe I'll tell my father! He'll have the police up here in minutes and arrest the bloody lot of you!"

Elijah wandered up to the scene, strangely unaffected, where the sight of these two boys sparked a very different reaction. "It's okay, let them in," he said calmly.

William whirled round and gaped at him. "Are you mad?"

"No," Elijah replied. "There's just one thing I want to say - do you remember when you got me chucked out of Mickey's party?" his eyes bore into him. "You've made my life hell, Gary. So if we let you into our party, can we stop being enemies?"

The other boy's eyes narrowed, before he let out a bray of laughter. "Are you trying to make a deal, Jansen?" With a sigh, he thrust out a meaty hand which Elijah had little choice but to grasp. The next thing he knew, Gary was tilting his head close. "Any chance you know where we can get some of this 'e,' mate?"

Elijah could not help but smile and with a joyful thumbs-up, he went in search of Andrew.

He found them in the chill-out tent, sharing another joint. Without a thought, Andrew passed it to him. Eli could not resist an experimental drag before he calmly explained his quest.

"Can you imagine what Boswell's gonna say?" he spluttered, handing Andrew the twenty pound bank note, Gary had stuffed into his hand.

"Well he can hardly arrest us for drugs if his son's off his face!" Andrew smirked. "Just don't tell 'em you got it from me, okay? Here - you might as well take the lot."

He handed him the tiny, polythene bag which now contained just three ecstasy pills.

The music continued to reverberate all around them. Angel was taking a break and was last seen engaged in a passionate snog with Lara. The crowd had grown so huge by now that Elijah was beginning to feel overwhelmed - thankful to catch up with Avalon, who was still in the throes of dancing. The next person to appear was Margaret, gulping down a bottle of water. Then finally, they spotted William strolling out from the 'Portaloos' installed in another area of the forest.

A gentle smile sprung to his face as he spotted them too, wriggling his way cautiously through the gyrating mass of revellers to reach them.

"What do you think of it so far?" Elijah shouted above the din.

"Fantastic!" William laughed. "Joshua's done an amazing job!"

"We need to stick together!" Avalon joined in. "We don't want to lose each other!"

To Elijah's unparalleled delight, she clasped his hand. He wasn't sure if it was the dreamy state of his mind from the ecstasy - but the moment their eyes connected, her face radiated an expression of such fondness, it seemed unreal. He found himself smiling back, his heart racing. He risked an affectionate squeeze of her hand, even more delighted when she returned the gesture. It was in that pivotal moment, Elijah realised that anything he had ever felt for Holly was nothing compared to this; lost in Avalon's beauty - her huge shining eyes. An intense feeling of love surged through his veins like a powerful electric current.

William glanced at Margaret. They had clearly witnessed the exchange and with a smile lingering on her own face, she reached for William's hands. He let out a light laugh.

"How long do you think this party will go on for?" she hollered.

"For however long you want it to!" William shouted back, sidling up close to make himself heard. "Are you tired?"

"Not at all!" Margaret sighed, closing her eyes. "I'm having a great time!"

She breathed deeply, savouring the sweet, musky scent of him. The four of them were bunched in a tight circle and before they knew it, Angel was back on stage for his next set. It was with no hesitation, he upped the tempo - blending in some hard-hitting 'acid house' which had the crowd reeling. The strobe light was going crazy. A heavy, almost violent beat shook the forest, infused with an echo of synthesisers. It was at that moment, the rave had almost hit fever pitch.

Joshua, stood slightly back from the crowd and watched, a cool smile glued to his face as he conversed with the organisers. He was going to be leaving soon, unsure how long the event would continue. Right now he was having the best time of his life. The crowd were going wild out there as Angel's skilful mixing brought them to even higher levels of euphoria.

At the same time, he was thinking about the Hamptons - trying to imagine the scene at Westbourne House, hoping this party would deliver the kick up the arse they deserved! Perry would be apoplectic with rage - though he also couldn't help wondering how long it would be before the police were called.

What Joshua could never have known was that two transit vans were speeding towards the rave; vehicles whose occupants had been lured from London and Nathan was among them.

Angel smiled across at his audience, arms raised like some sort of preacher - aroused by their joy as the music rocked them with its energy. Elijah's eyes followed him before they were drawn again to the lasers - back to Avalon's face which glowed from blue to green in the spectre of light. All four of them were dancing in a circle, hands joined. It was like something out of a dream - trails of smoke were threading their way through the trees, reflecting the shimmers of light. It was almost hypnotic. His gaze followed the writhing clouds then paused on Gary Boswell. He was caught up in a frenzy of manic dancing - clearly off his face and gurning away with the best of them.

Elijah started laughing - he simply couldn't help himself. It was in those final precious moments when everything seemed surreal. And then all hell broke loose.

The two unfamiliar transit vans charged into the neck of the woods where they screeched to a halt. Joshua watched in disbelief. The doors flew open and about a dozen dark-clothed figures exploded from the back. They looked like demons from hell - black balaclavas disguised their faces and to his horror, they were wielding baseball bats.

It was no co-incidence, he had just been talking to one of the event organisers - a heavily built man who had been roped in to provide security. Yet there had been no sign of any trouble-makers; at least, not until now.

"Hey, what the hell..." his companion bellowed, pitching himself forwards.

His words were cut short. One of the assailants swung his club and slammed it into his kneecaps. The man buckled to the ground with a cry. Joshua gaped in panic as the whole gang then thundered into the forest where the mass of dancing revellers were inevitably their next target.

A volley of screams rose from the crowds as they began to retreat from the stage. They had no choice. One minute, they had been swept up in an incredible wave of bliss; the next, it was as if armageddon had been unleashed.

Elijah froze, staring at Angel as the nightmare unfurled. Two hellish figures had closed in on him from both sides; followed by a horrific crash as the masked men launched into a frenzied attack, weapons raised as they smashed them over the turntables again and again, killing the music. Everyone watched in stunned shock - the absence of sound was terrifying.

"Me fuckin' records!" Angel screeched as stacks of vinyl were shattered into fragments. "What the fuck you doing, man…?" He broke off, staring at his attackers in dread.

A tall, skinny character was braced right in front of him, arms dangling by his sides like some sort of Neanderthal. There was something about those pale, reptilian eyes staring through the holes of a balaclava that turned his blood to ice. The figure bared his teeth - a hideous grin stretched across his face. "Well, look what we've got 'ere, boys!"

The character swung his club, striking a vicious blow across Angel's shoulder. He fell to the ground with a sob, as several more youths joined in the attack.

"You've had this coming to you for a long time, you black cunt!" the ringleader hissed.

They rained down blow after blow. Lara let out a scream, unable to believe what was happening.

"Help him, somebody!" she started howling.

Joshua was the first to hurl himself into the melee, grabbing one of Angel's attackers before flinging him against the stage. It was the catalyst everyone needed. One after the other, people started rushing towards the scene, Andrew and Matt among them. Between them, they managed to save Angel from any further violence. He lay slumped on the ground, unconscious, his arms still coiled around his head as if to protect himself. His headphones had become dislodged, a rivulet of blood running down from his temple. Lara was sobbing hysterically.

"Call a fucking ambulance!" Andrew hollered above the screaming masses.

A second security guard was quick to respond - bellowing into his mobile phone as revellers began streaming from the forest. The reception was awful yet he still managed to get the message out; describing the assault with outrage, just as a second van started spilling out its assailants. The man shrunk fearfully into the shadows as they swarmed by the forest entrance. At least an ambulance was on the way - and he had notified the police.

The scene inside the forest continued to erupt in violence. Half the crowd were trapped inside, at the mercy of the masked fiends attacking them. Small knots of people started to gather, some cowering in fear, others brave enough to challenge them. And somewhere in the middle of that crowd, William and Avalon's party clutched each other - powerless to know what to do.

"Bastards!" William breathed as they were jostled deeper into the woods by the moving mass of people. The dark trees closed in all around them - the yobs still wreaking havoc.

Another lot seemed to be loitering by the entrance, despite the continuous stream of revellers who were at least managing to flee.

William watched the scene in horror, his heart in his mouth. The strobe light and lasers had been deactivated, yet the area was lit up like a stadium; enough to expose the shadowy figures. They periodically slapped their clubs into their palms as if to flaunt their menace - while every so often, some innocent reveller was being halted and examined. William frowned. Something didn't seem right. These thugs were here for another reason than to break up the rave.

The answer hit him in seconds as a tall, black shape loomed nearby.

"That's enough, lads," the character growled. "Just find the boy..."

William turned cold. He would have recognised that swaggering, broad shouldered silhouette anywhere and it was with little hesitation, he grasped Elijah's shoulders and hauled him behind a tree. Avalon followed numbly.

For several seconds, they just crouched there. William put his finger to his lips, waiting for the man to pass. Then finally he spoke, his eyes wide with panic.

"It's Nathan!" he gasped, "I know it!" His bottom lip trembled as he stared at his friend. "Put your hood up! It's *you*, they're looking for, Eli - you have got to hide..."

Elijah's mouth dropped open in shock.

"Come on," Avalon whispered. "William's right, we need to find a place to lie low."

Together, they slithered across the forest floor, in search of better cover. It wasn't hard. The trees and bushes were in full leaf, the paths submerged in the long grass; within a few yards, Avalon had stumbled across a circle of bushes. They snuggled into the centre and lay very still, as the unwavering shouts and screams echoed all around them. From a distance they could hear the piercing wail of an ambulance. Help was on its way.

"Where's William?" Elijah dared himself to say.

"He's gone back to round up the others," Avalon replied in the softest of whispers. "We never saw where Margaret went..." she broke off and the two of them stared at each other.

Even under the cover of darkness, Elijah could see her eyes; two polished stones in the centre of a ghostly white face. She looked terrified - a situation which impelled him to wind a protective arm around her shoulders. He could feel her trembling, as the horror of this night was finally beginning to take its toll; a bolt of intense love shot right through him again.

He closed his eyes and took a deep breath, the urge to kiss her too powerful to fight. In precisely the same moment, she raised her head. A magnetic force of emotion bloomed between them, drawing them closer, until their lips tentatively made contact. For the first few seconds, Elijah thought he was dreaming. He knew he loved her - he was only just beginning to realise, he always *had* done! It seemed incredible that in the throes of an attack, Nathan's army of thugs brought raining down on them, they would discover each other in this darkest of hours.

There were only about 50 people left by the time the police arrived and William was among them. He rushed up to Joshua just as Angel was being lifted onto a stretcher - watching in hope, as the ambulance men attended to him. Several revellers had been checked for injuries. A couple had suffered broken bones, though most were afflicted with minor cuts and bruises.

"It's okay, he's breathing," they heard one of the medics mutter to a sobbing Lara. "Stay with him if you want, love..."

"You'd better get yourself away too," William whispered to Joshua. "Best no-one sees you."

Joshua's face was steeped in anguish. "I dunno what to say," he choked, "I never thought it was going to end like this..."

"No, neither did I," William spat. "I expected them to call the cops - I never imagined they'd drag in a bunch of thugs to attack us. Now for Christ's sake, get yourself home before someone recognises you!"

The next people to emerge in the woodland clearing were Andrew and Matt.

William gawked at them in disbelief. "Where's Margaret?" he spluttered.

"We thought she was with you!" Andrew rounded on him.

For a second, the three of them stood paralysed, mouths dropping open as the truth hit them like a sledgehammer. Their youngest companion was missing.

"Shit!" Matt gasped, just as a police car drew up to the forest.

"Come on," William muttered crisply, "we have got to go back and look for her."

IV

Margaret was still running - her staggering steps pulling her deeper and deeper into the heart of the forest, away from the boots thundering after her. She was sobbing in terror, glancing back at the stage where the light had been gradually fading dimmer.

One minute they had all been dancing. It was so beautiful; those magical seconds when she had snatched William's eye. It had been like a dream, a transitory flicker of time where he had materialised like an angel. The joining of hands, the pulse of brilliant music where all she could see was flashing lights. Everything glowed, the entire forest effervescent with movement and with the lingering effects of the ecstasy, she had felt sublimely happy.

Then came the screams coiling up from the crowd. Margaret thought she was hallucinating; staring in disbelief at the demonic, hooded figures with their black masks. They rose out of no-where like evil spirits about to destroy their enchanted forest. Margaret blinked, praying it wasn't real - but the music had died, the screams spiralled louder and Angel had been set upon as the monsters pounded him with their clubs.

Their circle was broken, the bonds between their hands severed. Margaret wasn't even thinking straight when she had turned and ran. Something or someone had propelled her in the wrong direction. She gaped at her surroundings in shock - where was William? Elijah? Avalon? With a sob, she tried to turn back but everything happened so quickly - and just at the point, she couldn't believe her situation could get any worse, she had come face to face with two of those nasty men. Even from behind the black masks, she could feel their menace.

"Stop right there, darling," a voice slithered into the silence. "You're coming with us!"

With a shriek, Margaret spun into the forest. She had never been a fast runner. Yet she surged on and on, diving in and out of the trees for cover in her desperation to escape.

It was to her increasing dread, she discovered she had practically crossed the entire forest. She crept up to the edge of the trees. She could see the shadow of the valley rolling out below her; the magnificent shape of Westbourne House silhouetted in the distance. Margaret stumbled onwards, clocking the twinkle of light in the windows - completely oblivious to the lingering presence of a man stood just meters away.

An invisible arm surged from the darkness and coiled itself around her waist. She tried to scream, wary of the soft palm being pressed over her mouth. She breathed in the woody scent of aftershave; a fragrance which sent her mind spiralling back to the day in the pub and her unexpected encounter with Ben... He called out suddenly; his voice razor sharp and commanding authority.

"That's enough, lads!" he barked. "Leave her alone!"

It was with little hesitation, the two masked thugs turned and sloped back into the forest.

Margaret felt her body go limp as his grip loosened. She whirled round in shock.

"Shh," he whispered, "it's okay, you're safe. I am not going to hurt you."

"What are *you* doing here?" she gasped.

She studied his statuesque face which shone pale in the moonlight. She couldn't quite make out his expression as he pinned her with his stare.

"I live here," he snapped softly. "You could hear that row from our house! I wandered up to see what was going on and just in time by the looks of it."

His lips twisted into a smile.

"Thanks for saving me," Margaret spluttered and suddenly she couldn't keep the tears out of her voice. "W-we were having such a w-wonderful party... until those m-men attacked us. They smashed up the PA system - they b-beat up our DJ..."

She started sobbing - powerless in the wake of such horror. Ben stepped forward and to her utter bewilderment, he gathered her into his arms; a situation which seemed almost unnatural.

She stared up at him in confusion. "I-I should go back a-and join the others," she shivered. "They'll be wondering where I got to..."

With a sigh, Ben reached into the pocket of his waxed barbour coat and pulled out a mobile phone. Margaret watched - filled with a sense of hope, as he punched in a number.

"Did you call the police?" he muttered. "Yeah? Well, I've found the girl..." The crackle of conversation was indistinguishable. But whoever Ben was speaking to, his next words turned her cold. "Yeah, that's right - I'm bringing her back to Westbourne House."

"What?" Margaret squeaked.

Ben thrust the phone back into his pocket. "Sorry Margaret, you have to come with me," he sighed. "My father's not happy. He wants answers. Your friends can come and collect you later."

She felt a sense of utter helplessness as he steered her up the woodland path. She had little choice - recognising the familiar wooden gate which led to the grounds; pleased to see the same configuration of James's gardens. They radiated their beauty even beneath the stars. By the time he guided her towards the entrance however, her heart started pounding again - conscious that it was inside this exquisite house, the real ogre awaited her.

"Please," she whimpered. "I can't go in there..."

He slipped his hands around her shoulders and turned her round. "Be quiet," he whispered, a smile playing around his lips. "Stop worrying, you're with me now..."

He stroked her face in a way that was strangely tender. Margaret gazed at him, unable to make sense of it all as he leaned in to kiss her. His lips brushed against her own, sending little shivers down her neck; his grip on her arm strong, while his other hand slid a little lower, grazing the side of her jaw. He lifted up one of her plaits and chuckled.

"Love the hair," he muttered, "you look like a little schoolgirl..."

It was with a complete lack of control, Margaret surrendered to him. She felt her inner resolve crumble, grateful for the affection - yet at the same time, petrified.

"Come now, little one," his voice pulsed into the silence. "You have *got to* face him at some point..." and it was with no further hesitation, he pulled her up the steps towards the door.

She was back in Westbourne House - gaping at the familiar surroundings in shock. Margaret took a gulp of air as Ben momentarily abandoned her. Seconds later, she flinched to the sound of slow, forbidding footsteps emerging from the end of the hallway and before she knew it, Perry had materialised. She met his eyes, chilled by the ice in his stare.

"Fetch us some brandy, Elliot," he snapped brusquely, glancing towards the bar.

Margaret felt her terror abate a little, as the kind face of James's former butler appeared in the doorway. He was desperately trying to avoid looking at her - yet it was impossible.

"Margaret? Goodness, you've grown up…"

"Enough, Elliot," Perry interrupted. "I have some questions for this young lady!"

Elliot mumbled some incoherent reply before Perry directed his furious stare back at her.

"Bring her through!"

She felt numb as Ben took her by the arm again, pulling her towards the library; dimly aware of a pair of suited gentlemen wandering up the staircase, conversing over '*the disgraceful behaviour of modern youth…*' She hung her head in mortification.

By the time she was propelled into the library, she was shaking. The room had changed - the walls a macabre ox-blood red, beneath a glittering chandelier. Even the dark leather furniture seemed uninviting. Ben coaxed her into a chair. Perry extinguished the main light, which left the subdued glow of a table lamp. She was captured in its glow like a prisoner under interrogation. Elliot flitted in and out of the library like a moth, leaving a tray of drinks. Perry closed the door.

"Right, Miss Bailey," he began, lowering himself into a sofa. He leaned forward to hook her gaze. "Just what the devil do you and your friends think you're playing at, holding a rave in the woods at the back of my hotel!"

"I-it was only a party, S-sir," Margaret began apologetically.

"Whose party?" Perry snapped.

Her eyes glanced from Ben to Perry, unsure what to tell him. "I-it was my brother's 21st last month. William's 18th is coming up too. We wanted to do s-something special."

Perry's eyes narrowed. "Was this William's idea?" he whispered softly.

"No!" Margaret gasped in denial.

"Oh come, now," Ben intervened in a tone which seemed equally chilling. "It's no secret how much William despises us and those are *his* woods." He waved his hand towards the windows, as if to indicate the rolls of countryside concealed in the darkness.

"This was designed to cause as much disruption as possible, wasn't it?"

Perry's voice lashed.

"There were loads of people involved," Margaret shivered. "Not just William - okay, so he agreed to let us use the woods - but - but..."

"But what?" Perry sighed. He grabbed the brandy bottle and to Margaret's amazement, sloshed a hefty measure into all three glasses. "Drink this. It will make you feel better. You must be feeling a little chilly, my dear."

He studied her light, flowing cardigan. It didn't quite cover her chest. Her skin was dotted with goose-pimples which had nothing to do with the cold. She took a gulp and nearly choked.

"Oh come now, don't tell me you haven't already been drinking," Perry added, "though I don't suppose that's *all* you've indulged in..." He gave a cruel smile. "Look at me!"

She slowly lifted her face, struck by the jab of his eyes. They reminded her of shards of ice on a stormy day as he examined her like a specimen. Her eyes wavered - she was finding it unbearable!

"You've been taking drugs," Perry sneered. "Your pupils are dilated and you look spaced out of your mind. So let's start again shall we? Tell me who organised that rave or I will inform the police about your condition." His smile faded. "I could have you tested. Imagine the embarrassment for your father! His sweet little girl not only drinks herself senseless, but pops pills and likes raves. I'll inform your school, the Community Centre; destroy your family's precious reputation..."

"Stop it!" Margaret whimpered, covering her ears with her hands.

Perry grabbed her wrists and pulled them apart, his evil face looming closer. "Who organised that rave?" he snarled in her face.

"Oh come now, Dad, go easy," Ben drawled. "She's only 14!"

"I told you - lots of people helped organise it," Margaret gasped.

"Event organisers from London?" Perry pressed. "People with ties in the music industry - such as your friend, *Joshua Merriman!* Now answer my question!"

Margaret gaped at him in horror - his face blurred behind a glaze of tears.

"That's it!" Perry snapped, lurching to his feet. "I'm going to talk to the police - and as for you, you little hooligan, I'll see to it that everyone knows about the state we found you in - a condition which will no doubt be confirmed by a single drugs test..."

"No!" Margaret sobbed. "Please!"

"Did Joshua Merriman organise that rave?" He pounded his fist on the back of her chair, causing her to flinch in terror - her eyes were fixed to his club like fist and before she even realised it, she had started nodding, the tears tumbling down her face.

"Thank you, Miss Bailey," Perry smiled, before downing his own brandy. He let out a satisfied sigh. "Notify the police, Ben - tell them she's here. I think it's time we had a word with the rest of her little gang, don't you?"

"I-I thought the police *knew* I was here!" Margaret spluttered. She turned to stare at Ben in disbelief - yet the smile on his face chilled her.

"I'm certain they do," he said softly, "but I doubt if the message has reached your friends."

Perry mirrored his smile. "Don't worry. We'll get the police to round them up and escort them here. I'm sure they'll be very pleased to be reunited with you, my dear…"

Margaret felt faint. She stared at the clock. It was nearly 2:00 in the morning and with every chance her friends were still out there looking for her.

She wasn't wrong - her friends were growing frantic as they systematically combed the forest, searching.

"Margaret!" Elijah cried out again and again, his throat hoarse from yelling.

The intrusion of police torches caught their attention, their bright beams flickering through the trees. Elijah froze, recognising the powerful bulk of Inspector Boswell.

"If you're looking for your little friend, we know where she is!" Ian hollered into the woods. "We'd like you to come out now! This party is well and truly over!"

The minutes dragged by painfully. It was in the last hour, the stage had been dismantled, the catering vans had left and all that remained were the portaloos, lonely in the woodland hollow.

The area had finally emptied of people, including Andrew and Matt - desperate to know if Angel had survived. The formidable gang of thugs had long gone; having abandoned their hunt, the instant the police had arrived. It was to William's heartfelt relief, they hadn't found Elijah

The air was eerily drained of sound as they marched from the woods in the direction of the farm track. A soft breeze spiralled around the tree tops, the air invigorating. Elijah swallowed nervously, conscious of the heavy plod of Inspector Boswell's boots. He spotted several police cars in the distance, positioned by the barns.

No-one spoke. There was a crackle of police CB radios where several officers lingered.

"Okay people, we may as well call it a night," Ian addressed them gruffly. "You three, on the other hand, are to follow me! I've sent word to Westbourne House - I think the proprietors might want a little word with you, young William."

"Fine!" William snapped, stalking past him and into the barn where the blueish gleam of his MG was just discernible in the shadows. "Just as long as Margaret's okay."

He unlocked his car and leapt inside, violently slamming the door. Elijah and Avalon stared at each other, unsure what to say. Elijah took her hand and coaxed her into the back seat.

"Try not to worry," he whispered as the rumble of William's engine ruptured the silence.

An enduring sense of affection wound its way into the atmosphere - maybe the mind altering effects of the pills had unlocked their true love. At least, Elijah liked to think so.

Within minutes, he found himself staring at the familiar gates of Westbourne House as William turned towards them. He felt a chill of fear. Hadn't William already saved him from the claws of Nathan's gang? Perry would relish a chance to get his hands on him. It was only now, he was grateful of the escort of police cars - one in front, one behind, forcing them up the drive.

Though they were hardly going to abandon Margaret. He couldn't bear to imagine the state she would be in - a frightened 14 year old in the clutches of their enemies...

They pulled sharply into the parking area and William killed the ignition. Elijah reluctantly started to open the car door before tugging up his hood.

"You don't have to come..." Avalon whispered.

"Yes I do!" he protested. "Besides - we're with Boswell..."

"Out!" Ian ordered, "and that means you too, Jansen. As far as I'm concerned, you're in this together. So let's go and see what Mr Hampton has to say about this little 'acid house party' of yours shall we?"

Once again, Elijah's hand slipped into Avalon's and as if to mirror their camaraderie, William fell into their ranks, linking arms with his sister. They formed a picture of solidarity as they advanced towards the house. Before Ian had a chance to knock, the door was thrown open, revealing a square of light. The solid frame of a man awaited them. Elijah froze - and yet, he wasn't afraid. He sensed his vulnerability as Ian nudged him forwards; simultaneously fuelled by a surge of confidence he just couldn't explain! Perry's steel hard gaze drilled into them. William broke gently away from the chain and took his first bold steps towards him.

"I might have known," Perry's voice hissed into the silence. "William Barton-Wells! Determined to make a nuisance of yourselves were we?"

Avalon was next to wander up to the door. "It was written in the stars that William would celebrate his 18th in the grounds of his ancestral home," she said dreamily. "It seemed a fitting place to have a party..."

"You had no right to organise a rave in those woods!" Perry thundered.

"Why not?" Avalon taunted. "It's our land!"

Perry bristled with fury.

"Let's just try and keep this civil, shall we?" Ian interjected coolly. He clamped a fleshy hand on Elijah's shoulder, the only one who seemed hesitant. "I think we'd better *all* go inside!"

Elijah found himself unwittingly being herded through the door. He lowered his head, wary of Perry lingering. A creamy glow emanated from a small desk lamp, illuminating the floor tiles - it would perhaps explain the gloomy web of shadow they were encircled in.

"Follow me, all of you," Perry snapped, waiting for him to shuffle past. He wrenched down his hood where the soft light enhanced the reddish gleam of his hair, "and don't bother to disguise yourself. I know who you are, Elijah Jansen!"

Elijah's eyes flitted towards him, studying his face. A thousand questions flew through his mind but it was William's shout that broke through his stream of thought.

"Okay, where is she?" he yelled, striding into the corridor. "Where's Margaret?"

"Keep your voice down, boy," Perry snarled, turning towards the library, "I have guests trying to sleep! Haven't you caused enough disruption for one night?"

He opened the library door where William jammed to a stand still. Margaret materialised in front of them. She was frozen in fear, her face pale and tearstained - yet it was the company of Ben that seemed more sinister, a caressing hand on her shoulder.

"Hello, William," he taunted, "and Avalon! What a pleasure…"

William's eyes smouldered. "What's going on?"

"Oh, your little friend has revealed everything," Perry retorted smugly. "We'd already figured, it was *you* who sanctioned that rave. Though I gather you had some help - from *Mr Merriman!*"

A sob escaped Margaret's lips. "I'm sorry!" she croaked. "I never meant to tell them!"

"It's okay Margaret, don't cry," William said coldly - his eyes shifted to Ben. "Why's she upset? What did you do, you fucking sadist?"

"Mr Barton-Wells that is completely uncalled for…" Ian tried to intervene.

Ben stepped away from the chair, his face twisted in hatred. "How dare you!" he seethed. "What gives you the right to make such an accusation?"

"You know why!" William shot back.

"That's enough, William," Perry barked, "and before you proceed to demonise us any further, no-one has laid a finger on her! We were protecting her! Unlike you lot - subjecting a 14 year old to acid house parties - drugs… Did you know she was nearly set upon by a pair of hooligans? It was *my* son here, who saved her!"

William's face blanched. "Is this true?"

Margaret nodded, a tear spilling from her eye. It was the shock on his face that finally stirred her into motion - she struggled from her chair, crumpling into his arms. William held her tightly as she sobbed - though he was still glaring at Perry.

"We were doing nothing wrong!" he thundered. "It was supposed to be a party, a joyful occasion, not a riot! Even if the police *had* turned up, we'd have left. You didn't have to send a gang of masked thugs to terrorise us!"

"I have no idea what you're talking about," Perry drawled.

"Don't you?" William intervened, "well that's strange - because I could have sworn I spotted your security guard, Nathan!"

"Rubbish!" Perry snapped, "and besides, I thought you said they were masked!"

"William, just leave it," Avalon begged him. "I want to go home!"

"He's not wrong though, is he?" Elijah finally dared himself to say - he was gazing at Perry directly. "I believe him, Mr Hampton. I think one of those men *was* Nathan. We heard him say, they were *looking for someone...* That person was me, wasn't it?"

"Shut up," Perry retorted, "don't you dare start that again! Whatever went on tonight had nothing to do with me, do you hear?"

An angry mauve flush spread across his face and for a moment, Elijah was reminded of the photo his mother had shown him: same face yet in a dramatically different scenario. It was in that split second, he knew they had him in a tight spot. Perry turned to Ian.

"Well, are you going to arrest them or what?" he said nastily. "They've confessed to organising an illegal rave and I remain convinced, they've taken drugs!"

"You can't arrest us!' Avalon breathed. "We haven't committed any crime!"

"In the eyes of the law, I'm afraid you have," Ian said firmly. "Your activities constitute *a breach of the peace* - and we'll be talking to Mr Merriman too."

"You'd arrest Joshua?" Avalon squeaked. "That's outrageous!" Her eyes flitted towards Ben, "you didn't arrest *him* for the way he threatened Lucy!"

"That was due to a complete lack of evidence," Ian sighed.

"So what evidence have you got against Joshua?" William gasped. "So you forced a confession out of Margaret! Joshua wasn't the sole organiser! All our friend agreed to do was to put out some feelers and can you blame him after the *disgusting* way they treated Lucy?"

"I'm afraid we still have to talk to him," Ian sighed, "though if it's any consolation, no arrest will be made tonight."

"You what?" Perry whispered, his face as dark as Bordeaux wine. "These kids are drugged up to the eyeballs! Can't you see it?"

"If you can't arrest them," Ben added silkily, "won't you at least have them tested?"

Ian let out a sigh. "Mr Hampton, with all due respects..."

Elijah suddenly released a volley of laughter.

Perry whirled round in fury. "What the hell do you think you're sniggering at, boy?" he barked.

"I-I'm sorry, but this has got to be a joke, right?" Elijah spluttered. "If you want to test someone for drugs, w-what about your Gary!"

"I beg you're pardon?" Ian rounded on him.

Elijah shrugged, fighting to suppress his laughter. "I-I saw him at the rave - he looked as if he was completely off his face, same as everyone..."

For a moment Perry looked so murderous, Elijah swore he glimpsed a flash of teeth - finally his laughter waned. "We were having a great time, M-Mr Boswell," he shivered. "The only ones who caused any trouble were those thugs! They put our DJ in hospital. Will you be arresting them?"

The whole room fell into a stunned, horrified silence. Yet before Ian had a chance to say another word, Perry spun to him angrily.

"Get them out of my sight!" he ordered, his voice a hiss. "I for one, am *not* going to forget this. There will be repercussions, I warn you!"

They needed no further persuasion. With his arm casually slung around Margaret's shoulder, William guided her through the door, followed by Avalon.

Only Elijah hesitated, as he threw Perry one final backward glance. He had no concept of the glitter in his eyes; only Perry's which remained icy with threat.

He waited until they had gone before he lowered himself into a chair, glass of brandy in hand.

Twenty minutes later, he checked his watch - casting his son a long and dangerous stare. "It is time we liaised with our friends," he muttered.

Ben showed no hesitation. He knew where Nathan had taken them, conscious of a derelict barn about half a mile away, close to their favourite vantage point. Ben had sobered up considerably since the gala dinner, yet said nothing. He knew when to keep quiet. His father was fuming, his face a mask of stone as the events of the evening festered.

The truth was, Perry was finding it difficult to keep a grip - despising those Barton-Wells brats for the bedlam they had caused. Yet it was the Jansen boy who had rattled him most; to think, he had been stood right there in his house, a static target. His comment about Nathan had enraged him. He could still picture that final spark in his mesmerising eyes. In fact, he could no longer deny that Elijah was a highly valued prize - someone he would pay a fortune to have captured, if only he could find an opportune moment.

Perry clenched and unclenched his fists as the caravan hovered in the field below. He was convinced it was empty. No light twinkled in the windows and there had been precious little sign of Joshua's Land Rover lately.

"So, you didn't spot the boy at the rave," he snapped at Nathan.

"No, Perry," Nathan muttered. "He must have been lying low! We combed through the crowd as best we could - though you have got to credit the boys. They did an excellent job!"

"They did indeed," Perry whispered where at last, his face broke into a smirk. He met the pale eyes of the young man braced next to him. He had a lean, rat-like face, enhanced by his skinhead hair cut. "Trevor, isn't it?"

"Yeah," the youth grunted without an ounce of respect. "DJ turned out to be that Ray Engel. Been looking for 'im for months, we 'ave! Gave him a proper good thrashing!"

"Good," Perry nodded, as much to himself as to the violent-looking youth gazing back at him. He averted his eyes. Eleanor's caravan lurked on the periphery of his vision again, isolated in its field. "I take it, Mr Merriman has left, Nathan."

"Correct," Nathan affirmed. "No-one's seen him for weeks!"

"Then best it stays that way," Perry said. A chilling silence bit the air and he was still glaring down at the caravan; he met the youth's eye again. "See that caravan? I want you to come back in a couple of weeks time and torch it! Do you think you can do that for me?"

The look on Trevor's face was pitiless, his lips twisting into an almost inhuman grin. "Yeah, you're on, Mister."

Nathan remained silent as the temperature dipped even lower.

Chapter 21

I

Even before dawn broke, the stories had started flowing. It began from the moment an overspill of shell-shocked revellers poured into Bella's. For some reason, Dominic had chosen to hang around - yet didn't seem that surprised by the outcome.

There wasn't a person in Rosebrook who didn't eventually pick up on the news of some earth-shattering rave in the forests around Westbourne House; a covert operation which had ultimately ended in violence. Journalists were swarming around town, desperate to interview the Barton-Wells siblings. Eleanor meanwhile, had received an ominous call from Inspector Boswell.

At first, the kids were oblivious to the furore they had caused, where the luxurious trappings of Avalon's home felt like a sanctuary. They had flopped down in the living room in a state of turmoil - minds buzzing as they picked over each chapter; though Elijah was of a mind to leave the discussion on a positive note. "Let's forget how it ended," he yawned, "hang on to the best memories. We were having a brilliant time... I hope we'll have a chance to do it again, one day."

He closed his eyes which were heavy with love. Given the choice, he would have liked to have spent the whole day, cuddled up in a big, soft bed with Avalon. His heart swelled with longing - except their peace was unexpectedly shattered by a frantic banging on the door.

It was Andrew - unshaven, sallow faced, his eyes filled with dread. "You've gotta come back to the almshouse, now! Dad's doing his nut!"

He wasn't wrong. Charlie was speechless and for the first few minutes, he couldn't bring himself to even look at them. Eleanor on the other hand, felt haunted. She studied their smooth complexions; a painful depiction of their youth. Elijah did at least have the grace to look a little remorseful, his eyes deep with shadows as he sheepishly met her gaze.

"Thank God, you're all safe!" she whispered huskily.

And so the story unfolded. Eleanor sat in silence - unable to believe they could have chosen to throw a party in such a remote location and so close to their deadly enemies!

"How could you be so stupid?" Charlie finally roared, unable to contain his fury for any longer. "Have you any idea what might have happened out there? Someone could have been killed!"

Andrew couldn't remember a time he had seen his father so angry - inclined to let him have a good rant until he ran out of steam. Except he didn't - it seemed to go on forever, his face crimson, his eyes two cauldrons of boiling, black rage.

"Oh for God's sake, give us a break!" he finally shouted. "We're sorry, okay? It was more than a party, it was a protest!" He stared at his father through pleading eyes. "We're pissed off about what happened to Lucy and Joshua! What better way to use that land than to have a bloody good rave? Those bastards deserved a wake up call!"

It seemed to do the trick - gradually, Charlie's anger began to dissipate. By the time he sank into his chair, it was as if all the energy had been siphoned out of him, his eyes fixed on Margaret - appalled to think what she had been put through.

"You have *got to* be more careful," Eleanor urged them. "You put yourselves in terrible danger, last night! Maybe, you could have just told us!"

"I know," William said guiltily, "but you'd have only tried to stop us..."

The discussion shifted around the lounge until every detail was extracted. They had never expected an army of masked men to break up the event - appalled by the sheer savagery of Angel's beating. Just the slightest hint that one of those thugs had been Nathan brought back Eleanor's worst fears - the notion that Elijah's safety had been compromised. She turned to William in horror.

"There isn't a shadow of a doubt, those thugs were connected to the Hamptons," she finished miserably. "Didn't you know Ben had connections with the criminal underworld?"

She pressed her eyes shut, leaving them to ponder over that last chilling revelation.

It took a while for the fuss to die down. For several days, their lives were besieged by a relentless barrage of calls from the press and visits from the police, where they were urged to make statements. It seemed, Inspector Boswell was particularly interested in this case for reasons which Eleanor didn't quite understand - but then she had no idea of the state, Ian had found his son in when he had finally got home.

These thoughts came to Ian now as he accompanied her to the hospital; fully intent on getting some answers out of the enigmatic DJ known as 'Angel' and hoping Eleanor's presence would put him at ease. It appeared that her stepson, Andrew, was a close friend. He too, seemed particularly keen to visit; though Ian was finding it difficult to divorce his mind from the disturbing manner the night had ended, as visions of Gary kept pricking at his mind.

In truth, he could have killed him! As if Elijah's accusations hadn't been shameful enough. Yet he had crept into his son's bedroom to find him plugged into a computer console, engrossed in some game - chomping chewing gum, swigging coca cola... It was obvious he was high on something and firing on all four cylinders, despite the lateness of the hour.

"You stupid little sod!" he remembered yelling, before he belted him across the back of his head.

Little did he know that when Elijah had slipped him Andrew's last three ecstasy tabs, Gary had hogged two for himself. He had always been greedy - completely unaware of the effects.

Ian released a tortured sigh. His son was 16. He couldn't really blame him for sneaking off to the rave with his friends, though it appalled him to think, he'd experimented with drugs.

At least he hadn't been harmed; which was more than could be said for the helpless black youth stretched out in a hospital bed. Angel had suffered multiple bruises and two cracked ribs, as well as internal bleeding. Right now, he was hooked up to a drip, his head wrapped in bandages. He gazed up at them through startled brown eyes, one so badly bruised and swollen, it was almost shut.

"Angel!" Eleanor gasped. "What in God's name did they do to you?"

"S'okay," Angel mumbled, forcing a smile which didn't quite reach his eyes. "It probably looks worse than it is. At least I'm alive..." he touched the side of his head and winced.

He had taken a vicious blow where fortuitously, the cushioning of his headphones had saved him; but they had shattered on impact, causing a deep cut to his temple. He had suffered a mild concussion in the aftermath and yet it could have been so much worse.

His eyes locked with Andrew's. It wasn't the first time they had spoken; Andrew had already grasped some theory of who his attackers were - never able to forget the yobs who had set upon him last summer.

'It was them, wasn't it?'

The terror that flashed across Angel's face had said a thousand words - but he begged him to stay silent. Once again, Andrew agreed to conceal his secrets; now wondering if Inspector Boswell was going to have any more joy dragging the truth out of him.

"Do you have any idea who your assailants were, Mr Engel?" Ian probed.

"Nah," Angel sighed, closing his eyes, "like everyone says - they were wearing balaclavas, man. Time you guys arrived, they just scarpered!"

"You're from London," Ian continued where his tone was beginning to sound a tad accusing. "I've spoken to your parents. They seem to think you had enemies."

Angel shrugged. "Yeah, maybe - but it was a long time ago. I don't think they'd drive all the way to Aldwyck to settle some score, do you?"

"They would if they were allied to the right people," Ian said stonily. "Have you ever come across a man named Alan Levy?"

"No," Angel frowned, feigning surprise, "ain't never heard of him!"

Both Eleanor and Andrew experienced a shiver of unease. Angel's eyes remained closed as if to disguise the fear that lurked there; yet they hadn't failed to notice the sudden tightening of his jaw. It left them with little doubt, he was hiding something.

The one thing they could never have known, was that Alan Levy had got to him first.

For now, Angel lay in a cocoon of darkness. Even as he deflected their questions, he couldn't forget the terrifying moment, late night, Sunday, when his notorious boss had crept up on him.

Visiting hours were over. How he'd managed to sneak past the nurses station seemed impossible, yet there he was, staring icily down at him through those pale slivers for eyes.

"You stupid fucker!" Alan hissed, pressing his face close.

"What's up, boss?" Angel mumbled in his innocence. "I done everything you asked..."

"I told you to buddy up with Bailey, not organise a fucking rave," Alan whispered. He gripped Angel's collar, pressing him hard against the pillows. "My paymasters ain't happy - reckon you deserved that beating! Not my fault they called the heavies in, but seein' as they did and you were targeted..." he tut-tutted like a teacher scolding a pupil.

"It was Trev Deeley's gang, weren't it?" Angel whispered fearfully.

"Serves you right for working with the enemy," Alan smirked, "I 'ope you ain't said nothing!" His chilling smile bore into him, before he whipped out his scalpel. Angel felt his blood run cold.

"Sharp as anything you'd find in this place," Alan continued to taunt him. The blade was very close to his face, forcing Angel to cringe against the pillows.

"Please boss, I ain't said a word," he sobbed.

"Make sure it stays that way," Alan whispered, "'cos if the fuzz ever trace any of this back to me..." and with the scalpel hovering just inside Angel's nostril, he gave a light flick of the blade.

Angel let out a gasp - a warm trickle of blood slid into the groove of his lip.

"You just lie there and keep your trap shut!" Alan finished evilly. "Looks like you're gonna be here for a while - but we're keeping an eye on you. No-one trusts you any more, see..." and that was how it had ended.

Angel shivered, the memory as sharp as the incision in his nostril and all the while, Boswell was bearing down on him, digging for details.

"He's telling the truth, Mr Boswell," Andrew finally intervened. "If we had anything to tell you, we would. We wanna see those bastards charged as much as anyone!"

"Any news on Joshua Merriman?" Eleanor quizzed him.

"Mr Merriman was let off with a caution," Ian answered without expression. "It seems there are worse problems with acid house parties in London than *your* little gathering. But he needs to watch himself if he hopes to make a success of his career. I gather he's a journalist."

"Yes," Eleanor said and finally, her face folded into a smile. "I'm glad they didn't press charges - seems unfair in the light of what happened recently…"

Ian gave her a cool nod and left them. There was no denying, he looked troubled - but before Eleanor had a chance to reflect any further, Lara breezed up to the bedside.

"Hi, sweetie," Angel smiled up at her.

She swooped down and kissed him. "Angel," she sighed, gazing tenderly back - her features buckled into a frown. "What happened to your nose?"

A line of encrusted blood betrayed the tell-tale wound. Angel shrugged. "Dunno, babe. I had a shave this morning - must have nicked it with me razor."

Eleanor didn't quite know what it was about that statement that left her cold - but before the day ended, the answer came to her as she drifted towards the Community Centre. How could she have forgotten those two sinister characters who had turned up last summer? The man with a scar running down his face: *'Happen, I just cut meself shaving.'* It was almost precisely the same flippant remark as Angel had made in reference to his own injury!

Eleanor stood very still. Angel was clearly a victim of the same people; thugs who worked for Ben Hampton whose ties with the criminal underworld had originally been leaked by Dominic: *'Sounds like one of London's top hard nuts.'* It all fitted with everything Inspector Boswell had insinuated and now a name had crept into the equation; Alan Levy.

"I don't think I can take much more, Charlie," she found herself murmuring, that night. "It seems, our enemies are more powerful than ever…"

"I'm aware of that," he snapped. "The burning question is what are we going to do?"

"We have to do the right thing," Eleanor shivered. "This business has gone on for long enough. It's time we brought Perry to justice."

Charlie couldn't help but wonder if she was bluffing. Even *he* was aware of the pressure she had been under; first from Joshua and now the Barton-Wells kids, whose confrontation inside the walls of Westbourne House had resurrected the full force of their hatred.

"It's got to be done, Charlie," she kept whispering. "So I've spoken to John Sharp. He has found us a barrister and next Monday, I am travelling up to London to see him."

"Good," Charlie responded, inspired by the fire in her eyes. "I knew you'd see sense." He was thinking about Margaret - struck with a bolt of loathing over the way the Hamptons had interrogated her. "I'm not happy about you going to London though," he added thoughtfully. "How do you know you won't be followed?"

"There's always a risk," Eleanor sighed. "I suppose I'll just have to take it."

It was a decision that inspired him to wrap his arms around her. "Then why don't I come with you?" he murmured into the silky curls of her hair. "I can't bear to think of you putting yourself in danger."

She smiled seductively and stroked his face. "I couldn't possibly be putting myself in any more danger than I'm in now - and this is what they've always relied on..." Her eyes retained that glitter. How could they forget the remorseless campaign against the Barton-Wells family? Wherever the Hamptons trod, they carved deep, psychological scars. "I'm tired of living in fear, Charlie."

Charlie nodded, his caresses turning more passionate - empowered with a sudden love for this woman who was prepared to risk everything to take on that *monster*.

"Okay," he whispered, his hands moving to her breasts as he kissed her again. "I meant what I said though. I *am* coming with you!"

"What about Peter's housing trust?" she whispered. "Haven't you got some liaison officer from the council visiting - to talk about the landscaping?"

"Hmm," Charlie smiled. "So, maybe I could leave it in Andrew's capable hands..." and with the decision left hovering, he snuggled up close to possess her delightful body.

II

They set out early. The aftermath of the rave had left Eleanor especially tense - never sure who was who, any more. There always seemed to be someone lurking around the Community Centre; whether it was an unfamiliar workman sitting on a bench - or some faceless stranger in a car, smoking a cigarette. Her eyes flitted from one side of the road to the other. Already, some youth was poised outside the fish and chip shop, reading a newspaper. He looked up as they crossed the road. Eleanor met his neutral stare. Seconds later, she swivelled her head around - and oddly enough, the man had disappeared.

"That's it, someone's on to us," she snapped, quickening her pace.

"You seem jumpy," Charlie muttered, grabbing her hand. "He could have been anyone!"

"So where is he now?" Eleanor added. "We're on foot, it's 8:00 in the morning and this road leads directly to the railway station - it's fairly obvious where we're going. I'm sorry Charlie, but we can't trust anyone! I said pretty much the same to the kids."

It was no exaggeration. Eleanor had virtually worn everyone down with her perpetual warnings. Even the neighbouring building site seemed to have attracted an unusual amount of attention lately; the very location where Charlie and Andrew spent most of their time, as Peter's housing trust entered the first phase of its development. They had seen so little of Robin Whaley -

yet suddenly, he was taking an interest again.

"Try not to worry," Charlie kept reassuring her. "You said there was a chance we'd be followed. We might as well just try and act normally."

Eleanor gave a shifty nod, though she still wasn't happy. With the exception of Andrew, the kids were at school - but it was inevitably Andrew, her thoughts turned to now, wondering if he would take her warnings seriously. Everyone had a weakness, especially when they were drawn to the various pleasures in life and none so much as her step-son.

By 11:00, Andrew was engrossed in his work - unaware of the predatory eyes zooming in on him. An attractive girl stepped cautiously over the threshold, scrutinising the scene. Straight away, she recognised the roguish, dark haired young man caught up in the throes of bricklaying. This had to be Charles Bailey's son, she mused - her lips curving into a smile.

"Hello! I'm looking for Mr. Bailey," she called across the building site.

Andrew stopped dead and whirled round.

She had pale skin and deep-set, blue eyes. Her reddish brown hair fell softly to her shoulders.

Finally, he found his voice. "I'm Andrew Bailey. Are you from the council?"

"I am indeed," she smiled pleasantly. "Naomi Chandler - Parks and Gardens department."

She had a soft, breathy voice, Andrew noticed. She extended her hand. Andrew shook it tentatively - conscious that his own hands were dirty with cement.

"It's actually my dad you were meant to see," he said somewhat apologetically. "He asked if I'd cover for him…"

"He's not around?" Naomi probed.

"H-he's in London," Andrew blurted, forgetting to be careful.

She was keen to begin her assessment, clip board in hand as they proceeded to amble around the site. Occasionally, they paused. It appeared, the council were scrupulous in their intervention.

"The development will have a lot more appeal if you plant a screen of trees," she piped up. "You need to get the saplings planted soon, if they are to have a chance to mature…"

"Sure," Andrew grinned, scribbling it all down on his father's notepad.

By the time they had covered the entire site, he felt drained - craving a drink. It was nearly lunch time anyway. He turned to Naomi anxiously.

"Do you fancy going for a drink somewhere?"

"I would love to," she breathed, gazing deeply into his eyes.

Andrew's face split into a cocky grin, convinced she'd just fluttered her eyelashes. He knew his rugged good looks appealed to the ladies; tousled dark hair - where a little 'designer stubble' only added to his sex appeal.

In fact, he couldn't believe his luck! This lady was class - perfect hair and makeup, a nicely tailored suit - an icon of the professional modern woman.

He chose a nearby pub where several tables had been set up outside against a backdrop of flowering hanging baskets. He ordered prawn sandwiches, crisps and two bottles of light beer. In fact, it was surprising how quickly he found himself drawn into conversation. She seemed particularly interested in him - his life, his family, their involvement with the Community Centre.

"You should see my step-brother," he added with a sigh, "he's the creative one! He spends a lot of time helping out in those gardens."

"Is that so?" she whispered with sudden passion. "Is he still at school?"

The smile on Andrew's face slipped abruptly. "Yeah! Just taken his GCSE's. Another week and he'll be on work experience..."

For a moment, Naomi became very still. She picked up her glass, running her forefinger around the rim. "What sort of placement?" she pressed. "Do you know where he's working?"

Andrew shrugged. "It's not decided. I suspect he's a difficult one to place..."

"We can always use someone in the Parks and Gardens department," she added smugly. She drained her drink - eyes narrowing. "They'll work him off his feet! We could even get him to plant some of those saplings for us!"

Andrew released a snigger, sensing the discussion had turned a little conspiratorial.

"Yeah, great idea," he nodded. "Knowing Eli, he'd jump at the chance."

"I'll talk to my boss," she finished, flashing her most alluring smile. "Shall we wander back? You haven't shown me your house yet..."

She guessed he wouldn't be able to resist her and if she played things carefully, it wouldn't be long before she had him completely ensnared. The almshouse beckoned. They sauntered up to the horse chestnut trees where Naomi paused to a standstill.

"What dear little houses," she gasped. "Love the trees! I moved down from London recently!"

"So how long have you been working for the council?" Andrew frowned.

"About a year," Naomi lied. It had been four months and largely down to her uncle's careful intervention, she had already been promoted. "I have to go back to the office soon - but could I trouble you for a coffee? It might be an idea to go through the paperwork again."

Andrew didn't hesitate. He unlocked the door, never once considering the slightly unorthodox nature of her request, knowing the house would be empty.

"It's so quiet," her soft voice kept piping. "Is it always like this?"

"Only when my folks are out," Andrew disclosed as he crashed noisily around in the kitchen, making coffee. "Eleanor's a nurse. She's only around half the time."

"I see," she smiled. She lowered herself onto the sofa and crossed her perfect legs. "Come and sit down. Thanks for the coffee by the way. Now - let's go through the final details of the landscaping, shall we? I'll ask one of the secretaries to type up a schedule..."

Andrew was beginning to look bored; nodding away to everything, as he quietly sipped his coffee. If she had suggested banana trees, he would have agreed to it! Finally, she put down her clip board, tilting her head in a way that was designed to be provocative. She peered up at him from beneath her long, black eyelashes - and all the while, she was smirking inwardly.

To a rough, working class labourer, this must have been a dream! Their eyes locked. For a moment, he seemed uneasy. It was Naomi who took the lead - moving towards him, her lips slightly parted, where any lingering trace of shyness was blown from his mind. He responded with the exact passion she had been hoping for - his lips drawn to hers like a magnet.

It was like one of those kisses in the movies! It seemed to go on and on. By the Naomi broke away, her perfect hair had turned messy, her lipstick smudged.

"Wow!" she spluttered. "Isn't it a bloody shame, I've got to go back to work!"

"So what are you doing tomorrow?" Andrew blurted. "D'you wanna come round for lunch? I'm sure the house'll be empty..."

"I'd be delighted," Naomi beamed, pausing by the mirror. She hastily tidied her appearance and gave him a peck on the cheek - she slipped him her phone number. "Give me a ring if anything changes. Otherwise I'll be round at about 1:00." She threw him a last, devious smile, before letting herself out of the door.

III

Eleanor collapsed into a train seat and closed her eyes. It had been a particularly exhausting meeting - they had finally sifted through her secret file, one section at a time. Only on this occasion, they were joined by another lawyer; a Barrister who came highly recommended.

His name was David Edgar and Eleanor had no doubt, they had made the right choice. Not only was he a close ally of Cyril Fortescue, but had been well acquainted with James Barton-Wells. He moved in the right circles.

David assured them, it would take no more than a few weeks to prepare his case and swore to chase up the Metropolitan Police for Jake's original murder case. He had even promised to track down Norman Hargreeves; his senior position in the police force was vital to this case - never to forget his unorthodox role in Jake's killing. David left Eleanor with the hope that he would contact her again soon, the moment he had a copy of the crime report. Though they agreed, any correspondence would be done by post.

"I don't trust telephones," John announced warily. "You never know whose listening."

They did not return home immediately. Charlie felt a compulsion to head straight over to the building site - curious to discover how his son had coped with the Council.

Eleanor, on the other hand couldn't wait to confide in Peter. There was a sudden charge to her heart, no longer caring if Perry's spies were watching her as she drifted boldly up the steps.

"We're going ahead," she whispered ecstatically. "The attack at the rave was the final straw!"

Peter looked troubled; but then again, she had no concept of the treachery he was about to reveal to her.

"I think you're very brave," he began, "but there's something I have to ask you..." His gaze flickered towards the door. "I'm not sure how to explain this - but have you ever met Rowena?"

Eleanor's frown deepened, not liking this shift in conversation. "Of course I've met her. Has this got anything to do with the day she sent Elliot here?"

"No - it's this!" Peter gasped. He appeared to be sifting through a pile of paperwork, until at last, he discovered what he was looking for. It was a small, charity flyer. "Read what it says. The Swanbourne Trust is an anti-drugs charity. I *knew* there was something a little odd about this fund raising event..." He shook his head in horror.

"What?" Eleanor exploded. She grabbed the flier, absorbing its contents. 'Patron, Rowena Hampton invites supporters of this worthy cause to a fund raising garden party, in the exquisite grounds of Westbourne House...' Dots swarmed in her vision, the rest was a blur. This was one of Hilary and Reginald's most favoured charities. Yet as the truth struck home, more memories were flooding back - that fateful day when Hilary had caught her in her disguise. "Oh my God."

"I know," Peter sighed, "how could they *not* be in communication?"

"Rowena's the enemy," Eleanor shivered. "Does this imply they've been in contact with Perry?" She broke off, her face rigid, already thinking about Elijah. She stood up shakily. "We have got to go and confront her," she finished numbly. "Will you come with me?"

It was with no hesitation, he swung his slender frame from his chair and followed her. Yet it seemed more than a co-incidence, that Hilary was already looming at the top of the staircase; her mouth twisted into a sneer.

"Those kids should be ashamed of themselves!" she accused, in her high pitched, piercing voice. "Organising an illegal acid house party! And in such an idyllic location!"

"What if they did?" Eleanor hissed. "They were only having fun!"

Hilary turned white with fury. "Fun?" she squawked. "Is that what you call it? There were nearly 1,000 people up there - hideous loud music - drugs - it's an absolute disgrace! I might have known, your son would be involved - along with that wicked Barton-Wells pair!"

"Wicked?" Peter breathed. "After all the money Avalon raised to buy that land for us?"

"Maybe," Hilary sneered, "but I always knew that *William* would turn delinquent! According to my contacts, *he* was the main culprit. They were drugged out of their minds on ecstasy!"

"And what contacts would those be, Hilary?" Eleanor whispered in hatred. She took a few more trembling steps - before flinging out the leaflet. "Not your friends, *the Hamptons*, surely?" She watched with pleasure as a flush of colour poured into Hilary's cheeks. "You stupid bitch! Have you any idea how evil they are?"

Hilary let out a sniff. "So you say! All Rowena ever wanted to do was to support one of our anti-drugs charities."

If the situation wasn't so lamentable, she would have laughed. "Anti-drugs," she breathed, "and yet her psychopathic son snorts coke - liaises with criminals - keeps handcuffs in his pocket!" Her eyes flashed as the true depth of her anger came coiling to the surface. "You call William a *delinquent!* Have you any idea of the horror those kids were subjected to?" she let out a sob.

"Shh, Eleanor," Peter leapt in quickly, "don't upset yourself."

"Perry always said you were determined to ruin him," Hilary drawled callously.

"So that's why Rowena sent Elliot here, was it?" Eleanor shuddered, "she was *so* worried about Perry's paranoia! He sees ghosts - shows signs of being mentally and dangerously unstable!"

Peter surged forwards - it was with every ounce of his strength, he managed to coax her away before she had a chance to say another word.

The next time Naomi faced her uncle Robin, she was smiling.

"Success!" she murmured in her breathy, little girl voice. "The Bailey boy was an absolute pushover - very soon, I'll be going round to his house to seduce him."

"Well done," Robin sighed, lowering himself into his chair. "Just make sure you play the next part carefully - there's an awful lot riding on this and he mustn't suspect a thing."

"That won't be a problem!" Naomi scoffed. Her expression was quite disdainful. "He thinks he's God's gift! Though you have got to admit, he is quite dishy..." She let out a sniff of laughter. "Didn't take long to get him blathering about his step-brother."

Robin stiffened in his chair. "Go on," he urged her.

Naomi was revelling in it; the waves of jealousy she had detected - the careless disclosure about Elijah's work experience. By the time she had finished, Robin's eyes contained a glitter of such excitement, Naomi knew they were on to something.

"We have got to make this happen," he whispered evilly. "Let's move *heaven and earth* to make sure the council agree to a work placement and together, we are going to make Perry very proud of us, my darling."

It was over the next hour, they embarked on a strategy more devious than Perry could have ever dreamed of. It engorged them with a sense of power - where Robin could not wait to phone him. He initially wanted to gloat over Naomi's success - but more importantly, he was relying on his network of criminal contacts, to fulfil the most crucial stage of their plan.

IV

Andrew found himself craving Naomi's company like a drug; nerves tingling as he relived their second encounter - the kissing which had been more passionate than ever... He gave a shudder, struck with a last minute attack of anxiety. She was late! Though it allowed him time to give himself a nice, close shave, wary of the scratch of his stubble against her lovely skin. He smeared on some of Eleanor's luxurious day cream, just as the clang of the doorbell pierced the silence.

"Hi," she smiled coquettishly, head tipped to one side.

She had swapped her suit for a close-fitting summer dress. It had buttons all the way down the front, Andrew noticed - imagining the thrill of unfastening them. His mouth turned dry. It had been a long time since he'd pulled such a stunner!

"Can I get you a drink?" he muttered hoarsely. "I bought some sparkling wine..."

"That would be lovely," she murmured.

They hovered in the lounge, staring at each other. Andrew swallowed - then spun towards the kitchen. By the time he returned, she had draped herself over the sofa, stretching out her long legs. One of the cats had sidled up to her. Naomi slid her hand over her fur, though her eyes never left Andrew - a naughty expression hidden in her eyes.

"That's Sukey - the other one's Moss," Andrew grinned, desperate to make small talk.

Naomi flexed her body in a way which reminded him of a cat - one polished, stiletto dangling from the end of her toe. She let it drop to the floor. Andrew tapped her glass and took a gulp; heart hammering as she pinned him with her penetrating eyes.

"Andrew, relax," she smiled, stroking a hand over his thigh. "We haven't got very long."

"Would you like something to eat?" Andrew mumbled.

Naomi released a sigh. "I'm not hungry," she purred. "In fact, let's forget about lunch. We both know the real reason I'm here - show me your bedroom!"

Andrew didn't hesitate. His bedroom lay conveniently on the ground floor. At least it was tidy, not that anything seemed to bother Naomi as she clutched him greedily and they immediately started kissing.

He sensed her urgency; his fingers fumbling with her buttons, easing them undone - relishing the touch of her silky skin as her dress was peeled away. His heart crashed against his rib cage; the sight of her poised in her underwear sent his senses spiralling. Yet nothing could have sparked more lust than the moment her hand swept past his groin.

"Naomi, are you absolutely sure about this?" he whispered.

Her fingers closed around his erect organ, drawing a groan from his throat - if only the moment hadn't been shattered by a second clang of the doorbell.

"Shit!" Andrew spluttered in horror, "who the fuck...? Sorry!"

He omitted to catch her chilling smile, as he leapt from the room to answer it.

Naomi sensed his frustration - listening with intrigue as a volley of conversation drifted from the doorway. The timing could not have been more perfect.

"What do you mean, there's a fault on the line…. No you can't come in! I'm busy, you'll have to come back tomorrow…"

"This will only take a minute, Sir," a male voice was heard protesting.

Andrew flicked a glance over his shoulder - she was peeping through a gap in the door. Their eyes met. She gave a shrug, following it with a nod - as if consenting to the intrusion.

Andrew exhaled a sigh. "Okay, check the bloody thing," he sulked, "but don't be long..."

She was watching avidly as a man in dark overalls marched across the threshold; an engineer from British Telecom, no less. Andrew turned and shot her a look of panic. She blew him a kiss - desperate not to waste a single, precious second as she eased the door open a crack wider. She waggled a forefinger to beckon him, her lips pursed - an open invitation for another sneaky kiss. She guessed he'd find it a turn on. Andrew twisted his head around, leaning towards the door frame. His lips brushed her own - she slipped her tongue inside his mouth to distract him.

Another minute passed - which was all the time the 'telephone engineer' needed to unscrew the handset and slip in a tiny recording device. He clipped the mechanism back together.

"There you go, Sir, all done!" he smiled gleefully. "Sorry to disturb you."

"Cheers, mate!" Andrew grinned, before hurrying him out of the door.

He barged his way back into the bedroom to find Naomi sprawled across the bed, practically writhing with pleasure. She unzipped his flies and with her hands cupped around his buttocks, coaxed him towards her. She had already taken a mouthful of the chilled, sparkling wine as she lowered her lips to his penis - relishing his cry of ecstasy. The tingling bubbles inside the cavern of her mouth must have brought him spiralling to a whole new level of bliss.

"You're fantastic!" he breathed. "Where the hell did you learn a trick like that?"

He wriggled from her grasp - intent on satisfying her with as much skilful precision as he could manage, as he pushed his way inside her. The mattress bounced beneath them; his lips sought out her nipples with as much eagerness as his hand burrowed between her thighs. It was to his ultimate satisfaction, they came together. His eyes searched her face where he was rewarded by her deliriously happy smile; woefully oblivious, it had little to do with their lovemaking.

"Perry, I have some excellent news," Robin announced. "The Bailey's telephone has been bugged. We have access to all their calls now and the transcripts will be faxed to you directly."

"Very well done, Robin," Perry responded smugly. "It seems, I underestimated you..."

Robin closed his eyes: *see, I am useful!* Finally he was back in Perry's favour - a notion which left him suffused with an almost dizzying sense of power.

"And how is the lovely Naomi?" Perry purred.

"Feeling very pleased with herself!" Robin smiled. "She's got her hooks right into Charlie's son! He tells her everything, you know. He even leaked it, the couple went to London..."

Perry released a chuckle. "Yes, I thank you for that, Robin, but we knew! Anyway, pass on my congratulations will you - and if she could secure the Jansen boy a work placement... that would be even better!"

"A letter's been sent to the school," Robin said coldly. "She'll follow it up with a phone call."

The smile on his face turned hard, knowing that without Naomi, none of this would have been possible. Even *he* had never realised quite how cunning she was; the ultimate Femme Fatale. She was as beautiful as she was deadly, virtually a female version of himself - and he hadn't been entirely sure about her sexual orientation either.

A flash of memory shot through his mind - a time when he had crept upstairs, alerted to the sound of orgasmic panting resonating from her bedroom. Yet nothing could have shocked him more than to see the long, sculpted back of another girl writhing around in bed with her.

'So you are a lesbian!'

Her smile had been icily calm. Of course, she knew he was a closet homosexual - his marriage to Theresa, nothing but a scam! Naomi on the other hand, was attracted to both genders and strangely enough, Robin found himself respecting her even more for it.

"She'll keep an eye on Elijah, have no fear," he added, snapping out of his reverie. "If all goes to plan, his work placement starts on Monday. So what are you going to do about his mother?"

"Oh, you have no idea what we have in the pipeline," Perry's voice pulsed from the other end of the telephone. "Just you leave Eleanor Bailey to me, my friend..."

IV

Come Friday, Elijah found himself drawn to the Community Centre gardens, filled with a powerful urge to tend to the flower beds. He guessed, Eleanor would be joining him, hoping to surprise her. He dropped to his knees, savouring the pungent scent of lavender as it wafted across the borders. His hands worked quickly, clearing away the few stray weeds that had smuggled themselves in among the flowers. It had been raining for much of the day. He breathed in the subtle fragrance of damp earth, reliving the nicer memories of the rave. Almost on cue, he heard a patter of sandals. He glanced up with a bright smile, expecting it to be his mother - overwhelmed by an even greater sense of joy when he spotted Avalon.

"Hi!" he chirped, jumping to his feet. "How are things?"

They stood facing each other, their eyes level. Avalon retained a thoughtful expression. She looked graceful and feminine, Elijah thought - loving the pretty summer frock from Laura Ashley with its delicate cotton fabric fluttering around her ankles. She let out a sigh.

"It hardly seems a week ago, we were getting all geared up for our party."

"We haven't really talked about it much, have we," Elijah replied softly. He cautiously took her hands. "Us, I mean..."

"No," Avalon sighed, unable to resist squeezing his hands in response. "I've been thinking about you a lot, Eli - but I don't think we should rush into anything just yet."

Elijah's hands stiffened, sensing the clouds of doubt. "I-it's okay, I understand," he mumbled. "You don't have to explain - I guess it was the pills we took." He lowered his eyes, his cheeks tinged with the first flush of colour. Of course, he would never forget that kiss!

"Eli, it had nothing to do with the pills," Avalon smiled. "I think this could be the start of a wonderful relationship. I-it's just - you're so very young..."

"Does it matter?" Elijah protested.

Avalon gave a light laugh. "Yes, Eli, of course it matters. You've only just turned 16 and I'm 19. Think of all the hassle you've had in your life. What if people started calling you my toy boy?" Her smile was fading. "I think it's important, you finish school - college, or whatever else it is you're planning to do with your life. I'm not saying, I could never love you..."

"So how long will I have to wait?" Elijah teased. "What if you meet someone better?"

"What if you do?" Avalon shot back, letting go of his hands.

Another set of footsteps had materialised and on this occasion, it was Eleanor.

"What are you two talking about?" she grinned.

"We were just reminiscing about the rave," Avalon said dreamily. "It really was the most *amazing* party, Eleanor - the weather was perfect!"

"I know," Eleanor sighed, "and nobody's angry with you - well, other than that vile Magnus woman! I'm just upset about the way it ended - that you had to face Perry..."

"Don't be," Elijah smiled smugly, "I'm sure we had the last laugh!"

"Ssh, Eli!" Avalon gasped in horror, "you mustn't speak too soon. Don't forget what Margaret said. He could still send some scathing report to your school!"

"Well, nothing's come to light," Elijah insisted, "and talking of school, I've got some news, Mum. You're gonna be chuffed to bits when you hear this!"

"Well go on then," Eleanor urged him.

"They've found me a work placement," he whispered feverishly. "Rosebrook Council. I'm going to be working in the Parks and Gardens department, as part of a team."

"Eli, that's great news," Eleanor gasped.

"I know." Elijah added, throwing another joyful smile at Avalon, "even better, I'll be helping out with the landscaping for Peter's housing trust. I'll be on site with Charlie..." He broke off with a shiver - convinced the pretty gardens were smiling back at him.

He had no concept of the evil about to infiltrate its way into his world...

Andrew couldn't resist mentioning the Telecom engineer; yet said nothing about Naomi. Charlie checked the phone nonetheless, satisfied it was working and thought no more about it.

In truth, Andrew was perplexed, unable to fathom Naomi's behaviour. He knew she had secured Elijah that work placement - yet he hadn't seen her since. He had even tried phoning her house where the sound of some silky, male voice had instantly compelled him to hang up. Andrew couldn't deny he felt uneasy, now wondering if she was married.

By the time Monday came round, he shoved his troubled thoughts aside - uplifted by the more significant news that Angel had been discharged from Hospital.

Eleanor imparted the news, just as she was leaving, to escort Elijah to the Council office. At least the sunshine had returned, draining away the cloud.

She couldn't have felt more proud. At 16, Elijah reminded her so much of Jake. The blaze of sunlight brought out the auburn glints in his hair as he sauntered along beside her with that familiar, swinging stride.

Naomi awaited his presence with a spark of anticipation.

Just before 9:30, a call came through from the switchboard. Naomi shot from her desk before hurrying her way to reception. Gradually her footsteps slowed. She already had some notion of what he looked like from Robin's description.

"Would you happen to be Elijah?" her girlish voice tolled into the reception area.

He whirled round. Naomi caught her breath, having never quite expected such youthful beauty and for a moment, her predatory eyes feasted on him.

Elijah smiled politely. "Yes, that's me," he answered.

There was a moment of tense silence as Naomi and Eleanor surveyed each other.

"I'm his mum," Eleanor announced. "I hope you didn't mind me escorting him today."

"Not at all," Naomi smirked, "it's a pleasure to meet you, Mrs…"

"Bailey," Eleanor smiled warmly. "Jansen was the name of his father."

Naomi's face tightened as she fought to retain her smile. She clocked his appealing eyes - intrigued by the unusual muted green, scattered with fragments of blue and gold.

"Naomi Chandler," she added. "Elijah's supervisor. I suppose, we should get started."

"Good luck, Eli," Eleanor murmured anxiously, "I hope you get on okay…" and recognising the dismissal, she delved into her handbag. "Here's a list of contact details in case there are any problems. Not that I'm expecting any. Eli's a good worker - but *please* look after him. I'm sorry if I sound like a typical, nagging parent, but I'd really appreciate it if he was supervised at all times - never left on his own."

"Of course," Naomi smiled. "We won't let him out of our sight, I swear!"

"Bye, Mum," Elijah muttered softly, "see you later…"

Eleanor felt a twist in her heart, agonising over the thought of leaving him. She hadn't dismissed the concept that it was in this very same building, her arch enemy, Robin Whaley, worked. At least the Leisure Services department was on the ground floor. The chances of Elijah bumping into him were minimal - yet still a possibility. Elijah had already been forewarned that should the situation arise, it was essential to offer him the same courtesy as any other member of staff.

Eleanor sighed, clutching her bag. In some ways, she couldn't wait for this to be over - for her son to complete his final week of term. Then maybe they could escape for another holiday.

They had already promised they would go camping; excited by the prospect of packing up the tents again and heading for the Continent. Charlie wanted to return to the Moselle Valley but they were also planning a detour to Holland - where Elijah would finally discover the beautiful city of Nijmegan, the place of his father's homeland.

She could hear the piercing ring of the telephone before she let herself into the almshouse. It rang on and on - the sound had a persistent, almost nagging quality.

"Hello?" she said breathlessly.

"Eleanor! I-I don't know how to tell you this," a familiar voice shuddered from the phone.

Eleanor froze, jarred by the panic in her voice. "Marilyn, is that you? What's the matter?"

"Somebody torched your caravan last night!" she sobbed. "It's burnt to a crisp!"

Chapter 22

I

Eleanor felt the warmth of the sunshine drain from her blood. She dropped the phone, watching as it tumbled to the floor with a crash. She closed her eyes as the words played over and over; *'somebody torched your caravan!'*

It was with a deep swallow, she snatched the phone from the floor. For several seconds, she just stared at it wondering if she could get a message to Charlie. She decided to track him down on foot in the end. It was essential to drive to Aldwyck - and if Charlie couldn't accompany her... Eleanor blinked as she toyed with the idea of asking Inspector Boswell.

As it happened, she needn't have bothered. Ian, along with a few colleagues were already congregated in the field. Eleanor stepped shakily from Charlie's Vauxhall and gaped at the scene. A large area of the field was cordoned off and there in the centre, stood her caravan; a blackened, burnt out shell. Eleanor started to cry. Charlie swooped to her side, gathering her in his arms. At the same time, a man in a light summer suit was marching towards them, flashing an ID card.

"Detective Harrington," the man said gravely as Ian too, sauntered over to join them.

"Does anyone know what happened here?" Charlie mumbled in shock.

Ian let out a heavy sigh. "Some time, at around 4:00 in the morning, several residents were alerted by a noise. A few came out to investigate - only to find your caravan up in flames. They got straight on to the fire brigade."

Eleanor gently broke free from Charlie's embrace and stared at him in panic. "Was it arson?" she spluttered.

"It looks that way," the detective answered her truthfully. "Obviously we need to wait for the exterior to cool down, not to mention the fumes - but the forensics are here now; they think the explosion was caused by a gas bottle."

"It's possible," Charlie found himself nodding. "There was a gas cooker in there, wasn't there, love? But what about the interior - is there any chance we could take a look?"

Eleanor could already guess what he was thinking, but the detective shook his head.

"I'm sorry - no-one is allowed anywhere near this vehicle until officers have carried out a thorough investigation. We need to discover the cause of the blaze. Even the slightest disturbance could impair the evidence..."

"I see," Eleanor sniffled. She wiped a tear from her face, unable to tear her eyes away; trying to imagine the idyllic haven where Elijah had spent his childhood - now burnt to a cinder! She turned to Marilyn who had also joined the assembly.

"Who do you think could have done such a thing?" she breathed.

Their eyes locked. A small part of her already knew.

"Mrs Bailey - er - Eleanor..." Ian intervened.

She reluctantly met his eye. Yet his face seemed softer; the piercing jab of his eyes reflecting more sympathy than she would have imagined. He took her to one side.

"When are you going to tell me what's going on?" Ian sighed. "You see - Marilyn and I had a few words, earlier. She has little doubt that Ben Hampton might be behind this and I have to admit, I'm becoming more and more suspicious of an enduring vendetta..."

Eleanor said nothing. She held his stare, her eyes refilling with tears as he started reeling off the crimes: Elijah's near abduction, the burglary, the mugging, the threat to Lucy...

"The younger generation of your community threw a rave..." Ian waved a hand in the direction of Westbourne House. "Even *they* came under attack; and now this! You can't deny the truth forever. It's obvious you have enemies - and we need to know who they are."

He placed a comforting hand on her shoulder, the guilt on his face heavy. Eleanor could sense what he was thinking. It had been almost 2 years since she had imparted those early warnings. He hadn't taken her seriously - yet his expression was sobering. It came as some comfort to realise he was finally on their side.

"Mr Boswell," she begun shakily, "in a very short time, everything will be explained. But you're right, this *is* connected to an *enduring vendetta* - one which began in 1972."

There was nothing they could do. It was with the greatest reluctance, they eventually left the scene and after a quick half in the 'Olde House at Home,' they headed straight home. Perry was in London. So was Ben - which once again, exonerated them from any blame. Though Eleanor guessed, Ben would never sully his own soft white, city hands. This was undoubtedly the work of the same criminal gang who had stormed the rave. Her enemies were upping their offensive.

The next person to telephone was Joshua.

"I've heard!" his voice shot from the receiver. "Aunt Marilyn told me. Shit, Eleanor! I don't know what to say!"

"There's very little you can say," Eleanor whispered as the shock of the situation continued to tear at her senses. "Just thank God, you weren't still living there!"

A furious sigh resounded from the receiver. "Look," Joshua continued, "I'm still agonising over that rave. It was a silly idea! It's just... everyone was so up for it. We had enough contacts to pull it off - w-we just never thought our enemies were gonna react like that…"

"Joshua, no-one is blaming you…" Eleanor interrupted.

But it seemed he hadn't quite finished. "We guessed they'd call the cops. We were prepared for that… and I had a visit from the police, by the way; told 'em everything…" Eleanor heard the shudder in his voice. "I suppose this is how those bastards took their revenge!"

"What? By setting my caravan alight?" Eleanor squeaked.

"It was our home, Eleanor," Joshua sighed, "but there's something else." He took a deep breath, his voice lowering to a mumble. "Has the caravan been moved yet?"

"No," Eleanor muttered anxiously. "You're thinking about what we buried there, aren't you? And yes, the file copy is still there - which is where it has to stay. Forensics want to carry out a thorough examination. They won't let us near it - though I suppose it will have to be retrieved at some point." She broke off suddenly, her heart pounding. "Do you think we should get it out sooner?"

"I would," Joshua finished darkly. "You wouldn't want it to end up in the wrong hands."

Eleanor was left in even deeper turmoil. Joshua was right - as soon as the burnt out remains of the caravan were removed from that field, her file was going to be vulnerable. She raked through her mind; reliving the night they had buried it. It had been so dark! Yet there was no way of telling what the ground would look like - already imagining a tell-tale mound which might indicate something was buried there.

"Charlie, we have got to go back," she heard herself mumbling, a little later, that evening.

"What tonight?" he echoed in sympathy.

"Yes, tonight."

Shadows slid across the grass, as daytime lapsed into evening. They were settled in their own back yard, where the aroma of grilling sausages gently permeated the air. The kids had wanted a barbecue in the event of such fine weather - Elijah craving an opportunity to celebrate his first successful day's work experience.

Margaret on the other hand, had returned from school, grim-faced, having picked up the news from the scattering of kids who lived in Aldwyck; kids like Gary Boswell's younger brother, Mark. Eleanor and Charlie had kept a very close eye on her since the rave, sensing her inner trauma.

Eleanor saw the tremor in her lip and sighed. "What is it, love?" she muttered, momentarily breaking her conversation with Charlie.

"Th-this is all my f-fault," she sobbed, "if only I-I hadn't told them about Joshua… none of this would have h-happened…"

Charlie clocked the first glitter of tears and felt his blood boil. "Stop it, love," he soothed. "You're talking nonsense! No-one's to blame. The police haven't even discovered if the fire was deliberate yet!"

"Let's not dwell on it," Eleanor said gently. "Peter's coming over for a beer in a minute."

Charlie had invited him over beforehand. Though given Eleanor's sudden fears, he was toying with the idea of asking him to stay a little longer; to keep the kids under protection while he and Eleanor headed back to Aldwyck...

A few hours later, they ventured into the darkness. Peter was more than happy to remain in the almshouse, knowing the risk they were about to take; whereas Andrew needed no explanation. Now Angel was out of hospital, he was hankering to spend some time with him. Charlie guessed he probably wouldn't be home before midnight.

They entered the village, wary of several people milling around outside the pub as they drove past its luminous, white walls. It brought back fond memories of the time they had lived here - the usual regulars lingering by the same tables, nursing empty glasses. A warm glow of light illuminated the familiar hanging baskets. Charlie couldn't help but wonder if the Hamptons were around on this cool summer evening, as he gently cruised his car up to the field.

Eleanor hopped out and flitted across to the door. Charlie was at her side within seconds and using a screwdriver, gently eased it into the frame to prise it open. His hands came away black with soot. Yet the door fell open easily. It was practically hanging off its hinges.

"Careful, Charlie," Eleanor whispered in his ear.

They found themselves gazing sadly into the shadows where little else remained. Fabrics, furnishings and all the pretty, handmade shelves had been completely consumed, leaving a litter of burnt debris. The moonlight emitted a faint gleam - the floor disintegrated to a gaping hole where the flames had licked away its surface. Eleanor peered deep into the recess. All she could see was the innermost framework of metal bars which formed the caravan's main chassis. Yet she knew that right there, in the centre of that frame, lurked the exact spot where her file was buried.

She stepped over the rim of the chassis as her eyes gradually became accustomed to the gloom. Charlie followed - his feet rooted firmly on the bare earth. She could just about make out his features in the heavy mantle of shadow before he flicked on a tiny torch.

"Okay, so what now?" he muttered under his breath.

She crouched low, feeling the ground. Her hand explored the dry soil, until she discovered an area which was slightly raised. The earth possessed a crumbly quality. Eleanor stared at Charlie in panic, knowing what had to be done.

"I think it's here," she whispered, "we'll have to start digging..."

Charlie lowered himself to his knees. He removed a trowel and a garden fork from his satchel and it was with no further delay, he immediately began to attack the soil. They worked in synchrony - Charlie gouged at the soil with the fork, whilst Eleanor shovelled it away with the trowel. They had forgotten how deep the hole was and it took several minutes before Eleanor hit something solid.

"Got it!" she gasped, catching a first glimpse of the strong polythene bag they had concealed.

They tore away at the earth more frantically and together, they managed to extract the parcel. Charlie grabbed it. It was within a few more seconds, they made a hasty getaway.

They drove in silence, leaving Aldwyck behind. Eleanor stared numbly ahead, her breath coming in shallow gasps as the winding ribbon of road uncoiled itself. Never in her life had she imagined she would be caught up in something so clandestine.

She clutched the package - hit with the thrill of their success. It was not until they were on the outskirts of Rosebrook, however, that she finally examined it. She delved inside the bag to reveal the enveloping layers of newspaper; but as she gradually peeled away the wrapping, she was jolted by a sudden sense that something wasn't right.

She started tearing at the newspaper with a growing sense of fear.

"What's wrong," Charlie said tightly.

"It's gone!" Eleanor screeched, as her hand closed around something unfamiliar. She let out a sob, staring with dismay at what appeared to be an ordinary household brick.

It felt as if the world had been wrenched apart at the seams - her sobs coming harder as the awful truth started swirling in her mind, bringing a suffocating blackness.

"It can't be!" Charlie yelped in horror.

He floored the accelerator, just as they reached the main road, thankful there was so little traffic as he swerved into Rosebrook - he was sharply aware of Eleanor's rising hysteria.

"No!" she kept whimpering, between the sobs, "Oh no, no, no, please God, no!"

"Eleanor, try to stay calm," Charlie snapped. "We're nearly home..."

He tore up the high street, praying there were no cops around. He could see the fine architecture of the town hall - the Community Centre, whose yellow walls reflected the street light. Eleanor was crying openly - unable to deny the most obvious and terrible scenario.

"Ssh, my love," he whispered as he jammed to a halt at the back of the almshouse. "The kids are in bed - we don't want to wake them. There could be another explanation, like - supposing the forensics discovered it...?"

"They w-wouldn't have r-replaced it with a fucking brick and buried it again!" Eleanor shuddered. Her voice was dry, husky with terror.

It took him nearly all his strength to drag her to the back door.

Peter was there in seconds - conscious of their staggering footsteps. Eleanor was shaking like a leaf, her face soaked with tears and she was blubbering incoherently.

"I-it's gone, Peter - my file's b-been stolen..."

She never had a chance to see his reaction. Stars spun in her vision, thickening to a cloud as she completely blacked out.

II

From another side of the county, Perry had never felt more smug. He had not long returned from London where finally, he had in his possession the one thing he desired more than anything. To think how that first crucial clue had unwittingly slipped from the lips of Eleanor herself! But of course, she had no idea her telephone was bugged; nor that her earlier conversation with Joshua Merriman would be to her ultimate disadvantage.

Perry had stared at the fax rolling from the machine in his office, his heart beating like a drum; and yet it was Ben who had mustered up the courage to speed to the village on his motorbike; Ben who had hidden himself in the trees, waiting for the creeping descent of dusk, until it obscured the ruined caravan. He could picture it now, crouched like a shadow - barely visible against the night sky. Perry smiled. Ben could have just exhumed the package from the ground and sped away but he had brought up his son up to be a little cleverer than that. He would so loved to have seen Eleanor's reaction. It was a moment he would have cherished.

The next obstacle they faced was to open the box. Perry tried every combination he could think of, starting with 3573 (Elijah's birthday.) Ever undeterred, his next goal was to open the box by force - which was where Nathan came in useful. It eventually took the strong blades of a power saw to carve through the metal where a thick padded envelope was revealed. Perry's eyes glittered. This was it, this was the file which concealed all Eleanor's secrets - and probably Jake's.

"Well, aren't you going to open it?" Ben snapped.

"I've waited 16 years to see this file," Perry murmured, "but seeing as you're here, I think it is time I explained the truth..."

Ben smiled in anticipation as Perry pulled out a thick sheaf of papers. He unfolded them carefully, flattening them out with his hands. The first pages were scrawled in Eleanor's own fair hand - notes written in the aftermath of Jake's murder and furnished with several news clippings. He briefly scanned the sheets where he spotted only 3 names: Theakston, Hargreeves and Whaley. Perry let out a sigh. This first section appeared to be *safe territory* - enough to introduce his son to the concept of Jake's killing but without yet revealing his own part.

There was only one thing troubling him. The story began with the news shattering headline of the car bomb at Enfield's party. A separate account had been stapled to it; one which revealed that Jake had been present - and it included a resume of everything *he'd* witnessed: *Jake didn't really get a proper look at his face, but described him as being stocky, with blonde hair and wearing dark glasses...*'

Perry experienced a sudden chill before he passed this first section to Ben.

"Jake Jansen," Ben whispered. "Eleanor's lover, right? The father of her child..." He threw his father a cold, accusing stare. "Theakston... she claims he was the killer - *you* told me you hired him to get her out of London! Does this mean you sanctioned the murder?"

"You're quick to cotton on, Ben," Perry answered with unashamed frankness. He felt the contours of his face harden - reading the shock in Ben's.

"So why was he killed?"

Perry jabbed his finger at the news clipping. "That's why," he hissed. "Jansen was a rock musician who's band were hired for entertainment. He witnessed something, just hours before the explosion. Unfortunately, he chose to take his evidence to Scotland Yard - evidence which was particularly damning..." Perry's eyes narrowed as they impaled him. "You do of course, realise the significance of the name *Enfield*, don't you?"

Ben's hands were shaking as they clutched the news clipping. It was Enfield's son, Michael, he had terrorised at prep school - a boy who's tragic death, they both knew he was responsible for; a death which had led to an enquiry, followed by his expulsion.

"Shit," Ben gasped. He dropped the papers as if they were on fire. "Don't tell me you had something to do with that car bomb..." He stared at his father in horror.

Perry shrugged. "What if I was?" he whispered. "I did it for us, Ben - for you! I had to protect our family."

Ben shook his head in denial. "I'm not sure I can handle any more of this..."

"You were the one who wanted the truth," Perry sneered, "now just read it!"

Ben read and re-read those first few pages - where it didn't take long to figure out the identity of the *stocky, blonde haired* man, Jake had seen by the roadside. The rest was a blur; from the carefully planned ambush, to the daring mission Eleanor had tackled in order to rescue him. So they had gone into hiding - and all the while, Theakston's men had been hunting them.

"Stupid bitch," Ben hissed. "Why couldn't she have stayed out of it?"

"My sentiments entirely," Perry muttered with an element of satisfaction. "So now you know why I despise her. But this is just the tip of the iceberg, Ben. There is so much more!"

He had chosen the room which had been James's office. It suited his purpose well; situated in the west wing of the house and separate from the guest accommodation. It was a room where they wouldn't be overheard - not even by Rowena, who he imagined would be sound asleep. Perry turned the page. It seemed, Ben had sufficiently absorbed the contents of the first section to understand what lay at the core of his secret. It was time to move on.

It was in the next section, Perry found himself staring at his own photograph. His heart started hammering - the photo had clearly been taken at the press conference.

"This is where the little bitch finally confronted me," he snarled under his breath.

It was a memory that haunted him - the reason for driving her out of London, thinking he would be safe. He had even resigned from politics.

He kept searching - any clues of his involvement had been scant, up until now. Regrettably, those clues were unfolding before his eyes in black and white - as chronicled in the transcripts. *'All I know is that his friend Andries spoke the truth, when he told you that Jake witnessed something. Just follow the clues...'*

The journalist had added a particularly damning description of his reaction; a blast of intense rage that was clearly reflected in that photo. *'Get her out of here. Don't let her say another word.'* He had possibly consumed a little too much red wine - so enraged, he had completely lost control.

"Where the hell did she get these notes?" Perry whispered, his voice shaking with hatred.

"NME, I guess," Ben sighed, gazing back at him with a pained expression.

"See - I was right all along," Perry seethed, "and your mother thought I was being paranoid!"

"So *this* is the reason you went after her kid?" Ben added.

"Indeed," Perry finished evilly. "I knew, from the moment she appeared in Aldwyck, there'd be repercussions..." he broke off with a shudder, clasping one of the sheets. As if the contents of Eleanor's file weren't damning enough - here he was, glaring at some extract from a diary written by that stupid old fool, James Barton-Wells. "She must have told him! Why else would he give her a page of his fucking diary?"

His eyes were slicing across the sheet with growing speed. Ben watched - squirming with anxiety as Perry started clawing at his collar.

"Christ, he told her about Evelyn," he hissed. He thrust the papers aside in shock.

"Who's Evelyn?" Ben probed.

Perry threw back his brandy. "The only other witness who saw me! And yet I thought I had guaranteed her silence!"

He glanced at the page in dread. *'I couldn't believe what I was hearing, as Evelyn described this gentleman she bumped into, known as 'Perry.'*

It seemed that fate had dealt him a very cruel card. Perry felt sick, tortured by the memory of his old adversary, James. It seemed, Avalon had finally achieved her wish - where even now, James was haunting him, tugging at the strings of his destiny beyond the grave.

"How the hell did he know Evelyn?" Perry spluttered.

"Enough, Dad," Ben intervened. "Leave it! Revisit it another time..." Perry let his head fall into his hands. "C'mon, don't give yourself a coronary. You've spent years searching for this file. For God's sake don't let it be the death of you!"

Ben couldn't deny, he felt a little concerned for his father. To stumble across a copy of Eleanor's file had been an amazing coincidence - and at first, they had revelled in their triumph. Yet it had never occurred to him, the effect this would have; the truth Eleanor concealed, so damning, it might actually push him over the edge.

Fearing for his health, Ben did manage to coax him into bed. It was past midnight. Though, by the time he returned to his own room, he could sense the build up of tension, knowing he had his own demons to wrestle with. How could he forget Michael Enfield?

He could still picture that timid little boy who had been his friend - but as soon as Michael started befriending other boys, he had turned his back on him. Even now, Ben could never forget that hurt. It was in a desperate bid to cling to their friendship, he had made his life hell! Ben experienced a moment of agony. He knew full well, Michael's tragic fall from that bell tower had been purely down to him alone.

The aftermath was a blur. Perry might have hushed up his atrocities, but even he had some inkling of the evil that festered inside him. There had been talks of medical assessments which his mother fought with an iron will. So his father took matters into his own hands. Ben would never forget the nights locked in a chilly, dark cellar - the merciless beatings...

He suppressed a shudder, pushing aside his traumas. In the light of how his life had panned out, it no longer mattered. He gazed at his opulent surroundings and sighed - adoring the rich leather and walnut furniture, the fur rugs, the glittering chandelier, as he luxuriated in his 4-poster bed. He felt his tension drain a little and smoked a joint, knowing sleep would be hard tonight.

So Enfield had kicked up a bit of a stink; and it seemed, his father had finally dealt with him. It seemed impossible to imagine. A car bomb! How the hell had he managed to get away with it? Except he very nearly hadn't. Ben's eyes narrowed, thinking about the troublesome witness known as Jake Jansen. The rest was obvious - where finally, he'd grasped some notion as to why his father despised Eleanor so much! And now they had seen her file - albeit, only a copy but enough to realise just how essential it was to track down the original.

Perry meanwhile, lay slumped in darkness, listening to the various creaks and groans which emanated from deep within the timbers. The ghosts of his victims flitted in and out of his mind like shadows. Of course, he was never going to get a wink of sleep, all the while that file lay smouldering in his drawer. The brandy had momentarily warmed his chest, yet it was impossible to relax. It was 2:00 in the morning when he finally crept out of bed again.

He switched on a tiny overhead spot lamp. It enveloped his surroundings in a pool of light, his face set like stone as he slowly extracted the file from its drawer. He poured himself another brandy and lit a cigar, before flipping back the pages to read on. Every section of the file had been dated, he noticed - it proved just how swiftly Eleanor had proceeded to update it after that unforeseen clash in James's bar. The extract of his diary had emerged in October 1986; Albert Enfield's political manifesto, six months later - a time when he could vaguely recall, Alesha had been watching them. But time had raced on and just at the point when Perry believed he held the whip hand, he had discovered the deception of Eleanor's disguise.

July 1988. He was looking at the section, right now. Even that Peter Summerville had stuck his oar in with his ramblings about the IRA. His eyes flared with hatred, as he puffed on his cigar. So she had confided in him too: James Barton-Wells and now Peter… it left him with absolutely no doubt, she must have told Charlie. He had accompanied her on at least one of those trips to London. But worse was to come - where the flap of one more page led to a section where she had finally met Evelyn Webster. Perry experienced a moment of dizziness, the pain shooting through his heart. He read her letter - followed by the most appalling testimony, dated October 1988.

The blaze in his eyes intensified, as they flew across the lines of type. Dear God, the silly mare had told her everything! He slammed the file shut, heart pounding, knowing that if this document went public, it would destroy him. His emotions flickered from panic, to murderous rage. Eleanor's file not only contained enough clues to suggest he'd played a major part in Enfield's murder - but was substantiated by an indisputable motive.

Perry's hands were shaking as he reached for the decanter again, dismayed to see it was nearly empty. He rose to his feet, dropping the file back into the drawer and locking it - then made his way silently downstairs. He no longer needed a light to see where he was going, as he felt the chill of floor tiles beneath his feet. He wandered through reception in a daze - but instead of making his way to the lounge, where a second decanter of brandy beckoned, he found himself drifting towards the kitchens.

Perry flicked a switch, flooding the clean, white-tiled room in a dazzle of light and as he stared across the work surfaces, his eyes stopped dead on the knife rack. He took a few more steps, barely understanding what possessed him any more, as he reached for one of the knives; it was long handled with a heavy blade, narrowing to a point. Already he had begun fantasising. He ran the blade lightly across his fingertip. It sliced neatly through his skin as if it was butter. Perry watched as tiny beads of blood swelled on both sides of the incision - imagining the gleaming, soft throat of his enemy. "Time for you to die, Eleanor…" he whispered.

Except, she couldn't die yet - oh no, that would be way too risky. They had to initiate the final stage of their plan and procure the original. They had to capture her son.

III

Eleanor hardly slept a wink, that night, either.

Peter and Charlie managed to calm her down with drop of whisky and it was fortunate, Charlie kept a few sedatives. Yet her mind refused to switch off as the consequences of the missing file kept raking at her thoughts. It was around 7:00 in the morning, when Charlie appeared by her bedside with a cup of tea.

"I'm so scared, Charlie," she croaked, "what if Perry's got it?"

"Ssh," he sighed, running a hand over her thick hair. "Look at it this way, if Perry *has* got it, he's the one who ought to be scared! He wouldn't dare harm you - otherwise we'd have good reason to go public with the original."

"It's the original, I'm worried about," Eleanor yawned, sinking back into the pillows.

"Stay in bed, love," Charlie said warmly. "I'll phone you in sick."

He wandered downstairs, confused. There was no way someone could have stumbled across that file by chance - they must have purposefully gone there looking for it. The burning question was how the hell could anyone have known about it?

He picked up the telephone to contact Rosebrook Hospital. It rang several times - yet the instant the call was answered, he detected a click somewhere deep within the phone mechanism. Charlie frowned, unsure what it was about the sound that unnerved him.

"Rosebrook Hospital switchboard…" a bored voice drawled from the earpiece.

Charlie's voice was heavy with regret as he reported that Eleanor was too ill for work. He bit his lip, lowering the phone back into its cradle - his earlier troubled thoughts creeping back to him, as he tried to make sense of it all. First the fire and now this… though before he was able to grapple any further, he jumped at the phone's piercing ring.

He grabbed for the handset, pressing it against his ear: *'click.'* There it was again! "Hello?"

"Charlie, it's Peter," a familiar, Irish voice piped into his ear. "How is she...?"

"Not good," Charlie interrupted, "look, Peter - I-I'm a bit busy, right now and I don't mean to fob you off but is there any chance we could meet up a bit later?"

"Of course..." Peter answered. Straight away, Charlie heard the frown in his voice. "Just one thing and I'll make it quick. We've got a team of consultants coming over on Thursday, to discuss the interior design of the flats. Meeting's at 4:30. I was wondering if Eli might like to attend..."

Charlie felt himself relax slightly. "I'm sure he'd love that!" he sighed. "Though it depends on his work placement and whether they'll let him out early. Anyway, I'll see you in say, 30 minutes?"

He held his breath, waiting for Peter to hang up. The phone went dead - though for a second, he pressed the handset to his chest. He had a hundred things on his mind, but something had just leapt to the forefront. He couldn't shake off the memory of what Andrew had said - something about a fault on the line - a telephone engineer... He experienced a sudden shiver.

Andrew was undeniably furtive. "He showed me an ID card," he insisted. "He definitely looked like he was from BT. Are you gonna check?"

"Later," Charlie said tightly. He didn't want to push it. His son looked terrible, his face pale, eyes heavy with anxiety. "What's wrong, son?"

The shocking truth was that Angel had been ordered to leave town. It seemed, his much-feared 'boss' was determined to yank him back to London so they keep could an eye on him.

"He's one of us, Dad," Andrew desperately tried to explain. "Those bastards in London think they own him!"

Charlie nodded, having already figured out some 'gangland' connection from what Eleanor had said. Angel had clearly been on the run when he had first arrived here.

"Lara's heartbroken!" Andrew continued. "What about his DJ job? He loves working at Bella's."

"So, have you thought about talking to Theakston?" Charlie sighed. A small part of him was already wondering if Dominic was the best person to deal with this.

They snatched a hasty breakfast of coffee and toast, then gradually made their way to the building site; but not before Charlie had called in on one of the neighbours - shocked to discover, they knew nothing about this mysterious 'telephone engineer.' It was with growing trepidation, he was beginning to wonder if their telephone hadn't just been tampered with - it had been *tapped*. He froze, just as they drew up to the building site. Joshua had called! It was in the aftermath of that conversation, Eleanor was hit with a sudden fixation to return to Aldwyck.

"You go ahead, son," he said softly. "I'll catch up with you in a little while."

He shoved his hands into his pockets, marching back towards the Community Centre, head down, now hankering to talk things over with Peter.

"Look, I'm sorry if I seemed cagey," Charlie began in the privacy of his office, "but in the light of everything else, I've got an awful suspicion our phone might be bugged."

"You're kidding!" Peter spluttered.

"I wish I was," Charlie sighed and suddenly, he was afraid. "Whoever took Eleanor's file knew exactly where to look. She and Joshua were talking about it." He shook his head. "We need to be so careful what we say in future - which is why I need to ask a favour…"

It took just a few minutes to explain that he needed to contact Eleanor's solicitor - and of course, Peter was unwavering in his consent.

"It's important, he realises the file copy's been stolen," Charlie whispered. "I've got no doubt, they would have forced the box open by now - and if so, they've probably seen the contents!"

He fought off a second shudder, remembering John Sharp's words. It seemed ironic, he had voiced his distrust of telephones. Maybe he knew the type of enemies they were dealing with, better than he thought.

IV

Elijah meanwhile, was ever keen to appease his supervisors as he immersed himself in his work experience. There was only one tense moment when he had crossed paths with Robin Whaley. Although, he had no reason to feel scared - the man had thrown him a most engaging smile which momentarily put his mind at ease.

What Elijah could never have known, was of the dark undercurrent of whisperings behind the scenes. Robin's smile lingered - fully aware of a meeting soon to take place at Westbourne House. Finally, Naomi was about to meet Perry - along with Ben, Nathan and another two 'contacts' from the criminal underworld. Robin almost shivered, gripping the boy's gaze with a feeling that bordered on obsession - then slowly wandered on.

Elijah thought little more of it. He threw himself into his work, which at least took his mind off the more troubling events in his personal life; fully aware, his mother's file copy had gone missing - which in the aftermath of the fire, had brought a darkness into their world.

He took a deep breath, focusing on his next task. He couldn't deny, he was loving it here. He couldn't have wished for a nicer supervisor than Naomi, who had been openly amenable from day one. His first job had been to assist her with some paperwork. Then, to his ultimate delight, she had taken him on a walk around town where they had ended up at his favourite park - a rolling expanse of lawn, threaded with paths and flower beds.

The sun was bright, illuminating the flower beds and it was here, he had been assigned his first task. Naomi gently handed him over to a team of gardeners before leaving him in their care. It surpassed all expectations; a delight to tend to the flower beds, alongside a team of healthy lads, some perhaps just a little older than himself. Together, they had pruned shrubs, dead-headed roses and weeded - filling the gaps with a profusion of petunias. Elijah smiled. Everything was so uniform, so different from the rambling cottage style borders in the Community Centre gardens.

The day passed quickly; a day he had revelled in the praise Naomi showered him with and not only that - she had treated him to tea and cake in the Council cafeteria. He was moved by her passion; her undisguised interest in his life and especially his love of art.

"Play your cards right, Eli, you could land yourself a job here," she breathed, blue eyes heavy with adoration. It was day 3 and as Elijah studied her sweet smile, he felt himself relax slightly.

There was something he had been hankering to ask - but it was not until they were half way through the week, he finally banked up the courage to approach her.

"I was wondering," he said softly, "you know the new housing trust - the site where we're gonna be working today, doing some tree planting...?"

She tilted her head to one side, her expression pensive. "Yes?"

"Mr Summerville invited me to a meeting," he blurted with unsuppressed glee. "They've got a design team visiting. Thursday 4:30. W-would it be okay if I went along?"

"You're asking me to give you time off?" Naomi frowned, the smile dropping from her face.

Elijah braced himself - picking up the shift in her mood. It was without another word, she guided him into an office - he found himself staring at an empty desk, a tweed jacket slung casually over the back of a chair, indicating that her boss had disappeared on one of his lengthy tea breaks. She closed the door, her expression cold.

"Elijah," she snapped, "have you any idea how lucky you were to get this work placement?"

"Of course..." he started to mumble.

"Really?" she sighed. "Only - Mr Manning wasn't too happy about having to mollycoddle some school boy. If it had been up to him, he'd have shunted you off to the photocopying room. Yet I've offered you some really interesting assignments."

"I know that!" Elijah retorted, feeling the colour sweep into his cheeks. He lowered his eyes, scraping one toe over the carpet. "I-I didn't mean to sound ungrateful," he added miserably, "I've enjoyed working here, really I have. I-I guess that's a 'no' then..."

"Correct," Naomi snapped - a muscle flickering in her jaw. "You are our responsibility from nine until five, Elijah - we can't let you go galavanting off on your own."

"I'm sorry," Elijah whispered and suddenly, he couldn't meet her eye.

He put in a considerable amount of effort that day, mortified to think he may have offended her. Shirt off, with the sun blazing down, he slogged away relentlessly, shovelling the earth as if his life depended on it, as one after the other, a seemingly never-ending chain of Silver Birch saplings were planted - and this was just the first lot!

"What an absolute cow," Eleanor gasped. Charlie was on site and so was Andrew, hoping to catch a glimpse of Naomi.

"It doesn't matter," Elijah panted, without breaking his work flow. "Maybe I'll just turn up a bit later. Otherwise, I'm sure Peter will fill me in..."

Eleanor stared at him in disbelief. "Eli! You've got your heart set on being an interior designer. What difference does half an hour make?"

"I don't want to annoy her," he protested, finally pausing for breath, "not when I'm this close to finishing my work experience; and I *do* want a glowing report!"

He studied her face, feeling the first stab of anxiety. His mother had lost weight recently - her cheek bones looked sharp in the unrelenting glare of sunshine. At last, she nodded her head.

"Fair enough, Eli, I hope it goes well. Two more days then maybe we can escape for a bit."

Come Thursday, Elijah wasn't entirely sure if Naomi had forgiven him - at least, not until the moment she floated over to greet him. She ran a caressing hand down his arm.

"Okay, little soldier?" Elijah turned to her in disbelief. The expression in her eyes seemed gentle. "Sorry, if I was a bit hard on you yesterday - but I've got a real treat lined up for you today. Did you bring your sketchpad?"

Elijah couldn't deny a tiny flicker of confusion as once again, she led him from the Council building. On this occasion, they wandered towards the back of the town. The houses seemed to thin out, the area more remote, where row upon row of sycamore trees guarded the driveways of houses, larger and more grandiose than any he was familiar with. His confusion crumbled into anxiety as she ushered him towards a set of ornamental, wrought iron gates.

"Bevington Gardens," Naomi whispered. "Rosebrook's best kept secret! These are the oldest gardens in town - they're steeped in history and still open to the public."

Elijah felt the onset of a shiver, not liking this place. As if to add to his sense of desolation, it wasn't so sunny today - a series of grey clouds had threaded their way across the sky, allowing only an occasional shaft of light to pass through. He gazed ahead in awe as Naomi unlatched the gate. It swung open, releasing a groan of hinges before they were drawn down a narrow path, banked by thick laurel hedges on both sides.

The area was surrounded by high flint walls. The feathery branches of a mature cedar stretched overhead, reminding him of a tree in James's grounds. Yet before he knew what to expect, he found himself staring at the most extraordinary configuration; a large area, paved in stone, embracing a series of sunken banks. It sloped down towards a circular fish pond - four sets of steps were dug into the banks, supported by ornamental balustrade, mossy with age.

"Come and take a closer look!" Naomi smiled, as she strode up to the edge.

Elijah followed numbly. He began to descend the steps, spotting the muted shades of succulents packed in amongst the paving stones - the whorls of spiky leaves looked strange. This garden was completely devoid of the conventional flower beds which distinguished other parts of the town and lined with rambling rockeries.

"Beautiful, isn't it?" Naomi sighed, just as Elijah was running his hand over a mound of purple heather. "These are more commonly known as *sunken gardens.*"

Elijah nodded, unsure what to say as his eyes travelled further. He noticed a few ornamental urns, tumbling over with ivy - thinking they might look prettier if they had a few bright begonias in them. Then finally, he saw a man positioned by a wheelbarrow, watching them.

"Good morning, Arthur," Naomi greeted him politely.

The man offered her a shifty nod. Elijah placed him in his fifties - a tall, somewhat dour looking man whose straggly grey hair and unsmiling face did nothing to ease his nerves.

"Good day to you, Miss Chandler," he answered her coolly - his dull, blue eyes swivelled towards Elijah, "and who is this?"

"I've brought you a little helper," Naomi continued. "You said the garden was getting unruly. This is Elijah Jansen - on work experience for a week."

"And not before time," Arthur grunted. "Damn place is a mess - could do with a hand!"

Naomi turned to Elijah and beamed. "Eli, this is Arthur Morecroft, who manages this place. It features on the 'Gardens of Kent' tour and tends to attract Coach parties - same as Westbourne House did. It's paid entry. There's even a little tea shop."

It was the mention of Westbourne House that finally drew a smile to his lips and suddenly, he guessed her reasons for bringing him here. It was in the last couple of days, she had insisted on seeing some of his sketches, where his beautifully drawn pictures of James's gardens had impressed her beyond belief. His pad was tucked in his satchel, just as she'd suggested. Given the chance, he was hoping his manager might spare him some time to make a few sketches.

Before he knew it, Naomi had launched into a glowing testimony of his talent. Arthur nodded again, though he seemed preoccupied - keen to get him working on the rockery.

"You get a tea break at around 11:00," he snapped, before turning back to his wheelbarrow. "Café will be open for soft drinks and ice creams…"

He waved a wizened hand towards an oak stained summer house where a couple of flimsy tables were perched outside. They were tinged green with algae and didn't look particularly inviting. Then finally, Elijah glanced back at Naomi - she seemed to be retreating.

"I'll be working on my own?" he said nervously.

"You've got Mr Morecroft to look after you," she breezed. "Don't worry, you'll love it here. I'll come and collect you a bit later."

The moment she was gone, Elijah was hit with a sense of dismay. For all her good intentions, he didn't really relish the idea of being stuck here with this miserable old man, who seemed incapable of making any conversation other than barking orders.

"I want every weed dug out of that rockery! And make sure you use a fork."

Elijah had no choice other than to throw himself into his task. Yet it was in the stark solitude of this place, he started thinking about their troubles again; struggling to imagine who would set fire to their caravan. The police were convinced it was arson. Traces of petrol had been discovered on the grass and while Charlie reassured him, they could claim on the insurance, it would never compensate for the lovely pine shelves cluttered with nick nacks, the beautiful rugs and furnishings his mother had collected, to fill it with warmth and colour.

He ran a hand over his forehead and sighed. Within two hours, he had filled two giant garden bags. Though it wasn't until 11:30, his boss finally released him for a break. The man seemed as hostile as the terrain he was working on. He found himself craving the company of the younger labourers. If only he had been stationed in one of the other parks. This place might have possessed an unconventional beauty but there was something about the atmosphere that struck him as forbidding. There was so little colour; the surrounding walls were making him feel trapped, adding an unsettling darkness to his environment.

The day passed slowly, though he was grateful to get a lunch hour - enough time to produce three breathtaking sketches, before making a speedy dash to a nearby shop for a sandwich. By the time he returned, Mr Morecroft was engrossed in a cross word - then immediately got him working on the shrubs and topiary. It wasn't until nearly 4:00 that Naomi finally reappeared.

Elijah felt his heart lift, never more pleased to see her.

"Sorry Eli, I got held up!" she gasped, rushing over. "How are you getting on?"

"Okay," Elijah said, squeezing a smile. He glanced at Mr Morecroft, who's reassuring nod suggested he didn't mind him pausing to liaise with Naomi.

He took off his gardening gloves and massaged his wrists. It was only after a few moments however, that Arthur bit his lip - he begrudgingly moved over to join them.

"He's been a good lad," he muttered in earnest. "Done a jolly good job. Shame there weren't more folks around to appreciate it..." It was true. Only a scattering of people had visited and even those had been mostly elderly folk. He gazed at Elijah with pity - it was almost as if he sensed the day hadn't been much fun for him.

"Tell you what then," Naomi said with a conspiratorial smile, "supposing I let you off early, after all. Say about 4:30? You might even make that meeting of yours!"

Elijah's heart gave a sudden leap of joy. "Do you really mean that?" he gasped.

"Of course," Naomi replied sweetly. "I hope it goes well."

It was without another word, she drifted away, leaving Elijah in stunned silence. The only thing left troubling him now was that Peter wasn't expecting him until 5:00. A bright smile shot across his face - he would surprise him.

The last half hour passed quickly and from the moment Arthur retreated into the summer house to finish his crossword, Elijah was inclined to follow him.

"You can get off now, lad," he mumbled. "Thanks for your help."

Elijah offered him a warm smile, feeling his excitement soar. He wasted no time - grabbing his light summer jacket and satchel. He gave the man a final, cheery nod before rushing towards the exit. He could see the wrought iron gates ahead. For some reason, they had been left wide open, almost inviting his escape.

He thought nothing of it, desperate to get to the Community Centre. His footsteps drew him down the same path and deep into the shadows of the laurel bushes. He was only yards from the gates however, when he tensed to a sudden rustling sound. Elijah glanced round and froze, as two evil looking youths emerged from the thicket of bushes. He instinctively quickened his pace, intent on reaching those gates. Already, he was overcome by a wave of fear - a sense that these boys had been hidden there, just waiting for him...

Elijah broke into a run. The road beckoned; but within a split second everything changed. It was like the shifting scenery on a stage. A dark transit van pulled right up to the gates, blocking his exit. Elijah skidded to a halt. He watched with dread as a man leapt from the passenger side - broad shouldered, narrow hipped, a vision that sent his mind spiralling back to a scene, two years ago. His spiky hair might have been bleached blonde and he was wearing dark glasses - yet there was no mistaking where he had seen this character before: *Nathan!*

He was no longer thinking straight as he spun round and charged in the opposite direction; regrettably, it was straight into the path of the youths who savagely grasped his arms. He let out a sob, wanting to scream - but of course, Arthur was conveniently tucked away in the summer house, oblivious to it all. Elijah wriggled in their grip, kicking wildly with his feet - his panic spinning out of control, as Nathan kept on marching towards him.

Finally he found his voice. *"Help!"*

Something hard and blunt was whacked across his shoulders. Elijah released a shriek, as a second blow sent him to his knees. It took just seconds to realise, one of his captors had extracted a small but deadly club, pounding him without mercy. He momentarily cowered on the ground. Yet the seconds passed quickly. It was within a few terrifying strides that Nathan finally caught up with him. His accomplices yanked him to his feet. Elijah attempted to scream again. Only this time, he was hurled into Nathan arms; overcome by a suffocating chemical smell as a cloth was clamped over his face, smothering his nose and mouth. He tried to hold his breath, choking as the powerful fumes entered his lungs. He saw stars - the evil men around him seemed to disintegrate, before the entire world turned black.

At around the same time as Elijah was leaving Bevington Gardens, Eleanor had hidden herself in Peter's office to sort out a few outstanding legal matters.

She had received a fax from her barrister, David Edgar. At last, he had obtained a copy of the crime report which she read with morbid curiosity. Jake had not been shot in the temple as one would have thought; the fatal wound had been discovered in the back of his head, just below his right ear. The killer had used a jacketed bullet with low grain ammunition to reduce penetration - the bullet lodged inside Jake's head as discovered in a post-mortem.

She could hardly bear to picture him in death - the lustrous sheen of his beautiful auburn hair. Tears sprung to her eyes as the truth sunk in, the images racing back... It was the angle of the shot which had ultimately ruled out Dominic as the killer. He had been stood to Jake's left - she had deduced that much from the echo of his voice above the floorboards. Yet Dominic was evidently left handed. According to another report, his right hand had been crushed in a vice at the age of 17, leaving it so badly damaged, it was impossible for him to hold a gun, never mind fire one.

Eleanor's heart felt heavy yet there was no time for sentiment. Jake had been gone for 16 years and it was time to bring his real killer to justice: *'I never saw who killed him. I only assumed it was Theakston, given that he had been hunting for us. But he was after me, not Jake, due to some vendetta against my father. I was hidden below the floorboards on the night of the murder. I could have sworn I heard his voice - though, I have to confess, the sound was muffled...'*

Eleanor kept writing until she was satisfied she had cleared his name. Reliving the night of Jake's death had been a moment of pure torture - yet somehow, she felt cleansed - pleased to think that Perry no longer had such a hold over Dominic. It was safe for her file to go public.

Just as she was cherishing the idea, a loud knock shook her out of her musings.

"Come in," she called out nervously, stuffing the sheets into her handbag. The door flew open. Peter materialised in front of her, his face pale. "What's wrong? I thought you were supposed to be having a meeting..."

"We decided to postpone it," Peter snapped, "but that's not the point. Where's Eli? He was supposed to be joining us at around 5:00 and he hasn't shown up."

Like everyone else in her close-knit sphere, Peter was constantly on guard - especially now. She stared at the clock: 5:15 - and yet her son had always been punctual. Eleanor swallowed back her fear, praying there was a perfectly logical explanation.

"Let's go to the almshouse and check if he's there," she mumbled.

They wasted no time. Side by side, they poured from the office, down the stairs and straight through the exit. They were oblivious to all who watched them - gaivanised by their concern.

As soon as they reached the almshouse, Eleanor sensed the emptiness that was about to greet them. Charlie and Andrew were working. Even Margaret had vanished for an end of term school trip. She rammed her key into the door and rushed inside. Peter followed, where the well of silence had never been more startling.

"Oh my God," Eleanor whimpered, gripping Peter's arm.

"Phone the council!" he urged her. "They're bound to know if he's left..."

She shakily moved towards the telephone, just as her thoughts crept towards *Naomi*. She felt a spike of anger - she had been resolute in her refusal to allow Elijah to attend Peter's meeting. Was it possible, she had taken her campaign one step further by deliberately keeping him behind? She never had a chance to find out. The ring of the telephone tore into the silence.

"Hello?" she snapped.

There was a brief pause, before a chilling voice hissed from the ear piece. "Missing your son, are you, Eleanor?"

Chapter 23

I

Her eyes dilated with terror as she gripped the handset more tightly. "Who is this?"

"Shut up!" the same voice spurted. "Listen carefully - follow our instructions and the boy will be quite safe. You got that so far?" They didn't wait for a reply - she was too numb to speak. "You are not to contact *anyone* and that includes your husband. In case you didn't know, your phone is bugged. Try anything clever and well... I don't need to spell it out."

"Okay, I understand!" Eleanor gasped. "Please don't hurt him!"

From the other side of the lounge, Peter turned ashen. Their eyes locked.

"Do not even *attempt* to contact the police," the sinister voice continued, "otherwise he dies! Now here's what you do. You pack a bag, you take the next train to London and go straight to the Grosvenor Hotel. A room has been booked for you. Do not tell anyone where you're going and make absolutely sure no-one follows you..."

"Alright," Eleanor nodded, "just one thing - what am I supposed to tell my family? They're going to know something's wrong! What if *they* call the police?"

"Leave a note!" She heard a menacing chuckle. "We gather you spoke to your friend, *Avalon*. Didn't you say something about *disappearing for a few days*? Say you decided to leave a bit earlier - you were feeling *scared* and you didn't want to hang around..."

Eleanor felt chilled - the voice possessed an evil, mocking quality. She could even sense the smile in it. Threads of cold passed over her skin, bringing her out in goose-bumps.

"Okay," she relented, "but they'll *still* be suspicious..."

"Then I suggest you act normally and get yourself to London, right away!"

The voice had resumed its nasty quality. Eleanor wished she could work out who it belonged to but her heart was sinking fast. All that mattered was Elijah.

"They've got him," she shuddered, the moment the phone clicked dead. "Peter, h-he's been abducted and this time, it's for real..." she let out a sob.

Peter flew to her side. "Okay, just try to stay calm," he soothed, "what exactly did they say?"

"I have to go to London and book myself into the Grosvenor Hotel. God, the irony - this is the place I first bumped into Perry..." She couldn't help herself, she started to cry.

"So Perry is behind this!" Peter hissed in outrage.

"Of course he's behind it!" Eleanor squeaked. "Or someone connected to him - possibly some criminal gang. This is the exact same tactic he used when

Jake was killed!"

It was with no hesitation, Peter scooped her into his arms. She sobbed into his chest. Yet the moment passed quickly - as soon as she had released that initial deluge, she found herself struggling out of his embrace.

"I should leave now before they do something awful! Poor Eli - he must be terrified."

"I want to come with you..." Peter started to say but she pressed her finger to his lips.

"You can't! They gave strict instructions, I was *not* to be followed..." her face crumpled in misery as she studied his gentle features. "Stay here, Peter. Look after the others e-especially Charlie. He's the one who's going to need the most reassurance. You might have to explain what's happened - if only to stop him charging to the police. Tell him I love him..." a tear rolled down her cheek, "and as for you... You have always reminded me of Jake, you know. Same height, same build - even the way you walk! You are so very much like him, Peter."

"Eleanor, please," Peter whispered, "I can't bear to let you go off on your own."

"I have too," Eleanor protested, "otherwise they might kill him..."

She stared at the clock - it was 5:30.

Peter followed her gaze, where his eyes were unwittingly drawn to the photo of Jake on the mantelpiece; his mesmerising green eyes smiled back at him as the echo of Eleanor's words sank in. *You are so very much like him.* He felt a shiver of cold.

"Sneak out the back," Eleanor whispered, "best no-one sees you..."

Peter sighed, his heart heavy with woe. Yet he had little choice - studying Jake's photo one last time, before he reluctantly slipped out of sight.

Eleanor sped up the stairs to change, abandoning her thin cotton top and shorts. She selected a long summer dress whose olive green shade was sufficiently muted. The one thing she did not want to do was stand out. She slipped on Jake's pendant where the coolness of the stone felt comforting. She started hurling a few clothes into a small overnight bag with no concept of how long she would be away for; that was, if she was ever meant to return...

Thrusting aside her heartache, Eleanor rushed downstairs and unearthed a notepad. There was a sudden clench to her jaw as she began writing - determined not to break down.

'My darling Charlie, don't despair but Eli and I needed to get away. I'm sorry to do this. I will call you as soon as I get a chance. Keep safe. I love you very much xxx'

She swallowed back her tears and leaving the note on the table, glanced at her reflection. Her face was devoid of colour, her expression glazed - only the gleaming dark ripples of her hair drew attention; she found a velvet scrunchie to tie it back with then stepped out of the door.

Eleanor kept walking, praying no-one would see her. It was only as she stood on the curb, waiting for the traffic to pass, that her eyes inadvertently wandered towards the Fish and Chip shop and up to the window. Peter loomed behind the glass, staring back at her, his expression fearful. Eleanor clung to his gaze, then delved into her handbag and slipped on a pair of sunglasses. It was with no further hesitation, she made her way hurriedly to the railway station.

5:45: the train started to glide along the tracks. Eleanor felt every muscle harden like steel, determined to keep her emotions under control as her fear for Elijah twisted inside her. She had no concept of what had happened - or the conditions he was being held in. He could be anywhere! It was the not knowing that made this situation so horrible.

The stations flipped past, one after the other. Eleanor knotted her hands in her lap, gazing sadly out of the window as a familiar screen of pine trees towered on both sides of the tracks. It was only now that her mind started to wander.

It was fairly obvious, Perry had the file. He had absorbed the contents; a truth which must have sent his twisted mind spiralling towards insanity. Eleanor felt the sting of tears. To think, they had been on the verge of initiating a prosecution. Was it even possible, Perry had discovered this too?

It was ironic how she had only just cleared Dominic's name - yet she had got him so wrong! Memories of every warning crashed into her mind: the hint that Avalon was under threat - the meeting at his night club; *'Concentrate on the future, especially your son's future!'* It was Dominic who had dropped the first clue as to how dangerous Perry was; the warning, his son was hooked up with some particularly evil faction of the criminal underworld. In fact, it was only now that she realised he had been on their side all along - careful to keep their true enemies from double guessing. If only she had known - but now it was too late.

Eleanor shivered as the train pulled into Waterloo Station. She was fighting to control her tremors where deep in her heart, she knew, the real nightmare was about to begin...

Peter chewed his lip as he watched her disappear, knowing he couldn't abandon her.

Charlie could not be left in the dark! If Eleanor really *had* made a decision to run, she would have told him; and it was for this very reason, he had scrawled down the threads of an idea.

He dropped a few clothes into a carrier bag and slipped on a jacket, before striding across to the building site. He carried an envelope which contained the outline of his plan - keys to his flat, confident his own phone would be safe for any communication.

Almost as soon as he reached the building site, he spotted Charlie. He was just leaving, his son wandering off in the opposite direction, probably to see his mates. He let out a sigh, grateful to grab Charlie on his own.

"Hi, Peter," he frowned, his footsteps dwindling. "How did the meeting go?"

"Charlie, there is no time to explain," Peter whispered, sidling right up to him. "I have something for you. Don't ask questions. Our enemies could be watching us - but you'll get the gist when you read it. Where are you off to anyway?"

Charlie's eyes narrowed. He knew better than to draw suspicion - picking up the pace, just as Peter fell into step beside him.

"School," he snapped, his expression stony. "Just off to pick up Margaret - they told us to get there at six. Now what's going on, Peter?"

"Just walk," Peter said in as casual tone as he could manage.

Finally they reached the almshouse, now swerving towards the path that led to Charlie's car. Anything said in the open could be overheard; yet as soon as they were in the solitary confines of a car, he was going to spill out the whole story - and it was not going to be pleasant.

II

At about the same time as Eleanor was rushing to make the next train, Elijah was just beginning to regain consciousness, with no concept of the nightmare he was about to wake up to. He would think he was dreaming, Perry found himself musing - until the horror of his surroundings gradually took shape and he would wonder if he was in hell!

These ideas slid easily into his mind, as he gazed at the prostrate figure slumped on a worn leather settee. From the moment of his capture, they had bundled him into the transit van and charged up to London, consumed with an urgency to get him delivered to this house. Perry smiled, as he reached down and stroked Elijah's cheek, relishing the softness of his skin - it symbolised his fragile youth. This was such a highly prized specimen; the only child Jake Jansen had ever fathered and ever would. Perry displayed a sliver of teeth as his hand closed around his throat. It would be so easy to kill him. Except young Elijah was of far greater use to him than that.

"When do you suppose he will come round, Nathan?" he whispered.

They were hidden inside Nathan's house; a gloomy terrace guarded by a boundary wall, set far enough back from the street to shield them from prying eyes. They hovered in the lounge. Nathan knew no-one could see in. Net curtains veiled the windows whilst a canopy of overgrown shrubs cut out any light which might have penetrated the shadows.

"Shouldn't be long," he muttered, glancing at his watch. "He's been out cold for nearly an hour. He should start to stir at any minute."

"Then best we move him," Perry snapped, rising to his feet. "We don't want to leave him in too much comfort. I want him to be scared..." He gave a cruel smile. "Is everything ready?"

Nathan gave a nod, his eyes narrowing. There was a basement in the house in which he had set up a small gym. His face and torso were glistening with sweat from a frenzied weight lifting session; it was a vision that would have left any young boy fearful - yet Nathan had planned so much more. The stage was set and it was with an element of pleasure, he hoisted him off the sofa and carried him down to the basement. Perry followed.

Eventually Elijah began to stir, his mind thick with fog. At first, all he could recall was some distant thread of memory just prior to leaving Bevington Gardens. He must have fainted. An image of the mysterious sunken gardens momentarily swum in his mind's eye - the shadow of an imposing cedar tree. Then slowly the clouds began to part, unravelling the moment he had left. His arms and shoulders throbbed, he was immersed in a syrupy darkness. He was remembering the two evil-looking skin heads who had crept out of the laurel bushes - before an even more terrifying image of Nathan tore through the shadows. He let out a whimper of fear - his arms were stretched high above his head, his wrists shackled in hand cuffs.

Elijah struggled instinctively, hearing the clank of chains. He let out a gasp, forcing his head upright - a mass of pain splintered through his brain. He pressed his eyes shut. But the next time he opened them, they gradually adjusted to the gloom where the reality of his situation was horrifying; the cruel, iron cuffs which constrained him, the heavy ceiling beam they were attached to. He cried out in panic, tugging against the chains - aware of some subtle shine of light, lingering a short distance away. Elijah carefully inched himself round, startled by the image of a man lounging in a chair, observing him. Their eyes met and Nathan smiled.

"Hello, Elijah," he muttered in a low, mocking voice.

Elijah struggled against the chains again, wincing as the hard metal cut into his skin. He let out a sob, unable to hold back his fear a second longer.

"Wh-what's going on, why am I here?" he shivered.

"Bait!" Nathan smirked and holding his stare, he sat up slightly.

He was seated in a swivel armchair, next to what appeared to be a work bench. A heavy iron vice was clamped to one end - but worse was to come. Nathan seized the edge of a dark cloth and carefully peeled it back. The bench was illuminated in the glow of a spot light - a vicious looking set of clubs revealed, from what appeared to be a policeman's truncheon to a long, gleaming baseball bat. Elijah swallowed, staring at the collection with dread. Among the gruesome display, lay a smaller club - no doubt the same type those skinheads had used to bludgeon him with. He winced again, conscious of the pain in his shoulders and back from all those merciless blows.

"Nice collection, don't you think?" Nathan kept taunting as he slid the cloth back a little further.

Elijah's heart started to pound, unable to tear his eyes away from Nathan's growing inventory. Next to be unveiled was a set of lethal looking knives - a pointed stiletto, a curved hunting knife whose serrated edge glittered. As if he wasn't terrified enough and yet all the while, the cloth kept slithering back, drawing his gaze to more weapons - screwdrivers, a hammer, pliers... Elijah squeezed his eyes closed again, the sight was making him feel faint.

"Tools of the trade," Nathan whispered, rising to his feet. "Been a long time since I've had a fresh, new victim to experiment on..."

Elijah gritted his teeth, knowing the time had come to face his ordeal. This was the scenario his mother had always feared; the ultimate threat they had used to control her.

"I guess I'm in for a lot of pain then," he shuddered, just as Nathan ambled up to him.

"That very much depends on your mother!" a new voice rang from the shadows.

Elijah twisted round, wrists burning - and there in the dim glow of light, materialised the solid frame of a man he knew only too well, his face not quite visible.

"M-Mr Hampton?" Elijah gasped.

The echo of Perry's footsteps closed in, sending another rush of fear sweeping over him.

"That's right," Perry sneered, circling round to face him. "Not laughing now, are you, boy?"

Elijah stared at him, instantly struck by the predatory gleam of his eyes.

"Look - I'm s-sorry about the rave," he whispered miserably, "y-you wanted Boswell to arrest us... I-I thought it was funny." He caught his breath, despising himself for grovelling.

Perry let out a hiss of laughter. "You think this is some kind of punishment? My dear boy, this has got nothing to do with the rave! This is to do with a diary your father made, many years ago when he first hooked up with Eleanor! Surely, you must know about it."

"No," Elijah gasped. "I-I d-don't know what you're talking about..."

"Really?" Perry kept delving. "You've never wondered what became of your father?"

"He was murdered," Elijah sighed, "b-but Mum was always very tight-lipped about it - said it was for my protection a-and now I know why..." He broke off with a shiver. Perry's eyes narrowed. "It was you, wasn't it? Did you kill my father?"

Perry gave a shrug. "No, Elijah. I did not *kill* him. Though over the years, I became increasingly concerned about something he may have said about me! Which is where you come in..." He glanced up at Nathan, as an expression of evil crept across his face. "Your mother has 24 hours to give me what I want. But should she fail, I will allow my friend here, to practise what he does best and yes - you will be in for a lot of pain!"

Elijah hung his head, resigned to his fate. It was in the same moment, he sensed Perry's triumph; the notion, he had finally consummated his deadliest threat.

"Okay Nathan, I think we can let him down for now," he finished icily.

"Yeah, right," Nathan muttered, his voice lowering to a growl, "except there is just one thing I think I owe you..." He reached up to unfasten the chain then paused, glaring at Elijah with an expression of unparalleled viciousness. It was without warning, he drew back his fist and lashed out, delivering a cruel blow to his groin. He casually unclipped the chain.

Elijah crashed to the floor with a gasp before releasing a inescapable wail of pain.

"Oh come now, Nathan," Perry chastised. "That was quite unnecessary!"

"Now he knows how it feels," Nathan snarled. "I've waited a long time for this."

"Fuck you!" Elijah whispered under his breath. The pain that spiked between his legs was excruciating, filling him with hate.

Except he did himself no favours. Nathan reached down, clawed at his shirt collar and yanked him to his feet, practically choking him. "Shut up, you little shit!"

"Enough, Nathan," Perry warned. "He is not to be harmed - not yet!"

"You were the one who wanted him softened up a bit," Nathan grinned.

"Later," Perry snapped. "We have a long night ahead - it's time we moved him."

Nathan's fist was like steel as it closed around his arm. Before Elijah knew what was happening, he was hefted into the air like a rag doll and flung across his shoulder.

Moments later, he had been transported up the steps and into a lounge. He blinked as Nathan dropped him onto a sofa - drinking in the next unfamiliar set of surroundings; a tidy but shabby room where the greying net curtains hung in the window like cobwebs, sapping away the light.

"What now?" Elijah dared to ask, as he cowered against the back rest.

The two men appeared to be putting on their coats.

"We're taking you to my house," Perry said coldly, "where you'll eventually be reunited with your mother. Provided she plays ball, of course!"

"She will!" Elijah blurted. "She'd never let me come to any harm..."

He felt the chill of Perry's eyes before he was hauled from the sofa. "You'd better hope so," he muttered, "otherwise I've got something very nasty in store..." He examined his wrists, which were now chafed and coloured with bruises - he ordered Nathan to remove the cuffs.

Seconds later, he found himself being escorted towards the door and onto a driveway. He blinked, struck with a sense he had seen this sleek, black Mercedes somewhere before. Yet with no time to ponder, Perry was whispering in his ear again.

"Get in the back, duck down and make sure nobody sees you."

Elijah found himself unwittingly being pulled towards the car, where the door swung open.

"Shouldn't be too hard," Perry's voice mocked, "skinny little rat like you..." Elijah numbly obeyed, sliding himself into the back seat, but it seemed, Perry had not quite finished: "and don't you *dare* do anything to draw attention. Try anything clever and I'll tell you what will happen when your mother arrives. You see, my son has always lusted after her."

Elijah turned cold. He already had a sense of how depraved Ben was.

"Now keep out of sight!" Perry kept hissing, "otherwise I will present her to him as a gift..."

Elijah needed no further warning. Nathan started the engine, his cruel face still visible in the reflection of the wing mirror. He took a deep breath, before he folded himself into a ball, covering his head with his arms. The car finally eased its way out of the driveway where for the next few minutes, he sunk into a world of silent oblivion.

10 minutes later, they had arrived in a very different part of London.

Elijah sensed the car being squeezed into a side road where it finally drew to a halt. The window was open. Yet the first thing that struck him was the tranquillity; a silent coolness which reminded him of a park. There was a distinct absence of traffic. He could even hear a ring of bird song.

"Right, we're here," Perry's voice broke into the silence. "Let's get him inside."

Elijah opened his eyes just as Nathan was unlocking the car door - he felt the grip of a fist on his arm as he was hauled out onto the street. He had little choice but to comply - absorbing the image of a small, leafy side street before he was ushered a few yards further and pushed through an iron gate. The towering walls of a house blocked out the sun, filling his locality with shadow. They were in a back garden; an eerie place where nothing grew other than a dark landscape of topiary balls and crisply manicured hedges.

Perry shoved him forwards, filled with a relentless urgency to get him inside the house. They completed the last few yards in silence where the back door opened slowly.

Elijah froze as Ben loomed in the doorway - pale eyes latching themselves to his face. He barely had time to blink before he was thrown into the house and the door clicked shut behind him. He shivered, staring at his new prison with dread - though it appeared to be considerably more luxurious than the last place.

"My London residence!" Perry stated pompously, steering Elijah into a large and beautifully designed kitchen. "Say hello to our house guest, Ben. Any news of Eleanor?"

"She knows what she has to do," Ben smirked. "Hopefully, she'll have checked in by now." He glanced at his watch - it was 6:30.

"Good," Perry nodded. He opened the fridge, extracting a bottle of chilled white wine.

Elijah said nothing. So his mother was somewhere in London - they must have relished breaking the news of his capture. The house was bathed in a glow of soft light though it brought him no comfort. He felt cold - watching in subdued silence as Perry poured out three glasses.

"Here," Perry smiled, handing him one. "A drink to set your mind at ease…"

Elijah took a nervous sip - its clean, crisp flavour was refreshing.

"Did our housekeeper leave a buffet as I instructed?" Perry snapped.

"Oh yes," Ben replied smoothly, "you know Carlotta, she doesn't do anything by halves."

Perry peered into the fridge again; only this time, he unveiled a platter of fine food. His eyes locked with Elijah's. "I expect you're hungry."

Elijah felt the onset of a shiver. He so much wanted to refuse their hospitality - except just as the thought struck him, his stomach betrayed a lengthy rumble.

Perry's smile turned cold. "Come now, Elijah, relax. If it makes you feel any better, we'll leave you alone for a while - now follow me."

The next room he was funnelled into was a dining room. Elijah glanced at the exquisite furnishings in awe; the most beautiful, polished oak table nestling beneath a sparkling chandelier - a wall of mirrors which made the room appear double in size. Trails of shimmering drapes covered the windows; but while the house seemed elegant, it lacked cosiness. The evilness of its inhabitants breathed a chill into the air. Perry guided him into a chair and lowered down the platter.

"Thank you," Elijah answered. His voice was a dull monotone - but he could no longer ignore the appetising feast set before him; a mouth-watering filet of salmon surrounded by a beautifully prepared salad - quails eggs, creamy coleslaw, a pile of buttery, golden potatoes. He picked up his fork and tentatively took a first mouthful.

"Enjoy your supper," Perry said softly. "I'll leave you in peace for now…"

He let his words trail off before he silently withdrew from the room. Elijah heard the click of the key turn and knew he was trapped - and although his new conditions were considerably better than the basement, he couldn't quite shake off his terror; plagued with a sense that they were playing with him.

III

A few miles north, Eleanor too, was settling into surroundings as opulent as those in which her son was being detained. A uniformed porter showed her to her room, yet her heart twisted in pain. This was where it had all begun. The Grosvenor Hotel. It was as if they had come the full circle.

She was unsure what to do at first, wishing there was someone she could talk to. She unpacked her overnight bag before exploring the splendid en-suite bathroom; but its gleaming marble interior brought no solace as she agonised over her son. She eased herself onto the bed, unable to dispel the fear of what he was going through - hit by an involuntary tremor, just as the phone rang.

"Ah, Eleanor," a deep voice throbbed from the receiver, "I gather you've arrived!"

"P-Perry?" she shivered.

"Yes, Perry," he echoed. "You have been a very foolish woman, Eleanor Bailey. I warned you never to cross me and now your precious little boy is about to pay the ultimate price... that is, unless you do *exactly* as I tell you!"

"You know I will," Eleanor croaked. "H-how is he? Please tell me you haven't hurt him."

Perry gave a sniff. "Your boy is fine - perhaps a little bruised from his capture, but he knows the score! We made it perfectly clear what would happen if anything went wrong. He is very scared, Eleanor, as you should be."

She felt a stab of panic, before clutching the bedspread - the slippery satin felt cool between her fingers, yet she had broken out in a cold sweat.

"Please go easy on him!" she found herself crying. "He's only sixteen!"

"I am aware of that," Perry seethed into the earpiece, "though, quite a feisty little soul. I cannot believe he had the gall to swear at my security guard..."

"Your security guard," she repeated. "Not N-Nathan?"

"Yes, Nathan," Perry confirmed, "I do not have to remind you of what he is capable of."

His voice dripped with contempt, Eleanor felt sick.

"Where are you holding him?" she begged. "When can I see him?"

"All in good time," Perry snapped. "If it's any consolation, your son is being held captive in my home with all its luxurious trappings - but that could very quickly change. I will call you again later. But for now, understand this..." his voice thickened nastily. "I have my own people hanging around the hotel to keep an eye on you. You are not to speak to anyone - nor step outside the building! Because if word gets back, that you have betrayed me..."

He did not have to finish; the chilling threat was left dangling as he abruptly ended the call. Eleanor shakily replaced the receiver, paralysed with fear. Memories of her son hurtled through her mind; all she could picture was his gentle eyes, his innocent beauty - never able to forget what Nathan had subjected William to.

The phone rang again. Eleanor opened her eyes, easing her troubled thoughts aside as she reached across the mahogany bedside cabinet to grab it. She was already wondering if it was Perry again - praying she might be connected to her son, this time. Though nothing astounded her more than to hear a soft Irish voice on the other end of the line.

"Peter?" she whispered.

"Eleanor, I couldn't leave things... I had to call. How are you?"

"Peter, I shouldn't be talking to you," she shivered. She closed her eyes - flooded with a sense of gratitude yet at the same time, terror. "How did you get this number?"

"Well, I knew you were staying at the Grosvenor Hotel," his sunny voice piped from the telephone, "so I phoned directory enquiries. I'm sorry - I just couldn't bear for you to be alone."

"Where are you calling from?" Eleanor pressed anxiously.

Peter let out a sigh; his voice turned grave. "I'm a little nearer than you think..."

"Peter!" Eleanor whimpered, "have you any idea how much danger Eli's in?" She let out a sob. "He's being held captive by that monster of a bodyguard. Perry will have no qualms about hurting him if he finds out I've been in communication with *anyone!*"

"You've spoken to him?"

"He phoned. He's got people on surveillance. This could be terrible for Elijah..."

"Eleanor, ssh," Peter whispered. "I am not about to show my face anywhere where they will see me. I have a friend in London looking out for you. You won't know him and neither will they. I've even discovered a way we can communicate - but tell me what Perry said."

His words emanated down the phone in soothing waves, massaging away her sorrow. It was over the next few seconds, she rapidly explained the exchange - wary of spending too long on the phone. Perry had made his intentions clear - and he was planning to call again.

"You can't stay on the phone long," Eleanor finished woefully, "just in case..."

"Say you were ordering room service," he argued, "'cos I've got a surprise. At about 7:00 there'll be a knock on your door - a package. Read the instructions and get back to me."

"How will I know how to contact you?" Eleanor bleated - but Peter had already hung up.

Five minutes later, she was alerted to a tap on the door.

Fearful of Perry's spies, she sprang across the room. Her bare feet were light on the deep pile carpet, making no sound. She paused for one more second, then carefully opened the door. A young man stood before her - no-one she knew. In fact he appeared to be a member of staff; his smile was cool but polite as he presented her with a tray.

"Room service," he announced.

At first glance, it contained a silver domed platter - yet right there, nestling among the napkins, lay a small padded envelope. Eleanor forced a smile, gratefully accepting the tray. She slipped him a pound note and closed the door. Her heart was thumping; thankfully, there had been no-one else in the corridor. Finally a smile touched her lips - the platter contained a round of cheese and pickle sandwiches which could only have been ordered by Peter. How thoughtful! Although she resisted them - intrigued to know what the package contained.

Within seconds, she found herself staring at a small electronic device; it was roughly six inches wide with a tiny numeric key pad and screen. There was even a note tucked into the belt clip. *'Eleanor - in case you didn't know, this is a pager. Use the key pad and call the number written in my message. My own pager will bleep. I'll know when it is safe to call. Leave a number you can be contacted on (if different to the hotel.)'*

She recognised his handwriting, her heart racing faster; so he *was* somewhere nearby! It was with a furious sigh, she grabbed the pager and switched it on. Gradually, the small digital screen flickered to life. Eleanor entered the number in Peter's message and waited.

Seconds later, her telephone rang again. "Hello?"

"You got it then," Peter laughed.

"Peter this is crazy!" Eleanor gasped, "I know you mean well but… there could be someone listening outside my door, right now."

"So we keep communication to a minimum," Peter advised her curtly. "Use the pager whenever you need to talk - nothing more. Just keep me up to date on what's happening."

"Okay," Eleanor sighed. "Just don't do anything risky and *please* keep your head down…" she felt the breath drain from her lungs, every muscle tensed. At the same time, it was lovely to hear a friendly voice. "Thanks for the sandwiches," she finished, her voice cracking slightly.

The moment the call ended, she took a bite out of one of the dainty sandwiches. She had been too numb to even consider eating. Yet she felt faint with hunger, sensing a need to replenish herself as she wolfed down the rest. She could no longer deny, she felt better. At the very least, Perry had divulged that Elijah was being kept in his home - inspired by his talk of *'luxurious trappings.'* She tried to imagine him now, knowing Perry had a taste for the finer things in life - where the only threat left dangling was the hint that his situation *'could quickly change.'*

Elijah consumed his meal slowly, unable to finish it. He couldn't deny, the quality of food was excellent, savouring each delectable flavour as it mingled inside his mouth. But the scene in the basement had stayed with him, striking a fear which lingered deep. It was a feeling that left every muscle braced, his stomach taut, where gradually his appetite had begun to waver.

The door swung open before he was expecting it. Perry stared at him with disdain.

"What's the matter with you, boy?" he sneered. "You've hardly touched it!"

"I-it was delicious - thank you," Elijah stammered, "I'm just not hungry any more."

He despised himself for crawling. Yet what was the point of being cocky? He was completely in their power - a feeling that was reinforced, the instant Nathan loomed in the doorway.

"Get up!" Perry snapped.

Elijah obediently rose, his head swimming slightly. He stole a glance at Nathan who he had never really seen until now. There was something inherently evil about his face - those hard, angular features, matched by splinter-like eyes. They looked almost black - though on closer inspection, he noticed they were a dark shade of blue. He suppressed a shudder.

"Is it okay, if-if I use the loo?" he whispered. "I'm bursting."

"Of course," Perry said icily. "We're taking you to your living quarters."

Nathan retained a firm grip on his arm, before he found himself being dragged up several flights of stairs to the attic. Ben was already up there, his expression smug. But what Elijah saw surprised him; a stunning en-suite apartment whose decor was reminiscent of the mid-eighties - stylish and mono-chrome with an abundance of black ash furniture. The flat was stripped of all personal belongings apart from a few motorcycle magazines stacked along a shelf. He stared at the swivel desk chair in leather and chrome - the double divan in one corner whose sturdy metal frame was screwed into the hardwood floor.

"This used to be my room," Ben smirked as Nathan shoved him into the centre. Elijah caught his breath, his fear spiralling as he spotted the heavy metal cuffs dangling from a robe hook. Ben picked them up and gazed at them lovingly. "Hold out your hand."

With a sigh, Elijah obeyed, knowing that brief respite of kindness was over. His captors had transformed back into their true evil selves; his wrist ruthlessly clamped in iron.

"Bathroom's there," Perry said softly.

Elijah gave a grateful nod - but it was not until he had finished relieving himself, he sensed they had accompanied him here for a reason.

He met Perry's hate-filled eyes. "Time we had a little chat, Elijah..."

They pushed him onto the divan, while Nathan was fixing the end of a chain to one of the sturdy metal bed legs. It was long enough for him to reach the bathroom but no further. He couldn't even see out of the window, never mind escape.

Perry lowered himself onto the divan and faced him. "I have spoken to your mother," he began, "and in a very short time, I will explain what she has to do."

"What's going on?" Elijah pleaded. "When can I see her?"

"Never mind that," Perry hissed. "Tell me what you know about her file!"

"I-I told you - I don't know anything," Elijah shivered. "Mum's always been very cagey."

"You're lying," Perry accused.

Elijah shook his head. "I'm not! My father was killed before I was even born."

"Oh come on!" Perry barked. "She must have explained *some of it* to you! Any normal boy would be curious. I know I would be, now spit it out!"

Elijah sighed, the cogs in his mind working. It was over the next few seconds, he started babbling - anything he could think of that might satisfy them: his father had been a singer, a song-writer and a guitarist - a prominent member of the Dutch band, 'Free Spirit' from Nijmegan... "I-I don't think he was a bad person - a-and I don't know what he saw..."

"Saw?" Perry jumped in quickly. "What makes you say that, Elijah?"

"I-I think he may have witnessed something..."

"I see," Perry sneered, "so you *do know* about the file."

"I know there's a file," Elijah echoed numbly. "Mum wrote down their story. She said it would protect us, but I have never, ever seen it."

Perry's expression turned crueller. He grasped the front of Elijah's shirt, pressing his face close. "Well, I hope you never do," he growled, "because it has come to my attention *exactly* what's in that file..." Elijah turned cold, remembering the caravan; the terrible news of the fire and the theft of his mother's file copy. He stared at Perry in panic.

"Why are you so worried?" he whispered before he could stop himself.

"I want her testimony against me erased once and for all!" Perry ranted. "Now who else have you been talking to?"

"William Barton-Wells, perhaps?" Ben intervened with a sneer.

Elijah spun round, his panic spiralling - he had almost forgotten his presence.

"He said something very revealing on the night of the rave," Ben smiled. "He accused Nathan of 'looking for you,' an opinion you agreed with - now why would he say that?"

Elijah found himself stalling, his mind struggling for answers. It was obvious why Perry had given him the wine. "I-I heard him too," he shivered, locking with eyes with Nathan. "I was nearly grabbed before, remember? Two people identified him - and they were right weren't they?"

"Enough!" Perry barked. "This is getting us no-where. The fact is, we needed you to fulfil our plan. I have waited many years to acquire your mother's file and you were the only bait!"

Elijah struggled in his grip, wilting beneath his glare. So Perry had read the file copy. Their situation could not have been worse.

"It's almost time to speak to your mother again," he finished harshly, "so you had better pray she goes along with my wishes or you'll find yourself straight back in Nathan's basement."

Elijah gulped, unable to escape Nathan's scrutiny. His sadistic smile lingered; and it was the last thing he remembered before they filed from the room, locking him inside.

Dusk was beginning to creep in and the room felt cooler. It was only now, he started to recall what Eleanor had revealed to him: the secret behind his father's killing. *'A future Prime Minister was blown up in a car bomb? And this is what my father witnessed?'* Her file had the potential to expose a terrible truth.

And if Perry obtained the original, he was going to annihilate it.

IV

As time wore on, Eleanor became restless as she paced her hotel room. Peter's communication may have created a breath of reassurance but the feeling was short lived. She wanted to see her son, craving the moment when she would hear his voice - anything to prove he was unharmed! Deep down, she knew what Perry wanted. It was simply a matter of how quickly she could get it.

She momentarily left the room to stretch her legs. Perry might have ordered her not to leave the hotel, yet he couldn't prevent her from wandering down to the foyer - a chance to admire the magnificent architecture, where the tawny, gold pillars and rich carpets brought back reminiscences of the press conference. She found herself unwittingly drawn to the bar. The decor might have changed, though an establishment as fine as this was bound to undergo refurbishment.

She stepped into the lounge which possessed a warm and contemporary atmosphere - breathing in the scent of leather and polished wood, as staff and guests skirted around her. It was only as she began to focus, she became more and more aware of the predatory eyes swivelling in her direction. Eleanor swallowed back her fear. There was no doubt that everywhere she turned, unfamiliar men seemed to be watching her.

The constant stab of eyes unnerved her. Eleanor ordered a drink from the bar, only to disappear as quickly as she had emerged and back to the seclusion of her room, where she had to confess, she felt safer. An unexpected knock shook her out of her reverie. She shot forwards, to find a different waiter hovering in the doorway - a bottle of fine wine balanced on his tray.

"I've had a request to deliver a complimentary bottle of wine to you," he announced.

Eleanor frowned, staring at the bottle with dismay - a rich, burgundy red. There was little doubt in her mind who had ordered this.

"Thanks very much," she muttered and with no choice other than to accept it, she gently lifted the tray from his hands.

Already, she had spotted a tiny envelope resting against the bottle - staring as if in a trance, before she prised it open. It was hand written in a slanted, spidery script. The exaggerated downward stroke of each letter depicted an impatient, almost aggressive mentality.

'Dear Eleanor, I will call you in 20 minutes. In the meantime, enjoy my gift of wine. You may need it, to steady your nerves.'

Eleanor's eyes wandered towards the clock. It was obvious he intended to call at 9:00. Yet his note left her floundering, wondering why on earth he imagined she needed alcohol. Right now, nothing could eradicate her terror for Elijah. She poured herself a glass, holding it to the light where its ruby red gleam was illuminated. She drank slowly, savouring its robust flavour. Yet it only took one glass for the alcohol to surge straight to her head.

Five minutes before the hour, Elijah found himself being dragged down from the attic. Perry awaited him in the lounge. He was enthroned in one of his resplendent oak framed armchairs, observing him with a look of cruel satisfaction. Nathan wrestled him forwards. He hadn't failed to notice a smaller, upholstered chair stationed next to him into which he was unwittingly forced.

"Constrain his wrist," Perry ordered, holding his stare.

Nathan grabbed his wrist roughly which was still shackled in iron; a chain was slipped through the clasp and sequentially used to bind him to the chair arm.

He watched as Perry calmly lit a cigar then picked up the telephone.

"Eleanor!" he announced pompously, "we speak again!"

Elijah closed his eyes, despising the drama he was creating out of this.

"Hello, Perry," a husky voice piped into the room. Elijah blinked - he had left the phone on speaker. "How's Eli? When are you going to let me see him?"

"All in good time," Perry snapped. "First, I want you to know this. A couple of years ago - when I discovered that *cassette* inside our Orangerie, I made an oath. I swore that if you brought me any more trouble, I would make your son wish he had *never been born...*"

"Perry, please tell me what you want from me!" Eleanor exploded.

"You know what I want!" Perry retorted. "You created a file - a very dangerous file which contains some serious allegations. Now tell me where it's hidden!"

Elijah felt a stream of hatred uncoil itself from deep in his heart - listening with mounting horror as his mother meekly surrendered.

"I-it's in a secure bank vault in L-London," she faltered.

Perry fired a glance at Elijah. "So you are to retrieve it!" he ordered. "I will meet you at the hotel, where you will hand it to me - and only then, will you be reunited with your son."

"Alright, Perry, I'll do as you say," Eleanor's voice chimed from the speaker, "and when all this is over, what then? You see - I never meant to cause you *trouble*. I wrote Jake's story to protect myself. Yet no-one in our community feels safe! If I give you my file, can *you* promise we will be left alone in future?"

"Eleanor, you are hardly in a position to bargain with me," Perry laughed. "I'm calling the shots here!" He took a puff of his cigar, blowing a long coil of smoke into the lounge. Elijah's fists tightened, loathing his expression of triumph.

"I am sick of living our lives in fear," Eleanor whimpered, "yet I am prepared to forget everything that ever happened - I realise there will never be any justice for Jake."

"There was never meant to be," Perry said brutally.

"Then leave us be," Eleanor pleaded. "I don't want this threat hanging over us. Can't you understand that? I'm about to give you the one thing you have always wanted..."

"So how can I trust *you*?" Perry snapped, rearing up in his chair. He flicked a lump of ash from his cigar before taking another deep drag. "I've waited a long time for this moment. How can I guarantee that *you're* going to co-operate?"

"You know I will," Eleanor sighed. "You've got my son - his well-being means everything, now *please*, Perry - is it possible I could speak to him?"

"In a moment," Perry muttered, "just as long as you fully understand what will happen if you dare try to deceive me - like drop any clues to the police - or tell your loved ones..."

Elijah felt a strange, dizzying fear. Perry's face was engorged with colour, his eyes like two burning splinters and it was a vision that took him sailing back to the scene in James's bar. *'Don't ever dare to cross me again, Eleanor! You've already seen what I can do!'* This was the question. What was Perry going to *do*, once he had destroyed her file? He had organised the death of his father, but with nothing left to incriminate him, was this the fate that awaited her too?

Perry's head snapped round. "Elijah," he murmured, his voice thick with menace. "Would you like to have a word with your mother now?" He rose from his chair, his eyes never leaving his face as he calmly passed him the handset.

Elijah grabbed it swiftly, his heart charging. In the same moment, he saw Perry flick Nathan a nod - aware the man was still lurking behind his chair. Something was about to happen and it was already making him feel uneasy.

"Mum!" he gasped into the telephone.

"Eli, is that you?" Eleanor said tearfully. "How are you? How are they treating you?"

"I'm fine, Mum," he blurted. "I'm in a house - a beautiful house. I-I've got my own room and I had a lovely meal..." He could hear the tremor in his voice but how could he tell her the rest? He didn't want to think about the basement, Nathan's tools, the punch in the balls - no more than he wanted to described how his wrist was chained to the arm of this chair. Nathan loomed close and taking his hand, turned it over - palm facing upwards. Elijah stared up at him in dread, sensing danger.

"I'm so glad to hear you're okay," Eleanor soothed, "hopefully, this will be over soon. I am going to give Perry my file. All that aside, I can't wait to see you again..."

Elijah felt a stab of fear - watching as Perry took another puff of his cigar. The hatred inside him was boiling now, having long recognised the threat in his words. The man was a monster. There was no doubt in his mind, what was about to happen.

"Don't give it to him, Mum, just don't!" he shrieked. "This is the only thing that protects you! There has to be another way out...!"

Perry snatched the telephone, his eyes blazing. "That was very stupid, Elijah!" he snarled into the mouth piece.

He glared at Nathan, whose grip tightened brutally around his fingers, stretching them out, practically breaking them. Elijah cried out.

"Eli?" he heard his mother gasp.

"I warned you what would happen if either of you tried any tricks!" Perry's voice tolled dangerously, "and this is just a little taster..."

It was without mercy, he plunged the glowing end of his cigar into the palm of Elijah's hand whose agonising scream went on and on.

"Goodnight, Eleanor," Perry whispered in hatred before he slammed down the telephone.

Elijah stared at him in shock, the sobs of pain shuddering out of him. *"You bastard!"*

Perry's hand sliced through the air without warning, delivering a ferocious, back hand blow across his face. His head flew backwards on impact - his chair momentarily wobbling.

"Insolent brat!" Perry roared.

"Why should we give up everything we've been fighting for?" Elijah screamed, "and it wasn't Mum who left the cassette in the Orangerie - it was me!"

"Enough!" Perry retorted, struggling to compose himself. His gaze shifted to Nathan. "Get him out of my sight!"

Nathan was icily calm as he unchained him. Elijah was shaking; the pain in his hand so unbearable, he felt faint - though it seemed, Perry had not quite finished.

"I expected you to be a lot more scared," he whispered nastily. His eyes flashed towards Nathan. "Maybe it's time you told him what *really* happened, on the night you evicted the Barton-Wells pair!"

"I thought we agreed to say no more about that," Nathan sneered.

"We did," Perry shrugged, "but it's his *own* fate he needs to worry about now..."

Nathan's grip tightened as Elijah found himself being hauled up the stairs. Ben materialised on the first floor landing - his face alight with curiosity.

"What the fuck's going on?" he whispered. "What was that scream all about?" he glanced anxiously towards an open window. Elijah was clutching his hand in misery.

Nathan said nothing, jaws clenched like iron as he continued to yank him up the stairs.

"Don't you think Dad's gone a bit far?" Ben added coldly.

"Stupid kid knew the score," Nathan answered, "and now he's made him angry!" He turned and glared at Elijah, who collapsed weakly onto the divan. "You should have known better! When Perry's angry, everyone suffers!"

Elijah let out a sob, his world so dark, he was unsure whether he could take much more. Nathan crept towards the divan. There was something particularly nasty hidden in his expression.

"Please..." Elijah whimpered, as he grasped him by the roots of his hair.

"Shut up!" Nathan hissed in his face. "See - when we rode up to Westbourne House, that night, Ben wanted revenge on the bitch!"

Elijah's face crumpled in agony. "Not Avalon..."

A smile curved Nathan's lips. "She scratched him didn't she? Left him scarred. It was pay back time; a night she was finally gonna get her comeuppance - 'cept that stupid kid brother got in the way. So we decided to have a bit of fun with him instead!" Elijah's eyes shot wide open. "That's right," Nathan smiled, his narrow eyes boring into him. "I screwed him!"

"No!" Elijah gasped in horror. "That can't be true...!"

Memories rained into his mind - never able to forget the state his friend had been in. Elijah knew Nathan had hit him, yet could never understand why William had been in such deep shock.

"He's not lying," Ben added casually. "I made her watch. I confess - Avalon was the one we really wanted. Yet they escaped - I never did get to fuck her..."

"Stop it!" Elijah gasped, clamping his hands over his ears. "Just leave me alone...!"

Nathan released his hold, his face simmering with pleasure. "So now you know," he finished evilly. "Your little friend was no match for us and neither are you..."

Elijah shied away from him, knowing what was coming. Nathan bent down to retrieve the chain, left coiled on the floor like a snake. It was firmly padlocked to his wrist, his imprisonment complete. But he felt too dazed to move - curling himself up on the bed, as the surreal horror of this day finally caught up with him.

Eleanor sobbed into her pillow. It had been several minutes since Perry's call; yet she couldn't drive her son's scream out of her mind. It rang on and on like a siren, tormenting her with ghastly visions. She knew her son. He had been so brave to stand up to them - *if only he hadn't tried to interfere with Perry's plans*. Eleanor grabbed another glass of wine, quaffing it back before she could stop herself. She so desperately needed to talk to someone - then she remembered Peter's pager.

He responded immediately.

"Eleanor, calm down. Tell me what's wrong."

"They tortured him!" Eleanor shuddered into the receiver.

It was over the next few seconds, she relayed every horrific detail - Peter listened carefully, struggling not to interrupt.

"The poor child!" he mumbled in shock. "So you're going to give them your file?"

"I have no choice," Eleanor sniffed, sloshing another drop of wine into her glass.

"So what about your law suit? I suppose that's off too, is it?"

"Peter, my son is being held under the most horrific circumstances... How can I possibly fight them, knowing how much they could hurt him?" She bit her lip, before taking another draught of wine. "I have to do the right thing. Tomorrow, I'm going to phone my solicitor and arrange for the collection of my file. It's the only way I'll ever see him, surely you must understand that."

"Of course," Peter whispered, "I pray you get him back safely, Eleanor."

There was a pause. Neither of them knew what to say any more, knowing the situation had become drastic.

"I have to go," Eleanor slurred. "I'll contact you again soon..."

She slumped back against the pillows, her head muzzy from the wine. She was even beginning to feel sleepy - wondering if maybe the best idea was to drink herself into oblivion; but suddenly the phone was ringing again, dragging her from the bed.

"I had to call," Perry's voice pulsed from the telephone. Eleanor sat bolt upright, almost knocking her wine over. She had never expected any further contact from him.

"What do you want?" she hissed with loathing.

"To see how you are," he drawled, "wondering if you've had long enough to mull over that last conversation."

"How is my son?" she demanded. "What did you do to him?"

"Your son took a cigar burn to the hand," Perry snapped. "He is back in his room now..."

"You piece of shit!" Eleanor shouted before she could stop herself.

He let out a cruel chuckle. "Oh Eleanor, that was just the tip of the iceberg! Elijah knows he's in for a lot worse and this is the reason for my call. Are you going to comply with my wishes - or has your son swayed you in another direction?"

"Of course I'll comply," Eleanor retorted. "Do you really think I could live with myself, if he was forced to suffer any more pain? I'll get you the file, you sadistic bastard!"

"Good," Perry muttered in a voice which oozed satisfaction. "In that case, I will meet you tomorrow evening at the Grosvenor Hotel - I believe they have a very nice bar. Be there at 5:00 and make sure you have your file with you."

"Alright," Eleanor finished bitterly, "there is just one thing I beg of you - don't leave Eli's hand untreated! Burns are serious. Couldn't you at least give him some antiseptic cream?"

"You expect me to show him mercy?" Perry responded, his voice soft. "Very well. I intend to speak to him anyway - now get some rest, Eleanor and I will see you tomorrow."

Perry's steps were heavy as he plodded up the stairs. Of course, he had guessed Eleanor wouldn't waver in her decision and yet he had to be sure. All along, he had hoped the boy's scream would be the last thing she heard. The sound would play over and over in her mind, all night, ravaging her darkest hours with nightmares. Right now though, he needed to make one final check on his prisoner. Nathan followed - though on this occasion, he carried no weapons, just a mug of hot chocolate laced with sedatives, a first aid kit and a wash bag.

Perry unlocked the door and strutted into the room. His charge was huddled on the bed, his head bowed, arms curled around his knees. He did not look up. Perry felt a heady flood of excitement - there was no denying, the poor boy looked terrified.

"Hello again, Elijah," he greeted him coolly.

Nathan lowered the mug onto the bedside table, dropping the other items on the bed. He hovered by the door, while Perry lowered himself to the mattress. The boy gave an involuntary flinch, adding further fuel to his spiralling sense of power.

"Not so cocky now, are you?" he drawled. "Learnt your lesson, have you?"

He detected a nod, though still Elijah refused to meet his eye. He was nursing his hand which Perry noticed was wrapped in damp tissues. He let out a sigh, reaching towards him. Elijah instinctively shied away, yet his back was pressed against the wall, allowing him no retreat. Perry clasped his chin and tilted his head back, intent on making eye contact. Still, his eyes flitted sideways, sparking with terror.

"Look at me," he ordered him.

Elijah blinked before reluctantly meeting his stare.

Perry fought against the urge to smile. "That was a foolish thing to do, Elijah. You should have known better than to jeopardise my plans. I've fought long and hard to get hold of your mother's file. So don't you *ever* try a trick like that again, do you hear?" He felt the flush of colour rise in his face, as his victim clung to his silence. Refusing to be ignored, his grip tightened. "Well?"

Elijah gave another nod.

"Show me your hand," Perry ordered.

"Please..." Elijah whimpered, "d-don't hurt me any more!" He gingerly held out his palm.

Perry peeled back the tissue, where a most appalling scorched and angry crater was exposed; the surrounding area reddened, as if it had absorbed some of the heat. Perry tutted.

"Nasty! But then you really should have kept your trap shut, Elijah. You may be interested to know, I had another word with your mother. She seemed to think you needed medication." He let go of his chin, momentarily rummaging through the first aid kit. "I brought you this," he added, handing him a tube of ointment. "See - I can be merciful."

"Thanks," Elijah whispered, taking the ointment.

Perry watched him tentatively smear some of the cream into his palm. He winced - but then the pain must have been awful. There was no doubt, his spirit was crushed and it was a feeling he wanted to keep reinforcing.

"There is nothing you can do, Elijah. Tomorrow evening, it will all be over. I will be meeting Eleanor and she has assured me she will give up her wretched file, once and for all!"

"I'm sorry," Elijah choked. "I just couldn't let her do it!"

"There is no point apologising," Perry answered. "Just don't try any more tricks..." his eyes narrowed cruelly, "or you'll be back in that basement faster than you can blink - and next time, there will be no mercy. Nathan has my full consent to do his worst..."

An expression of intense fear spread across Elijah's face. His bottom lip trembled, just as a tear trickled down his cheek. Perry felt a surge of power, a feeling he enjoyed immensely.

"Not so tough, after all," he smiled, "in fact, you're just a frightened little boy." His voice thickened in a way which bordered on perverse - though he could guess what he was thinking. Physical pain, he could handle - but the final veiled threat, his abuse could turn sexual... it had elevated his fear to an entirely new level.

Chapter 24

I

Eleanor had no idea where she was, at first. A tiny beam of light shone through a crack in the curtains. It cast a soft glimmer across the bedspread, causing her to blink and turn. Yet what she saw snatched her breath away - staring in amazement at the sleek waves of auburn hair trailing across the pillow, bright against the crisp white linen. Jake opened his eyes and smiled.

Eleanor froze. She studied his face where every detail was accentuated - his clear white skin, his beautiful bone structure... "Jake?" she gasped, reaching towards him.

"It's okay, my love," he murmured, folding her into his arms, "everything will be fine..."

She closed her eyes and breathed deeply, savouring the musical slur of his Dutch accent. A warm and loving feeling radiated from her core and her limbs tingled. She curled up against him like a kitten.

"Oh Jake," she whispered, smoothing the hair away from his face. It slipped through her fingers like silk - just as she remembered. "What are we going to do?"

Their mouths came together in a lingering kiss and for a few precious moments, Eleanor clung to the sensation. His lips felt like velvet against her own. Then finally, he broke away. His eyes seemed dark in the shadow of the hotel room and he was staring at her intensely.

"We have to protect our child even if it means sacrificing ourselves..."

"Eli," Eleanor smiled teasingly, "his name is Elijah - we have a son, Jake."

She ran her hands over the bumps of his shoulders, absorbing the dream-like melody of his words. Yet at the same time, they brought an element of fear - the notion, their child was in danger. Eleanor sat bolt upright.

"Eleanor, listen to me," Jake insisted, grabbing her arms. "You have to save him. We swore we would protect him and time is running out. Forget about me - he is the one who matters."

"What are you talking about?" Eleanor whimpered. "Of course I'll save him!"

She stared at him in panic, wary of the hazy early morning light rolling across the bed - it illuminated the greenness of his eyes. They flashed a multitude of colours. It was almost as if she had forgotten she was about to offer up her file to Perry; and once it was destroyed, he would have no qualms about killing her. Eleanor nodded, finally understanding Jake's warning.

"I'm sorry, Jake - I so much wanted justice for you."

"I wanted justice for Enfield," Jake responded sadly, "but it's too late for us. It is our son who has to live on to fight this..."

She felt the onset of terror - Jake's voice was starting to fade.

"I love you so much," she mumbled.

"And I love *you*..." he finished tenderly, pulling away from the sanctuary of her bed.

The scene dissolved in a swirl of mist and the next time Eleanor opened her eyes, he was gone. She let out a gasp, her hands feeling frantically for any lingering sign that he might have been lying there - but the empty space in the bed felt cold.

"Jake!" Eleanor cried out.

It was no use. Jake was gone, he'd been missing from her life for almost 17 years and the entire scene had been a dream. Eleanor stared at her surroundings, her senses restored - recognising the elegant hotel room with its beige walls and heavy damask drapes. Her mind flipped back to her current life and to Charlie, who she loved dearly. He had been so desperate to rid their lives of Perry's evil - but they had been fools! They should never have tried to fight him, he had always been too powerful. He had obliterated Charlie's life to ashes - pursued James's ancestral home like some kind of war lord. Even as a united group, they still weren't strong enough. Eleanor sighed, knowing they had reached the end of the line.

She dragged herself out of bed, creeping towards the bathroom for a shower. Her head felt groggy and thick, her mouth dry. She had drunk too much red wine and it had left her stomach burning. The pounding spray of hot water was soothing as it bit into her skin. Eleanor soaped herself all over, using the complimentary miniatures of shower gel and shampoo. By the time she stepped out of the cubical, she felt clean and revitalised.

She dressed quickly, stepping into a casual tunic and trouser suit, made from soft, draping fabric. By the time she had dried her hair and applied makeup it was 8:00, but she saw no point in dithering - desperate for a cup of strong coffee, she began to make her way slowly downstairs.

Several business men populated the restaurant, impeccably groomed in their sharp suits. The area felt pleasantly light and spacious - the creamy walls adorned with the most intricate plaster mouldings. One of the uniformed waiters glanced up coolly, then disappeared in the direction of the foyer. Eleanor frowned before another materialised in his place, his smile friendly. He ushered her towards a table and scrawled down her order. Yet she felt uneasy - having glimpsed the suspicion in the first man's eyes. Was it possible Perry's spies included the hotel's employees?

From another side of the restaurant, a man's eyes seemed to follow her. Eleanor turned her chair sharply, to block out his stare. Right now, she didn't want to speculate how many of these strangers were monitoring her, conscious of her mission. The waiter returned, pouring freshly brewed coffee from a jug. Its pungent aroma wafted pleasantly past her nostrils bringing a clarity to her thoughts. She was going to have to telephone John Sharp and arrange a meeting. It would mean leaving the hotel - but then, how else was she supposed to retrieve her file?

Her stomach felt queasy, though at the same time, she was desperately hungry as she sank her teeth into a buttery croissant. As far as she knew, Perry was picking up the tab. Filled with a sense, her days were transitory, she requested smoked salmon and scrambled eggs.

By the time Eleanor wandered through the revolving glass doors, her strength was restored, knowing it was time to contact John. She wandered a little further up the street. Several shop fronts loomed opposite before she saw something which froze her in her tracks. A slender young man shimmered in one of the wide glass panes. He possessed the same long hair as Jake, slung casually back in a ponytail - its auburn sheen illuminated like a flame in the early morning light. No! It was impossible! Eleanor rubbed her eyes, wondering if she was hallucinating.

She spun round but there was no-one there. The next time her eyes shot back towards the shop window, the refection too, seemed to have vanished. Yet he had looked so much like Jake!

A sense of fear crawled over her. She would never forget something Rosemary had said about the fine veil which hung between the physical and spirit world. Eleanor felt a shiver, struck with the possibility she was being drawn to the other side. Perhaps this was the reason Jake had visited her in her dreams - it was as if he was beckoning her.

She fought off her panic and quickened her pace. By the time a bright red telephone box had sprung into view, she was practically running.

"John!" she gasped into the handset. "I need to see you urgently! Is there any chance you could fit me in for a meeting - preferably this morning?"

"Of course," John muttered anxiously. "What is it? What's wrong, Eleanor?"

There was no time to explain. Eleanor was fighting tears as she ended the call, unable to believe she was doing this! She wasted no time. She rushed towards Victoria tube station to make her way to Holborn - and 20 minutes later, she found herself staring at the bank of white offices which had become so disturbingly familiar throughout this entire crusade.

John shook his head, his expression grave. "I can't believe you're asking this of me! Are you absolutely sure, this is the best course of action?"

"How easy is it to retrieve my file?" Eleanor persisted.

"I have it here," John confessed. "I removed it from the bank vault, as soon as we agreed to instigate legal proceedings. David has been making notes from it…"

"I'm afraid we are going to have to drop the case against Perry," Eleanor added softly.

John looked crestfallen, his sad, brown eyes reminded her of a Labrador.

"How can you give up when we're so close to bringing that fiend to justice? What's going on, Eleanor?"

"It's my son, John," Eleanor replied, her voice wavering with the first hint of tears. "He's in danger. He faces a terrible ordeal if I don't go through with this."

"Dear God," John gasped, shuffling in his seat. "Isn't this the exact scenario Mr Theakston threatened, all those years ago?"

"Yes," Eleanor nodded, "but Theakston only ever *voiced* that threat. It came from Perry. He was always the invisible force behind it."

"Didn't you ought to inform the police?" John urged her.

She shook her head. "It's too dangerous - but there is just one more favour I need to ask you. I've been communicating with someone in private. Is it okay if I page him your office number?"

"Of course!" John sighed, spinning from his chair.

Eleanor fumbled with the pager, tapping in the telephone number. Within a few seconds, the phone rang.

"It's good to hear your voice," Peter said warmly. "How is Elijah?"

"I don't know," Eleanor sighed. "Hopefully, I'll see him later. Perry promised we'd be reunited. Once I've given up my file, of course."

"You're meeting up with him?" Peter's voice piped from the telephone.

"Yes," Eleanor replied in a resigned tone. "He asked me to meet him in the bar."

"What time?" Peter asked.

Eleanor paused. "He-he said 5:00," she faltered, "why?"

"Do you have any idea where they're holding your son?" Peter kept probing.

"Perry's house," Eleanor gasped, "but that could change - you're not about to do anything stupid are you? After everything I've said? They really hurt him, last night!"

"Eleanor, calm down," Peter whispered. "I would never do anything that would compromise Elijah's safety, I swear…"

"Then go home, Peter," Eleanor finished, feeling her anguish take root. "Comfort Charlie and the others - tell them we'll be home soon!" Those earlier thoughts of mortality slipped back to her; that mirage of Jake. "I have to go through with this. If there's any opportunity to make contact, I will. Though please understand that once I'm with Perry, it's impossible."

II

Elijah gradually stirred at 9:00 - roughly around the same time as Eleanor had been standing outside the snowy white offices, reminiscing over her days with Jake.

He too, opened his eyes, feeling muzzy. The last thing he remembered was the chill of Perry's stare - Nathan leering in the background - the inescapable sting of tears. Everything that followed was hazy. Then he remembered the hot chocolate. Perry had been insistent on making him drink it, before he lapsed into a heavy, dreamless sleep. Obviously, it was doped with something.

Light flooded in from the attic window, so dazzlingly bright, he was forced to squint. He sat up where the clank of a chain reminded him he was shackled. Elijah clenched his teeth, staring at the chain with contempt. It was in the same instant, he noticed his bandaged hand. Memories of his ordeal came tumbling back to him. He turned cold, unsure what to do; except there was nothing he could do. He was a prisoner - and although this sunny attic room was undeniably chic, it was nothing short of a glorified prison cell.

He eventually struggled from the bed to use the bathroom; grateful the chain at least, allowed him that freedom. He couldn't help wondering how long his enemies had been plotting this, as the fragments of memory drifted back; the ambush in Bevington Gardens. It was the first time he had really thought about it, now wondering how they could have known he was there. But Perry had spies crawling all over Rosebrook - and his defences had been low that day, exacerbated by the grumpiness of his supervisor. He remembered popping to a nearby shop for a sandwich. Maybe this was the pivotal point, where someone might have recognised him.

He flinched to the sound of footsteps. They had obviously cottoned on to the sound of the toilet flushing, a notion that compelled him to slither back under the satin duvet cover.

The door swung open and he opened his eyes drowsily.

Perry towered over him with an air of supremacy, mug of tea in one hand and some dark item of clothing draped over the other. "You're awake then!" he barked.

Elijah shielded his eyes with his arm, to block out the glare of sunlight - oblivious to the bruises blemishing his delicate skin. Perry observed him stonily, then tossed the garment towards him.

"Put this on," he added coldly. "It will hide the bruises!" He placed the tea on the bedside cabinet. "I trust you slept soundly."

"Y-yes, thank you," Elijah mumbled, acknowledging the tea.

He wriggled himself upright, wincing from the grip of the hand cuff. He was still wearing a thin, short sleeved shirt, wondering what had happened to his jacket and satchel. Perry reluctantly unfastened the manacle so that he could dress, studying him like some sort of specimen. Elijah pulled off his shirt, where the aftermath of his beating was gradually revealed. It had left him black and blue - though in the light of his more recent ordeal, he had almost forgotten about it.

"What happens today?" he dared himself to whisper.

Perry gave a sniff. "You're to keep quiet and behave yourself! Just remember that Nathan and I are here to keep an eye on you. Ben is at work.

He's a stock broker, you know. I asked him to purchase some clothes for you and drop them in later."

Elijah slipped into the long-sleeved, black polo shirt he had given him, but of course it was miles too big - hanging off his willowy frame like a sack.

Perry displayed a sneer. "What size are you?"

Elijah gave a shrug. "Extra small. 12-14 generally fits me. H-has anyone seen my jacket? I was wearing it when I was captured."

"We've got it, have no fear," Perry drawled. "Nathan stuffed all your belongings into a carrier bag before he chained you up in his basement..."

His eyes glittered cruelly. Elijah felt a flutter of fear, not wanting to be reminded of that hellish place.

"I'll send him up in a while," Perry taunted. "You'll no doubt be needing some breakfast. Is there anything else you want - something to read, perhaps?"

Elijah swallowed, dreading the thought of seeing Nathan. Though, right now, it seemed they were at least, being a little more humane. He took a gulp of air. "Yes, please," he whispered timidly, "and i-is there a chance I can have my sketch pad? It'll be in my satchel..."

"A sketch pad," Perry muttered, eyes narrowing. "I see no harm in it. Just as long as you're not up to any tricks, boy."

"Not at all," Elijah placated him. "Drawing's my hobby. It'll make the hours go faster."

Eventually, Perry left him, his attitude frosty as ever. Elijah watched him go as the fear churned inside him - traumatised by the events of yesterday, where the burn on his hand still throbbed.

He sipped his tea slowly. Yet it seemed only minutes before a second set of footsteps materialised from the staircase - they lacked the solid stamp of their predecessor, definitely more of a swagger. Elijah huddled in terror as the door banged open and his worst nightmare loomed before him. Nathan's muscular frame blotted out the light, the stubble of bleached hair illuminated.

"Here!" he barked, hurling his sketchpad onto the bed, "just don't do anything stupid. Much as it would be my pleasure to drag you back into my basement, Perry doesn't want the hassle!"

Elijah flinched, reluctant to meet his eye.

"I brought you breakfast," he added with a snarl, "not that I'm your fucking servant."

"Ta," Elijah said coldly. He massaged his discoloured wrist, just waiting for him to go.

The moment couldn't come quick enough. Elijah stared at the Danish pastries set down on the bedside cabinet and gobbled them down hungrily, grateful for subsistence. At least his head had cleared a little by now, as he flipped through his sketchpad. Those last drawings of Bevington Gardens tugged his heart - how he wished the day could have ended differently. Yet he didn't really feel like sketching, filled with a hankering to explore his surroundings.

It was the first time he had really thought about his location; balancing on top of the divan and stretching himself out as far as the chain would allow. He felt a tug of resistance, straining to drag himself a little closer to the window. A line of dark rooftops was only just discernible behind a spray of foliage. Elijah attempted to creep forwards one more inch but the restraining chain impeded him. He craned his neck. He felt like an animal chained up in a zoo!

With a sigh, he retreated. If only he could nudge the bed a little closer but it was impossible. He gazed at the heavy screws pinning it to the floor with dismay, then flopped against the pillows. He took a sip of water. It was only as he settled the cup down onto the cabinet however, he noticed a tiny drawer. Elijah opened it instinctively, driven by his unrelenting curiosity; surprised to see it contained a few personal belongings - cotton buds, a pot of hand cream, condoms and lastly, a leather manicure set. He extracted it numbly, conscious of his grubby fingernails - he saw the usual array of scissors and nail clippers, yet there in the centre lay a long metal nail file. Its pewter handle possessed a flat end. Elijah felt a tiny ray of hope as he ran his finger over the edge.

His mind started ticking as he carefully gouged the soil from under his fingernails. He never did have a chance to clean his hands after that gruelling day of gardening - and yet he was struck with an idea. Elijah slid down from the bed and stared at one of the leg brackets. It was with no hesitation, he positioned the flat end of the nail file into one of the screw heads then carefully tried to turn it. It wasn't easy. Compared to a real screwdriver, the file was flimsy. It skidded out of the groove, inspiring him to try again. Elijah focused harder - until at last, the screw started to turn a little. He released a gasp; and with an entire day ahead of him, he systematically got to work.

Progress was slow. His captors checked up on him every hour. It was almost as if they expected him to find some way of deceiving them, thereby compelling him to get a few sketches done. He set to work, thankful it wasn't his right hand they had burned. At first, he concentrated on a sketch of Bevington Gardens; honing in on one of the ornamental urns to recapture its detail - from the trailing fronds of ivy, to the circles of moss that clung to its timeworn stone.

Perry returned with a couple of newspapers, rewarding him with further inspiration. Finally, he delved into Ben's Harley Davidson magazines - captivated by the photography. One of the images displayed the most sexy female model; her dark hair streaming out like a Valkyrie against a fiery sunset. Elijah periodically worked on this sketch throughout the day, adding more shading, accentuating every detail; from the gleam of lipstick, to the powerful bike on which she sat provocatively astride.

Come lunchtime, it was Ben who breezed into the room, armed with a carrier bag which contained a brand new set of clothes.

"Nice," he murmured lasciviously, snatching up the sketch pad.

Elijah watched him cautiously, though his very presence chilled him. He felt inside the bag. It contained a pair of black jeans and an olive green, checked shirt in soft brushed cotton.

"Matches your eyes," Ben added, his smile taunting. "Do you like them?"

"They're great, th-thanks," he faltered, wishing he didn't have to be so polite to this psycho.

He watched him go, waited a few minutes, then got straight back to work on the screws.

Predictably, Perry visited him twice more. A second interruption arose just moments after Ben had left. The unexpected crash of steps alarmed him, forcing him to slip the nail file inside his sock before rolling onto the divan to launch himself into the pretence of sketching again.

By the time he delivered sandwiches, he was left for another hour - but the hands of the clock turned faster. 4:00 came quicker than he expected and on this occasion, Perry lingered.

"Right, time to get yourself cleaned up and changed!" he snapped, unlocking the manacle. "I'll be bringing your mother back soon and I expect you to look presentable."

Elijah was ushered into the bathroom, where he showered and washed his hair. It was good to feel clean - conscious of Perry lurking on the other side of the door. Eventually he emerged, a fluffy towel wound around his slender hips, his hair damp. His ribs and collar bones stood out like iron bars. Perry eyed him with scorn then passed him the second bag Ben had delivered, which contained new underwear. Elijah used the towel to shield himself from the constant bore of his eyes while he quickly changed - relishing the feel of the fresh clean fabric against his skin.

"That's better," Perry muttered. "I wouldn't want her to think we've been neglecting you." He smiled coldly. "It's time I met her. So you'd better pray, she has the file in her possession!"

Elijah said nothing. He felt numb, oblivious to how this terrifying scenario was going to pan out. It was over the next hour, Ben and Nathan kept him under almost constant scrutiny, denying him any further opportunity to continue his quest. The day was fading fast. He had succeeded in unfastening the screws on just one bed bracket - two on the next. Yet he was barely half way through his task - and with another fearful evening yet to unfurl.

As 5:00 drew close, Eleanor changed into a new dress. It had caught her eye as she dragged her way slowly back through London, unable to resist the draw of the lovely fashion shops. There was something about this elegant black dress that had appealed to her - three quarter length sleeves, padded shoulders and a long skirt. It enhanced her slender figure; not dissimilar to the evening gown she had worn on the night of the press conference and almost designed to depict the fatalistic nature of the evening.

It was in the next few minutes several things happened.

Eleanor's hair tumbled loose as she floated into the lounge. She momentarily lingered on the threshold, charmed by the decor; the bar carved from rich wood, complimented by sumptuous leather and velvet furniture. Stepping up to the bar, she froze as she met the pale blue eyes of a man propped up on a stool, reading a newspaper. He possessed a flat, deadpan face, dusted with freckles, his dark hair slightly tousled - and yet she had definitely seen him before. Eleanor swallowed. She retreated from the bar just as Perry materialised in the doorway.

She braced to a standstill again - clocking his sinister face. His eyes contained a demonic, almost crazed glint and for once, his face was devoid of its ruddiness.

Eleanor had no idea what had just occurred. Perry had been wandering towards the hotel; jolted by the vision of someone who looked disturbingly familiar. A slender youth had been ambling past those same beige walls, hands in pockets. He observed his swinging stride, the shimmering auburn ponytail. Perry clutched his chest, feeling the onset of panic - unable to deny who the figure reminded him of: *Jansen!* His heart began to palpitate, bringing a rush of giddiness.

By the time he strode into the hotel, he felt well and truly unhinged - and there lingered his second nemesis. Perry clenched his teeth as his eyes clashed with Eleanor's.

She shot another glance towards the man at the bar, observing his smirk as he returned to his newspaper. That was it - he was clearly one of Perry's look-out posts! She gripped her bag as Perry took those first few menacing steps towards her, conscious of her file tucked inside.

"Perry," she greeted him coolly, forcing her lips into a smile.

He gave her a nod - though the insane loathing in his expression hadn't faded. "Eleanor," he drawled. He loomed close as if to peck her cheek. "Do you have it?" his voice hissed in her ear.

Eleanor recoiled - assailed by the earthy fragrance of his aftershave which discharged so many memories. This was not going to be pleasant. Already, she felt sick with nerves.

"Yes," she said softly. "So what now?"

"Sit down," Perry ordered. "I think this calls for a glass of wine, don't you? This is, after all, a momentous occasion…" he stood back and observed her - his eyes travelled wolfishly over her figure. "A new dress. Enjoyed your little shopping excursion, I see."

She read the disdain in his face, wondering how much she resembled her 17 year old self - from the glossy waves of dark hair to the sweep of her dress, as black as a Raven's wing.

"I thought a special occasion deserved a special dress," she murmured in a voice of silk.

His square-jawed face clenched like stone before he turned to the bar. "A bottle of your finest red," he snapped.

"I would prefer white," Eleanor taunted. "Why not just order a glass?"

For once, Perry didn't argue. He reiterated her wish - then turned and took her arm, steering her into a corner seat. It was far enough away from the other guests to communicate in private.

"So you obtained your file - from your solicitor, I understand?" he said.

Eleanor blinked in shock. So someone *really had* been tailing her.

"Give it to me," his voice hammered relentlessly.

"All in good time, Perry," she murmured. "I want to see my son first…"

She broke off as the waiter sashayed over to their table, laden with drinks - a hefty glass of red for Perry whilst a delicate flute of white lingered next to it.

"Thank you," Eleanor said politely. She took a sip of the cool wine before her eyes drifted inexorably back to Perry's. "How is he?"

"Elijah is well," Perry informed her bluntly. "Though I am sure I don't need to remind you how quickly his situation could change. Now stop playing games. I want to see that file. I have to be sure you're not about to trick me."

With a sigh, Eleanor opened her shoulder bag and pulled out the file - a professional looking document, spiral bound in black leather. She positioned it carefully on her lap so he could see it, then idly flipped back the cover. The fateful lines of her original script were revealed. Perry leaned forward and squinted to get a closer look: *Jake saw someone parked by the roadside, right opposite the minibus hired to take Mr Enfield's party home…'* An angry flush of purple seeped into his face.

"I gather, you've already read it," Eleanor stated boldly.

Perry lifted his eyes. "You played a very clever game," he whispered. "This file would have ruined me if it had gone public." His expression was cold, as he turned the page - his hand momentarily grazing against her own. He glanced at the news clippings before proceeding to the next section: the press conference with NME. "Where did you get these notes?"

"NME had archives," Eleanor answered him frankly.

Perry knocked back his wine, draining almost half a glass in one swallow. He was clearly agitated, Eleanor realised - knowing it would be dangerous to provoke him.

"Perry, I'm sorry," she whispered. "I discovered a trail of clues and I had to follow them. I never intended to incriminate you in quite the way this file suggests..."

"You went to see Evelyn Webster," Perry broke in icily, "do you really expect me to believe, you were simply 'following clues?'"

"Yes!" Eleanor gasped.

"Finish your wine," Perry hissed under his breath. "There seems little point in wasting time. If you wish to see your son alive and unharmed, then I suggest we move on to my house! And maybe I can get rid of this malicious document once and for all!"

Eleanor didn't hesitate, now fearing for her son's safety. Maybe if she allowed Perry to destroy her file then at least, Elijah could go free. As for herself... she had kept her part of the bargain. She had given Perry what he most desired and with some luck, maybe they could disappear for a while and pick up the threads of their lives. Eleanor left the hotel with no concept of the future that lay ahead, as the crowds buzzed all around them.

Perry sidled up close. "Take my arm," he ordered.

Eleanor quietly obeyed as his elbow jutted towards her. Obviously, he didn't want to raise suspicion; although it took only minutes to reach Victoria Station car park where his black Mercedes awaited them. Eleanor slid into the passenger seat, her mind on Elijah. The last 24 hours had been awful - she could feel the waves of love pounding through her even before Perry started the engine, yearning for the moment when she would see him. She closed her eyes, paying little attention to her locality as the car purred into life.

Perry's face was granite hard as he turned into Buckingham Palace Road. He shot one last fleeting glimpse towards the Grosvenor Hotel and caught his breath, his hands almost slipping on the wheel. He gripped it harder, forcing himself to concentrate as the traffic converged on all sides. Yet as he peered in his driver mirror, he could still see him; that same auburn haired character, lingering right on the corner. He could feel his eyes boring into him.

A cloud of dots momentarily swirled in his vision. He paused by the traffic lights, yanking on the hand brake. He felt almost faint. Eleanor looked at him sharply.

"Is everything alright, Perry?" she frowned.

He glared directly ahead. "No-one followed you here did they?" he spat.

"No!" Eleanor gasped. "Absolutely not! Why? Have you seen someone?"

"It's nothing," he said icily. He screeched away, the moment the lights changed.

She had no idea of his numbness - a sense that Jake's ghost was hovering. For several minutes, they drove in silence. Veils of ice swept over him, where he couldn't quite shift that last troubling vision. He was too preoccupied to notice a white transit van which had been tailing them ever since they had left the car park.

Eleanor kept quiet, wary of the crash of her heart. She was thinking about Peter; he had told her he was *a little nearer* than she thought, despite her warnings. For now, his pager was hidden in the hotel room. She stared ahead, observing the changing backdrop. Perry turned left and headed towards Pimlico - the traffic thinned out, drawing them into an area that was strikingly residential. Everywhere she looked, she saw wide streets lined with cars - row upon row of elegant, regency terraces until finally, Perry turned into a side street.

A stunning square rolled out before them; two terraced rows of the most grandiose, creamy white houses flanking the opposite sides of a park. Perry eased his car into the curb, next to an enclosure of black railings. Eleanor peered through the gaps, clocking the lush foliage and the scattering of mature trees, just as he extinguished the engine.

"Come along now, quickly," he urged her.

He wasted no time, circling around to the side of the car to let her out. Eleanor paused, absorbing the beauty of her surroundings - dimly aware of Perry taking her arm again, before she was steered towards the steps of one of the houses. It featured the same uniform, pillared entrance as the rest. She had already spotted box balls outside the windows, where topiary seemed to be the prevalent form of horticulture.

Perry unlocked the door and thrust her into a hallway - the click of their footsteps echoed. So this was his London residence? The very place where her son was imprisoned. They kept walking. A moment later she was propelled into a lounge. Eleanor froze on the polished wood floor - barely able to take in the furnishings as her eyes fell upon Ben. He was lounging in one of the oversized sofas, his face twisting into a leer.

"Hello, Eleanor," he drawled, hauling himself upright. "What an absolute pleasure." Eleanor turned cold, hating the way his eyes crawled over her.

Perry lingered behind her. She was trapped - and yet another set of footsteps was emerging from the stairs before Nathan strolled into the room. Eleanor let out a gasp - there was no mistaking those rough-hewn features; the glare of his eyes seemed almost deranged.

She spun to Perry in outrage. "You left my son in the custody of these two *monsters?*"

"Eleanor, calm down," Perry smirked. "Your boy is quite safe. Neither of them have laid a finger on him - isn't that right, boys?"

"Your son is quietly relaxing upstairs," Ben added softly. "He's been sketching for most of the day. Quite talented, isn't he?"

"I want to see him," Eleanor snapped, ignoring Ben completely.

Perry turned to Nathan. "Perhaps you could bring him down now."

Eleanor sighed, dismayed to imagine the nightmare this had been for him. Ben wandered up to them, his eyes never leaving her. She started trembling, she just couldn't help it; unavoidably dwelling on Avalon - Lucy - knowing exactly what this man was capable of. He slid his fingers through her thick hair, sweeping it away from her neck.

"Don't touch me," Eleanor shuddered, cringing away from him.

Perry let out a mocking laugh. "Did you not realise, my son had developed quite an obsession for you? I even warned Elijah. I said I'd let him *have you*, if he dared step out of line..."

"Did you now?" Eleanor said tightly, golden eyes blazing as she glared at Ben. "And?"

"I'm disappointed," Ben drawled, "I was looking forward to having the pleasure of you to myself for a night - but Elijah chose to behave himself."

Eleanor swallowed, feeling her insides churn. Every second ticked by slowly - until finally the sound of footsteps materialised again.

Her son in all his innocence appeared in the room. For a moment they just stared at each other. A lump rose painfully in her throat; she couldn't deny he looked clean and well-groomed, dressed in new clothes which he definitely hadn't possessed before. Yet there was something in his demeanour which seemed *broken*. His eyes harboured a haunted look, his face pale - the trace of a bruise lingered beneath his eye where Perry had hit him. The manacle around his wrist registered, as did the bandage on his hand. Nathan gripped the end of the chain with a look of cruel satisfaction. Her son reminded her for all the world, of a frightened bear cub being paraded around a circus ring.

"Eli!" she sobbed, stumbling forwards. She coaxed him into her arms as if she feared he might shatter. "Oh my God, are you okay...?"

Elijah sunk into her embrace, his fear so pronounced she could almost smell it. "Mum," he mumbled into her shoulder as she clung to him.

"How very touching!" Perry sneered.

Eleanor momentarily broke away. "What the hell did you do to him, you bastards!" she shouted. "He looks terrified!"

"Your son has been threatened," Perry said icily. "He is well aware of the ordeal he faces should you *dare* go against my wishes. Fact is, you've seen him. Now give me that file!"

It was with no further delay, Eleanor pulled the file from her bag and rammed it into his hands. "There! Do what you want with it, destroy it for all I care!"

"Good," Perry muttered, teeth gritted. "I'm pleased we've finally reached an agreement. Now let us relax, a while. We must have another drink, some refreshments..."

They eventually found themselves in the dining room where another sumptuous buffet had been laid out; fresh salads, quiche, accompanied by

427

slices of succulent turkey breast.

Elijah shivered, recalling the previous night. There was no denying, the food was delectable. But it in no way compensated for the terror he was experiencing. Eleanor sipped her wine nervously as if fearful of Perry's looming shadow. Another hour dragged by painfully.

The moment Ben cleared the plates away, Eleanor seemed restless. She wanted to explore the garden and maybe the park. Though naturally, Perry forbade it; determined to shield his captives from the eyes of his neighbours.

"Can't I at least see his living quarters?" she bleated. "I just want to get some picture of what it's been like for him here..."

In the end, Perry saw no harm in it, releasing Ben to pursue his own pleasures. He needed to hit the town, visit one of his sleazy clubs - anything to divert his lust from Eleanor. He had never wanted his son to become involved in this kidnap and the more he thought about it, the more he realised, Ben had become increasingly antsy over the last few hours. Finally, they reached the attic. Perry stationed Nathan outside the door, knowing his presence would unnerve them.

"What a stunning room," Eleanor said numbly, as Perry dragged Elijah across the floor and chained him to the bed post. She clocked that flash of fear in his eyes - just as Perry was binding the chain around the leg, clipping it into place with a padlock.

"I appreciate your wish to be alone," Perry said in a voice of ice, "but I cannot allow it! You may converse freely with your son, Eleanor, but do not think for one moment I am going to abandon you. There has been quite enough scheming..."

He stepped away from the bed and moved to the other side of the room. He shot a cursory glance out of the window, Eleanor noticed, before lowering himself onto the sofa.

She released a shiver as she settled herself down next to her son.

"It doesn't matter, Eli. At least we're together. I've missed you so much. Now let's see some of these sketches. You do realise, you haven't told me about your last day..."

Elijah gazed back at her in desolation, then slowly began to describe it; from the moment he had stepped inside Bevington Gardens - to the terrifying ambush on his exit.

"I thought I asked that *Naomi* not to leave you on your own!" Eleanor breathed.

Elijah spoke quietly. "I wasn't on my own, I had a supervisor. His name was Mr Morecroft." He ran his fingers lovingly over one of his sketches. "Naomi said it was supposed to be a treat. I showed her one of my sketchpads - she thought I'd love it there..."

"But it looks so remote," Eleanor gasped.

"If anyone's to blame, it's me!" he confessed bitterly. "I couldn't wait to leave - especially when Naomi let me off early. I wanted to get to Peter's meeting. I should have asked Mr Morecroft if I could use the phone - arrange for someone to pick me up. I just wasn't thinking..."

"Ssh," Eleanor soothed. "You were grabbed by a gang of thugs, Eli, how can it be your fault?"

She stroked his cheek, feeling her heart melt with love. History had almost repeated itself. This was how it had begun with Jake; the same form of capture!

He seemed reluctant to say much more, although Eleanor sensed he was hiding something. She tended to his hand, insisting he take off the bandage to aid its healing; where the atrocity of the wound brought a dizzying rage to her senses.

"How's Charlie?" Elijah blurted quickly.

"Charlie has no idea what's going on," Eleanor sighed. "I left a note - I told him we decided to run away." Tears welled in her eyes. "I'm sorry, Eli."

Their conversation had started to dwindle. They had so much to say - but it was impossible to relax with Perry sitting there. Elijah slid into her arms again, sensing their time was nearly up. It was a feeling that was reinforced, just as Perry rose to his feet.

"You've had quite enough time for now," he announced crisply. "I wish to share a few private words with your mother, Elijah."

He clung to her fiercely, reluctant to let go. "Please..." he mumbled, as Perry swooped close.

"It's okay, Eli," she whispered, planting a kiss on his forehead. "Perry's right - we need to talk. Hopefully, I'll see you again very soon..."

The final vision of his face haunted her - pale as a ghost, his eyes dilated with terror. For that moment, he had looked so much like Jake. Memories of her dream sailed back to her: *We have to protect our child. Even if it means sacrificing ourselves...* ' Perry had her file; the copy *and* the original but would it be enough to secure them their freedom, *as well as* their safety?

IV

"Who else have you told?" Perry began coldly.

They were back in the lounge where the silence was eerie. The glittering pendants of an overhead chandelier cast a spray of clear gold light. Eleanor turned to him.

"Perry, this has always been *my* secret. I never wanted to put anyone at risk."

"You're lying," Perry sighed. "You spoke to James Barton-Wells. Why else would he have given you a page of his diary? Or told you about that *meddlesome* woman?"

"Evelyn," Eleanor said dreamily. "Okay, James was curious. After that confrontation, he knew straight away that you and I had history. He begged me to explain it." She shook her head sadly. "If only you hadn't showed up, that day! I might never have recognised you!"

"So you told him!"

"About the press conference?" Eleanor nodded. "Yes, I'm afraid I did and this naturally led us to a conclusion; maybe you were the man Jake saw on the day of the car bomb."

"So you spoke to Evelyn," Perry accused dangerously.

"I'm sorry," Eleanor whispered in fear. "I just had to know."

"Why?" Perry demanded.

She let out a sigh, fearful of what to tell him. "I was devastated by what you did to James and his family. To Charlie's. It all came back to me at James's funeral! You had to be stopped and for some silly reason, I thought I held the key. If I could prove you were the man behind Jake's murder, then maybe it would give me an edge..."

"You intended to bring me to justice?" Perry's voice lashed.

Eleanor paused. How could she confess, she had begun legal proceedings? It would be like signing her own death warrant. "I hoped I'd never have to. My secret file was only ever meant to protect us. If I could gather enough evidence, then maybe you'd back off." Her eyes narrowed. "Why Perry? Why did your family have to be so *evil*? Take James's kids - you destroyed their lives! No-one was safe, you just had to keep hurting people."

"I had to protect myself and *my* family," Perry hissed back.

"So that's why Ben got himself hooked up with the criminal underworld is it?" Eleanor challenged. "You see, I always knew Eli was in danger..."

"Capturing your son was the only way I could be certain you would give up your file," Perry hissed. "Have you any idea of the risk *it* posed? A sword of Damocles! I already know what it feels like to be threatened - I had to get rid of it!"

"So we've reached a truce have we?" Eleanor challenged, clocking his carved, cruel profile. She gripped the arm of her chair, heart thumping. "You have my file, Perry - you can finally destroy all the evidence I ever found."

"What is there to stop you making another?" he contested icily.

"I won't do that," Eleanor sighed. "The last few hours have been hell. Do you honestly think I would put my son through this again?"

"So you're prepared to drop it," Perry taunted, "despite everything you know about me?" Eleanor could hear the cynicism coiling into his voice.

"Strange though it seems, Perry, nothing is going to bring Jake back." She touched his pendant where all of a sudden, the stone felt lifeless - it was as if his very essence had been drained out of it. "The question is, are you going to let *us* go?" she added fearfully.

"Seems I have little choice," he sneered. "Though I'm sure I don't need to repeat my warning. You are never to cross me again!"

Eleanor found herself nodding. He had won! How Charlie and the Barton-Wells kids were going to handle this, she didn't know. All that mattered was Elijah's safety. It was the only hope she could cling on to - though regrettably, his next words chilled her.

"You may return home, Eleanor, but the boy is to stay a little longer."

"What?" Eleanor squeaked. "I thought we had a deal..."

"Ah yes, a deal," his voice grated. "Yet how can I be sure you won't go straight to the police? Do you really expect me to trust you after you've gone to *so* much trouble to plot against me?"

"Perry, you have my word," she whimpered, "Elijah's suffered enough. Please let him go!"

Perry gave a shrug. "Elijah is my insurance. I realise *you* understand the need to stay silent, but does he? He said something very disturbing, you know - he confessed that *he was the one* who left that cassette in the Orangerie. Now why do you suppose he did that, eh?"

"Eli knows nothing!" Eleanor protested. "He only *suspects* you were involved in Jake's death!" her world crumpled to misery as she assimilated the polished elegance of this house; yet it represented nothing but a cold, harsh prison. "You can't do this," she sobbed.

"Elijah needs to know the score," Perry sighed, "so I wish to detain him for another week. He will not be harmed - I might even show him around London, take him to a few art galleries. Come nightfall, however, I will work on his fear. You see, I have to be sure that he too, never repeats what happened this week."

"How?" Eleanor whispered. "He is already terrified of you, Perry."

"Terrified, all the while he is my prisoner," Perry smirked. "The moment he's back home, things will be different. He needs to understand my power - which inevitably means threatening someone *he* cares about."

"Who are you talking about?" Eleanor shivered.

Perry turned to her, his silver eyes calculating. "Avalon! I will never forget the night of the rave. There was definitely something between them; holding hands, gazing at each other like a pair of love-sick teenagers - and of course, we *had* to mention the night of the eviction. Nathan told him everything. It nearly drove him crazy..."

Eleanor shook her head as the dark reality unfurled. "No!" she spluttered.

"I saw that dreamy expression in his eyes, every time we mentioned her," Perry kept taunting. "I think your son is in love, Eleanor! Everyone has an *Achilles* heel!"

"How can you be so cruel?" she breathed.

"People will do whatever it takes to guard their loved ones," Perry finished triumphantly. "It worked on you. You fulfilled your role very well, my dear and now it is time for you to leave."

Eleanor could barely move - her golden eyes steeped with anguish. Perry smiled inwardly, as he momentarily left her to ponder. The next time he appeared, he was carrying a tray, laden with two glasses of brandy and a mug of hot chocolate for Elijah.

"One last drink to bolster your courage," he drawled, handing her the glass. He watched with pleasure as she sipped the brandy - observing the tremor in her hand. "Drink up! I'll escort you upstairs to say goodnight to your son."

Eleanor rose shakily, before taking another slurp of brandy. Perry raised his glass, then tipped it down in one go - he emitted a satisfied sigh, waiting for her to do the same.

By the time he led her up the staircase, he could feel a slight flutter in his heart as he prepared himself for the final stage of his game plan. Eleanor put up no protest. She seemed to have accepted his decision, as she dragged herself up to the attic floor. Nathan was still stationed outside the door, his smile filled with mockery. Eleanor lowered her eyes. Perry could sense her desolation. Who wouldn't feel intimidated by this giant of a man, knowing what he was capable of and young Elijah was still very much at his mercy.

"Mum!" Elijah shrieked. He wriggled across the divan towards her before the yank of the chain restrained him. "What's going on?"

Eleanor gazed at him in despair. A tear plummeted down her cheek. "Eli," she began softly, "Perry has agreed to let me go - but you have to stay a bit longer..."

"No!" Elijah exploded. He fought against the chain again, his arm reaching out to her.

Eleanor glided forwards and scooped him into her arms. "I'm sorry," she gasped, her voice husky with tears, "it seems, Perry doesn't trust us. Please darling, just go along with this. The sooner you accept it, the easier it will be for both of us."

Elijah stared at Perry in outrage.

He placed the mug of chocolate next to the bed. "Your mother is right," he snapped. "She played her part well - but I have to be certain *you* will keep quiet. When you return home, people are bound to ask questions. They'll want to know why you disappeared for a week and this is going to be the scenario."

He lowed himself onto the divan, invading their personal space. Deep in his heart, he knew the boy would be a problem. He could see it in his face - his eyes blazed with hatred.

"Let's say, you were feeling rebellious," Perry continued. "You were *pissed off* about the way the rave ended. So you took flight to London, went on a jolly and stayed in a fancy hotel. Several days later, you finally saw the error of your ways and came skulking back. There was no ambush and no kidnap; and there will be no further mention of *my name* in connection with your father's death! Do you think you can live with that lie?"

Elijah's face twisted into a frown - his forehead scored with lines. "How am I going to explain this?" he protested, holding out his hand.

Eleanor stared at it, her heart pumping faster. It was obvious, he'd be left with a terrible scar.

"I'm sure we'll think of something," Perry drawled, "but for now, I suggest you go along with my wishes. Your mother has finally seen sense which is why I'm prepared to let her go. It's just a few more days, Elijah - after which time, you may continue your life as normal."

Elijah stared at Eleanor, his face ashen. There was a spark in his eyes that alarmed her; it was almost as if he had realised, something far more sinister lurked behind the veil of Perry's intentions. He was shaking his head, his grip on her arms tight.

"M-mum," he whimpered, "don't go..."

Eleanor lifted her eyes, staring directly at Perry. "Does my son have *anything* to worry about?" she levelled at him.

"No, Eleanor," Perry smiled benignly. "You're to return to the hotel and collect your things. Stay another night if you wish! I'll give you my phone number." His eyes locked with Elijah's. "You can speak to her again in the morning."

"Goodnight, Eli," she whispered, hugging him. "Drink your cocoa and try not to worry. Do whatever Perry tells you - I'll see you again very soon."

It seemed he wouldn't let go, the tears falling freely from his eyes as he gazed sadly back at her. He traced his finger tips over her eyebrow and down her face. Eleanor could remember Jake doing this once. It was almost as if he was trying to memorise every detail.

But Perry's patience was beginning to waver. He shot a glance towards Nathan, summoning him closer. It was with no hesitation, he strode forward and seized Eleanor's arm.

"Please!" Elijah started sobbing, the squeeze of his fingers tightening.

Eleanor smiled at him dreamily. "Hush now, Eli," she murmured. "Don't make a scene... I love you very much." She kissed him tenderly, her lips brushing against his cheek. Moments later, she found herself hauled from the room, her arm ensconced in Nathan's iron grip.

Elijah meanwhile, heard the click of the key in the lock and his whole world sank into desolation; plagued with a sense, he might never see her again...

Perry's face betrayed nothing as he picked up Eleanor's file. He dropped it into a drawer for now, to read again later - but first he had to deal with the woman. He closed his eyes as a deluge of thoughts stabbed at the core of his fear - reliving the moment he had viewed its ruinous contents. There was no question in his mind what *really* had to be done tonight. Eleanor had to die.

He turned and gazed at her, forcing a smile. "Are you ready, my dear?"

"Mmm - yes, Perry," she murmured. "Maybe I *will* spend another night in London. I'm very tired…"

Perry's smile intensified - she had no idea that her brandy had been heavily spiked with sedatives. Her head would be feeling quite leaden by now and in a very short time, she would barely know what was happening to her.

"Nathan will drive you to Victoria," he added coolly.

The words momentarily brought her to her senses. Her eyes flickered with panic. "No, not him, Perry - please," she mumbled. "Couldn't you just phone for a taxi?"

"I'm afraid not," Perry sighed. "I can't run the risk of anyone knowing you were here. Not even a cab driver. Now pick up your bag and follow me."

Eleanor did as she was told as Nathan loomed in the hallway. She looked uneasy. Even now, Perry hovered on the brink of a decision.

"He is not about to molest you, have no fear," he continued. "His orders are simply to take you back to the Grosvenor Hotel."

"Okay," Eleanor sighed. She brushed a hand over her forehead. He witnessed the same flash of fear in her eyes, as she stole another backward glance.

Only then, did Perry hesitate. He felt a twist of pain, wondering if he dared go through with this. She was a very beautiful woman. Charlie would be heartbroken, poor man! And what of Elijah? As soon as he received word of the unaccountable 'disappearance' of his mother, there would be a raft of suspicion. Although his future too, hung in the balance.

Perry had lied. Elijah would remain here for a lot longer than 'a week.' He was probably never going to set foot outside this house again. Perry experienced a final tremor of anxiety - recalling the mysterious, auburn haired man who had flitted in and out of his vision; Jake's ghost. The image served as a warning. If he went through with this murder, he ran a risk. His days would be forever haunted, his mind tortured.

Perry looked into Eleanor's eyes one last time. She may have possessed an unworldly beauty but she was lethal. She was the thorn that had gouged into his heart, more than Jake Jansen ever could - he had made his decision.

"Good-bye, Eleanor," he whispered. She didn't seem to notice the icy sweat that had broken out on his forehead. He glared at Nathan. "Take care of her," he added icily.

He gave a subtle thumbs up, feeling like an emperor - one more roll of the dice would seal Eleanor's fate. Another second passed - he jabbed his thumb downwards, just as she was staggering into the car. Nathan understood the gesture and smiled.

Eleanor's head rolled back against the head rest as Nathan pulled out of the square.

She felt so sleepy now, she could barely keep her eyes open. At the same time, it was impossible to shake off her fear; conscious of the man sat braced in the driver seat. His muscular frame seemed especially threatening, the chiselled planes of his face like stone. This was Perry's right hand man, his deadliest thug and she was completely in his power.

She forced her eyelids apart, trying to stare at the road signs. The words blurred into meaningless squiggles - the street lights swaying. Eleanor blinked, unsure where they were even heading now, as Nathan steered his car out of Pimlico and headed south towards Vauxhall Park.

Their journey continued in a tight knot of silence.

Nathan cruised his car across Vauxhall bridge where the inky waters of the Thames lurked below. She didn't even seem to notice. He shot a glance in his wing mirror, conscious of the continuous tide of traffic - mindful there may be police around. Though fortunately, he saw none.

The car edged deeper into the maze of streets where his own house awaited them. A few youths loitered on the corner, kicking a beer can around like a football; other than that, there was a comforting isolation to the area - still a few cars around but for now, Nathan ignored them. He eased his car into the driveway and killed the ignition.

Nathan turned and allowed his eyes to crawl over the motionless figure slumped next to him. He took a deep breath, knowing what had to be done. The moment he slid out of the car, he strode quickly round to the passenger side, opening the door. He leaned in and grasped Eleanor's shoulders, then dragged her from her car seat.

She let out an incoherent murmur as he forced her onto the path. She was just conscious enough to stand - if anyone asked, he would say she was drunk. Once again, his eyes darted towards the road, just to be absolutely sure no-one was lurking. He thought he heard a shuffle of footsteps. Nathan braced himself, waiting. Still, no-one appeared. Wasting no time, he tightened his grip and marched Eleanor towards the alleyway which led into a small back yard. The echo of her shoes seemed unnaturally loud - Nathan quickened his pace, desperate to get her hidden from view before anyone knew they were there.

A square of lawn was barely discernible beneath the cloak of stars, the brick walls of the house blotting out every last trace of street light. Nathan hauled Eleanor across the grass. He was heading towards a stone sink fixed in the furthermost corner of the lawn - it was filled with aquatic plants and murky water. No-one could ever have known that he and Perry had already discussed this scenario; the notion that Eleanor's death would be quick and clean with no incriminating marks. Drowning her would be easy - especially in her befuddled state.

Once he had dropped her lifeless body into the depths of the river

Thames, this was going to look like a suicide. For a moment, Nathan faltered. This was a first; he had never killed another human being. He felt a sudden charge of excitement - teeth clenched as his face twisted into a sadistic grin. They had finally reached the stone sink, where he thrust her to her knees. Waves of pleasure pounded through him - God, he even had a hard on! Nathan could have laughed, as he curled his fingers around her soft neck, already toying with the idea of what it would be like to shag her, whilst he was drowning her.

The moment passed, his smile vanished. No - there was only one job he needed to concentrate on right now and that was to end Eleanor's life, before any further distraction got the better of him.

Eleanor moaned, dimly aware that something was wrong.

Seconds ago, they'd been in a car - now suddenly it was as if the entire world had spun on its axis; the cold, suffocating darkness, the sensation that she was kneeling and finally, the cold, damp grass beneath her palms. She jerked, just as Nathan's hand around her neck tightened and her head was plunged into the icy, stagnant water. Her limbs flailed as he held her - one final, frantic struggle as the water gushed down her throat and into her lungs. Nothing made sense any more. She even thought she saw Jake's face again. It hovered in the tunnel of her mind like a tiny, welcoming light before the world hurtled into oblivion…

V

In another corner of London, Dominic watched with disdain as Ben Hampton came prancing out of the club, arm in arm with some blonde, before slipping into a taxi. He narrowed his eyes, waiting for him to disappear - then turned back to the establishment known as 'Scarlet Moon' whose neon lit sign bled into the brickwork with a sinister red glow.

He forced his hands into his coat pockets, knowing exactly who he wanted to talk to. It was unusual for Dominic to visit the city on a Friday but tonight, he had decided to abandon his own club - infuriated by the absence of his most popular DJ for a third week on the trot.

Dominic paid the entrance fee and strode into the club. His eyes tore through the crowds. It was a sleazy joint at the best of times, a magnet for every lawless toe rag. The air was foggy with cigarette smoke, the shadows dark. Captured in the spotlight, he could see a scantily clad dancer weaving herself around a pole. But Dominic wasn't here for the entertainment. He threaded his way around the dance floor, eyes like lasers as he scanned every corner - then finally, they found their target. Dominic saw Alan Levy before he spotted him and it was with no hesitation, he forced his way through the crowd to get to him.

He was lounging cockily in a horseshoe of leather seating. The cut of his waistcoat suggested a designer label, as did his two-tone silk shirt. He glanced up, just as Dominic approached his table and for a moment, the two of them surveyed each other.

Alan gave a twisted smile. "Well, fuck me! Would you 'Adam and Eve' it! Dominic Theakston!" He stretched out his hand which Dominic firmly shook.

He patted the seat next to him with a look of defiance. Dominic clocked the cigarette dangling from his fingertips and lastly, the brawny West Indian man stationed right next to him.

"'Dis man gonna be any trouble, boss?" the man grunted.

Dominic resisted the urge to laugh; with his wraparound dark specs, medallion and unsmiling face, he reminded him for all the world of 'Mr T.'

"Nah!" Alan grinned, taking a drag of his cigarette. "This is the guy my dad used to work for! Used to be one o' London's top men. What brings you to this neck of the woods?"

"Just a word, Alan," Dominic said icily. "See, I've got me own club now - nice little gaff in Rosebrook. Bella's - named it after me daughter but that ain't the point. This is about Angel, who happens to be my best DJ."

"Yeah, sorry about that," Alan sneered, "but that kid works for me!"

"Alan, I've known you since you were a snotty-nosed kid," Dominic muttered, his voice lowering dangerously, "all I'm asking is for you to cut him some fucking slack! He's a good kid. I gather he was involved in a bit of drug dealing - but you can't just drag him back to London."

"Yes, I can," Alan smiled. "That kid's mine. I planted him in Rosebrook to suss out their dealer network which I now supply. Thing is, he overstepped the mark! Pissed off some of the people I work for - and that caused a bit of shit."

"The rave," Dominic nodded knowingly, "and who are you working for?"

Alan ground his cigarette into the ashtray. Suddenly, he looked furtive. "Not sure I wanna tell you that," he responded coldly.

"Stop pissing around, Alan," Dominic sighed, his voice soft as it brushed past his ear. "It's that cock-sucker, Ben Hampton! Just saw him leaving..."

Alan's eyes flashed as he shot round to glare at him. His colossal, black body guard was already braced and about to stagger to his feet, but Alan held up a restraining hand.

"Don't bother to deny it," Dominic smirked.

"What's it to you?" Alan hissed, his pale eyes threatening.

"It's me who gave him your name, you twat," Dominic confessed. "Never imagined you'd end up as fucking partners! What's he got you working on now?"

Alan sagged into his chair. "Thing is, Dom, he hob-nobs with a fuck lot o' them rich bastards! Yuppies who like a bit of 'Charlie.' We've been shifting tons of the stuff and making a fuckin' fortune! Is that so wrong? So, he asks a few favours in return…"

"Like breaking up a rave?" Dominic pressed coldly, "those were your boys, weren't they? You must know they attacked Angel. Beat the shit out of him!"

"He shouldn't have got involved," Alan argued. "Bad luck, them lads came from some skinhead gang he pissed off a year ago. I dug him out the shit. He landed 'imself right back in it. Ain't my fault! As for all the other stuff - happens Ben's old man went right behind my back, there."

"What *other stuff?*" Dominic probed, keeping his voice even. "Come on Alan, you can tell me. This ain't gonna go no further."

Alan smirked where Dominic sensed a sudden evilness. He wasn't that different from himself at that age; he knew he was a nasty piece of work - and couldn't resist bragging.

"The boys torched some caravan in the village," he scoffed. "Seems old Hampton 'ad a few scores to settle. Last I 'eard, they were involved in some kidnapping malarky…"

Dominic felt every muscle in his body clamp with tension. "You what?"

Alan laughed, enjoying his reaction. He lit another cigarette. "Don't ask me what it's about! Just some kid, Hampton's been after for a while now! Word is, they got him!"

Dominic clenched his teeth. "And you went along with this?"

Alan shrugged. "Ain't got nothin' to do with me! They roped in the boys - that's all I know."

"Was Wadzinski involved?" Dominic kept fishing.

"Maybe," Alan sniffed. "Anyway, 'nuff said. Can I get you a drink?"

"Don't bother," Dominic snapped, lurching to his feet. "Said what I came to say - just want me fucking DJ back. Do you have a problem with that?"

"I'll think about it," Alan smiled. "No reason he can't keep 'is job! He can commute can't he?"

Dominic gave him a nod, followed by a slap on the back, then made his way out of the club as rapidly as he'd fought his way in.

He found himself lingering in the brightly lit quarter of China Town before he even knew it, his mind ablaze. There was only one 'kid' Perry had ever been after and that was the Jansen boy. It sounded as if the bastard had finally succeeded which didn't augur well.

For the first time in his life, Dominic felt torn down the middle. On the one hand, he wanted payback for that bastard, Hampton. On the other, he was consumed by his own *personal* vendetta against Eleanor as well as her bloody file!

Dominic headed through the streets, engrossed in thought. He had no idea where Perry lived but he had a pretty good idea where Nathan did, having scrutinised his gym membership - guessing this was the most likely location they were holding the boy.

Chapter 25

I

Elijah opened his eyes to find himself trapped in the same contemporary attic suite. Today there was no sunshine glaring through the window. The sky was as cheerless and black as the clouds swimming in his head. He guessed they must have knocked him out with sedatives again. His mouth felt dry, his senses groggy.

He struggled into a sitting position where the room felt chilly. He started to shiver. Then finally, he recalled the events of the previous evening. Elijah let out a gasp as he dragged himself out of bed. He was wearing nothing but a thin pair of cotton boxer shorts, his skin dotted with goose pimples. He dressed, straining his ears for any sound. The whole house seemed uncannily quiet - where yesterday there had been movement. Yet at the forefront of his mind lingered the worst fear of all; where was his mother? Perry had sworn she would ring.

Elijah tugged against the chain, his heart racing - it was as if something ominous was lurking and he couldn't quite put his finger on it.

Struck with a sense the house was empty, he downed a mug of tap water and quickly retrieved the nail file. He had tucked it inside one of Ben's magazines, praying they wouldn't find it and to his eternal relief, it was still there. He slid to the floor and got to work, concentrating on his task. After nearly an entire day of practice, his nimble fingers worked quickly until he had unfastened every last screw. He paused for a second, where the stark silence was reassuring.

Elijah took a swallow and grasped one of the metal bed legs. He gave it a gentle shove.

It moved. His heart could have burst with joy. Now all he had to do was carefully ease the frame across the floor, little by little. It was the only way he was ever going to reach the window - then at last, he might be able to attract someone's attention.

Seconds later, he felt his heart sink as the boom of the front door echoed from below. Elijah caught his breath - icy jets of panic shot through him as he carefully began to nudge the bed back. Deep down, he dreaded the thought of his strategy being discovered. The ordeal of the last 36 hours had rooted itself deep inside his mind, where the memory of Nathan's basement delivered an immediate groundswell of fear. Elijah pressed his eyes shut. He could still picture his ghastly array of weapons; never able to forget the pain from Perry's red hot cigar tip. It was a concept that turned him cold, forcing him to abandon all hopes of escape for now - especially as the familiar thud of footsteps began to advance up the staircase.

Perry had in fact, been awake for some time. He couldn't relax, his emotions in shreds.

He too, had been reflecting on the events of last night, from the moment Eleanor had left to face her subsequent doom. He was surprised he felt so icily calm about it. Yet he had settled down with another brandy, resigned to read her file, until he had inevitably stumbled across that final section; the crime report in reference to Jake's murder, followed by the most alarming addendum, ruling out Dominic to be the killer. Pain spread across his chest like fire. This was a twist he had never expected.

The rest was a blur. He could vaguely remember lighting a fire in the grate. It was with no further duress, he dropped Eleanor's contentious file right into the heart of it, watching as if in a dream as the flames greedily devoured it. Pages curled like leaves, the flames dancing from blue to orange. They were reflected in the sheen of his face as an expression of intense loathing swam across it. He had fallen asleep in his chair shortly after, then finally shuffled off to bed.

It was around 1.00 in the morning when Ben had returned. Perry could have smiled, guessing he had hooked up with that sluttish girlfriend of his, Sasha. Ben had been relishing the prospect that Eleanor would spend the night here - but that in itself would have been risky.

Come morning, everything seemed different. Perry opened his curtains to a hostile, thunderous sky. He paced around for at least an hour, downing cup after cup of strong coffee - every nerve stretched tight with tension. He had hoped Nathan might have called but the eerie silence mocked him. Eventually, he took a walk around the square in the direction of the shops; a trip to the delicatessen to replenish the day's food supplies.

Conscious Eleanor would be dead by now, he always knew this day would be difficult. By the time he ambled back into the square however, he was plagued by a different sense of fear - mindful of several unfamiliar cars parked along the curb, which included a white transit van. Perry felt the grip of tension. He thought he knew this neighbourhood pretty well. But worse was to come as he snatched a cursory glance across the park; and there, materialised a familiar auburn haired youth.

Perry ground to a halt. He could see him through the railings, embraced in a cloud of foliage - a vision guaranteed to send him into a frenzy of panic. He turned and rushed up the steps leading to his own front door, then threw himself inside, slamming it behind him. For the next few seconds, he could barely move, giddy with shock - and he remembered the boy.

Perry's hands shook as he carefully unpacked the groceries. He downed a glass of red wine almost without thinking - knowing he needed to get a grip before he faced Elijah.

The alcohol momentarily numbed his senses. He checked the answering machine - dismayed to hear a few innocuous messages. They included one from Rowena; demanding to know when he was returning to Westbourne House. Perry clenched his teeth. Still nothing from Nathan! He might have called if only to leave a message.

He eventually plodded up the staircase, his mood flipping from overwrought anxiety, one minute, to fury the next. He paused outside the door, listening for any signs of activity - then barged into the attic where the sight of Elijah shimmered in front of him.

He was fully dressed and sprawled across the divan, flipping idly through one of Ben's magazines. The moment Perry entered, he looked up. His face seemed pale - abruptly reminding him of Jake's ghost again. He struggled painfully into a sitting position.

"Good morning, Elijah," Perry said stiffly as he placed a tray of tea and pastries down on the bedside cabinet.

Elijah gave him a nod. "Thanks, M-Mr Hampton... um, has there been any word from Mum yet? D-do you know where she went last night?"

With any hope, a watery grave, Perry thought evilly. He forced a benign smile. "Your mother stayed another night at the hotel. I expect she'll be on the train by now."

Elijah lowered his eyes. For now, he seemed satisfied with his explanation. "What's going to h-happen to me today then?" he added sadly.

Perry sucked in his breath: *blasted boy with his confounded questions!* He felt the heat pour into his face as he glared down at him; clocking his frightened young face - that chilling resemblance to his father. It was impossible to shift the last sighting from his mind - possibly no more than a fragment of his imagination and yet the boy's questioning eyes begged for answers.

"I haven't decided," Perry snapped. "Right now, I suggest you enjoy your breakfast and keep quiet. I have to go out." Elijah frowned as he began to back towards the door. "My son is around to keep an eye on you," he added coldly. "I'll visit you again in a while."

Perry closed the door - reassured that Elijah was secure inside his prison as he resolutely turned the key and made his way downstairs. He could no longer ignore that sharp tug of instinct. Nathan *still* hadn't contacted him. He was beginning to feel irritated. It was with no further hesitation, he stepped outside and climbed into his car, intent on visiting his house in person. Maybe the man had committed the deed, gone out and got himself blind drunk - but he just *had* to know the truth.

Perry was not the only one plagued with fear. For Elijah too, the 'not knowing' was unbearable. It hadn't taken long to register that something was wrong. Perry had been pale when he had first intruded on him; there had been a few snappy words and then his face had turned that thunderous shade of purple. The fury in his eyes served as a warning where right now, Elijah was too frightened to work on his escape plan; the consequences of being discovered would be awful!

He nibbled his pastries in silence. His stomach churned but he couldn't seem to find an appetite. The same worries tore at his mind and for the next hour, he didn't dare move.

Eventually, Ben made his acquaintance - though he too, seemed jumpy as he marched up to the window, glaring down at the square.

"Is something wrong?' Elijah plucked up the courage to say.

"Fuck knows!" Ben whispered through gritted teeth. "Dad left a note, telling me to check up on you. Not that I need this shit!" He spun round and glared at him, his eyes cold. "I never wanted to be involved in this, you know!"

"S-so, why d-didn't you just say?" Elijah muttered nervously. He bit his lip - he despised Ben more than anyone yet sensed he was on the verge of revealing something.

Ben let out a mirthless chuckle. "Get real! When my father wants something he usually gets it! And he was determined to get his hands on *you*. D'you know, I even feel a bit sorry for you. My father can be a bastard..." He gave a snort. "I heard you scream. I was worried, someone might have heard and called the cops. They could be staking the place out right now..." he shot another glimpse out of the window. "There's a lot of cars down there."

Elijah frowned, his heart skipping a beat. He was already thinking about Perry again, wondering if this was the reason for his volatile mood.

"On the other hand, they're probably Dad's spies," Ben added nastily. "He's got men crawling all over London, you know - men you wouldn't want to be acquainted with!"

Elijah froze. "Do you have any idea what's going on?" he mumbled.

"Not sure," Ben taunted, "but you're going to be kept prisoner for a while yet, so get used to it! Do some sketching or something. In fact, do one for me!" He dipped into his pocket, fishing out a photo and tossed it onto the bed - watching with amusement as Elijah turned it over.

He flinched, startled by the image of a glamourous blonde wearing a pair of stiletto boots and nothing else. She was poised before the lens, legs splayed wide open, labia and clitoris shamelessly exposed in the glare of the flash. Elijah felt his cheeks burn with embarrassment - it was like something out of one of William's porn magazines!

"Bit strong for you?" Ben jeered, "how about this one?" A second polaroid was flung across the bed; same girl, only this time she was lying on her front where the sight of her soft buttocks didn't seem quite so offensive. "She's my girlfriend and she can be a right slut! So if you don't mind... I could give it to her as a present."

"Okay," Elijah agreed, picking up the photo. "I-I can certainly give it a go..."

"Good," Ben finished smugly, "in that case, I'll be downstairs, chilling out to some music. How long is this likely to take?"

Elijah sensed his spark of opportunity. "About an hour," he said wistfully.

He was left in blissful solitude - still a little numb to move, as the fear for his mother surged back to him. On the other hand, could he really afford to waste this precious hour?

A distinct thump of rock music resonated from several floors down. Elijah leapt to his feet where any thoughts of Ben's explicit photos were forgotten. He rammed the nail file into that final cursed bed bracket again and started untwisting the screws, hoping it would be for the last time. Then at last, he began to nudge the frame across the hardwood floor, inch by careful inch.

Every so often, he paused - checking for any tell-tale signs of movement. His heart was racing faster. He was so very close to the window now, with only a couple of feet to go until finally, the bed butted up against the wall, just beneath the window ledge.

Elijah stood up and eased himself onto the sill. He was no longer so restricted by the chain, though regrettably, it was still secured to the bed frame. At least he could see out of the window where for a moment, he studied the area. He saw it through the same eyes as Eleanor but from an elevated position; a rectangular park scattered with trees, whose light caps of foliage had only just been discernible. They were rooted amongst glossy banks of laurel bushes, enclosed inside a fence of black railings. His eyes travelled further - seeing the elegant terrace on the far side; a continuous row of creamy white buildings constructed in a beautiful regency style. The sight took his breath away as he struggled to imagine which part of London he was hidden in. He counted the ornate windows arranged on four levels.

He experienced a sudden wave of giddiness as he pointed his eyes down to the park. Even if he *did manage* to escape, it would be impossible to jump. He had to find a way of drawing attention to himself. He craned his ear - at least, the muted thud of music reassured him.

Elijah shuffled himself round slightly, raised his feet, then rammed them against the window pane. His first experimental strike had no effect. He lashed out again, harder. It wasn't until the third attempt, his shoes finally broke the pane, filling the room with an explosion of splintering glass.

He gasped, hit by a gust of cold, harsh air. It made him falter slightly but with a nervous swallow, he managed to drag himself just a tiny bit closer to the edge. His face leaned out of the aperture, his heart pounding so violently, he felt faint.

"Help!" Elijah yelled hoarsely, spotting a few people wandering around in the square below. He raised his wounded hand - the other still gripping the window sill. "Up here! Help, somebody!"

Everything happened at once. Elijah froze as a man surfaced from the dense foliage of the park enclosure. He appeared to be an icon of the 70s;

flared jeans - long, brown hair, slung back in a ponytail. Even beneath the cloudy gloom of the sky, Elijah could detect an auburn tone - unable to shake off the bewilderment that he carried a haunting resemblance to his father! The man stared up at him intently, his steps graceful as he darted across the ground. He raised a hand to wave - then pressed a finger to his lips. Elijah couldn't move. He was paralysed with shock.

Several car doors flew open from where a number of men began to emerge. Elijah's breath came faster. They were casually dressed and unrecognisable yet they too, seemed to be glaring towards the attic - the very spot where he crouched, rigid with terror. They were making a beeline towards one of the houses - *this house.*

Elijah shrunk back from the window. There was an urgent hammering on the door from below, just as Ben's words flew back to him; *'they're probably Dad's spies.'*

He started shaking, aware of the burn on his hand and now a sting of pain in his ankle from where he'd cut himself on the glass. He was thinking about Nathan's tools again - those vicious looking knives: *'He's got men crawling all over London - men you wouldn't want to be acquainted with...'* Elijah couldn't help himself, he started sobbing. It was with no hesitation, he slid down from the window sill before ramming the bed back in place.

He had no concept of the scene about to be unleashed; only that the pounding was becoming more incessant, followed by the continuous chime of the doorbell.

Ben turned rigid. He had been lounging on the sofa, smoking a cigarette, whilst enjoying the powerful belt of heavy metal - yet there was something about the commotion which could no longer be ignored. He struggled to his feet and crept towards the door.

"Okay, I'm coming!" he yelled, reaching up to unlock it. "What the fuck...?" He never had a chance to finish. The door burst inwards as several men came piling into the hallway.

He found himself staring at the first man who's casual attire disguised a demeanour of authority. Ben stared at his cold, deadpan face, just as he was whipping out a police badge.

"Sergeant Wilkinson, Metropolitan Police!" the man barked. "We have reason to believe a teenage boy is being held captive in this house!"

"Rubbish!" Ben spluttered. "Y-you're not to go any further! Not until my father's back!"

"Your father is under arrest," Wilkinson said coldly, "as is your friend, Nathan Wadzinski!"

Ben watched in dread as two more men started to advance up the stairs. The notion that these were plain clothed policemen hit him with a sudden dizzying force.

"Stop!" he hollered without thinking. "You can't go up there..." The next thing he knew, he was being thrust against the wall, his wrists snapped in cuffs. But little did he know that his panic was nothing, compared to spiralling terror of the boy trapped in the attic, three floors above.

Elijah huddled on the bed. Perry must have had men stationed outside his house all along, just waiting to see if he would attempt any escape.

He heard the crash of the door - the pounding of feet on the stairs, drawing closer. This was it. They had caught him in the act. They knew of his treachery and within a very short time, word was going to get back to Perry. Spikes of terror shot through him. It was with no further doubt, he would end up in that basement where his torture would be relentless. Elijah heard the key in the lock being turned. He let out a moan of fear.

He was dimly aware of two shadows; two heavily built strangers materialising inside the attic. He couldn't bear to look at them, knowing the reason they were here.

"Elijah Jansen?" one of them demanded.

His hands shot up in front of his face. "Stay away from me!" he gasped.

"It's okay, we're police..." He made a grab for his arm

Despite all those assurances, Elijah's first response was to lash out. He couldn't bear it. This had to be a trick. He was already panting heavily, his stomach heaving.

Within a split second however, everything changed, as he clocked the expression of the second man. He appeared to be staring at his foot - his eyes widening.

"Get a WPC up here, Ron. This kid's injured - and he's in shock. He needs medical attention quickly!"

The urgency in his voice had an instant calming effect. Elijah followed his gaze, where he too saw the blood seeping through his sock. It was as if a curtain had been drawn back, revealing two men who no longer seemed so threatening. One of them was waving a police badge. Elijah could see it was genuine. Finally his breathing began to slow itself as he lowered his trembling hands.

II

A crowd gathered in the square as Elijah was gently coaxed out of the house. He massaged his wrist, finally free of its manacle. A short distance away, Ben stood fuming. It had taken a lot of persuasion to finally coerce him into surrendering the keys. It was the last Elijah saw of him before he was bundled into a police car.

Elijah meanwhile, shuffled slowly down the steps, barely able to believe how this quiet and elegant corner of London could have concealed a crime of such horror. He felt giddy. The outside world seemed huge, though he froze to a standstill as the mysterious, auburn ponytailed man wandered up to him.

"Eli," he greeted him softly. "Are you okay?"

Elijah frowned, recognising the voice. The man smiled then tugged at the crown of his hair, peeling off a wig where a mop of tousled silver hair was revealed. Elijah let out a gasp.

"Peter!" he breathed. "What are you doing here?"

"We've been keeping a lookout," Peter sighed. "This is Seamus, me very good friend. He's been hanging around the Grosvenor Hotel, where your Ma was staying..."

Elijah turned to the man, loitering by a white transit van. He possessed a flat, freckled face and blue eyes - he struck him as being somewhat aloof.

Peter's expression turned sombre. "I wore the wig so no-one would recognise me but there's a little more to the disguise than that. Eleanor said I reminded her of your dad..." he lowered his eyes, hesitant in his explanation. "Over the last few days, Perry may have seen a man who very much resembled Jake. It was meant to unhinge him - yet it was me all along..."

"That's brilliant!" Elijah interrupted.

It took a while for the fog of confusion to lift as he desperately battled to make sense of it all. He let out a sigh, his eyes fixed on Peter.

"What now?" he whispered fearfully. "Have you heard from my mum?"

A look of alarm flashed in Peter's eyes and all the while, Elijah was dimly aware of the sputter of a police radio. *"We've just arrested a third suspect. We've found the boy - over..."*

A sense of misery poured into his heart. "Sh-she's not dead..." He whimpered. "Please don't tell me they've m-murdered her..."

"He needs to see her!" Peter broke in quickly, whirling round to face the police officers. "Is there any chance we can go to the hospital?"

"Of course," Sergeant Wilkinson nodded curtly.

Elijah had turned numb - compelled to forget about his injuries as he sank into the front seat. They drove in convoy: Peter and his friend, Seamus, accompanied by an unmarked police car. Its blue light flickered ahead, as they surged through the busy streets. He could feel an ocean of tears welling up behind his eyes which remained unshed for now. All that mattered was his mother whose lovely face was etched on the canvas of his mind. He would never forget the way she had looked at him on that last fateful evening, her expression laced with such tenderness - the way he had traced the outline of her face as if moulding it to his memory. He had felt a grip of terror even then, knowing something bad was about to happen.

No-one spoke as they made their way through the corridors. Elijah paid little attention to where they were going, his mind consumed with fear. He had no idea where they were, nor even which hospital. He stared ahead, eyes carving through the throngs of patients and medical staff whose faces didn't register until eventually, they reached a ward.

Elijah blinked, shaking himself out of his reverie. One of the police officers was speaking again, as they guided him into a private room - the whole scenario possessed a dreamlike quality.

The next person he saw was Charlie; his chair pressed close to the bedside, both hands clasped around one of Eleanor's. He glanced up as soon as the door clicked open and straight away, Elijah read the anguish in his eyes. Even now, Eleanor lay still - barely alive, her face devoid of colour. Her dark hair straggled across the pillow like seaweed, lacking its usual gleam; then finally, he saw the cruel purple bruises around her neck. He let out a sob, breaking away from the others.

"Eli!" Charlie croaked, struggling to his feet. "Thank God you're okay!" he stared at the police constable who had rescued him, his eyes full of questions. "How did you find him?"

"It's a long story," he sighed, "but first, we need to tell him what nearly happened to his mother…"

The story tumbled out piece by piece.

Peter had known Perry was due to meet Eleanor at the Hotel. It was practically the last thing she had told him, before reluctantly disclosing where Elijah was being held.

Of course, Peter had no idea where Perry lived but he was struck with a feeling, the Barton-Wells children might. He had telephoned Avalon and she in turn, had scoured her memory; vaguely recalling some house in Pimlico.

Peter relished the next part. He had sauntered past the hotel, moments before Perry arrived, guessing he would be punctual. He would never forget his face - grey as a ghost as he gripped his chest. The disguise had been more than effective, it had been devastating.

But now was not a time for self-adulation. Peter suppressed the feeling - relating the rest of the story, which now involved Seamus.

He had been at the hotel all the time, keeping watch. There were times, when he thought Eleanor had detected his scrutiny yet most importantly, he had seen them leave. He had followed them to the car park prior to retrieving his van - careful to keep a safe distance behind, before Peter reappeared in the guise of 'Jake's ghost' again as he lingered on the corner, waiting…

"The traffic lights were red. As soon as Perry moved off, Seamus pulled into the curb and I hopped into the van. We headed for Pimlico which is where we caught up with them."

Peter described the square. He had no concept of the events unravelling behind those chalky white walls, which was where Eleanor's testimony would fill in the gaps. Eventually, a mantle of darkness had spread across the square and nothing much had happened - at least, not until 11:00.

Peter was hit with a bayonet of fear, the instant he spotted that thug of Perry's. He had been hauling a woozy-looking Eleanor towards a car while Perry watched from the doorway. He was captured in a glow of light, his face simmering with evil; Peter had watched in dread as he turned his thumb downwards. It was a vision that turned him cold and once again, they had followed. Peter was desperate not to lose them, knowing the situation had become critical.

"I so much wanted to call the police," he shivered, "yet they were there already…"

They arrived in that dingy terrace with no concept that some of those stationary vehicles were unmarked police cars - where it later transpired, they had been lured to the area in advance.

Peter had been oblivious to it; his principal concern being Eleanor, as she was roughly dragged into an alleyway. He had sneaked into the garden, ready to face his worse nightmare and it was a scene that would haunt him forever.

"He forced her head underwater," he shuddered. "She struggled - then became very limp. Something inside me just snapped…"

He closed his eyes where the remains of a rockery leapt into view. It was almost as if his body had become detached from his mind as he grasped one of the rocks and shimmied across the grass. Nathan had had his back turned, where Peter glanced at his bleached blonde head for one more second before slamming down the rock.

"I feared I might have killed him - but do you know, I didn't care!"

It was at this point, the police had swarmed into the garden before shoving him aside. He watched; helpless to do another thing as they swooped towards the woman lying half dead on the grass, flipped her over on to her belly then frantically started pumping the foul, black water from her lungs. Peter couldn't remember much else after that.

Elijah took it all in as a jumble of different voices crowded his mind. He moved towards Eleanor - careful not to disturb the drip attached to her arm. Her skin felt clammy, her eyes closed. So they really had meant to kill her. This was the scenario he had been dreading all along - crucified by their treachery. He turned to stare at Charlie.

"S-so what about *you*, Eli?" he stammered, gazing woefully back at him.

"Never mind me, I'll survive," Elijah whispered through gritted teeth. He felt faint - his mother had never looked closer to death.

"You're not okay, Eli," Peter argued, "Eleanor said they hurt you!"

Elijah shrugged. "My injuries are superficial."

"My colleague insisted you needed treatment," the accompanying WPC intervened bossily. "Look at your trouser leg! That wound needs stitches!"

The moment Elijah looked down, he wondered if this was the reason he was feeling so faint. The glass must have cut deeper than he thought. He was losing blood - the hem of his jeans as well as his sock were now saturated with it. He gaped at Charlie in panic.

"Go on, son," he urged. "I'll stay here - Eleanor won't be too happy if we sit here and let you bleed to death will she? Now go and get yourself sorted!"

The moment they vanished, Charlie turned his attention back to Eleanor whose limp, motionless body slumped in the hospital bed. It brought back his worst fears; those final hours spent with Anna, before her failing heart had finally given up the battle and the fine thread which anchored her to life had been severed. Now here he was again - gazing down at the woman he loved more than life itself. The scenario was horribly familiar; her lungs poisoned with whatever foul substance they had tried to drown her in.

Charlie clenched his fists as his mind spun in a vortex of emotions. On the one hand, he felt murderous - he could quite happily kill Perry for this ultimate act of evil *as well as* that bastard, Nathan! He was glad they had been arrested - he hoped they'd rot in jail forever! Yet somehow, it didn't seem enough.

He had endured 48 hours of hell, from the moment Peter had taken him aside to convey the disturbing news. Returning to the almshouse had been painful. Though despite his innermost instinct, he could see the logic in Peter's plan especially if he could pull off the disguise. Charlie had periodically slipped across to his flat to use the phone - though it pained him to hear of Elijah's torment. In fact, he could never understand how he kept so calm - but he had no choice, if only for the sake of pacifying his own kids.

He arose on Friday, fired up with enough strength to carry on life as normal; a day when the sun had poured through the windows, filling the almshouse with a warm, rich light. The weather had been glorious - the trees ringing with birdsong. But his heart felt like stone. It didn't take long for Andrew to realise something was amiss either.

He had enough problems of his own. He had finished a shift at the 'Cat's Whiskers' where he was soon to be promoted as bar manager; and in his haste to visit Angel, he had been shocked to discover the flat empty. His friend was gone - it was as if he had vanished in a puff of smoke.

Charlie shuddered. At least the kids were on their way, including William and Avalon who had insisted on driving. He gazed tearfully down at Eleanor, wishing he could tell her how much they had missed her. That was, if she ever regained consciousness.

Andrew stared out of the window as the first graffiti sprayed walls and drab factory units signified the outskirts of London. But he wasn't taking in the view - he was agonising over what had happened, still thinking about that phone call! Andrew fought back a shiver. Even *he* detected the prickly atmosphere malingering in the almshouse, last Friday.

"Don't say anything," his father had whispered, "but Eleanor and Eli had to go away! They left on a mercy dash - probably some ailing relative they haven't seen in years…"

Andrew nodded coolly. His father couldn't pull the wool over his eyes. He had guessed something was up for a while now and it had spiralled from the aftermath of the rave. He remembered the day, Charlie and Eleanor had rushed up to London before the caravan had been torched. Eleanor had been on tenterhooks - and now she had taken flight!

Andrew's mood smouldered, wondering when it was ever going to end; the burglary, the mugging, the threat of some sinister gangland influence… then just as his frustration reached fever pitch, the telephone rang.

"Hello?" chirped a familiar voice.

Andrew gripped the handset - his heart gave a sudden leap. He would have recognised that soft, breathy voice anywhere. "Yes?" he answered wistfully.

"I was after Elijah?" Naomi's voice berated him. "It's the last day of his work experience and he hasn't showed up!"

"Um - sorry b-but Eli and his mum were called away," he stammered almost apologetically. "Is that Naomi? This is Andrew…"

"Oh hi, Andrew," the voice drawled dismissively, "sorry to have bothered you. Bye-eee!"

The call ended abruptly, leaving Andrew gaping at the telephone. Yet by the time he caught up with his father, he was fuming. Bloody bitch! How dare she flirt with him, seduce him, circle her lips around his dick and then blank him for two weeks! Andrew couldn't drive the fury out of his mind. He was still agonising over Angel's departure but this was the ultimate kick in the balls. He tried desperately hard to concentrate on his work until the moment he had caught a glimpse of his father.

Andrew felt something inside him twist. Charlie might have portrayed his usual lionhearted demeanour - at least superficially. Yet he didn't miss that flicker of anxiety. It was reflected in the inky dark pools of his eyes as he periodically glanced around the site in despair.

"What's really going on?" Andrew challenged him.

"Andrew, you have to swear to keep this secret," Charlie begged. "I know what you're like, especially when you've had a few - b-but Elijah's been kidnapped."

Andrew nearly dropped his cement trowel. The world had turned suddenly very cold.

"Please, Andrew," Charlie kept whispering. "You mustn't tell a soul! We're not supposed to know. If word gets out, Eli could be tortured… they've been working on him already."

Andrew could barely take it in, hit with an unexpected bombshell of horror. Come teatime however, his earlier concerns crept back to him, his mind on Naomi. It was with no further delay, he marched towards the council headquarters, ready to have it out with her.

Naomi's glossy hair bounced around her shoulders as she came strutting out of the office. She was absorbed with an air of such confidence, Andrew faltered. He was barely thinking straight when he began to follow her; but five minutes later, she paused outside a terrace of smart town houses, a short distance from the centre. Andrew's eyes narrowed, drinking in the multi-tone brickwork, creeping with honeysuckle - wondering how on earth some 'council worker' could afford such a place. Then he remembered that silky, male voice on the phone. Andrew lingered in the shadows, wondering if he dared confront them. Except everything changed in a flash, as a man came to the door. Andrew's mouth ran dry. Robin Whaley? A sense of horror came snaking up from his stomach as the two of them embraced.

Fragments of truth were peeling back in his mind like onion skin; the day at the building site, her unrelenting curiosity about his step-brother and she had been particularly keen to get him that work placement! Even Andrew had the intelligence to figure out that Whaley was the enemy, where one particular memory stuck: *'I'd be very careful what you say, Charlie. I'm not a man you want to pick a fight with…'*

By the time he caught up with his father, he was distraught; mindful of Charlie's mood which had darkened like thunder. He had not long received news of Eleanor's meeting with Perry.

The atmosphere had been barbed with tension and it was a feeling that anchored Andrew to his home that night. "Best I stick with you," he whispered. "You're right - I might give the game away!" He shuddered, thinking about Naomi again.

She had purposely seduced him and this was the only secret he couldn't bear to impart, feeling his innards twist. Only he knew the truth. It had been nothing but a ploy to distract him, whilst some bogus telecom engineer had tampered with their phone. Andrew could have throttled her - but for now, the discovery of her relationship with Whaley was enough to keep him on tenterhooks.

Elijah limped back towards the ward. He had been thoroughly examined; every scratch and bruise registered, as well as the hideous cigar burn on his hand. The gash to his ankle had been the direct result of ramming his foot through the glass, leading to a sustained blood loss.

He crept back into the room, where the first person he locked eyes with was Eleanor.

Finally, she was sitting up - though she was barely recognisable; her face grey, her complexion waxy. Heavy black shadows encircled her eyes where even their golden light seemed subdued.

"Eli?" she muttered, her voice cracked and barely audible.

"Mum!" he gasped, dragging himself slowly forwards. "You look terrible..."

He touched her hand, shocked by its icy stiffness as he stared into her eyes - willing that sparkle to come back. Then gradually, he began to notice there were other people in the room. Margaret's face registered, pale as she clung to Charlie; Andrew, his face tight with anxiety - and William. Elijah blinked. It was as if a dark cloud descended - the knowledge of what Nathan had done to him; but William smiled back warmly, banishing the horror from his mind. Finally, he met the beautiful, hazel eyes of Avalon. They glittered with tears.

"Eli," her voice wobbled. "Are you okay...?"

Elijah felt a stranglehold of emotion. It seemed a very long time since he had seen them all.

"I'll be fine," he muttered stiffly, "but what about Mum?" he turned to her sadly. "They nearly killed you..."

"D-don't worry," Eleanor whispered, "I'm *determined* to survive this. Nurse says my temperature's going down. Now come here - it's such a blessing to see you safe again!"

One hand was locked into Charlie's - the other clinging to Jake's pendant. Its power might have momentarily faded but right now, its greenness had never been more pronounced.

It was all the energy she needed to get through the next stage.

The following days proved to be a relentless struggle; the lengthy police interviews where both she and Elijah had been obliged to give statements. Finally, they were permitted to return home - although Eleanor couldn't quite dispel the horror of what had happened to them.

In another part of London, Perry was detained in custody. Nathan had been granted a brief respite in hospital to recover from a superficial head wound; though it was inevitable that he too, would be dumped in police custody and charged.

In fact, the only one of them released was Ben. But then Perry had been quite insistent.

"My son played no part in this," he pleaded to the arresting officer. "The house in Pimlico is his *permanent* residence. He had no choice but to be there."

Sergeant Daniel Wilkinson loathed the decision to discharge him but held no authority. Elijah's statement had made little mention of Ben. As far as they could fathom, he was not a willing participant in the abduction - nor the physical abuse he had suffered. It was with a sense of painful irony that even Elijah was forced to confess, he had never wanted to be involved.

Perry on the other hand, had his own reasons for demanding his son's release.

He needed someone on the outside to carry on fighting. Right now, he had no choice other than to bide his time, all the while he remained in the grip of police custody - yet his emotions were boiling over. *Someone* had interfered despite his most malevolent warnings. He had no idea who but he had reached an unwavering decision; that person was going to pay.

He was shaking with hatred as he relived the events of that final morning; from his walk to the shops, to a third sighting of that mysterious auburn haired hippy. He remembered visiting the boy shortly after. His resemblance to Jake struck painfully at his heart and suddenly, he couldn't bear to be in the house for a moment longer. He could *never* have known about Nathan's arrest - nor that the neighbourhood would be crawling with police...

"We are arresting you on suspicion, you are involved in a kidnapping - you do not have to say anything, but anything you do say…"

He felt dizzy as he stumbled against the police car, wary of the icy snap of handcuffs. What had the police been doing there anyway?

Detectives meanwhile, had started furrowing for evidence. Regrettably, they had discovered the basement in Nathan's house as well as his macabre display of weapons - laid out exactly as he had left them, ready for use. The chain to which Elijah had been suspended was left dangling from the joist; a sight which left the officers outraged - yet substantiated everything the boy had told them. There were even traces of blood on it, where his wrist had been badly chafed. Finally, several strands of chestnut coloured hair were collected from a sofa in the lounge.

But the search went further where the trail eventually led to Perry's house. Police had been horrified to re-examine the bed shackles left in the aftermath of Elijah's rescue; droplets of blood on the window sill, on the bed and lastly, a sketchpad lying on the bedside cabinet - evidence which was irrefutable and from which Perry knew there was no escape.

Worse however, was to come. Not only was he charged with Elijah's kidnapping but the more serious crime of attempted murder. A wine glass bore smudges of Eleanor's lipstick. Finally, they found traces of the powerful sedative, obtained forensically from her brandy glass. Perry cursed himself; he should have been more careful and his next task would be to find himself a bloody good lawyer. Yet thoughts of a far more dangerous nature were festering in his mind.

"I warned them," he whispered. "I swore I'd make him wish he had never been born…" It was as if he was communicating with Jake alone - remembering that last eerie sighting. "I'll be granted bail, have no fear - and then I'll deal with every last one of them…"

No-one was safe - not even with Perry behind bars. His quest for revenge gnawed deep into his soul: the only fantasy that prevented him from completely slipping over the edge of sanity.

PART 4
THE TRIAL

Chapters 26-29

June 1990 - June 1991

Chapter 26

I

June 1990 - 11 months later

Elijah glared down from the public gallery in hatred. They were seated in a row; William and Avalon, one side whilst Charlie, Peter and Eleanor lingered on the other. He caught his mother's eye. She smiled gently, though anyone could see how much the last year had taken its toll. At 35 years of age, she may have retained her fragile beauty but no-one could miss the faint lines etched across her forehead - nor the tiny threads of silver in her hair. Only she knew how close she had come to death, never mind losing her only son. Charlie squeezed her hand. They listened with increasing dread as the judge passed sentence.

Eight years! What a bloody joke! Elijah thought to himself.

He watched as Perry turned and stepped from the dock, escorted by two police officers. Nathan followed, dark eyes smouldering. There was some consolation in knowing that both men were about to be shipped back to Prison to begin their official sentence - and yet it seemed so little.

Both men had pleaded guilty to the charges of kidnapping and attempted murder on the grounds of overwhelming evidence. There had been no jury - just a gruelling trial whereby a long list of offences had been recited before the judge.

Elijah shuddered, conscious of the circle of glossy scar tissue embossed in his palm - a constant reminder of that nightmare. Perry's eyes flickered towards the public gallery where they finally clashed with his own. Elijah experienced a sudden chill - there was no denying that flash of triumph. Perry could no longer escape punishment from his recent atrocities but even Elijah knew, the trial was by no means over. This was just the beginning.

He turned away, practically quaking with horror; away from that smug face, away from the poison those men breathed into the air as it continued to swirl all around them.

"Eli?" Avalon gasped as he staggered to his feet.

He escaped from the public gallery without another word; peeling himself away from the courtroom where they had been forced to relive the entire ghastly episode. By the time he stormed his way into the foyer, he was practically hyperventilating.

He felt the pressure of a hand on his shoulder and glanced up - relieved to see it was their barrister, David Edgar whose crumpled features disguised a look of concern.

"Are you alright, Elijah?" he whispered.

"Not really," he sighed, "I'm sorry, I don't feel there's been much justice.

It seems hard to imagine, that man was nearly responsible for the death of *both* my parents…"

"I know but we are getting there," David placated him. "The wheels of justice turn slowly. Yet think about what we *have* achieved." His blue eyes twinkled. "Two very evil men are about to spend the next eight years behind bars. We on the other hand, have plenty of time - as well as an indisputable motive."

"But I thought they burnt Mum's file…" Elijah mumbled.

"They did," David sighed, "but they had no idea, we'd initiated legal proceedings beforehand. I saw the file. I made notes from it - there are even sections I took copies of."

"Yet it's not enough to prove he killed my father," Elijah added gloomily.

"Not yet," David snapped, "but even the authorities agree, the procurement of that file was the most obvious motive behind your kidnapping."

Elijah nodded, knowing he was right. Despite a bitter sense that Perry might still get away with murdering his father, justice *had* in some way been served.

There was a sense of atonement as they congregated outside and just in time to see an armoured police van sweep through the gates. William sidled over, unable to erase his smirk. It was obvious he would feel a certain degree of *Schadenfreude* - perhaps even more so than he did, knowing that Nathan was about to be ferried back to Wormwood Scrubs alongside Perry.

"Okay, mate," he muttered, "you still up for a celebration?"

They had agreed to stick around London - a chance to hook up with Angel for a couple of beers, before heading further afield to a rave.

Elijah gave a shrug and delving into his coat pocket, he extracted a pack of Silk Cut before lighting one. He felt the jab of Eleanor's stare, averting his eyes. It was obvious she didn't really approve of him smoking although she was prepared to cut him a bit of slack.

He blew out a ribbon of smoke. She looked away - although he already had some notion of what she was thinking.

Even Eleanor was startled as to how *swiftly* Perry must have planned her murder. She had surrendered her file - yet her life had nearly been extinguished from the moment he'd seized possession of it.

Eleanor shivered. She too was filled with a horror that eight years for a long list of crimes, that included ABH, kidnapping, GBH, extortion and attempted murder, wasn't anywhere near enough. But as usual, Perry had been clever. A guilty plea was bound to ensure a shorter sentence and given the judicial system, there was even a chance he could be out in less.

It left her with a sense, they were in as much danger as ever - unable to ward off that enduring chill as she stole another glance at Elijah.

She was so proud of him - perhaps a little disappointed, he smoked and went to raves (where she was certain he indulged in other substances). Yet she could hardly blame him, given the ordeal he had suffered; an ordeal for which she felt partly responsible, since her file had always been at the root of it. It was a feeling that delivered a surge of guilt - which in some way defended her in allowing him this freedom. She loved him more than ever, her only concern to keep him safe.

Charlie sidled up to her, his arm warm around her shoulder.

"C'mon, let's just get out of here," he muttered, "there's nothing more we can do..." He cast another nod towards David with whom he had shared a few closing words.

Given what David had gleaned from Eleanor's file, this trial had ignited a spark. It was about to resurrect the more *historic* crime of Jake's murder and ultimately, Albert Enfield's. She could almost sense the swell in Charlie's heart as he revelled in their triumph. He was steering them towards the exit; a magnificent stone parapet which enclosed an arched iron gate.

"Beautiful building," he murmured to himself.

Elijah took another drag of his cigarette and followed, conscious of Charlie's admiring glances as he studied the architecture. He could have smiled - the warmth of his tone bringing back echoes of their holiday where they had finally discovered the historic city of Nijmegan.

It was only as they jumped into a taxi, he found himself reminiscing...

The homecoming had felt strange. There were isolated moments when his escape from the attic seemed unreal and yet somehow, he dragged himself through the aftermath. People were overwhelmed with concern over what had happened - and none more than Peter who feared the long term effects. He had suggested counselling but Elijah refused. He was determined to get through this his own way; to focus on the positive where for the first time in his life, he cherished his freedom.

Yet it was impossible to evade the continual invasion of journalists, hankering to hear his story; nor the entanglement of the law whose attention to detail seemed relentless. His life had turned into a whirlwind which made it virtually impossible to return to school. Given that his capture had occurred on the penultimate day of his work experience - and with less than a fortnight until the end of term - even his teachers had agreed, it was pointless.

The rest was a blur. He knew Nathan and Perry had been arrested and were now incarcerated in a high security prison somewhere. Bail had been refused and with nothing left to restrain them, the family had finally taken off to the Continent.

Returning to the Moselle Valley had been a pleasurable interlude - but his true calling lay in Nijmegan, where the rolling fields of a campsite allowed him a feeling of complete escapism. It was here, they had hired bikes. They explored the long straight roads which criss-crossed the city, loving the eclectic blend of architecture.

If anyone was delighted to see his safe return, it was Margaret - dreamy-eyed and in love with her very first boyfriend (who she had begged to drag along too). Charlie could hardly refuse. Margaret had been traumatised by the events of that summer, where the enduring effects of Perry's evil had only just sunk in. Elijah smiled, remembering her ceaseless enthusiasm - golden hair swaying as they flew around the cycle paths to the top of the town. They had discovered a most idyllic park. A stone bridge stretched across a moat; its cool, pea green surface reflecting the fronds of a weeping willow and at the core of its setting, squatted a tower - a single circular turret built in brick, where the crenelated battlements evoked images of fairy tales.

"Kronenburg Park. It's just the sort of place I can imagine my dad chilling out - I wonder if he wrote some of his songs here..."

Margaret had looked at him through eyes glassy with tears. "Did Perry *really* kill him?"

It was in one of the rare moments, her blonde, blue-eyed boyfriend, Phil had momentarily disappeared. Though all Elijah could do was nod, not wanting to think about the pending trial.

He was inclined to concentrate on the finer things - where the buzz of this place couldn't have brought more pleasure. They cycled further - adoring the cobbled streets packed with shops, the towering, pastel buildings. Everything was so uniform and neat. Beauty and colour leapt from every corner and as the afternoon wore on, so the streets came alive with music. Casual buskers drew a smile; but it was the live bands that brought the crowds flocking to the taverns, an ambience which never failed to evoke a passion in his mother: *"There would have been a time when Jake played in these pubs, back in the 70s..."*

Elijah remembered feeling a slight shiver.

He recalled the evening they had taken a leisurely stroll, where the shade of the trees was cooling. The path had drawn them right up to the city wall from where they soaked up the sublime view across the river Waal - the graceful bridge which spanned it. It had taken his breath away, a time when he found himself wondering if any members of his family still lived here.

This had consequentially set Eleanor on a quest and before the holiday ended, she had approached the town hall. It nestled in the oldest part of Nijmegan, a vision of medieval charm with a gabled roof cut into intricate, curling shapes. Charlie was in raptures.

It was also in this quarter, they had settled down for an evening meal. To his glee, Andrew had discovered one of Holland's notorious 'coffee shops,' thrilled to *legally* purchase a lump of cannabis. It was only a little later that Elijah had shared a joint with him - far from Eleanor's eyes; a time when he could hear singing from one of the nearby caravans and as his mind wandered, so the distant reverberation of Eleanor's words started to permeate.

Few members of the Jansen family lived here any more; a situation which inspired Eleanor to tell him about the one and only time she had visited in the aftermath of Jake's death.

"I met his parents. They seemed cool and detached - as if they didn't really want to talk to me. I guess they were grieving for their son. Yet I was the only person who could have explained the truth to them..." The husky rasp of her voice alarmed him - years of unshed misery finally oozing out of her. It seemed even more strange how they had never shown any interest in *him* - Jake's only son!

"I will never know if they blamed me for his death," she kept explaining, "that maybe I enticed Jake into some sordid criminal underworld - at least, that's the story Whaley wanted people to believe... Perhaps it stuck."

Her eyes glittered with tears before they coursed down her cheeks. Elijah's heart twisted. He hated seeing his mother cry. He even wondered if there was a way *he* could make contact with his grandparents - but the most disappointing news was yet to come. Rutger Jansen and his British born wife had left Nijmegan many years ago. There was only one consolation. Jake had a younger sister named Marjolein. According to records, she still owned a house here - though it was regrettable, her family had been on holiday in Greece, that summer.

"I sent her a letter," Eleanor had finished warmly, wiping the tears from her face. She clasped his hands. "Who knows - maybe she'll write back to me some day..."

Elijah blinked, conscious of William's elbow in his ribs as the taxi chugged its way through London. For the last five minutes, he had been lost in another world where those final reminiscences had rekindled a strange and stirring warmth. Eleanor *had* heard from Marjolein. In fact she had been quite vehement in her plea for them to revisit. She wanted to invite them to stay in their house set on three levels - even camp in their large back garden.

"Jesus, what planet are you on, Eli!" William laughter rang in his ears.

"Sorry," Elijah sighed, "just thinking about Nijmegan. D'you know they had some really cool art shops. Avalon would have loved it."

William smiled warmly, casting an affectionate gaze towards his sister. She wouldn't be joining them tonight - she was just yearning to see them off before travelling back home with the adults. Out of everyone in their community, no-one had been more supportive than the Barton-Wells kids. He felt his stomach tighten - remembering what Nathan had taunted; it was impossible not to mention it, where sadly, Avalon had confirmed everything. Elijah would never forget her face; *Yes, it happened...* the memory of that humiliating rape was still haunting her! She wished William could have gone to the police - although Elijah could fully understand why he hadn't.

"There's no way he's gay," he remembered whispering.

"With his track record?" she smiled, "I doubt it! He just didn't want people to know..."

Elijah sighed softly. It wouldn't have mattered anyway - he loved William, just as he loved Avalon. The enduring pain they had suffered had bonded them closer than any siblings, forging a deep and lasting attachment.

Looking at her now, he couldn't understand why she was still single. It was months since she had jacked in her job at the antique shop; a situation which left her slightly unsettled. Eventually, she had enrolled in a course to study art history and at the same time, had landed a new job as PA in one of Rosebrook's larger advertising agencies - but it was here, she had been swept into another fruitless romance. This time, he was some suave, good looking account executive, who had cheated on her not once but twice. Elijah lifted his gaze. How was it that a girl as beautiful as Avalon could fall for such *utter* bastards?

She caught his eye in the mirror. The courtroom must have brought back her worst horrors, especially when Ben had been loitering. Yet the adoration in her eyes was unmistakable, reminding him of their own special love bond. He knew he was too young for her. Avalon needed a man - and he was still very much a boy with so much education ahead of him. But at least they had something to look forward to; at the end of September, she was opening a little shop of her own. It had been Peter's idea. A unit had become vacant in the same parade as the Fish and Chip shop, leaving her with an insatiable desire to open her own art and antiques gallery.

Elijah closed his eyes, momentarily distracted by his own goal. He had followed his dream by enrolling in an art foundation course. It would take 2 years to complete the qualification he needed to move on to University. But in the meantime he was happy; relishing the chance to fine tune his own talent and by the end of the first term, he had produced a number of outstanding paintings - some of which Avalon had already promised to exhibit for him.

"Right, I suppose this is where we part company," William piped up, just as the taxi squeezed itself into a rank outside Victoria Railway Station. He slipped another glance at Elijah who had barely said a word for the entire journey - still lost in his reverie.

"Yeah," he sighed, "look - I'm sorry. This stuff has left me in a bit of a daze..."

"That's fair enough," Avalon said as they stepped from the car.

He watched as if in a dream as the other taxi pulled in behind them. Charlie and Eleanor emerged from the back seat followed by Peter. Eleanor looked as white as a ghost - but then again, they had just cruised past the Grosvenor Hotel...

"Alright, kids?" Peter called out, wandering over.

Avalon embraced both boys tenderly; it seemed as if William had shoved the drama of the trial aside already, hopping with excitement in anticipation of the night ahead.

"Please, *please* take care of yourselves," Eleanor whispered, her grip tight around her son's shoulders. "I know I don't need to say this but stick together - don't get separated..."

"We won't," Elijah sighed, his cheeks flushed, evoking poignant memories of his boyhood. He wriggled out of her arms. "Stop fussing, Mum. You know I'll be careful!"

He pecked her on the cheek and suddenly, he couldn't get away fast enough.

Eleanor was left rooted to the pavement, watching them go. Her stomach churned. It was impossible to cast aside the torment of the last year but he was no longer a child.

Elijah had undergone a complete transformation in the last year, as if determined to honour the life of his father. He had adopted a look that was trendy yet typical of an art student; his hair slightly longer - tousled, messy layers, flopping around his chiselled profile. His clothes were mostly dark. Though tonight he wore a blue striped boating jacket; a jaunty twist to his usual black jeans, studded leather belt and Doc Martens.

"He'll be okay," Charlie sighed, "he's got William to look after him..."

William looked particularly well-groomed with his 'short back and sides' haircut. He had joined the territorial army in the last year, having successfully completed his 'A' levels - now destined to attend a Regular Commissions Board, where he hoped he'd be accepted for training at the Royal Military Academy Sandhurst.

"Growing up fast aren't they," Charlie's voice was murmuring. "C'mon love, let's go home. They'll be meeting up with Andrew too, don't forget. Everything'll be okay..."

II

Within a few minutes, they were racing up the steps of the London Underground to reach Sloane Square. They instantly hit a bar - a trendy Chelsea establishment where they were scheduled to meet Angel. William had to fight his way through a swirl of cigarette smoke before he spotted him lounging in one of the neon-lit alcoves. He was sipping a cocktail. Andrew, perched next to him, seemed a little guarded.

"Hey! Over here!" Angel called, clocking their arrival. "William! How you doing, man?" He had already sprung from his seat, palm raised for a high five.

William obligingly slapped it before Angel's warm eyes travelled to Elijah. His face split into an even wider grin. "Yo! How's tricks?"

Elijah forced a tight smile - conscious of Andrew's stabbing eyes as he clasped Angel's hand and tumbled into a chair. He shook his head, the words trapped in his throat.

"So what happened?" Andrew chipped in just as William sank into a leather sofa beside him. "How many years did they get?"

"Eight!" William snapped.

"You're joking!" Angel spluttered, "that's fuckin' mental!" It was his turn to sag into his seat. "Eight years for nearly killing your mum - he could be out in five!" he rolled his eyes and took a deep slurp from his cocktail. "Anyway, can I get you boys a drink?"

"I'll get them," William grinned, intent on lifting the atmosphere. "I was going to get a few beers in. Unless you're into cocktails like this flash git! Who do you think you are, fucking Del Boy?"

Angel let out a loud laugh. "Watch it, bro! But no - nothing for me."

The instant William skipped over to the bar, Angel gazed fondly at Elijah again.

"C'mon, spill the beans... what was it like seeing them bastards go down?"

They locked eyes. A wave of secrecy loomed between them which Andrew didn't fail to notice. His face tightened - yet he had no idea what Angel was thinking.

The truth was, Angel felt indebted to Dominic for tackling Alan Levy.

He still managed to work the occasional shift at Bella's - but only as a guest DJ. His life was very much anchored to London now.

But Dominic had discovered something else that night. He had finally sussed who Levy was working for and it was a truth which left him cold. *The Hamptons.* How could Angel forget the rumours he had picked up about those people? According to Dominic, it was on that same night, Alan had tactlessly disclosed what they were *really* up to - where the fate of Elijah had been very much in his hands. For some unknown reason, Dominic had been hankering for some sort of retribution against Perry and it was only after he had dripped the right words into the ears of those in authority, he had drawn Angel into his confidence.

Angel guessed the police must have sorted it.

He lit a cigarette and offered one to Eli, his attention focussed as he continued to drag the details of the court case out of him. He flicked the pack towards Andrew almost as an afterthought.

"They went over the gruesome details? Shit, man..."

Angel shuddered. Despite everything he knew about Alan's gang, he was shocked by the brutality that lurked behind Elijah's kidnap. He despised Nathan - convinced he had engineered the attack at the rave. And from the moment he'd spoken to Elijah, he had no qualms about identifying the two skinheads either, who were undeniably involved in his ambush!

So he too, had spoken to the police. Trev Deeley and his worthless brother were consequently arrested and charged with assault, as well as conspiring to aid and abet a kidnapping. To his everlasting relief, Alan had done nothing to defend them - highly pissed off, they had gone behind his back. Even better, he had disassociated himself from them completely.

"Here you go," William broke in, back from the bar with a tray of beers. "You okay, Andrew?"

"I'm fine," Andrew said quietly, taking a draw from his cigarette. He narrowed his eyes, wary of the bond which had blossomed between Angel and Elijah; a secret rapport he felt excluded from and it irritated him beyond belief. He had become very possessive of his friend of late. "So how come you're not drinking?" he added coolly as Angel sucked up the last dregs of his cocktail.

The answer unfolded before Angel said a word. Two black men sauntered into the bar, making a beeline for their table. Elijah stared up dazedly - unable to tear his eyes away from the first one; a tall, skinny youth dressed in a black shell suit, whose dreadlocks hung to his waist.

"You're not coming to the rave?" William breathed.

"Nah, 'fraid not," Angel sighed, rising to his feet. "Been good to catch up though…"

"He's wanted elsewhere, boys," the second youth said, his voice laced with menace.

Elijah was still looking at them. An expression of woeful intuition clung to his face. It was obvious Angel was still very much under the control of this mysterious 'King Pin.'

"'S'okay," Angel kept smiling. "They're brothers! See you again some time!"

They had already guessed he wasn't talking about *siblings*.

"Wankers," Andrew hissed, the moment they were out of the door.

"Aw come on, lighten up will you," William smiled. "We might as well stay and have some grub. We've got ages until the rave starts and I'm famished."

"I'll get another round in shall I?" Elijah added softly.

They stayed for an hour where the conversation seemed forced. William started shredding his beer mat - conscious of Elijah sat one side and Andrew braced on the other, feeling very much like a referee at a football match as the atmosphere pulled tightly between them.

It was gone 9pm when they finally sauntered out of Chelsea, just as a swelling crowd of revellers poured in. The plan was to head for East London where they had agreed to rendezvous with Joshua. They slouched silently in their seats, conscious of the train surging from station to station. Elijah met Andrew's eyes in the reflection of the window pane, unable to understand why he was still glowering at him. Andrew had always been a bit jealous, even more so in the aftermath of his kidnapping. Elijah looked away with a sigh. It was hardly his fault, he had been put through that ordeal - no more than it was his fault that Angel couldn't join them tonight.

He could never have known the *real* reason for Andrew's simmering resentment.

Andrew lowered his gaze. He clocked the desolation in his stepbrother's eyes and it spiked him with guilt. That was half the trouble. Andrew was assailed with guilt. It was a feeling that clung to his gut, making him feel grubby on the inside. There was *no way* he could have told Charlie what he really knew at the time of the kidnap. He had to confront Naomi first.

It turned out to be the worst decision in his life.

If only he had bypassed that step and gone straight to the police. But no, he had to go marching round to her house, almost from the moment they arrived home from hospital - unaware of the bomb about to explode in his face.

"You scheming cow! You knew about the phone bugging all along, didn't you?"

Naomi's blue eyes had flickered furtively. "What are you talking about, Andrew? Okay, so I'm sorry if you feel jilted. Y-you're a very nice guy and that but..."

"This has got nothing to do with being jilted!" Andrew remembered screaming. He wished he hadn't lost control - wished he hadn't grasped Naomi by the lapels of her pin-striped suit and slammed her against the wall of her own living room.

"I would stop right there if I were you," a silken voice drifted from the staircase.

Andrew glanced up, just as the flash of a polaroid camera blinded him in its glare - blown away by the sight of Whaley whose look of cruel satisfaction had been disturbing.

"What the fuck is going on?" Andrew gasped, stepping away from the wall. "In this together, are you? You - him - those bastard bloody Hamptons?"

Robin raised his eyebrows. The tension in the room thickened. "What's the matter, Andrew?"

Andrew turned back to Naomi, heart charging. He had been completely unprepared for this, conscious of the developing photo Robin held deftly in his fingers.

"You're trying to tell me, you had nothing to do with my step-brother's kidnap? I'm not stupid, Naomi. You're shacked up with *him* for Christ's sake! Are you married to this creep?"

She let out a light laugh - almost revelling in the betrayal that Robin was her uncle. It painfully mirrored everything he feared. Naomi had been *so* keen to get Elijah working in the Parks and Gardens department, where his ambush in Bevington Gardens was undoubtedly planned in advance - a desolate place where any witnesses would have been scarce.

"You can't prove anything," she taunted. "The council are always sending letters to the school, inviting pupils for work experience. Why do you even care? You were just as keen!"

Andrew felt the heat flare in his face, as he remembered their first clandestine lunch - they had surreptitiously flitted back to the almshouse without a second thought.

"You seduced me on purpose," he spluttered, "what about that telephone engineer?"

"So how are you going to explain this?" Robin intervened. He brandished the polaroid. It revealed a terrified looking Naomi pinned against the wall - the hovering threat was unmistakeable. "Naomi's right. You feel no loyalty towards your step-brother, in fact you despise him. Do you really want your father to know how stupid you were, the day you tumbled into bed with my niece?" He smiled coldly. "Yes Andrew, we bugged your phone. An associate of mine wanted Elijah *very* badly and you proved to be a useful pawn."

"Hampton!" Andrew spluttered in misery. He stumbled away from the wall. "They tortured him, you bastards!" He had experienced one final burst of courage - he had been so very close to defying them. "That's it, I'm going to the police!"

"That's up to you," Robin smiled. "In which case, you might as well face up to your own flaws. You're a drug addict, Andrew. You are bitterly jealous of your step brother's success. As far as his safety's concerned, you couldn't give a shit about him and this is the reason you were so careless. And as for the telephone - that was primarily *your* fault!"

"Shut up," Andrew hissed, backing away from them.

But Naomi had touched his arm. She had gazed into his eyes in a way that was almost hypnotic, her smile comforting. "We won't say anything, if you don't," she finished seductively.

Andrew closed his eyes, giddy with shame. They were right. The fact they knew about his drug problem came as something of a shock but did he really want his father knowing how easily he had been 'used' in their phone bugging strategy? He had breathed in her perfume. She pecked him on the lips in a way which had turned his insides to jelly and he despised himself for it.

Nothing else was said about the photo, yet how could he forget? Nothing could drive away the hurt of what that *tart* could do to him, together with her creep of an uncle. Andrew took a deep breath, grateful when the train finally lurched to a standstill. He felt oddly detached as Elijah jumped onto the alighting platform, struck with a sense, he had shown precious little interest in the trial. He took a deep swallow.

The truth was, he had always known that *something* was going on; a secret he had been excluded from and because it concerned Eli's father, he had never really cared. He couldn't believe that all this 'bad stuff' might be linked

- hacked off that Angel too, had been dragged into it. But nothing could compensate for the way he felt about Naomi. They had exploited him, leaving him feeling an idiot. He lit a cigarette, hoping he could forget for a while; maybe try to be a bit nicer to Eli, especially in front of Joshua. At least he had another rave to look forward to, a chance to get completely off his face and lose himself for the night.

It was getting darker, where the rush of cool air felt invigorating. They were following Elijah. He seemed to know where he was going as he led them into a pleasing suburban neighbourhood. A typical East London pub lurked on the corner and straight away, they spotted Joshua's Land Rover. Elijah broke away from the group with a shout, just as a familiar silhouette loped into view, distinguishable by his wavy shoulder length hair and trilby hat.

"Eli!' he laughed, catching him as he threw himself into his arms.

For a moment they grinned at each other, a raft of history flowing between them. Joshua looked well - a father himself now, with an adorable baby daughter. They kept any greetings brief before they were hastily shepherded into the pub - wary of the cloak of darkness which seemed to encroach on every corner.

"I'm coming to the rave too, by the way," Joshua announced. "Mum's worried about you, especially around London…"

"We can look after ourselves," Andrew grunted.

"I know that," Joshua placated him, "but she insisted I was to take you there *and* bring you home. You can stay the night. There's plenty of space. It's just - she was pretty shocked about the attempt on Eleanor's life. You know what she's like…"

Elijah smiled his thanks. He adored Rosemary, she was what he would describe as a real 'Earth Mother.' He had to admit, he felt a lot safer here; enjoying the comforting ambience of this pub far more than that pretentious place in Chelsea - never knowing who anyone was, an influx of coked-up yuppies, not to mention the all pervading sense of threat.

A thudding beat emanated in the background which Elijah recognised as 'Ride on High' by Black Box - a last remnant of 80s dance music.

"When did music ever get this shit!" William muttered, mirroring his thoughts.

"What are you into at the moment?" Elijah piped up.

"Mostly Techno and New Beat," William answered. "You?"

"I like the Levellers," Elijah sighed, fumbling for his cigarettes again. "They remind me of Free Spirit. Andrew's mad on Ozric Tentacles," he added, determined to draw him into the conversation.

Finally a smiled curved its way onto Andrew's lips. "Yeah, they're cool. Eli got me their latest album, 'Erpland,' for my birthday. It's brilliant, especially if you listen to it stoned."

"Good choice," Joshua nodded indulgently, "aren't they a bit psychodelic? Reminds me of the 70s when I was your age. Now tell me what happened in court…"

They loosely went over it again.

It was only after William and Andrew disappeared into the Gents to swallow their ecstasy tabs, that Joshua drew Elijah to one side. "You look troubled," he muttered.

"I am," Elijah confided. "I mean - I'm glad those fuckers are behind bars but…"

"I expect there'll be another trial, right? For the murder of your father?"

Elijah nodded, his expression pained. "He'll get away with it, I know it. Angel thinks he could be out in five and then what? They'll come after us again. How are we ever gonna prove what he *really* did? He burnt my mum's file…"

Joshua clung to his stare. "You're right. Perry Hampton will lie through his teeth to escape justice and probably get that sly bastard, Whaley, to back him up. Thing is, Eli, I remember the press conference. Some of it's starting to come back…"

"And?"

"Have you thought about any other witnesses?" Joshua probed. "What about Inspector Hargreeves? Didn't Eleanor say you were particularly keen to find him?"

Elijah felt a sudden release, reflecting on everything she had told him. Yes, there was a time when he had been hell bent on tracing Hargreeves; a time when he felt a certain distrust for the police. Though it had to be said, Inspector Boswell had done everything to secure their safety - one of the main protagonists who had ensured that Perry and Nathan were refused bail.

"Tell me what you remember," he said dreamily.

"It was something Eleanor said," Joshua kept meditating. "She thought he was a *good man*. He visited her in hospital after Jake was killed, he was kind to her. Maybe you could appeal to his better nature. He's bound to be a bit cagey about it - but supposing they had some power over him? You'll never know, unless you talk to him."

The rave was held at a farm just a few miles outside London. Joshua eased his vehicle onto a field. There were thousands of people already in attendance.

Elijah twiddled his ecstasy tablet between his finger and thumb, reluctant to take it. On the one hand, he knew he'd enjoy himself - get swept up in the music, see beauty all around him and temporarily blot out everything that was sordid. On the other hand, there was always the possibility of a downer. Elijah closed his eyes. Without warning, Perry's sneering face tore through the darkness, filling him with fear. Sod it! He threw the pill into his mouth and took a glug of water.

A light show was already underway as the lasers shot spikes of purple, pink and green across the landscape. Elijah felt his lips twist into a smile, gazing up at a huge smiley face before recognising it as a balloon filled with helium. It bobbed and swayed in the breeze, reflecting the merging beams of light. He wove his way through the masses, drawn towards a wide screen, onto which a mosaic of computer generated images was projected. Splinters of grey and white exploded into rainbow fractals. Elijah remembered they were called 'Mandelbrot sets.'

"It's gonna be okay," Joshua whispered. "There'll be justice one day, you'll see..."

Elijah found himself nodding - even though a tiny part of him still walked in terror.

III

October 1990

Eleanor finally brought her private prosecution against Perry. It was fortuitous that David Edgar had logged some of the evidence beforehand - without it their case would have been flimsy. Yet no-one could ignore the lengths to which Perry had gone to procure and destroy her file - it did him no favours. In the light of Elijah's kidnap, coupled with his ruthless determination to kill her, he had virtually sealed his own fate; and it was for this reason, he was initially charged with the conspiracy to murder Jake Jansen.

The crime report detailing the assassination of Albert Enfield was considered even more serious; a situation where police feared they were dealing with not just one death but several, including the driver of the minibus. David knew the police had their work cut out - obliged to carry out a thorough investigation for which both sides would be given sufficient time to collate the facts and evidence. It was a complex case which was likely to drag on for many years.

For the time being, David managed to console them: he had made rigorous notes from Eleanor's file. He had also taken photocopies of the relevant sections; transcripts from NME including the photographs and most crucial of all, the manuscript typed by Evelyn.

"Thank God you recorded it!" Eleanor found herself gasping. She gripped her son's hand.

"These are the most vital clues from the 70s," David elaborated, "which coincides neatly with the era the crime took place. As for the rest - you will have to supply your own testimony."

"That won't be hard," Eleanor muttered. "As if I could forget..."

"There is plenty of evidence you gathered in the 80s," David added. "We can bring up the confrontation at Westbourne House. Perry approached and threatened you - as was witnessed by a number of people. There has been an ongoing campaign of intimidation ever since."

"And what about Robin Whaley?" Eleanor whispered in hope, "is there any chance we could prove *his* involvement?"

A look of woe was already drawn into David's features. He shook his head. "There is no evidence which links Mr Whaley to this conspiracy, I'm afraid."

"But we know he's involved," Elijah gasped. "He attended meetings at Westbourne House! Elliot saw him!"

"It proves nothing," David snapped. "They were friends. As far as we know, he played no part in your kidnapping, Eli and I'm sorry but I don't think we have a speck on him." He glanced down at his notes again, his brow furrowed with an expression of deep concentration. "There is however, one person we can investigate. I understand you were very keen to meet Mr Hargreeves…"

David raised his eyes and this time, they connected directly to Elijah's.

"Joshua met him!" Elijah spluttered. "He remembers him from the press conference. He said I might be able to appeal to his better nature."

Already David was nodding shrewdly. "You're Jake's only son. Norman Hargreeves could be vital to our case if he was prepared to confess his part in the conspiracy."

"But why would he do that?" Eleanor frowned.

"Why?" David smiled, snapping his ledger shut. "Because he is already serving time at 'Her Majesty's Prison Service.' He has nothing more to lose!"

Eleanor and Elijah stared at each other - and it was over the next half hour, David enlightened them. The truth which emerged suggested that Norman Hargreeves had never been a particularly honest man. He had been ousted from the police force for corruption, as Eleanor had already discovered from John Sharp. But it was over the next 12 years, he had been employed by a number of blue chip companies, ever keen to claw himself up to the top; until eventually, he became a senior underwriter for one of London's top insurance firms and where a number of fictitious claims had led to his ultimate downfall.

"He extorted a ridiculous amount of money over the years," John sighed, "but in 1988, he was finally convicted of fraud and sentenced to six years."

"Where is he now?' Elijah insisted, hands gripping the edge of the desk.

"Ford Open Prison," John replied. "It's in Sussex. Close to a town named Arundel."

Elijah was resolute in his decision to go there, despite Eleanor's anxiety. She watched him from afar - recognising the set line to his jaw as he stood before the mirror, combing his hair. There seemed no point messing it up with gel today. He needed to look smart and presentable if he ever hoped to reach this man's heart.

It was a meeting that left Eleanor with mixed emotions. Joshua was right; Hargreeves was the only one at the press conference who had ever expressed any remorse. Even the transcripts proved he had been tactful and sympathetic; where Whaley displayed little more than a cold-hearted tenacity to defend their positions. Eleanor sighed. If only there was a way they could nail that sly bastard which was where Hargreeves came in - he was the only one capable of blowing the whistle.

Two hours later, Charlie found himself gazing fondly towards Arundel: a tiny, hilltop town with streets packed with charming medieval buildings beneath the magnificent 'Motte and Bailey' Castle that surmounted it. There was no question he would be returning here, once he had safely delivered Elijah to Ford Prison. It lay a little further south in a remote setting. Charlie steered his car down a relatively quiet ribbon of road, where their first perception was an expanse of flat fields - the accommodation set out in tidy, regimental rows.

Surrounded by a high security fence with a manned security barrier at the main gate, the prison accommodation was never locked. There were no bars at the windows; just row upon row of white painted 'barrack' style huts.

"Well, here we are," he whispered. "Good luck, Eli. I'll be back to collect you at 2.00. Do you think that will give you enough time?"

"Hope so," Elijah shrugged, "that's if he even speaks to me."

His fears turned out to be unfounded. Almost from the moment a prison officer had escorted him to the visiting area, he was struck by a pair of piercing blue eyes. Norman gazed up at him and smirked. It was as if he had known straight away who he was.

"Elijah Jansen? It's alright, son, I've been reading about your plight in the papers. In fact, I've been expecting you. Won't you sit down?"

"H-how did you guess," Elijah faltered.

He lowered himself shakily into a chair, unable to drag his eyes away. Norman Hargreeves had changed very little; receding silver hair, the same stony expression set in a granite hard face. Elijah nearly shivered. This was the one time, he was finally about to glimpse a snapshot of his father's life as seen through his mother's eyes. He could imagine him now; trapped by the same interrogatory stare as on the day he was summoned to Scotland Yard.

"How?" Norman echoed. "What, you think I'd forget? I can see the resemblance! So you're hair's a little darker. You're not as pale as he was - but the shape of your face, your eyes, your build... you couldn't be anyone other than Jansen's son."

There was an uncomfortable lull of silence. Elijah could already feel himself wilting and he was finding it hard to meet the man's eye.

It was Norman who shattered the silence. "What did she tell you? Come on, don't be shy."

Elijah opened his mouth as if to speak, wondering where to begin. He had come here full of accusations, reliving the moment Eleanor had explained it all. If only he could recapture that feeling now - but in the light of everything since... He let out a sigh, conscious the anger was still festering somewhere. He could feel the words forming - they rolled onto his tongue like a ball of bitter phlegm until finally, he spat them out.

"Y-you were the only police officer who interviewed my father on the day of the car bomb. You held him for ages - destroyed his statement and b-by the time he left, there was a van waiting. He was grabbed by a gang of thugs - men who plotted to kill him!"

"And she has proof of this, does she?" Norman retorted calmly.

"Not yet," Elijah hissed, "but nothing stays buried forever, not in this day and age. It might have been easy for police cover ups in the 70s - but this is the 90s. If there's any proof, we'll find it, even if it takes us a lifetime."

"I see," Norman drawled, "do continue..."

"*Someone* must have seen him," Elijah kept whispering, "only there was never a thorough investigation was there? At least, not until now. You were hooked up with the criminal underworld, Mr Hargreeves, you liaised with gangs, contract killers - how can you deny it? You were thrown out of the police force for corruption!"

For all this time, he had retained a cool demeanour yet his heart was pounding.

Norman smiled. "Impressive. You seem like an intelligent young man. Though do you seriously think I'm about to confess any of this?"

Elijah felt the heat spread across his face. He lowered his eyes. "No - but there's more," he blurted. "You attended a press conference. There were witnesses - people who thought there was something very *fishy* about the way you handled my father's murder..."

"Go on," Norman added guardedly.

"It all goes back to that party where an MP got himself blown up," Elijah kept ranting. "Jake's band performed a gig there. Several people knew he *witnessed* something - but he vanished. His murder had nothing to do with drugs. Yet this is the story the police wanted people to believe and it was a pack of lies!"

"Calm down, Elijah," Norman sighed, "I remember it well. By *witnesses* I assume you're referring to the NME journalist - as well as those *kids* Eleanor was lodging with?"

Elijah gaped at him in panic. "M-mum saw copies of the transcripts."

There was an unexpected clatter of crockery as two men lurched into the area, hauling a tea trolley. Their dialogue was momentarily stifled. Hot drinks were offered. Elijah breathed deeply, blessed with the opportunity to compose himself.

But it didn't seem long before Norman was staring at him again - his eyes had resumed their penetrating quality. "Why did you come here?" he demanded. "What is it you want from me?"

"The truth," Elijah shrugged. "You say you read about me in the papers - so you must know I was kidnapped. I was chained up, Mr Hargreeves - threatened with torture." He raised his hand. "This is what Perry Hampton did to me - he branded me with his cigar..."

Norman shook his head, a look of contempt creeping into his expression. "You had the pleasure of meeting Peregrine Hampton," he sighed.

"He is the most evil man I've ever known," Elijah shuddered, "and as for that sadistic thug, Wadzinski... You *do* realise, he nearly drowned my mother!"

"Eleanor," Norman nodded, "how could I forget her?"

Elijah glared at him - ready to deliver his ultimatum. "Perry's in jail now, which is where I hope he stays for good - and *that* is why I came here, Mr Hargreeves. You are the only person left who can prove his true crime - that he conspired to murder my father."

"And why should I do that?" Norman sneered.

"What have you got to lose?" Elijah pressed. "You're already doing time! What difference would it make?"

"Confessing to what you're asking could add years to my sentence," Norman replied silkily. "Why should I sacrifice my freedom to help you?"

"I got the impression, my mother thought you were a good man," Elijah sighed. His face softened slightly, remembering Joshua's words: *Maybe, you could appeal to his better nature...* "I believe her. I don't think you're evil. Not like the other two - not like Hampton or Whaley..."

Norman's eyes narrowed - and suddenly, it was *his* turn to take the centre stage; wishing for nothing more than Elijah to grasp some semblance of the truth.

"So let me tell *you* something," he muttered, his voice lowering to a hiss. "A few days after your father was shot, I visited your mother in hospital..."

"I know, she told me..." Elijah started to interrupt but Norman raised his hand.

"She was being sedated - prone to hysteria and on the brink of a nervous breakdown. I was ordered to detain her. Fact is, she could have ended up in the same place as your father but she told me she was pregnant - it changed everything." He gritted his teeth, his face writhing with indignation. "I protected her! God only knows, the others condemned me for it. They wanted me to hand her over to the same thugs who dealt with your father."

"Theakston's gang?" Elijah whispered fearfully.

"Yes, Theakston!" Norman spat. "His gang were recruited for the murder. He was cleared! But if your mother had ended up in his hands - there's a slim chance you might never have existed! I refused to hand her over, in order to protect her."

Elijah's lip started to tremble. "I-I don't know what to say," he mumbled, "except that we're still in danger! If Perry walks out of jail in a few years time, there is nothing to stop him coming after us again."

"I know, lad," Norman said stonily. "Which is why I need to explain something else and I hope you won't think too harshly of me. Knowing someone like Peregrine Hampton had its advantages. He was a wealthy, powerful man who hailed from the public school system. He attended university and later Westminster - established connections with those in authority; high court judges, politicians. It was to my own personal gain, he was also a friend of the Deputy Commissioner of the London Police..." There was a certain flash in his eye as he gripped Elijah's gaze. "Enough influence to get me a promotion."

Elijah swallowed painfully. "He bribed you?"

"Oh yes. You see, I too craved power - I was hungry for it. I took my job in the police force very seriously, but I wasn't satisfied with being a lowly Inspector. All Hampton had to do was drip a few encouraging words to the right people. I jumped at the chance."

"And he expected you to abuse your powers in return," Elijah said disgustedly.

"He did," Norman smirked, "powers to have certain *trouble makers* removed. He also offered me an enviable sum of money - which brings us back to the politician, Albert Enfield. I don't know what you've heard about him, Elijah, but people in our circles didn't like him! He was a left wing socialist who's plan was to destroy this country's power structure. He condemned the police, the public school system - despised those in authority."

Elijah nodded but said nothing - refusing to be drawn into a debate. Norman had no concept of what he *really* knew about Perry, nor his hatred of this particular politician.

"I knew there was a plot to kill him," Norman whispered, "though between you and me, boy, I was appalled by the method. The IRA were a convenient scapegoat..."

"You knew?" Elijah breathed, "but you did nothing?"

"What did I care?" Norman responded evilly. "He was nothing to me. I'd already agreed to use my powers to protect those responsible. It was regrettable, Jake spotted that car on the road but we couldn't afford to take any risks, I had to get to him first." For a moment, he almost shivered. "I made a pledge and I promised to fulfil it. There were to be no witnesses."

"So what did they offer you in return?" Elijah demanded, feeling his hatred rise.

"I told you," Norman barked. "Wealth and power. It was shortly after your father's death, I rose to the rank of Chief Inspector - then finally, Superintendent."

The proceeding silence could not have been more strained. Deep down, Elijah was fuming, his earlier loathing finally struggling to the surface. He was horrified to imagine how anyone could be so corruptible - glaring at the middle-aged man slouched in front of him; wondering whether it had been worth it!

"I know what you're thinking," Norman scoffed. "Fat lot of good it did me!"

He sagged in his chair as if all the stuffing had been knocked out of him; his chin resting above his knuckles, his head drooping. It only took a split second for Elijah to spot the twinkle of a crucifix behind the neck of his overalls; and just at the point where there seemed little else to say, the conversation took a peculiar new twist.

"You're a Christian," he frowned. "Do you go to church?"

"Yes, I seek solace in God!" Norman snapped. "Is that so wrong? Why do you look surprised? You think wicked men like me are incapable of salvation?" He let out a mirthless sniff. "My wife thinks the same; I'm beyond redemption. She despises me and who can blame her? I used to hit her, you know! I've always been violent towards my women. Three times I've been married..."

Elijah could no longer disguise his shock. "Three times," he echoed.

"First wife was a cow," Norman grunted, "we got divorced. She took me for every penny. Then I married Felicity. Blond, pretty... but she never failed to catch the eyes of other men. She loved the attention - had a tendency to flirt. It drove me wild, so I ended up punching her too. She buggered off abroad in the end, no thanks to Maxwell! Your grandfather's boss in case you didn't know!"

"You knew my grandfather?" Elijah mumbled, "Ollie Chapman..."

Norman lifted his chin, his eyes turning stony. "Yes, I knew him. He and Maxwell considered me something of a laughing stock - the archetypal 'bent cop' but I digress. I didn't have much to do with women for a while - too busy pursuing my career in the police force and you already know how that ended! Then finally, I met Mary - we got married and had a son. He's a little younger than you, Elijah." He swallowed visibly, already his voice had started wavering. "They're glad I'm in jail. They're hoping it will teach me a lesson and when I finally get out, maybe I'll be a better person. If there's anyone I want to redeem myself for, it's them..."

Elijah detected the crack in his voice. He leaned a little closer; seizing the opportunity while the man's defences were down.

"It's not too late. There *is* something good you could do. You could help us convict Perry Hampton for the murder of my father!"

Norman gripped Elijah's wrist with sudden force, pinning it to the table. "Don't you try to manipulate me, boy. I agreed to talk to you - but I am not going to drop myself in any more shit!"

"So I'm willing to make a compromise," Elijah said quickly. "There's only two things I want you to confess..." He breathed deeply, ready to broker a deal. "After the car bomb - you purposefully went to the hotel to check if there were any witnesses. You spoke to my father. You know exactly what he saw, but you destroyed his statement. This is *all* I am asking of you. If you can agree to that, then I swear I won't mention the van *or* the capture. I know you didn't actually kill my father. Hampton *used* you. He coerced you into abusing your powers."

"Which is still a major crime," Norman spat.

"Maybe," Elijah nodded. He sank heavily in his chair, his optimism sliding. "Yet if you could confess to this much, it'd go a long way to securing the imprisonment of a very dangerous man. This could be the only decent thing you will ever do in your life..."

He closed his eyes, exhausted - just waiting for the wrath to come pouring out. Yet there was nothing but cold a empty silence. Norman let go of his wrist. Elijah blinked.

"I-I'm sorry," he spluttered. "I am not trying to *manipulate* you, I-I only want justice."

"And lucky for you, I've decided to give it to you." Norman hissed. His eyes emitted another flash. "Talk to your lawyers. I'll make a statement. Just as long as you know, I'm not just doing this for you. I'm doing it for Mary and for my son, Robert, who's only just started talking to me again. Last of all, I'm doing this to redeem myself in the eyes of God."

Elijah nodded, where a flood of affection exploded in his heart. "Thank you," he whispered, "and whatever you did in the past, I reckon I can forgive you too - I am really grateful."

He stretched out his hand, heart hammering. Norman shook it quickly. His face hid an element of fear, but Elijah sensed his pledge was genuine. They had gained a crucial witness.

As soon as Elijah had won him over, he felt no desire to walk away - curious to know a little more about this enigmatic character who had only ever featured in his mother's story as the corrupt police officer. Norman explained a little about the 70's - his role in the police force, particularly during an era when London had been overrun by criminal gangs. They took a walk around the prison grounds. Norman seemed completely in tune with his surroundings - happy to show him the accommodation as they sauntered around the barren fields and all the while he kept talking.

He told him about Sammie Maxwell - a powerful influence who ran several brothels in the East End, along with gambling dens, pubs, a snooker hall and of course the diamond of his empire, the Malibu Nightclub. He had always known about the protection rackets for which his grandfather, Ollie Chapman, was notoriously associated. Finally he explained the turf war - the infiltration of a much feared gang leader named Dominic Theakston.

"Theakston," Elijah whispered, feeling his mouth run dry, "who now owns a nightclub in our home town! He's scary, though he doesn't seem as evil as people make out."

"You wouldn't have liked him in the old days," Norman sneered. "He took over 'Sammie's Patch' as you know. He even ran your grandfather out of town."

"Why?"

"Ollie killed one of his top men."

"Really?" Elijah whispered - dimly aware that he was also the man who had been enlisted to threaten his mother. "Tell me - was it Theakston who shot my father?"

"Not him personally - though it would definitely have been one of *his* men. Maybe you should talk to him."

Elijah nodded, stunned by the mysterious criminal underworld Norman had evoked; but time was running out. Charlie was due to collect him. It was with another firm shake of the hand, he expressed his final mumblings of gratitude. "I guess I'll be seeing you in court then," he finished gently. "It was good to finally meet you, Mr Hargreeves."

Later that night, Norman lowered himself onto his knees and began to pray.

There was no denying the surge of guilt that assailed him; reliving the time he had met Jake personally. He recalled his own prejudice. He had not lied to Elijah. Perry really *had* been a man worth knowing with his connections in parliament as well as the various gentlemen's clubs. As a staunch supporter of the establishment who stood against everything Enfield campaigned for, all Norman had ever wanted to do was to appease him - even if it meant abusing his powers to get rid of *troublesome people*. Or more specifically, Jake.

Norman squeezed his eyes shut, fighting tears. He had viewed Jake as nothing more than some long haired hippy who he had no qualms about dispensing with. Yet there were times when he wished he had never got involved - struck with a sense that Jake's killing would haunt him forever; and today, his son had plucked some tiny string in his heart, he had never known existed.

"Alright, Norm?" a voice clanged into his thoughts. "What's up?"

Norman hauled himself to his feet, conscious of the prison officer loitering. It was over the next few minutes, he found himself babbling out the entire ugly dilemma he was faced with.

"That kid's father was murdered," Norman sighed, "and I know who was behind it. He's asking me to testify in court..."

"And will you?" the other man challenged.

"Oh yes," Norman nodded. "I think I owe it to him…"

"Goodnight, Norman," the officer said softly.

He never saw the cunning glint in his eye as he turned and closed the door.

Chapter 27

I

November 1990

What Elijah could never have realised was that in addition to 'bent cops' there were 'bent screws.' He was still of an age where integrity prevailed; not yet fully aware of the corruption that blackened the ranks of nearly every profession and none so much as the prison service.

Perry gazed up from his paper and smirked.

In the last fifteen months, he had become gradually accustomed to prison life but it had taken a while. Those early days incarcerated in a police cell had been insufferable. He had never imagined he could handle it and yet somehow, he had dredged up the will to survive.

He could clearly remember the day he was refused bail - so convinced it would be granted. This was perhaps the first time in his life, he had no control over his fate. He had stood there in that court room trembling with fury, pale eyes sweeping across his audience - and he had never seen more hatred in a man's eyes than in the moment they had locked with Charlie's.

His heart felt heavy as lead when they had returned them to the remand wing and of course, no-one could have been more devastated than Rowena.

Still, at least life in the remand wing had been tolerable - permission to wear his own clothes, where the caress of pure cotton and Savile Row tailoring seemed a remote luxury, compared to the fabric of his customary prison uniform. He had kept himself very much to himself to begin with, wary as to how he would fit in - wealthy enough to afford a few luxuries such as the rich coffees and fine cigars which over time, he had generously offered to other inmates to *buy* their friendship.

Eventually, he had started to earn respect. An avid reader of books and newspapers, he had even started watching a lot more television, ever keen to keep abreast with current affairs. He was delighted the Conservatives were still in power - even more amused to watch the opposition making fools of themselves in the House of Commons. It was during a recent Labour Party conference that Perry could have laughed; referring to each other as *Comrades* - ranting on about the new Poll Tax initiative that Margaret Thatcher was keen to introduce. According to the news, there had been an outcry; how scandalous that wealthy citizens such as himself would be charged little more for council run services than the average worker!

It had drawn his thoughts to Rowena, wondering how she was coping, rattling around in that vast mansion of theirs - a memory which drained the smile from his face and where the echo of her voice still lingered...

"You fool! How could you have been so stupid?" Her voice had shuddered to a

whisper. *"Why in hell's name did you have to try and kill her?"*

"You never saw what was in that file, Rowena," Perry hissed. "She met Evelyn Webster."

"But you were caught, Perry - and now you've landed yourself in jail. How on earth will I ever survive?" she had been crying openly, utterly shattered.

"This was never meant to happen, darling," he conceded, "something went wrong…"

He clenched his teeth as a wave of hatred passed through him.

Everything should have been perfect. It had never occurred to him that his enemies might have a contingency plan. *Peter Summerville:* a name that never failed to charge him with sparks of wrath, especially since he'd discovered what was *really* going on behind the scenes, at the time of Elijah's kidnap. It had all come leaking out when the lawyers had been preparing for his trial - how some *friend* of Peter's had been drifting around the Grosvenor Hotel, just watching. Seamus O'Flaherty. There was another name which sent shivers running down his neck. He had already feared some IRA connection from what he had gleaned from Eleanor's file.

So Peter had evolved into the true enemy and Nathan felt a similar, violent loathing; consumed with his own nasty fantasies of what he would like to do to him, given the chance. They had known nothing about the pager either - yet another Machiavellian deception.

Perry had hugged his wife, that day and watched her go; grateful that Ben was still around to support her - and of course, there was always Elliot. Nothing had changed there, Perry thought. He allowed himself another pitiless smile.

He had never trusted James's former butler and even from the confines of a prison cell, he was damned if he was going to let him escape. The last thing Perry wanted was for some bitter old employee of James to go sneaking back onto enemy territory, especially now he knew the truth.

He had no idea, Elliot had gained some inkling of his mental state; the paranoia, the hauntings, which Rowena had finally owned up to sharing with him. '… *I was so worried about you, Perry.'*

He exhaled a bitter sigh - she had timidly confessed to their trip to the Community Centre. It left him wondering what had *really* been said - and whether Elliot had sewn those first seeds of treachery. He closed his eyes, savouring what had happened in the aftermath…

Rowena had returned home from the Magistrates Court court, to find him hovering around outside with a jacket slung over his arm. She had lowered herself onto a bench, just as the sun dipped behind a cloud. The grounds had been momentarily swept in shade. It seemed almost like an omen as she sat there in a trance. For once, her beautifully made-up face was frozen - where any lingering guests had avoided her.

"Where do you think you're going, Elliot?"

"I'd like to take a trip to Rosebrook," he answered her coolly. "I think it's time I visited Eleanor and Charlie - given what they've just been through..."

Rowena's head snapped upright. "You can't. Perry forbids it!"

"Perry's in custody," Elliot had taunted. "He no longer has any authority."

"No," Rowena sighed, "but I do. Let's not fall out over this - surely you must realise this isn't sensible. Your loyalties lie with us now - those people are our enemies."

He had lowered himself onto the bench next to her. "Rowena, I may as well tell you, I have never felt any such loyalty. The Baileys may be *your* enemies but they are not mine! Despite everything your husband threatened, I care very deeply for them. Eleanor nearly died last week."

Rowena closed her eyes, she started to tremble. "Elliot, don't go, please," she whispered. "I need you more than ever..."

"I'm sorry, but you can't stop me," he replied, slipping on his jacket.

The shadow had spread itself further across the grounds and the air felt chilly. Several minutes later, she had watched him go tearing down the wooded drive like bird escaping from its cage.

Perry's eyes narrowed. This was the only occasion Elliot had stood up to them, a situation where it was useful to have Ben around to take care of things.

Even better, he was still allied to Alan Levy - along with his secret gang of thugs. Orders had spread fast and by the time Elliot came sloping back to Westbourne House, no doubt to collect the rest of his belongings, Ben had been waiting for him.

He had marched into his room uninvited and closed the door.

"I wouldn't even bother to pack," he whispered nastily, reaching into the pocket of his leather motorcycle jacket.

The expression on Elliot's face must have been priceless! Ben had narrated the story with relish; describing how he had flaunted a photograph in front of the man's terrified eyes.

"You were warned what would happen if you stepped out of line..."

The truth that emerged was that Ben had engineered a violent assault. Elliot's illegitimate son, Alex, had been on his way home from work, that day, when he had been unexpectedly set upon; repeatedly kicked and punched. Apparently, a number of shocked onlookers stood, frozen on the pavements - powerless to do a thing. Eventually, the police and ambulance had been called; the young man rushed to hospital where he lay in a terrible condition, his face a mask of hideous black and purple bruising. Elliot had leapt away from the photo as if it was on fire.

"We've got thugs spread all over London," Ben kept taunting. "I gather he's a *friend* of yours..."

"A relative," Elliot sobbed in horror. "How could you be so evil! What is it you people want from me, haven't I served you for long enough…?"

"You are not going to abandon my mother," Ben hissed. "She *said* she needs you. So don't you dare bugger off and leave her like that again, do you understand?"

It was indisputable that Elliot would remain in their power, his wings well and truly clipped.

He had even been permitted to visit Alex in hospital - but only with Ben as an escort.

The moment they were back inside the car however, he continued to torment him with his threats - reiterating the warning of a dangerous gang leader renowned for being 'creative' with a scalpel; and they were banking on Elliot's unwavering loyalty if Alex wanted to keep his good looks.

Perry nodded to himself, triumphant he still held an element of power.

The following months however, had not been pleasant; the looming trial, the statements of his victims from which it was impossible to escape - and where a 'guilty' plea seemed the most obvious strategy in the light of the overwhelming evidence.

The ensuing trial had been speedy and uncomplicated; there was no need for any cross examination - just a lengthy recital of their villainy, while his enemies sat watching from the public gallery. He had felt the burn of their eyes, right up until the moment the judge had passed sentence.

Eight years seemed a hell of a long time but it wasn't forever. Perry relived the moment he had glanced up and met Elijah's eye, clocking the panic etched into his tender young features. It was as if a fire had erupted in his heart, a sense they could easily be out in less - and that in itself, had brought a warm and satisfying glow of amusement.

Now all he had to do was survive - to prepare for the next stage.

The 2nd chapter of his imprisonment had been harder to adjust to.

In the first instance, it meant having to endure longer hours in a cell where the repetitive clang of metal doors left him startled. It was fortunate, he shared a cell with Nathan. The two men had always got along well and as partners in crime, they had bonded even closer.

Yet there were times when prison life filled him with dread; the lack of space and privacy - the cloying stench of disinfectant and prison food. The lack of inhibitions in other men irritated him - his peace violated by the unsavoury sounds of belching, farting and snoring.

Nathan on the other hand, faired better - a lifetime of mixing with criminals had proved to be an advantage, not to mention his height and strapping build.

In addition to physical work and weight-training, Nathan continued to behave as his personal body guard. Thus, despite Perry's social standing, his obvious wealth and plummy public school accent, he was left well alone. In fact, it was over the next few months that he too, started to bond with the criminal community - amused by their anecdotes which he found educational as well as compelling. He had taken a particular shine to a former gangster named Eddie whose advice turned out to be priceless.

"Shouldn't 'ave tried to kill 'er out in the open," he muttered evilly, one night. "Better would 'ave been to lock 'er up somewhere, where no-one could interfere…"

Perry smiled sagely, praying for a day when they might be able to heed his words of wisdom.

Now sixth months down the line, a second trial was imminent.

He had been formally charged with conspiracy to murder, where the face of Jake Jansen reared up to taunt him yet again. Perry shuddered, knowing he needed to retain a sense of calm. By this time, he and Nathan had penetrated a far deeper network - one which embodied the inmates and prison officers of other establishments.

It was through this very network, they had effectively come to learn of Elijah's visit to Ford Open Prison. It had triggered an alarm - where his chosen 'contacts' had rapidly gleaned some forewarning of Hargreeves's treachery.

But there was no way he was going to allow this to happen. There would be no statement from Hargreeves. They *had* to get to him first.

Perry gazed down at the headline with shiver. The news that Norman Hargreeves had been found hanged in his prison cell could not fail to deliver an immense swell of pleasure.

The only challenge facing him now, was to prove that he was *not* the man Jake had seen by the roadside. At least, the wheels were turning in the right direction, supported by an ever expanding web of allies inside and out - and where his son's criminal connections had never been more crucial.

II

There were days when Elijah focussed on everything that was good in life; thankful he had escaped the horrors of his captivity and blessed that his mother was still alive, even though the ordeal had never stopped haunting him.

Despite his inner turmoil, it had been an interesting year. At 17, Elijah was beginning to show an interest in current affairs. It started in January when he was unavoidably drawn to the news of a protest march campaigning for the 'Right to Party,' a reaction to the government's first draconian attempts to ban illegal raves. The notorious 'Anti Poll Tax riots' followed in April which also featured prominently in the news.

Finally in tune with British life and politics, Elijah was also loving college.

It marked the second chapter in his life where a radical change had taken place and so different to being at school; no uniform, permission to smoke - an institution where tutors treated him like an adult, not a child. It was his art foundation course which ultimately gave him the scope to expand his creativity - and by the summer of 1990, he had produced a number of remarkable paintings in all types of media.

The sketchpad recovered from the Hamptons' attic suite felt like some sort of memoir. It had sparked up the inspiration for his most famous work to date; a watercolour titled 'Pimlico Prison' which had attracted media attention. It was a contemporary work which depicted the atrocity of his kidnap. Peter described it as a form of catharsis; a pale regency terrace shimmering behind a shattered window pane and where the reflection of a shackled wrist in the background was almost subliminal. The piece hung proudly in Avalon's art and antiques gallery which had finally opened its doors to the public. She had been glad of the publicity.

Elijah cherished his friends and none more than Avalon. At the same time, he was enjoying the first flush of a new relationship. He was drawn to Caitlin because of her individuality - a sultry blonde, who wore clumpy Doc Martens with the most feminine, floral dresses. Her long, sleepy grey eyes reminded Eleanor a little of Alison Merriman. Small and petite, Elijah adored her.

Sadly, there were darker days: days where his life seemed like a wasteland of destruction and chaos - especially as they prepared their case for the imminent trial.

It was only now, the truth was finally unravelling. Photos of Jake had started to appear on the TV and in the media. His *own* father - and yet, he seemed like a stranger! It came as a painful blow; a father he revered but had never actually known - a father his enemies had taken from him.

There were times when Elijah couldn't help but speculate on what might have been. His father could have been famous. He might have had beautiful groupies hurling themselves at him. It was even possible, he might have *left* his mother. But in another context, he imagined what it would have been like growing up in Holland - having brothers, sisters and being part of a normal family. It was a life he had been denied, a childhood stolen.

The ugly headline glaring up at him now however, was the final straw.

He slammed the paper down on the kitchen table, his face ashen. Margaret gazed up from her grapefruit half, her pretty features drawn into a frown.

"It's not your fault, Eli," she whispered.

"Yes it is!" Elijah snapped. He quaffed back half his coffee, banging the mug down next to the paper. "I mean - how can it not be? I only saw him last week! Our discussion must have been the final thing that pushed him over the edge!"

He closed his eyes as the image of Norman Hargreeves flickered like a dying flame. For a moment, he had truly believed that justice would prevail -

where this tragic news brought another black cloud hurtling into his world.

Eleanor tiptoed into the room - she had just been discussing this latest atrocity with John Sharp. She too, was visibly shaken, her head spinning from the horror of it all. Elijah stood up, an unlit cigarette already clamped between his lips as he put on his coat.

"Elijah, stop this!" Eleanor gasped. "I'm as upset as you are but I cannot believe his death could have been suicide!"

She touched his arm, wary of his mood swings. Her son was a text book case of teenage angst, these days and it was obvious the news must have floored him.

"I've spoken to John," she added quickly. "Hargreeves might have been a little depressed but according to those who knew him, he was of sound mind…"

Elijah shook her off irritably. "What - so you're saying this was murder?"

"Yes," Eleanor answered him numbly, the volume draining from her voice. "There's going to be a thorough investigation. It was an open prison, Eli, the doors were never locked. Anyone could have got to him - even someone allied to Perry."

Elijah shook his head. There was a slight glitter in his eyes which could have been tears. "So it *was* my fault. He promised to be a witness, Mum, a very important witness. He never even got to give a statement to the police…" he broke off suddenly, his eyes widening. "That's it!"

He turned towards the back door, an element of steel working its way into his expression.

"Where are you going?" Eleanor gasped.

"I'm going down the nick!" he snapped, reaching for his lighter. "Norman might not be able to make a statement but I can! I'm going to tell them everything he told me and then *I'll* give his testimony in court!"

"Elijah, you don't have to do this," Eleanor begged. "If you go marching down to the police station, you'll put yourself straight back in the firing line…"

"I already did that when I walked into Ford Prison," Elijah sighed. "I'm sorry, Mum, but I have to do this! Not just for us - but for him!"

Eleanor knew she had no choice other than to let him go, watching helplessly, as he lit his cigarette and stormed off. She was right, nothing had changed. Even with Perry incarcerated, her son was still in danger - oblivious to the hidden eyes that were monitoring his every move.

****

In another part of the country, a woman found herself staring down at the same headline. Her bottom lip trembled. Despite the ruin of their marriage,

Felicity had still loved him. But she had been young and vulnerable, her heart shattered; Sammie had smuggled her over to Italy and she had never seen her violent husband again.

A man hovered behind her. He possessed a tanned, heavily lined face, racked with an element of suffering which made him appear a lot older than his 61 years.

He lowered a comforting hand on her shoulder. "Who would have thought it, eh? C'mon Felicity, love, don't cry."

"I know he was a bastard, but I cannot *believe* he could have hanged himself," she whispered. "Do you remember him, Martin?"

"Yeah, I remember him!" the man sniffed. "I met some bent cops in my time, but none so bad as him; says here, he was chucked out of the police force. He was doing time for fraud…"

He broke off his eyes still darting across the lines of print - Felicity followed his gaze where the mention of a trial in the last section had captured their attention.

'*…the possibility that his death was murder, not suicide, cannot be ruled out. It has recently come to light, the former police officer may have been involved in the conspiracy to murder Dutch born musician, Jake Jansen, as mentioned in a historic dossier written by Eleanor Bailey (35). He was due to appear in court as a result of these allegations. He had sworn to make a statement, during a recent visit by Mrs Bailey's son (17).*'

For a moment, he stood very still. He tore his eyes away from the paper.

"Eleanor," Felicity recited - she raised her pale, tear soaked face. "Y-you don't suppose…"

The man squeezed his eyes shut, his hands already shaking as he grabbed for a half bottle of scotch left on the sideboard.

"Leave it, Flick," he growled. "Don't go dredging up the past. It's not her! We both know that's impossible!"

December 1990

III

Perry's expression was cold as he stared across at his son. On this occasion, they had managed to secure a private room on the grounds they had *personal family matters* to discuss.

A lone prison officer lingered in the room, despite his heart-felt plea. Fortunately, he didn't hang around for long - especially as the conversation hedged around Perry's health:

"I still suffer from nightmares, you know. They say, I talk in my sleep - my continual ramblings are keeping other inmates awake… at least the sessions are helping…"

The prison guard was starting to look uncomfortable. It was no secret that Perry was undergoing a rigorous program of counselling and psychotherapy to help him prepare for the next stage. Rowena had been insistent - fearing the strain of all this could kill him. It had taken the skilful intervention of a private family doctor to finally get them to agree to it.

Perry released a sigh as the door clicked softly shut, finally granting them solitude.

"Thank God for that," he hissed. "Now hurry up and update me. I've spoken to my lawyer, I need to know the score."

"It appears, the police are treating Hargreeves' death as murder, not suicide," Ben whispered back - he drew his head close, "but I've got some other news…" He swallowed, shooting a sneaky glance over his shoulder almost by instinct. "Elijah Jansen was seen marching into the police station last week." Ben spoke quickly, his eyes flickering with anxiety.

Perry kept very quiet at first, absorbing the information - and all the while, thoughts of a different nature were ticking away in his mind.

There had been a new inmate recently. His name was Adrian and he was a habitual thief, mainly to fund his relentless addiction to crack cocaine. His real value lay in Rosebrook or more specifically, a flat Ben had rented to accommodate the man's girlfriend. The couple had an eight month old baby. No-one would suspect anything of a typical young mother wheeling a pushchair around in the high street - nor the fact that she periodically lingered outside the Community Centre which lay so conveniently close to the almshouse.

Perry looked at Ben and smirked. "Well done," he responded, keeping his voice soft. "So now we know why the police are treating this as a *murder enquiry.*"

"Indeed," Ben sneered, "there is no doubt he would have told them about their meeting. There's even a possibility he might testify in court - repeat everything Hargreeves told him."

"Yes," Perry responded icily, "and speaking of which, I have something to tell *you.* According to my lawyer, our enemies are trying to bring this bloody court case forward. It could start as early as May next year. So we need to up the offensive."

Ben's eyes revealed a glitter of excitement - it had been many months since he had been absorbed in the thrill of organised crime and he was clearly missing Nathan.

"The fact is, we've just got rid of a very damaging witness…" Perry added spitefully.

"Ssh!" Ben hissed, wary of the possibility they were still being monitored. "Just tell me your plan." He craned his ear to one side, waiting for his father to drip feed his instructions.

"It's over to you, Ben," Perry whispered. Even to a close observer, his voice would have been barely audible. "Time we injected a little more fear into their community - and this time, I want Elijah to be targeted."

"Are you sure..." Ben faltered but his father cut him off brutally, his hand tightening around his wrist like a claw.

"Yes," Perry kept spitting, "just do whatever it takes to keep him out of the courtroom. I always knew that boy was going to be trouble! I'm beginning to wish I'd let Nathan work on him a little more... but no. It's too late! Time to put the frighteners on him instead and if *he's* not scared, I'm damned sure his mother will be - enough to stop him from testifying."

"So what about *her*?" Ben frowned. "Isn't *she* the one you should be worried about? She's the principal witness - I wonder who else she's got lined up."

Already, Perry was shaking his head. "Be careful Ben. At the end of the day, there is no question that Eleanor *is* the most important witness, not to forget those Merriman boys. If any one of them is targeted, the police are bound to point the finger of blame at us. We can't take unnecessary risks. They might start investigating *your* networks..."

Finally Ben nodded, his instructions clear and understood. He pulled away from his father.

Perry was right. If the police started tailing him now, there was a grave possibility his movements could be tracked back to Alan Levy and that would be disastrous - especially given how much they were relying on him. Ben fought against the urge to smile as he settled back in his chair. Perry had changed the subject - alerted by the click of the door, just as the prison officer made a sudden reappearance.

Yet Ben's heart was racing. He craved a line of coke - anything to give him that extra buzz. In fact, he was hardly listening to his father any more, conscious of him rambling on in the background. His mind was on other matters; the notion that a new campaign of fear was about be inaugurated in Rosebrook and he couldn't wait to work on a plan.

May 1991

IV

It started on the morning of Elijah's 18th birthday. He watched as Sukey raced across the back of the lawn, alerted to the chirping of birds in the nearby trees. There was a flurry of wings as she leapt gracefully up into the branches. He hadn't seen Moss but could only assume he was somewhere in the neighbourhood, placidly doing his rounds.

Eleanor had shot up to London for another meeting with the lawyers. The court case was drawing very close now and scheduled to commence at the end of the month.

He experienced a momentary flutter of fear but shoved it aside as he sauntered up to the bus stop on his way to college - determined not to allow any thoughts of the trial, nor Perry to intrude on this momentous day.

It wasn't difficult. He had plenty on his mind right now, compelled to concentrate on the final stage of his art foundation course. He was immersed in project work and building up his portfolio in readiness to start a university degree course.

Elijah jumped onto the bus where a familiar sea of heads swayed into view. He was overjoyed to have been offered a place at two academic institutions; Kingston University which was his mother's preferred choice. But he had also been offered a place at Trent Polytechnic, in Nottingham - about 130 miles to the north of London.

The challenge of living in a different town excited him - somewhere far away from their enemies, where he might actually feel a little safer. He sensed they were still around; wary of Robin Whaley's presence - and never to forget Ben. He gathered he was spending a lot more time at Westbourne House these days, while Perry festered in jail. Yet the fear of retribution was never far from his mind, especially if Perry was to incur a life prison sentence. Yes, it would be nice to get away from it all - to explore somewhere new.

The remainder of the day passed in a blur and by 3:00 he was on his way home again, content to chill out for a few hours before the main celebrations began.

Elijah had wished for nothing extravagant - just a small intimate party at home, where they would be joined by Peter, Avalon and his long standing girlfriend, Caitlin. He was heartily disappointed that William couldn't be there, but William was at Sandhurst. He had sailed through his Regular Commissions Board - finally committed to endure an intense five month training course, from which he would emerge a 2nd Lieutenant.

Elijah kept walking. The air felt cool for the time of year with an icy breeze spiralling around the tree tops - but he didn't go home straight away. He found himself drawn towards the Community Centre Garden and eventually, the site of the new housing trust - inspired to do something he hadn't done for a long time. He pulled out his sketch pad. It suddenly occurred to him that he had never sketched this idyllic development of houses - the result of three years hard work.

Elijah shivered, pulling his jacket tight around his chest as he threaded his way down the path towards a horseshoe of wrought iron seating. He settled himself down before allowing his gaze to wander. It was almost a miniature village - clusters of family homes surrounded by a screen of silver birch trees. He could even remember planting some of those saplings - it had been just before his abduction…

He blinked, refusing to dwell. His hand was already working, capturing the beauty of the architecture - the diverse shades of brickwork, the tapering roof tiles. To think, Charlie and Andrew had invested hundreds of hours in the construction of these houses. There was a central green, a cluster of shops and a children's playground teaming with mums and toddlers. What's more, he knew that every single dwelling had been filled.

He felt a smile slip onto his face as he flipped the page to start a second sketch; now focusing on the magnificent apartment block to the rear of the development.

These stylish flats had thrown so many young couples a life line - even more so, given the gloom of the recent recession. There had been mass redundancies - homes repossessed, as people struggled to meet mortgage payments. But in the midst of this economic hardship, Peter had achieved his vision. He had inspired something wonderful for the hard working citizens of Rosebrook. These dwellings were pulling in an income of over £20,000 a month in rent now, which sufficiently cleared the loans of investors, including the council.

By the time Elijah had completed his second sketch, he rose to leave. He was still thinking about Rosebrook - hit with an appreciation that if anything good had come out of the recession, it was the gradual slump in property prices. For the first time since the 80s, there were some really affordable flats around. Even Andrew was looking for a place to do up. He was still doing well financially and ever since the new housing trust had reached completion, he and Charlie had resumed their own building projects.

Andrew was still working at the 'Cat's Whiskers' which formed a major part of his social life. He guessed he would be heading there now, although he had promised to join them later. He was resolute on dragging everyone to Bella's as part of the ongoing celebrations - firm in the opinion that you couldn't celebrate a proper 18th without getting hammered!

Andrew was in fact, as passionately immersed in his role as bar manager as ever - happy to join his colleagues for another night of pint pulling and cocktail shaking, intermingled with the usual cheery banter of fellow staff and punters. He was a familiar face now.

There were still times when he missed the company of Angel by his side - yet nothing could have astounded him more than to see Naomi Chandler strutting into the lounge.

She threw him a cool smile but Andrew did not smile back. She appeared to be with a group of friends - not to mention the smarmy, suited slug who had an arm plastered around her shoulder. Naomi muttered something in his ear, to which he expelled a bray of laughter. Andrew shuddered. He hated these yuppie types at the best of times!

"Bit downmarket for you, isn't it?" he said lightly. "What can I get you?"

Naomi gazed at her companion and smirked.

"I'd like a 'slow comfortable screw against a wall,'" she said with a giggle.

Andrew said nothing, unsure whether it was meant as a jibe as he reached for sloe gin and Southern Comfort. He grabbed an orange, hacking it into quarters somewhat savagely - secretly wishing she would just bugger off and find a table or something! Already her presence made him feel uncomfortable - but unfortunately, she chose to linger.

The night wore on. Eventually he turned to Patsy, one of the barmaids. She was also his latest girlfriend; a foxy, green eyed goddess with a glittering nose stud, her long straight hair dyed an inky black. It was all symbolic of the early 90s fashion craze known as *'Grunge'* which showed no signs of abating - a look that even Elijah and his girlfriend still embraced.

"I've gotta go in a minute, Pats," he sighed, pulling her up for a kiss. "Told you I was knocking off early - should just about get back in time for the party…"

"Celebrating something are we?" Naomi's voice shot across the bar.

Andrew froze, having briefly forgotten her presence.

He clocked that same disdainful look and it suddenly got him thinking. What must it be like for her and that slimy uncle of hers? Waiting in the wings - powerless to do a thing, while Perry was incarcerated behind bars, especially now another trial was coming up. It was obvious where *their* loyalties lay. Was it even possible, Whaley would be summoned as a witness?

Andrew felt a tiny ripple of cold. He wound his arm around Patsy, holding her tight. "Why are you so interested?" he said in a monotone. "It's Elijah's 18th birthday."

"How nice," Naomi said sweetly, "are you going anywhere special?"

"It's really none of your business," Andrew snapped. "After all - we wouldn't want him to go *missing* again would we?"

He watched Naomi's face turn white - her eyes emitted a sudden frost.

"See you later, baby," he grinned at Patsy.

Moments later, he left - hands buried deep in the pockets of his leather jacket as he swung left and proceeded to march up the High Street. It was 8.00. He broke into an unexpected jog, not wanting to be late - unsure what it was about that minor encounter that left him uneasy.

Elijah raised his glass, a bashful glow to his cheeks as he took a long draught of champagne.

It was very dark outside by now, the air chilly. Yet he was reminiscing - his day had been filled with joy; the hours spent at college, joshing around with his fellow art students - the peaceful walk home via Peter's housing trust - and now this hearty celebration. He breathed in the mouthwatering aroma of Italian pizzas, immersed in the company of all the people he loved. He was still gazing into his glass, watching the champagne bubbles fizz to the surface. Most wonderful of all was the exquisite two-tiered birthday cake, hand decorated by Margaret who at 16, would soon be leaving school to start Catering College.

"Happy birthday, Eli," Avalon's voice chimed in accompaniment to the tinkle of glasses.

Her eyes wandered in his direction, just as Caitlin had snuggled up to him - she planted a kiss on his smiling mouth. The warm glaze of candlelight accentuated his beautiful bone structure and the copper glints in his hair. Avalon looked away.

Elijah felt his heart squeeze. He hadn't missed that subtle, secret glance.

She was 21 now, as he lingered on the cusp of adulthood; aware he would be starting University soon. Three years down the line and then what? Maybe they would finally face up to their feelings; that lingering sense, their hearts were entwined - despite his devotion to Caitlin...

But first, they had to get through the trial - the next unsurmountable hurdle.

He noticed Peter's eyes had been drawn to Jake's photo. Eleanor followed his gaze. She was curled up in Charlie's lap, cocooned in his arms. It was obvious she was never going to forget their ordeal - and suddenly, it felt like yesterday. Elijah thought he saw her shiver - horror-struck to think how close Perry had come to fulfilling his evil plan. And where would *he* be now, if it hadn't been for Peter's clever intervention?

"Cheers!" Peter chorused, "and congratulations, Eli! There are times when I thank the Lord, you made it home..." It was as if he had been reading his mind.

Charlie smiled. "I don't suppose Hampton will ever know what was *really* going on in the background," he muttered. He tilted his eyes towards the same photo. "Best he never does - your plan was ingenious, Peter. We've never really talked about it much, have we?"

"Peter disguised himself as my father," Elijah whispered to Caitlin.

"Perry genuinely believed he was haunted," Peter added. "I confess, I acted on his weakness. I knew Eleanor wasn't supposed to be followed - I had to find a way of deceiving them."

He turned from the mantelpiece where his face betrayed a devious smile. Elijah could clearly remember him telling him about the wig he'd purchased from Selfridges in Oxford Street - the 70's style jacket and flares from a vintage clothes shop.

"Have you still got the wig?' he chuckled, already starting to feel a little drunk. "I dare you to turn up in court wearing it! Perry will shit his trousers!"

Everyone in the room collapsed with laughter and none so much as Andrew.

Elijah wondered if he was stoned; he could never have known about

Naomi - her ability to make him feel so worthless.

"Hey come on, we mustn't laugh," Avalon whispered anxiously. "I can't deny it - I'm worried about you, okay? The thought of you having to face that monster again..."

"We'll be fine," Eleanor sighed. "We've got Charlie to look after us. Adam Morrison'll be there too, along with Luke and Joshua..."

Her eyes shone with that strange faraway look whenever she was reminiscing; she was no doubt, thinking about Lucy and Joshua's baby-naming ceremony.

They had named their daughter Rhiannon Rose. Elijah felt a tiny tug of emotion. At 15 months of age, she was an adorable brown-haired cherub with glossy pink limbs and plump cheeks.

"I wonder who else could vouch for you?" Peter started pondering. "I've often thought about asking Reggie. He met Jake, didn't he? He told me - I'll never forget the shock on his face, the first time you walked into the Community Centre."

Elijah sat up sharply - he too was remembering something. Reggie had always seemed guarded in his presence and none so much as that chilling moment in church; a time when he'd been dating Holly. He locked eyes with his mother, recalling something even more poignant; and with everyone focussed on the aftermath of the kidnapping, it was time to bring it out in the open.

"I'll never be sure exactly what Reginald knows," Eleanor whispered. "if anything..."

She picked up her champagne glass.

There had been a day after their homecoming - a day when they'd clashed with the Magnus couple. They had wandered into the Community Centre, unprepared for the attentive crowd hovering by the tea bar; oblivious to their presence to begin with until finally, their shadows registered.

Eleanor had braced herself. Elijah would never forget the blaze in her eyes. "So what do you think of your precious Perry now, Hilary?" she muttered, "seeing as you were *so* convinced I was out to ruin him! Did it never occur to you, he might be hiding something?"

The hall had been gripped in a chokehold of silence. Hilary started to cry. *"How was I supposed to know, he would do something so wicked?"*

It seemed incredible that despite everything that had happened, Hilary was ever determined to cling to her 'high society friend,' Rowena; insisting, she needed her more than ever and that she too, had no idea what her husband had been plotting.

There was no question there would be a conviction - where the judicial system was finally faced with the prospect of an even more serious crime: the unresolved murder of Jake. It was the point when her eyes had swivelled towards Reggie, who had turned ghostly pale.

"Even if he did know anything, he'd never tell us," Eleanor finished bitterly. "There's only one other person who could have backed up my story and he's dead..."

"Bernard James," Peter nodded. "Don't worry - me and Charlie will be there! You have nothing to be scared of. Now come on, this is supposed to be a celebration. Who's for a top up?"

A second bottle of champagne was opened and eventually the cake was cut, but not before Elijah had snapped up a few photos of it. He was over-awed by the tenderness and skill his stepsister had poured into it - the warm, honey coloured icing, the intricate scrolls and most touching of all, the musical notes piped in black icing.

"It's fantastic, Margaret," he breathed. "You'll be on Master Chef, one day, I bet!"

With laughter drawn back into their conversation, he felt he could relax; forget about the trial where his mind had momentarily wandered. Their lives had been a tempest when he thought about it - remembering the rave. It seemed a lifetime ago; although it was undeniably the catalyst that had detonated the power of Perry's evil. He couldn't help reminiscing - his eyes dreamy. They flickered towards Avalon's lovely face again as he recalled their sensational kiss in the forest.

"Has anyone heard from Angel, lately?" he piped up.

Andrew cleared his throat. It seemed that he too, had an announcement to make.

"Angel's off to Ibiza. He's sick of London and needs a break - Lara's going with him..." He broke off, turning his wine glass slowly around in his hands.

Apart from a soft thud of music, the room had fallen silent. Andrew let out a sigh, wishing he could explain; but how could he relay Angel's fears, especially with the trial coming up? His notorious 'boss' was using him as an errand boy - whether it was to pass on messages or traffic drugs, he wasn't sure! But he was scared for Lara - controlled by the constant fear of what they could do to her if he didn't tow the line.

"I wouldn't mind going, too!" he suddenly blurted. He locked eyes with Charlie. "Maybe six months - get away from it all. I could get a bar job..."

Already, Charlie was nodding.

"It's okay, son, you go," he smiled. "You're right - a change of scenery will do you the world of good. I won't deny, I'm going to miss you. We make a good team, you and me."

"It won't be forever," Andrew grinned.

"No," Charlie said softly, "and we'll still be here when you get back."

"Brilliant," Andrew whispered to himself and with nothing left to say, he knocked back his wine. He shot a cursory glance towards the clock. "C'mon, you lot! If we're going clubbing, we should get off soon... it's half past ten!"

One by one, they struggled out of their seats, feeling so thoroughly chilled by now, they didn't really want to move - but a good night's clubbing had always been on the agenda.

Elijah slipped into his new black suede jacket - a family present. He had been touched by everyone's generosity; the beautiful cards, the gift vouchers to spend on new clothes, music and books. Margaret met his eye and beamed, delighted to be joining them. With her shiny, ruler straight hair and sophisticated make-up, she looked old enough to smuggle herself in among their ranks.

She darted quickly into the kitchen to grab a glass of water. Straight away, she spotted Sukey crunching away at her biscuits; yet Moss's remained on the other side of the mat untouched. It was a sight that made her frown. No-one had seen him all day.

Next morning, Elijah chose not to malinger in bed. His head was pounding from an excess of alcohol, cigarettes and dope, his senses foggy, not to mention the foul taste left clinging to the inside of his mouth. His ears were still ringing from the club's powerful sound system. In fact, the only thing that would make him feel better right now, was a strong coffee followed by a bracing walk in his favourite park. The air temperature felt icy despite the glare of sunshine. He wandered downstairs, flexing his arms and shoulders. Another card lay invitingly on the doormat.

Elijah scooped it up before he collapsed onto the sofa. He had no idea where Charlie was, though he could hear raised voices echoing from the kitchen - his mother and Margaret, engaged in some heated argument.

"He's gone missing, Eleanor! No-one saw him at all, yesterday!"

Elijah bit his lip, tearing open the card. He craned his head towards the kitchen, conscious of the friction snapping the atmosphere.

"Margaret, love, calm down!" Eleanor said firmly. "Will you please just hang the washing out for me! Then I promise, we'll ask the neighbours..."

Elijah frowned as he extracted the card. It possessed the outer appearance of a typical birthday card, the sort that was usually left blank for the sender to write their own message. He idly flipped it open and turned completely cold. He was staring at a pencil drawing of a hang man. It was reminiscent of some word game they used to play at school. Yet the words underneath were not hand written - each letter had been crudely hacked from a variety of different newspapers and magazines, forming a macabre collage of words. Elijah leapt to his feet, just as a loud scream tore into the air from outside.

Margaret was sobbing, pointing at something dangling from their rotary washing line.

Elijah followed the direction of her finger. The world started spinning as he absorbed the horrific sight. Moss; their beautiful cat, Moss - his tabby coat devoid of its lustre as he swayed lifelessly in the breeze from the rope knotted around his neck. Elijah clamped his hand over his mouth and retched, staring at his mother. Her arms were wrapped around his shuddering step-sister and all the while, the words on that card were tearing at his thoughts:

'b-A-d T-h-i-N-g-s h-a-p-P-e-N i-n T-H-R-e-e-s'

Norman Hargreeves and now Moss... There was no doubt as to the threat behind that message. He was next on the list.

V

"Hmm, I wonder what sick individual dreamt that one up," Perry sighed, wary of his audience. Several prison officers were flocked inside the canteen as he closed the paper, their eyes like blades as if anticipating some sort of reaction. It was obvious, everyone was going to think that *he* was behind this. "Whatever you think of me, I don't approve of cruelty to animals..."

"No, only humans," one of the prison officers sniped, "like burning that kid with a cigar."

"That was a long time ago," Perry drawled, rising from his seat, "and I was provoked."

"Whatever," the other man retorted coldly. "You sure you had nothing to do with this? Especially since *that kid* was supposed to be a witness in court? It's reported he's under police protection. Left the country!"

Perry was forced to bite back his smile. "Yes, I know and probably for the best..."

It was without another word, he left the canteen and crept quietly back to his cell for some peace. Nathan was already in there, having evidently read the same news story.

"I gather, they killed Elijah's cat," he muttered. "Sent him a birthday card - it had a picture of a hang man inside it."

"They did," Perry said, keeping his tone neutral.

Even *he* could never have envisaged the extent of Ben's cruelty; his ability to inject terror into a community. Adrian had been released last week - back on the crack cocaine where £1,000 would buy a lot of rocks! He was convinced he must have played some part - whilst the only other person who could have identified one of the cats was Naomi. Or maybe she had sent Elijah the card.

But Perry was not the only person to acknowledge that this atrocity had his son's hallmark stamped all over it. There came a turning point - where Avalon's recollections of the rabbit skull incident began to rake at the minds of the authorities.

Finally, Ben was about to be investigated. He would be under very close observation now, his day to day movements monitored. Only Perry knew, their precautions had come too late. The trial was due to start in two weeks time and without the incriminating evidence of Norman Hargreeves and now the Jansen boy, Eleanor had nothing! It was simply a case of her word against his and he could already sense who wielded the more power.

Chapter 28

I

The Baileys struggled their way through the next few days under a mantle of anxiety. There was never any question the incident would leave them traumatised, especially Elijah - this latest act of barbarism had exceeded anything the poor boy had ever lived through.

Eleanor kept a careful watch over him - Margaret too, since she was prone to frequent outbursts of tears. She was hardly eating again while Elijah sat as still as a statue, pale, tight lipped and withdrawn. His eyes harboured the same tortured look Eleanor remembered from almost two years back; a time when they had briefly been reunited in Perry's house. His tender spirit had been crushed, any lingering memories of his 18th reduced to a nightmare. Eleanor clenched her teeth - a feeling of suppressed hatred coiling its way to the surface like smoke.

The police were outraged and none more than Inspector Boswell - vehement in his opinion, the family needed better protection; it was a discussion which had finally pushed Eleanor into a decision. '*Do you know of anyone you could stay with - somewhere abroad perhaps?*'

She had no hesitation in contacting Jake's sister and after a lengthy, somewhat fraught conversation, Marjolein had urged them to revisit Holland. Elijah would stay with her for the next three weeks or at least, until the trial was over.

At first he was reluctant. He didn't want to abandon his family right now, nor his girlfriend - not to mention his studies.

"Under the circumstances, we're prepared to allow him some leeway," his tutor had tactfully explained. "Just as long as he completes his portfolio."

Caitlin, though devastated by this macabre twist of events, had smiled sadly into his eyes.

"We can still phone each other," she whispered. "I just want you to be safe, Eli!"

Over the next couple of days, Elijah was resigned to suppress his misery. He so *desperately* wanted to attend court - shout out to the whole world what Hargreeves had confessed to him!

Yet it took the iron-will of Inspector Boswell to convince him otherwise.

It was after all, Ian who had taken his statement - Ian who now insisted on providing his testimony; not only to step in for Elijah, but to describe the prolonged ordeal of terror the family had been subjected to, over the years. The business with the cat had sickened him - a scenario which made him think twice about the chilling stories Avalon had imparted. And how convenient that Ben happened to be in Spain at the time of the offense; some impromptu *jolly* with his rich stock broker friends. Ian was still suspicious -

especially given Eleanor's warnings that he was hooked up with the criminal underworld. It was for this reason, the police had finally decided to question him before placing him under close surveillance.

Right now however, Eleanor and her son felt relatively safe as they rolled aboard a ferry in the back of an unmarked police van. The rear windows were blacked out, concealing them from view; though it didn't prevent them looking out - watching the disappearing coast line as they headed across the Continent. On this occasion, there were no stops in the idyllic beauty spots of France and Germany; just a lengthy haul down the motorways of Belgium and Holland where gradually the landscape became more rural.

Five hours later, the roads were at last, beginning to look familiar. Elijah felt himself relax a little, recognising the fine steel arches of the bridge spanning the river; the roads teeming with cyclists under the gaze of the towering buildings.

Eleanor met his eye and smiled. "Nice to be back, isn't it?" she sighed, "and to think, you're finally going to meet Jake's family."

Elijah felt his sorrow lift. She was right. Maybe he couldn't be in court to watch his father's killer go down, yet he was blessed in another way. This was an opportunity to pay homage to Jake; familiarise himself with the city he'd grown up in and spend some quality time with his sister who he was thrilled to be meeting. She would be able to tell him so much about his father - fill in the gaps, Eleanor could never hope to. She might even have photographs.

They continued to thread their way through the city, using a map that Marjolein had faxed to Rosebrook Police Station. Two plain clothed officers accompanied them. PC Les Johnson and WPC Jemima Kelly. They had promised to remain in the neighbourhood for two days until it was time to escort Eleanor back to England. At this point, Elijah's 'safe house' was to remain under close guard, as agreed by the Dutch police authorities. There was no question that his horrific birthday card represented nothing other than a death threat.

Eleanor sighed with pleasure, forcing herself to push those dark recollections aside. They were cruising gently down a narrow street where the shops petered out and the buildings had begun to take on a residential look; tall, undeniably elegant, they possessed narrow bay frontages and balconies, walls stretching towards an unusual array of dormer windows in differing shapes and heights. Eventually, the van twisted into a network of roads before being squeezed into a parking bay. Elijah was the first to jump out, relieved to stretch his legs.

"Oh wow," he breathed, "it's so peaceful here!"

He wasn't wrong. Eleanor was next to ease herself out of the back, gazing at her surroundings in wonder. Her feet landed on cobbled brick paviours. The air felt clean - the streets lined with trees whose lush foliage offered a comforting cloak of shade. They scuttled quickly up the pavement where more of the same beautifully styled houses towered above. They were built from a lighter, golden brick and capped with red roofs. Elijah breathed in the smell of leaves. Everywhere seemed so green, from the gardens heavy with shrubs to the thick banks of ivy crawling over the tree trunks and up the walls of some of the houses.

The police officers steered them up a small path then rapped on a door.

It was opened instantly - the residents had obviously been expecting them. Eleanor blinked as a woman shimmered before them and her heart took on a strange, almost dizzying beat. She possessed a round face and curly auburn hair - yet her green eyes were almost identical to Jake's. They were glittering with tears in a way which exposed their multiple facets of colour. She felt a chokehold of emotion as they gazed at each other.

"Marjolein?" Eleanor gasped.

She let out a sob as they slid into each other's arms - her eyes had just fallen upon Elijah.

"Jake's son?" Marjolein shuddered, gripping Eleanor even tighter.

"This is Elijah," Eleanor answered huskily.

"Perhaps we ought to get ourselves inside," Les muttered cautiously.

It was with no hesitation, he nudged them gently into the hallway. They had not been followed, but he couldn't resist one final glance at the neighbourhood, before pulling the door firmly shut.

They stepped into a dimly lit hallway. Marjolein couldn't seem to tear her eyes away from Elijah. At 18, his resemblance to Jake must have been startling, despite the longer eyes and the soft swell of his lips. It was his facial composition, Eleanor realised, recalling every detail of Jake's lovely bone structure as well as the sweep of his eyebrows.

"Come - meet my family," Marjolein mumbled, fighting tears. The musical slur of her accent brought a smile to Eleanor's lips, "and then you must tell me everything…"

II

"I swear by Almighty God that the evidence I shall give shall be the truth the whole truth and nothing but the truth." Eleanor closed her eyes, her heart heavy as she stood in the witness box, her fingers locked around Jake's pendant.

It had been two long weeks since she had left her son in the custody of Marjolein's family and in all that time, the trial was drawing closer. Now finally here they were, enclosed within the wood panelled walls of one of the 18 courts inside the infamous Old Bailey - about to begin a trial for justice which had taken nearly 2 decades to be inaugurated. There was a moment of chilling silence as the courtroom swam before her, but Eleanor's mind had lapsed into another time and place.

She was picturing the park in Poplar, the day she had said goodbye to Jake; a spray of white carnations left lying on top of the stone. Even now, she could recall her profound, departing words. *'I swear that one day, I will find out the truth - I'll discover the real reason why they killed you and I swear to you that those responsible will pay.'*

Eleanor blinked. Her eyes fell upon Perry seated several rows back and whose expressionless face seemed pale. It struck her as uncanny that he could be so icily calm as her barrister opened the case.

It was in that first tense hour, David had reeled off her story.

It began with a summary of the previous trial; from the meticulously planned kidnap, to that last-ditch attempt to kill her. David kept his voice steady as he ended his indictment. *'It seems an incredible effort to go to unless the file contained evidence so incriminating - there was a real possibility that charges would be brought against him...'*

David paused for a few more seconds, knowing it was time to begin. He was armed with the notes he had prepared for his original case; notes which he was finally about to present to a judge and jury. Perry stiffened in his seat, his face tight - and all the while, Eleanor had been observing him before she took her place in the witness box.

"Jake was a prisoner when I found him," her voice rang into the courtroom. "I never knew the reason why until later - when he told me his story..."

Eleanor had never wanted to relive the terror of their escape across London but it was inevitable that Perry's defence lawyer would pick over every minor detail like a vulture tearing at a carcass.

"You describe your pursuers as some *criminal gang*, Mrs Bailey!"

"Those men were recruited to kill him," Eleanor whispered. "Jake told me everything. They accused him of 'telling stories.' He had only just given a statement to the police..."

"A statement which does not exist!" the barrister snapped brutally.

Eleanor gaped at him, her mouth dry. The horror of Norman's death slashed into her mind like an axe and it was suddenly so obvious why he had been 'silenced.' Only *his* testimony could have bourn out this first section of Jake's story. She shook her head sadly.

"I'm only trying to explain what Jake told me."

"Is it possible we could move on to what Jake is reported to have witnessed?" David requested, keeping his voice light - as if wary of the defence barrister's delaying tactics.

He was glancing at him shrewdly. His name was Darius Bentley - possibly in his early 50s. He was a handsome man whose sharp features depicted a predatory nature, as did the pale green eyes set beneath thick eyebrows - eyes which seemed dazzlingly bright behind the lenses of his glasses. It was obvious Perry would choose the best lawyers money could buy - primarily this highly skilled barrister with an unbeaten track record of getting his clients acquitted.

"Sustained," the judge nodded approvingly, his eyes fixed on Eleanor.

"Jake told me about an incident *before* he was captured," she said quickly, determined to spit the words out before Darius could bar them. "My barrister has already explained. He was one of the musicians at Albert Enfield's party. He described the venue - a hotel in a remote country setting and yet there was a car lingering on the road; a-a gentlemen in the driver seat, smoking a cigar…"

"And did he describe the car?" David prompted her.

"He recognised it as a Daimler - a black one."

"And the man?"

"Blonde haired and stocky. Smartly dressed in a suit and wearing mirror sunglasses. He had a companion…"

"Objection," Darius sighed, springing to his feet before another word could escape her lips. "I find your description somewhat *misleading*. Did Mr Jansen actually see the man's face?"

Eleanor swallowed. "Yes," she answered him truthfully, her gaze drawn towards Perry.

"You said the man wore mirror sunglasses," Darius added. "To be honest, I am finding it hard to imagine Mr Jansen would have recognised him again! His story would have been completely unreliable in a court of law, wouldn't it?"

"But he saw the car!" Eleanor cried out, "and this is the one thing Inspector Hargreeves was skeptical about. A Daimler - not many people own them. This was probably the biggest clue as to the identity of the man behind the wheel."

She clocked the glitter in his eyes. "Mr Jansen was Dutch, wasn't he? I gather, he spent much of his life in Holland. A Daimler is predominantly a British car. How could he be so sure?"

Eleanor pressed her eyes shut again, unsure what to say. She detected the sneer in his voice - hit with an intuition of how Jake had felt, levelled with the same type of interrogation from Hargreeves, as he repeatedly ransacked his memory for the same details.

"I don't know!" she finally gasped, "but he seemed pretty certain!"

Eventually, the trial had to move on. Eleanor had doggedly tried to explain everything Jake had witnessed, including the man in overalls under the minibus. It seemed obvious, no-one would ever grasp the truth of what he'd *really* seen - especially in the absence of Norman Hargreeves. There was little to debate - at least, not until Inspector Boswell took the stand - and after a short adjournment, Eleanor returned, determined to push ahead.

It was in the next hour, she was forced to relay the most agonising part of her story.

They had finally reached the night of Jake's murder; both sides listening in silence as her voice piped tearfully into the chamber. How could she forget that nightmare?

"They were hammering on the door. Jake could no longer ignore it. He thought it was the police so he hid me under the floorboards…" She gripped the edge of the witness box to stop her hands shaking. "I heard a group of men force their way in…"

Both lawyers waited until she had struggled her way to the end. She had barely mentioned the pop of a gun shot however, when Darius was on his feet. Eleanor's heart pounded, knowing what was coming.

"Mrs Bailey - is it not true, you recognised the voice of Mr Jansen's killer, that night?"

She stared at him in dread, choked by the truth of her original testimony.

"Could you kindly answer the question," Darius coaxed in a tone that sounded unusually soothing. "I realise this is distressing - but did you not inform the police, a man named *Dominic Theakston* shot your boyfriend?"

"I-I did b-but…"

"Objection!" David shouted, spinning towards the judge. "Mr Theakston was acquitted of that crime based on indisputable forensic evidence supplied by the Metropolitan Police!"

"But he was there wasn't he, Mrs Bailey?" Darius pressed, the earlier spark now searing through his lenses. "Mr Theakston *was* arrested. I understand, you changed your story. Is it not true, this same man threatened you…?"

Eleanor shook her head, consumed with panic. This was the one scenario she had been dreading - the fear that if she attempted to bring Perry to justice, Dominic would be dragged into it. It was a scenario that took her right back to that terrifying meeting in his nightclub: *'Hampton's gonna let loose it was my gang recruited for the killing.'*

Dangling on the edge of her mind was his second threat! If he went down, it was Charlie who would end up being hurt; the reason she had buried her file for all those months. Even with her amendment, it was inevitable the accusation was going to resurface. There was nothing she could do, they had her trapped. Eleanor started to cry. She just couldn't help herself.

"I'm sorry," she spluttered. "I-I thought I *did* hear his voice - directly above the place where I was hidden, beneath the floorboards…"

"Eleanor, please - take as much time as you need," David intervened kindly.

Eleanor sighed. She had sworn an oath - to tell the *whole* truth. It was with no hesitation, the words came spewing from her lips unrestrained. She rapidly recalled the chair they had chained him to - how Jake had nudged it across the floor to conceal the treacherous squeak of one of the boards. She knew, without question, that loose board was located a couple of feet away and to her left; that Dominic had been facing Jake in the moment he was shot.

"I could hear every word he was saying," she shivered. "He said that Jake was *'a marked man.'* He was *'never going to escape'* and th-then finally I heard the shot..."

"Forensic evidence proves that Jake was shot from behind," David added hastily, "evidence which is yet to be presented to the court. My client speaks the truth, your honour. Jake was shot in the back of the head. Mr Theakston was *not* his killer!"

Eleanor felt the breath pour from her lungs, almost giddy with relief; but Darius was staring at her intently again, his eyes like lasers.

"All you've confessed, Mrs Bailey, is that Perry Hampton was *not* Jake's killer. I must therefore ask - why is it, *Mr Theakston* hasn't been summoned here as a witness."

Eleanor sighed - a tear plummeted down her cheek. "All I know is that Jake was murdered by a contract killer. Dominic may yet be able to identify him..." she raised her eyes to stare at him, "but he may also confirm the identity of the man who *enlisted* their gang for that murder."

It was to her greatest satisfaction that Perry lowered his eyes - and suddenly, he could no longer look at her. They had him trapped.

"God, that was horrible," Eleanor shuddered.

It was midday and David had whisked her away for a discreet lunch. The area near the Old Bailey was hectic, already thronging with people flocking to the various cafés around Paternoster Square and St. Paul's, including an abundance of stockbrokers and white collar workers.

"Don't worry," he smiled, "you're doing really well! I cannot believe you deflected those questions so cleverly - especially the part involving Mr Theakston."

"I don't want him to go down for this," Eleanor mumbled.

She sipped her tonic water, deep in thought. It seemed a *very* long time since she had made the amendment to her file. She had hoped it would be enough. But Dominic was entangled in the conspiracy as much as any of them - as Darius suggested, he might yet be called to testify.

"So where are we going with this?" she sighed.

"There is only one place your story is heading and that's the press conference - the night you came face to face with Mr Hampton. Your friends will back up everything you say, so don't let Mr Bentley unhinge you. This is the most important part of your testimony."

It was just as David suspected. So far, every chapter of Eleanor's tragic story had been extracted, from the moment Jake was captured to the terrible night of his killing. There was little left to disclose other than the time she had malingered in hospital, suffering from shock; the visit from Inspector Hargreeves and the months of self preservation - her pledge to protect their unborn child, knowing her enemies were still out there.

"Can you tell the court why you organised the press conference?" David led her in gently.

Eleanor felt the touch of a smile. She could clearly remember the day they had cottoned on to the idea; the scene in the Merriman's sitting room unravelling. She had not long given birth. The heady tempo of 'Free Spirit' had been thudding away in the background and there had been a snippet of news in NME, after a report of Jake's murder had filtered its way to his homeland.

"The press coverage was particularly damning," Eleanor continued sadly. "No mention was ever made of Jake's band, nor his musical talent. We just wanted to put the record straight."

"The conference was designed to honour Jake's life," David nodded.

"NME contacted a man named Jordaan Van Rosendal; manager of the record company who signed up his group..." She spoke softly, momentarily glancing at Perry - searching his face for a reaction though still, he remained icily composed. It was almost as if he had lapsed into some sort of meditative state. Eleanor took a deep breath. "Jordaan called the press conference, hoping to get some answers. Jake's band were on the verge of success."

The memories were ticking through her mind like a tape. She could clearly remember the moment Perry had appeared; some *companion* of Whaley's. And yet his presence had drawn attention - stockily built, thick blonde hair. There was something in his demeanour that conveyed power.

Eleanor kept talking, guided by her barrister. It was David's careful prompting which kept her on track, whilst Darius pounced at every opportunity.

"You had no idea who he was though, did you?" he cross-examined. "Is it not the case, he was merely a companion of Mr Whaley's - invited for no other reason than to support him?"

"Yes, they were friends," Eleanor nodded. "Though we had to ask ourselves, *what was he really doing there?*"

"I'll ask the questions," Darius hissed with sudden coldness. "You on the other hand, weren't supposed to be there at all, were you? You hid behind a curtain purely for the purpose of eavesdropping!"

"This is irrelevant!" David snapped. "We are just trying to establish how *my* client ultimately came into contact with Mr Hampton! These people were her enemies..."

"Can we have some order please," a third voice clanged into the proceedings.

Eleanor gazed at the judge. It was impossible to gauge the thoughts mirrored behind that stern, impenetrable mask. She hoped he would be fair-minded.

"I apologise, your honour," David muttered with a small bow. "May we continue?"

It was over the course of the afternoon they combed through the finer points of the event.

David felt blessed he had taken a copy of that transcript! It would have been impossible to have recaptured the same level of detail. Eleanor felt exhausted. They took a break, in which time the jury were left alone to absorb the burden of information. By the time the session was resumed however, Eleanor knew they had reached the most critical part of her story.

Darius scrutinised her beadily. "So this is the point you jumped out of hiding - where I gather you made a series of outrageous allegations."

"They were not outrageous," Eleanor gasped, "I was speaking the truth!"

"You disputed the word of a senior police officer," Darius scoffed, "a local ward councillor. You accused them of reciting lies and yet what proof did *you* have?"

"Jake was not a drug dealer!" Eleanor started shuddering. "That story was a cover up!"

David shook his head in dismay, wary of how cleverly he was trying to derail her. They were hedging towards the moment Perry had lost control; a situation Darius was desperately trying to avoid. Yet they had covered so much ground. Now if only they could end this first session with Perry's explosive reaction.

"Your honour, we have *three* witnesses who attended this event," he jumped in. "Is it not possible, Mrs Bailey could just finish her story?"

"Do continue," the judge drawled. He too, was beginning to show signs of fatigue.

Eleanor bowed her head, shoulders slumped as she gripped the brass rail in front of her. "Yes, I made an appearance. This was the first time I came face to face with Mr Hampton and he went berserk! He tried to have me removed..." She closed her eyes, recalling the moment she had passed Jake's song lyrics across to Jordaan - the air had been frothing with hostility, propelling her from the table. "Adam asked if there was *anything* I could tell them. I think they already knew the truth. Jake *had* witnessed something..." she broke off, staring resolutely at Perry. "He was practically choking with rage! Purple in the face, clawing at his tie, accusing me of slander. I thought he was having a heart attack. Last of all, I told them about my secret file..."

"I understand, this was the first time you spoke of it," David nodded. He seemed visibly relaxed, pleased it was out in the open.

Darius on the other hand, looked furious. He shot to his feet, drawing right up close to the witness box. Eleanor gazed fearfully back at him, waiting for him to rip her apart.

"And what exactly did this 'secret file' of yours contain, Mrs Bailey?"

"I wrote down everything I could remember," Eleanor said, "from the moment we met - to the night Jake was shot. I added some news clippings - the bomb explosion for example."

"Did it contain Mr Hampton's name?"

"Not then," Eleanor added fearfully, "but…"

"Mrs Bailey - you stand there, glibly accusing Mr Hampton of the most monstrous crime and without a shred of proof to substantiate it!"

"I didn't know who he was, back then!" Eleanor exploded.

"No," Darius echoed nastily, "and there was no mention of him in your file."

"I object," David defended angrily. "This was the first time my client had ever met this man."

"There was no mention of him then, nor for the next 13 years!" Darius continued. "In fact, Mr Hampton's name was not added to your file until 1986."

"I - I can explain," Eleanor mumbled.

"I cannot help but wonder if Mr Hampton was a convenient scapegoat in your campaign for justice. You met him again didn't you? Many years later and in an entirely different confrontation."

"Yes," Eleanor said miserably.

"Your fiancé made mention of a man with blonde hair and that is all. Mrs Bailey, your testimony is flimsy. In fact, I suspect this entire prosecution is based on some spiteful vendetta; one where you sought to avenge your friend, James Barton-Wells, am I right?"

The intensity of his glare left her trembling. Eleanor could not speak.

"Your honour, I object," David kept spluttering, "this is completely unjustifiable…"

His words echoed across the courtroom, a meaningless jumble. Yet she could see the pattern of the defence. It was connected to something *she had* said; words on that fateful evening in Perry's house. *'I was devastated by what you did to James and his family. To Charlie's… If I could prove, you were the man behind Jake's murder then maybe it would give me an edge.'* She had accused Perry of being evil and now those same words were being cleverly used against her.

"I only warned him, that if I ended up dead like Jake, my file would be published!"

"But it seems clear, you did a lot more research in the years that followed, Mrs Bailey."

"I vowed I would bring his killers to justice," she finished numbly.

And this was how the first day ended.

Eleanor stepped from the witness box, her head spinning. She met Darius's eyes once more; but already, her evidence sounded dubious, granting Perry a dangerous advantage.

A taxi cruised into the curb outside the forbidding grey walls of the Old Bailey. Eleanor shuffled into the back seat and David followed, his intention to escort her to a hotel in High Holborn.

She was allowed no contact with Charlie since he was later due to stand witness; but they had agreed to meet John Sharp who was particularly curious to know how things were progressing. Eleanor stole a final glance at the imposing archway where a cast iron grill protected the entrance. An Ionic column towered above - a cloaked statue crouching between the two which reminded her of the Grim Reaper and as her eyes travelled upwards, they scanned the motto: *'Defend the Children of the Poor and Punish the Wrongdoer.'* Eleanor turned away, unable to fend off a shiver.

"What a nightmare," she gasped. "Thanks to Perry's barrister, everyone must think I'm a complete liar."

"Hush now," David said airily, as the cab began moving. "He's only doing his job. Don't take it personally. I expect Perry paid a fortune for his services. It will be his head that rolls if he doesn't get a result!"

She glanced out of the window, her heart sinking. "What if they find him not guilty?"

"We'll cross that bridge when we come to it," David snapped. "On the other hand, what if they find him guilty? He could go on to stand trial for the murder of Albert Enfield! Now try to relax, Eleanor, today's session is over."

"So what happens tomorrow?" she pressed.

"Adam Morrison will give his testimony," David replied, "followed by the Merriman brothers. That should just about round up everything from the 70s era..." he trailed off, his eyebrows pinched into a frown. "It's a terrible shame Norman Hargreeves couldn't testify," he finished sadly.

The taxi pulled away from the Old Bailey to join a traffic queue. They hadn't spotted Ben Hampton sidling into the building just as they were leaving.

Ben's face wore no expression as he marched resolutely up two flights of stairs. He was hoping to catch up with his father. A security guard accompanied him - and eventually they found them conversing in one of the offices.

"Ah, Ben," Perry greeted him softly. "I'm glad you came..." he turned to Darius. "Is it possible we may have just a few words in private?"

Ben fidgeted with his tie, impatient for his father's barrister to leave - he had been hankering to impart some news of his own.

"I saw them," he sneered, the moment Darius had vanished, "having lunch together..." He drew his head close, his eyes narrowing.

It was no lie. How very convenient that the London Stock Exchange and Paternoster Square happened to lie such a short distance from the Old Bailey.

He had been tucked in the shadows of a pillared archway - his eyes never leaving them. He could never have failed to recognise Eleanor, lovely as ever as she sat braced at one of the tables - her golden eyes huge with trepidation.

"I couldn't hear what was said, but it appeared to be the barrister doing most of the talking. He looked quite pleased with himself. So how's everything going?"

"It's difficult to say at this point," Perry said coldly. "I have no idea which way the wind will blow. Why don't you spend some time in the public gallery tomorrow? Invite your mother. There are going to be several witnesses, including that journalist from NME."

Ben nodded, unsure what to say. He was watching his father carefully, conscious of the chill developing in his eyes.

"The name *Theakston* came up," he said disdainfully. "She finally confessed to his part. I must therefore ask you to do something very important for me..."

Ben's face tightened - he was thinking about the past. It took him right back to the aftermath of the kidnapping; Alan's casual confession that he had bumped into Dominic at the 'Scarlet Moon.' Alan might have had a bit too much to drink. Yet he could clearly remember the man challenging him about their alliance - moments before he let slip, he knew about Elijah's capture.

Ben shuddered. If only the stupid cretin had kept his mouth shut! Yet it gave him a sudden insight; a concept that left him reeling. Was it possible, it might have been *Dominic* who'd revealed Nathan's address to the police? There had been so many cops crawling around that night.

Of course, Ben would never dare to criticise Alan. The man was lethal. Further more, Ben needed him; he had been relying heavily on his criminal networks. How else could they have got to Hargreeves and ultimately Elijah? Throughout time, however, his father too had learned of Alan's indiscretion; but regrettably, Perry's hatred had spiralled to alarming new heights - where *Theakston* was yet another name added to his growing list of adversaries. It had reminded him of an earlier threat he had once made...

"Do you remember me giving you the key to my bureau?" Perry kept whispering. "The place we hid the *copy* of Eleanor's file?"

"Of course," Ben hissed, already picturing the leather topped desk in Perry's office.

"There is a page I want you to retrieve," Perry added, "a page written in Eleanor's own fair hand. She states with no uncertainty that Theakston was Jake's assassin."

"I remember," Ben murmured. "Why is this important?"

"This is the file she wrote *before* she changed her story," Perry said evilly, "*before* she saw the crime report, ruling him out to be the killer. I want Darius to see it. I want him to understand how certain that bitch was, before she started adding *my name* to her file."

"Isn't that a bit risky?" Ben questioned.

"Not if I'm convicted," Perry snapped. "Many years ago, I warned Theakston that if I went down for this murder, I'd make bloody sure he went down with me! There's a good chance, he'll be called in for questioning. And if there's any mud, I want it to stick."

"Okay," Ben nodded, glancing at his watch. "I'll bring it tomorrow - but what if they reach a verdict of *not* guilty?"

"It gives us an incredibly powerful hold over him..." Perry smiled thinly, just as the click of the doorknob shattered the peaceful seclusion.

III

It was past midnight. Swanley lay 20 miles to the east, where the very subject of Perry's spiteful reverie lay wide awake, his emotions in turmoil.

Dominic had spent very little time in Rosebrook over the last two years - instead choosing to pour his energies into improving his health club. He still had his finger on the pulse - all too aware of everything that was unravelling behind the scenes.

Fortunately, Pippa had stood by him. She was sprawled alongside him right now, her expert hands running over his bare skin. Four years they had been together and she knew him possibly better than he knew himself. The touch of her fingers was light as they traced over his many scars - but then again, he had confessed everything; the years of gangland violence, organised crime, killings and an incident of manslaughter for which he had served time. Secretly, she was thrilled by it; and as immersed in the management of his nightclub as she had ever been.

She smiled down at him, her eyes filled with adoration as she studied his many war wounds: the bullet wound that grazed his hip - a more serious stab wound to the thigh, added to a mosaic of cuts sustained from the razors and flick knives of rival gangs. Neither could she dismiss the pattern of cigarette burns trailing down his forearm. They were artistically concealed by a tattoo, although Pippa knew damn well what had happened to him as a teenager - her expression tender as she savoured the veneer of his skin, taut and polished, despite his 46 years.

"C'mon honey, relax," she whispered. "It's not like the police are battering down the door."

"Not yet," Dominic muttered, "but it ain't gonna be long..."

Pippa kissed him on the lips to silence him, thinking about the blissful life they shared; the hours of lovemaking where they must have covered every position in the Karma Sutra! She lowered her head where her lips brushed against his cock, flicking out her tongue in the way she knew he loved and hoping it might distract him.

She could sense his anxiety. She couldn't bear the thought of him being flung into prison; impressed how a man like him could have turned his life around. His two children, Anton and Bella, stayed with them nearly every weekend now, allowing Dominic's ex-wife the freedom to indulge in as many girlie weekends and health spas as she desired. He would have loved them to have had a child of their own but Pippa wasn't keen, a little too career orientated to feel any such urges. No, she wanted to cling on to the wonderful life they had - fearing a baby might ruin things. She could feel the pound of his heart beneath her palm as she stroked his chest - struck by a sudden tidal wave of fear. She raised her head.

"Do you really think you're going to go down for this?"

"Dunno," Dominic said tightly. He ran his fingers through her hair with a sigh.

They had heard news of the court case. Peter, of all people had kept them in the loop - not to mention, he had a man on the inside; a very old friend from London with whom he'd downed many a whisky in his crime boss days. He'd been tucked away in the public gallery from the moment the trial got rolling... but news of Eleanor's testimony had left him on a knife edge.

"Pity the stupid bitch couldn't have kept my name out of it!" he hissed.

"Hey, come on," Pippa soothed. "I thought it was the bastard defence lawyer who brought this up. Sounds as if Hampton's trying to nail you for this."

"I fucking knew he would!" Dominic retorted, his voice thickening with hatred. "If he went down, he'd swear it was *my* gang they recruited for the murder."

"But you were cleared!" Pippa argued. Her grip on his arm tightened as the terror began to spear through her mind. "Besides - I thought that woman *changed* her story!"

"Doesn't matter," Dominic snarled. "Fact is, the lawyer knows I was there. I *was* involved. I accepted a contract - I could still go down for *conspiracy* to murder..." he broke off, his jaw clenched in a rigid line. "Fucking cunt! I knew Hampton wouldn't back down. I told Eleanor but she wouldn't listen!" Dominic sat up, his dark eyes narrowing. "She'd better pray Hampton gets off, otherwise she knows damn well what's gonna happen..."

"What are you talking about?" Pippa whispered. She froze, her hands clamped around his arms, not liking the nasty undertone woven into his voice.

"She went for me once, you know - said I'd done the worst thing any man could do. I killed the man she loved!" He let out an unpleasant laugh. "Ironic, ain't it! 'Cos if I get convicted, her Charlie won't know what's coming to him!"

"Stop it!" Pippa shouted, the points of her fingernails digging into him. "I don't like it when you talk like this - you're starting to scare me!"

"I am not gonna let that bitch get away with screwing up my life,"

Dominic retaliated.

"Then get yourself a lawyer," Pippa snapped, "'cos *whatever* that Hampton fucker threatened, you are not gonna take the rap for this!"

If Eleanor had known of that conversation, she might have dropped all charges against Perry, there and then. By 10:00 next morning however, she was back in the witness box. She couldn't wait to see Charlie, knowing it would only be a matter of hours.

But first, they had to wrap up the relentless saga of the press conference.

Eleanor repeated her allegations with renewed passion. Yes, this was the first time she had clashed with Perry, oblivious to who he was at the time. His similarity to Jake's description of a blonde man had drawn suspicion; but she had been bewildered by his reaction - the irascible fury at the mere mention of her file. She had never discovered anything more; threatened by Dominic and finally ordered to leave London, where she had spent the next 12 years in woeful ambiguity.

At last she stepped down, from where Adam Morrison was about to take her place - relieved this first part of her testimony was over.

Adam on the other hand, looked ecstatic. His brown eyes emanated a certain glow as he began ruminating over the same press conference.

On this occasion, there could be no dispute. David had circulated photographs which clearly depicted Perry's thunderous face. The accompanying transcripts recaptured the moment when Robin had addressed him as 'Perry.' Judge, jury and court officials scrutinised the documents and for once, Darius sat in stony silence, letting the information wash over him.

"We were never able to print any of this stuff," Adam sighed. "Inspector Hargreeves ordered us not to. I believe they may have issued a 'D Notice.' Although we always suspected Jake's murder was a cover up. I'm pleased the truth is finally coming out..."

The next person to stand witness was Luke; confident in his recollections of the time he had briefly conversed with the two men.

There was little more he could divulge other than his initial impression of Perry. He had struck him as a man suffused with self-importance - 'a politician' with a powerful desire to stand for parliament. He couldn't quite explain why both men had disturbed him - yet there was no question, they had behaved in a manner which seemed shifty.

Luke vanished from the courtroom, only to be replaced by his younger brother.

Joshua appeared a lot more nervous. He had not only locked eyes with Perry - but a man in the public gallery whose cold blue eyes never failed to resurrect a spark of fear. Ben watched from above. He seemed to be lapping up every word of his testimony. Yet there was little Joshua could add, other than the fact that the two men seemed unusually aggressive - especially when they had attempted to stop him from leaving.

Before the morning session ended, Adam was brought back into the witness box. He felt compelled to bring up the subject of Jordaan Van Rosendal whose tragic death had effectively stalled any further investigation in Holland.

"He knew the band had been booked to play at the 40th birthday party of the late Albert Enfield," he said bitterly. "He mentioned it at the press conference."

"What happened to the band?" David injected into the examination.

Adam hung his head, his eyes filled with sorrow. "Someone put the frighteners on them which came as a terrible blow. I am sure at least one of them could have confirmed what Jake saw - a musician by the name of Andries..."

Perry froze in his chair, his face tightening. His thoughts turned to Ben, wondering if he had followed his instructions.

A bubble of activity arose - a moment, he could not resist a hasty upward glance, gratified to see his son gazing coolly back down from the front row of the public gallery.

"All rise!" the voice of the law clerk clanged into the hubbub.

There was to be another adjournment. The distorted mumblings in the background were gradually fading as the jurors filed out of the courtroom - but the lawyers were still talking.

"All we have established so far, is that my client attended a press conference," Darius was heard angrily protesting, "and precious little else!"

Ben smirked as a security guard let him back into the public gallery. Only this time, Rowena accompanied him, her grip tight on his arm. The afternoon session hadn't quite got underway, though it did at least give her a chance to acclimatise herself. She gazed over the rail, her eyes lowering to the court enclosure. She drank in the solid wood furniture, the jury stands, the witness box and finally, the large richly coloured crest which rested behind the judge, an official representative of the crown: *Dieu et mon Droit*.

"Dear God, I don't think I can bear this," she whispered dazedly.

"Just relax," Ben sighed. "Dad could really do with our support, right now."

His smile faded as his thoughts turned to Perry. He had been distinctly pale when he had seen him last, his voice curt, the light in his eyes subdued with some troubled emotion. Maybe all these accusations were finally taking their toll. Yet he had done as he had asked. He had passed Darius that vital section of Eleanor's file copy, urging him not to reveal how they had come by it.

"I'll keep it on ice," Darius whispered, "though I seriously doubt we're going to need it."

Ben nodded. His father's lawyer seemed confident. Although he had no idea where the trial was going. Little seemed to be happening as jurors and court officials settled back into their positions. Perry followed, escorted by two security guards. Ben heard his mother catch her breath as the vision of his thick white hair shimmered below - she gripped his hand tightly.

It seemed, the barristers were addressing the judge, indistinguishable in their flapping silk gowns and horse hair wigs. There followed a brief period of discussion as David began to summarise the events which had brought Eleanor back into contact with Perry. This inevitably led to the conflict at Westbourne House. Ben listened with intrigue. Though nothing could have delivered more surprise than to see William Barton-Wells strutting into the witness box.

Rowena froze, equally dumbfounded to see this impeccable young man whose calm, self-assured manner evoked chilling memories of James. But before the cross examination had even begun, she flinched to the click of the door. Ben whirled round, just as Peter slipped into the public gallery. Their eyes clashed. Peter momentarily braced to a standstill - undoubtedly floored by the raw hatred in his eyes. He inched himself into a chair as far away from them as possible.

The session was rapidly underway now, as David guided William through the momentous altercation in James's bar. William would never forget the hostility that had befouled the atmosphere - right up to the point when Perry had finally spotted Eleanor.

"It was a horrible confrontation," William narrated coolly. "Mr Hampton said something I will never forget. He warned Eleanor never to *cross him again,* although none of us had a clue what he was going on about."

Darius faced him with a patronising smile. "Mr Barton-Wells," he began. "How old were you when this confrontation took place?"

"I was 14," William informed him truthfully.

"Do you not think you may have been a little young to remember such detail?" Darius taunted. "You describe this as a *horrible confrontation.* Your father was unwell - forced to give up his home to save himself from bankruptcy - yet it was Mr Hampton who turned out to be the buyer. Surely you must have despised him!"

William gave a shrug. "We always knew he was evil," he said tactlessly, "it's irrelevant."

"Irrelevant?" Darius echoed. He gave a cynical lift of the eyebrow.

"I know what I heard!" William shouted. "I'm not making this up!"

"William, calm down," David intervened. "No-one's accusing you of lying..."

"I'm *not* lying," William said through clenched teeth, "I just don't like the way he's twisting things. If you want back up, speak to Elliot Simpson." His eyes gleamed coldly as they held Darius's stare. "He was our butler and he is *still* employed by the Hamptons."

Darius on the other hand, kept himself icily composed - revelling in the prejudice Eleanor's witnesses were finally revealing in themselves. The next one turned out to be her husband.

"Eleanor hid, the moment he walked through the door," Charlie began slowly. "I have never seen her look more terrified…"

It was over the next 30 minutes, every detail was thrashed out. Darius quizzed him remorselessly; honing in on his own bitter feud, certain it would unhinge him. Perry had ultimately destroyed his life - there were times when Charlie's eyes boiled black with loathing. Yet he managed to keep his voice soft without losing control.

"Yes, I had my reasons to hate him," he stated coldly, "but none of this had anything to do with what I saw, that day… I was as confused as anyone. I had no idea, Eleanor and Perry knew each other - though it was obvious, they had history. You could tell - not from the way she reacted but the way *he* did! He was blatantly aggressive towards her."

"Thank you, Mr Bailey," David concluded. "I must now ask you to repeat what Eleanor told you afterwards. From what I understand, Mr James Barton-Wells was *also* present."

"Indeed, he was," Charlie said sadly. He ran his fingers through his dark hair, devastated by the memory. "Did she tell you about the press conference?"

"Yes," David said softly. "I think we have sufficiently covered the press conference."

Charlie nodded, the gears in his mind spinning. "Okay - well she tried to explain what happened *beforehand*; we ended up discussing the Enfield car bomb atrocity. She spoke of the mysterious man, Jake had witnessed - someone we all agreed, sounded a little like the man she met at this press conference. By the end of the conversation, *even James* was left wondering if Hampton had anything to do with it - both the car bomb, as well as the contract on Jake's life…"

Darius erupted towards the stand, just as expected.

"Objection," he snapped. "These testimonies are completely groundless. We are basing this entire case on speculation, not fact and I have yet to hear any hard evidence which may prove that my client was the same man Mr Jansen saw…"

"Given the way *your client* has behaved ever since, I cannot understand how anyone can dispute it!" Charlie thundered. "My step-son was abducted! My wife nearly murdered!"

"Order!" the judge bellowed. "Mr Bailey, would you please refrain from commenting on any evidence that is yet to be discussed."

"I'm sorry," Charlie spluttered, "but I don't think anyone realises the effect this has had on us."

"Mr Bailey, please," David begged him. "Try to stick to the story in hand. Was there anything else your wife was able to tell you at that time?"

"No," Charlie snapped. "The fact is, we *all* heard Hampton threaten her and we were desperate to understand why! Eleanor was frightened, your honour - and this is the reason she tried to explain her story to us."

IV

By the time the second day of the trial had ended, the atmosphere was barbed with acrimony. Perry breathed deeply as a familiar flush crept back to his face. Six months of psychotherapy and stress counselling had helped keep his emotions at bay - but today had been challenging; concluded by one final exhibit which unveiled an extract from the diary of James Barton-Wells.

Tomorrow threatened to be worse. There would be no further witnesses for now - only the dreaded attendance of the Metropolitan Police along with Inspector Boswell.

They had reached a critical part of the trial where a series of statements were about to be recited. This included the original crime report detailing Jake's murder; evidence which had finally eliminated Dominic to be the killer. Perry also had a pretty good idea that Boswell would be broadcasting Elijah's statement - even though there was nothing to prove what Hargreeves had confessed. He had covered his tracks well.

He stood and glanced up at his wife. Her face appeared ghostly pale behind a sheen of tears. Ben was braced next to her. Yet there was something in his eyes that bordered on insanity; some deep, simmering fury which left him cold. Perry looked away, wondering what might have transpired to provoke such a look; but he had not seen Peter Summerville.

Ben gritted his teeth. Summerville had possibly been tucked just a little too far back to be visible and now he had disappeared completely.

Peter had crept his way out of the public gallery, long before Perry had a chance of spotting him.

He could sense the judge had been about to wind the session down, almost from the moment Charlie had let go of his emotions. Though he could understand Charlie's frustration. So the case appeared to be based on little more than hearsay - yet Jake had been silenced almost two decades ago, leaving nothing to prove Perry's conviction; now *if only* they could just uncover something!

Peter had agreed to consort his friends though right now, he needed some air. He had listened to the trial in silence and in all that time, he had detected

Ben's loathing. It was emitted into the air like a toxin, reinforced by the occasional glare. Peter didn't know how he had clung on to his composure. Any lesser man would have dissolved under the power of those stabbing eyes. He rushed his way out of the building almost breathless - escaping before anyone had a chance to follow him, having already gained some forewarning of Ben's criminal connections.

He was unsure where he was even heading as he leapt onto one of the prominent London red buses. Then suddenly he remembered Seamus. *Seamus* who he had been hankering to talk to for a while now. It was as if a veil was lifted, drawing his mind to a conversation they had shared, many years back. It had been 1988 - a time when the IRA had grown more active. How could he have forgotten?

Peter closed his eyes. There had been so many incidents in the news and as the bus chugged its way through a sea of rush hour traffic, he started recalling them. He blinked, just as they were passing the London Stock Exchange - clocking the sharp grey walls, the columns of tall windows. It was hard to imagine, an IRA bomb had blown a massive hole in that building in July 1990.

Peter felt the onset of a shiver. Wasn't it in that same month, an IRA car bomb had claimed the life of Conservative MP, Ian Gow - a hefty Semtex device whose effects were nearly as devastating as the one which had blown up Albert Enfield's minibus.

Peter felt sick, waiting until the bus paused by a tube station. He decided to jump off. He didn't want to leave Charlie and the others for *too* long, knowing it would be quicker to get to his friend's house by tube. Yet the memories kept rolling. There was no question, the IRA had upped their offensive. Earlier that year, they had fired a mortar bomb at 10 Downing Street - a shocking attack which had left the entire Conservative cabinet reeling!

Peter bit back his anguish, as he sped those final few yards towards Seamus's flat. He stopped at a nearby off-licence to pick up some Guinness then resolutely pressed down the doorbell.

"Peter!" Seamus gasped. "What brings you here? Not another lady in distress, Oi hope!" His face broke into a grin.

Peter threw his arms around his friend, before following him up the stairs. The flat was undeniably spacious - high ceilings adorned with decorative plaster corbels, green painted walls and tall sash windows which allowed the light to flood in. The lack of furniture seemed minimalist compared to the clutter of his own flat. Yet it was a sight which brought a knot of anxiety - never able to forget the day he had travelled here before. It had been in the aftermath of Eleanor's sinister phone message; the day her son had gone missing.

Once again, time was of the essence as he rapidly imparted the news of the trial - but it seemed only seconds before Seamus started shaking his head. His blue eyes darkened.

"Enough, Peter," he spluttered in his thick Irish accent, "I know what yer gonna ask o' me and I sincerely don't think Oi can help you!"

"Yes, you can," Peter sighed, cracking open one of the cans. "You told me someone confessed to his part in the Enfield killing. A lone mercenary, you said - someone you reckon would kill anyone for the right price and I need to know who he was!"

Seamus's face was tight as he clung to his Guinness - a metallic pop was emitted into the silence as if the can had been crushed slightly.

"Look - things are not going well," Peter added gently. "Even with the evidence they *have* got, there is nothing to prove what Jake actually saw…"

Seamus emptied the last of his Guinness into his glass and sighed. "Why are you doing this?" he demanded waspishly. "We saved her life once, didn't we? Rescued the kid! What is it with you and this woman? Are you in love with her or something?"

"Don't be daft!" Peter laughed. He took a long swig of Guinness, savouring its intense roasted flavour. He contemplated his next words carefully. "The thing is, Seamus, I'm scared. The Hamptons are a very evil family and that man is a killer! I want to see him convicted - not just for the murder of Eli's Da, but for the seven people destroyed by that bomb."

Seamus fixed him with a cold, blank stare. "So?"

"Jake saw *two* men by the roadside," Peter persisted. "Not just Perry, there was someone else. Someone in overalls lying under the mini bus who Jake believed to be a mechanic. This is where your contact comes in." He took a deep breath. "Seamus, if he was to confess his part in the conspiracy; that Perry hired him for the job… we might possibly have him nailed!"

"No," Seamus growled, hurling his empty can across the floor. "No way!"

Peter gaped at him in disbelief. "Seamus, I'm begging you! You know who that person is don't you so why in the love of God, won't you talk to him?"

"He's me feckin' cousin!" Seamus hissed. He lowered his glass to the table, his hand shaking.

Peter turned very still. "Oh no," he muttered, "not Declan…"

"Yeah, Declan!" Seamus spat. "Remember him, do yer? There was a time when you were one of us, Peter! That same boy who used to run errands, riding around Dublin City on yer bike, deliverin' parcels to Finnegan's…"

"Stop it," Peter gasped in horror. "That was *before* me parents were murdered. This isn't about me, anyway. I seriously want to do something! I'm sick of all this violence - the bombs, the explosions, the killings…"

Finally Seamus's face softened. "Oi know and sorry - but you must realise this is hard. Declan copped a 20 year prison sentence for his crimes. Convicted in 1974, he was and coming up for parole. He could be out soon - and you're asking me to do something that's gonna put him behind bars for *another* 20 years? Oi can't do that, Peter…"

"I understand," Peter said miserably. "You can't betray family."

"No," Seamus added, "Oi can't. But all that aside, it's good to see you. Now stop worrying about the trial - it'll be foin, you'll see! Oi'll lay bets, they're gonna find him guilty!"

"We'll see," Peter said. He studied his freckled, Irish features and forced a smile.

"So what are you up to now?"

"We're staying in Holborn. That's me, Charlie and William. They've done their bit in the witness box so I expect, we'll go out for a meal or something. I was wondering if you might like to join us…" but regrettably, Seamus was shaking his head again.

"Sorry, Oi can't! Seeing a lady friend. Some other time, perhaps…"

Peter could feel the disappointment dragging his heart down like a millstone, knowing they had reached a dead end. There was only one thread of evidence remaining and that was Evelyn's testimony - but was it going to be enough?

V

If anyone was grateful for an opportunity to reel off a long list of crimes against the Bailey family, it was Inspector Boswell. He hovered in the witness box with a demeanour of self-importance - conscious of the jury to his right as he eagerly addressed the judge.

A detective from Scotland yard had already given a resume of the crime report from the 70s; the tragic details of Jake's murder finally released. The public gallery was scattered with journalists, Ian noticed. This story would be hitting the news soon.

20 years in the police force may have hardened Ian's heart but there was something quite unnerving about this conspiracy. He had no idea, Elijah's father had been murdered - recalling his own prejudice, when he viewed Eleanor to be just like any other single mother: a naive teenager who had foolishly got herself pregnant in the 70s, no doubt by one of those nomadic hippy types.

How wrong he had been.

"The first attempt to abduct Eleanor's son happened in February 1987," he began gravely.

He swallowed back the lump that bit painfully into his throat. *If only they'd done more to investigate that thug, Nathan Wadzinski.* It was only now, he had finally recognised the ongoing threat that was destined to bind Eleanor's silence.

Once Ian began talking, it was impossible to stop; determined not to lose momentum, despite being under constant fire from Perry's defence lawyer.

He breathed deeply. "There is no doubt the burglary was a highly professional job. But no, unfortunately, the police were unable to find any evidence to trace the perpetrators..."

Elijah's near abduction, Avalon's stalking, the burglary... the list went on and on. No-one could have been more baffled, if not embarrassed that these crimes had remained unsolved.

By 12:00 noon, even the jury were finding it hard to take it all in. Photos were distributed which showed the burnt out caravan - an undeniable result of arson.

He told them about the rave, two weeks prior to that incident. William had been vehement in his opinion that he had spotted Nathan among those thugs - a trail which had ultimately led to the arrest of the skinheads enlisted for Elijah's ambush. Ian could have smiled. This was perhaps the only lead that linked Nathan to the criminal underworld; Perry's right hand man.

"Of course, we do not need to repeat what happened in July 1989," David added coldly. "The court is familiar with the details of Elijah's kidnapping; a crime for which Mr Hampton and his accomplice, Mr Wadzinski, are currently serving an eight year jail sentence. But it is Elijah I wish to turn to now, your honour..." He stared at Ian with a look of heartfelt woe. "I understand he would have testified - am I right?"

Ian nodded curtly. "It is to my utmost regret, this boy was yet again targeted." He cleared his throat before dictating the most crucial elements of Elijah's statement.

"I spoke to Norman Hargreeves on October 29th 1990. He was the only man who could have told me anything about my father's murder. He interrogated him. It was in 1972 after the death of Albert Enfield...

"... Mr Hargreeves confessed this much. He also admitted he attended a press conference where questions about my father's murder were discussed...

"... eventually, he told me other things. He spoke of a man named Peregrine Hampton. A man who was influential - had friends in high places. He mentioned the public school and Westminster. Mr Hampton had enough power to get him a promotion but he expected him to abuse his powers - to have certain 'trouble makers removed.'

"... he finally agreed to do the right thing. He was a Christian. He wanted to redeem himself, to win back the respect of his family by proving he was capable of doing something good. He swore he would make a statement to the police - to confess everything he knew about my father's murder - and last of all, he promised he would testify in this trial..."

Ian raised his eyes. "The following night, Norman Hargreeves was found hanged in his cell. It was a Sunday. He was unable to make a statement until the next day…" He cleared his throat again where the impact of this saga was beginning to bear down heavily. "This is what Elijah wanted to tell you but unfortunately he was scared off. The boy received a veiled death threat, shortly after his 18th birthday. We had no choice other than to grant him police protection."

By the time Ian's report drew to a close, a chilling silence lay suspended in the courtroom. Ian studied the faces of the jury as the depths of evil sunk in. Despite everything else, there was no question, Eleanor's family had been subjected to a merciless campaign of intimidation.

Eleanor settled into the lounge of her hotel, grateful for a reprieve from the Old Bailey. The building may have appeared outwardly striking; the architecture a feast for Charlie's eyes. Yet the atmosphere was menacing. Those walls had absorbed the echoes of some hideous crimes, she found herself thinking - imagining the villains who had walked those same corridors...

It had been a joy to see Charlie - the lingering warmth of his arms had brought a strength to her heart. They had spent the day exploring London, knowing the session in court would be mostly taken up with police statements. Eleanor had no desire to be there. She knew what those statements contained, seized by the gnawing pain of her son's absence. She could barely wait to see him and for this exhausting trial to be over.

It had nevertheless, been good to catch up with William. He had been granted a two day reprieve from Sandhurst; his attendance in the Crown Court was a legal commitment - one which even Her Majesty's Armed Services couldn't breach. Peter had agreed to deliver him safely back to the academy before returning home with Charlie. But the weekend was approaching and with no idea how long the trial was likely to drag on for, Eleanor ordered herself a large glass of wine.

She closed her eyes, listening to the gentle rumble of voices. The hotel John had recommended turned out to be a pleasing establishment in Lincoln's Inn Fields, just a short distance from his office. She had caught up with him a little earlier where David had brought them up to speed with the trial. Both men offered to take her out to dinner. Yet Eleanor felt too tired to venture out into the lively hub of the Capital. The emotional upheaval of the case had drained her and for now, she was content to relax with a magazine, allowing the events of the last few days to trickle through her mind like water.

She sank her feet into a richly patterned carpet and sighed, luxuriating in the embrace of a wing backed chair. By the time she had finished her wine, it was 9:00 and after a few last words with one of the young waitresses, she decided to head back to her room.

She had just wandered into the hotel foyer, when her heart nearly stopped dead. A man lingered by the marble reception desk, scribbling out a cheque. His face was turned sideways but already Eleanor recognised him; clocking the deep gold shine of his hair, no longer concealed by a barrister's wig - the twinkle of steel-rimmed glasses. He glanced up. Eleanor recoiled, almost blown away by the penetrating strike of his eyes.

"Ah, Mrs Bailey," Darius greeted her smoothly.

Eleanor ground her teeth together in fury. "What are *you* doing here?"

"I'm sorry," he sighed, "I had no idea you were staying at this hotel - but please, there is no need for any hostility. In fact, I'm glad I bumped into you. Is it possible we may talk?"

Eleanor was perplexed, unable to make sense of it. Her initial reaction was to tell him to back off. He had no right to approach her like this. On the other hand, his unexpected presence had unsettled her, leaving her wondering what on earth he could possibly want to say to her.

"We shouldn't be talking to each other," she snapped as he led her back towards the lounge. "We're on opposing sides."

"I know that," Darius coaxed her gently, pulling out a chair. His manners were impeccable, considering his high court status; a QC like David, a man who had taken the silk. "If anything, I am concerned about you. I've been listening to the police statements and there is no question, your family have suffered the most terrible harassment."

Eleanor nodded, unsure what to say. A tiny part of her wondered if maybe he had cottoned on to the true evilness of his client. He ordered a coffee, then turned to her and smiled. She declined his offer of a drink. There was something about this situation that felt wrong.

"What exactly *did* happen to your son?" he asked her. "Inspector Boswell said he was targeted; received some sort of death threat..."

Eleanor hugged her arms around herself in fear. "H-he received a card with a drawing of a hangman inside it. One of our cats was found hanged from the washing line a-and there was a message; *bad things happen in threes*. We'd barely got our heads around Norman Hargreeves' death..." She was seized by a shudder. "Losing Jake was painful but I couldn't bear it if something happened to our son - it would destroy me."

"I know," Darius whispered. He reached out a hand as if to comfort her then slowly withdrew it. "It is difficult to know what to say - except what a shame he never had a chance to testify. I sensed, he would have liked to - I heard his statement."

"And?" Eleanor prompted him.

He let out a sigh. "He made some very serious allegations. I apologise if I seem callous but I would have challenged him on every one of them! I'm sure you must have some idea..."

"My son despises corruption," Eleanor interrupted icily.

"So I understand," Darius conceded. "Though I cannot see what possible advantage my client could have gained from keeping him out of court. We all heard his testimony."

"My son would have convinced people," Eleanor said. She gave a cool smile despite the irony of this encounter. "You seem to have forgotten his kidnapping ordeal. You must know what Perry did to him. Elijah was chained to a chair when he burned him..." Darius stiffened but she hadn't quite finished. "We were talking on the phone. I'd only just accepted that there would never be justice for Jake - and do you know what Perry said to me? *There was never meant to be.*"

"I cannot comment," Darius sighed.

"Of course not," Eleanor whispered, turning her head away. "You're being paid to defend him."

"So what do you hope to achieve from this trial?" Darius levelled at her.

This time it was Eleanor who stiffened - jarred by the cynicism coiling into his tone. "I told you. We've fought long and hard for justice..."

"But this is a case you cannot win," Darius said silkily.

Eleanor blinked, unsure she had even heard him right. "How can you say that?" she breathed.

"This is no longer about a kidnapping," Darius replied. He picked up his coffee cup, his movements slow as he stirred it. "This case concerns conspiracy to murder. The judge needs to hear evidence and you have none. You should seriously consider dropping all charges."

"No," Eleanor retorted angrily. "Absolutely not. Why should I listen to you anyway? You don't care about justice, all you care about is winning."

Darius sipped his coffee. "Perry Hampton already faces several years in jail for foolishly trying to destroy your file but there is *nothing* which connects him to Mr Jansen's killing. I'm sorry but you cannot prove this crime. The jury are likely to find him 'not guilty.'"

Eleanor politely excused herself, wondering whether to contact David. It seemed almost a breach of confidentiality for Perry's defence lawyer to disclose such opinions - but in the end, she declined. She was due to return to the witness box the very next morning to continue her story; from the months that followed her unforeseen clash with Perry - to the day she had met Evelyn Webster. David had a copy of her manuscript, the one thing Perry had been unable to obliterate. Eleanor smiled, thinking about Darius's handsome, self-assured face - his confidence that Perry would be acquitted. The court had yet to hear Evelyn's testimony and she was due to attend the Old Bailey, later next week.

The next time David faced her, his expression was grave. Eleanor's footsteps slowed.

"What is it?" she muttered anxiously.

"We have a problem," he whispered, tugging her to one side. "It's Evelyn. I tried to contact her last night…"

Eleanor turned rigid. "And?"

"She won't be testifying after all," he kept whispering. "It appears, she flew off to some place in South Africa to see her ex-husband. To be honest, the timing could not have been worse."

"Does this mean she's been threatened?" Eleanor breathed, sensing a familiar thread of fear.

"I don't know," David pondered irritably, "though I suspect she's worried about repercussions. I'm beginning to wonder if Perry still has some hold over her - maybe these tax fraud allegations could be used to incriminate her husband." He let out a snort. "The police are looking to question her anyway in relation to the car bomb! The anti-terrorist squad in particular, want to ask her about the man in overalls. I imagine she must have just panicked…"

"But where does this leave us?" Eleanor whimpered.

"We carry on as normal," David snapped. "We've got this far. We cannot back down now."

They had been ambling along the main passageway that led to the court, when Darius breezed into their path almost on cue. There was no mistaking the cunning glint in his eye. He too, must have known! Eleanor felt sick.

"Eleanor, relax," David murmured. "This is your chance to reveal *everything* that was contained in your file. The jury will surely speculate as to *why* Perry went to such lengths to destroy it. We can still address your meeting with Evelyn - and I will recite her manuscript."

"Okay," Eleanor said numbly as she followed him into the court; but her mind was focused on Darius. His triumphant expression had unsettled her. He was right, they had nothing!

VI

The sun shone down warmly, easing away the earlier mist before it spilled across the front of the 'Olde House at Home.' Boris was opening the door just as a car crept into the parking area.

Two girls jumped out, causing him to stop and stare. They were dressed in similar clothes - cropped jeans and floaty cotton tops. The first he recognised instantly. Avalon's burnished brown curls were pinned up messily in a manner which drew attention to her slender neck and the pearl drop earrings dangling from her ear lobes. Boris's face split into an ecstatic grin.

"Well stone me, I must be seeing things," he muttered.

His eyes wandered to the second girl; she was about the same height but with straight blonde hair that shimmered in the sunlight. She turned towards him and flicked back her tresses - there was something about her movements which appeared ultra feminine.

"Avalon!" Boris greeted her with pleasure. He clasped her hands. "Who's your friend?"

"You don't remember Charlie's daughter?" Avalon laughed.

His eyes widened. "Not Margaret, surely! Goodness, look at you. You were just a little girl when I last saw you - what a beauty you've turned into!"

Margaret smiled coquettishly and lowered her eyes. Avalon hooked arms with her as they sauntered towards the door. She looked troubled - but then, Boris had no concept of the lingering angst she was suffering, in the aftermath of losing their beloved cat, Moss.

"Come inside," he cajoled her. "What brings you to this neck of the woods?"

"You must know, Perry's standing trial this week," Avalon whispered excitedly. "William phoned. He and Charlie have been to the Old Bailey to give evidence. Apparently he saw both Rowena *and* Ben lurking around in the public gallery!"

"I see," Boris smiled shrewdly. "In other words, there's a distinct absence of *Hamptons* in the village. Shall I call Elliot? I know he's been desperate to talk to you. Things are not good."

"I know," Avalon mumbled. "They've been threatening him again haven't they? Marilyn passed a message to Luke, Joshua's brother. A member of his family was hospitalised, two years ago, not long after Perry was arrested..." she broke off, the colour draining from her face. "I guess they're scared he's going to turn up in court. They must have repeated their warnings."

Boris nodded. "So where's William now?" he questioned, pouring them each a glass of cider.

"Back at Sandhurst," Avalon sighed. "Margaret's staying with me at the moment. Charlie's in London to give Eleanor a bit of moral support. She's back in the witness box today..." She let out a sigh. She was not the only one horrified to imagine what Eleanor was going through.

Boris shook his head. "Terrible business! You must have seen the papers. The news is full of it! The police have been presenting statements, I hear - Ian Boswell was among them."

"I know," Avalon shuddered. "We were going to buy a paper..."

She slipped a glance at Margaret who hadn't said a word. It was obvious, the news would only reinforce the terror of the last two years; everything that had happened since the rave.

"Anyway, it's great to see you," Boris sighed and as if by telepathy, he released a little smirk. "You're not thinking of planning another *rave* are you?"

It was a statement which finally drew a smile to Margaret's lips. "Of course not."

"We thought it would be a good opportunity to catch up with the villagers," Avalon added lovingly. "Have a drink, a pub lunch - take a wander round the woods and revisit the allotments. And I bought some flowers for

Dad's grave..."

She broke off, giddy from the wave of emotion that swept over her. Almost 5 years had passed since that shocking confrontation in Westbourne House and yet she could sense her father's spirit lingering, as the beautiful village shone all around them. The pub's hanging baskets were as splendid as ever - tumbling with fiery red geraniums against a profusion of pale pink fuchsias. Aldwyck hadn't changed - a place suspended in time where the memories had never faded.

The day seemed to pass in a blur as they resolutely stuck to their plans. They hiked across fields and hills foaming with cow parsley and golden buttercups - it wasn't long before the clouds of green forest loomed in the distance which had once again grown thick with foliage.

They even managed to steal a glimpse of Westbourne House; pleased to see the same peachy brown walls which had stood solidly for over 2 centuries.

Peter was convinced she'd get it back one day and maybe she would. If Perry was found guilty, he would be facing life imprisonment. And what would become of the despairing Rowena? Was it too much to hope that she could no longer bear to face life on her own? Forced to face up to the shame of her husband's evil - the contempt of the villagers? Avalon exhaled a sigh, just as they were returning to the allotment field.

They spent the next half hour there. The allotments were scattered with locals, busying themselves with their plots. The only thing absent was Eleanor's caravan; a denuded patch of grass served as a constant reminder of its torching. She felt the onset of a shiver, moments before a car came sweeping through the village. She turned - feeling her blood turn to ice, as the familiar pale blonde head of Rowena shimmered in the car window.

"Oh my God, it's them," she heard Margaret splutter. "Good job we *didn't* call Elliot!"

"I know," Avalon mumbled.

The car began to slow. She hadn't noticed Ben in the driver seat but she could feel the blades of his eyes. He leaned forward, determined to catch her eye. In fact the more she thought about it, the more she gradually came to recognise the unpleasant sneer glued to his face. Rowena too, looked infuriatingly smug.

"This doesn't look good," Margaret added. "I mean, why are they even back?"

"I don't know," Avalon mumbled. "I'm going to phone Eli, a bit later - find out what's going on."

Ben started opening the car door - a notion that forced them to turn from the allotments and make a hasty return to the pub. Avalon had no desire to speak to them, whatever they wished to say.

Only Margaret lingered. She couldn't help it. Ben had seized her attention, compelling her to glance over her shoulder. He flashed her a smile and followed it with a wink.

She felt the familiar flutter of wings in her stomach, wishing he didn't have this effect on her.

Chapter 29

I

"I suppose you've heard," Elijah said numbly. "Mum told me. Perry's horrible lawyer totally destroyed her in court today - she's terrified Perry's going to win."

He was curled up on one of the baggy, velvet brown sofas in his aunt's lounge, listening to the soft patter of rain against the window pane. The lounge was light and spacious - tall windows looked out onto a sprawling back garden where a conifer hedge guarded the rear. Yet the dark clouds seemed oppressive, leaving the room steeped in shadow. Elijah turned and flicked on a table lamp, wary of Marjolein's glances. 14 year old Lars was snuggled up next to her, too engrossed in a comic to pick up the tension building in the atmosphere.

It was over the next few minutes, Elijah spilled out the news to Avalon.

A vital witness had pulled out, leaving Eleanor's testimony starved of evidence. Yet how could anyone dismiss the truth that Evelyn had exposed? The bitter feud that had erupted between Perry and Albert Enfield which in time, had evolved into an obsessive hatred?

Eleanor had desperately tried to explain it - but even with the backup of Evelyn's manuscript, which David had doggedly presented to the court, it was predictable that Darius would repudiate her claims as fantasy! It left the entire case teetering on the brink of collapse.

"I was wondering why they looked so smug," Avalon sniffed. It was with no further delay, she told him about their day in Aldwyck.

By the time the call ended, Elijah felt a tiny glow ignite his heart. Marjolein smiled fondly.

"Avalon," she reflected. "Beautiful name - you love her, don't you?"

He could feel the colour in his cheeks flaring brighter. "A little," he mumbled, "I always have. We've known each other since we were kids..." he broke off, remembering Caitlin. He couldn't deny that he loved her too. They had enjoyed a lengthy conversation, the previous night.

Marjolein's smile faded as she turned her eyes back to the TV to catch the weather. Elijah studied her profile, noting the soft outlines which he had captured in so many sketches; the straight forehead, the shallow indent that dived into the sweep of her nose, the delicate point of her chin. He had long recognised her profile as being uncannily similar to his own; a legacy of his father. Even to an outsider, it was obvious they were related.

Right now however, his mind was consumed with worries of the trial. He couldn't escape from it. Reports of the court case had filtered their way to Holland - the media emblazoned with stories. Dutch by birth and a legendary musician, Jake was one of Nijmegan's unsung heros and people remembered him. It was over the last week, Elijah had been curious to know as much about his father as possible and Marjolein didn't hold back.

She described him as a loving person who adored his music and this was what Andries couldn't understand. Jake would *never* have abandoned them. She spoke painfully of the era when he had gone missing: his fellow band members had returned from England in shock, initially devastated by the car bomb they had witnessed - but it was overshadowed by something far more sinister. Jake had visited Scotland Yard to disclose a crucial piece of evidence and never returned. It had been impossible to get on with their lives, all the while his fate lay unresolved.

Elijah could imagine their frustration. He had spent many an afternoon with Marjolein, flipping through family photo albums; absorbing the pictures of his father as a baby, as a small child, interlaced with the typical photos taken throughout his school days. They twisted his heart.

By the time Jake was 18, he had developed into a strikingly good looking youth. It was also around this time that he and Andries had experimented with song writing, prior to starting up their own rock band. The photos as well as the stories brought tears to his eyes.

Yet there were darker aspects to Jake's life which Marjolein had struggled to explain. Her voice was choked with tears as she recalled the aftermath of his death. Her world was left shattered - desolate without the aura of her brother. But her parents attitude had perplexed her; their icy dispassion of the truth. It was a concept that forced her to accept, they had never really approved of their son's *hippie* ideology; that Jake had been too happy touring around with his band to knuckle down to a 'proper job.'

She described their father as a powerful man: Rutger Jansen - high ranking executive of an International engineering plant. Nijmegan was renowned for its thriving business in science, technology and engineering and although the corporation was no longer around, she had some inkling it had merged with another organisation who manufactured weapons.

"What, you mean they didn't care?" Elijah couldn't help asking her.

"Papa was angry," Marjolein sighed, "Jake might still be alive, if not for that band!"

Elijah couldn't help but feel embittered, remembering his mother's story - the one occasion she had met Jake's parents. *'They seemed cool - detached, almost.'*

Marjolein wiped away her tears, before moving on to describe their mother, Elspeth. She had loved Jake dearly, despite his disappointing choice of career where the news of his murder had left her numb. She had become silent and withdrawn - right up to the year they had eventually moved from Nijmegan. Marjolein however, felt no such desire - very much attached to this ancient city where she had lived life as a student. It was at University, she had met and fallen in love with Pieter who she had later married.

In between reminiscing, Elijah had settled into a relaxed and pleasant lifestyle which momentarily allowed him to forget about the traumas back home. He had bonded with the whole family and together, they had drifted into a pleasing harmony. He liked Marjolein's husband, a somewhat pensive man with small neat features and receding brown hair. Further more, he had taken a real shine to the kids: Lars, a sprouting adolescent, teased him like a younger brother. Though it was 16 year old Viebeke, he cherished the most - tall, as pretty as her mother and blessed with the same lustrous auburn hair that Jake had possessed.

Ever since his arrival, they had spent many pleasurable hours together. On the days the kids were in lessons, he occasionally attended a class at the 'Arnhem School of Arts.' Tutors kept in regular contact with his college, happy to allow him use of their facilities and to expand his portfolio.

It was later in the afternoons, he met up with Viebeke to explore the various labyrinths of Nijmegan - mindful of the cautious gaze of the plain clothes police officers who continued to keep him under guard. Yet their protection allowed him a certain freedom; a chance to enjoy shopping, watching films at the local cinema and visiting the charming street cafes to enjoy burgers and ice creams. Viebeke loved nothing more than to show him off to her friends - proud of her artistic cousin who had unwittingly captured the attention of some of the townsfolk.

There had been a day when they had cycled up to Kronenburg Park. He had started sketching again, charmed by the soft and chalky medium of pastels. In fact, he had been yearning to set up his easel - to capture the legendary tower perched against its scenic backdrop; astounded by the scattering of passers by who had paused and tossed coins onto the grass.

"You're getting famous!" Viebeke breathed, "it is in our family!"

Within a fortnight, he had produced some beautiful sketches; from cobbled streets and shaded parks, to the famous bridge streaming with cyclists. He couldn't deny, he was impressed with this town, the well organised lanes clearly laid out for cars, cycles and pedestrians. He found himself wishing Rosebrook ran this efficiently. Although, he could never completely divorce his mind from home; wondering how his family were coping - especially Margaret.

The drama of the trial crouched darkly in his mind like a harbinger; and it was only after the kids were in bed, he had gradually divulged the horror of everything that had happened to them.

Marjolein switched off the television and sighed, wary of his sinking mood as he perched anxiously on the sofa. At least the rain had subsided, the clouds thinning, allowing a little more light to permeate the sky. Right now, she was reluctant to watch the News, certain Jake's face was about to flash up at any minute. She sensed the trial must have been harrowing.

"Is something wrong?" she piped up softly. "Was it not good news?"

Elijah raised his eyes, from where his mind had momentarily drifted. Of course! He had only just ended his call with Avalon…

"She saw them," he sighed, "Perry's wife and son - looking incredibly pleased with themselves. I bet that means the bastard's going to get off."

"That is maybe not true," Marjolein argued, rising to her feet. She gave her head a gentle shake, auburn curls bouncing as they were captured in the light. "Come, don't be so gloomy!"

"A really important witness pulled out," he added sadly, "which means Mum doesn't have a shred of proof any more…"

"Hey shut up will you!" Viebeke yelled, making him jump. She had crept into the lounge unnoticed, before grabbing a cushion and flinging it at him. "Are we going out tonight?"

"Yes," Marjolein nodded. "I think we must. Cheer ourselves up, Eli, would you like that?"

He smiled, feeling a familiar rush of delight as he caught his cousin's eye. He grabbed the cushion as if to hurl it back at her, then squeezed it against his chest.

"That'd be great! So where are we going, Vie?"

"Hey, we could take him to Boom Feesten!" Viebeke gasped. She smiled at her mother.

"Boom Feesten?" Elijah echoed, frowning.

"Sure," Marjolein shrugged. "Good idea, why not? You will love it, Eli, it is small concert."

"It's a mini rock festival!" Viebeke breathed, rolling her eyes. "Havanna on the Waal! You know, the beach by the river? Six bands. They will play a few songs each. It's fun. The whole family can go and if it rains, there's a big tent."

So it was settled. By 8:00 that evening, Elijah found himself being shepherded into an enormous green field which overlooked the river. It was almost dark. A red and white striped marquee stood at its core, resplendent against the final phase of a sunset. Streaks of fiery pink and orange were feathered across a descending indigo sky. The air was cold tonight and with the possibility of rain, they had all worn waterproofs. The first band were already underway - a couple of musicians in their 30s, one hammering away on a keyboard while the other played electric guitar.

The second group were more vocal - a deafening roar of heavy metal. Elijah had already noticed a few students he recognised from art school, hopping about at the front.

Marjolein kept her family a little further back, fearful of how easily Elijah might get himself sucked into that crowd and lose himself. She knew there were a couple of police officers around; she had seen Pieter conversing with them. By the time a third band took to the stage, they headed to the beer tent.

Elijah seemed happy. It was an evening where he had lapsed back into his reverie, probably thinking about Free Spirit. This was just the sort of open air concert, Jake would have loved - watching the happy faces swaying all around him, clapping in time to the music.

"Jake played in many places," Marjolein enlightened him. "Taverns, concert halls - he liked to tour, especially the festivals…"

"Did you know he was invited to play at Albert Enfield's party?" Elijah asked distractedly.

She turned to him and frowned, before taking a thirsty gulp of beer. She wasn't even that sure, wondering if Jake had ever mentioned it.

Already, they were drifting towards the stage again. The river gleamed in the distance - the waters reflecting the lights from the stage as they bobbed and shimmered on the surface. Elijah watched as if in a dream, as a woman and two men took to the stage, fumbling with their instruments. They seemed older than the previous performers - possibly in their 40s. He also noticed the crowd had parted slightly, leaving a winding river of space. He crept closer to the stage, just as the group started playing. He would have described their music as folk - the woman had a beautiful singing voice, sweet against the chords of an electric piano. Elijah's eyes were gradually drawn to a guitarist, his head bowed, his face barely visible within the hazy gloom at the back of the stage. It was only when they had finished their final song, he eventually looked up.

Marjolein's hand had been resting upon his shoulder when he felt her fingers stiffen.

"What's up?" he mumbled, glancing round.

It was only then, he realised that she too, was staring at the guitarist.

He was an emaciated looking man with shoulder length straw blonde hair. He possessed a strong, yet bony face. Shadows rested in his sunken cheeks - but what captured his attention were his eyes; dark, slightly down-turned, they harboured a look of intense sadness.

"It cannot be…" he heard Marjolein gasp and suddenly, the man met his eye.

There was no mistaking the shock that flickered across his face. He turned pale. He was attempting to unfasten his guitar strap and yet his hands appeared to be trembling. All the while, Marjolein was edging her way forwards, desperate to reach him as he staggered from the stage.

She had momentarily broken away, leaving him rooted to the spot in bewilderment. He was dimly aware of Viebeke tugging at his sleeve. She too, had clearly assimilated the tension but Elijah shook her off lightly, easing himself closer to catch their conversation. The man was pointing, mumbling something in Dutch. Elijah could never have understood what they were saying, yet he distinctly overheard the word *geest*. He felt a strange chill, remembering what Eleanor had told him. Free Spirit - Vrije Geest. The word literally translated to 'ghost.'

"Nee, niet een geest!" he heard his aunt splutter. "Hij is Jake's zoon…"

"What's going on?" Elijah demanded, his eyes transfixed to the unravelling scene.

"Elijah, this is Andries!" Marjolein whimpered, startled as she spun round to face him.

They wandered from the area in a daze, resolutely threading their way back to the beer tent, Andries among them. Pieter pushed his way to the bar, keeping a firm grip on the children. It was almost as if he had sensed the need for secrecy. Elijah faced the man who had been his father's best friend and shivered. He had seen photos of the band tucked in amongst Marjolein's collection - recalling the fresh-faced blonde youth who had also periodically popped up in Jake's childhood pictures. They had virtually grown up together. Yet the man stood before him now was a shadow of that person - skeletally thin, incapable of shedding that haunted look. Elijah wished there was something he could say to make him smile.

"I'm sorry," he sighed, conscious of his eyes pricking into him. "I didn't mean to alarm you."

"Jake had a child?" Andries croaked, "I never knew…"

It was over the next hour, Elijah bravely poured out Jake's story - though it was torturous to have to explain it. Yes, he had been abducted on the day Andries had last seen him. He went on to describe the criminal gang recruited to murder him before his mother had found him; their frantic escape - the weeks spent in hiding and their intense love resulting in his conception.

By the time they returned to the car, Andries looked as if he could have wept. Elijah offered him a cigarette. He turned to Marjolein, his expression wistful.

"I know," she whispered, "and yes - he can stay tonight. I think he has something to tell you too."

Elijah nodded, his heart pounding; already wondering if there was anything Andries would remember before he'd said that final farewell to his friend…

II

After a temporary respite, Eleanor was dreading her return to London. They had survived the May Bank Holiday, which had allowed her an extra two days. But on Wednesday, the case was due to resume; Eleanor about to endure one final session of cross examination before a closing statement from the Police Officer in charge. They were approaching a phase known as 'Half Time.'

David had already forewarned her, there was a grave possibility that the case could be stopped at this point: a situation Darius might use to his advantage especially if he could convince the judge, *there was no evidence that the crime alleged had been committed by the defendant.*

She felt a familiar creeping chill as she approached the Old Bailey. David took her aside.

"We may yet be in with a chance," he whispered feverishly, as soon as they were tucked out of earshot. "John Sharp received a fax from South Africa last night..."

"Evelyn?" Eleanor whispered in hope.

David nodded, his blue eyes glittering. "She spoke to her former husband. Basil reckons he paid millions to the Inland Revenue in corporation tax over the years. If there ever *was* any insider trading, it happened so long ago, it would be impossible for Perry to prove!"

"So Perry no longer has a hold over him," Eleanor mused.

"Possibly not," David smiled, "and if he has... Basil is prepared to stand up to him - but don't you see what this means? Evelyn is no longer afraid. She is willing to bear witness after all."

"That's wonderful," Eleanor gasped. "So there'll be an adjournment?"

Her eyes smouldered as she gazed at him where finally, their fire had returned.

Unfortunately, it didn't take long for those flames to be well and truly doused as a familiar face loomed outside the court. Eleanor was repelled by Robin's icy gaze as he turned and met her eye. It was inevitable he would be here to defend Perry - ready to repeat his lies. Rivulets of cold swept down her neck as she suppressed a second shiver.

Robin on the other hand, was feeling extremely pleased with himself.

He had been rehearsing his story over a number of weeks now and it had started long before Elijah had received his 18th birthday card. He almost smiled. The entire scheme may have arisen from the twisted mind of Ben Hampton, yet it was Naomi who had delivered that card - their last ditch tactic to unhinge him.

He hadn't fully approved of snatching their cat - nor that Ben's criminal accomplice had heartlessly strung the unfortunate creature to the washing line. But that was in the past, Elijah safely out of the way and denied any opportunity to sway the jury. Now finally, it was his turn.

Robin took a deep breath and straightened his grey silk tie. His appearance was flawless as usual, from the pristine cut of his suit to his neatly combed, silver streaked hair.

It was over the long Bank Holiday weekend, he had engaged in a lengthy dialogue with Darius Bentley - now revelling in the prestige of being Perry's first defence witness. Robin smiled, listening to the click of Eleanor's heels as she disappeared into the alleyway known as Warwick Passage; and all the while, his well rehearsed testimony was ringing in his mind.

"Yes, I met Jake. I warned him, the police were desperate to talk to him; I had already picked up rumours of the criminal gang who were hunting him..."

He wasn't lying. He had sent them to Toynbee Hall to help them; praying the police would catch up with them before the criminal gang did. His story would bear out Eleanor's own testimony.

Darius Bentley had clearly felt a need to familiarise himself with whatever evidence he could bring to the case. So Robin went on to recount the weeks when Jake and Eleanor had slipped back into hiding: *"I had lost the one and only lead I could have given to the police. I urged the manager of Toynbee Hall to reveal their whereabouts but he was reluctant."*

Of course, Bernard James *had* eventually divulged an address.

Darius feared this would be the only grey area. David would demand to know what had originally triggered the rumours that Jake was *alleged* to be a drug dealer. Robin held his breath - he had his lies prepared well in advance. In fact, he had been thinking about this for years, even though he was never expected to reveal his sources before - not with Hargreeves on the inside; Hargreeves who had spawned the idea of framing Jake in the first place. It was largely due to *his* influence, the Police had swallowed the lie whole.

As for the press conference... Robin let out a sigh. There was no denying Perry had been in attendance, but how he was going to explain his behaviour presented a challenge.

"Perry was renowned for being hot-headed. We'd just consumed a bottle of wine when Eleanor jumped out. He found himself being unjustly associated with the murder without understanding why. And he didn't appreciate being photographed. He panicked, nothing more..."

It was with the help of Darius, Robin knew he would interweave his own part carefully; compelled to recall the night he had originally intended to back up Hargreeves over the drug dealing allegations - knowing they were about to come under fire.

For some reason, Darius was convinced the court would want to know why he'd chosen *Perry* to accompany him. Inspector Hargreeves had been there for a reason but why Perry? This was the point where Robin would embellish Perry's good character - the crucial role he had played in his own life. He closed his eyes, allowing his speech to roll through his mind again.

The man had been his friend and his mentor. *'Perry was like the father I never had. He coached me in politics - drew me into important social circles and encouraged me to stand for election. Without him, I would be nothing...'* It was for this reason, Perry had been the most obvious choice to champion him - and what a privilege it was to defend him in a court of law!

But he was still thinking about Eleanor's lawyer - wondering how else he might cross examine him; never able to shake off the fear that he was bound to grill him over that final showdown. There was nothing to suggest Eleanor had pointed the finger of blame when Perry had threatened her.

Robin blinked, he could no longer fend off that tiny dart of anxiety. He longed to convince them that his friend had been innocent of any wrongdoing; and that ever since that night, Perry lived in constant fear, people would mistake him for the 'mysterious man' Jake had spoken of: '... *and he was right, wasn't he? People knew he despised Enfield for his politics...*'

He could remember Darius's smile, an indication that he was pleased with his performance. If Robin could retain the same icy calmness inside the courtroom, then no-one would have any reason to doubt him - there was just one more question he needed to test him on.

"Mr Whaley," Darius had drawled, "did Perry know anything about Mr Enfield's party?"

"No," Robin snapped. "It is my understanding, it was for friends and family only."

"Was it publicised? Was there any way my client could have found out about it?"

"Not to my knowledge," Robin reinforced, bracing himself. "Albert Enfield's party was a private event and no, it was never publicised."

Darius gave a conspiratorial nod, his eyes bright. *"If it was never publicised, how would Perry have known of the location?"*

He could not have been more pleased with that final disclosure.

Perry meanwhile, was panicking. He had been suffering palpitations all night, unsure as to whether he could cope with much more. From the day he had stepped into the court, he was confident there was nothing that would connect him to Jansen's murder. So far Darius had been convincing. Now he wasn't so sure. The next time Perry faced him, he did so angrily. Spots of colour burned in his face, his expression filled with loathing. Yes, he'd heard more than enough! *How dare that bitch bring charges against him for something she could never prove?* The trial had been excruciating. Now he just wanted it to be over.

"Calm down," Darius whispered in the same solicitous tone a doctor might use. "There is every chance we can win this. Your friend, Robin Whaley, has shown himself to be an extremely compelling witness - and more are coming forward..."

It was no lie. Perry had his own circle of friends to vouch for him; heavy weight company directors, professional colleagues such as Edward Booth, friends he had met at university and Westminster. Among them loomed a knot of eminent politicians; people who had supported him in the 70s - a time when Albert Enfield's politics had been ridiculed, especially his flimsy defence strategy. Politics had always been a dicey game, yet there was one thing Perry's associates were convinced of: Perry would never have embroiled himself in a conspiracy *so dangerous* as the one being suggested to the court in this instance.

"I am going to defend you whatever it takes," Darius pledged. "There is just one more option I would like to put forward to you…"

Perry breathed deeply, fighting to suppress his rage. "What exactly are you proposing?"

Darius took a deep breath. "I am going to ask the judge to rule that this case be terminated. In legal terms, this is known as a *Galbraith submission*."

David had not been wrong in his supposition; a situation, Darius was about to explain.

"I can show the judge that this entire saga has been fabricated, based on your one minor appearance at that press conference."

"Really?" Perry spat. He narrowed his eyes. "Do continue…"

"The evidence presented to the court is tenuous. The judge may agree that it is insufficient for the jury to make a proper conviction - in which case, it is his duty to stop the case. He should consider the reliability of the main witness, Mrs Bailey. My view is that a group of people collaborated; people you wronged in the past. Eleanor's husband for example and the Barton-Wells boy. They conjured up this outrageous story based on nothing but speculation."

"You think the judge is going to believe they tried to frame me?" Perry sneered.

"Yes," Darius snapped abruptly.

Perry's eyes narrowed. He was gazing at his lawyer as a falcon might observer a shrew before devouring it. "What about her file?" he muttered. "The police report, the kidnapping?"

"We can only suggest that you were scared and you panicked," Darius kept insisting. "Eleanor was using that file for revenge. There was never any mention of you in it for 13 years then suddenly, she started adding to it. She was digging for dirt, *anything* to incriminate you."

"And if the judge refuses your application?" Perry kept baiting him.

"It doesn't necessarily imply, he suspects you are guilty," Darius smiled, "only that there is *still* a possibility the jury can convict…"

"Except the case for the prosecution has left me looking like a monster," Perry growled.

"It is over!" Darius said breathlessly. "She has no more witnesses."

"Apart from the lovely Evelyn," Perry sighed, "who might yet turn up and surprise us."

Darius swallowed back his fear. "In which case, I'll portray her as an embittered woman - one who colluded with Eleanor. Were you not lovers once? You accused her husband of fraud… now please. I am doing everything in my power here. The case for the prosecution is weak."

"So you keep saying," Perry hissed.

Darius had spent the last few minutes cowering beneath his gaze, yet he had one final trump card. "Eleanor Bailey has presented no proof that you were connected to this alleged *contract killing*. We on the other hand, have Mr Theakston. She named him as Jake's killer as can be verified in her original file. We could still have him summoned to this court."

Perry's eyes never left his face, his expression veiled with threat. "So why not just do it?"

"Let's see if we can stop the trial first," Darius interrupted. "Failing that, I will insist that the case cannot continue *unless* Mr Theakston is cross-examined! He may yet be charged for his part in the conspiracy to murder Jake Jansen."

"I see," Perry nodded. "If it's looking like a 'guilty verdict' in other words."

Darius sighed, his throat dry as the malice in Perry's eyes flared brighter.

Perry on the other hand, was unable to share the complacency of his barrister. He took a long, shuddering breath, desperate to compose himself.

Something was troubling him - a sense of growing anxiety squeezing around his heart like a fist. It brought his mind back to his enemies. He closed his eyes, filled with a sense that his life was never going to be the same again - regardless of whether they found him guilty or innocent.

The case for the prosecution however, was not quite over. Before Darius could make any last ditch attempt to apply for his so-called 'Galbraith submission,' the jury had yet to hear the closing comments from the Police Officer in charge, along with Eleanor's defence lawyer.

Eleanor too, was about to answer any final questions from the judge before the case for the prosecution was summed up. Yet she was terrified. It had started from the moment she had seen that odious bastard, Whaley. How could she forget his propensity for lying? That silky, silver tongued voice of his? Such a contrast to her own emotional outbursts.

She dabbed her eyes and topped up her makeup, determined to stay strong despite the waves of aggression swelling outside the courtroom. A female court usher flashed her a nervous smile as she vacated the lavatories. Eleanor forced a smile in return before she began to drag her way up the staircase. She had only got half way, when she was alerted to a sudden flurry of movement.

"Eleanor!" David called up to her.

He was flapping his way towards her, eager to catch up. Small and birdlike from her elevated position, his eyes glittered with unsuppressed glee.

"Eleanor, get yourself down here, now," David muttered, "your son has just arrived and we have another witness…"

30 minutes later, the courtroom erupted into commotion.

"This is highly irregular!" Darius could be heard spitting. His cheeks had taken on a crimson flush, Eleanor noticed. "How can you possibly spring a new witness at this stage? This case is a farce! I must implore you to end it…"

The judge pointed his lugubrious face towards him and sighed. "Mr Bentley!" he exclaimed in a voice of authority. "This is about justice! And I for one, would like to hear what this witness has to add *before* we proceed any further."

Eleanor felt a pang of sympathy as he backed away from the bench. He looked terrified. It seemed unnatural for a barrister to display such fear - which was the point, she glanced at Perry. She clocked the venom in his expression just as the side door swung open.

David strutted nimbly inside, accompanied by another man.

Eleanor had joined Charlie in the public gallery as advised. Charlie glanced at her with a frown, while Elijah perched tensely in the chair right next to him.

"He finally agreed to come forward," Elijah was heard whispering, "said he owed it to Jake."

"Eli, what the hell is going on?" Charlie spluttered in his confusion.

"Shh," Eleanor chided him. "You'll see."

Andries manoeuvred his emaciated frame into the witness stand, wary of the shocked glances of his audience. He raised his head before he latched his deep set eyes upon Perry.

"Hello again, Mr Peregrine," he began slowly. "We met once before."

Darius turned to the judge, open mouthed, clueless as to know what to do.

David on the other hand, looked confident - urging him to continue. "Just tell the court, what you know, Andries."

Perry turned white - his knuckles tight on the table top in front of him.

"You *are* the man Jake saw," Andries continued, "you knew where that party was, didn't you?" His Dutch accent curled into his voice with every damning word.

Perry started writhing in his chair - already the air was turning black.

"My mother told him. She was nuclear scientist - member of some - some *group*. They used to meet in the Netherlands. I met Mr Peregrine when he came to our house! I thought they were maybe having an *affair*…"

"This is highly irregular," Darius could be heard muttering.

Only the raised hand of the judge could restrain him. David looked ecstatic.

"He was very interested in our band," Andries added, his voice slurring a little as the memories came back to him. He closed his eyes. He could still hear the desperation in his mother's voice: *'Andries, please! Just tell him what you said to me!'* "Interested - because we were invited to play a gig at this birthday party! A party for Albert Enfield, a man who Mr Peregrine hated…"

"Enough!" Perry snarled from his position in the courtroom. "Get him out of here! Don't let him say another word - this is slander!"

Eleanor spun to Charlie in shock. Everyone could sense the volcanic tension brewing. Perry was struggling to rise from his chair, where it took the restraining grip of two thick set police officers to prevent him from flying towards the witness stand.

"Could we have some order, please!" the judge commanded, belting the table with his gavel.

Andries raised his face, the power in his voice growing. "I told him! I told him where we were playing; the name of the hotel and the village. It lay in some quiet little road. I know what Jake saw when he went to get an amp from our van. It was before this horrible explosion and I believed him; a blonde gentleman in a black Daimler..." he was pointing his bony finger directly at Perry now, who was turning gradually purple. "It was him..."

"Shut the fuck up!" Perry roared.

"Jake said we had t-to stay the night in England!" Andries continued shakily, despite the rumpus. "Police wanted to talk to him! They wanted him at Scotland Yard. I told him he *had to* go - a-and it was the last time I saw him." A tear plummeted from his cheek, his bottom lip trembling.

"Enough," Perry spluttered, struggling wildly in the grip of the police officers. "Get that bastard out of here!"

"Would the defendant keep quiet, otherwise I will suggest the officers remove him," the judge drawled. He gave another thump of his gavel. "Please continue!"

"Can you tell the court what happened later," David coaxed him.

"Many months later, we heard news Jake was dead," Andries sobbed. "Jordaan wanted answers; he demanded press conference! Finally, he told me about this - this *blonde man* and then I knew! Jake *was* murdered... and all the time, I know who is behind it!"

Eleanor was staring down at the unravelling scene in horror. Perry was tearing at his tie in the same manner she remembered from the press conference. He seemed to be struggling to breath.

Yet Andries was still speaking. He wiped a tear from his face as his voice shuddered across the chamber. He had already mentioned Jordaan - the terrible hit and run accident that had killed him. Then came the death threats. It was only in the aftermath of meeting Jake's son, he had finally agreed to break his silence.

Eleanor turned to the others with a smile - *surely* the court must have cottoned onto Perry's guilt by now. At the same time, she was aware of her hated enemy in the dock below - a strange feeling crawled over her as she glanced back down.

She felt her initial hubris swept away, as fast as the colour was blanched from Perry's face. The blaze of purple had vanished, leaving two tiny spots of pink - in fact, his face had turned grey! Eleanor let out a gasp, clocking the glistening perspiration on his forehead. He slumped forwards, one hand gripping the table edge, the other clawing his chest.

"Oh shit," she whimpered.

"Dad!" Ben shouted, leaning over the rail.

"Humph!" Charlie grunted, "great bit of acting - give that man an Oscar!"

"He's not acting..." Eleanor gasped in panic. "Call an ambulance!" She hollered down from the public gallery. "He's having a massive heart attack!"

Ben whirled round to glare at her but Eleanor wasted no time - inclined to ignore him as she surged from her seat. It was only the light grip of Charlie's hand that restrained her.

"What are you doing?" he breathed. "Just leave it."

She shook him off irritably. "I'm a nurse, Charlie," she reprimanded him, "my duty is to save people's lives. I have to do the right thing..."

Moments later, she was kneeling by Perry's side. The court was gradually emptying, the jurors restless as they began filing their way out of the stands. Eleanor was dimly aware of the judge gazing down despairingly - of Darius who had crept right up to her. She met his mesmerising green eyes for the last time.

"What happens now?" she dared herself to whisper.

"The case will have to be suspended," he answered her frankly. "U-unless my client makes a rapid recovery, there seems little point in continuing..." He broke off quickly.

Eleanor nodded, guessing what he might be thinking. A guilty verdict was inevitable. This must have been the first case he had ever lost. She almost felt a bit sorry for him yet at the same time, she sensed his relief. She turned back to Perry, hands balled into fists as they steadily pumped his chest to keep the heart muscle working. He was still conscious. Though by this time, she was beginning to suspect he had suffered a full blown cardiac arrest.

She shuddered, chilled by the intense malice in his eyes; but she was also thinking about Andries - that final, damning testimony. It had resurrected the full horror of the press conference as her final words came rushing back to her: *all I know is that his friend Andries spoke the truth, when he told you that Jake witnessed something...* Eleanor had been firm in her belief, it was the word 'witness' that had pushed Perry over the edge. Yet it had nothing to do with the word *'witness.'* It was the name *'Andries.'*

There was so much she wanted to ask him but right now, she felt obliged to fulfil her moral duty; at least until an ambulance arrived. There would be time to reflect later.

III

10 minutes passed before Perry was carted into an ambulance and sped to

the nearest hospital in Westminster, leaving a wake of unsettling silence.

News reporters had crowded outside the Old Bailey, desperate for news of this tempestuous court case. Ben shoved them angrily aside before clambering into the back of the ambulance. His mother was on the way - though right now, he couldn't take his eyes of the motionless figure pinned to the stretcher. This man no longer resembled his father. Gone was the fight, the aggression and the ruthless energy he was accustomed to. Ben wandered along in a state of numbness as they arrived at the hospital, virtually oblivious to his surroundings.

Even as he lingered by the bedside, he was surprised how devoid of emotion he felt. He should have felt something; fury, desolation, even hatred but he felt nothing. The whole scenario had a surreal quality. His hand closed around his mobile phone and for a moment, he felt a compulsion to call someone - he badly wanted to talk to Nathan or even Sasha. Except Nathan was in prison - Sasha, he hadn't seen for over a year. They had drifted apart from the moment he had submerged himself in the criminal underworld, shortly after his father's arrest in 1989. Strange though it seemed, he hadn't particularly missed her - Ben had no time for relationships any more.

He had been far too busy running around for Perry, directing their criminal allies - from silencing witnesses to terrorising people. He had no choice but to oversee the management of Westbourne House either, whilst commiserating with Rowena - all this, squeezed into a tiny window of time between surging to and fro in his capacity as a stockbroker. Ben should have felt exhausted but he enjoyed life in the fast lane - and he never went short of kicks either.

These days, Ben turned to fetish clubs to satisfy his urges - inspired by Alan Levy who had long recognised his dark side. These shady establishments provided an avenue of thrills where he could live out his sadistic fantasies, whilst hiding behind a black leather mask. He gave a shiver as he glanced down at Perry. He really shouldn't be thinking about such perverse pleasures when his father was so ill. Then at last, he opened his eyes.

For the first few seconds, they just stared at each other.

"Ben?" he spluttered, "what's going on, what the hell am I doing here?"

"Shush," Ben said curtly. "Try not to move - you've had a serious heart attack..."

They were barely left alone as nurses kept popping in and out, checking his pulse, his blood pressure, before administering more drugs to clear the potential blood clots from his arteries. Perry glanced up at him with a look of panic, desperate to spend some time alone with him - but it was possibly another hour before the opportunity arose.

"Where's Rowena?" he demanded.

"She'll be here soon," Ben snapped and suddenly he felt a stab of fear. His father didn't look good. He was alarmingly pale. Yet Ben clocked the obsessive flare creeping back into his eyes, sensing he was about to say something crucial. He seized Ben's hands.

"What was the outcome of the trial?"

"It's been suspended," Ben said. "They haven't discussed a verdict - but then how can they? You're in hospital for Christ's sake."

"Which is where I will probably stay," Perry added coldly. "I fear this could be the end, Ben."

"Don't say that," Ben gulped. "You're only 55!"

Perry's grip tightened, despite his frailty. "It doesn't matter," he hissed through gritted teeth. "Death would be preferable to a life prison sentence! I've had enough! I miss my life with Rowena and I miss Westbourne House... Everything I've fought long and hard for has been taken from me. Better to go this way - but don't worry, I've put my affairs in order."

Ben frowned - he actually felt quite sick.

"Westbourne House is willed to your mother," Perry kept whispering, "but I've left you the house in Pimlico - half my money. You won't go short." He attempted a smile. "I know I haven't always treated you very fairly, Ben, but you've been a good boy. I'm proud of you. There are just two things I must ask you to do in the event of my death - now come a little closer..."

Ben leaned his head right up to him, assailed by the fumes of anti-sceptic from the electrode pads on his chest. He stroked his thick, white hair - still a little damp with perspiration. Then Perry spoke again, his voice lowering to a snarl.

"That man who attended court. Find him - track down his mother. I want you to continue a secret mission I began in the 70s. My solicitor has orders to pass on a set of highly confidential documents..." he coughed as if he was short of breath.

"Calm down," Ben whispered, glancing towards the door, "I'll do whatever you ask, I swear. Now is there anything else? It's just - I think Mum's arrived."

Perry tilted his head back and fired him a long and chilling stare. This time, there was no mistaking the hatred in his eyes - they seared into him like steel blades.

"Avenge me," he whispered evilly. "Make them pay - all of them!"

Ben was unsure whether he had even heard him right as the commandment sunk in - guessing they were intended to be his final instructions before Rowena swept into the room.

IV

"Well, I never expected it to end like that," Charlie muttered.

"Nor me," Eleanor sighed.

They were congregated inside a traditional pub, close to St. Paul's, where the richness of the polished oak tables and burgundy carpets offered an ambience of comfort. Elijah had hardly moved; a bottle of ale sat in front of him untouched as he stared dreamily into space. This was an outcome no-one had anticipated - and although Perry's collapse was the best result they could have hoped for, not one of them felt like celebrating. It didn't feel right.

Eleanor turned her eyes away from her son, whose glazed expression disturbed her.

"It's good to meet you, Andries," she smiled gently. "So what was this *consortium?*"

Andries shook his head. He could barely remember - but ever since his fateful meeting with Elijah, tiny threads had started to come back to him: visions of a sinister, blonde-haired man loomed in the fog of his mind. *Mr Peregrine* - an English man who had turned up at their home on more than one occasion. His mother, Angelien, had always been secretive - the reason he imagined they were lovers. Yet she too, had suspected him - right up until the day she had pressed an irrefutable warning: *'You must never speak of him again, Andries...'*

"I never really knew," Andries murmured, fumbling for his cigarettes. "They were a group of scientists and engineers. They met in secret. I think maybe some were military - but there is something else I must tell you. One of them was Rutger Jansen."

Eleanor froze. *Rutger Jansen* - Jake's father. She raised her head slowly, meeting his pained brown eyes. "What did you say?"

Andries gave a shrug. "Is all I can tell you," he whispered, "but yes. It is possible, he met Mr Peregrine too! I think he was very powerful man - people were scared of him."

Elijah finally snapped out of his trance and blinked, reaching for his beer. No-one could ignore the tremor in his hand as he poured it carefully into a glass, as if fearing he might spill it.

"Are you okay, Eli?" Charlie said gently.

"Yeah," Elijah answered. "I was just thinking about what Andries said."

Eleanor pressed her eyes shut in horror - could *this* have been the reason Jake's parents seemed so detached? It wasn't grief they were suffering from, it was guilt!

Jake had naively attended Enfield's party like a lamb to the slaughter. He had inadvertently witnessed something he was never meant to see and Perry must have understood the risk - not just from Evelyn's sighting, but through the fear of what Andries knew. So he had ruthlessly arranged Jake's murder. Was it possible, even *Rutger* knew who his son's killer was?

"This takes me right back to a meeting I had with Adam from NME," Eleanor shivered. "The idea that Perry's network spread further." She gazed at Andries with pity. "I understand you received death threats - one of you committed suicide."

"Yes," Andries said, his voice breaking slightly. "Youf suffered depression. The threats were terrible; he was scared he was to be murdered like Jake. He end his own life." His knuckles were almost blue as they gripped the glass. "Matthias - he choose to leave the Netherlands, travel the world, find a new home, somewhere far away where no-one would find him. As for me…" he took a deep draw of his cigarette, his expression drawn in pain. "I too, choose to hide. Better to be invisible."

Eleanor nodded, conscious of his plight; he had plunged into a downward spiral of alcohol and drugs where he had spent the next 10 years trying to blot out his misery. Yet eventually, he had managed to turn his life around - joined a folk group which was how Elijah had met him.

"I'm sorry," Eleanor said numbly. "Perry has got a hell of a lot to answer for."

She lowered her eyes, feeling the slow burn of anger. Elijah forced a smile as he too grabbed for his cigarettes - though she suspected he wanted to forget about Perry, right now.

"I'm so pleased I-I met Andries," he faltered, "is it possible he could come back and stay with us for a few days? There's a bit more space, now Andrew's in Ibiza…"

"Of course!" Charlie grinned, "and now this bloody trial is over, I want to hear about your time in Holland. I gather you had a great time."

"I did," Elijah responded warmly. "Marjolein's family were great. I'm missing them already…" he broke off, his smile brightening.

They had been discussing his unscheduled return almost from the day he'd bumped into Andries, wondering if there was any way they could shatter the court case. After three long days of discussion - never mind negotiating with the police, they had finally set out in a camper van, Andries included.

"We stayed the night in France," Elijah sighed, recalling the emotional farewell in Calais. "The police escorted us the rest of the way. That's how we happened to be in London - and just in time by the looks of it."

"The case for the prosecution was about to be wound up," Eleanor mused.

Elijah rested back in his chair, beer in one hand, cigarette dangling loosely in the other. "I know. But I can't help thinking, it was a bit sudden. It would be nice to go back and see them again; all of us - maybe go camping and spend another week there!"

"I can't argue with that!" Charlie sighed. "We'll have the best holiday ever - especially with that bastard out of our lives. Now come on, drink up. There's nothing to keep us in London any more, so let's just go home."

"Well you three can," Eleanor announced, "but I'm going to have to stay a bit longer."

Charlie turned to her in outrage. Not one of them could decipher the grit in her expression; her lips were tightly pursed, her eyes glittering with some undefined emotion.

"I'm sorry, but the case still has to be wrapped up! The judge wants to deliberate over *all* the evidence - decide if there's enough material for the jury to reach a verdict."

"And then what?" Charlie muttered irritably.

"Charlie, stop worrying," she sighed. Her expression softened slightly. "If Perry's found guilty, he'll be sentenced in *another* hearing - depending on whether he makes a full recovery, that is."

She felt a powerful force of energy uncoiling, knowing she couldn't just leave things. *Perry has got a hell of a lot to answer for.* They hadn't seen the way he had looked at her in that splinter of time before he lost consciousness. His eyes had burned with loathing; an aura so intense, it had left her scared and with an all pervading sense, the fight wasn't quite over.

It was 1:00 in the morning when Eleanor sneaked her way into the hospital. She had changed into the pale blue nurse's tunic, she carried at all times - her gleaming dark hair coiled up with pins. To the unknown observer, she looked just like any other nurse employed by an NHS hospital. She flitted stealthily up the stairs towards the Cardiac Ward, knowing exactly where she was heading. He had demanded a private room of course - tucked away from the scrutiny of other patients.

She wandered past the nurses station, barely acknowledging the lady on duty. The area was dimly lit, the corridors veiled in shadow - his room lay just a little further. She craned her head towards the window, spotting a night nurse by Perry's bedside. Eleanor observed her lank black hair and sallow complexion - dark shadows ringed her eyes. These nurses worked long shifts, she realised, the poor girl looked shattered.

Eleanor gently turned the door knob and slipped inside. "Here, let me take over," she said in the softest of whispers. "You look like you could do with a break."

"Aw cheers, mate," the girl grinned and a second later, she was gone.

Eleanor crept towards the bedside. For a few moments, she stared down at the man she despised more than anyone in the world, her face hard with contempt. Despite his chalky pallor and the tube peeping out of his nose, he appeared to be sleeping peacefully. The sheet was rolled back just sufficiently to expose his bare shoulders - the tufts of white chest hair sprouting between the profusion of clamps and wires, designed to monitor his heart rate. Eleanor made a few adjustments to his surroundings before studying his chart. Then finally, she sat down.

"Comfortable are you, Perry?" she muttered.

Perry's eyes sprang open, alerted to the soft and husky tone of a voice he knew only too well. Their eyes locked. She read the shock as it gradually spread across his face.

"Dear God, I'm in hell," Perry wheezed.

"Not yet," Eleanor taunted, "but that's probably where you're heading."

Perry glanced towards the door in panic. The monitor blinked faster but Eleanor had not quite finished. "I wouldn't try to move if I were you. You're a very sick man. I suspect your heart muscle is damaged." She let out a sigh. "You do understand the nature of cardiac failure do you? Your arteries have become narrow from a gradual build up. There will be blood clots. It may even be the case, an arterial wall has torn..."

"What the hell are you doing here?" Perry finally found the energy to snarl.

"What do you think?" Eleanor snapped. "I want answers, Perry. I want to understand why you were so desperate to end Jake's life."

"You - you know why," Perry faltered. He pressed his eyes shut - it was as if he was finding it hard to speak. "H-he saw me..."

"Saw you?" Eleanor echoed. She let out a tiny laugh. "Even in court, his story was *unreliable* as your expert lawyer so aptly pointed out. Jake didn't even get a proper look at your face..."

"Whatever," Perry hissed, "now get out!"

"No," Eleanor whispered, "I won't." She leaned her head a little closer. "You destroyed the life of a wonderful human being without a shred of remorse; a talented musician who brought nothing but joy to people's hearts and that's not all - how about we talk about what Jake *really* witnessed..."

Perry gritted his teeth - he was clearly finding the entire business painful.

"You brought about the death of seven people," Eleanor hissed. "You murdered Albert Enfield along with everyone else in that minibus. So why? What could he have possibly done to you?"

"You expect me to atone for my sins?" Perry sneered. "Didn't Evelyn explain it to you?"

"Not all of it," Eleanor said coldly. "There was a secret - something deep in your past that gave Albert the edge. A private consortium, *now what was it?*"

He made a strange sound which could have been a chuckle. "Oh Eleanor, that secret dies with me. I am never *ever* going to tell you. Is that the reason you came here?"

Eleanor felt her mouth turn dry. There was so much more she wanted to say to him, yet the spikes on the graph were dropping, his heart struggling with the effort of keeping the blood pumping. At the same time, he appeared to be smiling.

"You bastard," Eleanor hissed under her breath. "I should have left you to die in the courtroom! Even Charlie told me to leave well alone, yet I tried to save your life."

"Charlie was right," Perry mocked, "you were wasting your time. You will never discover my secrets, my dear. There is nothing more you can do - and I am yet to be avenged..."

Eleanor shook her head, her eyes burning with tears. She couldn't back down, not now, determined to battle her way into the darkest depths of this mystery. She could no longer deny, it was *Andries* who had sparked this outrage; the thought that Perry concealed a secret, even Jake's father could have been a part of... She couldn't bear it, she had to know the truth.

"You're evil," Eleanor snarled. "You're a murderer and a sadist and I am not going to let you get away with this. I can't stop thinking about all the others you *destroyed* - Jordaan Van Rosendal for example... and what about those band members you terrorised? I bet you even played some part in Hargreeves' death! I always knew you had to be stopped."

"So what are you going to do about it now, you bitch?" Perry whispered back nastily. His eyes flashed with enmity as he clung to her stare. It was almost as if he had won!

Eleanor breathed deeply, fighting bitter, angry tears. Seconds later, she slipped her fingers into her pocket before drawing out a syringe. Perry watched as she slowly removed the cap - the glint of a needle was reflected in the spot lights.

"What's that?" he demanded.

She offered him a cold smile. "I'm a nurse, Perry. It's my job to make patients comfortable. On the other hand, I could make you very *uncomfortable*... and you thought you were in hell."

The look of cruel satisfaction was wiped from his face instantly - he stared at her in terror.

"It must be time for your medicine," she taunted, looming menacingly close. He cringed against his pillow. "What if I were to tell you, this syringe contained hydrochloric acid? I could inject it into your stomach - watch you spend the last moments of your life in unbearable agony."

Perry let out a whimper. One hand clawed the bed clothes as he fumbled frantically for the pull cord of his panic switch - grabbing nothing but empty air. He glared up, horrified. Eleanor had looped it over the curtain rail where it dangled infuriatingly out of reach.

"No," Perry breathed, "don't do this..."

"You're asking me to be merciful?" Eleanor quizzed. "What mercy did you show my son?" She twisted her head away and suddenly, she could not bear to look at him.

Already the nightmare had resurfaced. Elijah's scream had always stayed with her. It lurked in the data banks of her memory like a tape recording: *'Oh Eleanor, that was just the tip of the iceberg! Elijah knows he's in for a lot worse...'* She felt her innards twist.

"You threatened him with the most appalling torture," she whispered, "you and that sick bastard, Nathan. My son was physically and psychologically scarred!"

A tear plummeted from her eye as she turned back to face him. Elijah may have forced a brave face in the years that followed but only *she* knew about the nightmares. It was reflected by the torment in his face, the smoking and the erratic mood swings. Perry had damaged their lives beyond repair.

"And you wonder why I seek revenge?" she shuddered.

"Eleanor, don't do this," Perry pleaded softly, "don't sink to my level. You are not a bad person... if it's any consolation, I'm not proud of what we did and I'm sorry."

"It's a little bit late for that," Eleanor retorted, brandishing the syringe.

"N-no, it isn't," Perry was struggling to say, "it - it is something I truly regret and for which I have already been p-punished. You seem to forget, I was sentenced to 8 years in prison..."

"8 years is nothing for the hell you put us through!" Eleanor spat.

Her lip trembled as the full force of her emotions thrashed inside her. On the one hand, she felt a little sorry for him - a feeling that conflicted with her spiralling hatred. How could she forget how close they had come to killing her?

"I would have died if Nathan hadn't been caught," she sobbed, "and what fate did you *really* have in store for my son?"

She tilted the syringe, watching with pleasure as the horror crept back into Perry's face. She eased the plunger forwards, expelling any last trace of air. A tiny bead of liquid glittered at the tip. Perry's face blanched - already turning the same disturbing, putty grey as she remembered in the courtroom. Then finally she met his eye.

"Would you have kept him prisoner? Or did you plan to kill him too? You would have destroyed us all in the end, Perry Hampton - and this is your last judgement."

It was with no further hesitation, she swooped to his side. She gripped his wrist - sliding the needle into a cannula fitted to his hand. Perry let out a gasp as she pushed down the plunger. She thought she heard him splutter one final word: *"Clarissa..."* Yet he was sweating and shaking; about to suffer another heart attack - only this time, it would be fatal.

There was a final flare in his eyes as they tore into her soul, no longer pale as icicles but black with the threat of vengeance. Eleanor stepped shakily away from the bed, unable to bear the last visions of his death throes. She backed out of the room.

"We need a doctor!" she whispered to the shadowy figure on reception, "better still, a crash team! I think he's having another attack..."

"Hang on a minute, will you?" the woman called out, as Eleanor resolutely marched her way into the corridor.

"There isn't time!" she cried out, breaking into a run.

Eventually she hid herself inside a different ward, just as a crash team came hurtling into the corridor.

She waited for a few minutes, heart pounding. There was a rapid flurry of movement from somewhere - though it gradually died down, allowing her the freedom to make a hasty get away. Eleanor scuttled down the steps of the hospital and into the night where the cool, dark air seemed to embrace her. She had walked nearly half a mile before she returned to her hotel, fumbling for the guest keys - conscious of the syringe still tucked inside her hand.

She finally allowed herself a smile. The syringe had contained no more than tap water, blended with a measure of liquid paracetamol. When doctors performed a postmortem, they would discover nothing suspect in Perry's bloodstream other than a standard pain killer. Only Eleanor knew the truth; Perry had quite literally been *scared to death*.

V

"Charlie, you are a truly amazing man! What an accomplishment - just think, generations of Rosebrook citizens are going to love you for it."

They had been ambling arm in arm through Rosebrook, admiring the town. Gradually they found themselves immersed in the pretty Community Centre gardens - gazing over the new housing trust as it reared up on the other side of the fence.

Two weeks had passed since the night of Perry's death.

The announcement had been sprung in the Old Bailey, shortly after Eleanor's arrival. David was flabbergasted. Although even the judge was prepared to concede that in the light of Andries' revelations, they were already considering a guilty verdict. David guessed that if Perry had survived, he would have been transferred straight to a prison hospital wing. Only they had never reached that point. The trial was no longer suspended, it was *over* due to the untimely decease of the defendant.

The complex case of Albert Enfield's killing was far from over; the news besieged by insinuations of a huge cover up. As a result of the fracas, the authorities were about to embark on a new investigation - the only fortuitous outcome of this turbulent trial. Even Evelyn's secret testimony was finally about to come into play.

No-one could have been more relieved than Eleanor. It had taken 18 long years for Jake's evidence to be drawn into the light and his cold-blooded murder had finally been acknowledged. It was inevitable, the police would be just as keen to resolve *his* assassination. Perry's trial had rekindled their interest; rumours that Scotland Yard were particularly keen to root out the criminal gang, alleged to be behind the killing - where the name 'Dominic Theakston' was already beginning to roll into people's memories.

It was the only matter which left Eleanor unsettled - a notion that had sent her shooting over to Forest Haven to visit the Merrimans.

"Perry might be dead," she whispered in horror, "but what if they arrest Theakston? I couldn't bear to make an enemy of him again - not after this nightmare!"

Rosemary gathered her into her arms as she wept, unable to understand such overwhelming fear. It hadn't taken long for her to realise that Eleanor was hiding something and it inspired her to explain her reasons. A few years back, Theakston had levelled her with yet another deadly threat - only this time, it had been directed towards Charlie.

Eleanor turned her eyes towards her husband as he continued to gaze over the pleasing housing development; his dark hair windswept, the contours of his face strong beneath the tanned veneer of his skin. She squeezed his hand, feeling the waves of love rippling through her.

"So," he grinned, "seeing as I'm so popular, do you think there's a chance we can live here in safety now? Not to mention, I am dying for a drink. Didn't we agree to meet Peter at the Castle Donahue?"

Eleanor's lips curved into a smile. She gave a grateful nod, swallowing back her terror. "Okay, you're on!"

They wandered down the path, hands entwined. Margaret's herb gardens still flourished in their own special little corner. The mature flower beds were exploding with towering delphiniums in delicate shades of blue and lilac - in fact, it had taken only a few years for the area to evolve into something more reminiscent of James's formal gardens; another legacy Eleanor hoped would be maintained. Finally, they meandered past the pale, butter coloured walls of the Community Centre.

Eleanor glanced over her shoulder, drinking in its splendour; the rusticated blocks cleaved into the walls, the columns of mullioned windows - never able to forget, it was her son who had instigated its redesign. Together, they had made some valuable achievements and with the menace of Perry finally eradicated, she hoped it was a place where they would put down roots.

Peter beamed as they gathered in the bar, his face partially masked in shadow. Charlie was gazing around the familiar surroundings with pleasure - the wood-panelled walls lit with the glow of brass lamps. It embraced them in an ambience that was dark but cosy.

"Isn't it your wedding anniversary soon?" he greeted them.

"Next week," Charlie smiled. "What are you drinking, love?"

"I wouldn't say 'no' to a glass of white wine, Charlie," Eleanor answered him.

"And why not?" Peter added with a wink. He swooped his head a little closer. "I can't help thinking about that *pledge* we made at your wedding..."

"Hmm," Eleanor murmured, recalling the joining of hands across the table: *we will stand up against our enemies and destroy them*. "Seems a little soon to rejoice our victory, though."

"True," Peter whispered, "we never did get to the bottom of the mystery..." He broke off, unable to avoid lapsing into his own reverie.

He could never quite dispel the despair he had felt over Seamus's confession.

It troubled him even now. He had already deduced, the police were about to launch an inquiry into the Enfield car bomb atrocity - where the testimony of a man known as Declan O'Flaherty would have gone a long way towards resolving it.

He squeezed a smile onto his face, just as Avalon floated through the door with Margaret.

Elijah and his girlfriend were ensconced in another corner - one of the reasons they had decided to congregate here. Elijah was desperate to get a summer job in advance of starting his degree course and the landlord so happened to be looking for a kitchen assistant. Peter was hoping he might be able to put a good word in - though right now, his eyes were on Avalon.

Margaret was already lamenting about the absence of boys in their posse; with Andrew in Ibiza - never mind that William was still at Sandhurst.

"We all miss him terribly," Avalon added. "Our gang just doesn't seem the same any more..." then finally, her eyes flickered towards Elijah.

He flashed her a smile. His green and gold eyes sparkled with renewed energy; it seemed as if a dark cloud had been lifted, now Perry was gone.

"He'll be home soon, won't he?" Charlie quizzed. "When's his passing out parade?"

"July," Avalon sighed, "he'll be a fully commissioned army officer."

"God knows where he'll be posted," Margaret shivered. "What if they send him to the Middle East? I don't think I could bear it!"

Both men nodded sagely.

The Gulf war in Kuwait had been triggered a year earlier and showed no signs of abating as Prime Minister, John Major, released more British troops to expel Iraqi forces.

"I wouldn't worry," Peter sighed. "As a newly commissioned officer, I'm sure he'll be posted in Britain somewhere. I can't imagine, they'll throw him straight into the firing line."

"I hope not," Avalon sighed, locking eyes with Peter.

Eleanor witnessed the exchange - warmed by yet another momentous revelation. Peter was finally about to abandon his cluttered flat and move in with Avalon as a lodger.

The more Eleanor thought about it, the more she acknowledged, Peter had always been the rock in their community; unable to forget his tireless support throughout all they had suffered. The suggestion to move in had come from Avalon - she finally had to admit, she no longer felt safe in William's absence. The house seemed uncannily empty - where no-one in the world could offer a more powerful sense of protection than Peter.

"So when's he moving in?" Eleanor murmured.

"Sunday," Avalon breathed. "It'll be great to have some company - and there's nothing fishy going on, I swear, despite what everyone thinks. I'm just lonely."

"It wouldn't bother me if there was," Eleanor smiled saucily. "Peter's lovely. I can't believe you're still single. Isn't it about time you found yourself a decent guy?"

Avalon's smile dropped - a moment where she couldn't prevent her gaze flicking towards Elijah again. "I think I already have," she faltered, "h-he's just a little out of reach..."

They stayed for another hour. Eleanor's head was already swimming after just one glass of wine, filling her with a yearning to slip back to the almshouse and lie down.

"I'll come with you," Charlie murmured seductively.

The warmth of his breath sent little shivers down her neck, evoking her desire.

They had only just stepped outside, when they came face to face with Dominic. Eleanor stopped dead, floored by the penetrating jab of his eyes. She gripped Charlie's hand.

"Congratulations," Dominic said, his voice a monotone, "heard you won your case."

"Well not exactly," Charlie muttered. "Perry's dead! Though no-one ever doubted he was guilty."

"Really?" Dominic drawled. "Well I've got news. Seems that prick of a lawyer was determined to prove him innocent - so *yours truly* is probably gonna end up in court..."

Eleanor's grip on Charlie's hand stiffened. "No," she gulped. "Surely not!"

Dominic took a menacing step towards her. "Police wanna call me in for questioning," he added darkly. "Told you Hampton'd dob me in. 'Spect you'll be standing witness again soon, love..."

"So I'll defend you!" Eleanor stressed, "I said I wouldn't implicate you..."

"Yeah, you do that," Dominic smirked. '*You owe me,*' he very nearly added.

She was still clueless as to who had *really* tipped off the cops over her son's kidnapping.

Even *Peter* could never understand why the police had been sniffing around Nathan's house, on the night she had come close to her death. Pippa had urged Dominic to tell her - especially if he was about to be hauled through the court. Yet this was a paradox he chose to keep to himself - at least until the day he decided to call in a debt. Yes, Eleanor owed him big!

"She said she'd vouch for you, Dominic," Charlie added coolly. "Now is there any chance we can put this behind us? I realise we've got the obnoxious *Mr Whaley* to contend with, but Perry is well and truly gone! The battle is over."

"Oh yeah?" Dominic sneered. His eyes narrowed, still pinned on Eleanor. "Don't kid yourself. This ain't over by a long shot. You've got no idea what his nut-case of a son might be planning - I wouldn't get too complacent..."

By the time they reached the almshouse, Eleanor was trembling.

"Hey, don't let him get to you," Charlie smiled, drawing her into his arms.

"I'm going upstairs," she spluttered, "weren't you going to come and join me?"

Moments later, they were in the bedroom. Eleanor wasted no time as she sank into his arms, tugging at his shirt buttons. She slid her hand into the opening, savouring the tickle of chest hair as it curled around her finger tips. The musky scent of his skin sent her senses spiralling as she buried her face in the hollow of his neck.

"I love you so much," she said tearfully. "I can't bear the thought of losing you."

"You won't," Charlie laughed, "what's got into you? You've been jumpy ever since that bastard, Hampton, suffered another heart attack..."

"I just *so much* want our lives to be normal," Eleanor shivered, raising her face.

To Charlie's horror, it glistened with a trail of tears. She kissed him hungrily, her mouth travelling downwards, following the path of his shirt buttons as she unfastened them one by one.

"It will be," Charlie insisted, burying his fingers in her luxurious hair.

"Okay," Eleanor sighed, "in that case, didn't you promise *me* something? Once the kids were grown up - we might think about having a baby of our own?"

She smiled up at him wistfully, happy to see the love that flooded his expression. *A new life would be the ultimate victory*, she thought to herself, *what better way to celebrate?*

Epilogue

June 1991

A small service was held in a London cemetery just a short distance from Pimlico. The peaceful grounds shimmered, verdant with ivy; and there amongst the assortment of graves, stood the most exquisite new memorial stone sculpted in white marble - his final resting place hidden beneath the shadow of a beech tree.

"Whatever thy hand doeth, do it with all thy might; for there is no work, nor device, nor knowledge, nor wisdom, whither thou goest."
In Loving Memory of Peregrine Alfred Hampton
January 1938 - May 1991

It was everything he could have wished for, Rowena found herself explaining, as mourners came flocking to Westbourne House for the wake.

A small scattering of villagers watched in silence as four gleaming black funeral cars swept past the pub - Boris tucked in amongst them.

"Didn't want to be buried in Aldwyck then," he muttered cynically.

"Probably frightened James's ghost might come visiting," Toby smirked.

It was a beautiful day, given the occasion. Banks of puffy clouds gleamed above, their outlines sharp against a brilliant blue sky. The grounds of Westbourne House had never looked more pleasing. James's roses still bloomed in the neatly maintained flower beds; water trickled gently from the tiers of Perry's fountain, harmonised by a distant chirp of birdsong. Rowena stood gazing across the gardens. She wiped her tear reddened eyes - a desolate figure, frozen in silence as the crowds tip-toed carefully around her; Hilary approached her tentatively.

"I'm sorry, Rowena," she whispered, "this must have been such a terrible shock."

"I cannot even begin to explain," Rowena started sobbing. "Do you know the worst thing of all? I never had a chance to say goodbye to him! We were already in London, for God's sake. By the time the hospital got in touch with us, it was too late - he'd gone..."

Hilary touched her hand before coaxing her into an embrace. "You poor thing," she whispered. "You know you can always count on me and Reg for support - and you've still got Ben..."

She broke off, clocking the gleam of white blonde hair as he loomed in the parking area. He was pacing around, smoking a cigarette and for a moment, Hilary followed his gaze - astounded to see a prison van roll up. She watched as if in a dream, as Ben approached it. The doors flew open and two prison guards stepped out - the next person to emerge was Nathan. He was handcuffed to one of the guards, menacing in a black suit. Hilary released Rowena and squinted into the distance. She blinked - unable to understand what that *thug* could possibly be doing here!

Rowena clocked the horror in her eyes and glanced round. "Oh, don't worry about him," she sniffed. "He was quite insistent about paying his last respects."

"I see," Hilary responded stiffly, loathing the idea of having to breath the same air as some prison inmate.

"He was one of Perry's most faithful employees," Rowena added tearfully, "I cleared it with the authorities. It's what he would have wanted - they were soul mates in the end, you know..."

Nathan met Ben's eyes and smiled.

"Hi," Ben muttered, turning to the prison guard. "It's okay, he's with me. Any chance we could lose the handcuffs? Only - people are staring at us."

They seemed reluctant. Nathan was only permitted to spend half an hour here, since he had already attended the cremation service. Yet his manners were impeccable. He knew how to behave in polite society, a fresh-faced 24 year old 'rookie' known as Jamie had noticed.

"Nice service by the way," Nathan growled softly. "Very touching."

Already the guard felt unnerved by his hard features - those searing, midnight blue eyes.

"Can't see any harm in it, can you?" he double-checked.

It took the subtle nod of his superior to reassure him.

"Let's walk," Ben finally snapped. "How are you coping without my father being around?"

Nathan gave a shrug. "Bearing up, I suppose."

They wandered past Robin Whaley; he was visibly grief-stricken and accompanied by Naomi. She threw Ben a cool smile - flicking her gaze towards Nathan, who winked.

"So what's really going on?" Nathan murmured beneath his breath - the tinkle of Perry's fountain shielded any conversation from wagging ears. "You still under surveillance?"

"Yeah," Ben announced loudly, "still at the London Stock Exchange. An old friend rang me up, you know. D'you want to hear what he said to me?" Ben sniggered. He drew his lips right up to Nathan's ear as if to impart some dirty secret. "Alan reckons he can *spring* you."

The whisper was dropped into Nathan's ear undetected, prompting him to raise his eyebrows. "So why would he want to do that?" he smirked.

Ben turned sharply where his pale eyes adopted a sudden chill. "I told you my father's last wishes, didn't I?" he hissed, tipping his head sideways. "He said '*Avenge me...*'"

This is the end of 'Pleasures'
Watch out for
'SAME FACE DIFFERENT PLACE Book 4 - Retribution'
A story of love, power and revenge.

Also by Helen J. Christmas

Book 1 - Beginnings

A thriller and a love story set in the criminal underworld of 1970s London.

Book 2 - Visions

1980s Psychological thriller set around the restoration of a country house.

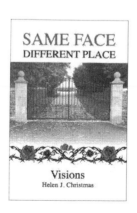

Made in the USA
Charleston, SC
06 November 2015